Etched

Etched

A Novel

Annette I. Smith

Ione Publishing
New York

Cataloging-in-Publication Data is on file with the Library of Congress

Published in the United States by Ione Publishing

First Edition: December 2010
ISBN 978-0-557-73131-2

Ione Publishing
P. O. Box 25523
Brooklyn, NY 11201-5523
Visit our Website at www.annetteismith.net

Dedicated to Irene Margaret Smith

*My mother, my best friend, my confidant - my
"Aunt Bess"*

*Thanks for dreaming, waiting, and praying right along
with me.*

Rest until I see you in God's house

Alfred Leo Smith

My father—unique parenting style but still—father

Contents

Acknowledgements ix

Foreword... xi

Book One: Gina Pearl Fields (Promise Greenwood)............................ 1

Book Two: Momma Mae and Lil' Mae................................... 43

Book Three: Molasses 57

Book Four: Chauncey Street: Aunt Bess & Cousin Thea..................... 91

Book Five: Cornbread 97

Book Six: Milkweed 129

Book Seven: Lilly Greenwood... 307

Book Eight: Andrea Matti Hirsh Greenwood........................... 351

Glossary...447

Acknowledgements

My most important and heartfelt "Thank you" goes to my Editor, Angela at Angel Editing. Angela did an amazing job, smoothed out the rough edges and told me, "Annette, stop cleaning the house for the maid." I left the manuscript alone and Angela cleaned it up perfectly. Angela also brought me to tears (happy and heartfelt) more times than I can count. Those reasons are between Angela and me. I can truly say that Angela is an incredible 'mid-wife' and I couldn't have had a better birthing coach. I feel as if Etched is our baby.

My three children: Richard A. Smith - (Anika); Zenoebia A. Washington-Cohen - (Tony); Kevin D. Roberts - (Sheryl) and grandson Kye D. Roberts.

My younger brother Gradfil C. Smith "Gray" for always believing that I could do anything I put my mind to except using a penname—he said, "Are you ashamed of the name that muh Ma and Tata gave you." That was it, my penname went out the window and in its stead—Annette I. Smith—the name that our Ma (my Keba) and Tata (my father – "Mickey") gave me.

My sister Imega Florence E. L. Smith, who believed right along with me, called me a GREAT writer and had me on her vision board.

My remaining siblings: Edmey O. Rose, Zeta O. Adamson, Wesley L. Smith, Charles H. Smith, and Frederick E. L. Smith.

Richiedenne Cooper who asked the most important question anyone ever asked while I was writing this book. She said, "Arlene where her (Leela) kin at?" (Arlene is Richie's name for me. When we first met she said, "You don't look like an Annette you look more like an Arlene— I've been Arlene, and only for her, ever since). The question of 'kin' for Leela gave Leela kin and an amazingly rich history.

Judith Lovell who asked me for Thea's and Crawford's love story and with that simple request, got me to produce, in ten (10) hours, something that I didn't even know was there. Judy also thought it not robbery to write the Foreword.

Cherryl Walcott who one day, when I was feeling my lowest and tears were streaming down my face said to me, "Annette my Pastor said the other day, "A delay is not a denial so although it may not be happening now doesn't mean it's not going to happen." I held onto those words. Also for every time you made me laugh, every time you listened even when you didn't feel like it; thank you.

Tim Moses—your friendship over the years, your continued belief in my dreams, Cornbread and Molasses and all my other, sometimes, far-fetched dreams have been and is deeply appreciated.

Dr. Kathy Bishop (NYU) who many years ago said to me, "Annette, don't ever let anyone tell you that you are not a writer; you are a writer and a good one." Those words resonated within spirit and have kept me going when I felt I couldn't or shouldn't bother.

Theodore Lewis—your word is your bond and your bond—your word. Your kind, caring and thoughtful nature is deeply appreciated.

Chris Devonish— a friend and fellow country man who believed so deeply in this project that he paid me for a copy when Etched was still an unedited manuscript.

Karl Victor Robins—for allowing me to use your original song: **Promised Land**.

Maurice Clarke—a true and living testimony of what being a Christian young man is. On that day you saw me struggling with a big rambunctious, not listening-to-me-dog you said, "Miss, do you need help with that dog?" I wanted to cry but I didn't I said, "Yes." Almost every day since you've given of your time, efforts and energy to come and get August to take her running, for walks, to play basket ball or to just give me time to work on Etched without interruptions.

Stephanie Clarke (Maurice's wife)—Thank you for being a dear Christian who so freely shared your time and thought it not robbery each time Maurice came and took August walking for me. You (Queen Bella and Sir Barkley Jones) are truly appreciated.

August Chance Smith my 85 pound Mastiff/Labrador mix, my very best friend. No human can possess your caring nature, your ability to love me despite my many failures and short-comings—which you never seem to notice. I wish I could be the kind of person you think I am. Thanks for your high hopes in me, the calluses in my right hand from trying to hold onto your chain as you grew bigger and stronger, the tetanus shot I had to get because you'd never heard, 'don't bite the hand that feed you'. The hand that just happens to be the one I need to write amazing books so you can get that big back yard to run and feel the wind in your face. I'm also working on forgetting the numerous black and blue marks, the popped knee and oh yeah the broken tendon in …that's right—my right hand. How can I not thank you? At least I know for sure where you're coming from—land of the big goofy dogs.

Foreword

I first met Annette Smith, the author of *Etched*, about twenty years ago. Both of us were enrolled in an employer sponsored management certificate program in New York City. Annette was, and still is, passionate about life, love, and learning. She is a brilliant story-teller and an extremely gifted writer with a magnetic personality. We shared many things in common and became friends immediately. Like the paternal side of my family, Annette and her family hail from Barbados, West Indies. Though Barbados is a relatively small island with few natural resources, its contributions to world history is enormous. Numerous internationally renowned individuals call Barbados home.

It was on the shores of "Little England," as Barbados is also known, where Annette learned to appreciate her rich heritage in the African Diaspora. She understood the power of a closely knit family that knows its history and cherishes its roots. She emulated the strong black women who despite their trials and tribulations stood tall and confident. According to her mother (Irene Margaret Smith), Annette is the seventh child of a seventh child of a seventh child. Understanding that the number seven symbolizes God's perfection in work, she stays firmly rooted in the word of God. Annette embraces her divine legacy and honors her spirituality not only with this novel but with her life. She spiritually uplifts and enlightens readers, especially in Chapter 1, *"A Time for Everything,"* where she masterfully entwines Ecclesiastes Chapter 3 of the Bible into the storyline of *Etched*. Her divine connection with the Creator can be experienced throughout her entire collection of writings.

Etched is a novel that tells the multi-generational stories of colorful characters. They enrich the lives of readers through their pain, suffering, wisdom, and the life-lessons they have learned. Beginning on the Beauford Plantation in Promise Land, Greenwood, South Carolina, *Etched* embraces history and stresses the importance of passing down one's story to the next generation. It is evocative and leaves its imprints on your heart and soul: you will cry and laugh, get angry, jump for joy, feel loneliness and disgrace, and experience love, lust, hate, fear, shame, and despair.

Not only does Annette exquisitely tell a story about family and keeping the family story alive but she creatively uses words to describe her characters. She perfectly paints pictures. Her main character *Cornbread's* hair is described as burnt butter running down the sides of some good cornbread. *Molasses, Cornbread's* soul mate, is said to have skin matching the color of midnight and molasses all rolled together. Readers can close their eyes and the characters of *Etched* come alive.

This novel is to be devoured, savored and passed down from generation to generation. It is a story that will elicit much needed conversation about slavery and self-determination and one's own story of struggle and survival.

Judith C. Lovell
Adjunct Professor
Brooklyn, New York
October 10, 2010

"Milkweed let ev'ting I tell yuh sink in yer brain. Mark it on yuh heart. 'member ev'ting. Fer wat we dun been through—sep'ration, beatings, and sights our eyes, brains, and heart nots ever gine fergit—yuh, meh, we gots to 'member but more dan anyting, fer what I dun seen dem do to yuh and all dem tings dat too hard fer yuh to tell me; we must 'member. All dat sufferin' nots to be fer nuffin'.'member book learning is de most special ting. Dat's wat yuh must do; 'member and tell yuh own; 'specially yuh daughters dem. Tell 'em book learning 'fore anything—even love. Yuh hear me, Milkweed, let nuffin' but de good Lawd come 'fore book learning."

Jennie Etta Mae "Cornbread" Litchfield - Slave

Book One

Gina Pearl Fields
(Promise Greenwood)

Chapter 1

A Time For Everything

Gina Pearl Fields

"Everything got its time." That was my Aunt Bess' favorite saying. It didn't matter what life threw her way, she always said, "Everything got its time." It didn't make sense to ask her when that time was 'cause all she would say was, "God's time. His time is not ours. Have faith."

It was all about faith for her; faith and Ecclesiastes 3:1-8. If you ever appeared to question God and His timing, she would snatch her bible, which was always within arm's reach, turn to the page and point. No one ever read where she was silently pointing. We knew what it said. Those verses described the women in our family. We'd lived every line.

A time to be born (Giving birth is what started most of the women in this family down one rough road or another).

And a time to die (When the women of this family died, they took your heart and soul with them, leaving you to re-evaluate living).

A time to plant (We were gardens always ready to be planted. None of us ever refused a baby seed. It was one of these baby seeds that was responsible for bringing the curse on us).

And a time to pluck up what is planted (I was the only one ever to be plucked up and sent away from Promise Land. Before that, every female in this family grew into her own right there. The curse was there. They all knew about it. Was told about it yet none escaped it. Every woman did her fighting and struggling, trying to break the curse right there in Promise Land. How could they not; the place was called Promise Land after all. To hear my Aunt Bess tell it, the place, at times was their Canaan as well as their wilderness).

A time to kill (God kept His hands on us. If it wasn't for Him, a few men, and some women too, would have met Him through us).

And a time to heal (Since everything had its time, we knew that eventually the hurt would heal, but until then we licked our wounds, nursed our pain, and prayed the H-U-R-T prayer. **Help Us Run This** race. We prayed our H-U-R-T prayer 'till healing showed up).

A time to break down (The breaking down started with my daughter; after that it hung in the air waiting for the next one whose hurt ran deep and for whom escape seemed impossible).

And a time to build up (Aware of the "break-down" hovering over us, we stayed strong 'cause we knew the journey back was rough).

A time to weep (We wept so often, I'm sure there's a river in heaven called "The Mighty Greenwood").

And a time to laugh (We laughed to stay one step ahead of the "break-down").

A time to mourn (Mourning is never easy. Once you get pass the first one, it gets a little easier; never easy, just easier).

And a time to dance (We danced; it kept us from mourning too, too long).

A time to throw away stones (My mother treated me like a dirty stone. She didn't have a glass house so she didn't worry, nor look when or where she threw me).

And a time to gather stones together (I was never gathered back. I promised myself after that no daughter of Promise Land would ever know what it feels like not to be gathered back home).

A time to embrace (We embraced and how).

And a time to refrain from embracing (Some of us, because of those hard life lessons, learned quickly about refraining from embracing, but others…).

A time to seek (And did we seek. Not all the seeking was done by us, sometimes people sought us out).

And a time to lose (Those losses made us thankful for our gathering place).

A time to keep (Some of us failed to recognize when something was a keeper).

And a time to throw away (Not all of us got *'A time to keep'* right so we often kept what should have been thrown away).

A time to tear (Sometimes we, the daughters of Greenwood, did this and it wasn't always strangers we tore up).

And a time to sew (Love of family is the best thread to use to repair tears of any kind).

A time to keep silence (If we'd gotten this right, our journey to peace would have been much quicker and quieter, a lot less kicking and screaming).

And a time to speak (Because we never learned when the right time to be silent was; tearing, temper, and temperance kept us talking even when we should have been quiet).

A time to love (We lived to love even though it sometimes caused us agonizing pain. That's where that H.U.R.T prayer came in handy).

And a time to hate (No one in particular taught us to hate. However, living, loving, and losing did. Losing and weeping kept it around).

A time for war (Mine started with my mother finding, gathering, and clinging to a husband and tossing me to the wind so she could get her "Happy Ever After". She and I never battled, but the pain of that rending stayed with me forever).

And a time for peace (There's no moment like when you realize that you've found it. It's like walking in warm summer rain).

Chapter 2

Leaving Promise Land

That morning when I woke, it was raining as I'd never seen it rain before. Heaven was throwing everything at us but angels. I started wishing my mother would rethink her plan to send me to New York. I started to believe God and all the angels were angry and upset at my mother for sending me away. This wasn't one of those times when God was part of the plan. This was all about my mother and her plans. My mother had found herself a husband and she needed to get on with the life he'd promised her. He'd promised her a "Happy Ever After" but had told her there was no room in it for me; Ma wanted her "Happy Ever After". She'd seen other women with theirs and felt it was time, her time, and nothing was goin' to get in her way; not even me.

With everything for her wedding arranged, my mother took me to the bus station; as people milled around and rushed from place to place, my mother waited with me. There was no milling or rushing in her, just a slight nervousness. She was waiting to place me on a bus. Actually if I told the whole truth, it wasn't really a bus the way you picture a bus with fresh paint, clean white-walled tires, shiny bumpers, and shining bright head lights. Instead, it was a rusty tin can, rust was and had been a constant passenger, the lights didn't look as if they were goin' to come on when it got dark down the road, and all the places that used to shine were mud-spattered, chipped, dented, or missing.

This pile of tin was doing everything it could to pass itself off as a bus. What it looked like didn't matter to my mother. The only thing that was important to her was that this tin can was headed out of Promise Land: Greenwood, South Carolina, for New York City. When it left, I was goin' to be on it. She was sending me to live with my Aunt Bess, her sister. The fact that I'd never met Aunt Bess also didn't matter because Ma had made up her mind and, like it or not, I was goin' to be on that tin can headed to New York City.

With the silence between Ma and me getting thicker than the clouds overhead, I stared at the tin can. I wanted it to be a bus but it made no pretense to be a bus. It was just what it was: a consolatory tin can trying real hard to be a bus and I started to think that if I wished hard enough, it was goin' to become whatever everyone wanted it to be. Today, by the look on my mother's face and the nervous way she shifted from one leg to another, she desperately needed it to be a bus and so… it was a bus. I looked with my mother's desperate eyes and I saw a bus. I took a deep breath and let it be the bus she needed it to be.

The rain didn't let up. It was as though those angels that hadn't fallen out of heaven with the first downpour were shaking a big wet silver blanket all across the sky. The drops were big and silvery looking. My mother, who had said nothing to me all day, suddenly seemed to notice it and decided to add her two cents. When she spoke, she made no sense. She said, "September rain sure can be funny. The way it be raining, you would think it be getting ready to bring flowers or something, but you know that ain't the case 'cause spring done gone; everything done grow that was goin' grow."

I wanted to tell her that her ramblings weren't helping and could she just shut her mouth unless she was fixing to tell me something that was goin' make my being sent away hurt less. I looked at her and knew that although she had nothing to say that would take away my hurt; I also couldn't tell her to shut her mouth. So I replied, "Yup, there's something special about a September rain."

When Ma answered, "You think so too?" I knew that she wasn't really thinking about me at all. She was talking to fill the space the silence had created, or she was just talking until they said the tin can was ready to roll away from Promise Land. Knowing that this wasn't a real mother and daughter talk, I stated, "Yes, Ma, I do. There's something special about a September rain."

Then Ma looked at me as if she'd been thinking about rain forever and agreed, "Yup, yup, yup, there sure is something special 'bout this September rain." Then she went quiet. It was as if she was goin' let the falling rain talk for her. I got quiet too and let it. It filled the void between us and just when I'd gotten used to the rhythm of the rain beating on everything outside and touching every sad place inside of me, it was time to go. The tin can was ready to roll away from Promise Land. We didn't say goodbye, well not the way a mother and daughter, especially a daughter who had never been away from home before would say goodbye. I said, "Ma, they said it's time to get on the bus."

And Ma, without looking at me, replied, "Yup, yup, yup, that's what they said."

I waited for her to hug me, touch my hand, reach up and touch my face, say she was goin' to miss me, wish me a good trip, start crying and telling me she was sorry about sending me away, that she couldn't do it and she'd changed her mind… something, anything. However, she didn't say or do nothing. I looked at her, waiting, expecting, and when it didn't seem like she was goin' say or do anything, not even hug me, I moved slowly pass her and made my way towards the bus. When I'd taken about three steps pass her, she repeated, "Yup, yup, yup, there sure is something 'bout a September rain."

I slowed my pace. I didn't want to walk too fast and miss the hug, touch, or pat she was getting ready to give me; you know, that soft tender moment that always came just before the tearful goodbye that two people who were goin' to miss each other go through when it was time to finally say goodbye. I waited. It was coming. It had to be. I was goin' away, leaving her. Nothing came. She did nothing. As I walked pass, I picked up my pace and continued my walk to the tin can. When I reached it, I turned to see if she was at least watching me board. She wasn't. She wasn't even in the spot where I'd seen her last. She'd just walked away. I found her retreating back in the crowd of people who had waited with family and friends to board the tin can. I watched her as she walked away from me. Her walk had purpose. Her head was turning from side to side: she was searching for something or someone. Since she wasn't looking in my direction, I knew it wasn't me. Her head stopped moving. I looked in the direction it was facing and that's when I saw him: Earnest Threadwell. He'd followed her. Came in his truck and now he was waiting for her to take her away to her new life with him: the promised Happy Ever After.

I turned my head to look away. I didn't want to see her now walking with a bounce in her step as she hurried towards him. I wasn't fast enough. I noticed as he smiled at her. She quickened her step. My mother was now almost skipping as she hurried to him. Her steps became so light she was almost floating towards him now. My legs stiffened. I could feel the stiffness as it moved pass my knees to my thighs; I'd looked back and now I was turning to a pillar of salt like Lot's wife. I begged God not to let me stay stuck there in the bus depot. He heard me. My feet lightened up. I willed myself to make a step. My feet moved. I thanked God and boarded the tin can bus, promising God I'd never look back at her or think of her and Ernest Threadwell ever again.

The minute my whole body was in the bus, I felt something in my belly I'd never felt before: longing. I was already missing my mother and yet I started to hate her for what she was doing to me. I hoped time and distance would change that. As I moved down the aisles, the feeling grew deeper. I couldn't help it. When I felt it was safe, I took a sideways glance out the window in the direction of the truck. Since I wasn't actually looking back, I had no fear of turning into a pillar of salt. The truck was gone. A cloud of dust was in its place. She, he, and the truck, were all wrapped up in this thick dust cloud.

I stayed watching until the dust cleared. She, he, the truck, and any trace of her was gone. I started to think he'd performed a magic trick and had stolen her away from me, but the truth was he hadn't. She'd volunteered. I turned my head back inside and continued looking until I found a seat next to a window. I was hoping he'd do another magic trick and when I looked out the window she would be standing there smiling and signaling to me to get off. I wanted him to bring her back. I took another quick sideways glance to see if my wish had come true, it hadn't. They were still gone. Accepting that she'd gone off to her Happy Ever After and there was no chance of me turning into stone since they were gone, I decided to look out the window. I wanted to watch Promise Land as I was being taken away from it.

My mother had been my Promised Land and for the sake of a big house, land, a car, and a promise made to her by a man she just kind of halfway knew, she'd sent me away so she could become his wife. I promised myself to hate my mother for a long time and as for Ernest Threadwell my hatred for him would stretch over time. I would let it search, stretch, and wrap itself around everything until it found forever. Once I'd found forever I was goin' to let it wrap itself around it so tight that forever would feel as if it was being shortened. It wasn't... it would just feel that way. I knew that nothing, not time, not distance, not a new city, nothing was goin' change the way I would feel 'bout Ernest Threadwell. I was goin' to hate him forever, I didn't mind. I had time. I was goin' live one day pass forever just so I could be sure that I'd hated him the longest hate ever. I smiled at the thought. I was satisfied with the idea of living one day pass forever.

As I made my way to the back of the bus and found a seat on the raggedy, falling apart tin can passing itself off as a bus, I never noticed, or simply didn't care that it was Fall outside. To anyone who cared to look, the trees were now a multi-colored spectrum of reds, oranges, yellows, and burgundy, sprinkled with greens and browns, all drizzled and some drenched by the earlier downpour. All of this, like many other things in my life, was second place to what my mother had just done to me. I had only two thoughts at that moment; surviving this trip, and finding a way to make a good life for me and the child growing in my belly once I reached New York City.

The bus filled up with white people at the front, and all the rest of us Negroes at the back. That's the way it was; no questions, just know your place. Our place, every Negro's place was at the back of everything. As tightly packed as the back was, I started to wonder why everyone was sitting away from me. Then I guessed: no one wanted to go all the way to New York City sitting next to a girl who had turned into a crybaby. They left me alone. I started to be glad then my joy was over. A large Negro woman rushed onto the bus like she was being chased by the devil himself; looking around for a seat and finding no place else to sit, she took the only available seat: the empty one beside me.

Already feeling sad, lonesome, and a little homesick, I started feeling a little sicker. It was the woman and the way she smelled. She smelled like a mixture of fear and sweat and dirty clothes, the way clothes smell when you've been in them too long. When you have passed the day when you ask yourself if it's too dirty to put on and shouldn't you be washing this and have it on a line somewhere drying in God's hot sun. But if that's all you own and it means being naked for a while, then perhaps it should be cooling under some moonlight somewhere as you wait for the night air to work like sunshine. I took a quick look at the woman and I could see that she never got around to asking herself that question. She looks uncomfortable yet still comfortable in her dirty dress.

In the unrelenting heat of the bus, other trapped and slightly sour smells on the woman started to free themselves. They reached my nose and brought on a wave of nausea. I started to think, not that I wanted to be thinking about this woman, that perhaps she had either gone unwashed for a while or might not have had an opportunity or reason to change her clothes. I didn't want to care about her or feel sorry for her, but the way she was looking around nervously and anxiously made me wonder why. She looked more nervous than any other Negro squeezed in the back of this tin can. We were squeezed up in the back while the white people, and some of them poorer than a lot of us, but 'cause they be white, they get to sit in the front and even have a few empty seats. I let my wondering about this woman and why she was nervous and anxious leave my head. I was curious but not enough to let my wondering about this woman get mixed up with the way I was wondering about Ma and the way she just went off to her Happy Ever After and left me.

My stomach gave an unforgiving lurch. Spit filled my mouth. Clenching my teeth, I swallowed, forcing the soon-to-be vomit back down my throat. The force hurt my throat. I tried to get my mind on something else but I couldn't. The woman started to fidget and because the bus was hot and I was sad and hungry, the thickened air on the bus was more than I could take. My stomach lurched again. The bus, which I hadn't noticed pulling out and away from the station because of this nervous smelly woman, swayed. The contents of my stomach rose; I feel as well as taste it. I was goin' to vomit. I covered my mouth with my hands and turned my head away from the woman so that I wouldn't vomit all over her.

The woman, realizing that I was about to throw up said, "Miss, is you fixing to throw up?" Unable to answer because my mouth was filling up too quickly, I clamped my hands tighter over my mouth nodded. The woman turned to me and said, "Put your head out the window quick. We at the back of the bus so none of it goin' come back in the bus and get on the white people because of the wind and how the bus goin' fast. Go on, miss, put your head out the window, quick."

Without a word and as quietly as I could, I put my head out the window and opened my mouth. All that was in my mouth and the little bit that was in my stomach, that is everything except my baby, came out. I was glad that my baby wasn't about to change the way babies are born. My belly had tightened from the force of throwing up, but since I was only two months pregnant, I didn't have to worry about the baby being born on this rusty tin can somewhere between Promise Land and the City of Promises.

Weakened from my effort to empty my stomach and still keep my baby from coming up, I kept my head out the window so the cool breeze could wash over my face. I had heaved and heaved and the only thing that came out of my stomach was some bile, regret, and sadness over what Ma had just done to me. None of the hate I was feeling for Earnest Threadwell had moved. I was glad. I didn't want it to. I still had that one day pass forever to get to. I was also glad that all that had come out my stomach had been outside the bus because there would be no lingering smell of vomit to make its way to the driver and have him get mad and put us off his tin can bus.

Soon as I was feeling better, I brought my head back in. I turned to the woman and said, "Thank you." She looked at me but didn't say anything. It was in that look that I noticed her eyes: they were sad. I looked away from her and closed mine. I didn't want to look into her eyes. I didn't want to know why she was sitting beside me smelly, sad, and yet able to look pass her own troubles long enough to help me. I didn't want any more pain; she looked as though she had a lot. It was goin' to be a long ride and if I started talking to her, I was sure I would find out about her pain. I had enough of my own with my man Milton dying so unexpectedly, Ma finding her Happy Ever After, and me on my way to New York City. I'd only heard about New York and now because of the accident that had robbed me of my Happy Ever After; I was here on this falling apart tin can sitting next to her and headed there.

Nope, I wasn't goin' to try and become her burden bearer. I was sad, tired, and what I didn't need was someone else's sadness or the reason for it. Milton, because he was his mother's only everything and was tied to her apron string until he met me, always had a scab for every cut. If I said I was tired, he would say, "When you feel too tired and sad, take some time and look at all the troubles that got you feeling burdened and sort it all out. When you get done sorting, take only your troubles and then look at what's left. All that's left belongs to somebody else and since you already know that God will never give you more than you can handle, give what's left back to the person you took it from.

"If you can't put the other person's shit down 'cause you done promised them that you goin' fix their shit, then take it all to God. Tell him that because you love other people's troubles, you've picked all their stuff up and now you don't know how to give it back or put it down because they are depending on you. Listen and you'll hear God say, 'Give it to me. I'll sort it and because you love as deeply as you do, I'm goin' to give you a double portion.' He's not goin' to tell you what the double portion is, but when you look around, you'll notice that he's given you a double portion of His grace, joy, love, mercy, and kindness, and if you need them, He'll send a pair of arms that will know how to hold and love you double and above what others may think you deserve."

So with Milton's voice in my head I said a silent prayer for this woman and whatever bad or sad things that had happened in her life to bring her to where she was. I closed my eyes tighter and prayed, "Dear God, please send this woman sitting beside me somebody that will want to hear what she has to say. Somebody that is goin' to care about what has happened to her and if it's Your will, Lord, someone who will hand her a whole bunch of kerchiefs or towels for her tears if she goin' be crying. And also, Lord, send the kind of person that won't ask her why she needs them. That, dear God, is my sincere prayer for this woman. It's coming from the deepest part of my heart because I understand... I understand sadness and lonesomeness. Dear God, please forgive me for not wanting to be the somebody she tells it to. Lord, you know I got my own troubles and I got to admit, though you already know, my heart can't take on anybody else's pain. Thank you, God. Amen."

Chapter 3

A Change Is Needed
Promise Greenwood

After I said the prayer for the woman, I kept my eyes closed. I wasn't sleeping but soon I heard her. She was snoring softly. She'd fallen asleep. God had taken her stuff or enough to let sleep come to her. I was glad that he understood that I couldn't take to hearing her. I started to wish for some sleep for myself, but it wasn't coming, at least not yet. My stomach still wasn't quite settled, but I knew there wasn't anything to come up. I hadn't eaten and so somewhere between Promise Land, throwing up, dry heaves, and the City of Promises, I put my head back, closed my eyes, and made a life-changing decision. I would change my name. Right there behind my closed eyelids, I went from Gina Pearl Fields to Promise Greenwood. Nothing good had ever happened to Gina Pearl Fields or anybody with that blighted Fields name. Changing that name might just be what I needed to change my future and break the curse that had followed all the women of my family who were either Beaufords, Litchfields, or just plain Fields.

The curse that had started back in the days when my Great-Great-Great-grand-nana was a slave still hung over our heads. It hung there like a halo yet there wasn't one godly thing about it. It was, after all, a curse and for one that started way, way back, it still managed to affect us just as strongly as when it got started.

As the tin can bus rolled further away from South Carolina, my stomach quieted. There was nothing else I wanted to bring up, the hate for Earnest Threadwell had to stay and whatever I was feeling for Ma had to stay too 'till I could figure out quite what it was. I closed my eyes and did all I could not to notice the woman next to me and her assorted smells. It was hard but after a while, I got used to it and almost didn't notice, well, not as much. The tin can bus rolled forward, sure of where it was headed, unlike me. Not knowing what was really waiting for me and not wanting to think about how Ma could just give away her daughter for a man, a house, a truck and some land kept pricking at my heart. I could feel the tears wanting to come back. I couldn't afford to cry. I had to think about something else. I decided to think on the women in my family and how they pressed on and forward as Ma would say, "Never mind how much they had to suffer."

The sound of the wheels crunching on the road seems to be repeating one constant song: "Want something. This family's been through too much, suffered too much for the rest of us Negro people to think life easy now that we can find a little work and eat what and when we feel like." As I listened, I promised myself I would want something and want it bad enough for me and my child. I'll want something bad enough that I'll be willing to make any sacrifice to get it. I heard the tin can's message and let it sink it.

That was about the one thing Ma remember about what the women in my family said. It was enough for me and now it was helping me to not cry. I listened to the sound of the wheels crunching on the road and I knew that with each turn of the wheel, I was getting further away from Promise Land and closer to the future waiting for me, uncertain as it was. Ma, her soon-to-be new husband, Ernest Threadwell, and Gina Pearl Fields were my past. I wasn't looking back. Gina Pearl was my past; Promise Greenwood was my future. I closed my eyes and the rhythm of the tin can bus helped me to relax. Peace and sleep came. I welcomed both.

The tin can bus and my belly held together. We'd made it. New York City. Promise Greenwood was in the Land of Promises. As soon as I got off the bus, I started looking around. Not so much at where I was, but I was looking for Aunt Bess. Momma had said, "When you see a woman fatter and taller than me and looking just like me and you, same thick long dark brown hair, lightish brown eyes, medium brown skin, but with fuller lips; that be your Aunt Bess."

No one like that passed by. I watched as the Negroes who were on the old tin can bus along with me got swallowed up in hugs and happy screams from family members waiting to welcome them to the Land of Promise. I waited for my happy scream and my welcome but no one was there… no Aunt Bess. Fear started to rise up in my belly.

Soon no one but me and the woman who had rushed onto the bus with fear and sweat dripping from her were left. Turning to me, she said, "Ain't no one coming for ya? My people soon come for me. You goin' be OK waiting here by yourself?"

"Don't know. I think my Aunt Bess goin' be here soon though."

"Aunt Bess? Bess Fields? You waiting for Bessie Fields?"

"Yes. She's my aunt."

"Good Lord, child, then you be kin to me. Bessie Fields is my third cousin, twice removed on my grandfather's mother's side."

"So what does that make me and you?"

"Kin; that's all we need to know. Look how the Lord works. He put me next to you so I can, without my knowing, take care of you and now you turn out to be my own kin. The Lord be something else." She smiled a big smile and in that smile some of her stink got sucked up. It was a sweet smile.

She came closer. "Ain't it something that me and you waiting for Bessie? I ain't goin' be living at Bessie's though. I goin' be just down the road a piece from her. You been to New York before?"

"No, I ain't been here before."

"Me neither, but I hear that here in the North, a Negro don't get treat near as bad as in the South."

"I don't know 'bout none of that, miss."

"Gina Pearl! Gina Pearl!" The woman calling my name was as Ma described; a woman, taller and fatter than she, but looking every bit like she and I. I knew who it was. It was Aunt Bess.

"I be Gina Pearl."

The taller Momma swallowed up the space between us with two long strides. Her arms were opened and she had a big smile just like my new third cousin on my mother's side twice removed, and she was coming to and at me. Before I could brace myself for our collision, she had her arms wrapped around me and I was buried in the folds of her flesh. It was the first time someone was touching me and pulling me to them since Milton had died. I started to cry. She folded me deeper into her. My heart, which had longed for this hug from Momma and didn't get it, exploded with a mixture of joy and sadness.

She spoke into the top of my head. Her breath was warm and made its way to my heart. She was speaking right into my longing. The same spot, which I believed to be closed 'cause I wasn't expecting this kind of love or gentleness from anyone anymore, opened up. I wrapped my arms around the place where her waist was supposed to be. She was soft and warm. My arms got sucked and sandwiched in. The space my arms had gotten swallowed up in felt like it had happiness, joy, hope, and wishes buried deep within. I was sure once I'd pulled my arms out, they were goin' to be covered with happiness. I cried even harder.

"Hush, child. You ain't got no reason to cry. I is here. That's all you need remember. Your Aunt Bess is here. There ain't goin' be no more separation for you, so hush and dry your tears."

I felt myself being pulled away from her warmth. I wanted to beg her to let me stay. Not forever, but just for a few minutes more. Fully pulled away but not quite separated, she looked at me and smiled. That smile said, "You're safe. I'm goin' to take care of you; you in peace's open field right now."

I looked at my arms before I looked at her. I was right; all over my arms were little flashing stars. I knew they weren't really there, but it was how she made me feel. Aunt Bess reached out and touched my face. Her hands were soft. "I know you scared but you ain't got reason to be. I done been thinking on this. Got my own thoughts but we goin' talk about that at the house. Now where your bags? She did give you some clothes to start you off at least?" I nodded.

"Bessie Fields, is you forgetting 'bout me?"

"Lord! Lord! Thea Louise, if you ain't said nothing I'd be well on my way with this child 'fore I remember you."

My newfound kin two or three times removed on my grandfather's mother side of the family stepped towards Aunt Bess. It was clear she intended to hug Aunt Bess, but the minute she was within breathing distance, Aunt Bess said, "Thea! Tell me you got this sour smell on that long ride. Tell me that you ain't start out like this from home."

My new kin, whose name I just found out was Thea, stopped. The expected, hoped for hug hung suspended in the air. I felt bad for her. I know what it's like to want something as badly as she seemed to have wanted one of Aunt Bess' hugs and not get it. Aunt Bess noticed. She opened her arms. Thea and all her scents rushed into Aunt Bess' arms. I looked at my kin two or three time removed on my grandfather's mother's side and realized that like me, she'd been yearning, not just for someone to hold her, but for someone to want to hold her.

Standing there and watching her try to transfer all her wanting into Aunt Bess, I felt really, really sorry. I was sorry to see a grown woman so hungry for holding. I was sorry that I had had all those bad thoughts 'bout her. Then I felt sorry that when she'd first said we were kin, I was sorry that I had something joining her with me. Looking at this hungry woman now, I was glad in a way that I couldn't get away even if I wanted to; she was kin. Kin was kin. It don't really matter how many times they are removed from where you are. You didn't get a chance to throw kin back and pick ones you weren't goin' to be ashamed of.

Just as Aunt Bess' hands had put me out of her folds, she did the same to my new kin. As my new two or three times removed kin stepped back from Aunt Bess, I could feel her longing. It reached back and hugged Aunt Bess just a little longer.

"Thea, if I didn't love you or if you weren't kin to me, I won't have let you near me and God knows not hold onto me and press yourself into me the way you just did." Smiling a little, Aunt Bess said, "Now, even though I can't see one, I know you done stain the front of my clothes just as if you was wearing a dress made out of soot."

"Bess, I'm sorry." Thea looked as though she wanted to cry. Aunt Bess noticed. "Don't cry, Thea, I goin' thank God with you that you was able to get away from that stupid fool. So we just goin' get on our way. Come, Gina Pearl, this be your kin. Both of you in the same boat: she running from a man and you from the memories of one, now we all in the same man-less boat, so let's go and row this boat together to a better shore."

Aunt Bess turned to go and stopped. She turned and said, "Gina Pearl, I can see you got that travelling case there. What 'bout you, Thea? You got anything?"

"No, Bess. I just took me and ran first chance I got." Thea looked like she was getting ready to cry again.

Aunt Bess said, "Girl, you ain't got time for all that crying you fixing to do. Them tears inside of you goin' have to wait 'till you find your own two feet and standing firm on 'em. So let them tears go back to some place or somebody who can afford them. In your situation, you can't afford them. So treat it like something you want bad, but ain't got the money for. Walk 'way from 'em. Now come. Follow me."

Having said that, Aunt Bess picked up my bag and started to walk. I, with all my memories, and Thea, with all that was trapped in her clothes, spirit, and soul, followed too. One of Aunt Bess' church people had come with her to fetch us. Thea gave Aunt Bess the address where she was goin' to be staying. We would, according to Aunt Bess, drive there first, see Thea settled, and then we would go to her house: home. The woman, Mrs. Mornings, as Thea called her, didn't really know Thea. Thea told Aunt Bess that the woman was an aunt of a distant cousin of a distant cousin of hers on her mother's grandmother's cousin's side.

By the time Thea got done explaining how distant the woman was related to her, she sounded like the woman was holding on to our kin-tree by the thinnest of threads. A bit more distant and the woman wouldn't be kin to us at all. All Aunt Bess said was, "Ain't never heard of her but if she feels more like kin to you than me, then I'm to goin' see to it that you get to her safe."

Thea was quiet after Aunt Bess said that. It was as if she was thinking 'bout what Aunt Bess had said 'bout her feeling that this very far removed distant kin was more kin to her than to Aunt Bess. There was no doubt how Aunt Bess got onto our family tree in the first place. Aunt Bess was my Momma's sister; that wasn't far removed at all. Actually, she wasn't even removed. We all knew where she was on our family tree, in the center holding all of us up and on. As Thea dragged her feet behind, it was clear she was wondering if she'd hurt Aunt Bess' feeling with what she'd said. Aunt Bess turned to her and said, "Child, this is New York; you don't have time to be second guessing what you done. You want to go to this woman house and I said I'd take you to her so let's go. If you're thinking 'bout how I might be feeling, let me tell you how I'm feeling. I'm feeling that you grown. I'm feeling that you needed to get away from that hell you was living in and if this woman can give you a slice of anything better than what you had, go and get your slice of better and stop worrying 'bout my feelings. I'm your kin and always goin' be your kin."

Thea looked at Aunt Bess and it was clear that she was glad Aunt Bess had said all that she had. We walked on in silence but it was different. This silence had a kind of peace about it. When we got outside the man pointed to his car, and with as much pride as if he was introducing his new baby to the whole family, he said, "That, ladies, is what you call a Ford Model T Sedan. Ain't she a beauty? Had me a Tin Lizzie back in '27 but my heart stayed with the old girl and I had to go back and get her. She was my first car and my first love. She 'bout four years old now, but I'm keeping her, we know each other. She starts real easy for her papa." Touching the car as if it he expected it to smile, purr, or turn over for him to scratch its underside, he added, "Don't you, baby?"

I looked at the jet-black car and then back at Aunt Bess' friend and I could see that he was waiting on somebody to say something so I said, "It's a very beautiful car; never seen one so pretty and shiny 'fore now."

He smiled and when he turned to open the door, Aunt Bess looked at me, smiled, and winked. No sooner were we in the car than the rain that I'd left behind in Promise Land caught up to me and started afresh. The man, whose name I didn't quite get nor got a feeling from Aunt Bess that I had to know or remember, drove slowly. He said, "This is New York city. A Negro with a fancy car like this takes his time. Don't want nobody stopping me thinking that this car too beautiful for me to have."

We arrived at Mrs. Mornings' house on Hart Street. Aunt Bess walked to the door with Cousin Thea. She said she wanted to see who she was leaving Thea with. As soon as they were at the door, which was on the same level as the street, Aunt Bess pressed the bell. The door opened and from the car I heard, "Jesus Christ, girl, you come all the way from Promise Land stinking like that? Child, that smell ain't no promise, it threatening to kill somebody, God damn."

I heard as Cousin Thea started to cry. Then I heard Aunt Bess' deep voice filling the spaces in between Cousin Thea's sniffles.

"What kind of unfeeling unchristian heathen woman are you? You don't get off a hello, a how are you, come in out the rain, or nothing before you insult the girl; ain't like you don't know of her circumstances."

"She stinks!"

"She may stink, but you don't have to be so heartless. She got circumstances that put her in this condition, but that don't make her less human. She's human like anybody else with feelings."

"Feelings or no feelings, she stinks and she should have thought 'bout coming to somebody's house smelling like that."

"You may be the aunt of some distant cousin of hers on her father's mother's side or whatever mistake put you on our family tree, but from the way you acting towards this girl, I know for sure that you ain't no kin or can be no kin to me. I ain't goin' stand here and let you speak such unkind words to Thea. Now, if you taking Thea in, take her in and do so with Christian kindness or me and Thea goin' over to Chauncey Street where kindness lives in every corner of my house. Now what you goin' do? What it goin' be?"

The aunt of the distant cousin looked from Aunt Bess to a now crying Thea and she replied in a loud brittle voice, "She can go with you 'cause I guess you use to stink smelling people. Maybe more than that kindness you mention living over at your house; maybe some stink, like your Negro ass living over there too."

The sound of Cousin Thea's crying reached the car. I started to cry with her, but the sound of Aunt Bess' voice now raised to booming drowned out Thea's crying and put a stop to the tears I was getting ready to cry for my new cousin. Aunt Bess' voice was a little loud before but when the woman said that she had a stink ass, Aunt Bess' voice started to explode. It sounded like thunder was being dragged down the sidewalk by a giant.

"Miss, if I weren't a woman working hard on my religion, I would tell you to kiss my Negro ass. It ain't stink now, but I'm sure once you put your mouth near it, it will stink from all the hate living in your soul. I would also tell you to kiss Thea's big fat stinking Negro ass. We know her ass stink, but that's only goin' be for a short while. Miss, I'm a sinner saved by grace and so I know it would be unchristian and un-ladylike for me to tell you that you are a cold unfeeling bitch. You are lucky, woman, that I'm working on making heaven my final destination or I would truly tell you what a poor excuse you are for a human. And that you and your thin, ugly nappy hair, wide nose-self can go back in your house 'cause even if you changed your mind, I won't let Thea step foot in your place.

"Thea goin' fix up right fine with a bath and a change of clothes, but you're goin' to stay the same: an old ugly dried up crispy bitch with nothing but hate running through your veins. Now, try to control yourself from wanting to run and kiss our big Negro asses when we turn to walk 'way from you and your ugliness."

Aunt Bess' church friend didn't even flinch as Aunt Bess' thunderous voice rattled the glass in his car. It was as if he'd heard Aunt Bess tell someone before about all the reason she couldn't cuss them as she cussed them like a sailor. As I sat there with my mouth hanging open, Aunt Bess said, "Come, Thea. Let's get away from this passageway to hell before her evil sucks us in."

As soon as Aunt Bess said, 'suck us in', I heard a loud slam. The cousin that was far removed from our kin tree had slammed her door and broke the thin thread that was keeping her on our family tree. She fell and rolled away into some unreachable ditch where, if Aunt Bess had anything to do with it, she was goin' to stay forever. Even if she crawled out and found her way back to our tree, she would never have hands long enough to reach even the lowest branch. The best she could ever hope for was to sit in the grass growing in the shaded area of our family tree and that was providing Aunt Bess didn't see her.

Aunt Bess and Cousin Thea walked back to the car. Neither said anything. Cousin Thea took a deep breath. I kept waiting to hear her let it out. I gave up waiting. We drove the few blocks to Aunt Bess' house in silence. The rain, which hadn't stopped falling since we left Mrs. Mornings' house, started falling harder. It was as if in her anger at Mrs. Mornings, Aunt Bess had grabbed hold of the cloud holding the rain with her thunder-loud voice and had shook out more rain than the good Lord Himself had intended.

Not only was it raining harder, it was also a different kind of rain. It was cold and damp. It made me want to cry but Aunt Bess was not one for tears; that much I'd learned from watching her with Cousin Thea. I kept my tears and thoughts to myself.

We stepped out of the car and the cold September rain instantly soaked through my clothes and made its way to my skin. I started to think the heavens seemed to be raining down sadness. God and the angels had to be feeling what I was feeling. We were all sad that I had to leave Promise Land. I started to cry and since Cousin Thea hadn't stopped since we left Mrs. Mornings' house, we were both now standing in the rain, looking at Aunt Bess and crying. She was watching us, and when it didn't look like we were goin' to stop or move, she said, "What the two of you think goin' get solved by ya'll crying and standing here making the rain soak through our clothes?"

Aunt Bess wasn't really looking for an answer. I think she just wanted us to know that she didn't plan on standing around in the rain with us. When we didn't move, she said, "One of the two of you make a move. Brother Theodore ain't got time to be standing around in the rain with the two of you. Now he got us here and his wife is home waiting on him. So the two of you figure out how ya'll goin' stop all this crying."

Brother Theodore, who hadn't said anything since he'd spoken about his car earlier, said good night to Aunt Bess and us, got back in his car, and waited. Aunt Bess looked and saw him in the car and said, "Here in New York, a Negro man not goin' drive 'way and leave no Negro woman just standing in her yard so ya'll make a move so Brother Theodore can go on home to his wife. He ain't goin' drive off from in front this house 'till we inside."

Aunt Bess stepped to the gate, pushed it, and stepped through. She didn't look to see if we were following: she knew we were. We stepped into the yard. She put her foot on the first step and then she stopped. She looked at the two of us and said, "It ain't like you all come on no special holiday. You're here, Gina Pearl, 'cause you pregnant and my sister, Etta Pearl, is stupid; picking up some ole' ass man to marry. What woman at her age, or any age for that matter, would throw 'way her only girl child over some old wrinkle up piece of man? What woman does a thing like that to her pregnant child?"

Although Aunt Bess was mad at Momma, I had enough good sense not to open my mouth and say anything 'gainst Ma 'cause in no time at all, Aunt Bess would be reminding me 'bout the respect that's due Ma. When she was done venting, she turned to Cousin Thea and said, "And, Thea you here 'cause you had to run from your man. So the two of you stop with the crying and come so that Brother Theodore can drive way from in front my house."

That was it. She was done. She started up the steps again. We followed in silence. Aunt Bess reached the door. After unlocking the door, she stepped in. Again we followed. I stopped crying but Cousin Thea couldn't seem to get herself to stop. Aunt Bess stepped back out and waved. I heard the car start up and drive away. Aunt Bess was right about Brother Theodore being a good Negro man. He didn't drive away until he was sure we were safe. We were safe. I felt it in my soul.

Chapter 4

Arriving in Bedford Stuyvesant, Brooklyn

As soon as we stepped into Aunt Bess' house, Cousin Thea tried to get her tears to stop. She wasn't fully crying but she was sniffling. I'd stopped and wasn't 'bout to start again. Aunt Bess' words had dried my tears. With only one of us crying, Aunt Bess paid Cousin Thea's crying no mind and soon I didn't either because of the warmth and smells that were all over the house. Cousin Thea's smells were no match for these smells. The smell of biscuits, yams, ham, and something else I couldn't figure out rushed at me and wrapped itself all around me.

I started looking around at the beautifully carved wood framing the door and the curved polished banister leading up the stairs. I couldn't take my eyes off the flowered cloth on the chairs. The chairs were made; it seemed, from the same polished wood as the banister. The wood was polished 'till it looked like there were squares of white here and there on them but that was just the reflection of the light bouncing off the polished wood. There were big thick pillows on the chairs, a fireplace that looked like it could just warm your whole heart, and on all the walls there were framed pictures everywhere.

Aunt Bess spoke and stopped my gazing. She said, "Now, Thea, I hadn't planned on you being here so I ain't fix a place for you so tonight, you goin' sleep on the extra bed in the room where Gina Pearl goin' be, and tomorrow we goin' work on something more permanent for you. Now come. Follow me."

As we'd done since the bus station, we followed Aunt Bess as she walked us up the beautiful stairs with the shiny curved wooden banister and all its carved rails. It looked like I should be coming down it in a beautiful wedding dress and, there, waiting at the bottom would be Milton. There will never be a Milton waiting at the bottom of any stairs for me. He will be waiting at the top of some stairs for me someday but since I have to see about our child, him and those stairs, heaven's stairs, goin' have to wait. Right now, I couldn't right think about getting into heaven with Milton. I have a lot of living to do; death was not part of my living plans. I got my mind free of Milton and heaven and got back to admiring Aunt Bess' house. At the top of the stairs, the rail continued down toward a wall where it looked like it just kept right on goin' even though you couldn't see it any more. Then my mind said, "That's just like heaven, you know it's there; you just can't see it." I smiled inside; it was painful but comforting to think of Milton in heaven.

Aunt Bess said, "Over here is the bathroom for this floor, you two goin' share it. Walking over to a room where the door was closed, she said, without opening the door, "This room here is where I does my sewing." We walked passed. It didn't matter at the moment what that room looked like inside or why Aunt Bess didn't open the door and let us see it. We walked over to another room, which wasn't too far from her sewing room. This room was almost as big as the room downstairs with all the beautiful furniture. It also had furniture but not near as pretty as the furniture downstairs. This looked a little older, but it was still pretty. There was a long chair that had one arm and a back. The back was uneven. It was high on the end where the arm was but lower on the other end, 'till it did like the banister that came up the stairs: it just stopped.

Right away, I wanted to be on that chair resting. It reminded me that I was tired. Aunt Bess, seeing where my attention was, said, "That chair that you staring so hard at is called a chaise lounge. When you start to work at the white women's houses, you'll see a lot of these chairs. You'll also see the white women wasting a lot of the precious time the good Lord have given them just lying there doin' nothing. They call that good waste of the Lord's time lounging."

Looking from Cousin Thea to me, she continued, "Neither one of you goin' have time to waste nothing the good Lord blesses you with. When the good Lord is ready for you all to have lounging time, He goin' make it 'cause everything got its own time; that's how the Lord works. Right now, this is the time for all three of us to be here together. Anyway, child, I'm getting ahead of myself. I just love the Lord for all that He's brought me through; setting up my time, fixing everything for me. Let me tell the two of you this; if the Lord sets your time, nothing can get in your way. The Lord, He has a time for everything and a purpose for everything. He might not have shown either of you yet what His plan is for you, but trust me; there are no mistakes in the Lord. Look what He says in Jeremiah 29:11: 'For I know the plans I have for you.' That's the Lord for you. He knows the plans He has for all of us. He just don't share those plans with us. You got to live and watch the Lord do His unfolding of all that He has in store for you. Live long enough and all will be made clear."

Aunt Bess stopped then raised her hands to the ceiling before continuing, "Lord, I thank you for bringing these two kinfolk of mine away from all that wasn't right for them and helping them to make their way safe to me. I ask you to bless them, Lord." She took her hands down and continued, "When the spirit moves you to do or say something you are to be obedient but 'fore you get me preaching a sermon with the two of you tired and hungry, let me finish this real quick tour so you all can get clean up and come get something hot in your stomach before we all go to bed.

"Now what was I saying before your staring at that chair took me down a different path? Yes, yes I remember. Over here is the sitting room for this floor, but it don't get use much since I got a right fine sitting room downstairs. It's here 'cause this is how I find it when I move in and so it be, but I guess, Gina Pearl, that you goin' be trying your hand at some lounging when you here by yourself; that's fine, just don't get too used to it 'cause soon as that baby gets its legs strong, you goin' out to work." Smiling she added, "So enjoy your white woman lounging time; it won't be for too long." We all smiled a little and following Aunt Bess, we walked away from the room.

She pushed a door. "In here is the room the two of you goin' share tonight." I stared inside the room almost a little scared to go in. I wasn't expecting nothing to be so beautiful. There were two beds. One was grand with four posts and a roof over it. The post holding the roof up over the bed had some fancy swirl goin' round and round all the way to the top, and when it reach the bed roof, it had a big ole' acorn sitting on the top. It was shining like Aunt Bess had used oil on it. There was a rug that looked like the first step you make on it you was goin' fall right in it was so thick.

"Don't you all just stand there, go on in. Look round and make yourselves comfortable. When you all get the travelling dust off come down to the kitchen and get something hot to eat." Cousin Thea started to say something and Aunt Bess told her, "Thea, I know you ain't got but the clothes on your back. Me and you 'bout the same size and if we ain't, tonight it ain't goin' matter none. I'll get you something fresh to put on don't fret yourself."

"Thank you, Bess. I didn't plan to be on your hands."

"You ain't on my hands. You is kin. Now go get cleaned up."

While Aunt Bess went to her room to get something for Cousin Thea to wear, I got some things out from my valise and went to the bathroom to bathe. Soon as I came out and while I dressed, Cousin Thea went in the bathroom. I finished putting my clothes on and went downstairs to join Aunt Bess to wait for her. When Cousin Thea came in the kitchen, I didn't recognize her. The stink that had been on her like a second skin was gone. She looked different. Aunt Bess announced, "Now that's the Thea I remember. I hope to Christ that I never see that woman that walked in here a little while ago."

Cousin Thea lowered her head and said, "Bess, she got washed down the drain just now. She gone."

"Good. Let's thank God for this food and eat." Aunt Bess blessed the food, thanked God for bringing us safe, and she also asked him to bless the baby I was having. Then she said, "Amen and pass me that dish of stewed beef."

Cousin Thea passed her the dish with the stewed beef. We ate well. Aunt Bess had made yams, stewed beef, boiled rice, string beans with great big pieces of pork fat, and ham hocks, there was candied yams, chunks and chunks of ham, and she'd fried enough chicken to feed everybody that had been on the bus a little while ago, Negro and white alike.

We ate and talked 'till Aunt Bess said, "Let's get up from this table and clean up these dishes. I got work in the morning and plenty figuring to do."

We helped Aunt Bess clean up and then we all walked slowly up the stairs. I don't remember nothing pass putting my head on the pillow. The next thing I know, the smell of bacon was pulling the covers off me and helping me to my feet. I smiled my first smile in a very long time.

Aunt Bess' voice came from downstairs, "This here ain't no hotel. Can't be wasting none of the Lord's Day. I got work to get to and the two of you got some figuring to do. Come."

I wasn't in Aunt's Bess' company a long time, but I'd figured out enough to know that Aunt Bess wasn't one for repeating herself. I knew I had to get downstairs and quickly, but I also had figured out there was no such thing as goin' to her table unwashed. I washed, dressed, and like the night before, was the first one in the kitchen.

That first dinner and breakfast became the way things were done from that day on. Aunt Bess cooked and either me or Cousin Thea cleaned up and put away the dishes. Before Aunt Bess went to her job, she showed Thea a room next to hers and the sitting room that was a storage room of sorts. She told Thea, "Thea, I got to go to work so today you and Gina Pearl make this room yours. You can put all those hatboxes in my room and the other things you all take down to the basement. Now don't just throw things every which way. Make them neat so I can find stuff when I start to look. Thea, if you want any of the clothes and things you find in here, take them; make them yours."

Cousin Thea's eyes filled with tears and it was clear she was goin' to cry again.

"Now don't go crying. That's goin' take more time than you got so dry 'em and start figuring how you goin' make this space your own. Today, I goin' ask 'bout work for you. If you lucky you goin' be working tomorrow." Thea smiled. The tears were gone.

Aunt Bess noticed. "That's all you got to do from now on. If you get the job, don't have too much talk for them white people. It's best if you just nod and smile. They goin' think you simple-minded and after a while, if all you doing is nodding and smiling, they goin' forget you there and just talk all their business 'round you. That, Thea, is your job when you at work. Learn from them, but don't ever look like you learning. Now do with that piece of advice what you will. Work calling me."

That day was the last day I had company in the house during the week. The next day, Cousin Thea went to a job that Aunt Bess got for her. As time passed and Aunt Bess was comfortable with the way I cooked and cleaned, —the housework and cooking became my work. By the time I started to show, we - Aunt Bess, Cousin Thea, and I - were family. Aunt Bess was in charge. She told us what she thought was best for the family and we did just that.

If either Cousin Thea or I started to talk 'bout Promise Land too much, Aunt Bess would bring us right back to Chauncey Street and remind us why we were here and not there. She was making us strong to stand on our own two feet. Cousin Thea acted like she was a mother to me even though she was only ten years older than me. In her free time, and there wasn't a lot of that since she worked six, sometimes seven days a week, she was knitting something either for me or the baby.

I learned over time from Cousin Thea about her man Crawford. To hear Cousin Thea tell it, she and Crawford had invented love and loving. I didn't want to hurt her feelings and tell her that I believed both of those things started with Milton and me, so I let her talk. I didn't have to say anything that would hurt Cousin Thea's feelings since it seemed as if Crawford had forgotten himself about hurting her feelings. He'd forgotten all the good and beautiful things they done to get to the point where she was pregnant and her feelings were raw, fragile, and it was important that he not do or say anything to hurt them.

Cousin Thea and I were sitting in the upstairs drawing room; we'd taken to using it but mostly if Aunt Bess was at church, down town, or visiting one of her friends. Aunt Bess didn't mind. She said the whole house was for living and she was glad that we were doing just that by using the upstairs living room. I'm not sure what Cousin Thea and I were doing, but for sure it had something with our hands and had to involve some kind of needle. We'd been doing our needlework quietly for a while with the radio playing for itself, as Aunt Bess called it when the radio was on and nobody was really listening when Cousin Thea spoke suddenly. "Remember that day we met on the bus; well it had taken me just a few minutes to get on that bus, but I'd waited weeks. As a matter of fact; three… three weeks of hiding and not knowing if I'd be able to get on and get away."

"Hiding? Who or what were you hiding from?"

"The police and Crawford."

"But why?"

"Before you ask a thousand questions, I'm just goin' tell you and when I'm done with this telling, I'm not telling it again because to tell it means I have to live it again and I don't want to do that. Living what I went through, the year leading up to those three weeks no woman should have to live through. You see, if Crawford had gone to her, don't ask me who her is, I'm goin' tell you or its goin' come out in the telling anyway. If I'd never known, you know, never saw the way he was loving up on her, I would have gone on maybe suspecting; if I had even suspected, hurting if I felt hurt. I would have just gone on loving him, loving him, loving him, but he went to her.

"The 'her' was my cousin. She was more than three or four times removed on my father's side, and no I'm not goin' to say her name, her name isn't important. What's important to the telling of this is that she was a nasty stinking whore, cousin or no cousin. She was a stinking, nasty, slimy bitch of a whore.

I brought her to my house. I was the one. I brought her the first time and maybe a few times after that, but it was the rest of times when she was in my house that I didn't know about that changed the way things were for Crawford and me. I mean, you shouldn't have to worry about bringing kin home even if they are more than three or four times removed on your father's side. I brought her to our house but it was Crawford who brought her to our bedroom. He brought her and she, forgetting that she was my cousin more than three or four times removed on my father's side, climbed into our bed: mine and Crawford's. It was she who did the climbing into our bed; that was wrong."

Cousin Thea started to cry but I could see she didn't want any sympathy or questions and now that she'd started, she was goin' to tell it and like she said, be done with it once and for all. I watched her fighting with her tears and her memories. I waited.

"The house, bedroom, and bed were mine, ours. We'd done it all together. Him doing the Chitlin' Circuit... Crawford was some kinda good with the Blues and a saxophone. You ever heard of The Blue Sun Rays? That was Crawford, Sonny Blue, Ripping Charlie, and Smoking Camie, they called him that for what he could do with a piano... made them keys smoke, black as well as white."

Cousin Thea smiled when she said that. It was like she could see him playing that piano 'till it smoked. I didn't ask a thing. She wasn't waiting on me to ask.

"They had a song called, 'The Kind of Girl That Men Forget.' Oh that was one lonesome blues song. I remember the first verse, it went like this, '*She's just the kind of girl that men forget they'll use her and leave her and never have regrets. She's just the kind of girl that men forget 'cause baby, baby, baby she make it so easy to please her and leave her. Forgetting her is easy 'cause you're not her only one...anyone can have her. She doesn't make it to your heart 'cause leaving her is easy...'cause she's just the kind of girl that men forget.'*

"Remembering that song is making me forget why I'm telling you this. I met Crawford when he came through Promise Land. I'd heard about The Blue Sun Rays and the fellow Crawford that could blow so sweet, angels lined up to sing back-up. Anyway, one Saturday night I went down to Miss Mavis' Sugar Spot where they were playing and I walked in and he was up there, girl, blowing that saxophone like I never heard nobody blow before and when he took that thing from his lips to catch a breath, he saw me and he smiled. Quick, quick he smile and went right back on to blowing and in that quick smile, every trouble I ever had left me. That was it: 'fore Crawford and the Blue Sun Rays were done playing I was his woman. He got down from the little platform they were on, walked over to me, and claimed me. He and The Blue Sun Rays might be popular with the song, 'The Kind Of Girls Men Forget' but I knew from the way Crawford was looking at me that he wasn't forgetting me.

"He didn't. Soon... every time he made it to Promise Land and was at Miss Mavis' Sugar Spot, he would want me to come and listen. I always went—never missed one night. One night after he was done playing, he said, 'I needs a place to stay when I come through.' I was fixing to tell him that he couldn't stay at my place 'cause my place was my momma's place when he said, 'I gots me some money, how 'bout you and me get a house so this way when I come through, I gots a place to call home.'

"I smiled. We got that place and while he was gone, I fixed it up and he had a place to call home every time he came through. On them nights when he wasn't doing the circuit, he'd sit on the porch and just blow that saxophone for me. The night critters loved it and I swear, even the lightning bugs came more and more to the porch when he sat in the swing just blowing our blues away."

"Smiling, Cousin Thea continued, "Now don't think all we did was sit on that porch and swing or blow saxophone for the night critters. Oh no we loved, a lot, hard and often. It was Crawford who said that I put the most steel ever in his manhood. That was our own word for what we did. Sundays when Crawford was home, we'd go down to the Baptist church down the road. Crawford would wait 'till Ole Reverend Sin-No-More, that wasn't his name but Crawford called him that because he said he remembered when Cuthbert Plumber, that was his real last name, was one of the biggest, lying, cheating whores around. But, girl, one day Cuthbert fell in the river. He was fishing, caught a real big catfish and when he tried to pull it in, it fought him fierce and dragged him in. Nobody was there with him so he struggled as much as he could with that catfish and when he realized that the fish was bent on drowning him, he gave up and made his way out. The minute he was able to stand up, he told everyone around that because of the catfish trying to drown him and failing, he knew it was the work of the Lord.

"Everybody that knew him then let him keep what he said he'd found in the river: the Lord and religion. A lot of men were happy they didn't have to worry about him stealing their women, cheating them at cards, or hearing his thousand and one lies about how he was running bootleg liquor for Al Capone anymore.

"But anyway, I was saying Crawford would wait 'till old Reverend Sin-No-More was sweating and spitting at the mouth and getting ready to climb into the rafters and then he'd lean over, squeeze my hand, and say, 'Tee Tee, I got the steel and it's a lot of steel, girl. I can't wait to get you home.' Once he said that, he'd pick up the bible, hand it to me like he needed help holding it, and then right there in the presence of the Lord, he'd take that bible and put it in his lap right on top of all that steel. Girl, more than once I would let him press that bible down on my hand and yes Lord, right there, I would slide the back of my fingers over his steel. People all around would hear either me or Crawford, as a moan would escape and they would think that it had something to do with Reverend Sin-No-More, but I knew that it was Crawford and all that sweet feeling steel.

"Gina, after that I wouldn't hear another word the preacher had to say; all I could think about was rushing home. Don't think we didn't and once we got in the house, girl, all his sweet steel was mine. Then we would eat our supper and when the sun go down, we'd sit on the porch, talk, he'd drink a beer, and I'd shell us some boiled peanuts. We both loved boiled peanuts. I mostly did the shelling and while I shelled, he'd sip his beer and sing me a whole mess of blue songs. We didn't eat them as I shelled them… we'd let them pile up for later.

"When later came and Crawford was done with his beer and the blues, I would sit in his arms and he'd tell me how much he loved me as we ate the shelled peanuts. Crawford loved me a fierce kind of love. Every time he said he loved me, I felt it in my belly. It was real and true. It was a pure love. I loved Crawford and he loved me back. He really did.

"Then she came. It's not like she came outta thin air. She was always around somewhere 'cause she was kin, but at first I didn't notice 'cause she was so poor. You know the kind of poor where even though you poor yourself, you feel sorry for them. Well, she was that kind of poor. I thought she came looking for kin, but I didn't know she'd come with her poor slimier than boiled okra self, looking for a man: any man. My Crawford was there, getting regular steel in his manhood and me, unable to take it now 'cause all that running home from church to take the steel outta his manhood had put a child in me. The baby was sitting real low and 'cause he was so big and strong, he was hurting me and I was afraid that the baby would get its head knocked in and fall out.

"At first, I didn't know why Crawford stopped begging or making himself happy just to rub his steel on my legs or anywhere near my 'Miss Mary', I called it that. I was so busy being pregnant I didn't even notice when Crawford started changing towards me. I would wait at night for him to come to bed and rub my belly, talk to my belly, or sit and sing the blues, but he didn't come and when he did, he didn't want to do none of the things that made us Crawford and Thea.

"I would cry and miss him but that cousin was there. She had taken to being around a lot. She was being more than a cousin far removed to me; she was being my friend. I was happy. She was there for me, doing things for me, gaining my trust, and I would talk to her 'bout how Crawford was changing and how much his changing was hurting me and making me miss him. She would listen and tell me not to worry 'cause she was there. I stopped worrying 'cause she was there. I started believing that she was staying around to help me once my baby was born. I was wrong. She'd gained my trust and taken my man and his steel from me.

"Then three weeks before my baby was due, I came home from visiting my Momma only to find that cousin, who was more than three or four times removed on my father's side, in my house, in my bed. To make matters worse, if not seeing them together naked wasn't bad enough, but the nasty cousin was on my side of the bed and Crawford was stroking and loving this far-removed cousin better and, it looked, from where I was standing, harder and sweeter than he'd ever loved me.

"I screamed and cussed. I tried to drag her wicked whoring behind out my bed and because I screamed, cussed, and tried to hit at that naked cousin who wasn't far enough removed to think twice about climbing into my bed with my man, Crawford got distracted by my noise and lost the steel in his manhood. Losing the steel, not my carrying on made him madder than hell. He jumped up from the bed naked and angry 'cause he was so close to claiming his sweetness and I'd made him lose it he said, with my foolish carrying on for nothing bullshit screaming. He kicked, punched, and shoved me trying to get me outta the bedroom.

"Because I was pushing against him trying to get to that far-removed cousin to beat her and he was shoving to me to keep me from getting to her and kick her in all her parts, I fell. My baby, who was already sitting low and now was in position waiting for the right moment to crown and come into the world, just dropped out right there in my bedroom where we'd made it. My stinking, slimy, whoring, naked, far-removed cousin started screaming and shouting at Crawford, to stop kicking and shoving me. I think she was remembering then that she was my far-removed cousin, but she was forgetting that she was naked in my house, in my bedroom, on my bed, and with my man. Crawford finally stopped kicking me because that cousin that should have been further removed than she was finally got him to see that the baby was out.

"The baby, a boy, lived for almost a day because Crawford, who hadn't noticed in his anger that the baby was coming out had missed, when he went as he said later to stomp some sense into my blasted stupid ass. He had, instead, stomped on the head of my almost out baby. The blow to the head was too much for the little baby so he died; killed by Crawford, his own father.

When I got on my feet after the birth and death of my baby, Crawford beat me for making him, as he said, kill his own child because never mind the fact that I was one big-boned bitch, I was a weak woman and mother who couldn't hold on to or protect his baby from being hurt as I was supposed to. More than Crawford beating me each time he saw my belly without his baby in it. More than him beating me if the sun came up on the day he felt it should rain, or beating me 'cause he felt like some sunshine on the day it rained. More than all of that, what hurt me the most hurt I've ever had in my whole life was when the unmerciful beatings stopped, and Crawford moved that stinking whore of a cousin into our house to live so that he could climb on her each time the steel rose in his manhood.

"You know, Gina Pearl, its one thing for a man, goin' through whatever men go through when his woman is making his baby and can't take the shoving and poking for him to go and find someone else to ease his tension. But it's another thing that would make them just up and not love the woman they couldn't wait to spend their days and nights with. That's one thing and it's a hurting thing, but it's one thing for a woman, same woman as you with all the same wants and wishes as you, to see nothing wrong with a man telling her to come live in his house where he live with a woman, and not just any woman but your kin… three or four times removed on your father's side and you come. It don't matter how far you are removed… you should think about how that woman goin' feel 'bout you bringing yourself and setting up house with her man in her house while she still there. What kind of heartless sluttish whoring woman would do a thing like that? What kind… the kind like my cousin; a stinking whore. She was the kind that made Jezebel and Delilah look like nuns.

"Gina, each time the steel came up in Crawford's manhood, and it was more often than it used to be with me, Crawford would make me go outside. Outside of my own house, Gina! Outside of the place where he used to sing me the blues and blow that saxophone 'till the lightning bugs would just sit on the porch, listen and flash their tiny lights to match his blowing. Gina, I had to wait outside and it didn't matter if the sun was up, if it was raining, or if it was a minute pass midnight; I had to go outside 'till he and she, my cousin too far removed from good judgment and pride to care 'bout how I might be feeling, were done.

"It was always the same, 'Bitch, get your big-boned, almost big as a man, fat couldn't hold onto my baby, stinking like old hot grease ass outside 'fore the sight of you make me lose the steel in my manhood.'

"This went on 'till a few weeks before the morning I got on the bus. A few weeks before that morning, I got up and knew I didn't love Crawford anymore nor did I care even the least amount about that woman. I also knew that I'd had enough of the two of them treating me like I didn't have any feelings. Like he didn't kick me and make me lose my baby because of her. I made a decision and once I made it, I fixed it in my heart to accept whatever happened to me after I was done."

I wanted to ask Cousin Thea what that decision was, but one cross-eyed look from her told me to shut up. I shut up and she went on.

"One afternoon, I prepared some things, and then the next morning, I went to our kitchen and poured all the old grease I'd been saving up in tins into a big old skillet. I lit the stove and watched as the oil got hot—almost to the point of boiling. In another pot, I had some grits cooking. I let the grits cook 'till it was bubbling and spitting all over the stove. I looked at the bubbling and spitting grits and it was then I realized where I was with my anger and hatred. I'd let my anger and hatred simmer and stew these past few weeks and now it was way past simmering. It was bubbling and spitting and I had to let it out or burst. I wasn't about to give them the satisfaction of watching me burst.

I hurried and poured the mixture in a big galvanized bucket where I'd been boiling enough water to scald a hog; if no hog was available, which was the case today, then my used-to-be man and a nasty whoring cousin who didn't mind taking the steel outta my used-to-be-man right in my own house and bedroom would have to do. The boiled water made an angry hiss when my bubbling anger and hatred got added to it. When the angry hiss of the grease and grits mixture settled down, I added in damn near a gallon of lye. The lye kicked up one stinking angry smell. I looked at all that bubbling and foaming stinking anger and hatred and I was satisfied. It would do the job, I wondered for a split-second how I was goin' to lift that big old galvanized bucket, with all that bubbling and hissing anger, and then I remembered that hateful nasty lie that Crawford had called me. He'd called me a big-boned, almost-big-as-a-man bitch and right in front of that far removed cousin and she laughed. Remembering the way she'd laughed at me, I grabbed the handle and lifted the bucket. It felt no heavier to me than one of those bottles of milk that I would never, because of Crawford and that nasty whoring bitch of a cousin, get a chance to feed my baby. I walked out the kitchen.

"I tipped to the bedroom.

"Listened for a second to make sure that nothing had changed. Satisfied that nothing had, I eased the door open made two steps towards the bed; I didn't look to see who was on top, if they were on their sides, or how they were. I wasn't there to watch the love they were making. I was there because of my dead baby, my hurt, shame, and most of all, the non-stop beating that Crawford was now giving me. I aimed the bucket in the direction where the screams and sounds of passion were coming from and because I am a big-boned bitch, I was able to easily raise and pitch the near full-to-the-brim bucket of hissing bubbling anger and hatred at the bed. I wasn't sure how much of my simmering revenge got on my far-removed cousin, but I knew that Crawford, my used-to-be man won't be getting no steel in his manhood no time soon.

"Just as my bubbling anger and hatred was sailing through the air, Crawford was turning around to find another position to put that too far-removed cousin in. His manhood, with all the steel in it and covered in passion that wasn't mine, came in full contact with the anger, hatred, and simmering revenge floating through the air. He had so much steel in his manhood that upon contact with my thick simmering revenge, it parted it in two with its hardness, just the way he'd parted my woman business so many times.

"But now, after it had parted my simmering revenge, it went from being a great big old blue-black piece of thickly veined steel tree-trunk-looking piece of manhood covered with that nasty cousin's passion, to a big old bouncing up and down piece of blue-black flesh dressed in thick grits, lye, and boiling old grease and revenge. The head was wearing a wig made of hot grits and a chunk of hot lye had landed dead smack in its eye, stopping it. It would never again be able to find its way to anybody's sweetness 'cause it had come with an eye and not a nose; what a poor choice his manhood had made. Eye or nose, none of that would have mattered; steel would never be part of his manhood again."

Cousin Thea took a deep breath and stopped talking when she realized I couldn't picture that much hate and anger. She let the breath out and said, "That nasty woman what was supposed to be my cousin three times removed on my father's side. She was supposed to care about me. I was her kin. Kin don't do that to kin. Her coming to my house, into my bedroom, and laying down on my side of the bed to ride my man 'till the steel went out his manhood gave me the right. 'Till she came along, he was my man and all the steel and sweetness in his manhood was mine; more than anything else, he loved me. Crawford was my … Gina, he was my saxophone-playing, blues-singing, steel-getting man. Crawford was my man and we, me, he, and the baby; we were goin' to be a family. A family Gina… a family."

Thea looked as though she was goin' to break down and cry. I wanted to know the rest but I wasn't goin' to push her, never mind how much I wanted to ask, "What happened next?" I didn't have to; Cousin Thea stopped her tears and continued her story.

"I heard them hollering and calling on the Lord, but this time it wasn't sweetness that had them. This time them was calling on him 'cause the water was burning their skin, the lye was eating through what holes the water was making, the grits was sticking to the holes the water and lye was making, and the oil was cooking the rest of them.

"I shut the bedroom door fast. Locked it and ran. As I ran, I heard them screaming, hollering, and banging on the door to get out. I knew them wasn't getting out no time soon 'cause the day before, when neither she nor Crawford was home, I'd gone and nailed the window shut from outside. As I ran down the street, I saw another cousin, he wasn't as far-removed as the cousin who was now cooking and peeling with Crawford back in my bedroom. I told him what I'd just done and he agreed that Crawford and the whore, who was also his far-removed cousin, deserved it. He drove me to his house and hid me.

Him and his momma got word to Mrs. Mornings, who was his far-removed distant cousin's aunt, telling her that I needed a place to be for a while. She said it was OK but since his wife was a woman only half my size, there was no clothes for me to change into. That's why I was in that dress for more than a couple of days and nights: three weeks. I was in that dress for three whole frightening weeks. It was fear of what I'd done sweated into that dress that made me smell the way I did, but I couldn't care 'bout how I was smelling I was hiding, waiting to get away and that was all that mattered."

"What happened to Crawford and your far-removed distant cousin?"

"I don't know, but those days of hiding was the worst for me 'cause if the police had find me, I was goin' rot way in jail for attempting to kill them."

"But you didn't attempt to kill them, did you?"

Cousin Thea looked at me and with her face straight as a razor blade, she said, "Yes."

We never talked about it again.

Chapter 5

Living With Aunt Bess

I liked Chauncey Street, not because of the framed houses with their porches and front yard gardens that started my block and, for a long time, became a constant reminder of the house I lived in with Ma back in Promise Land. Nor the way the large trees lined the blocks, buffering the noise from Fulton Street, or because fine upstanding Negro people lived there. None of that was why I liked Chauncey Street. I liked it because of the park; Robert Fulton Park. It separated my house from the rest of the world. It was my sanctuary.

During the day when I was alone, I would go there and let my mind drift back to those carefree days with Milton. I never cried because my memories of him were too beautiful. I missed him, but our child, a sign that we'd been together and that we had truly loved each other, was growing. This child was proof that I'd known love; a beautiful, unending love, even with Milton dead. I didn't have Milton but I had the park; there in the quiet of the afternoon, Milton lived and our love in the form of our child continued to grow. Milton was gone, but I hadn't lost him completely. Once our child was born, he would live again.

At night, when Aunt Bess and Cousin Thea came home from work was another reason I loved Chauncey Street. Aunt Bess made living on Chauncey Street the best place in the world to be because she talked about my family. Not just about when she and Ma were little, but the family years and years before even her and Ma's great-great-grandma Cornbread was born.

Once dinner was over and the dishes were cleaned up and put away, Aunt Bess would tell us about what the women in our family went through. Most nights, the story started the same way. "Gina Pearl (Aunt Bess never called me Promise), - if you think my ways are hard, then you need to make your way over the roads that the women in this family walked."

"Aunt Bess, I can't walk over where they've already walked. That road already closed off to me."

"Child, I don't mean it in the true sense of walking, but it's because they walked it we can sit in this house, have work to go to and even, schools we can go to if we want. Child, you with a baby growing in you and no man is nothing new or different to this family. You ain't but one lil' fine link in the chain that make up the long line of women in this family. But, Gina Pearl, I want you to know this: you ain't goin' be the link that breaks the chain. We done suffered too much hardship to let this chain break with you."

"Aunt Bess, I ain't planning on breaking no link, but Ma didn't ever really talk 'bout our family chain."

"That was something 'bout my sister I never fully understand. She and I ain't that far removed from what happen to us for her to choose not to tell you, her only girl child, the hell that the women in this family done suffer. I never did understand that 'bout your Ma."

"Aunt Bess, I shouldn't have said that Ma never talked 'bout it. Ma talked 'bout it but not in a way that you could get a good idea of how to learn from what they went through. Ma said it was, but wasn't her job to go on repeating some old-timey story that according to her, our Great-Great-Great-grand-nana Milkweed, I think she said, Milkweed, I'm not sure, had lived through."

"You see, Gina, that's where your Momma was wrong. Your ma ought to have held on to that story stronger and told it more and you won't be sitting here trying to remember your great-great-grand-nana's name. It was Milkweed. But that is your Momma. On the days when things were bright, she was only interested in good things, but on the days when it looked like every bad thing that could happen was happening, she always got to lamenting 'bout all the terrible, terrible things our grand-nana and those slaves that were in our family 'fore us had gone through."

I laughed a little laugh and answered, "I know what you mean, Aunt Bess, because on those God-Forsaken-Days, as Momma called them, she would talk and I, always anxious to hear the old-timey stories, listened hard. Whatever Ma told me I made sure it took root in my heart."

"But did your Ma tell you what Cornbread told her daughter, Milkweed?"

"She told her something special?"

"By the very fact that you asked that question, I know your ma ain't fully told you the story of our people."

"Well, I know that there was a lot of suffering."

"Well, that almost goes without saying if you was nigger back in them days, but do you know what drove this family?"

"Drove us where, Aunt Bess?"

"Child, what is wrong with that sister of mine? She ain't told you nothing at all. I'm goin' make it my business that you get a full understanding of what drove our people then and why it should drive you now. I'm goin' take my time and when I done, you goin' see that this family get what my momma's great-nana felt was rightfully ours. Once you get it, you got to promise me that you never goin' let go of our history or of telling why the women in this family should be through suffering by now. One person slipping on a family history is all it takes for everybody to go back to the place they already left. I got your promise, Gina Pearl?"

I could see that Aunt Bess was waiting on me to give her my promise. I looked at her and said, "I promise you, Aunt Bess, that I ain't goin' let what happened to us die with me."

"You see, Gina Pearl, everything has its time. This is your time to hear for real what happened to your kin. Nothing don't happen 'fore God's time. You see, God knew that as long as you stayed on in Promise Land with your momma that you was never goin' hear the full story. He needed you here in this house with me. It's sad that you had to go and lose your man, but God got a way of working everything out in His time. He wanted you and here and as Queen Esther said, 'For such a time as this and if I perish, I perish.'"

"Perish, Aunt Bess?"

"You ain't goin' perish none, girl. That's just my way of letting you know that even bible women had to make hard choices. Queen Esther's goin' into a husband, the king, without him asking her to come into his chambers was a big risk she was taking, but she didn't have a choice. Her people, the Jews, were depending on her, same way the rest of the women in this family goin' depend on you to tell them what happen. So no, you ain't goin' perish, but you can't let the story of us perish even if you perish."

I said nothing else. I sat where I could give Aunt Bess my full attention. She settled herself better in her chair and once satisfied that Cousin Thea and I were ready to listen, she started.

Book Two

Momma Mae
1760 – Unknown
and
Lil' Mae
1796 – 1813

Chapter 6

Lil' Mae and Momma Mae

"What happened before Great-Great-Great-Grand-nana, Lil' Mae and her people on the reservation is still a mystery to this family, but we know what happened to the women of this family starting with her.

"The men were mostly not around. I think the last man that stayed around was Great–Great-Great-Grand-Poppa Molasses and that was as long as the white people let him. If they'd let him, Great-Great-Great-Grand-Poppa Molasses would have stayed with Great-Great-Great-Grand-Momma Cornbread 'till they both turned into dust. Neither of them had anything to do with them being parted, but when he could, he found a way to join them back together again. I'll tell you 'bout that when the time comes. Anyway, even without men, the women in my family never let go of their wanting. It was always the wanting of book learning that changed things for us; all the time.

"Somewhere, when this country was digging deeper and deeper in slavery and planting, reaping, and selling whatever crops the white man could get to grow off the strength, sweat, and blood of nigger people; found, bought, or sold, that's when the history of our family started. Because of all this buying and selling, we didn't have simple names. We had names like Beaufords, Litchfield, and Breckenshaw."

I'd never heard that name before and without thinking, I asked, "Breckenshaw?"

"Yes, Breckenshaw, but it weren't none of the women in this family with that name. But if I tell you 'bout that, you goin' have me jumping all over this story and make me miss out something important. Now where was I?"

"You were listing all names that this family had already."

"Yes, and some like Great-Great-Great-Great-Great-Grand-Nana Lil' Mae didn't even have a last name when she first showed up; actually as best as I can remember, she didn't have a name at all. But now that all that buying, lending, and selling is done, we are Fields.

"Sometimes, through no fault of their own, our kin sometimes had three or four different last names, some of them even got the same last name twice 'cause they got sent or sold back to the same owner a second time. That happened to Great-Great-Grand-Momma Milkweed. The story doesn't start with her, but you might as well know now that she's the one the family remembers being on the same plantation twice, but there's an almost unreal reason behind her goin' back to that same plantation."

I wanted to interrupt Aunt Bess again, but one look from her told me it wasn't a good idea. She didn't want to be interrupted. I held on to my question and decided just to listen. "Four plantations in Greenwood owned our family but the Beaufords Plantation is the furthest that anybody in the family can remember our beginning. That's where Great-Great-Grand-Nana Jennie Mae was from and where Cornbread and Molasses was born. Jennie Mae was from the Seminole tribe and when she showed up on Beaufords Plantation sometime in the late seventeen hundreds, she didn't have a name and it was Momma Mae who called her Jennie Mae, and somehow along the way she became Lil' Mae; that name stuck."

Chapter 7

Where We Started

"Back in those days, nigger folk couldn't decide where they wanted to live, what they wanted to do, eat, or nothing. The slave master decided. Slaves didn't have no more value than what the slave owner could use them for and, trust me, there was never anything good involved; slaving was real hard work with shame, beating, and every kind of shaming that you could imagine. Jennie, like all other slaves, got up before the sun and by the time she and the rest like her lay down again, it was almost time for the sun to rise again. They lay down tired and them fortunate enough to rise, did so tired. Sometimes, situations and things being so hard and slaves being so tired from being tired, they just lay where they were and chose to die.

"Nana Jennie didn't had no choice 'bout living or dying, but she put the spirit in Cornbread and Willie made Nana Cornbread his reason for living. He had her to see 'bout and since he'd promised that he was goin' see 'bout her, he had no choice but to live. He was living for the both of them. At a time when most didn't had a reason to live, your Great-Great-Great-grandma Cornbread gave him reason to endure the harsh treatment and all the hardships plantation living can bring.

"He made it his business to watch after her, do for her, and see that nothing bad happened to her, 'cause he loved her. Now he didn't love her at first 'cause he was missing her mamma Lil' Mae too much to pay her mind. In his mind, she was the reason that Lil' Mae went away. But soon she started following him 'round the cabin and smiling and after a while it was as she was always there.

"At first, Cornbread was smiling at him with no teeth, then a few teeth, and 'fore he knew it, her mouth is full of teeth and she's done with the smiling and now she's trying those new teeth out on him all the time. He started to get real happy every time she was around. Soon he forgot 'bout his mamma and her mamma being gone and Cornbread, well she filled his whole life up and he doesn't want for nothing else, but to be with her all the time.

"Everything was goin' all right with them when them was children, a little bit less than you now, but soon things started to change. Well Cornbread started to develop, you know, get girl parts that were starting to look like woman parts and soon everybody concern that them like real cornbread and molasses. They can't be parted from each other for too long. Wherever Molasses is, Cornbread wants to be and wherever Cornbread is, Molasses wants to be; them two just be each other's best company.

"Soon Molasses start to see Cornbread different and she start seeing him differently too, but folk don't say anything to Cornbread 'cause she is a girl, but they say to him, 'Molasses, don't eye Cornbread, she be yer sister.'

"He was doing his best to obey but she was looking good coming into her womanhood. It was hard, but he was doing it. Then the master calls for her and they, not having any choice, fix her up to send to him. Nobody remembers that Cornbread is his sister, as they have been reminding him, and that it's goin' to hurt his heart to know that she's up there with the master. They tell him don't eye her, but nobody can say nothing to the master when he says, 'Send Cornbread up here to me after supper!'

"You know why nobody can't say nothing to the master, none of them brave enough. Aunt Bess suddenly changed the way she was talking and started to talk like a slave.

"Dem need suh to him, "Master, yuh not eye Cornbread, she be yer daughter." Why nobody not tell him that? 'Cause enough of them done seen kin and non-kin alike swing from tree 'cause the master felt like it. They done seen man, woman, boy, or girl beat to death 'cause them, in the master eye, did something so troublesome them just deserve to be dead. That's why nobody suh nothing to him. None of them can suh to him, 'But, Massa, according to yer good book, a man should not show his nakedness to his own kin, and Cornbread, though yuh dun acting like yuh either fergit or not know'd, is yer kin. She be yer daughter you breed off the lil' Seminole Indian you brung here.'"

I forgot not to interrupt Aunt Bess and I asked, "Seminole?"

"Gina Pearl, you just like me. Every time my momma would get to this part, I would ask the same question every time, and she would say the same thing. 'Your great-great-grand-nana Jennie, her and her people them was Indian. They was here on this great land of America when the white man showed up. And white men, as white men do wherever them be, them make slave out them Indian, but them Indian don't just become slave like that. They fight the white man but you had some bad ones in every group and in them Indian group, just like in nigger group, you had Indian that don't mind sell Indian to white man for lil' bit more than a handful of funny money, beads, buttons, and white man liquor.

"Lil' Mae ended up on Beaufords Plantation at the end of one of these mix ups somewhere 'round 1812 or 1813. I think, they said, the war was with the Lower Creeks and her people lost. She was what you call a spoil of war and so the Lower Creeks sold her to the plantation to be a slave. Lil'Mae was very pretty with long, long, soft black hair. Hair so black that it could throw back light just like river water when the sun or moon light hit it, and it was soft like white women's fine silky things. Her skin was almost like red clay, but not quite. Her eyes, I was told, were jet-black circles sitting there above her short but pointed Indian nose. You see the way your lips have that nice little dip under your nose, well it's believed that we, all the Fields women, got that little deep trench under our nose from her." Aunt Bess smiled and pointed to what she called the dip and then she nodded and said, "Did you think that only Fields contributed to our beauty? Remember, child, Seminole blood is strong, stronger than any white man's blood any day of the week.

"And before you ask me to tell you, let me just stop my storytelling and tell, as my Momma did about Molasses' people. His people them was big strong fighting African people; even other African people look up to them. They were from a place call Gambia. They were tall, strong, and dark, dark. It was said they carried everything to make a moonless, starless midnight in their skin. Their skin was so black it looked white when moon light bounced off it, and when there wasn't no light, well, they just became a part of the night--like shadows.

"They blend into night. Only difference is that night soft and you don't feel the softness of night all 'round you, but Mandinka nigger, they feel like they are carved from fancy marble. Every white man wanted a few Mandinka niggers on his plantation for stud, like a bull or horse. It was for this reason that the Dutch West Indian Trading Company sold so many of them.

Same way the white men paid what the slave sellers wanted for Mandinka niggers. A white man would fight another white man on price for Igbo nigger. Nobody really want those Igbos because they were called a slave's slave. No Igbo nigger ever got to see inside of the big house. An Igbo was a slave 'till they died and even then when they died and went to heaven, they be slave up there too."

I didn't know if I should laugh or not, but I couldn't help it. I laughed at the idea of them not even being able to be free in heaven.

Aunt Bess said, "Child, that ain't no laughing matter. Now you gone and confuse my mind again with your laughing. Where was I with my storytelling?"

"You was goin' tell me 'bout the day the master ask them to send Great-Great-Great-Grand-Nana Cornbread up to the big house."

"Yes, yes that's where I was. Well, Willie figure that if he can remember the day Cornbread was born, then all the other folk should remember since they were right there, praying for her mamma and getting washed in all that blood that Cornbread floated into this world on. That was what Willie was thinking, but there was no way he could know or fully understand what the women of that time had gone through and knew what they had to do just to live. Living was the most important thing. No one could tell the master that the slave woman or girl he'd picked wouldn't or couldn't come up to him so Momma Mae had to do what she had to do to keep her family living. She had to do what she had to do even if it meant fixing up this child that she'd raised as her own and sending her up to him. She'd done it before and she was able to keep that child alive and she would do what she had to so this one that he'd seen and called for would live."

"How did Momma Mae do that?"

"It started with Bertha Mae. No, the master didn't start calling for his slaves with Bertha Mae, but from Momma Mae's family she was the first. That tore at Momma Mae's heart, but there was nothing she could do to stop her goin', but she was goin' to do what she could to make sure of one thing. That was when the morning came, her daughter was still alive. What the master did was not the focus; the focus was on staying alive. That was the conversation that Momma Mae had with Bertha Mae as she readied her some fourteen or fifteen years before Cornbread was born. Master was older now but in many ways, he was the same. Actually, he wasn't the same; age had made him worse than when Momma Mae send her Bertha Mae."

Chapter 8

Your Turn Now

Bertha Mae

It fall to meh to comb and plait Cornbread hair. Dat be de part I do in fixing she up to send to de Massa. Momma Mae she busy 'round Cornbread too, but I know'd dat it be mek she heart bruk to know'd dat de Massa want Cornbread to come to him. Cornbread be jis't like Momma Mae pickney, and I can see dat it paining Momma Mae someting awful to have to send we Cornbread to him. I be de furst of Momma Mae pickney to go, and fer a long, long time him not call on none of Momma Mae pickney, but now him dun call fer Cornbread.

On de morning dat Massa furst send fer meh, it not be too long after him suh to send Channy up to him. Channy, she be pretty, pretty nigger gal pickney, and most dem dat 'member suh dat she be him pickney, but Channy not be de furst pickney dat be him pickney dat him suh to send. Far as Massa be concern, nigger pickney not be real pickney fer a white mans. Dem be jis't him property like him horse.

Channy and she muddah and all de rest of we niggers wuk in de rice field. Wuk in rice field be de hardest wuk nigger do. Standing in de water dat day, de mosquitoes dem be act like it be night-time. Dem biting, biting, and not giving nigger, driver, or overseer no peace from dem biting. De sun it no better dan de mosquito; it be hot, hot, hot. It so hot dat wen it be tired burning and scorchin' niggers all day, it jis't jump in de river to cool off and jis't like dat, dark—night and Channy gots to go to de Massa.

Her mighty frighten 'cause some of dem dat been up to him 'fore still fear and beg de Lawd not to let him call fer dem no mo'e. But Massa, him not have habit of wanting de same nigger over and over. Him most like dem dat not have man 'fore him. Not one nigger woman on him plantation get to she womanhood widout him poking in she pee-hole.

Channy her not wants to go. Wen it be time, her not jis't do like all de other nigger womans and stands on him porch fer him to jis't drag dem in. She go to her muddah cabin and she hide. De overseer, him send two nigger drivers to get she and bring she up. Wen dem gets to she muddah cabin, Channy be outside peeing. Dem grab she wid de piss still dripping out she pee-hole, and soon as dem seen de lantern on de porch, dem drag she and mek she stand under it so de Massa can see she, open de door, and snatch she inside.

Soon as Channy be inside, she start one big screaming and den her not scream but one more time 'fore it be quiet. Next mornin', Channy she be dead. Dem, de same two nigger drivers dat be drag she from she muddah cabin be de same two dat de overseer mek bring she out. She be naked and I see she jis't 'fore dem throw'd she dead body in de dirt. Dem not so much as give she box. I see she. Channy, she eyes dem open wide, wide. It be clear dat de last ting she see 'fore she dead be de devil himself. She skin be black and blue. It clear dat Channy suffer plenty, more dan any nigger womans dat be up thar 'fore. Channy suffer different kind of cruel at him hands.

As Massa be getting older, him a different kind a cruel. Him not cruel like to not give clothes to wuk in de rice field, or not give nigger a big piece of pork wen it be Christmas, but de way him cruel is to nigger womans. I tinks on dat all de while I be plaiting and combing Cornbread hair. I be sorry dat him suh to send she. I be begging de Lawd dat him let tonight be one of dem nights dat Him let de Massa cocky 'member wat it 'pose to do wen de Massa see young nigger gal. I wants it to 'member dat it 'pose to get like tree trunk or de flag pole dat Massa have in him yard wen him fly him flag. De one him call de Union Jack.

On most times, de Massa cocky be like potato sack widout potato in it and thar be nuffin' him can do to mek it full up de bag and stand like full sack of potatoes or like him flag pole ready to fly flag. Wen him be like dat, him tek wateva him can put him hand on and him be shove and poke it in nigger womans 'till him get to tinking dat it be him doing de shoving and poking. Sometimes, him poke and shove so hard dat nigger gals look like dem red river flowing. Some live and some do like Channy: dem dead.

Fer a long time; 'till I get wid pickney fer him, I be de one dat him 'call fer and call fer. Momma Mae, at furst she be plenty frighten and den she suh, "Bertha Mae, I know'd dat yuh not know'd no man but yuh be him slave and yuh be nigger, but yuh is muh pickney and I nots want de driver to come in de morning and tek yuh and throw'd yuh in de dirt 'cause yuh mek him kilt yuh."

I tink Massa be tek out him old man vexation on Channy 'cause she not know'd wat to do when him be jis't thar wid him mind young, but him cocky got de, wat dem call it? De dotage and him not able to get it to 'member dem good days wen dem both be young.

I looks at Momma Mae and I not know'd wat her talking 'bout so Momma Mae suh, "Yuh not fret yuhself no more dan yuh have to. Yuh got to go so dat part we pass. Wat yuh gots to do now is go to de Massa and live. I gine mek yuh live. Dat be de only ting fer yuh to have in yuh head wen yuh be thar. Yuh keep tinking, 'I gots to live.' Wen dat be do only ting on yuh mind, de rest of tings yuh gine have to do gine be easy. Live. Yuh must live Bertha Mae; live."

I know'd from de look on Momma Mae face dat I gine live. I gots to live 'cause dat be wat she want fer meh to do. I suh, "I gine live, Momma Mae. Wat yuh suh fer meh to do, I be do dat."

Momma Mae suh, "Thar be two tings I know'd and dat be food and bush. Right now, de Massa him hungry. Him hungry fer young nigger gal, muh nigger gal pickney. I not want yuh to go but dat not be matter. Wat matter is dat yuh go and yuh live to come back to meh. Yuh not gine give him 'cause to kilt yuh."

"I gine live Momma Mae. Yuh suh fer meh to live and I gine do jis't dat: live."

"Good. Yuh see, Bertha Mae, wen de Massa call fer Channy to come to him, she not wants to go 'cause she dun hear of him wicked white mans ways. Her fergit dat him be Massa and she be jis't a nigger gal pickney; him gots plenty gal pickney. Her not special to him. I gine mek yuh special to him. Yuh not gine to him smelling like stale piss, swamp water, and wet dirt. Yuh gine wash yuh fronts—yuh pee-hole, comb yuh hair, and yuh gine put on Annie Mae's dress. Her wuk in de cookhouse; yuh best smell like ham dan wet dirt. Den yuh gine drink dis here cup of bush tea wen it cool. Soon as yuh dun drink it, yuh tek dis leaf and yuh put it in yuh pee-hole and yuh put dis one in yuh mouth, and yuh chew it 'till him open de door. Wen him open de door, quick fast yuh get it out yuh mouth."

I look at Momma Mae and I tinking dat Momma Mae talking like she be getting meh ready to jump de broom. Momma Mae look at meh and she suh, "Tek de leaves and yuh rub dem all over yuh legs, yuh neck, and yuh arms." Den Momma Mae she pull meh, whisper some tings in muh ears and den she suh, "Go and live."

I see de driver walking to de house wid de lantern. I walks out de cabin and I go and I stand on de porch. De door it open and de Massa him be standing thar. Him not snatch me in straight way. Him look and den him turn and look 'hind him. Soon as him turn him head, I tek de leaf from muh mouth, throw'd it on de ground and I wait. Him not drag meh in, but him suh, "Come." Him step back and I step in. Him suh, "Follow me." I follow him.

Wen Massa open de door, I be gets muh furst look at him. I know'd all along dat him be old, but close as I be to him mek meh wants to run way from all de wrinkles dat him be have. Him face it look like it dun slip 'way from him forehead and it be jis't down by him neck. It be jis't thar soft; wrinkle sitting on top of wrinkle and swinging slightly wen him move. Him hardly have hair and wat him have be soft like white pickney hair. Massa him also got a bend in him back. It not bring him to de floor 'cause de bend it mostly sit at him shoulder. Like him got one of dem fancy pillow under de shirt him be wearing. Him not be wearing no breeches, so I can see him legs. Dem be still powerful legs to tek him up and down de stairs. Him start up de long stairs and I jis't follow him. I nots be frighten. I be tinking, I got to live. I dun promise Momma Mae dat I gine live.

At de top of de stairs, Massa push de door to a room. It be him bedchambers. Him step in and him suh, "Come."

Soon as I be in de room, I do wat Momma Mae suh. I suh, "Kind Massa, can Bertha Mae draw a baff fer yuh?"

Him, jis't as Momma Mae suh, nots be 'xpecting nuffin' but fear from meh so him surprise. Him suh, "Did I say for you to speak, nigger?" I jis't stands thar and I not suh nuffin'. Him suh, "Didn't you hear me ask you a question, nigger?"

"Yas, Massa. Yuh nots suh fer meh to speak, but yuh wants meh to draw de baff fer yuh?"

"I didn't bring you up here for any bath." Him turn way and den him suh, "Draw the bath." Him go and him sit in him chair.

I suh, "Kind Massa, I nots be here 'fore, now way de water be?"

"Its already drawn already. I simply didn't feel like taking a bath."

"I be here, Massa. Let meh do it fer yuh. Come. I give yuh good bath and rub."

Wen I suh rub, him get a little smile at de corner of him old white mans wrinkle face. Him get up and him walk over to way him baff be. Him tek off him shirt and him be naked underneath. Him step to de water and I follow like I be do dis ev'ry day. Him gets in de water and I gets to washing him. I wash and I rub him jis't like Momma Mae suh to do, and I mek muh hand to touch him cocky, and I mek it seem like accident. Weneva muh hand touch him, I quick tek muh hand out de water and I suh, "Sorry, Massa, I sorry."

Him smile and him suh, "You should wash my leg again. I believe you have missed a spot."

'I do wat I do 'fore and I let muh hand touch him cocky. Dis time I stay longer and near it and den I jis't tek it in muh hand and I suh, "Massa, yuh wants meh to wash it fer yuh?" I not give him time to answer. I do jis't wat Momma Mae whisper in muh ear. I wash it fer him like it be new pickney. Den it, him cocky dat been sitting in de water all dis time like branch dat fall off tree and floating in river, it start to grow'd.

It not grow'd sudden, but it grow'd; jumpy, jumpy like it surprise. Him reach in de water and him tek muh hand and mek meh hold it. I hold it like it be wat I need to not drown. Him quick stand up out de water and him suh, "Come here."

Him be walking fast cross de room and I be seeing him old white mans skin and I not wants to be near him, but I do jis't wat him suh. Him suh, "Nigger, take that dress off and get over here." Wen him climb up in de bed, I turn muh back to him jis't like Momma Mae suh and wen muh back be turn, I reach in muh pocket and I crush de leaves dat Momma Mae put in muh pocket. She suh, "Wen him ready, yuh tek yuh hand and yuh crush dese leaves. Yuh must not let him see yuh. Yuh crush dem and get dem all over yuh hand. Yuh not have to worry 'bout him smelling dem. Dem not carry smell no stronger dan de soap on him skin. Wen yuh gets in de bed wid him; yuh must quick fast rub yuh hand on him cocky and den yuh stand holding it strong. Yuh hold him like if yuh fall off side of de mountain and dat be de only ting dat gine keep yuh from falling off and deading. Him not gine mind.

"It gine mek him cocky tink it young again. Dat gine mek him happy. Wen him happy over him now-young cocky, yuh must reach in yuh pee-hole quick and tek out de leaf dat yuh got in thar. Drop it on de floor and wen him sleep, yuh must pick it up. Yuh must not let him see dat."

I do jis't wat Momma Mae suh fer meh to do and time I get in de bed wid him, him got a big smile on him face and fer de furst time since I set foots in de house, him grab meh. Him grab me and jis't like dat, him got him young cocky in muh pee-hole and him go on like him not know'd I be thar. I tek wat him be doin' like I not know'd him be thar. Dat mek him shove harder and harder and den him shaking and shaking. Den him cocky it like it spit at meh and him stop moving. Jis't like Momma Mae suh him gine do; soon him sleeping and I ease out him bed, pick up de leaf, and I puts it back way I be tek it from—muh pee-hole. It be wet from way him cocky spit in meh.

Morning come and him wake. Him suh, "Tonight you are to come back."

Dat be how I be de one dat get to go night after night after night and live. I go 'till I get wid de pickney. Him not call fer meh wen him find out I wid pickney. Him call fer different nigger womans and de screaming, beating, shoving, and poking wid whatever him can find to put him hand on start fresh. Nigger womans wants to know'd why him never beat or poke meh. Momma Mae, she suh, "Dat other nigger womans ought to find out on dem own how to live. When yuh know'd wat to do to live, den living not be so hard."

I know'd wat to do fer de Massa to live, but I wid pickney fer him again and now him calling fer Cornbread. Cornbread, she gine live 'cause Momma Mae be whispering in she ears.

Book Three

Molasses 1808 - Unknown

Chapter 9

No One To Talk Fer Her

Molasses

Somebody ought to have suh someting to de Massa de same way dem suh someting to meh. Most dem dun call her him pickney from de day she born. It be de same blood dat float she in on dat float she mamma out. One of dem ought to suh someting to Massa rather dan fixing she and looking at she sorry like. Dat be muh Cornbread and I be able to see dat she be frighten. De way I be figuring it, I able to see dat she be frighten den de rest be able to see dat she be frighten.

I be starting to feel a lot of tings as I watch Momma Mae and Bertha Mae busy, busy round muh Cornbread, and de more I watch dem, de more I can feel muh Mandinka blood getting hotter and hotter. It not be right dat Massa can mek him way down from de big house, look at any one of de nigger womans or gals and suh, "Send that nigger gal up to me tonight."

Or suh to put dem in de special lil' house him had some of dem very own nigger mans or fathers build. Most of de time, I not care which one de Massa want, but today I care. At nineteen years, I be wat de Massa call a big nigger buck and I not be call Molasses or Lasses jis't 'cause I like dipping most evryting I be fixing to eat in some warm molasses. Dat might be one of de reasons, but de reason most clear to ev'rybody 'membering be dat muh skin most match de color of midnight and molasses all rolled together.

It be Cornbread furst called meh dat wen she be 'bout five or six, and I be 'round nine maybe ten muhself. De furst time she call meh dat, it be late one evening and ev'rybody be fixing to leave de field. I gets it in muh head to hide from she so I run up a bit and I go 'hind some low bush. Cornbread, she come up, walk right pass de bush wid meh in it and all de while she calling, "Lil' Willie, where yuh is?" Where yuh is hiding yuhself?"

While Cornbread is calling muh name, I is hiding in de low bush laughing 'cause she not can find meh 'cause her not 'pecting meh to be hiding in de low bush. Wen she be jis't ahead of meh a piece, I den run from de low bush and I comes up 'hind she and I pounce, knocking she over. She gets up madder than a rattlesnake and she throwing dirt at meh and she suh, "Lil' Willie, it not fair fer yuh to hide in de low bush, 'cause dat be not right. Yuh know'd no evening sun reach de low bush. Low bush in de dark and yuh know'd I can't see 'lasses in de dark."

Ev'rybody that hear wat Cornbread suh fix demselves to laugh 'cause Cornbread call meh 'lasses. Dem older people understanding quick fast and time dey mek it back to de yard, all yuh is hearing is, "Yuh all hear wat Cornbread suh?" Cornbread tolt Lil' Willie dat him not play fair to hide in de low bush over thar by de cabin 'cause him de same as 'lasses, and him know'd she nots be able to see 'lasses in de dark."

By night-time, folk dun fergot dat I be Lil' Willie and ev'rybody suhing, "Yuh seen 'lasses? Where's 'lasses?" Or, "Wat yuh doing thar, 'lasses?"

Every time somebody called meh 'lasses, Cornbread be jis't throw her little brownish-red self down and squeal wid de laughter. It be funny to she and since Cornbread be happy, I be happy and join she in calling muhself 'lasses. I be run up on Cornbread and suh, "Cornbread, here's yuh 'lasses. Yuh wants meh get someting fer yuh? Yuh want come find meh in de low bush?"

Cornbread be jis't look at meh and shake she head of baked brown hair from side to side and laugh. Den she'd suh, "Yuh not 'pose to hide in de low bush no more, Lil' Willie, 'cause I nots see yuh in dem."

Den meh and Cornbread be go and play and I be hide where she can see meh. She be mighty scared of dark places.

We mek a fine pair; she yellow like a good piece of cornbread with her hair brown like the crust on top of cornbread. Her hair be brown so 'cause Massa hair be almost red. Her Momma, being Seminole and all, had hair like white peoples but it be different. It be all de way down she back and it be look like melt-down poured out tar. So all dat mixing wid de Massa and Lil' Mae mek Cornbread to have hair dat be red and brown, same time and it all de way down she shoulders and it not stop 'till it be down she back and sitting on she sit-down.

It be hard to look at Cornbread and not tink of slightly burn-up butter running down de sides of some good cornbread. Not dat nigger ever had cornbread with butter burn-up or otherwise running down no side of it, but dem dat wuk in de cookhouse dem be de ones dat seen de way white folks eat dem cornbread. It be dem dat tolt wat her hair be looking like.

As straight and soft as Cornbread hair be, mine be as rusty as de foam dat forms on top of some good molasses. Muh hair be dat way 'cause I be pure African nigger, so muh hair it be hard and tight to muh scalp. It dared anything to pass through it. Nuffin' tek meh up on it nor did I've to try to find anything to go through it. Dat rusty-looking hair on muh head jis't be thar. It be knotty knotty, it be tight and looking like it be brek if yuh tried to pull on it.

Muh hair and head match perfect. Both hard and nuffin' getting in or passing through. Momma Mae, who raise up meh and Cornbread be suh dat all de time. "Boy, yuh head so hard. I nots know'd which be harder, yuh head or yuh hair."

Meh and Cornbread, we be together from day she born and before folks got to calling meh Molasses or 'lasses. Dey used to suh, "Jis't look at dem two, little Miss Day and young Massa Night. Now dem never suh none of dat Miss and Massa nuffin' fer de Massa to hear dem. Dat be jis't 'tween nigger people. But meh and Cornbread, we be playing together from since we be lil' pickney and best friends we whole lives. We dun share secrets that nobody else know'd 'bout. We even had plans of running way from dis plantation. Plans fer being free and moving up North, or even to Canada and now dem be fixing muh Cornbread to send she up to de big house 'cause Massa suh so.

Well I know'd dat wen de morning sun rise up over dis place, one of we, meh or de Massa, not gine see it. If it had to be meh, den I best be mekking peace wid de only real Massa I belongs to. De one dat de white mans tolt meh received ev'rybody, even nigger dat be slave into heaven. De white preacher mans dat Massa let come by de plantation once a fortnight tolt meh dat if I be a good nigger and serve de Massa faithful and wuk very hard here on Earth, den de Lawd gine reward meh by letting meh gets in heaven.

De preacher mans suh dat I gine get to walk through dem big ole' gates mek from pearls and wen I walks through de gates, de angels gine meet meh and give meh milk, honey, long white robes, and wings. If too many niggers come to heaven and dem angels run outta wings fer niggers, den nigger dat not get wings goin' be able to walk on streets mek from pure gold, and ev'ry nigger gine be free in heaven.

All we nigger happy wen de white preacher mans suh 'bout nigger getting in heaven and we gine be free widout a Massa but thar not be one nigger tinking dat dem gots to be dead 'fore dem can pass through dem pearly gates. But de way Massa wukking nigger to death, I gets to tinking dat dis Massa at de plantation and de Massa up in heaven must got plenty reward fer nigger wen nigger gets to heaven, 'cause nigger not getting nuffin' here on Earth.

Sitting right thar in de low bush, which twan't no more low bush since it had grow'd right along wid meh and Cornbread, I gets to talking to muh Massa: de Lawd dat up in heaven. I had to let de Lawd know'd why I be fixing to brek one of dem Ten Commandments de white preacher mans tolt meh 'bout. If it not be meh dat brek de commandment, I be de one dat gine mek somebody else brek one.

I be ready to brek all ten of dem commandments and ten more if thar be ten more fer muh Cornbread. De way I be tinking is dat one outta ten twan't so bad. I promised God dat if He help meh to let dis bitter cup pass from de lips of muh Cornbread, dat I be never brek another one of His commandments and dat I be serve Him full well right here on Earth and wen I be dead and I get to tek muh rest up in heaven wid him dat I be de best nigger Him ever have in heaven.

Dat be muh Cornbread and no non-praying, non-God-fearing white mans, least lone a gin-drinking, foul-mouth cussing, slave-owning, beating and killing white mans gine jis' call fer muh Cornbread and have his way wid her and jis' walk away. It be over muh dead body and since I nots have no mamma to be crying over meh, I could 'ford leave dis plantation. One way or de other, leaving be leaving.

All de while I be in de low bush, I be tinking 'bout wat I gots to do and how I be gine do it. I dun figure dat I not have no real choice. I dun mek a promise and no white mans, Massa or not, gine mek meh brek a promise I dun give. I not gine let Massa tek de only two real things I gots: dat be muh word which be always good, 'cause it be all I gots in dis world to give anybody, and de other be muh Cornbread. I sits thar and I tinks dat I best be dead if I gots to sit by and watch de Massa tek muh two most prized 'sessions from meh.

I begs de Lawd to keep sitting high and looking low and while He be looking low, to see meh in de low bush. I begs de Lawd to understand why I be doin' wat I be doin'. De more I tinks on why I be in de low bush and why I be begging de Lawd to understand why I be doin' wat I be doin', I be begging de Lawd to keep a finger on de angry spirit dat rising up in meh. I begs him nots to let it get outside of meh. I gots to tink hard so dat it not gets outside of meh.

I gots to keep it inside 'till de right time. It be a lot of anger and hatred dat I be feeling. I not know'd full well why I be feeling like if I nots keep talking to de Lawd 'bout all de anger and hatred in meh gine mek meh catch on fire. Muh head suh dat I be feeling all dis 'cause de Massa be treating meh way worse dan him treat de animals round de plantation. De way de Massa have de overseer to wuk meh so hard 'till sometimes I feels like I be jis' drop down dead.

Dat mean evil spirit dat be creeping up in meh now I not even know'd dat I had it. It jis't grow'd and grow'd each time I tinks of de Massa wid muh Cornbread. It grow'd right along wid meh in de low bush and now 'fore I know'd wat be happening, all dat anger be gone and set de low bush on fire. It weren't no real fire to see, not like de way de white mans dun suh God had set dat other bush on fire to show Moses His strenf; no it jis't be muh hatred fer wat de Massa be getting ready to do to muh Cornbread dat be mekking meh burn up.

It not worry meh dat meh and de bush be burning. I get so I want to step out de bush and see de kind of fire dat de anger 'gainst de Massa be mekking. I starts to tink on Momma Mae and I wants to tell she not to worry 'bout de bush and how it be burning. I wants to tell she and ev'rybody dat I be de fire dat be burning in de low bush. Dat dis be muh furst and last fire. I wants to tell dem dat dis fire dat I got gine now gine be a everlasting fire, like de one de preacher mans suh dat fer nigger dat not listen to dem Massa, run way, or tinks 'bout running way.

I feel de fire burning in meh and I tinks dat even if Massa wins and him put out muh life fire, dis fire dat him be seeing be a different kind of fire. It not be de kind of fire dat need wood chips or whittle to keep it goin'. Dis fire be burning because of de love inside of meh fer muh Cornbread and nuffin', not Massa, not whip, not knife, or dem machete gine put it out.

Chapter 10

A Fire So Bright

Yes Lawd, I be wait right here in dis not so low bush and wait fer de right moment to come out and save muh Cornbread. Cornbread be jis't like meh; she not got no real kin of she own, she mamma, Lil' Mae dead and nobody know'd which parts Massa brung her from and even if dey know'd it not mek one lick of difference 'cause dey not able to leave de place to mek she kin know'd dat she be dead no how. She be Indian but she be slave like de rest of we and she got treat de same way. Kin not mean nuffin' to de Massa and his people unless it be dey kin.

Someting tolt meh long time ago dat Massa and him wife not tink dat nigger not be human either. I think dey never even stop to think dat we jis't might have feelings. Massa never rec'on on no molasses-black buck having any kind of feelings, least lone love, fer no cornbread-yellow gal. Sitting thar in de bush, I figure dat it not be muh fault dat de Massa not give dat no rec'oning.

Massa not think him ever did nuffin' wrong wen it come to him niggers, but him niggers dun know'd dat him dun dem and all him slave plenty wrong. Wen de lil' Seminole Indian gal jis't showed up on him plantation one morning looking scared, it not be hard to feel sorry fer she 'cause dey who been 'round thar long know'd dat it not be long 'fore de Massa be wanting she brung up to him. Him not de kind of Massa dat come down to de slave womans' cabin. Him be different. Him had dem brung to him.

I 'member Momma Mae wen she furst seen Cornbread Momma 'fore she be she Momma. Momma Mae she suh, "Look at dat poe' lil' lost Indian gal. It be plain dat she not know'd wat be coming down de road fer she. Soon she be wish dat it be a wagon wid a kinder Massa coming to get she. But de only wagon dat gine come tek she 'way from here gine be de one dat come wen she lay down to sleep and dream; dat be if she twan't too tired to sleep, far less dream."

If she be tinking 'bout de wagon or if she be missing she people, nobody know'd. Most times she jis't walk 'round looking at she foots.

She never tek she eyes from looking at dem and wen she do, it be de same always. She be look up towards heaven like she be praying to de Lawd to do something: answer some pray; anything. Den she stare at she foots real hard like she begging dem to move, to run and tek she way from dis place.

Wen she wait and no answer come from de Lawd, den she look at de trees dat be far way off. After a while, we all know'd why she look at de trees. It be de same reason we all look at de trees: dem be free to be trees. If dem be apple trees, dem grow'd apple, if dem be peach tree, dem grow'd peach. Trees on dis plantation even wid dem roots deep in de ground dem more free dan slave. Slave be man but him wuk like mule by Massa and him overseer. Slave woman be woman jis't like white womans be womans, but nigger womans she not be womans to de Massa and him friends.

Nigger woman be jis't like sow pig, heifer, or horse. Massa breed dem and wuk dem same way. Nigger womans not be womans 'long as she be slave:, tree more free dan nigger. Lil' Mae not got a soul she can look at and call kin, nobody she know'd since Massa brung her all by herself. Him tolt another white mans dat yuh nots ever bring two Indians to yer place from de same tribe 'cause dem be talking dem Indian talk and next ting yuh know'd, dem jis't up and vanish: Indian magic. Him suh if yuh want tings to go smooth, yuh bring one Indian and yuh tell de niggers dat dem Indians know'd Indian magic and dem dumb niggers gets scared and den dey nots mix dem wid de Indians.

Tings bad fer all of we, but I had Momma Mae. I be look at Lil' Mae and I gets to figure dat insides, she must be mighty lonesome fer someone like Momma Mae to sing she a song wen she feel lonesome jis't de way Momma Mae be singing to meh wen I gets to be feeling lonesome. Sometimes I be see de way Lil' Mae watch Momma Mae, and her eyes dey get to watering slowly and den she jis't look back at she foots dat nots tek she away from dis place and jis't real slow like she go back to watever it be she be doing to mek she ferget.

Den de day dat de rest of dem know'd be coming come. Massa him suh send fer she. Nobody but Massa had a choice in de matter. So dem who had ev'ting tek or beat outta dem fix she and she, well she jis't walk 'long way dem point fer she to go and she go in de house and up de stairs to him and de fate he had plan fer she.

Though I not ever see no sacrifice, Lil' Mae look jis't de way I figured dem sheep, goats, and bulls must look wen dem Israelites mek sacrifices to de Lawd to get his fergiveness fer de wrong things dey dun. I look at Lil' Mae and I wonder why Massa pick Lil' Mae fer him sacrifice. Massa never figure dat none of him niggers have no kind of feelings. Fer him, nigger no more dan another kind of animals 'bout him place and it be dat kind of tinking dat gine one day mek him pick de wrong kind of nigger animal fer him sacrifice and de animal den gine mek him de sacrifice.

Since I know'd dat us not be no animals, I figure dat Massa should be mekking sacrifices all day and all night fer all de wrong tings him dun and still doing to we. De way I figure things, Massa, well him should be having a steady slaughtering and burning goin' on 'cause him be cruel and mean on a regular basis. If Massa and him wife be to kilt one animal fer each wrong ting dey be dun to niggers, well pretty soon 'tween de two of dem, dey be soon kilt off all de animals in dese parts. Not jis't dey own, but more dan a few from de other plantations.

Though I be too young at de time to know'd wat Massa really want Lil' Mae fer, I know'd dat like all de other women dat be gone up thar, 'fore long she be looking like she dun putting someting round under she apron 'till it be big as a watermelon.

Chapter 11

A Better Understanding

Promise

Aunt Bess took a deep breath and she said, "That's enough of that story for tonight. Me and Cousin Thea got work in the morning. We can pick this up tomorrow or another evening." I wanted to tell her to continue but I was getting used to Aunt Bess. When she said she was done with something, she was done. She wasn't changing her mind. She'd also promised to continue another night and I knew she would. Aunt Bess kept all the promises she made; big or small. I knew it would only be a matter of time before she came back to what she called her storytelling. I couldn't wait to find out more about Great-Great-Great-Grandpa Molasses.

Molasses

If 'fore goin' up to de big house Lil' Mae had look up ev'ry once in a while, after Massa send fer she a few nights in a row, she never look up at all, she jis't sit off by herself. She be sad so long. Some nigger, feeling sorry fer she try to help she pick she share of cotton, but Lil' Mae be jis't look at dem real sad and suh, "I fear Overseer."

Soon she look like all de other women dat de Massa call fer; she gots a watermelon in she belly. De watermelon in she belly mek she even more sad; she spend more and more time wid she head bend looking at she foots. She not stop from doing she wuk, she wuk but she sadder dan even nigger. Ev'n wen she watermelon look like it be touch de ground each time she bend down, she keep right on doing she share of de wuk. Lil' Mae watermelon be pull she so close to de ground dat I gots to wondering if she be trying to put de watermelon back in de ground.

Sometimes wen she wuk, she be hold de watermelon belly and she sing. It twan't de same kind of singing as Momma Mae. Lil' Mae she sing songs 'bout big birds and arrows flying in de sky, or buffalo and people dat roam free. She never really sing loud. To hear Lil' Mae sing, yuh had to be right next to she. I always be right next to she 'cause she let meh. She voice it so pretty wen she sing. It be mighty sweet sounding. As de watermelon grow'd bigger, she sing songs 'bout meeting up in de sky wid other birds, running bulls, a teepee, and things I never hear 'bout 'fore. Wen I ask Lil' Mae wat she singing 'bout, she suh de song be 'bout Indian people and dem ways. She suh dat wen she sing she songs in de open, she people be hear and know'd dat she be on dis plantation.

I be next to Lil' Mae de day she stop singing and grab hold of she watermelon. I gets to tinking that she be feeling hungry and goin' cut de watermelon and let meh have some. So I waits, but she drop to she knees and start rocking and she suh, "Oh Great Chief, show lil' squaw some mercy."

I suhs to her, "Lil' Mae, yuh wants meh to hold de watermelon fer yuh?"

She suh to meh, "Lil' Willie, dis no watermelon, it be a lil' squaw pickney. Go yonder and fetch Momma Mae. Suh come help Lil' Mae. Fly swift like eagle, Lil' Willie."

I not know'd 'bout no flying swift like eagle, but I gots to running and calling Momma Mae from de time I turns muh back on Lil' Mae. I runs right cross de field shouting, "Momma Mae, Lil' Mae suh de watermelon it goin' be a pickney now! Momma Mae, come quick and help Lil' Mae, she on she knees calling fer a Great Chief to come and show she mercy. Come, Momma Mae, I'll show yuh where Lil' Mae be!"

Momma Mae she come running 'cross de field in a mighty hurry. Lou Etta Mae, Bertha Mae, and Annie Mae be right 'hind her, all of dem moving like shadows in de midday haze. Momma Mae not let meh go back to be wid Lil' Mae, she suh dat it be no place fer a pickney so I had to stay wid de mans. De mans, dey jis' keep right on wukking in de field. Ev'ry now and then, dem be stop wen de wind be bring de sound of Lil' Mae screaming right to where we be.

De sun be almost down 'fore Lou Etta Mae, Bertha Mae, and Annie Mae come back cross de field to get a few of de mans. Dey ask Preacher man, Big Willie, Whistler, and Short Foot to come give dem a hand. Wen Momma Mae come and get de mans, I know'd dat soon we be joining dem over by de tree calls de weeping willow. I nots ever see no tears come from de tree, but I figure it be weeping 'cause nigger always be digging holes under it, putting wooden boxes wid somebody in dem in de ground, and den crying, crying, crying. It be de weight of all dem nigger tears dat mek de branches 'pon de tree hang down low and touch de ground. Nigger tears plenty and heavy wid dey grief and pain from slaving, losing, and wanting to be free like tree.

I know'd dat Lil' Mae or she watermelon pickney dead. I be hoping in muh heart dat it be de watermelon pickney 'cause I love Lil' Mae and dem beautiful Indian songs. I twan't even sure why but I starts to cry. Inside muh head, I be tinking why de Lawd always be calling home somebody I love. Why he always teks dem very special ones and leaves people like de Massa behind?

De white preacher mans suh dat de Lawd know'ds ev'ting, den de Lawd must know'd dat Lil' Willie loves Lil' Mae. So if Him know'ds dat, why must Him tek Lil' Mae from Lil' Willie? I know'ds dat de Lawd know'ds wat I be tinking, so I begs him not to tek Lil' Mae from meh. Muh heart it hurting in a mighty painful way and I wants to stop from crying, but I nots be able. I can see Lil' Mae inside muh head and muh heart; well, it jis't up and brek, but it nots brek enough fer meh to dead, it jis't beat painful slow, slow enough to stop, but it nots stop.

We stay wukking in de field and we wait fer somebody to come suh which one of dem dead. Soon, Big Willie come back cross de field and widout, a word we follows him. We walks over to de cabin at de other end of de cotton field near where de low bush be growing and de Massa had de cotton gin. Inside be Momma Mae, Lou Etta Mae, Bertha Mae, and laying on some flat boards wid some dry grass be Lil' Mae. Lil' Mae, she nots turn she face to look at meh and I suhs, "Lil' Mae, it be meh, Little Willie. I is come to see 'bout yuh. Is yuh feeling better now, Lil' Mae?"

Lil' Mae she not answer meh so I looks closer and I sees dat she have she eyes shut. Lil' Mae she looks like she be sleeping. Den I feel someting in muh belly and nobody gots to tell meh. I know'ds dat Lil' Mae and de watermelon pickney dead. She look peaceful in she sleep and fer de furst time, Lil' Mae look like she might smile. I smile at she almost-smile. I wants to run over to where she be lying on de straw and touch her face, but I know'ds dat Momma Mae nots 'low fer disturbing de rest of dem dat gone on to be wid de Lawd.

Lil' Mae, her face looks like one of de wind queens she always be singing 'bout. She not have on de regular apron she had on wen she fell to her knees and asked meh go fetch Momma Mae. She had on one of Momma Mae's good apron, de one she wear wenev'r somebody jumped de broom. Momma Mae had dun fixed it round where de watermelon used to be and fer de furst time since she come, Lil' Mae not have no head tie either, and de most hair I ev'r seen in muh life be spread all over and around her. Lil' Mae hair be jis't like white people's hair and de same color as de polish dat Big Willie sometimes puts on de Massa' boots, and it all de way to her middle. She sure enough looked mighty smart in her eternal sleep.

I looks round fer de watermelon pickney to be in its eternal sleep too and wrap in someting 'longing to Lil' Mae, jis't de way other dead babies be, but I nots see de watermelon pickney. Den Annie Mae, who I not even notice be not standing around wen we all furst comes in de room, come from round de back and holding in she hand is a bundle wrapped up. I waits fer she to put de watermelon pickney next to Lil' Mae but she nots. She suhs dat it is only Lil' Mae who gone home to be wid de Lawd and datbirfing de pickney be more dan Lil' Mae be able to manage, so she gone and de pickney 'long to all of we now.

Preacher Man suh a few words and we sing a song 'bout de river and how well it be wid Lil' Mae's soul, den we leave her in de cabin 'till morning wen we goin' come back and put she in a box and put she in a hole under de weeping tree. Even as Preacher Man be talking, we hears Big Willie, Whistler, and Short Foot digging de hole and we hear hammering in de distance. It be Big Pete and Little Pete; dem be de ones dat Massa suh can use lumber fer mek de boxes wen nigger dead.

We walks out de cabin. Momma Mae she put a big rock 'hind de door and we leave Lil' Mae. Momma Mae tek hold of muh hand and we walks back to de yard. Furst she be quiet, like she tinking and den she suhs, "Lil' Willie, it be a good think yuh dun, coming so fast to get meh. I mighty proud of yuh and Lil' Mae she thanked sweet Jesus fer yuh and 'fore she went to be wid Him, she asked Him to bless yuh mightily."

Jis't tinking 'bout Lil' Mae laying in de cabin all by herself and seeing de watermelon pickney in Momma Mae's hand jis't mek meh start to holler. Furst it jis't in muh throat, but de more I tinks of how de watermelon pickney come and mek Lil' Mae go 'way, I holler out real loud. Momma Mae suhs, "I can see I is goin' have muh hands mighty full tonight wid yuh hollering all night like yuh is de one lost a mamma and not dis here pickney in muh hands. Lil' Willie, I know'ds yuh be awful fond of Lil' Mae and she be fond of yuh de way she let yuh jis't follow she 'round all de time, but Lil' Mae she not be yer mamma. She gone and left dis lil' one widout a mamma and now de two of yuh paddling de same boat."

I wants to ask Momma Mae 'bout de boat I be paddling since I nots ever seen a boat, least lone paddle one, but I keeps muh mouth shut. I know'ds wat happen if yuh cut Momma Mae's words off. Wen she gets to talking, and it not matter wat it 'bout, yuh jis't keep quiet 'till she done, den if yer have someting to suh, it better matter, if not, well yuh jis't keep yer thoughts to yerself.

Seeing how I be not ready to stop crying no time soon, Momma Mae stop talking and start to hum. No words, not opening she mouth or nuffin' like dat, jis't singing deep in her throat. I feel it all de way to muh heart and it mek meh lonesome fer muh own mamma who Big Willie, Short Foot, Whistler, and Preacher Man put in a hole last summer.

I starts to feel de song tying muh belly and muh throat in one big knot and I wants to tell Momma Mae dat it mekking meh remember muh own mamma crying all night 'fore she went home to be wid de Lawd.

I wants to tell Momma Mae dat I can hear Mamma suhing, "Where 'Lil' Willie? Somebody bring muh boy close 'round by dat I can see him face one more time. I wants to see him close, touch him face. I can feel I goin to be wid muh Lawd. I not long fer dis Earth. Meh and dis one in muh belly not goin' live. Momma Mae, muh lips be so parched, give meh some water please, Momma Mae, a little water."

Momma Mae, she nots know'd wat be in muh head so she keep right on humming and de more she hum, de more I hear and see muh own mamma. I see Momma Mae wen she give muh Mamma de water. I see muh Mamma as she swallow de little sip of water and den how she look at muh face. She watching inside muh eyes, but 'fore she do wat Momma Mae suh fer she to do, she suhs to meh, "Lil' Willie, thar is only one way fer a nigger to be free other dan be dead. It be book learning, book learning goin' free yuh, Lil' Willie."

I looks at muh Mamma and I know'ds now dat she sick real bad 'cause no nigger ever talk 'bout book learning and live. Book learning not fer no nigger; it only fer de white peoples.

She try again to do wat Momma Mae be telling she to do, but she suh, "Mamma, I nots have no strenf no more, jis't let meh go. I can go now, Momma Mae, I dun told Lil' Willie de only important ting in meh." Ma took a deep breff and she let her head sink deep down on de bed.

Momma Mae raise her head up and she suh, "Yuh is got to try one more time; de Lawd not ready fer yuh. Try one more time fer yer mamma."

She never answer Momma Mae, she fix she eyes on meh and she suh, "Promise meh, Willie, yuh gine figure out how to get book learning. Get it, Willie, if dey kilt yuh. If dey nots kilt yuh, den get it and pass it on. Promise meh."

I nots know'd wat else to suh so I suhs, "I promise yuh, Ma."

Wen I suh dat, Momma Mae suh, "Way yer get dat nonsense from dat yuh mekking dis pickney promise yuh? Dat burden be too big fer dis boy. Do wat I is begging yuh to do; try one more time. Try."

I hear wat Momma Mae be asking Ma to try, but Ma she looking in muh eyes and I suh, "I promise, Ma. I promise."

Momma Mae she stop fer a minute from talking to Ma and she suh, "Wat yuh promising, Lil' Willie? Wat yer promising yer ma? Yuh know'd?"

Ma, she talk real soft and she suh, "Wat yuh promising meh, Willie?" I speak real soft but I suh, "Dat I is goin' gets book learning and den I is goin' pass it on."

Ma look at Momma Mae and I follow she eyes and I look at Momma Mae too. Momma Mae her eyes dem wet and she look mighty scared so I get scared too. Den Ma she call muh name one more time and I suh, "Yes Ma." She fix she eyes on meh and never stop looking at meh, she and 'cause Momma Mae beg she to try one more time, she try. Dat try mek Ma come right up on she elbows. She stay sitting up and staring at meh like dat fer a spell den she fall back.

In a real tired voice, she call muh name softly, so soft I 'most not hear it. 'fore I able to suh, "Yes Mamma." Her crying eyes look inside muh own crying eyes, pass de knot dat be in muh throat wen I see how sad she be. Her crying eyes dem go on a journey in muh eyes dat only she and de Lawd know'd 'bout. Dey mek dem way pass muh breking heart and dem stop at muh spirit dat had start to dry up from all de sadness. Ma know'd dat muh spirit be drying, 'cause it be wanting to be dead right wid she. She reach right in and touch it wid she tears and mek it live again and wen she touch muh spirit, I think she see dat de promise I mek be sitting right thar; waiting fer meh to figure out how to mek it come true fer she. Ma plant she will deep in muh soul, I not know'd how I know'd dat Ma touch muh soul but I jis't know'd.

I cry out loud. I not know'ds why but someting in muh belly suh fer meh to cry out loud or it be brek apart and be in bits and pieces in muh belly, so I cry out loud, loud, loud. Den I want Ma worse dan I be ever want anything so I move from de spot where I be near she bed and I throws muh head on she. I can tell dat Ma want to hold meh tight, but she not have no more strenf left. I put muh hand near her watermelon and it move.

Ma look at meh and she mek she hand touch meh. I holler harder and Momma Mae she holler too and someting in meh know'd dat Ma know'd I be keep dat promise I mek she. Looking in muh eyes but pass muh eyes, she stop ev'ting. Quick, fast, and in a hurry Momma Mae had somebody tek meh out de room and den she be shouting and sniffling and sniffling and shouting. Den ev'rybody started to bawl, but Momma Mae she not bawling, she shouting 'bout dat she gots to save de pickney. She suh, "I can't do nuffin' fer Jennie Etta Mae now, but I can try to save Jennie Etta Mae lil' pickney."

Sitting outside, I wonder wat Momma Mae talking 'bout since I not see no pickney wen I be in thar. It tek ferever 'fore Momma Mae come out, but wen she come out she be holding a little wrapped up bundle and she suh to meh, "Little Willie, dis here is yer sister, we goin' call her Lil' Etta Mae after yer mamma." I looks at de little pickney and I nots know'd where she come from, but Momma Mae suh she muh sister, so she muh sister. Momma Mae she teks meh by de hand and move meh from where I be sitting and she puts meh to sit on de floor in de corner of de cabin. She suhs to meh, "Yuh sits here quiet like and hold onto yer sister. I got to go tek care of yer mamma. She goin' home to be wid de Lawd and I have to mek her right fer wen she walks through dem pearly gates."

Momma Mae she go back and leaves meh sitting on de floor wid de little pickney. De little pickney, she head turn muh way like she be jis't watch muh face, but she eyes dem not open so I jis't watch she face wid she shut eyes and I do jis't as Momma Mae suh; I nots move. I jis't sit still and hold she. Den as I sitting as Momma Mae dun tolt meh to sit, I see muh mamma' face all over dis little pickney face wid de shut eyes and I start to cry. I nots want her. I want muh mamma back. I want her to go back to where she come from and fer muh mamma to come back from being wid de Lawd. I want to put she on de floor and go be wid Ma, but Momma Mae suh sit, so I sits and waits. 'Fore too long, Momma Mae she come and suh I did a good job and teks de little pickney from meh and suh, "Little Willie, yuh must come suh good-bye to yer mamma."

I follow Momma Mae and go see Ma. Ma, she look real pretty. Her face, it nots have no more tears on it. All dem tears gone. Momma Mae wipe all de tears away dat muh mamma had cried wen she be looking at meh, and wen she not be able to do watever it be dat Momma Mae had want her to do. If Ma be ask meh, I be help push watever it be dat Momma Mae had want push. But Mamma gone 'fore she can ask Lil' Willie to help. Mamma looks real pretty 'cause Momma Mae even dun comb she hair fresh. Ma look too pretty to be suhing goodbye to and I not know'ds how to suh good-bye to a mamma dat not coming back.

De way ev'rybody sad, I know'ds Ma not ever be coming back. It not feel like de time wen Massa send Ma over to him son's plantation and we all hurry, hide, and suh good-bye to she. Dis time I wants to run and beg Mamma not to go to be wid de Lawd. I wants to ask Ma if de Lawd can tek somebody else mamma and leave she to be wid Lil' Willie.

I starts to cry and I want to lie 'sides she on she bed but Momma Mae nots let meh, she suh, "Let yer mamma sleep in peace, and nots disturb her rest. She at peace now. All she pain dun over wid. She in heaven now wid de Lawd."

I suh to Momma Mae, "Can I go wid muh Mamma?"

She suh, "Little Willie, if yuh is a good boy and do wat meh, Big Willie, and Preacher Man suh to do, yuh will go to be wid yer Ma someday, but now not be de time. De good Lawd gine decide wen yer time be. Yuh jis't have to be good and He will let yuh through dem pearly gates one day, give yuh a white robe, wings dat gine set yuh free to go and be way yuh want in heaven, and wen yuh nots wants to fly no more, him gine lets yuh walk on de roads dat got gold all over dem. Yuh Ma, she be good and I know'd dat she gine be sitting up in heaven rejoicing wid de angels."

"I wants to go wid Mamma and get muh white robe and wings too."

"De Lawd Him not ready fer yuh yet and 'sides, yuh dun mek yer mamma a promise."

"But, Momma Mae, yuh know'd dat not be a promise I can keep. How I goin' get book learning? It only de white peoples who can gets it."

"Nots let dat be a bother to yer head; now we gots to see yer Ma on she homebound journey."

"But how I goin' get book learning, Momma Mae?"

"Lil' Willie, I dun told yuh it nots fer yuh to worry 'bout now. If de Lawd mean fer yuh to get book learnin', He goin' mek a way fer book learning to come to yuh."

"But, Momma Mae, de Lawd must not intend fer nigger to get book learnin' 'cause Him only mek it fer de white people."

"Lil' Willie, shut up wid dis foolish talk 'fore Massa hear yuh and sep'rate yuh from here. Now yuh is to hush up wid all dis book learnin' talk. Nigger dun wait all dese years fer de Lawd to mek freedom come fer dem, and so if we dun wait all dis time fer freedom, we can wait fer book learning. If nigger is to get freedom and book learnin', den it's only de Lawd gine mek it so. Now hush up."

I can tell dat Momma Mae dun suh she final word so I hush, but not 'fore I suh, "But Ma mek meh promise she."

I nots see she hands move but I know'd dem move 'cause in de midst of Momma Mae sad over Ma dun bein' gone to be wid de Lawd, she knocks muh head and I know'd she mean fer meh to hush up. I hush up. Wen we quiet, Preacher Man suh a few words and dem rest sing a song dem sing in de fields wen dem wukking. I hear dem but I nots. I only hears Ma talking to meh. I want Ma back from heaven so I listen. After de song, we leave Ma laying down on de bed behind de sheet and Bertha Mae feed de pickney. Wen she dun, she lie down wid dis pickney and she own lil' pickney. Ev'rybody suhing, "Poor little pickney, come in de world and she mamma dun got took out, not be nuffin' like a motherless pickney, but she our pickney now, she and Little Willie."

Jis't like dat, Ma gone and I 'long to Momma Mae, Lou Etta Mae, Bertha Mae, and Annie Mae. Dem be Momma Mae pickney jis't like Ma. I gets to lie down wid Momma Mae and Big Willie 'cause Momma Mae suhs I nots be able to sleep on de bed wid Ma tonight. Dis de furst night I nots sleep wid Ma other dan de time dat Massa send she over to him son plantation.

Chapter 12

A Ma, A Box, A Hole, and A Lonesome Boy

Wen it be morning, we follows Preacher Man as him walk in front of de box dat got Ma in it. Whistler and Short Foot mek de box 'cause Momma Mae suh dat dey mek de best boxes and she want Ma to be in a good box. She suh, "Massa him nots like nigger to dead, but him nots mind nigger deading if nigger leave behind 'placement. So him give dem de wood to mek Ma box. It kinda exchange. Ma left behind a pickney; she be 'placement fer de wood."

Whistler, Short Foot, Big Willie, Little Pete, Big Pete, and Brother carry de box and den de rest of us we walk real slow behind. Momma Mae, she crying and humming. De rest dem sing field song dat 'pose to help Ma get to de Lawd faster. I not want join dem, even if I know'd dem words 'cause I wants to be back at de cabin wid Ma.

We reached de hole dat Whistler and Short Foot dun dig to put Ma box in and Preacher Man him suh dat Ma is gone back to dust and now dat she be dust, she can get her reward in heaven and sing wid de angels.

Dem puts de box in de hole and Whistler and Short Foot start to put de dirt back in de hole. Big Willie, him is holding a spade but him nots be able to mek de spade pick no dirt up, so Little Pete tek it from Big Willie and him help Whistler and Short Foot put de dirt in de hole. Big Willie, him jis't standing thar likes him wants to jump in de hole wid Ma. Wen dey be dun putting all de dirt back in de hole, Momma Mae put de flowers she be gather 'long de way. She put dem by de place where ma's head be and she lay on de dirt and holler.

Momma Mae starts to dig in de dirt like she wants to tek all de dirt back out dat Whistler, Short Foot and Little Pete jis't put in to cover Ma's box. Preacher Man and Big Willie try to lift she up and suh to she dat Ma in heaven wid de Lawd but dat not stop Momma Mae from digging in de dirt. She suh, "I wants muh pickney, I wants muh pickney, sweet Jesus, muh belly hold dat pickney. Dat muh pickney in dis hole. Lawd, Lawd, why muh pickney?"

Den ev'rybody gets to shouting and crying. I cry 'cause Momma Mae crying, but I cry mostly 'cause she muh Ma and I wants she back from way she be wid de Lawd. Den Momma Mae suh, "I curse Massa fer sending muh pickney over to him son place fer breed and I hope de Lawd let him get to see him wife dead birfing a pickney jis't de way muh Lou Etta dead. Dis is de second time him dun send she over thar and now muh Lou Etta, she dun dead."

Soon as Momma Mae suh dat, she get strenf 'cause she gets up from 'pon de dirt, reach fer muh hand and starts to walk slowly, but strong back to de cabin. We leave Ma in de hole by de big tree dat in got no choice 'bout nigger digging holes and burying dem peoples under it.

Chapter 13

One More Mouth

Lil' Mae's pickney start to cry and it mek meh stop remembering muh Ma, 'cause now Momma Mae starts to walk faster, each step suhing she got purpose. De purpose is de crying and hungry pickney. We reach de cabin and Momma Mae sit patient wid de crying pickney. Momma Mae keep dis up 'till Bertha Mae come from de field and she tek de pickney dat tek way muh Lil' Mae. Den she go and she feed she 'cause Bertha Mae herself jis't had a watermelon pickney.

Wen Bertha Mae dun, she puts de sleeping pickney on she bed and suhs, "Little Willie yuh keep yer eye on she while Momma Mae fix yuh some sometin' to eat." Bertha Mae nots exactly suh wat she mean by keep muh eye on de pickney so I sit still and I look at de pickney steady like, I nots blink 'cause Bertha Mae nots suh nuffin' 'bout blinking. I stays looking at de pickney 'till Momma Mae ready fer meh. Wen Momma Mae ready fer meh, she suhs, "Little Willie, in de morning we goin' put Lil' Mae to rest, jis't de way we did yer mamma. We gots to be stirring mighty early 'fore its regular time, so we can do right by her and den get to de field."

Momma Mae give meh some boiled yams, a ham hock, and some roots teas, and suhs fer meh to eat hearty. I tries to eat, but muh heart it beating too slow fer meh to eat and tink 'bout Lil' Mae at de same time. Momma Mae she nots mek no fuss 'bouts meh not eating, she jis't suhs, "Lil' Willie, sorry last jis't fer a night, but joy comes in de morning."

I tinking how we goin' have joy in de morning if we gots to put Lil' Mae in a hole under de tree? I climbs onto muh pallet and I feel de pain deep in muh heart 'cause Lil' Mae gone. Lil' Mae pickney she start to cry, and I wish she had dead right long wid Lil' Mae. Soon as I suh so, I sorry 'cause I can tell dat Momma Mae dun mek a place in she heart fer de pickney and Momma Mae not gine want she dead.

It not tek long 'fore it be morning and we heading up to de cabin where we left Lil' Mae last night. It not feel like it's Lil' Mae anymore, 'cause ev'ting is de same as it be fer muh Ma, only ting different Lil' Mae not got no kin to cry fer she, and Massa, him not care dat Lil' Mae dead, dat wat Momma Mae suh. So ev'rybody dat pick cotton wid Lil' Mac gather round de hole and Preacher Man him suh de same ting him suh wen dey put muh Ma in de hole. Dis time it be only Momma Mae dat singing. She close she eyes real tight and wrap she arms 'round she bosom and in a voice dat sounds like Lil' Mae, she starts to sing.

She sing real pretty words dat seem to come from de air right to she mouth and she sing dem as dey come in. Nobody else singing since de words only coming to Momma Mae. Momma Mae sings a long time but I not hear no more 'cause I starts to cry fer Lil' Mae and fresh fer muh Ma. Momma Mae not grab de dirt dis time wen de box get cover over wid dirt, she jis' stop she song, put de flowers same way as she do fer Ma, and heads back to de yard.

Jis' like wid Ma, we follow Momma Mae. Dis time some stop short of comin' full back to de yard 'cause de sun dun crack de sky and de few steps it tek to come back to de yard be put de sun higher in de sky. Dey jis' go to de field wid out nuffin' to eat and start dem wuk. Nigger wuk start wen de sun brek de sky and end wen de moon looking at de sun.

Wen Momma Mae and meh get to de yard, de Massa him stirring 'bout and suhs to no one in particular, "What you niggers doing stirring before daybreak."

Big Willie, since him tek care of de horses and not have to be in de field furst ting like de rest slaves, look at him foots and him suh, "Massa, de Indian slave she dead birfing a pickney. We is jis' buried she over yonder in de woods where yuh suh its ok fer to bury dead nigger."

Massa him suh, "Nigger, it isn't necessary for you to say bury dead nigger since you only bury dead. Are you really as dumb as the horses and mules you look after?"

Big Willie him not suh nuffin'. Him look at him foots and wait fer Massa to suh wat him to do next. Massa him not tell Big Willie nuffin', him suh, "And the pickney she was having. Did that die with her too?"

Big Willie him know'ds dat him 'pose to answer Massa dis time so him suh, "No, Massa, de pickney it living. Momma Mae and Bertha Mae dem got it."

Massa him not suh nuffin' else 'bout Lil' Mae or de pickney but him suh to Overseer Mulhuddy, who always like shadow watching nigger, "Mr. Mulhuddy, see to it that somebody gets to picking the share of cotton for the Indian bitch which up and died."

Massa Mulhuddy him suh, "Big Willie, since you are the one that disturbed my rest this morning telling me that the Indian gal dead, you'll be the one to pick her share."

Big Willie him jis't look at him foots and Massa Mulhuddy, always looking fer reason to strip a nigger and peel him skin from him back suh, "Nigger, did you hear me say you is to pick the Indian bitch share?"

Big Willie him suh, "Yes, Massa. I hears yuh, Massa. Big Willie pick wat de Indian 'pose to pick."

Den, jis't like him have different idea him suh, "That lil' pickney standing over there with Momma Mae; give him the bag. He was always next to her side. It's time he earned his keep. Big Willie, give the little nigger the bag. He, not you, will pick the Indian bitch's share."

All dis time, Momma Mae and meh we be standing a short way off 'cause Massa not be suh fer we to "Get a move on." So we, not. Momma Mae, she not tek to no cussing, but dat is de Massa and Massa Mulhuddy cussin' so she not suh nuffin' 'cause dey be jis't as soon swing she from a tree as dey be a dog, and den him and Massa Mulhuddy be mek Big Willie cut she down and den pick Momma Mae share of de cotton. It never matter to de Massa if yuh sick, tired, bruk down, old, hungry, or dead as long as de cotton gets pick.

Massa him suh, "You, little nigger, get on over here and take that bag. All you done wasted enough time already. Get a move on."

Momma Mae she give meh Lil' Mae's bag, de very one she had yesterday wen she watermelon pickney mek she fall in de field crying. I hold de bag and follow Big Willie to de field. I feeling hungry from not having no supper last night, but I know'ds better dan to suh anyting. Nobody suhs nuffin' 'bout not having nuffin' to eat fer de morning. We jis't go to de field. I never had muh own bag 'fore but I know'ds dat dis is muh bag from now on, so I follows and do wat de other do. I picks cotton right along wid ev'rybody and I tries very hard 'cause I sorry Lil' Mae not here, and she not got no kin to pick she share, and she pickney; well she be too small to help.

Chapter 14

From Watermelon Pickney To Cornbread

Even now sitting in de low bush trying to figure out how I goin' save Cornbread from de Massa and doing all de remembering I be tired. Muh days of picking cotton never stop from dat furst day Massa Mulhuddy give meh Lil' Mae's bag. I picked wid Lil' Mae's bag 'till watermelon pickney be big enough to pick and den Massa Mulhuddy him suh, "Tomorrow, Momma Mae, when you bring the little pickney gal out here with you, put her over yonder with Little Willie. She's big enough to earn her keep."

Momma Mae she nots suh no more dan, "Yes Massa."

Dat be enough fer Massa Mulhuddy. Momma Mae she suh to meh wen him gone, "Lil' Willie, tomorrow yuh give Cornbread her mamma's bag. Dat all left 'long to her mamma." I be de only one still tinking of she as de watermelon pickney, but ev'rybody calls she Cornbread. Her real name though be Jennie Mae 'cause Momma Mae gave she de name and if Momma Mae give yuh yer name, yuh be called Mae at de end since her name is Mae. It be good fer meh dat I be a boy 'cause Momma Mae be sure to call meh someting Mae.

I 'membering so much sitting in dis bush like wen Big Willie and ev'ryone else suh, "Molasses, yuh not eye her, she be yer sister." At furst I jis't do wat dey suh, but den I gots to figuring if her mamma not be muh mamma and de Massa him not be muh papa, den how come Cornbread be muh sister? So wen Cornbread be round fourteen or so, I ask Momma Mae and she suh, "Little Willie, she yer sister 'cause I raise up both of yuh and since I raise up both of yuh, dat mek her yer sister."

Den I suh, "But, Momma Mae, how come den I feel fer Cornbread more dan if she muh sister and she feel fer me more dan if I be she brother. I wants to jump de broom wid Cornbread and she wants to jump de broom wid meh."

Momma Mae she jis't suh, "Cornbread, she jis't fourteen years and yuh soon goin' be twenty. She dun spend her whole life running and playing wid yuh as her kin, she can't jump de broom wid yuh, Little Willie. Yuh and her be kin."

Cornbread be more dan muh kin I wants Cornbread and meh to jump de broom and have us own cabin and have pickney. Pickney dat not be like either of us 'cause dey be have a mamma and a papa. Cornbread be more dan muh kin, she be muh life.

De Massa not gine to do to Cornbread wat him dun to her mamma and never even one day look at his own kin as she run in de yard and now him suh, "Send Cornbread up to me after supper!" Dis be one Cornbread I be not meaning fer him to have or, if him had dis Cornbread, it be him last piece. I dun 'cided wat I goin' do while I be sitting in dis low bush. I'd also made peace wid de Lawd.

De minute Massa suh to send Cornbread up to him, I know'd fer sure I be goin' to be in heaven wid muh Ma and Lil' Mae. I dun all dat Momma Mae, Big Willie, and Preacher Man been telling meh muh whole life and now Massa him suh send him Cornbread and him not mean de one dat come from the hurf and now I headed to hell. I ask de Lawd to see all de good I dun. I ask him to be fair wen him weigh de one bad ting I be fixing to do 'gainst all de good things I dun. I figure dis one bad ting I be goin' to do be do a whole lot of people some good so it not be so bad. I hope de Lawd can fergive me fer it, but if I had to go to hell, well I guess I be go to hell fer muh Cornbread.

I watch Big Willie putting de lanterns 'round de front porch. Wenever Massa suh to send somebody up, Big Willie put de lanterns round de front porch but none on de back porch. I dun watch and help enough to know'd dat Massa be waiting fer dem to bring Cornbread up. Once de lanterns be all light and hanging, dat be de signal to bring up de one Massa dun ask fer and leave she on de back porch.

I gine wait fer Massa to open de door and den I be rush from behind Cornbread. I be figure de rest after I knocks him down. Massa be old and alone now since Momma Mae got her pray fer wish on muh Ma's grave. Momma Mae she wish dat Massa's wife dead like Ma and it twan't long after Ma went to be wid her Maker dat Massa new pretty wife need Momma Mae to help she wid de birfing of she furst pickney. Dis pickney, de furst Massa be having wid dis new wife, not have de good sense like de Massa's other pickney so it start to come out too early and it must be planning on goin' somewhere in a hurry 'cause Momma Mae suh it be fixing to put it foots on de ground.

De Massa him frighten 'cause dis pretty wife nots have no idea wat happening to she; she in a lot of pain and Massa him not know'ds wat to do fer she while she wait fer de white doctor to come help she. Massa, him not know'd wat Momma Mae wish over muh Ma's grave so him send to get Momma Mae 'cause him little white pickney dun ferget wen it be supposed to come and it nots warn Massa so him could send fer de white doctor ahead of time.

Her pickney, dem suh, got stick trying to come out and Massa suh give she gin to ease de pain and Momma Mae give she de gin. She still in pain, so Massa him suh, "Give her more gin, she's a white woman, only nigger birth pickney screaming and hollering."

So Momma Mae give she plenty gin wenever Massa suhs to give she gin. Soon Massa wife, she drunk and she not be able to help de pickney dat won't help she. By de time de white doctor come and him mek Momma Mae leave from 'round de drunk white woman, dey suh de blood more dan him can stop. Momma Mae she suh she look at de white woman and fer a half a blink she sorry fer she 'cause she be a woman, but wen Momma Mae 'member dat she own pickney dead because Massa put nigger man to she daughter like she be dog, she nots be sorry no more. She left de white doctor finding basins to catch blood and pickney; him gine need two; one fer de blood and one fer de pickney.

Massa's wife, well both she and de pickney she trying to birf, dem dead and dem go wherever white people go wen dem dead. And Massa, if him be a nigger, I be suh him had a broken heart, but since him be Massa and I know'ds dat him not have no heart, him jis't drink all de time and cuss himself fer giving she de gin.

Momma Mae not be sorry de white mistress dead, she jis't suh, "Eye fer eye and a teet fer a teet." I looks fer de white woman eye and teet in Momma Mae's special box where she keeps things dat precious to she, but I nots see de white Mistress' eye nor teet. I decide I better be mighty careful wen I eats, 'cause I's not sure if Momma Mae cooked de white mistress' eye and teet.

Right now, wid de Massa drunk most of de time, him no match 'gainst me. I wuks in de field all day while him sit on de front porch and drink, smoke, eat, and call fer different nigger womans or girls from de cabins. All de hard wuk Massa mek meh do give meh big muscles and I fit muh breeches jis't fine. Thar not be no space left on muh body fer de hard wuk or Momma Mae's fine cooking to fill out. And I mighty strong from helping Big Willie lift all dem cows, bales of cotton, and corn in de Massa's barn.

Big Willie finish hanging de lanterns, I blinks, and in dat little time, Big Willie him gone from 'fore muh eyesight. Momma Mae and Bertha Mae get dun wid Cornbread and I watch as dem open de cabin door and Momma Mae walk wid she to de porch and Momma Mae she lean in and suh sumting to muh Cornbread in she ears. Muh Cornbread she crying but she nod she head. Momma Mae she reach and hug Cornbread tight, tight to she and den she jis't leave she standing thar. Cornbread, well she crying 'cause her not been up to de big house 'fore and she scared of both Massa and de dark. I want to cry 'cause Cornbread crying, but if I start to cry, I not be able to think wat to do wen Massa open de door. So I nots cry, or let Cornbread know'd dat her Molasses in de dark, 'sides I right in front she and she not be able to see meh no how. I wait and Cornbread wait. More time dan usual pass but Massa not come to de door.

Cornbread jis't standing thar wid she arms at she side facing de door, waiting fer it to open and Massa to jis't grab she and jerk she inside jis't de way him do ev'rybody else. De door still not open. Dis seeming more and more unlike de way dat Massa be, 'cause de younger de gal him ask fer, de faster de door opens and jis't as quickly yuh be hear she crying and him beating she into being quiet. Den de only sounds yuh be hear be Massa grunting and groaning.

I not want to hear muh Cornbread cry, so I put muh hands over muh ears and hold muh breff, waiting fer de door to open. In de dark, muh hand finds a rock de size of small watermelon and I decide den wat I'm goin' to do. I goin' smash de Massa's head and me and Cornbread goin' run all night 'till we get off de Massa' plantation. But furst him must open de door.

Cornbread she tired standing so she stoops down to wait. She stoops down and I stands up 'cause I gots to be ready. De door still nots open and muh poor Cornbread real scared now, 'cause if she go back to Momma Mae's cabin and Massa have to come get she, him gine mek Mulhuddy beat ev'rybody in de cabin including Momma Mae. She nots want Momma Mae to get no beating so she stays on de back porch and I waits in de low bush.

She stoops long as she can manage, den she sit down. Still Massa nots open de door. Cornbread gets tired sitting and lies down; still no Massa. I can tell from de steady way Cornbread's body moving dat she dun fall asleep in de night air and now she goin' catch she death of cold and no Massa even come to open de door. I wants to go pick muh Cornbread up and tek she back to de cabin, but I nots be able to move from muh hiding place in case Massa open de door and I be near Cornbread.

I be never have to worry 'bout heaven nor hell 'cause him be sure have me swinging from a tree 'fore mornin'. I watch muh Cornbread sleeping on de back porch of de big house and Massa him never come to open de door.

I hear Big Willie him suh, "Lasses, wat yuh doing in dis bush? Yuh here all night? Yuh better get yer nigger ass back down by Momma Mae's cabin 'fore Massa figure out wat yuh be tinking and skin yer nigger hide."

I look at Big Willie standing thar in de early morning sun holding muh Cornbread and she halfway asleep. Him suh, "Massa him never open de door so I be tekking Cornbread back to Momma Mae so she can rest proper."

Him looked at meh and him suh, "Tek yer nigger self to de field and pick yer share and Cornbread's share 'cause Cornbread roasting wid de fever from being out in de night air all night."

I wants to ask wat happen, but I know'd dat Big Willie like Momma Mae nots tek to no questioning so I do as him suhs and get muh bag and Cornbread's bag. I picking de cotton but I wondering all de while why de Massa never open de door fer Cornbread, den de bell sound and it mean ev'rybody gots to stop picking cotton and come to de yard. Someting important happen.

Chapter 15

A New Massa

We teks de bags and wait in de yard. It be de son dat Massa had wid him furst wife 'fore de young one dat dead wid de pickney. Him be grown and have de 'joining plantation where Massa send Ma. Him suh, "My dear wonderful Poppa is dead."

Niggers start to cry like dem jis't lost dem pickney. Massa son him go on talking like if niggers not be bawling dem eyes out. Mayhaps him knowd's dat nigger jis't balling 'cause him, standing thar and mayhaps him also know'd that him faddah be wicked. Him suh, "If all the doors and windows were not properly secured from the inside when I arrived this morning, I would have swung every last one of you niggers without a second thought. However, it's clear in my mind that your Master must have been coming down the grand stairs and had a heart attack, lost his balance, and fell down the stairs.

"I, along with Mr. Mulhuddy came in the house when Big Willie, the nigger here, came and got Mr. Mulhuddy saying he hasn't heard the master stirring about." Big Willie him looks at him foots and him hang him head low. Young Massa him suh, "It's so sad the way I found your Master at the foot of the stairs; his neck was broken and twisted, twisted most off his shoulders at least I know that he didn't suffer long." Him even mek a little joke wen him suh, "Well there was a bottle by his feet so I know he died enjoying something he liked: having a stiff drink." Soon as him suh dat, Massa's son look like him gine cry when him suh, "Poppa's neck, it was so…" Him not be able to suh wat him want to suh.

Young Massa him tek a deep breff and him suhs, "Believe me, if I thought that any of you niggers had a hand in my father's death, I'll find trees and branches enough to swing every last one of you; young, old, man, woman, and child. You all would be like nigger decorations on a Christmas tree. Anyway, that will not happen today. Today, as a sign of respect for your Master, no more cotton is to be picked and all of you niggers can return to your cabins."

Wen de new Massa suh 'bout him faddah's neck twist off I looks quick at Big Willie and Big Willie him looks at de ground. Den I gets to tinking 'bout de passageway dat Massa had Big Willie, Whistler and Short Foot dig. De one dat went from de big house to a trap door under one of de cabins. De Massa had dem build it in case it be raining and him want to have one of de womans put in de cabin and him not want to get wet coming down from de big house. Sometimes, Massa him wanted to come down to de cabin and not let him wife know'd, so him be use de trap door dat opened from inside him fancy food storage house.

Massa, him keeps a rug over de door in de floor so nobody know'd de door thar. Big Willie him suhs even if yuh moves de piece of rug, de door it looks jis' like de floor. Nobody but him, Big Willie, Whistler, and Short Foot know'd 'bout de door since dey de once fix it jis' like him suh. But Massa him not need de trap door after him wife dead, so him have Big Willie seal it, but Massa him never check to see if Big Willie seal it or not. I know'ds Big Willie not seal it 'cause dat be how him gots to slip little things to Momma Mae from de big house. I also gets to think 'bout how many cow heads Big Willie dun twist off 'cause him so strong. Massa him used to mek Big Willie twist de cows' heads off to show other Massas on other plantations how strong Big Willie be.

We walks away from de young Massa and I go to Momma Mae's cabin where Big Willie dun tek Cornbread wen him picks she up from de back porch. I goes and I look at Cornbread and Momma Mae she watch me watch Cornbread and she suh, "Molasses, wen Cornbread is better and dey dun bury de Massa, I is goin' to ask de new Massa if yuh and Cornbread can jump de broom. I goin' ask him if Big Willie and Short Foot can help yuh build yer own cabin near over where Lil' Mae had she cabin. Yuh goin' look after muh Cornbread and one day soon, we goin' be free from plantation living. I may not live long enough to see de day, but yuh and Cornbread young and may leave dis place.

"I know'ds wat yuh dun last night, Big Willie tolt meh, but Lil' Willie, yuh must remember dat Big Willie and Momma Mae loves Cornbread too. We mights not be able to do nuffin' to stop him from harming she mamma, but dis is our Cornbread and we know'ds dat de Lawd is in de fergiving business; de white preacher him suh dat."

I smiles and I sit on de floor to watch muh Cornbread as she sleep and she sure enough pretty wen she sleep. I know'd dat wen she be better, we goin' be together like Momma Mae and Big Willie, 'cause Cornbread and Molasses 'longs together de same way.

Book Four

Chauncey Street
Aunt Bess And Cousin Thea

Chapter 16

A Change Taking Place

It took Aunt Bess the next couple of months to tell us the first part of the story. Each night we did everything in a hurry just so we could get our needlework out and listen to Aunt Bess. The way she spoke, you could hear Great-Great-Great-Grandpa Molasses and Great-Great-Great-Grandma Cornbread as if they were right there in the living room. Every word took you right back to the days they were in.

Some nights we laughed and some nights we cried, but nothing mattered more than hearing the story. Aunt Bess wasn't just telling it. She was like a sharp chisel and we, Cousin Thea and I, a piece of marble or granite or something hard like that and she was just etching it right into our being. Aunt Bess knew that I was taking it all in. I could tell from the expression in her eyes that she knew she wasn't wasting her time telling me the story. Even Cousin Thea wanted to hear. It was her history too, but I felt that since she was a distant cousin it wasn't as much hers as it was mine. Aunt Bess didn't see it that way. She felt that Cousin Thea was as much a part of this family as she and I. She would say, "Thea got some Fields blood so she family." There was nothing else to discuss as far as she was concerned. We accepted Aunt Bess' words as law and since she was the oldest one in the house, there was no arguing with her.

All around us things were changing. The air was starting to get a little cooler. Aunt Bess was preparing Cousin Thea and me for our first New York winter. I was excited. The park was looking so beautiful and I loved just goin' there sitting and breathing in the cool air. Both Cousin Thea and I were starting to change too. My belly was now a nice little mound and it was moving. Each time it moved I thought of Promise Land and Milton. I was missing Promise Land and Milton; I missed him a lot but I kept it to myself. Didn't want Aunt Bess reminding me of all the reasons why I shouldn't be carrying on about either.

Cousin Thea's changes were different. She wasn't as jumpy as when we'd first arrived. Before, every loud male voice would make her nervous. She looked around always expecting to see her used-to-be man,

Crawford, or her far-removed distant cousin, whose name I never learned, coming around the corner to kill her for what she'd done to them. Since no word ever came from Promise Land about what happened to Crawford and the nameless, far-removed cousin, Aunt Bess told Cousin Thea that it was time she put that behind her and get on with the business of living. Cousin Thea did as Aunt Bess suggested but she did so cautiously. As she went about her cautious way of living, her voice changed. It must be, Aunt Bess said, from being round them white people all day like that. Aunt Bess would say in her booming, yet gentle voice, "Thea girl, one of these days you goin' come in here sounding just like a white mistress and soon you goin' want me and Gina Pearl to be doing for ya." Aunt Bess was laughing so hard we couldn't help but join her in the laughter.

Thea continued to change. She didn't quite become a white woman, but she picked up more than a few of their ways. It was the dry toast and black coffee that always got the same reaction from Aunt Bess. Aunt Bess would say to her, "Thea I never thought I would live long enough to see a kin of mine eat white people food and like it. But now here I am living to see a Negro, from Promise Land of all places, sitting at my breakfast table with some dry burnt bread and some bitter coffee calling it breakfast. Chile, you don't have to punish yourself for some stupid sin you think you committed. The Lord, if He thinks its bad enough, will punish you. Now throw those two dry pieces of bread out the window so the birds can pick on them and reach right over here and get a few of these biscuits, a piece of this thick ham, make room for some grits, and, child, the eggs scrambled just right. Now what do you say?"

Thea laughed, threw the two pieces of dry toast to the birds and did just as Aunt Bess said that Sunday, but after that she went back to her toast and coffee; well, Monday to Saturday. On Sundays when we sat down to breakfast, it was a good old Promise Land breakfast; dry toast never made it to the table; actually toast never made it to our Sunday breakfast.

Aunt Bess loved her needlework. So she taught me and Cousin Thea how to knit, crochet, do latch hook, embroidery, and everything that had to do with a needle. Soon we had more beautiful pillows, kitchen towels, fancy bath towels, sheets, and pillowcases than we knew what to do with. We were also making things for the baby too but that wasn't the only thing we were doing. We were changing. We were becoming family; a quilt. Our life had its own heartbeat and breath. It even had a pattern. Each day was like making a different part of the quilt. There was no telling from day to day what the color was goin' to be or even the feel of the cloth. I didn't worry about none of that. I just added as much of me as days, times, and feelings allowed. I wanted to be a big piece of this new family quilt we were becoming. I wanted my colors to stand out bold and strong; just like Aunt Bess'.

On the days I missed Milton, the colors were black. It was a black so dense it was thick and I would think that part of the quilt would have a patch of cowhide 'cause of the thickness. When I wasn't missing Milton as much and my mind went to Ma, I would always see a deep purple 'cause I would feel like the brown of my own sadness was mixing with the black of what I was feeling for Milton and it would turn all those feelings into purple.

Aunt Bess stayed on me and Cousin Thea, keeping us, as she called it, "Mindful of life for Negro women who don't have men folk. We have to be our own man folk," She said. By that, she meant look out and provide for each other. "Bills always had to be paid; there's no free living."

She didn't believe in wanting what other people had. She said, "If Negroes was to watch the fowl of the air and stop setting their hearts on what other people had, they would be better off. Just look at all them small birds, like sparrow and cardinal, they don't try to fly with eagles. You ever see a turkey trying to be a swan? No. You know why not? They know where they belong and if Negro people would adopt their ways, we would be better off and life would be easier. It ain't ever goin' be easy for a Negro, but it can be easier."

I quickly learned where I belonged. I, like Aunt Bess, was a turkey and I belonged with her and Cousin Thea on Chauncey Street. Aunt Bess loved us and we loved her back. It was the love that we got from Aunt Bess that kept us goin' and added the pinks, reds, yellows, and soft colors to our quilt. Sometimes when I was alone, I would get to thinking about Promise Land and I would get all teary-eyed and sometimes wish to be back there with Ma. That feeling didn't last long because once Ma was sure, and, I never quite knew how, that I had made it to New York City safely, she didn't ever look back at me, not even for one day.

It was as if I'd fallen off the face of the Earth and there was no way Ma could find a way to get to me, her only daughter who was carrying her only grandchild. I knew in my heart that it wasn't true that she couldn't find me 'cause after all, Ma had found a way to get me here. And as far as I knew, no one had shut down that long road; rusty tin cans passing themselves off as buses were still bringing people to the mouth of this place and spitting them out. My mother, if she wanted to, could have found me. She didn't want to. About the time I stopped thinking about Ma, Aunt Bess had reached the part that she called the most interesting part of our history. Thoughts of Ma, if they returned, would have to wait. It was time to hear Cornbread's part of the story.

Book Five

Cornbread 1813 - Unknown

Chapter 17

Once Upon A Time In A Far 'way Land

In dem white people's story books dem story start... Once upon a time in a far 'way land... and den it tell some fancy tale 'bout princesses and princes. Dat be white people's story. Muh story not be nuh white people's story though it got plenty of white peoples in it and it starts wid a white womans and she fancy tinking to teach nigger pickney letters, reading, writing, and numbers. She be call it book learning. Dat be de biggest mistake a white womans ever mek. It, she giving nigger pickney book learning, be 'pose to be secret and know'd only to a few slaves on she Poppa's plantation: Litchfield Plantation. Even de name of dat plantation sum up wickedness and I wish dat I be not want de book learning fer muh pickney and I be jis't gone on wid de cooking, cleaning, and teking care of Mistress Henrietta and not listen to she fancy story of wanting to do someting good fer de little nigger pickney.

It be she wanting to do someting good fer de little nigger pickney dat 'cause all de pain fer we. She called it she Secret Schoolhouse Fer Nigger Pickney and she tek us, she slaves dat wuk in de house, lil pickney fer she secret schoolhouse to give 'em book learning. In Mistress Henrietta's school, thar be muh pickney Milkweed, Tadpole, Chem, Lil' Theo, and Tiny. Tiny him be fat, fat, fat, and ev'rybody call him Tiny. Ev'ry time somebody be call him dat, somebody else be laugh. In Mistress Henrietta's school, thar not be much of nuffin' be really happenin' 'cause dem pickney wants to run and play and dem not be trying to mek dem letters dat Mistress Henrietta be mekking dem wuk so hard at. I nots remember if it be a Monday, a Wednesday, a Friday or a Saturday, but what I know'd fer blessed certain is dat it be day time wen dem white mans come and it be a day dat nobody... white mans or nigger ever gine ferget. White mans dem may ferget 'cause dem be de ones dat do it, but nigger; nigger not ev'r gine ferget. But 'fore I tell wat happen dat day, it best to tell how I gets from Beauford Plantation way I be muh whole life, to way I be at Litchfield Plantation 'bout ready to face de day dat nigger never gine ferget.

Chapter 18

De Fever Dun Gone

I feels him 'fore I sees him. Muh eyes open and I nots be on de porch no more. I be in muh bed and 'Lasses, Momma Mae, Big Willie, Bertha Mae, Annie Mae, and jis't 'bout all dem I been knowing muh whole life be here watching meh. 'Lasses him smile and him suh, "Momma Mae, her full wake now." Momma Mae she come closer and she smiling too. She suh, "Praise de Lawd, dat fever dun bruk and it turn you lose."

I suh, "Fever? Momma Mae I not have no fever. I nots be sick."

Momma Mae she suh, "Yuh not have fever now, but fer three days and nights yuh be roasting wid de fever. I be mighty scared dat it tek over yuh brain, but it not. It turn yuh lose. De Lawd answer muh prays."

When Momma Mae suh three days, I gets to be 'membering dat Massa Beauford dun suh to send meh up to him and I be stand on de porch and wait and wait and him never come fer meh. I suh, "Momma Mae, does I have to go and stands on de porch now?"

'Fore Momma Mae can fix she lips to suh a word, 'Lasses him suh, "Yuh nots gots to go. Him dead. Him fall down de stairs in him house and him bruk him neck. Him dead. Dem bury him dis morning and now him son de new Massa over we."

"Dead?"

Momma Mae she suh, "Him dead and him bury. De Lawd him answer nigger pray. Nigger pray fer mercy and de Lawd give nigger mercy. Him dead like 'Lasses suh and dem bury him dis morning."

I looks at Momma Mae and I be fixing to ask someting, I not sure wat it be, wen 'Lasses suh, "Momma Mae suh dat she gine ask de new Massa if me and yuh can jumps de broom. Cornbread, yuh wants to jump de broom wid meh?"

Big Willie, who be standing off to de side wid all dem rest dat I know'd forever, suh, "'Lasses, dats not how yuh ask yuh special gal to jump broom wid yuh. Yuh waits 'till it be de two of yuh and den yuh ask, yuh not do wat yuh jis't dun. Yuh jis't tek all de special right out yer asking. Now wat if Cornbread suh no yer ready to hear dat in front of all we?"

'Lasses him bends him head and him start to swing him foots. I know'ds when him do dat him shame. I nots want him to be shame so I suh, "I be mighty please to jump de broom wid yuh."

Momma Mae suh, "Now dat de two of yuh have fix yuh minds on jumping de broom, it be up to de new Massa to suh if him tink it be good fer de two of yuh to jump de broom."

Bertha Mae, who not suh nuffin' 'fore, suh, "Momma Mae, 'Lasses here dun jump and ask Cornbread 'bout jumping broom wid him and him dun ferget dat Cornbread here been sick and not have no bittle fer all dem days. Him not suh, 'Cornbread, yuh wants fer meh to get someting fer yuh to eat,' No, all him tinking 'bout is jumping broom. Now 'Lasses, if yuh not feed her den her not have strenf to jump no broom wid yuh."

Dem all fix to laugh and 'Lasses him gets to swing him foots again. I suh, "'Lasses, wat yuh gots fer meh to eat?"

Momma Mae suh, "Go find someting fer she. It be up to yuh from now on. Yuh dun fix dat yuh be man enough to ask Cornbread to jump broom wid yuh, now yuh go find someting fer she."

'Lasses him jis't go to way de food be and him come back wid someting fer meh to eat. Wat it be it not matter none but wat matter is dat him fix and bring it fer meh. I smile wen I tek it from him. Him smile and den it be like ev'rybody smile. Dat be all I 'member 'bout dat day 'cause soon tings change quick. De new Massa him not suh nuffin' to none de niggers but ev'ry day, it be a wagon come to de house and tek way niggers from him place. Den de wagon come back and dem tek tings out de house. Momma Mae not suh nuffin' to nobody, but she go and wen de new Massa come to de plantation to tell dem wat to put in de wagon, she ask him if 'Lasses and meh can jump de broom. Him suh to Momma Mae dat it be ok but him not giving no nigger wedding feast. Him suh dat 'Lasses and meh can jump de broom and den gets back to de field. Him suh dat him be let de Overseer know'd.

Dat be how it be. De next morning, de Overseer him suh, "This evening when you two niggers come from the field, Master Beauford say that the two of you can have your nigger marriage. After, until he says otherwise, the two of you can take up in the cabin nearest to the rice field."

We wuk in de field and wen we come to de yard, de Overseer him be there and him suh to Preacher Man, "Master has said that you are to join these two niggers however you niggers do it. Now join them, let them jump the broom, or whatever you niggers do, but do it now and get it over with."

Preacher Man him call meh and 'Lasses and him suh a few words 'bout de Lawd and mekking 'Lasses and meh one, and dem him suh fer me and 'Lasses to hold hands and jump over de broom. Him suh dat we be two on one side of de broom 'fore we jump, but wen 'Lasses and meh jump over de broom, we be one." I smile at 'Lasses and I looks at Momma Mae, Big Willie, Bertha Mae, Annie Mae, and all dem dat be us family dat de Overseer suh can watch. 'Lasses and meh we do jis't wat Preacher Man suh; we holds hands and we jump over de broom. We go up in de air as 'Lasses and Cornbread, and wen we foots touch de ground on de next side of de broom, we be de same but we be not: I be him wife and him be muh husband. We gets to go to a cabin and be like Big Willie and Momma Mae.

De Overseer him suh, "Now all you niggers get out de yard." We go out de yard and 'Lasses and meh we go to de cabin dat de Overseer suh be us own from now on. It be like all de other cabins, no different but like wen we go up in de air and come back down de same but different, dis cabin be like dat. It be de same but it be different 'cause it be us own now. Momma Mae and Bertha Mae dem come soon after we be in de cabin and dem bring us food and dem suh dat dem be happy dat Massa let we jump de broom. Dem not stay long. Dem leave smiling like dem got secret.

Dem leave de food and meh and 'Lasses we eat de food like we be doin' since we be small, and dem wid de food dun eat, we not know'd wat to do 'cause us never be 'lone like dis 'fore. 'Lasses him suh, "Us still have to be in de field furst ting in de morning so I suh we best get some rest."

I climbs in de bed and 'Lasses him climbs in after meh. Him open him arms and I scoot over to way him be and I puts muh head on him chest and him put him arm 'round muh waist, and 'Lasses and meh we spend we furst night together. In de morning, we be up like all de rest of niggers but we different: we be one now. Him smile at meh and I smile back, shy remembering us furst night together. We gets someting to eat and we go to de field. We not in de field long wen de bell in de yard go off. Dat mean dat all nigger gots to stop wukking and go to de yard. Meh and 'Lasses do like ev'rybody and go to de yard. Wen we gets thar it be de new Massa and de Overseer. De Massa him suh, "My father has left me this house, land, horses, livestock and all you niggers. I have my own plantation and do not need to concern myself with so many niggers so I will be keeping a few but the rest of you have been sold."

Wen Massa suh dat it be like him suh dat all niggers gine swing from tree right now. Nigger starts to cry but dem not cry loud enough to block de sound of de wagons. It be like de wagons dem be waiting fer him to suh dat we be sold off. De wagons come in de yard and Massa Liverpool, de new Massa's Overseer, him start to call off names and jis't like dat, niggers haul off wid rest of him property. Momma Mae and Big Willie dem get solt off together. Dem happy but dem be sad. Dem not get time to suh nuffin' to none of we. De wagon wid dem on it jis't start to roll way. 'Lasses and meh we mighty scared 'cause soon Massa Liverpool him suh, "Lil' Willie, Piper, Jim the shoemaker, Reene, Left Foot, and Planter get up in that wagon."

I starts to cry 'cause Momma Mae, Big Willie, Preacher and now muh 'Lasses get solt way from meh and I be standing in de yard wid all de other frighten niggers. I wants to beg Massa Liverpool to lets meh go wid 'Lasses but him not listening to no crying niggers. Him jis't calling nigger after nigger's name and dem jis't gots to get in de wagon and be tek way and dem not know'ds way it be tekking dem way to. I waits and I waits fer Massa Liverpool to call muh name but him nots. Soon de yard empty but fer a few of we. Massa Liverpool him suh, "Those of you that are left standing are the one that Master Beauford says are to stay here until the new owners come in a few days. If when they come and they want you, then you'll stay and have a new master, if however when they come and they don't want none of you niggers, then you will be sold as well. All of you go back to your cabins, there will be no more work done today."

Him turn and walk 'way and fer de furst time in muh life, I be all alone. I go back to de cabin and I jis't cry and cry. I not have Momma Mae, Big Willie, or muh 'Lasses. I wants muh 'Lasses. I nots know'd wat to do. Thar be nuffin' fer meh to do but get through de day and den de night. I get through de day and night and many days and nights after. Den one morning de bell it sound. We go to de yard dem of we dat left,. De new Master and Mistress dem arrive. Massa Liverpool him talk and him suh dat de new Massa and Mistress gine keep a few of we, but de rest dun sold off. Him dun jis't like 'fore. Him start to call name. Him call and call. De wagon full up wid niggers and wagon after wagon leave. I looks 'round and I not know'ds if in I wants him to call muh name, but soon him suh, "Jennie Etta Mae." Muh heart it get happy and I tinks dat it be a good ting dat muh heart get happy. I not know'd way de wagon tekking meh but I glad to be gine from de place way I born and muh muddah dead. I gets on de wagon wid all de other niggers and it start to roll way.

De wagon it roll from morning to de sun high and hot in de sky and we still be gine. De wagon man him eat, but him not give nigger nuffin' to eat. We be on de same place, or it look like same place to meh. De sun it go down but 'fore it go down, de wagon man tie all we niggers to de wagon. We sleep like dat. Morning time dem start to move de wagon and it be de same as de day before. Wen de sun mek it high in de sky, dem give we some water, a piece of pork fat, and a sweet potato. Dem tie de niggers mans together so dat dem can piss and den dem tie de nigger womans together so we can piss. Soon as we dun piss, dem load we back in de wagon and we steady roll. I not know'ds how far we go but we sleep one more night and travel most de next day and den we be at another plantation. I be mighty glad wen dem suh, "Niggers, get down."

We gets down and a white mans him come to de wagon and him suh, "Are these the niggers from Beauford's plantation? How many did you bring?"

De white mans who be driving de wagon suh, "Twenty-five. There are twelve on this wagon and the others are on another wagon. That's them you see a little way off yonder."

De white mans from this new plantation suh, "Follow me."

We follow him to de yard. Him suh, "Niggers I'm the Overseer here. This is Litchfield plantation. We grow cotton, rice and indigo here. Some of you will work in the rice field, some will pick cotton, and some will work with the indigo. I take no foolishness from niggers, no running away, no stealing, and no lying. I am fair but if I have to swing a nigger, I swing a nigger or as many niggers as it takes to teach a lesson. I have twenty-five other niggers from Beauford's plantation here already. If any of you find niggers that you jump the broom with or find that your pickney is here, let me know. I will let husband, wife and pickney cabin together. No nigger is to take it upon him or herself to make any decision here. If you do and I find out, you will be whipped and sold off." Him point to some cabins and him suh, "All the women take the first five cabins and the men take the next five cabins. When or if you find someone that you jumped the broom with, then changes will be made." Him walk away.

None of us knowd's nuffin' but slaving so we go to de cabin and do what we do at Beauford's plantation. Look fer something to eat, rest and wait fer crack of dawn to start wuk. Dawn crack de sky a few blinks after I puts muh head down. But dat not matter, I be slave and so I goes to de yard and waits fer de Overseer. Him come and him suh dat we must follow him. We follow him. If yuh ever wuk in rice field picking cotton be like no wuk. Dem nigger dat wuk in rice field 'fore start to sing wen dem gets to pick cotton. I tink dem feel dat dem dun dead and dis be de heaven dat de white preacher mans talk 'bout. Dem happy and walking de field like it be mek from gold and gots milk and honey flowing on it.

I be at Litchfield plantation fer a few days wen I feel him. I not see him but I feel him. I looks round but I not see him and dem muh head it suh, 'call him name.' I looks 'round but I not see him, den muh head it suh, 'call him name, call him name. Suh 'Lasses." I do jis't wat muh head suh. I suh real soft, "'Lasses, 'Lasses, is yuh here at dis place?"

One of de nigger womans near me suh, "Is you looking fer a big black nigger dat come over from Beauford plantation?"

"I be. Him and me we jump de broom together. Yuh know'ds way him be?"

"Him be wukking in de indigo field?"

"Indigo, wat dat be and way it be?"

De nigger woman suh, "On de other side of de cotton, but yuh best not go widout letting Massa Livingston, de Overseer, know'd dat yuh tink yuh husband be here and dat it be him yuh look fer."

I smile and muh heart it nots able to wait. I jis't know'd dat him be nearby. I feels him. She looks at meh and she suh, "I keeps waiting fer a wagon to come and muh mans be on it too, but I be here a long time. I not tinks him gine come, but I be glad fer yuh dat de Lawd let it be so dat yuh mans gots solt to de same place you got solt to. Yuh got pickney?"

Still smiling at she, I suh, "We jump de broom and next morning him got solt way from meh. So we not have pickney."

"So mayhaps yuh mekking pickney and yuh jis't not know'd yet. I hope yuh mek pickney. I be mighty glad to be 'round a new pickney again. Dem solt way muh pickney. I still be mekking milk wen dem solt way muh pickney. Wen muh milk stop, muh heart it bruk 'cause I not able to give muh pickney she milk. Here at Beauford, dem not solt way pickney from dem muddah. If dem gine sell a pickney, dem sell de muddah too. Dem not care if de mans get sell way wid de muddah and de pickney, but dem keep pickney and muddah together."

Meh and she we talk 'till it be time to leave de field. Wen I gets to de yard, she suh, "Go to Massa Livingston and let him know'd dat yuh tinks yuh mans be here. If it be him, den Massa Livingston be ask him and if him suh dat yuh be him jump de broom wid womans, den Massa Livingston gine send him to yuh cabin or him gine send yuh to him cabin. Him be do dat fer nigger. Dat be one good ting 'bout him. De one good ting 'bout him."

'Fore I leave de yard I see Massa Livingston and I suh, "Begging yuh pardon, Massa Livingston, yuh suh dat if I tinks dat muh jump de broom wid mans be here fer to let yuh know'd."

Him not let muh dun, him suh, "And which nigger you think is your jump the broom with nigger?"

I start to suh 'Lasses and muh head suh dat not be de name dem solt him way by, so I suh, "Him name be Lil' Willie and him be from Massa Beauford's plantation; brung here 'bout a fortnight ago."

Him suh, "Lil' Willie, he's the big nigger that works in the indigo field. I'll be damned, Lil' Willie has a wife and he never came a looking; wagon after wagon pull up in here and he never came looking. I'll have to ask him if what you say is true. Remember what I said the first day you niggers came here; I don't take to no lying. So nigger what you just said to me better be the truth; for your sake. Now go."

Massa Livingston him jis't walk way from meh. I go to de cabin way de other womans be and I not suh nuffin' I jis't wait. I waits to hear de sound of Massa Livingston's boots crunching in de yard outside de cabin but de sound it never come. I sleep best I can den it be morning and time to get to de field. Muh heart it heavy 'cause I wants to see muh 'Lasses. Dat evening wen I mek it to de yard, I see Massa Livingston and I dun know'd better dan to suh anything to him. I jis't go to de cabin. Wen I gets inside de cabin, de womans dat be dey suh to meh, "Massa Livingston suh dat yuh not to cabin here no more. Yuh is to go to de cabin way over by de tree dem call de magnolia."

"Way dat be? I not know'd way dat be."

Soon as I suh dat, I hear de crunching of boots outside de cabin. All de womans dem look frighten so I gets frighten too. De door to de cabin it open and it be Massa Livingston. Him look at me and him suh, "Come." Dat be it, 'come.' I follows him outside and him suh, "Over yonder way you see that smoke coming up is where you are to go. Go now."

I walk to de smoke. I not looks back. I feel muh 'Lasses and I walk to way I be feel him de most. I see de tree wid de big white flowers on it and den I see some other flowers. Dem be look like cotton but dem not be cotton, jis't look like cotton. Den I feels him stronger and I starts to look from side to side and den I sees him. Muh 'Lasses him walking to way I be. I stops from walking and I starts to run and I suh, "'Lasses, 'Lasses, it be yuh." Him know'd its meh and him stops from walking and him running to meh and him suh, "Cornbread, it be yuh? It be yuh?"

We meet in de middle of we talking and him grab meh in him arms and I be crying. Him suh, "It really be yuh. I begs de Lawd to send yuh. Him hears meh." Him put meh way from him jis't a little and den him suh, "Massa Livingston suh fuh meh to come to de yard wen I be dun in de indigo field but him not suh dat it be be fuh yuh. Come, Come. We gots to go from de yard 'fore Massa Livingston mek yuh go back."

"Way we gine?"

"Massa Livingston him put meh in a different cabin yesterday. We be gine to dat cabin. Come."

I go wid 'Lasses and I be happy. Wen we be inside, him hold me and hold me and him cry. I cry too 'cause him be crying. Den him smile and him suh, "Yuh hungry? Yuh wants fer meh to get someting fer yuh to eat."

I smile back at him and I suh, "'Lasses, wat yuh gots fer meh to eat?"

Him suh, "Yuh 'member. I be glad dat yuh 'member."

"Dat be us special day. Dat be de day yuh suh yuh want meh to jump de broom wid yuh. Now de Lawd give we second day. I be mighty glad." Smiling I suh, "So, 'Lasses, muh jump de broom wid man, wat yuh gots fer meh to eat?"

I eats de food him give to meh and den it be time fer rest; still gots to get to de field in de morning. Like de furst night we be together, I gets in de bed and 'Lasses him gets in after meh. Him open him arms and I scoots into dem. I be so happy to be in him arms. I puts muh head on him chest and him wrap him arms 'round muh waist. We be one again. I close muh eyes and I begs de Lawd to not let sep'ration come 'tween meh and 'Lasses ever 'gain.

Chapter 19

Morning Come Too Soon

It be like 'Lasses and meh only be blink and den it be morning. Him head to de indigo field and I to de cotton field. I sees de nigger womans dat tolt me way 'Lasses be. Soon as she see meh and she mek she way to way I be, she suh, "Yuh gots a big smile on yuh face. Dat be good. I know'd dat suh dat de be nigger in de indigo field be yuh mans and Massa Livingston dun cabin de two of yuh together."

I smile and I suh, "Him be muh jump de broom wid mans."

I looks at Orpah, dat be she name, and she not smiling no more. I suh, "Orpah, yuh not be happy fer meh and 'Lasses?"

She suh, "I be mighty happy fer yuh, but I nots be happy fer meh. Massa Livingston him suh dat I gots to cabin wid de nigger Tember dat dem bring from Beaufort."

"Tember? Beaufort? Yuh nots want to be wid him?"

"I wants muh own mans."

"But yuh suh him solt way a long time. So who be Tember?"

"Tember him be big big nigger from Beaufort in the Low Country."

"So wat dat mek him… not good nigger mans?"

"Him nigger mans and mayhaps him is a good nigger mans, but him been solt and solt so many times dat him not have skin left on him fer brand?"

"Brand?"

"Yuh sure yuh nigger? Yuh not know'ds 'bout branding?"

"I be nigger plenty, but I only been on Beauford Plantation and all him slave be on him plantation since 'fore I be born. So I not know'ds 'bout no branding."

Orpah she look at meh and she suh, "Dem dat know'd Tember from long time suh dat him suh 'fore dem solt him to Massa Litchfield, dat him be on plenty different plantation and 'fore dat him come from a place call Barbados, and it be thar dat dem furst season him to be fine plantation nigger. Tember him suh dat him be in Barbados fer almost two years. I not know'd way Barbados be but him not born thar. Him be born in Africa. Him tolt dem dat him be from Gambia. I not know'd way that be either but to mek him good slave dem tek him to dis Barbados place furst so dem can mek him know'd how to be a good nigger and wuk on a plantation. Him suh dat de white mans call wat dem to do to niggers dem bring from Africa and tek to Barbados 'seasoning'.

"It be thar way dem furst brand him. Wen dem brand nigger, de mark suh dat nigger 'long to de one dat brand dem. Massa Litchfield him got brand. Him brand him new niggers so dat be why dem look fer skin on Tember dat not be got brand and dem brand him. Massa Litchfield him brand be big mark like stick standing and stick laying down. Dem got name fer it but I not know'd wat de name be. Brand be mek from iron and dem put it in de fire 'till it turn red and wen it be red, den dem put it on nigger. Nigger be brand den."

"But, Orpah, nun of dat be him fault. Him jis't nigger and slave like we be."

"Dat be true but dem bruk him spirit. Tember be nigger man widout spirit. Him jis't do. Him never ever tink dat someday tings be different. Dem dun season him good. Tember be de best 'sample of seasoning a nigger. Tember him wid him talking different-self be dead inside. Him rut wen dem suh rut, and him do him best to mek pickney. Dem suh dat wen him mek de pickney, him be like white mans."

"How dat be? Him be nigger."

"Him be like white mans dat mek pickney wid nigger womans 'cause him never look at de pickney. It be like de pickney not be him own. I not wants to mek pickney fer no mans and him not tek one look at de pickney. It be him pickney and him ought to look at de lil' pickney dat be him own."

I not know'd wat to suh to Orpah so I jis't bends muh head and I go back to muh cotton picking. Orpah she stop talking and she go back to picking de cotton too. I not no more talk or try to mek she talk 'cause she start back crying wen she dun talk 'bout Tember, and now she crying she stay 'crying. Wen it be time fer we to go to de yard, she try to mek herself not cry no more and suh, "I nots want to cabin wid Tember."

I nots know'd wat to suh so I suh, "Mayhaps it nots be so bad. Mayhaps Tember not want to cabin wid yuh and so de two of yuh be happy 'cause yuh not like one another and so yuh jis't gots to get through night to morning."

"It not be dat way. Massa Livingston put meh to cabin wid Tember so Tember can mek pickney wid meh. Dem suh dat Tember good fer mek pickney. Bruk spirit man not be able to mek good pickney. Good pickney need whole spirit and him spirit it bruk."

We go to de yard in quiet. I go to be with 'Lasses and Orpah, she go to cabin wid Tember. I mighty glad to be wid muh 'Lasses. I happy to scoot to him arms and have him hold meh and den we be one and stay dat way 'till it be morning.

Chapter 20

Indigo, Cotton And Tember

It be 'Lasses dat notice when I not have a red river and him suh, "Cornbread, I tink dat we gine have a pickney."

I look at 'Lasses and I smile. I be happy to have a pickney. I go to de field and wen I see Orpah I suh, "'Lasses suh dat I gine have pickney."

Orpah she look at meh and she suh, "I be tell Tember dis morning dat I gine mek pickney too."

I look at Orpah- I 'pect to see she crying but she not crying. She smiling. I suh, "Yuh happy 'bout de pickney?"

She suh, "Tember him be fine man. Him is a fine nigger. Him wants fer meh and him to jump de broom, but I not tink dat Massa Livingston or Massa Litchfield gine let we 'cause dem gine mek Tember have pickney wid watever nigger womans dem feel like. Tember suh him gine ask Massa Livingston today."

I look at Orpah and it be strange dat dis is same woman dat not wants Tember; now she not want other nigger womans to cabin wid him. I suh, "Mayhaps Massa Livingston be glad dat Tember gots womans to cabin wid dat want to cabin wid him."

By de time Orpah and meh ready to mek we pickney, Massa Livingston suh dat Tember and Orpah can jump de broom. Dem go up in de air Tember and Orpah and dem come down; Tember, Orpah and Safronia: dat be de name of de pickney dat born to dem dat night. Muh own pickney born a few days after Safronia. 'Lasses him suh dat her mighty pretty and her name gine be Milkweed. I look at de little pickney and I tinks dat not be a name fer a pretty gal pickney, but him suh she name be Milkweed so she name be Milkweed. Him suh dat she name be Milkweed 'cause she be born wen dem be blooming and dem be de most beautifulist flowers ever and all kinds of butterflies come to dem."

So she be Milkweed and her grow'd so pretty, but pretty not stop Massa Livingston from sending she to de field soon as she be able to drag a sack. Her come to de field and her nots want to wear dress so

Massa Livingston suh she nots have to wear dress she can wear de overall like all de boy pickney.

She be dragging de sack hind she one evening wen Mistress Henrietta see she and she suh, "That is about the prettiest nigger pickney I ever did see. Mister Livingston, have them to wash her and send her tomorrow to the house."

De next morning wen we come to de yard, Massa Livingston him suh, "Wash the stink off that pickney and send her up to Mistress Henrietta. From today she's to be Mistress Henrietta pet nigger pup."

Mistress Henrietta, she be Massa Litchfield's pickney, and him not have no wife no more; she dead 'fore I come to him plantation. Mistress Henrietta she tek muh Milkweed and ev'ryway dat she be she gots muh pickney like muh pickney be she dog. If she be sit on de porch; muh pickney be sit on de floor by she foots so dat Mistress Henrietta can pet she hair and tek she foots to rub muh pickney. Muh pickney she be true pet to Mistress Henrietta. It burn meh in muh belly to see dat, but she be Mistress of de plantation and I be slave.

Mistress Henrietta she show muh pickney off to she friends like she be puppy and dem touch she hair like it be hair on dog and dem suh, "Look, nigger with hair that doesn't need combing, look, nigger that be pretty. Henrietta, you picked yourself a fine-looking nigger pickney to be your pup." Soon dem all go off and suh dat dem want nigger fer dem pet. Mistress Henrietta she feel mighty proud 'cause she be de only one of she friends wid nigger pet.

Den one evening wen we come to de yard from de field, Mistress Henrietta be thar wid muh pickney and she look at me; it be a day wen de sun be proper hot and it drain meh, so I be tired; jis't wanting to take de load of muh body off muh foots and rest fer a spell. I not know'd how she know'd dat I be more tired dan I ever be, but she steady look at meh and den she suh to she poppa, "Poppa, I think it be best for my pet Milkweed if her momma doesn't work in the field anymore. Can she work in the cookhouse, Poppa? Can Keziah show her how to make biscuits and bread?"

I not know'd wat her poppa feel 'bout a nigger dat only know'd field wuk coming to him cookhouse, but de next morning wen I get to de yard, Keziah be standing thar and she suh, "Mistress Henrietta suh dat yuh is to come to de cookhouse, yuh not field nigger no more. I is to show yuh how to mek de biscuits, bread, and dem brekfast. Yuh is to come wid me. Come."

I follow she and she stop and look back at meh and she suh, "Yuh not gine need dat bag wid yuh. Thar not be nuh cotton to pick in de cookhouse. De only ting in thar dat be white be de flour but yuh not have to pick or bag dat." She laugh and start to walk way den she turn and suh, "Jis't put it over yonder or wayever yuh feel; jis't as long as yuh not bring it in Mistress Henrietta's cookhouse."

I puts de bag down and I follow Keziah in de cookhouse. She show me quick wat be in der and she suh fer meh to jis't watch wat she do and wen her dun serve Mistress Henrietta and Master Litchfield dem brekfast, she gine show me how to mek de biscuits, bread, and all dem tings dat Mistress Henrietta and her poppa be liking.

Wen Keziah be dun, she suh to me, "Dey be Rashell, Phebe, Clarasa, and meh dat tek care of wat dem need here in de house. Massa Litchfield not tek fer no mans to be in him house, nigger or white mans. So we does all de wuk; someting too heavy fer one we to move, den all we do it ever no mans in him house, womans only. Rashell she be de one dat wuk upstairs. She do de mending and fixing watever it be dat Mistress Henrietta suh fer fix. Phebe; she and Clarasa dem be wuk de rest of de house, but wen it be time to mek dem food, all of we, Rashell, Phebe, Clarasa, meh, and now yuh gine be de ones dat dem 'pect to have 'em food ready and jis't how dem want it. Now I nots have forever to gets yuh to way yuh can mek dem biscuits on yer own. So I gine tell yuh wat yuh need to mek biscuits and den I gine show'd yuh and yuh gine do wat I do. Dat be all de time I gots to show'd yuh and know'd dat yuh cants be wasting dem goods or putting too much of de clabber and potlash to mek de biscuits."

I not waits fer Keziah to dun suh wat she be suhing 'fore I suh, "Clabber and potlash? Wat dat be? I never hear dem words 'fore now. Wat dem gots to do wid mekking biscuits?"

Keziah look at meh and she suh, "Wen I come to dis house and in dis cookhouse, dem show me de white powder and de tick sour smelling milk and dem suh dat dem go in de biscuits. Dem also suh to me dat I gots to get it right or de biscuits not gine taste good. De nigger dat show me suh, 'Jis't do how I gine show yuh. I gine show'd yuh jis't de one time after yuh watch de way I mek some. Yuh gots to get it right or Mistress Emmaline gine puts yuh back in de field. Mistress Emmaline be Mistress Henrietta's muddah but she dead. Her not from here. Massa Litchfield brung she from a place call England, den him tek she to a place called Barbados way him gots 'nother plantation and den him brung she here. She dead when Mistress Henrietta be a lil' pickney. Dem dat here 'fore meh suh Mistress Emmaline left pieces of she heart in de England place and pieces in de Barbados place and den wen she pickney, Mistress Henrietta, born she look at she and give she de rest of she heart. Mistress Emmaline her frail from all dem sea voyages him tek she on, so she not strong wen she gets de dysentery and she not able to fight it and she dead."

I stands looking at Keziah and I starts to feel a little sorry fer Mistress Henrietta dat her not gots no muddah, but den I nots feels so sorry 'cause her keeping muh pickney to be pet to she and muh pickney she not got no muddah. I be lost in muh tinking when Keziah suh, "Cornbread, dat be yuh name, well all dat I dun tell yuh 'bout Mistress Emmaline not matter to de biscuit, bread, or cakes dat yuh gine learn to mek in dis cookhouse—'cause yuh gine mek plenty of dat in here. But so yuh know'd and 'fore I fergets to tell yuh wat de clabber be it be jis't milk dat be bad, but de Massa and Mistress Henrietta and all dem white mans and white womans friends like it in dem biscuits so I puts in and yuh gine do de same.

"As fer de potash is wat us must have to get dem tings we mek wid de flour to rise up some. It not jis't enough to have de potash; yuh is got to pound and fold de flour plenty once yuh mix it up. Yuh do dat to get de air to be inside dem right. If in yuh nots do it right, it not rise up and Mistress Henrietta be mighty displeased. Nigger never want fer white womans or white mans to be displease wid dem so yuh better watch meh good. Yuh gots to get de lard jis't right too. Dat be come easy 'cause once yuh hand get used to de feel of de flour, yuh gine know'ds when yuh gots it right. I not gine have to tell yuh; yuh gine know'd on yuh own. It gine tek time dat be true, but yuh not gots time. Yuh gots to get wat I show yuh to heart quick fast."

I watch Keziah and I do jis't wat she do and 'cause I dun wuk in de rice field; dat be de hardest wuk nigger can do. Wukking in de rice field be 'close nigger can get to deading. Yuh wukking in water near up to yuh woman parts so dat yuh can plant de rice. Dem put de mans, tank de Lawd, but sorry time fer dem, to wuk de sluice gate way. De mans let in and out de water 'pon de rice. Dem men, if dem be lucky, live. But dem dat not be lucky get eat up by de 'gators or bite by de snake and dem dead same way.

Sometimes dem drivers mek nigger womans hill up de ground and dat be de most hard wuk. Wen yuh hill up de ground from sun up to sun down, yuh jis't want to tek de hoe and dig one more hole in de dirt, crawl in it, and dead from tired. If dem see dat yuh live through dat, den dem mek yuh put yuh hand pon de sickle to help cut down the rice stalk. Nigger wuk never dun wen it be harvest time fer rice. Dem barrels gots to be full so yuh gets to beat on dat rice wid a big wood mortar and pestle.

I stands thar looking at she and I be tinking how tekking flour, lard, salt, dis ting she calling clabber and potash be wuk dat nigger nots be able to do. I dun know'd hard wuk but wen I gets to way I wuk in de cotton field it be hard wuk but it not look like wuk to wukking in rice field. I mek it in muh heart to mek de best tings dat ever mek wid flour. I tinks in muh heart dat dem nots be able to have sieve big enough dat I nots gine be able to pick up. Sieving flour be like dreaming wen I tink 'bout all dem winnowing basket I dun use to sep'rate de rice from itself.

Next morning, I be in de cookhouse jis't as de sun crack de sky and I be do jis't wat I see Keziah do. I see dat Keziah watching meh out de corner of she eye, but she not suh nuffin' to meh. Soon as de biscuits be dun, her come over and she tek one and bruk it and put a piece in she mouth, den she smile. She suh, "Meh show yuh jis't yesterday and now today yuh put yuh hand in de flour and yuh mek a better biscuit dan meh. Dem good. Yuh got good hand fer flour." From dat day, Keziah never look at meh wid de biscuits. Her even suh dat Mistress Henrietta mighty please wid telling her poppa to put yuh in de big house to wuk 'cause him like de way yuh mek biscuits."

Mistress Henrietta gots muh Milkweed following she like puppy. Milkweed she happy to follow Mistress Henrietta. Her not know'd better. Dat be wat she be doin' since her be a lil' pickney and now dat her getting bigger, she not mind, she her happy to be pet. Soon Mistress Henrietta not jis't happy wid jis't muh pickney. Her suh her like having nigger pickney fer pet so her tek Rashell's pickney: Lil' Theo, Phebe's pickney: Chem, Clarasa's pickney: Tiny and not much time pass 'fore she tek Keziah's pickney: Tadpole, too. Soon she like ev'ry way wid de pickney following she like she muddah hen and dem be she chicks. But she nots happy wid dat. Her come in de cookhouse one day when her faddah be gone to town on him white mans business and suh dat she wants to talk to all of we in de cookhouse. At furst we not know'd wat her want 'cause us wuk hard to mek sure dat nuffin' ever be wrong so us not gets send to de field.

Wen Mistress Henrietta suh wat she be wanting, ev'ry set of eyes in de cookhouse be open wide like spook dun suh, "Boo." She suh dat she want to have secret school fer us pickney. She, smiling and happy suh, "I even have a name for it. I'm going to call it Mistress Henrietta's Secret Schoolhouse For Nigger Pickney, and Cornbread, I'm going to start with Milkweed the very next day that Poppa goes to town. It's going to be our secret. I will, of course, tell Milkweed not to say a word to any of the other niggers. It will be our special secret. Hers and mine and yours, of course."

Muh heart it beat so hard 'till it hurt. I be frighten but den I 'member dat all muh life, I be hearing from Momma Mac and 'Lasses how him muddah mek him promise him be get book learning and now de Lawd mek chance to come fall in muh lap. I want muh pickney to get book learning. Mistress Henrietta, she stands thar looking at we and smiling. She know'd dat us not be able to suh no to she, but she be looking like she want us blessing on her Secret Schoolhouse Fer Nigger Pickney. Wen us not suh nuffin', she start to lose a little of her smile and she suh, "It will be a well-kept secret. No one will ever know. I'll do it only when Poppa goes to town and he does every fortnight and sometimes he doesn't go for months and months. It will be a special secret."

Mistress Henrietta den look at all of we and she suh, "My Poppa goes to town in about two months. He has business in town about the indigo so I will start that day and since all the pickneys are my pets, I will do what I want with them." She turn she head and walk out. Rashell, Phebe, Clarasa, and Keziah all be mighty scared fer dem pickney, but I talk to dem and I suh dat it be a good ting fer dem to get book learning. I suh, "I not know'ds when de Lawd gine mek it happen, but some day nigger gine be free. Nigger not gine be slave no more and dem dat gots book learning gine be de ones to help de rest of we."

Keziah suh, "But, Cornbread, yuh dun know'd dat dem suh dat no nigger is ever to get book learning. Wat if dem finds out wat her be doin'?"

"Dem not gine know'd. She suh dat it be secret and it not like she gine do it ev'ry day. She suh wen her poppa go to town wid him white mans business. We dun know'd dat wen Massa Litchfield go to town, him tek Massa Livingston wid him and it jis't be de drivers dat dem left behind. She not gine tek all day. I wants muh Milkweed to get book learning. I be mighty pleased with wat Mistress Henrietta gine do."

Rashell she suh, "I not like it, but she be de Mistress and we be de slaves but I nots like it. Deep in muh bones, I feel a evil over dis ting. Dis ting it not gine be good fer no nigger. Lawd, Lawd, Mistress Henrietta dun kilt all we pickney."

Rashell she start to cry fer she pickney and den Keziah suh, "Mistress Henrietta is de mistress of dis plantation. She dun suh wat she gine do and all dat is left fer we to do is do de wuk dat 'fore us. I gine beg de Lawd to be merciful and watch over dem pickney."

Dat night wen I suh to 'Lasses wat Mistress Henrietta suh, him suh jis't wat Rashell and dem in de cookhouse suh. I 'mind him dat him promise him muddah dat him gine gets book learning and dat muh muddah begs Momma Mae to teach me de ways of de Seminole Indians and since it not happen fer we, den it be good fer we pickney to get de book learning. 'Lasses him sad all night and so we not be one dat night. Him jis't hold me and him suh, "Cornbread, she be us only pickney, muh heart not be able to tek it if someting ever happen to she."

I holds him and I suh, "Nuffin', nuffin' gine happen. Mistress Henrietta know'd dat no white womans is to give nigger book learning so she gine keep it a secret."

'Lasses him suh, "White mans suh dat book learning not fer nigger so it not be a good ting fer nigger if it be a white womans dat suh she gine go 'gainst white mans fer nigger."

It not matter wat nigger feel 'cause soon Mistress Henrietta doin' wat she suh. On de days she poppa go to town, she and de pickney dem go to de shed and dem be in thar fer a spell and den she come out way 'fore time fer she poppa to come home. Dis go on ev'ry time she poppa go to town and soon us not worry no more and 'Lasses him stops talking 'bout it. It be jis't wat Mistress Henrietta be do. She even gets to mekking Milkweed wear overalls like dem boy pickney and she suh dat 'cause Milkweed gots hair like white womans, dat it not to be seen.

She suh, "Cornbread, your pickney and my pet, Milkweed, her hair is not napping up like nigger hair and since it looks the way it does, I don't want to see it anymore so I'm going to make her wear a cap like all my boy nigger pets. When you see her, you tell her to never take it off. If she takes it off and I see her hair, I'm going to put Poppa's shaving cream to her head and have Mister Livingston shave it off."

From dat day, muh Milkweed never have she head uncover. It get so as she grow'd her not even look like gal pickney. Her look like boy pickney, same as Chem, Tadpole, Lil' Theo, and Tiny. Her play wid dem same way. It be like Mistress Henrietta gots only boy pickney to follow she 'bout de yard.

Chapter 21

Wen A Secret Not Be A Secret

De white mans, six of dem, come wen Massa Litchfield be to town on him white mans business. Somebody and we never know'd who it be, tolt wat Mistress Henrietta be doin' wen her poppa be go'd to town to do him white mans business. Dem six white mans be de Patrollers. Dem kicks de door down to Mistress Henrietta's Secret Schoolhouse Fer Nigger Pickney. It be de shed fer de dry goods. It not be no real school. It jis't be way she be wid dem so nobody can see or hear 'em. Dem Patrollers come in all dress up so nobody can see dem faces, but we know'd who dem be. Dem be some evil white mans dat ev'ry nigger, free or slave, fear. Wen nigger see dem, nigger know'd dat wen dem gone it gine be a bad ending. Never be not one good ting left in de wake after de Patrollers come by.

Dem not suh nuffin', dey tek Mistress Henrietta by she hand and drag she outside. Dem push we pickney behind she. Wen dem be outside in de yard, de white mans mek we, de mommas of dem pickney who be in de shed wid Mistress Henrietta, stand to in de front of all de niggers dem dun round up. One of de Patrollers him tek a stick to Mistress Henrietta and him hit she plenty on she legs. I not know'ds muh numbers but dem hit she and hit she and one of dem suh dat dem gine give she a lick fer e'vry one of de nigger pickney she have in she school.

Dem white mans not really hit she hard, but dem hit she and den dem push, almost drag, she to de door of de big house. One of dem open it and shove she in. Den him suh, "Don't you come back out here now, Mistress. What goin' happen out here not for the likes of you to see. You stay inside. This here is Patroller and nigger business and it doesn't have anything to do with no white woman."

Mistress Henrietta suh 'fore dem close de door, "Please don't do the pickney harm, they don't really know anything. They are just dumb niggers and you and I both know that niggers aren't predisposed to learning; book learning being the least bit of which they are able to absorb. Please, you have punished me sufficiently. I've learned my lesson and I'm rightful sorry for bringing shame to my father's good name. I won't ever do such foolery again, but please, oh please just let the little nigger pickney go back to the field. They are hard-headed and none of them, kind sirs, ever got any learning; not the first letter or the first number. They are just what you see before you, kind sirs, a bunch of little dumb nigger pickney."

De one dat had drugged she to de door gave she one final push and pulled de door 'hind him. One of de Patrollers dat I not see 'fore now him come up to de porch and him put a rope over de door handle and den him tie it to de porch. Him stand thar to mek sure dat Mistress Henrietta not come back out. She shake and shake de door and den she stop. De mans who dun tied de door handle wid de cord to de porch suh, "Mistress, it's not a good idea to keep shaking that door. Now stop!" De door it not shake nuh more.

'Till today, I not know'd how dem Patrollers know'd dat we be de muddahs but one by one, dem drag we to de center of way all dem hate pile up. One of dem suh, "You nigger bitches that got it in your heads to think your nigger pickney can know what white children know are going to live to see what wanting what the good Lord means only for white children is going to cost you all. This, niggers, is what you get for thinking that your little nigger pickney is good as white children. Stand and watch and don't none of you dumb ass nigger bitches ever forget that it is your fault that these nigger pickney are getting what they are getting. God didn't make letters and book learning for no niggers. When we done here today, ain't going be one nigger in the whole of Greenwood going ever want book learning again, ever."

One of dem walk over to Chem and drag him hollering and screaming from way dem had all we pickney to stand. De one dat drag Chem tek a rope wid de biggest noose I done ever seen, not dat I'd seen dat many, and him put it 'round Chem neck and him pass de rope to one of dem dat be waiting fer de rope and dem swing Chem up. Rope and noose so thick, it 'most bigger dan him head. Him be small and light so him not hang right 'way so one of dem jis' walk over to where him legs be flapping in de air and him jis' yank on Chem and I hear dis crunch snap sound and Chem, him stop moving: him be dead. Him momma, Phebe, she pee and lose she bowels as she try to scream, but no sound come out. She lost she voice wen dem pop Chem's neck. She eyes, dem jis' be white like ghost scare she.

A next white mans, him not suh nuffin' but him walk over to way de lil' pickneys be and him grab hold of Tadpole, we be call him dat 'cause him fat and round in him middle. Tadpole him eyes near coming out him head from him bein' so frighten. Him watch where Chem be swinging and de Patrollers dey start to put another rope round him head but change dem mind. One of dem him tek out a knife from de waist of him breeches and quicker dan lightning can light up de sky, him had Tadpole slit from him boy parts clear to him chin.

Tadpole him eyes open wide like him trying to figure out what stick him in him belly, but 'fore him can figure out dat him belly cut open, him momma, Keziah, she crumble to de ground. Tadpole him turn him head looking where him momma fall and jis't as him go to mek one step to way she be, him guts dem fall to de ground and him wid dem. Tadpole, him tek more dan a minute to dead. As Tadpole buck and bend on de ground in what must be outright real pain, de other small pickney 'cept muh pickney, try to run under dem muddah's dress. I looks at muh pickney and I know'ds dat she be wanting to run under muh dress so I can hide she, but she not move. It not matter dat her not move. Muh dress it gots plenty of room, but I nots have enough room to hide she from de Patrollers.

A white mans pull out a gun and him suh, "If in any of you nigger bitches thinking to make one step toward these pickney, ya'll going hear just one sound and it goin' be the sound of your head being shot right off your fucking nigger shoulders. Now don't none of you niggers make one extra blink or I'll shoot you in your fucking eye."

Ev'rybody stop blinking.

A different white mans grab muh pickney, him drag she to where de ground be trying to drink Tadpole's blood fast as it be gushing out and failing. She look at meh and de white mans standing next to meh suh, "Nigger, you so much as look like you thinking to move and I'll shoot the piss right outta you."

I not blink nor move. I mek like I be rock and stands still, but I not be stone or rock 'cause I be jis't as sorry as Phebe and Clarasa. De Patroller him push muh pickney, she stumble but not fall but she step in Tadpole's blood. It still be coming from him body so I know'd dat it be warm. De blood dat mek it to de ground dun soak in de mud and so wen her foots step in de blood-soak mud, it full up de space 'tween she toes. I know'ds dat her want to stomp and mek it go way from she toes but she 'fraid to stomp and mek 'em kilt she 'fore dem ready.

If dis be a different day, I be do like Tadpole's momma and piss on muhself but dis not be a different day; it be today and white mans be here to kilt we pickney dat us send to get book learning at Mistress Henrietta's Secret Schoolhouse Fer Nigger Pickney dat somehow not be nuh secret nuh more. Another white mans, dis one tall and not way near as fat as de one dat be dragging muh pickney, grabbed she hand and pull she faster toward de tree where Chem be swinging. I wants to run 'way and scream, but I nots gine do none of dem things I want to do. I still staying like rock but I not be rock; she be muh pickney and if dem gine kilt she, den I gine be she muddah 'till dem dun. She not gine get to see dem kilt meh. I not want she to dead wid dat in she head.

At de tree, de one who had grabbed she 'way from de fat white mans starts to put a rope over she head. It mek de cap dat Mistress Henrietta mek she wear fall off she head and she hair, which I be tek muh time and stuff under dat cap she love so much, tumble out. Him stop and him rip at she shirt. Him see she little bub bub and him know'd now dat her not be a boy like de rest. Wen him find out dat she be a gal pickney, him stop. Him suh, "Wait a minute. This one is not a boy. This little nigger is a bitch."

De fat white mans him suh, "A lesson is a lesson. We are here to teach these niggers a lesson so put the rope over the little bitch's head and let's be on with what we came here to do."

De minute dat be turning out to be de longest one of we life it go on. De one who be find out she twan't a boy suh, "Stop. Go and get the next little nigger that was figuring on getting book learning." Him shove muh pickney 'way from him real hard and him suh to she, "Sit!"

De shove it mek she stumble forward fer a bit. She sit down right way she be wen him shove run out. It run out near way Tadpole be on de ground. She shut she eyes fer a blink and den she open dem again. She look at meh and I see all de fear in she eyes. I be she muddah and I nots be able to be she muddah and save she from dis wickedness dat de Patroller gots in dem mind to do to she. She head turn and I not able to look way she look 'cause I still be de rock de white mans wid de gun mek meh, but I know'ds way she be looking. She be lookin at she poppa. I not, 'till this time, tink on 'Lasses. Now dat I be tink on him, muh heart it do like a rock hit it: it bruk. It bruk 'cause I be de one dat got him pickney right way she be, sitting on de ground waiting to be de next or to be de last pickney from Mistress Henrietta's Secret Schoolhouse Fer Nigger Pickney dat gine get kilt by dese white mans. Muh pickney look 'way from way she faddah be and her look at meh. Muh heart, de little pieces dat it be when it bruk, bruk even smaller. De pain of all dat brekking too much; I stop from bein' rock, I be she living muddah and I wants to dead too, but not 'fore I know'd wat dem gine do to muh pickney.

Dem grab hold of Lil' Theo. Lil' Theo be de smallest one and de letters be hard for him to mek but Mistress Henrietta let him momma,

Rashell, keep sending him 'cause Mistress Henrietta suh dat she can see dat him be 'frail lil' pickney and field wuk gine kilt him quick fast. It clear dat none of dese white mans care 'bout none of dat. De fat one dat grab hold of Lil' Theo suh, "This little nigger ain't nothing to swing." No sooner dan him suh dat dan him put him fat fingers on top of Lil' Theo's head and grab him by him hair and tek him knife and quick fast him be drawing a thin deep line cross Lil' Theo's neck.

Lil' Theo eyes dem open wide in surprise from de sudden pain and him mouth open a little like him gine scream. I hears a scream but it not be Lil' Theo 'cause wen de white mans mek de line in him neck, it cut him head near right off. It be him muddah, Rashell, she be de one hollering. She start to holler from de time de white mans put de knife to Lil' Theo neck and she holler 'till jis't wen Lil' Theo knees bend, him head flopped to de side of him neck, near way by him shoulder. Him head swing back and forth a little and den it not move no more 'cause him dun hit de ground. Him jis't be thar wid de eyes wide open and de mouth wid de same little opening it had wen de white mans put de knife in him neck. Him head jis't be holding on wid one little string dat must be a vein or watever be in necks to hold dem to yer head, stopping it from jis't falling off him shoulder and rolling cross de ground.

De same fat white mans see de string dat holding Lil' Theo head to de rest of him body and him mek a quick step, bend down, put him knife under de string and him mek one quick pull up wid him knife and jis't like dat, de fat white mans finish cut Lil' Theo's head off. Him muddah she holler even more now and she suh, "Lawd, Lawd, muh pickney! Oh, Lawd, Lawd, muh pickney."

De same fat white mans dat jis't cut off Lil' Theo head suh, "Nigger, shut your fucking mouth and shut it now."

I can see dat Rashell want to stop hollering but her nots be able to get she hollering to quit 'cause she be looking at way Lil' Theo head and him body be and she jis't hollering. De fat white mans shout at she again, "Nigger, shut your fucking mouth now. You hear me? Shut your fucking mouth right now!"

Rashell put one hand over she mouth to keep de holler from coming out, but a holler still come out so she put she next hand on top of dat hand to hush de holler, but even wid all two of she hands pressing hard to she mouth, de holler still come out. De fat white mans who tolt she shut she fucking mouth jis't step right up to where she be and him tek him gun and him put it right way she hands be over she mouth and him shoot she right through de hands dat she got over she mouth. She eyes dem open wide like she surprised and den she mek as to step toward where Lil' Theo be but she fall down 'fore she mek de step; de hollering it stop.

It be meh pickney and Tiny left.

Him steps back from way Lil' Theo and Rashell be wid dem blood, same as Tadpole, feeding de ground.

De longest minute it be come to a stop. Time, it start moving again.

De white mans wid a gun in one hand and a bloody knife in him next hand walk over to Tiny and him suhs, "This fat nigger should swing for all de food his fat nigger ass dun ate from Litchfield. Tie him up!"

They tie Tiny up and pull on de rope 'till him foots be clear off de ground. Clarasa, she groan real soft and de tears dem coming out she eyes fast like dem all running to catch up wid de furst one dat fall out she eye. Her eyes dem be on de rope dat be choking off him life. I know'd that if not be fer dem ropes, Tiny be hollering. Him be choking so no sound come out wen him try to holler. Him twitch and jerk and den de one wid de knife dat had Tadpole's and Lil' Theo's blood on it suh, "This fat nigger ought to have his guts opened to see what was the last thing his fat ass ate from Litchfield."

Wen him suh dat, Clarasa she mek she fingers to lock into dem one another tight, tight, like she be praying and she look at she dead pickney and I can see on she face dat she not want dem to cut him. I know'd dat her know'd dat it not matter now if dem cut him or not 'cause him be dead already, but her be him muddah and her not want him to suffer no more. One of de white mans who had suh nuffin' 'till now suh, "The fat nigger dead already, leave him be. Let's be on our way; Litchfield should soon be returning."

De mans wid holding him gun and de bloody knife suh, "There's the matter of the little nigger bitch." Turning to de one dat had find out she be a gal pickney, him suh, "What you want dun with the little bitch?"

"Nothing. Cover her head and bring her."

"Bring her? What you want to do that for?"

"Don't you question me. I said bring her and that's all you are to do. Cover her head and bring her."

Jis't like dat she be tie like she be a hog and throw'd 'cross de yard and tied to a horse.

De one dat suh fer dem to tie she up get on him horse dat she be tie to and him look back at way she be and him suh, "Run!"

She start to run but dem be goin' too fast and soon she stumble, fall, and dem be still riding and not caring dat she nots be able keep up. She try to get back on she foots but she fall down again. Him not slow down. Him drag she. From de way she getting throw'd from side to side,

I know'd dat she skin gine be coming off ev'ry part of she 'cause him be pulling she over dry dirt, rough grass, and rocks, small and big. I beg de Lawd to tek pity on muh pickney and let she hit she head on someting hard; not hard enough to kilt she but hard enough to mek it so she not know'd de pain from her getting drag. Soon as I dun suh de pray, I see de big rock dat jis't jump up in front muh pickney and it be like de Lawd pick she up, tek she right to it, and hit she head 'pon it. Her go limp. De Lawd, Him answer muh pray.

De piss I be holding in since dem white mans start to kilt off we little pickney jis't come out. I stands way I be and I piss on muhself. It be a long, warm piss. Jis't as de piss be running down muh leg, I feels a hand touch meh. It be 'Lasses. I looks at him and I be mighty sorry. Him crying. I nots able to suh nuffin' to him. Him open him arms. I step in and him wrap him arms 'round me like de furst night we jump de broom. Dis time it be different. Den love and joy brung us together, now pain of sep'ration dun come 'tween us. Him hold meh as we jis't stand and watch at way dem dragging way we gal pickney. I looks at de dust dem horses leaving behind and I know'd dat muh gal pickney be getting drag way 'cause I be de one dat tolt him it be a good ting dat Mistress Henrietta gine do at she Secret Schoolhouse Fer Nigger Pickney. I turn muh head way from way dem be draggin' way muh pickney and I look at 'Lasses. Crying, I suh, "I sorry, 'Lasses. I sorry, sorry dat I mek we pickney get drag way and I be sorry in muh whole body fer Rashell, Phebe, Keziah, and Clarasa 'cause I be de one dat tolt dem it be good fer de pickney to get book learning. I kilt dem all. I kilt Rashell too. Oh Lawd, Keziah, Clarasa, and Phebe… I bruk dem heart. I kilt Rashell and bruk yuh heart."

Him suh, "I know'd dat yuh sorry, Cornbread. I know'd but it not be yuh dat kilt dem. Hate fer nigger kilt dem."

I cry even more wen him suh dat and den him suh, "Muh Momma ought not to have mek meh promise she dat I gine get book learning and yuh Momma ought not to have ask Momma Mae to learn yuh de way of no Seminole Indian when she know'd dat Momma Mae not know'ds de way of no Seminole. Momma Mae dun wat she know'd best and now 'cause of dem wanting fer we wat we not know'd wat dem be wanting and we be trying to get dem wat was promised dem all dem wanting, dun mek Chem, Lil' Theo, Tiny, Tadpole, and Rashell be dead and we pickney get drag way." Him tek deep breff and den him start to holler. Him holler and I start to holler too and den we holler it jis't like wat we be we whole life; one. We see dat dem not kilt we pickney fer we to see but we know'd dat her not gine live after dem drag she way. We not know'd way dem drag she to, but we know'd when dem dun she be dead.

All 'round, nigger mans, womans, and pickney hollering. We not moving. Us not know'd wat to do. While we standing round hollering, Massa Litchfield, de Overseer and other white mans dem come back from dem white mans business in town. Him see him nigger slave in him yard hollering, him see de dead niggers, pickney dat be swinging from him tree, dem dat be on de ground and Rashell, and him see all de blood and him run to him house shouting, "Henrietta! Henrietta!" It like him not even see or hear nigger pain. Him be true, true white mans. I know'd from de way dat him look at we, jis't a blink, dat him true belive dat nigger not have heart so nigger not know'd love so how can nigger know'd pain. Him eye on him tings. Him house and him pickney. Him mek it to him door and while him untying de rope, him calling, "Henrietta! Henrietta!"

From de next side of de door, I hear, "Poppa! Poppa!"

Him get de rope untie from de porch and him tek de rope off him door, open it, and Mistress Henrietta she run to she poppa, but not 'fore she hear and see all dem from she Secret Schoolhouse Fer Nigger Pickney, 'cept muh Milkweed, cut up, or swinging from a tree dead. She holler, "Oh my Lord! Oh my Lord!" Den she faint. Her poppa him pick she up and him go inside him house. Him shut him door on nigger and nigger hollering; him be true, true white mans.

Book Six

Milkweed
1831 - 1908

Chapter 22

Waking Up To A New Hell

Inside de already dark sack dat de white mans put over muh head, it be darker. Wid de extra darkness, muh pain from de dragging go away too. I not know'd how long or how far dem drag meh. I not know'd how long de dragging be go on fer 'cause soon inside de dark sack, muh head not able to tek de pain from de hit no more and all muh senses dey leave out muh head.

I not know'd how long I be way, but I be waking up. Waking up suh I be still living. De sack it off muh head and I be on a bed and I be wash and gots a clean frock on. Tadpole's blood it be gone from muh foots, but not from muh memory. I look 'round to see way I be. I be in a cabin. I start to come frighten all over again. Someting in muh brain suh run. I try to move. I nots be able to: I be tied.

"They said you would run or try to run when you woke. If you want to live, you won't try that."

I 'member de voice. It be de same voice dat suh to cover muh head, tie meh to de horse, bring meh, and fer meh to run. De one dat be find out I twan't a boy and tolt meh to sit. Him start to talk again and him suh, "When I speak to you, answer me. There are only two answers for you and that's either, 'Yes master or no master, or yes Massa or no Massa.' I don't need any more talk from you."

I suh nuffin' since I not know'd if him want a yes Massa or a no Massa. Him went on, "You've been here for almost three weeks now and you are the only nigger 'round here who isn't earning a moment of your keep. That doesn't happen at Fields Plantation. Every nigger on this plantation earns their keep. So now your eyes are open and it looks like you are going to live, get to your feet, nigger, and earn your keep."

Him step out de dark place where him be and him walk over to way I be. Him voice, which be big and sound like low thunder, not match him or him face. Him voice suh dat him should be de short fat man dat got de marks from de pots on him face and him belly should be big from too much wine, ale, meats and cake. But him not look like dat. Him tall like him not need help to get on him horse. Him belly not look like him ev'r been too full. And him face it not pot-mark. Him face it white but not white white. It be like dem dat spend too much time in de sun; white but brown fer a white mans.

Him eyes dem blue like de sky and de white part; well dem be like clouds. Him eyes look like sky floating on clouds. Him nose it long and thin, but it not be long and thin like Massa Litchfield. Him nose it be long, but it be long enough fer him face, and him mouth it be a little like nigger mouth but not all de way. It jis't not be thin de way white mans mouth be thin.

Wen him bend down to untie muh foot, I gets a good look at him hair and it be look like de very tip of a ripe ear of corn; de part dat hanging out. Him hair it be brownish red and it look like it be soft. It not straight like de way de corn hairs be, but it curly and it look like de curl all mix-up in one another.

Dis be de closest I be to a white mans dat not trying to kilt meh. I can smell him. Him smell like him fresh scrub ev'ting. Like soap and watever white mans use to mek dem smell almost like white womans. I stands still and him wuk on de knots on muh foots and 'fore him free muh foots, him suh, "Make like you thinking to run and I'll shoot you."

I can tell him mean it. I dun live dis long, it not mek sense fer meh to give him reason to shoot meh. I also know'd wat a white mans mean wen him tell nigger 'bout earning keep. It always mean hard wuk, more hard wuk, and if thar's be anything left in yuh, den thar be more wuk. De only ting white mans let yuh keep fer yerself is sleep and even dat dem mek sure it not much. It not matter dat it never enough 'cause by de time yuh get 'round to tinking yuh deserve it and goin' tek it. Yuh body it be so tired dat most times, yer body it refuse de little sleep yuh dun wuk so hard to earn.

"Nigger, you hearing me?"

I speaks furst to muh mind and I suhs, "Milkweed, him dun let yuh live dis long, yuh nots give him reason to kilt yuh now." Den I suhs to him, "Yes Massa."

"Stand up!" I raise up from de bed. I manage to stand widout falling. Him suhs, "Come."

Dat's wat him suh. I follow way him go. I know'd better dan to ask anything. De cabin small so we outside in no time. Outside, a woman looking like a momma, but a momma dat not know'd nuffin' 'bout pickney look at meh. De white mans suhs, "You got her to live, now get her to work. Find out what the nigger wench good for and if she isn't good for anything, you get her good at something or I'll take that new skin off her and then I'll strip the old one off you myself."

Him walks away.

De woman, she not suh nuffin' to meh. She jis't turn and walks way almost in de same direction dat de white mans had walk but her go to de back of de house. She not suh for meh to follow she but I follow. Muh whole body it hurt wid each step. It feel like somebody dun put shoe and nails fer de horse at de bottom of muh foots; dem so sore wen I step.

She inside de house 'fore meh. Wen I mek it inside, she suh, "Fer watever reason Massa Fields brung yuh here nots mine to question. White mans got white mans ways. Dat's white mans business. Him suh yuh is muh business. Muh business on dis here place is to do wat Massa Fields and Mistress Olivia suh fer meh to do."

I stands at de door where I dun follow she in and I look at she. De ma dat not be mine, look at meh and I can tell she know'ds I tinking 'bout trying to figure a way to get 'way from dis place. I not know'd how she know'ds but she know'ds and she suh, "If yuh tinking wat I tink yuh tinking, know'ds Nigger Gal, dat 'fore I let yuh turn muh back up to dem fer another beating, I gine poison yuh furst. Yuh nots de furst one show up here 'cause a Massa on dis place tek a wanting to yuh. Dat's white mans ways. Dem always want wat nigger womans got between dem legs and den dem hate yuh fer mekking dem want yuh. Him wanting yuh nots mek yuh special to meh over meh."

I stands thar looking at she and wid de same voice, she suh, "Field wuk hard. Let meh see yuh hands." She look and she suh, "Yuh hands suh yuh know'd 'bout field wuk. Massa Fields suh to mek yuh useful. Fer yuh, dat mean no field wuk less I suh yuh nots good fer nuffin' else. Yuh good fer anyting other dan field wuk?"

I stare at she. I not suh nuffin' 'cause I afraid I might suh someting and mek she poison meh. I jis't nod. She suh, "Fer now, yuh watch meh. I got to get Massa Fields and Mistress Olivia dem brekfast and I nots be able to have yuh slowing meh down. Yuh sit here. Drink dis."

Wen she give meh de tin cup wid some brown stuff in it, I not know'ds wat to do. Muh heart it get mighty fearful. She sees de fear in muh face and she suh, "Massa Fields dun seen yuh walking and living, him nots be listening to nuffin' dat I have to suh 'bout yuh jis't up and dead so I nots goin' poison yuh. Not gots no reason to now, do I, Nigger Gal?"

I speaks muh furst word to her on dis new plantation. I suhs, "No."

She suh, "Den yuh bets be drinking wat in dat cup. It dun mek yuh heal up dese three weeks. Him mek yuh walk in here, but yuh not dun heal on yuh inside. Best yuh drink 'cause him want yuh to be earning yer keep and sick nigger nots be able to earn de kind of keep dat de Massa of a plantation tinks is enough wuk. So if yuh nots wants to dead de furst day yuh stands on yuh foots, yuh best drink it."

I turns de cup up to muh head and I drink wat be in de cup. It be bitter but I know'ds better dan to ask de Lawd to tek dis bitter cup from meh. Dis bitter cup not be as bitter as some of de cups dat I tink gine come pass muh lips at dis place. I swallow and I not taste de bitter no more. De Lawd, him not tek way de cup, jis't de bitter. I be tanksful. I drinks it all and I stands wid de cup in muh hand. De Ma dat is no ma she point to a spot dat not got too much on it and she suh, "Yuh can puts it over thar."

I do wat she suh. She gets busy wid wat she have to do and she not suh nuffin' else to meh 'till she tinks dat I may be hungry again and den she suh, "Cornbread left over from dem brekfast dis morning. Tek a piece and puts a little molasses on it."

Wen she suh cornbread and molasses, I get a sinking in muh belly and den I feel de crying wukking it way from muh heart. I nots be able to help it. I starts to cry fer muh momma and poppa.

De ma dat not be a ma she suh, "Yuh see dem tears dat yuh crying? Yuh not have time fer dem. Wen yuh dun cry dat set, mek dem de last set yuh cry in dis cookhouse or anywhere else near meh. I hate crying. Nigger not have time fer dat. Yuh is a nigger so find a way to stop dem. Dem not worth nuffin' here."

I try but de more I try to stop, de more dem come out. She step to meh and she suh, "Yuh stop now or I gine give yuh someting to cry fer. Now stop dis crying. It not be someting yuh can 'ford. Yuh is a nigger. Tears and feeling sorry fer yuhself is wat white womans be do."

I jis't do as de woman suh fer meh to do. I gots to tinking dat mayhaps if I do watever she ask fer meh to do, I can get to go back to Mamma Cornbread. I miss Mamma Cornbread wid such a pain in muh belly but thar not be nobody to tell muh hurting to. I jis't do wat she suh and soon I not be crying no more.

She do wat she have to do and wen de sun start to go down, she suh dat we dun fer de day. I follow she back out de way I dun come in. Dis time she not tek meh back to de furst cabin where Massa Fields walk meh out. She tek meh to a different one and she step in furst. I stands outside. She suh, "Nigger Gal, I be tired. Yuh jis't follow meh in. Dis place is where Massa Fields suh yuh is to be from now on." I step in and de woman step out. Wen she step out de little cabin, it like she tek ev'ting wid she dat might be good. De only ting left behind wid meh be muh fears and dems filling up de little cabin and squeezing out de little air dat gets in wen de woman, who name I learn be Neala, open de door.

"Wat I's 'pose to do?"

She look at meh. She look sad. "If yuh can; go to sleep, I 'pose. Dat's all. Go to sleep." Turning away, she suh nuffin' more. She left and I be alone. I stands in de same spot she left meh in. I not want to lie down in dis place or on de bed over in de corner. I stands long as I can den I start to feel tired and muh mind it suh, 'Wat yuh jis't standing here fer, it not like yuh standing gine mek tings change fer yuh. Wat gine happen to yuh, gine happen, so yuh best meet it wen yuh rest some.'

I walks over to de bed and I sits down. I be more tired dan I reckon 'cause I not remembers lying down or falling asleep, but a hand on muh ankle wake meh. De ting I be fearing come to meh and I not be rested to face it.

Chapter 23

Wishing I Be Asleep

De hand on muh ankle it be hot, and clammy, but it twan't rough so I know'ds straightway dat it not be de no nigger hand; man nor woman. Nigger hands dem be rough from wuk. White mans dem hands not be rough since dem not ever do no wuk. I know'ds den dat de hands dat on meh 'longs to a white mans.

De way de hands grab meh mek meh jump and I right scared, but I refuse to open muh eyes. If I be sleeping, I wants to stay sleep; if I be dreaming, I want to stay dreaming; if I be wake, I want to be sleeping and dreaming. Dream or wake, another hand be on muh other ankle. Dat told meh I be wake. I pray to de Lawd real quick to let meh be sleeping. I feels de hands and dem feel real so I know'ds dat de Lawd not answer dis pray. I open muh eyes slow not dat I want to see who it be 'cause I dun I know'd.

It be Massa. Him be holding each of muh ankles in each of him hands and looking at meh like I dun him someting wrong. Him look jis't de way him look de day dem come and tek we from Mistress Henrietta's Secret School. Wid de same fear beating in muh heart, I mek muh eyes look at him and I seen in him eyes de same ugly hateful look dat be in him eyes wen him tied meh like a hog and drug meh half to muh dead.

Him be mad and worser yet. him be naked. I comes more frighten. Muh eyes shut tight on dey own. Dey not want to look at him and his naked white mans self. It not dat I never see no body naked 'fore. I dun seen plenty nigger pickney and boy naked, but I never seens no big man naked, nigger or white mans. I thank muh eyes fer closing and I let fear freely use muh heart as it please. De pounding not have no sense to it, it be beating boom, pound, rat tat, boom pat, rat-a-tat and den pound again. Fear be beating on muh heart so hard I expect it to beat a hole right through and bust muh chest right open. I start wishing fer muh heart to stop. It not. It continue beating like it would burst but it refused to stop.

In de darkness behind muh shut tight eyes, I hears him voice. Him suh, "Don't you go shouting to wake this whole place, alarm everybody, make them think that there's something wrong."

I suh nuffin'. I not ever been able to think and talk at de same time, and besides I nots want to give him reason to wish him had cut muh guts out. I be tinking though dat I had to get away from him and him hands. No one had tolt meh wat it be dat white mans want wen dem come to nigger womans, but I 'members dat Neala suh dat white mans want wat nigger womans got between dem legs. De way him be pulling on meh foots tolt meh dat him want wat I gots between meh legs and him nots care 'bout meh not wanting him to want wat between muh legs.

De look I'd seen in him eyes also suh dat him be goin' do wat him want and none of wat him be wanting had anything to do wid meh or wat I may or may not be wanting, which be fer him to not want wat between muh legs. Ev'ting inside of meh be sure enough frighten. I feels like one of dem rabbits dat bout it business and de next ting dey know'd, dey dun get trapped and somebody dat not know'd or care dat dey got feelings getting ready to strip de skin off dem and chop dem up and put dem in de pot.

Thar be no pot in dis cabin, but I be de rabbit dat him be fixing to skin. I had to get away. I nots want him skinning meh. I know'd once him touch meh, muh skin be coming off. Opening muh eyes, I turned muh head to see if thar be some place I can runs jis't in case I can get way from him. Him must have figured out wat I be tinking 'cause him suh, "There's nowhere for you to go, nigger. There isn't anyone for you to call and nobody's goin' come no how. You are a nigger, my nigger, and my slave. Here on my plantation, I take what is mine. Whatever Neala find for you to do in the daytime is Neala's business, but at night your job is to give me what I want; those are your duties."

Duties? Duties? What duties him talking bout dat I gots to be doing now? It be night time. All de wuk dat Neal suh fer meh to do and dun do and I nots have no more strenf fer no more wuk. Watever Neal could get outta meh fer one day and mayhaps two days she dun tek outta meh today. 'fore de thought can full muh brain and mek any sense, Massa start to move him clammy hand up muh leg. I tries to get 'way from him and him touch by pushing muhself back towards de cabin wall, but him grabbed meh and pull meh back to him and in de one move, him send muh legs wide apart from each other. It be as if muh legs not belongs to meh or muh body no more. I try again to pull dem back together but him tek him legs and pinned dem to de bed wide way dem be.

"Nigger, this will be easier for you if you stop fighting me and just let me have what is mine."

I not care no more if him cut muh head or not. I wants to suh to him, 'Wat yuh mean, Massa, 'bout wat is yourn?' But I dun know'd dat not be de ting to suh, not dat dey be anyting to suh. I know'ds dat I wants to live and if I open muh mouth, him gine kilt meh so I stop from fighting him. Him be de Massa and I be de slave.

Massa get a hand to de top of muh leg and grab at muh pee-hole. Wen him hand touch it, I scream and at de same time, I push hard at him chest and de fact dat I touch him surprise him. Him stop and this let meh get out him way. Him grab meh and drag meh back from de place on de bed where I be wen him furst come in. No sooner be I widin arms reach dan him raise him hand high as him head and wid de back of him hand, him slap meh right across muh mouth. I be getting ready to scream wen I seen de hand go up a second time and 'fore I can get de scream out, him slap meh again full in muh mouth. Muh teeth dem come down hard on muh tongue. Muh mouth it fill up wid blood. I swallow it. I be too afraid to spit it out on him or de bed.

De taste of de blood mek meh want to vomit. Fear mix wid it. It taste brown. Fear dun tek de natural red out muh blood. From dat day on I wen I tink 'bout blood, it never be red, it be brown. Him grab meh by muh foots and pull meh 'till where muh knees fall apart. Him stands up and put him naked white mans self 'tween muh knees. Wid him eyes on meh like him goin' use dem to bore a hole in muh head, him suh through him teet, "Don't move. Stay still and it goin' be easier for you; not that I care. I won't care if you died right on that spot once I'm done with you, nigger."

Before him started talking 'bout meh and meh deading and him not caring, I be tinking of begging him fer mercy but de look on him face mek meh shut muh mouth and not suh nuffin' 'fore him gut meh like Tiny.

Even if I be have a second thought and be trying to figure out how to mek wat I be tinking sound like someting kin to a good question, him start talking again. Him not be waiting on meh. Meh and nuffin' dat I want not matter to him. Dat be clear. It not matter wen I be on Litchfield Plantation and I be sure it not goin' start to matter none now.

Wid him legs close to touching meh, so near dat I can feel de hairs on him legs, dat feel mek muh skin want to walk 'way. Him start talking again, "Now get this through your nigger head, I don't care about you, I won't start looking out for you. You and your nigger Momma be the dumb nigger wenches who went looking for trouble by wanting what is never going to be for niggers: book learning."

I wants to tell him dat it not be muh Momma dat went looking fer de book learning. I wants to tell him dat it be Mistress Henrietta, but I not tink him care 'bout none of dat. Him put more of him weight on meh and him suh, "It was your stupid, feeling-for-niggers Mistress over at Litchfield who decide to teach you niggers to read that 'cause you to be here. If you were a boy, your nigger ass would be dead and I wouldn't be here struggling with you because somewhere in your mind you think you have something that isn't mine to take. Imagine me, a white man and the owner of this plantation, struggling with some nigger bitch 'cause she's a virgin and scared to get fucked. I brought you here to work, or to fuck when I feel like it so, my little virgin nigger, open these nigger legs and let me get what I dragged your ass all the way over here for: my first nigger and a virgin nigger hole at that."

Hearing wat him suh tek de struggle and fight right outta meh. I mek up muh mind not to move or open muh eyes. I not care no more wat him do. I be him property. Him see dat I not gine fight him no more so him come closer and push muh legs furder apart. I close muh eyes. I feels de warmness of him naked body on de inside of muh legs. De warmness remind meh of warm milk and de way de wind feel on yuh face wen it be hot. I fix it in muh heart to never have warm milk or to ever run so de wind can touch muh face wen it be hot outside. I gine only run wen it cold so de wind can freeze muh face and if I be lucky, it gine fall off.

Him lower himself on meh. I feel him weight, feel him and it remind meh of stepping in pig shit and having it come through muh toes. Dis time de pig shit be a white mans and him pressing himself 'tween muh legs, spreading dem apart. De next time I see pig shit, I gine step right in it wid both muh foots so dat I never ferget wat him feel like.

Muh spreading apart legs feel like him be forcing dem to go back to yesterday. Muh legs dem not want to be open like dis fer him so dey get stiff. I not want him between dem. I feel cold like it be winter time. I want to reach down and stop him, but someting suh dat touching him like dat will only mek him brek muh neck. I not want to be hit no more so I let muh hands stay at muh sides. I tink in muh head dat dey be pieces of dry wood waiting to burn on de fire.

I feel him hands, not forced to be dead logs like mine, reaching to grab meh by muh hips. Him hand dat not be dead wood raise meh off de bed. I close muh eyes tight. De little calico dress ride up higher over muh hips, leaving meh naked below muh waist. I start to sweat. I want to cover muh nakedness, scream again, beg him to turn meh loose or someting. I not know'd wat him gine do, but I not want him seeing muh naked body or touching meh.

Massa lower meh back to de bed and wid one hand him tear de dress off meh. I hear ev'ry stitch as it give way. Him mek him lips open enough to jis't let de words come out. Him suh, "As long as you live on this plantation and in this cabin, make this the first and last dress I ever have to tear off you. When you come in this cabin, you take off that damnable rag and lay your naked ass on this bed and wait for me, you hear me."

All de anger in him voice mek him grind up de words and wen him force dem through him teet, dey land on muh face, neck, and jis't above muh bub bubs as hot white mans spit. Dey bounced on and off meh like dey be rock skipping 'cross de lake. I be too scared to move or answer. Rightly, I not think him be waiting fer any answer from meh.

Massa fidget 'round fer a few minutes more and den him grab muh legs; one in each hand and in one movement, him had dem furder apart dan dey'd ever been in muh life and den I feel someting touch muh pee-hole. Him be shoving someting hot and hard in meh. Him pressing and shoving. It be hurting meh. I wants to pull muh legs outta him hands and shut dem; squeeze him out de space him mek 'tween muh legs; mek de hurt go way, but someting tolt meh I should be still or him gine kilt meh.

Massa lean him full weight 'gainst meh and dis time him shove and push even harder at muh pee-hole. I feel watever him be pressing against meh start to get in. Muh pee-hole feel like it gine burst right open. Wid a even harder shove, like him be trying to move a dead hog, Massa bore into meh. Muh pee-hole tear open and I feel someting warm come out de bottom of muh pee-hole, and I start to cry and scream from de tearing and de pain.

Grunting, him suh through him teet, "Hush your mouth, nigger."

I stop from screaming but I stay crying. Him shove harder and deeper. I not want to scream again, but all him shoving be tearing way muh whole insides. I open muh mouth and I scream loud enough to wake de whole plantation. I wait fer him to hit meh. Him not hit meh. Instead, him start to raise up off meh. I feel de air come out muh pee-hole wen him raise off muh belly. I also feel wat him shove in meh coming out as him raise himself up more off muh belly. I feel it coming out more and more as him pull back and, tinking dat him be dun and goin' leave meh alone, I starts to move way from under him.

Wid one hand, him push meh back down on de bed and den wid one hard push, him shove de ting right into muh pee-hole. De push it be sudden and hard I feel him hipbone hit muh hipbone. Den like him been running a race and be getting tired, him suh, "What I tell you?"

Him dig harder and deeper in muh pee-hole and again him suh, "What I tell you?"

Muh brain it suh him not looking fer answer. White mans dem not ask nigger question fer answer. I mek muh brain tink only on not screaming no more. Him face near enough to mine dat I kin feel him hot breff. It coming out him mouth in puffs and it burning muh face.

Him pull back again jis' like before wen I be tinking dat him gine leave meh be and jis' like before him, shove himself even harder back into meh.

"What…"

Him tek a deep bref and pull back out de ting.

"Did…"

Him breave out and shove hard back into muh pee-hole.

"I…"

Him breave in and pulled back out.

"Tell…"

Panting hot air through him nose like horse wen it dun run fer a long, long time, him slam even harder into meh. Him hip bone hit muh hipbone again and I tink dis time him dun brek it.

"You?"

Him pull out again, dis time so far de hot ting leave muh pee-hole. Muh pee-hole it burning meh and it feel like it rip wide open. I start to push muh back 'gainst de bed, trying to get away. Him lean him whole body on muh right side, pinning meh to de bed jis' where I be. Him be heavy and I nots be able to move and him know'd it.

From where him be on muh leg, him turn meh to him and raise meh a little off muh back and wid muh back raised up, wid him free hand him mek de ting touch muh pee-hole again and grinding and twitching rough and hard him got de ting to go deep inside meh. Den him start slamming him whole body against meh jis' de way I dun seen de slave beat dem big floor rug.

I shut muh eyes and mekking muh mind tink I be de rug, I brace muhself each time fer him belly to pound into meh and de hot ting to tear muh inside more and den him start to scream wat sound to meh like, "Ooooo-liv-veeee-aaaahhhh." Him whole body start to shake. No sooner him shaking and screaming, "Ooooo-liv-veeee-aaaahhhh, Ooooo-liv-veeee-aaaahhhh, Ooooo-liv-veeee-aaaahhhh." Den I feel someting hot and wet inside of meh like him pee in meh. Him stop moving and screaming, "Ooooo-liv-veeee-aaaahhhh."

Him raise himself up and wid one pull, him pull de hot ting out muh pee-hole. Him pull so hard it sound like pulling a stuck rock out wet mud. Den 'fore de echo of de sound can leave and muh pee-hole and I could be glad dat I feeling no more slamming and pounding into meh, I hear him wiping himself on de only ting in de cabin him can wipe himself on: de thin rag dat jis't 'fore him comes in and tear it off meh— de frock dat Neala had put on meh.

Den I hears de sound of him bare foots on de floor den de sound of him struggling wid him boots. I half way got up to go help him put dem on de way I seen other niggers be bending and letting Massa put him foots on dem back to get him boots on, but I play stubborn nigger mule and I nots move. Him not tell meh to come and be footstool fer him so I nots move.

Him gets him boots on and den him boots mek like two crunch sound and him go through de door. Him tek time to shut it behind him. Time Massa boots mek furst sound on de dirt outside, I already mek in muh heart to figure out a way to kill him. I gots to kill him. I not goin' rest 'till him crumble up at muh foots, raw, hurting, scared, and wet jis't de ways I be feeling now.

I gots to kill him and not jis't fer wat him jis't dun to meh, but fer wat him and him friends dun to Tadpole, Chem, Tiny, and Lil' Theo, and ev'ry nigger dat white mans dun treat like animal. Him gots to dead and by muh own hands. I gine kill Massa.

I wait without moving fer a long time to see if him be coming back. Wen it feel like him not coming back, I reach fer de rags dat 'pose to be a dress and even though I not want it to touch meh no more 'cause it be feeling wet and dirty and rip up, I pull it over meh. Now we both rip up, wet, and dirty. I starts to cry from all de pain in muh body and muh heart. I wants Momma Cornbread, but I know'ds she not be ever goin' come. Thar no be nobody to come. I belong to him and like all de other niggers on ev'ry plantation round here, we do wat dey suh and dem do to we wat dem want 'cause to dem, we jis't like dumb nigger mules.

Wen sleep come, it find meh in de same spot where him had left meh. Fear dat him be coming back mek meh stay right where I be. Wen I did move, de bed it be wet. I know'd I not pee on him and I didn't see him pee so I figure dat de wetness be wat a white mans hate fer nigger feel like.

I stay right in de wet spot and de more de wet soak through de lil' thin frock, de more muh hate fer him grow'd. I know'd I nots be able to let on dat I hate him 'cause if him ever figga dat I do, him gine skin meh. I had to 'member wat it be dat him dun to meh so I stays in de wet nastiness him left behind. I mek muh brain remember how cold and nasty white man's hate fer nigger is. I mix muh hate fer him wid him own and stayed right thar, tinking how it gine feel to kill him.

From dat day on, Massa treat meh like dat. Anytime him feel like it, him act like a midnight robber and force him way into meh through muh pee-hole and I nots be able to suh nuffin'. I learnt how to be still while him rut meh. Dat be muh life. Him brek through; dig 'round, grunt, and ev'ry time jis't 'fore him dun, him suh, "Ooooo-liv-veeee-aaaahhhh," and dem him pull out him business from muh pee-hole and him gone.

I never one day or night welcome him. No nigger woman in she right mind welcome white mans to she body. Massa him jis't brek in and robbed meh wen him ting get taste fer nigger gal, and wid each hate spot him left behind fer meh to sleep in, muh hatred fer him grow'd.

I hated Mistress Henrietta fer giving Momma idea 'bout nigger and book learning; I wanted to hate muh Momma too fer tinking dat dey ever goin' be a day wen nigger do someting other dan wuk white mans land, but I not able to get muh heart to do it. So I mek muh mind to only hate Massa.

I be never goin' see Momma Cornbread no more and hating she for trusting a white womans and wanting dat dream dat Mistress Henrietta gots she to believe 'bout someday nigger goin' be free not mek no sense, but hating him mek sense; dat be easy, him be here. I can see him and so I fixed muh hate on him.

Chapter 24

No Rest At Night; Ever

Every night or sometimes soon as I mek it inside de cabin, him step in right behind meh and it be, "Nigger, bring yourself over here."

I would go. Massa Fields him would sometimes not bother wid mekking meh lie down on de bed, but if him feel to stand up den him would mek meh bend over and stand like horse or mule and him would push himself in meh.

It get so it not matter to meh wat him do. Muh inside not feel no more pain and I come to expect him to poke 'round in meh most evenings or nights. I never suh one word. Massa Fields never miss one day; it be like him be glad dat him nots kilt meh dat day at Litchfield plantation. Ev'ry time him poke in muh pee-hole, I wish dat him had kilt meh and den I not be here fer him to poke, poke, poke; mek meh sore, and jis't left same way him spit in dirt and leave.

Ev'ry night wen him gone, I gets to be praying to de Lawd. I pray two pray since dat furst night when him come and shove him way in meh. One be dat de Lawd mek a hole to open in de ground and him fall in and brek him neck, and den de hole it swallow him. De second pray be dat de Lawd fergive meh fer praying de furst pray.

I not know'd fer sure if de Lawd gine fergive meh or not fer asking him to kill Massa Fields, but it not stop meh from asking. I be long pass de point of caring 'bout de fergiveness. It not matter enough fer meh to stop from begging de Lawd in all muh quiet times to kill him. I know'd him be de Lawd's pickney and it be hard to ask a faddah to kill him pickney, but I be de Lawd's pickney jis't de same and I get to tinking dat de Lawd not seeing wat one of him pickney be doin' to de next.

De Lawd be tekking a long time to kill him and dat not seems to be like someting dat be so hard fer de Lawd to do. De preacher man him suh dat de Lawd is a Lawd of quickness and wat tek nigger all day to do, de Lawd do in a blink of de eye. Well, de Lawd twan't blinking at Massa

Fields. Him be letting him live 'cause him know'd dat a nigger could never kilt a white mans.

Ev'ry morning dat I see him and him living, I know'd dat come evening him gine come and rut meh, and den I know'd dat de Lawd be not fer nigger. Him only be de Lawd fer white mans. De Lawd not care wat nigger be gine through; him not listening to nuffin' nigger had to suh.

De Lawd let Massa Fields live and ev'ry day dat de Lawd let him live, him come round and poke in meh. Den I gots to tinking dat as long as de Lawd twan't answering dis nigger pray, den I not have to worry 'bout if him be goin' fergive meh or not wen I figure out how to kill Massa.

De hate inside meh fer Massa Fields grow'd so big dat at night wen de plantation be quiet and it be jis't meh and muh tinking, I be figuring. I wants to run but I wants to kilt him furst fer all de different ways and times him put him cocky in meh. Den one day de hate it change. It not change to no happiness or nuffin' like dat. It jis't move. It move from muh heart to muh belly and it grow.

Massa Fields wid all him pushing round and stealing him way in muh pee-hole dun left someting behind: a pickney. De Momma dat twan't a Momma, Neala, she be de one tell meh dat I mekking a pickney, but she suh, "Nigger Gal, yuh having a pickney growing in yuh belly not change nuffin' fer yuh. Massa Fields and Mistress Olivia still gots to eat and, Nigger Gal, Mistress Olivia goin' mek yer life harder 'cause Massa Fields dun fill yer belly wid a pickney and she belly not be able to hold nuffin' but food, and wen she push dat out it not be nuffin' Massa Fields can show him white mans friends. Him goin' still be on yuh 'cause white mans not give Nigger Gal rest 'cause she belly full wid pickney."

It tek Massa Fields 'bout three months 'fore him notice dat muh belly getting big. Him suh, "I be God-damned. I've gotten something to grow beside infernal cotton."

Den Massa Fields him suh, "The child, when will it be born?"

I suh, "Dunno, Massa Fields. Five, maybe six months from now."

Him suh nuffin' jis't look like him tinking and den him suh, "I be God damned. It took all this time and now a woman is pregnant with my child again and it's a nigger: a nigger. My child is going be a nigger, a nigger baby; that some infernal hell, I'm going to have a nigger baby."

Dat night, Massa Fields him come but him not rut meh. Him lie down 'sides meh and him quiet. De next ting I know'd, Massa Fields him start to snore. Him dun fall asleep. I stays awake, not moving and hardly breaving. Jis't 'fore de plantation wake, Massa Fields him stir and wen him come to him full sense and see him dun stayed de whole night in a nigger cabin and wid a slave, him jump up. Putting him breeches and on and reaching fer him boots, him suh, "Why in infernal hell did you let me sleep?"

I looks at him and all muh fear of seeing Tadpole, Chem, Tiny, and Lil' Theo kilt come back to meh and I fear dat Massa Fields goin' kill meh now. I start to cry and I not know'd why but muh hand it be go to muh belly. I suh, "Massa, I sorry. I begs yuh not kill meh. I wants de pickney to live, Massa. Please let de pickney live. Fergive a nigger gal dat be too fright to wake yuh, Massa. I not know'd wat to do wen yuh gots to be sleeping, Massa."

Massa Fields him look at meh as him put him shirt on and it look like him figuring wat to do 'cause I dun beg him fer de pickney life and not meh own life. Him not suh nuffin', him jis't turn and him go through de cabin door. Him leave it open and I watch him go 'cross de yard and him mek big wide steps.

A chicken it come cross him path and him kick it so hard, it sail through de yard wid it feathers comin' loose. It land and it not move. Massa dun kick it so hard it dead. I look at de dead chicken and I know'ds dat chicken dead 'stead of meh. I keep muh eyes on de dead chicken, put muh frock on to get muhself to de cookhouse where I know'd Neala waiting on meh. She dun figure out wat I good at and ev'ry morning, I mek de biscuits fer Massa Fields and Mistress Olivia's brekfast. From de time Neala figure out I can mek biscuits, it's all Massa Fields want at all him meals.

Wen I get in de cookhouse, Neala she look at meh and she suh, "If yuh got to cough 'till yuh bring dat pickney through yer mouth, mek last night de last night dat yer nigger ass let Massa Fields sleep in a nigger cabin. Yuh and him not be no love nuffin'. Ya jis't a nigger gal dat sweet him cocky, and it only 'till another nigger gal, one younger dan yuh mek it to de size him can fit him cocky in she. Dat is all white mans do. Dem climb on and off nigger gal and full, dem dat can full, wid pickney. Yuh may be him furst nigger gal, but dat not mek yuh special and now 'cause yuh dumb nigger ass let him sleep whole night wid yuh, Mistress Olivia goin' hate yuh more."

Neala be dun talking. She went back to cooking dem brekfast. Neala not send meh in dat morning to help serve. After dat and as muh belly grow'd bigger, I jis't mek de biscuits and clean up. Massa Fields him still come most nights, but I never close muh eyes one blink not even wen him rutting meh. Anytime him stay too long and it start to feel like him may nod off, I get to coughing and him get up, put him clothes on, and leave.

One night, him suh, "Tell Neala, Sukey, and Eme to let me know when you have that baby."

Him left and never come back. Him might not have come back to poke and rob muh body no more, but him pickney and muh hate fer him grow and push at all sides of meh. In de end, only him pickney come out. Much as I be sure I gine hate it, ev'ting in meh melt wen I seen him. Him be de most beautifullest ting I ever seen. Even Neala's hard crust fall off wen she help meh get muh bub-bub in him mouth. I look at him sucking and I gets to tinkin' how strange; furst Massa Fields suck at muh bub-bub, and now him boy pickney sucking at muh bub-bub. Even nigger pickney wid white mans blood act like white mans, even if dey not know'd dat dey got white mans blood.

Wen it look like enough time dun pass fer one of dem to let Massa Fields know'd dat him pickney born, I suh, "Neala, yuh nots goin' let Massa know'd dat him son dun born?"

Neala reach and it seem like she reach back in yesterday fer de slap she snatch and let loose hard cross muh mouth. Muh eyes open wide wid de same fear and fright jis't as de day de white mans, including Massa Fields, kilt Tadpole and all de rest of dem. Wen de slap settle in muh face and head, Neala suh through lips dat not open, "Nigger Gal, Massa not got no son! Yuh not no white woman dun have she husband him long wait fer 'eir! Yuh is a nigger gal. Him slave who jis't mek a white man richer by adding to him property. Yuh hearing meh, Nigger Gal? Yuh jis't had another slave and it not matter dat him look like a white mans. Dat red-brown hair on him head, dem thin lips dat if him be a white man would call yer ass a nigger, him blue like sky eyes, and dat straight as chicken beak nose not mek him a white man; him a nigger and a slave.

"Yuh not get no different treatment from any other nigger 'round here. Massa Fields him let ev'ry woman 'round here who birf a male one day and a half 'fore she gots to get back to earning she keep and mekking money fer him. Tomorrow wen yer come to mek dem biscuits, yuh can spread a rag in a corner over by where de potatoes be and yuh can put him thar while yuh get back to mekking Massa Fields dem biscuits and bread him love. All anybody goin' tell Massa Fields is wen him food ready."

I suhs nuffin' and I not even reach up to rub de place where Neala slap meh. I bends down muh head wid shame and I hear dem dat help meh birf de boy 'long wid Neala talking 'bout how I dun ferget muh place. Dem laugh and look at meh like dem sorry fer meh. I sorry fer meh all by muhself, so I not need dem to feel sorry fer meh. I wants to cry, but I not wants dem to see meh. Dem busy wid morning wuk and dem not look at meh no more. It be only den dat I start to cry fer Momma Cornbread. I cry 'till I not know'd wat else to cry fer, and den de pickney him start to cry too, and it not 'cause him be Massa Fields' pickney dat I stop from crying and put muh bub-bub in him mouth. I stop from crying 'cause I not want him to get salt from muh crying in him milk.

I never had no more time fer crying after dat day. Thar be always sometin' needing to be mek outta flour. Neala no longer bothered wid de flour things. She find out dat ting I be good at: flour. I be good at wukking wid flour. In between mekking de bread and biscuits, I had to slip in a second or two to mother de boy. Him be growin' and although him be little, him be big. Him also look jis't like Massa Fields. I hated Massa Fields, but someting in meh moved to soft wen I look at him boy pickney.

Chapter 25

No Room Fer Fergivenss

It be almost three weeks 'fore Massa Fields find out dat de pickney be born and dat be just by accident since him no longer came to muh cabin to rut meh. Him be waiting fer somebody to tell him I had de pickney. It be early morning and I be on muh way back to de cookhouse to get started wid de bread and biscuit-mekking. I done be in de cookhouse already and had put de pickney in de corner where Neala suh to put him. I be outside to get some leaves for Neala to mek de special tea she mek fer Mistress Olivia. I be hurrying back not thinking 'bout nothing else but getting back to muh biscuit-mekking. Massa Fields, him be goin' wherever white mans go furst ting in de morning 'fore dem brekfast, and him stop almost just de way him had stop dat chicken dat morning. Him look at meh and den him look at muh belly and him suh, "When? When did you have the pickney?"

I stumble over words in muh brain and den I suh, "It be three weeks tomorrow, Massa."

Massa Fields him face went red. Him suh, "What did I say to you about letting me know when you had the child?" I look down at muh foots. Him suh, "I asked you a question! What did I say to you about Neala, Eme, or Sukey letting me know when the child was born? Did you not tell them what I said?"

I was 'fraid but I suh, "I tell she."

"You told her? Which one of them did you tell?"

"Yes, Massa. I tell Neala what you suh."

Massa Fields was looking more and more like the day him help kill Tadpole, Tiny, Chem, and Lil' Theo. Him den suh, "Why didn't Neala let me know?"

Den, 'cause I be frighten, I suh, "She suh yuh not to be bothered 'bout no nigger pickney born since it just be one more slave."

Massa Fields, him stop talking and him walk fast pass meh to de cookhouse. Him push de door and go in. I hurry up and follow him inside. When Neala, Sukey, and Eme seen Massa Fields come in de cookhouse, dem face get de same look as mine when I dun seen him in de yard a few minutes ago.

Before Neala can get she lips to suh anything, Massa Fields step toward and back from Neala at de same time, and I guess him went de same place she went fer de slap she give meh when I tell she dat him wants to know'ds when him pickney born. Him slap Neala full in she mouth. Although she head snap back, Neala she not move. She stand like she mek from stone. Massa Fields, him suh in de biggest voice I ever hear come from him mouth, "I, not anyone else on this plantation, am the Master and when I say that something is to be done, that thing, and nothing other than that thing is to be done! You, Neala, are not ever to second-guess what I say!"

De pickney pick dat minute to cry out. It be like him know'ds him father's voice. Massa Fields walk over to where de pickney be and him suh in de same screaming thunder voice, "Tell me, Neala, that that is not my child on the floor like some blasted puppy!"

Him face went even redder and him suh, "Pick my God-damn child up from off that filthy rag! That is a Fields. It is not some puppy waiting on a bitch to come and let it suck."

Neala rush over to where de pickney be on de floor to pick him up and Massa Fields, him shout even harder. Him shout at she, "Not you! Not you! Do not touch my child, Neala! You have already done enough! Don't you ever touch my child! Ever!"

Sukey rush over and pick up de pickney. Ev'rybody else stay still, not sure if to move or not. Den Massa Fields, him say, "Eme, you go and get some nigger to make a box or something to put my child in. What, by the way is the baby?"

Neala, trying to find a way to get back in Massa Fields' good grace, suh, "A boy, Massa Fields. De pickney it be a boy."

When Neala suh a boy, Massa Fields step over to she and again him reach back to de same place where him had gone fer de furst slap and him slap she in she face even harder dis time. Dis time, him use de back of him hand and him suh, "I have a son and, nigger, you decided that it wasn't worth my knowing."

Den him turn to meh and him shout in de same thunder voice, "Three weeks! Three weeks! I'm the father of a son and none of you told me. I told you to let me know."

I never see him hand move but it must 'cause muh brain tolt meh dat I be dun slap. Muh ears hear de slap last. De sound it stay back where him be, waiting fer meh to feel de pounding pain furst fore it ring out loud. It be acting like it be thunder.

"That child," him suh, "is mine, not yours. Do you hear me? He is mine! I will do with him what I want and when I want. Do you understand? You don't own anything around here Milkweed nothing! Don't make me regret not having strung your nigger ass up."

Him look at Sukey holding de pickney like him be white pickney and him march out de cookhouse same way him walk in. Him left de same way dat him be when him walk in, but none of we be de same. We frighten. We all be 'fraid him gine' come back and do more dan jis't slap we hard.

We jis't standing like him turn we into stone. Even de pickney it gone quiet. It be Neala who talk furst. She suh, "Eme, yuh go to de barn and tell Harold Joe to mek a crate. Tell him mek it more dan a peach crate, but less dan a trough. Tell him throw some clean dry straw in when him done. Sukey, yuh search and find something to cover de straw and yuh." She turned to me. "Yuh, Nigger Gal, gots to be de luckiest nigger gal ever live, a white mans own a child a nigger mek him. Yuh be de furst nigger woman I know'd mek a child fer a white man and him notice it. If yuh make 'em like a bitch mekking puppies fer him, or 'till yer woman blood dry up, I goin' mek sure dat meh find him and tell him."

Neala give meh a hard look, but it twan't so hard 'cause she know'd him slap meh jis't as hard as him slap she. Dat be how it be. Massa Fields come back dat night to rut meh, but 'fore him come to rut meh, him had Neala, Sukey, and Eme put out to de field two days fer as many days dat I had de pickney and him not know'd.

He had dem pick cotton, peaches, planting, and digging from de time light crack de sky 'till it be time to come fix him and Mistress Olivia dem brekfast. Den it be back to de field 'till time to fix dem lunch and so him do dem for forty-two days. Most times when dem mek to crawl to sleep, it almost not mek sense since it be clear dat by de time de top of dem eyelids mek it to de bottom part of dem eyes, it be using up what time de dark have 'fore de sun chase it 'way. At de end of de forty-two days, Massa Fields him come in de cookhouse and him suh, "Neala, if you ever disobey me again, I'll cut your ears off. This way, I'll know for sure you couldn't hear or didn't hear me. Do you understand me, Neala?"

'Fore Neala can get she lips to open and suh, "Yes, Massa Fields," de way she always answer… him raise up him hand and slap she again as hard as him slap she furst time. Again, Neala stay like she mek from stone. Him turn and walk out de cookhouse. Him never had to tell Neala, Sukey, or Eme again 'bout letting him know'd when I had a pickney fer him.

Over time, I mek five more pickney fer Massa Fields, and each one raise like de furst one. Meh and dem alone in the cabin. Him never put dem to de field and when dem learn to talk, dem call him Massa like ev'rybody else. Dat be 'till de next to last pickney be born. Dat one be a gal. De furst gal pickney I mek fer him, and she come out de whitest of dem. She not look like a nigger had nothing to do wid she.

Massa him look at she de morning after de night wen she be born and him smile. Massa Fields him never smile at none of dem rest. Dis one him smile at and him suh, "A daughter, Milkweed. I have a daughter. Can you imagine? A daughter and she's white just like me. There's no trace of nigger in her. I'll be God-damned."

Massa look at she and when him be sure dat she be de whitest nigger him ever seen, him suh, "Her name is Lilly Olivia Everett Fields."

Den Massa do something him not ever dun. Him bend and pick she up and him suh, "Hey, Lilly, I'm your Poppa."

De next day, Sukey she come and she suh, "Massa suh you is to give me Lilly."

I suh to she, "Fer what? What him want she fer?"

She suh, "Him suh she is to live wid him and Mistress Olivia up in de big house."

Dat be it, Massa Fields and Mistress Olivia dem tek 'way de only gal pickney I mek fer him. Mistress Olivia she suh to Neala to tell me to come and suckle de pickney, but I not to suh nothing to de pickney when I suckle it. She tell Neala to make sure I understand what Massa Fields suh 'bout me not owning nothing 'round there. And so I gots to hold muh gal pickney to feed and when she full, Mistress Olivia she tek she from me and I jis't leave wid muh heavy heart. I hates Mistress Olivia more dan Massa Fields.

It tek Massa Fields a long time 'fore him come back to rut meh, but him come back and, like all de rest of times, I get wid pickney fer him. One night jis't 'fore him rut meh, him suh, "Milkweed, Mistress Olivia says if that child you are having is a girl, she wants it to come and live with her sister."

I wants to beg him to let me keep de pickney if it be a gal pickney, but I know'd dat watever Mistress Olivia suh fer him to do, den him do. So if she suh to tek de pickney from muh, him gine tek de pickney. I cry but only inside. Him rut meh like him not suh nuffin' to break muh heart. I waits fer him to leave de cabin and when him gone long enough, someting in meh suh, 'Dis be yuh pickney much as it be him pickney. Mistress Olivia dun got muh furst gal pickney, she not gine get muh second gal pickney.'

Someting in meh 'mind meh dat I hate Massa and Mistress Olivia and I gets to tinking dat if I not be able to keep meh gal pickney, den I not want Mistress Olivia to have she. Jis't like dat, I beg de growing pickney dat I know'd in muh heart be a gal pickney to stop growing. I beg she to dead.

Ev'ry day dat I wakes and de pickney still growing, I begs it to dead. It not dead. It keep growing and him suh again to meh, "Mistress Olivia she says that she's seen your belly and it's the same shape as when you made Lilly so she's happy that Lilly is going to have a sister." Him not look at meh after him suh so. Him reach fer meh and him jis't rut meh and den him jis't left. A little bit of time pass after him gone and I falls asleep and some time in de early morning, jis't 'fore it be time fer meh to get up and go mek de biscuits, I gets a feeling in muh belly like wen muh red river flowing, but dis one is different. It feel like wen him rut meh hard and leave de bottom of muh belly hurting.

Along wid de pain, I feels like I wants to move muh belly. I nots be able to help it. It hurt meh all in muh back and den I feel muh belly get hard and I push and push and de pickney come out and it dead: it be another gal pickney. I cry wen I see muh dead piccinanny. It be a gal pickney and she even more pretty dan Lilly. She hair it curly like him own, but it not be brownish red. It like de top of she head on fire. Her got brown hair dat look red and she white white white. She skin it so thin like I can almost see de blood. I tek she in muh arms. She feel warm. I feel so sorry dat she dead. I cry and cry and cry and cry. Wen I not be able to look at she no more, I cover she over and hold she in muh arms 'till it be time to go to de big house.

Soon as I see Neala, I start to cry. She suh, "Nigger Gal, wid de mix-up head wat yuh gots to be crying fer so early on de Lawd's day."

I look at Neala and I suh, "De pickney, it jis't born and it dead. Neala, de pickney she in muh cabin and she dead. Neala, she dead." I start to cry even harder 'cause I know'd dat I beg she to dead and she dead.

Neala she look at meh and she suh, "Milkweed, I sorry de pickney dead. I truly sorry." Then she suh, "I gots to tell de Massa."

I suh, "Tell him dat it be a gal pickney."

I start to cry again and Neala she suh, "Dat not gine bring she back and Mistress Olivia gine still be looking fer she biscuits. She gine suh if yuh can walk, yuh can mek de biscuits so its best yuh jis't stay here and start on de biscuit-mekking. I gine go and tell de Massa now." Neala walk away and I, 'cause I can walk, I walk over to where de flour be and I gets out wat I need to start mek de biscuits fer Mistress Olivia and Massa.

I mek de biscuits but all I can see is muh dead gal pickney. I try not to cry 'cause I not want one tear of mine to be mix in wid de biscuits dem gine eat.

Soon Neala she come back in de cookhouse. She suh dat she wait 'till him by himself and she suh to him dat de pickney it come out too soon and it dead. Him ask she wat it be. She suh she tell him it be a gal and him suh, "Neala, you have Harold Joe to bury her in the farthest corner of the cemetery, the cemetery; not out in the woods with you niggers but with my family, just far over by the oak. You know where the oak is? Do this but you wait 'till it's night time proper so no one else here knows but me, you, and Harold Joe. Tell him to put this in with her and, Neala, Milkweed is not to go with you. Do you understand me?"

Neala suh dat Massa Fields reach and him cut a lock of him brownish-red curly hair and him give it to she to put in de little box wid de pickney. Wen she suh dat, I cry again fer muh dead pickney. I not cry 'cause him give she a lock of him hair. I cry 'cause him not want meh to see way him bury muh pickney. Even though she dead, him tek she way from meh. I tink now dat I do de pickney wrong and dat she dead 'cause I beg she to dead, and she only do wat I beg she to do. She dead jis't like I ask she to. I stop crying fer de dead pickney and I cry fer de living one dat Massa Fields and Mistress Olivia pretending to dem friends is dem pickney.

Chapter 26

Muh Tek Up Wid Man

It be easy fer Massa Fields and Mistress Olivia to pretend dat she dun mek a pickney since all she dun from de day I come and start mekking de biscuits and bread is eat and she even fatter now dan how she be furst time I see she. Nobody able to tell if she be fat or if she wid pickney, so wen she suh dat she and Massa mek pickney, all dem white mans and white womans friends happy fer dem. I watch muh pickney growing and not know'ds I is she real muddah. Mistress Olivia she gets to not wanting to see dem boys I mek wid Massa Fields, and she suh one morning, "Nigger, stop them nigger pups of yours from playing near 'round this house. Mistress Lilly is starting to get sense and she'll want playmates. I don't want you thinking that those nigger pups of yours and Mistress Lilly is kin. They aren't, you understand me?"

I suh, "Yes, Mistress Olivia."

Dat night, Massa Fields him come to meh and him suh, "Mistress Olivia she says it's time that you take up with a nigger and make nigger pickney with him so you won't get in your head that there's something special 'bout you because I've only made children with you. She says if I don't take care of it, then she will take Lilly and go to her mother's. I can't have her do that. I care little 'bout Mistress Olivia, but I love our daughter. Do you understand what I'm telling you, Milkweed?"

I jis't nod 'cause it nots matter none to meh wat him do. Den him suh, "I've spoken to the nigger Harold Joe, and you and your pickney are going be moving over to his cabin. I've told Harold Joe that if I ever find out that the two of you rut, even one night, or you bring a child on this plantation that doesn't look like the children you've made for me, I'm going to cut his cock off and shove it up his ass. Do you understand that, Milkweed? You and Harold Joe aren't to take up for real. It's just to look that way so Mistress Olivia will stop saying she wants you and your nigger pickney off this plantation."

I listen to Massa Fields tell meh 'bout Harold Joe and I 'member Neala suhing dat a nigger gal be nuffin' more to a white mans dan two legs joined in the middle by a pee-hole fer dem to rut and fill wid pickney and dat wen him dun use up she goodness him give wat him not want no more to a nigger man. Fer reasons I not know'd or understand, wat him suh cut meh deep. I starts to cry and Massa Fields him not rut meh or nuffin'. Him stay fer a lil' while jis't rubbin' him hand up and down muh legs den him get to muh pee-hole and wen him put him hand by it, him stop, gets up, and jis't leave meh.

De next day, Harold Joe him come early to muh cabin and him suh, "Massa Fields him suh dat I is to tek yuh, wat little is in dis here cabin, and yer pickney to muh cabin. Him suh dat from dis day 'till him suh otherwise, we is to tek up together and live in de cabin cross yonder."

I step 'side so Harold Joe, a nigger man dat until dis day I never suh a word to, can walk in de cabin dat I share wid muh pickney and gather muh tings and tek dem to him cabin; him muh man now; but not muh fer real tek up wid man. Him muh man 'cause Mistress Olivia suh it to be dat way. Wen Harold Joe dun mek de trip from him cabin to mine and him gather wat little things I had and set dem up in him cabin, I follows him to him cabin. I looks 'round Harold Joe's cabin and I not see nuffin' different from de one I jis't left. Meh and de pickney de only ting dat different, or Harold Joe be de only ting dat different; ev'ry ting else de same. I feel a burn in muh belly… it be de hate I gots fer Massa Fields and Mistress Olivia 'cause dem pushing and pulling meh ev'ry which way dem feel like and thar not be nuffin' I can do 'cause I be dem slave.

Harold Joe him jis't watching meh and muh pickney and wen de silence stretch de wiff and breff of de cabin, him look at muh pickney and him suh, "Dem some fine pickney yuh have. Wat be dem names?" Harold Joe in dem furst minutes I move in him cabin dun more dan Massa Fields. All dem boys 'long to Massa Fields and him not one day ask wat dem names be.

I point to de furst one and I suh, "Him is Isham, de next one be Juba, dat one be Zack," and pointing to de one dat most favor Massa Fields, I suh, "him be Tuck but I jis't call him Tiny and dat one over thar be Willie."

Harold Joe him look at meh and den him suh, "Tuck? Wat name is dat fer a nigger?"

I look at him and I not answer him but I suh, "Massa Fields him tolt yuh dat yuh not to rut wid meh?"

Harold Joe him turn 'way from meh and him suh, "Massa Fields him suh dat. Yuh not have to worry none. Harold Joe is a good nigger and I be do as Massa suhs."

Dat is de way it be fer Harold Joe and meh. Massa him not stop from coming to rut meh. De ting dat be different is dat wen him come, him mek Harold Joe go off somewhere and den him rut meh 'till him be tired. I never know'd how Harold Joe know'd wen Massa Fields left, but him always come back, tek a mat, and drag it by de door and him sleep thar. It be like him be looking after meh by sleeping by de door.

One day in de cookhouse, Neala she suh to meh, "Yuh rutting wid Harold Joe?"

I suh, "Massa Fields him suh dat Harold Joe not to touch meh 'cause if I bring a nigger pickney on dis plantation, him goin' cut off Harold Joe's cocky."

Neala she laugh and she suh, "Do yuh want to rut wid Harold Joe?"

Sukey and Eme dem laugh and Sukey she suh, "De other womans suh dat Harold Joe him got cock like tree trunk, and dat if yuh not rutting wid him, den it be a waste of good nigger mans to have him shut up wid a young nigger gal all night and him not be able to have no pleasure 'cause a white mans wants de sweet and juicy young nigger gal fer himself."

I laugh and I suh, "Hush up. I nots look at Harold Joe like dat. Him jis't be a nigger mans dat Massa Fields put meh to cabin wid."

Sukey suh, "Yuh know'ds, Milkweed, dat yuh can rut and not mek pickney. Why yuh think Mistress Olivia not be have no pickney of she own?"

"I nots know'ds why. I guess she red river dry up."

Neala suh, "Mistress Olivia not old enough fer she red river to dry on it own yet, but it dry up all right. I start to dry it up from dat day she had Massa Fields mek de Overseer tek de skin off muh back. Dat day I be de only one dat have reason to skin somebody and dat somebody be Mistress Olivia fer wat she dun meh."

"Wat she dun to yuh, Neala, and why she had dem to whup yuh?"

"White mans or white womans not always have or need reason to whup nigger but if a white womans gets hate in she heart fer yuh, thar not be nuffin' a nigger can do."

"Mistress Olivia gots hate fer yuh too, Neala?"

"Mayhaps jis't as much hate as she gots fer yuh. She be no more dan a few weeks here and it clear dat she come wid more hate in she heart fer nigger dan him muddah, and him muddah had plenty hate in she heart fer niggers. Wen she dead, niggers sing song and tank de Lawd and den dem beg de Lawd not to let she in heaven 'cause if Him let she in, she gine mek tings bad fer nigger wen dem get thar.

Mistress Olivia mek it in she heart to have de most hate fer meh 'cause Massa John, him be Massa Fields faddah, not mek meh wuk in de cotton fields. She suh to Massa John dat I be a big strapping nigger wench and I should be wukking out in de fields. Massa John suh dat I neva wuk in no field since I be on dis plantation and now dat I wid pickney, him not want meh in field."

I look at Neala and I want to suh to she, 'If yuh be wid pickney, way yuh pickney be?" I not get time to suh dat 'fore Neala suh, "Muh pickney him dead. Him dead 'cause of Mistress Olivia."

"Wat Mistress Olivia do to mek yuh pickney dead, Neala?"

Neala she suh, "De pickney I be mekking it be fer Massa Fields faddah, Massa John, and I be jis't like yuh. I had a mix-up head fer him 'cause him speak soft to meh and him treat meh like I be human, so wen him come furst time to rut meh, I welcome him. I be glad on dem nights wen him come to rut. I rut him wid all muh strenf and soon I wid pickney. I be happy dat I gine have pickney fer him.

"De other Mistress Fields, him wife and de muddah of Massa Fields, she heart it grow'd more bitter to meh 'cause her not mek but Massa Fields fer him, and him always want more pickney. Him rut slave and wen dem mek pickney, him happy. Him not suh dat dem be him pickney nor treat dem other dan slave, but wen de nigger woman wid him pickney, him not let dem wuk in field and dat mek Mistress Charlotte, dat be she name, full wid hate. I gets to know'd not to be way she be or way she can see meh. I mek de brekfast and Sukey and Eme dem tek it in to dem and dem serve dem 'till de pickney born. I, like all nigger womans, get one day and half de next after de pickney born 'fore I gots to be back in de cookhouse mekking de brekfast and all dem food. Mistress Charlotte she dead soon after I mek de pickney."

Sukey and Eme dem start to laugh and Neala suh, "She not dead 'cause of meh. I had mix-up head fer Master John, dat be true, but not mix-up enough to kill she. She dead 'cause dat wat happen to white womans wen all dem insides full up wid hate and wickedness; dem not even have room fer air. Master John him suh dat him not want no more wife."

"Him love she dat much?"

"Him not love she like dat. Him tolt him white mans friends dat him not want no more wife 'cause him too old fer de nagging and him since him not having no more wife, him not have to buy no more pearls or jewelry. Him suh, 'Niggers are not like white women; white women bargain their fronts for jewelry but niggers make no pretense at loving you. Never met a nigger that loved a white man. No sir, never did but for an extra ration of pork, cloth, sugar, or flour to take care of their pickney, they would rut you to death. For instance,' him suh, 'take pearls, you make a big show of giving white women the finest pearls you can find for them that says you love them, but with a nigger you never have to worry about giving her pearls, you just rut, breed, 'cause those damn niggers can breed, and you move on to de next nigger. Wife? Why would I ever want a wife with all the good rutting that's waiting for me without me ever having to hear, 'John stay away from me, you smell just like them niggers."

"All him old white mans friends dem laugh and one of dem suh, 'Niggers would never know what to do with pearls anyway and beside,' him suh, laughing even harder, 'didn't Jesus say that you should never throw pearls before swine. Now, not that I'm saying that niggers are swine, we know they are not, swine is too good to call niggers.'"

"Wat pearl be?"

Sukey suh, "Wat dat matter to why Mistress Olivia and she red river drying up?"

I suh to she, "I never hear word pearl 'fore now so I jis't want to know'd wat dem be."

Neala suh, "Dem be rows and rows of white marbles dat be tied together and white womans like to wear dem 'cause it tell other white womans dat dem white mans love dem someting special. Now can I get back to way I be 'fore all dis talk 'bout pearls?"

Neala not wait fer Sukey, Eme, or meh to suh nuffin', she suh, "Massa John him suh dat Massa Fields should go get him a wife to be mistress on de plantation since him set in him ways and him not 'bout to start looking fer no pearls fer nobody. Massa Fields him not tek long after him faddah suh dat 'fore him finds Mistress Olivia. Soon, she and young Massa Field dem marry. Him brings Mistress Olivia to live here at Almars Ville, dat be de fancy name dat dem give dis house. Him call all de nigger womans dat wuk in de house and de cookhouse to come and meet de new Mistress.

"Wen we go out to meet de new Mistress, I jis't be looking on a magra, white white womans. De whitest white womans I ev'r set muh eyes on and her hair it be white too. Her gots it pull back from her face and her whole face be open fer yuh to see. It be hard wid a long pinch nose dat look like her fall wen her be pickney and it bruk. Her lips dem be jis't to tin lines dat not look like dem ever move to mek a smile. Her ears dem be big and dem stick out from under her bonnet like her want dem under de bonnet, but her not know'd how to keep dem thar. Her eyes, dem be de deepest tings I ever see. Dem, fer de quick time I look at dem, look like dem sitting in wells at de back of she head. Dem so far under her high hard forehead dat dem look like dem need eyes demselves to see dem way to de front on she face. She be standing next to him and I be wondering if she be de best ting a fine-looking young man like him can find in all of South Carolina. De magra woman open she mouth and suh in a voice dat sound jis't as magra as she be looking ..."

I cut Neala off and I suh, "Neala, wat magra be?"

Neala look at meh like magra be someting dat I should know'd already but she jis't suh, "Magra be tin, tin, dry up... it be jis't skin stretch ova bone."

After Neala suh wat magra be, Sukey suh, "Milkweed, Neala be not have fer eva to tell yuh wat happen to Mistress Olivia, so mayhaps it be best if yuh jis't let Neala talk 'till she dun."

I suh, "Guh 'head, Neala, I jis't listen 'fore Sukey mek me look magra wid all dat wicked she got in she eyes." Sukey and Eme laugh but Neala she not laugh, she suh, "Mistress Olivia wid she magra lips suh, 'I am the Mistress and you nigger women have gone on long enough on your own without a Mistress on this plantation telling you niggers what to do. That is over. I am here and I will tell all the niggers that are allowed in my house how to be around me. I don't take for any insolence, talking when I'm around, or any eyeing me. No nigger is ever to take their dumb nigger eyes and look me full in my eyes. If you want to speak with me, you wait and once a week I'll come into this cookhouse and ask if you have anything to say to me. If at that time you don't have anything to say, then you will keep your nigger eyes downcast; dumb niggers that means you look at the floor or ground whenever I'm around, you are to keep quiet, and stay away from me. I never want any nigger near enough to touch me unless you are serving dinner to the Master and me. Do you, dumb as mule, nigger animals understand what I've said?'

"We stands and looks at de floor since she suh dat we not to look at she and we not suh nuffin' 'cause dat jis't be de way it be. We not care if Mistress be young or old, magra or fat, Mistress is Mistress."

"But, Neala, how she mek yur pickney dead?"

Sukey and Eme dem talk like one voice and dem suh, "Wait."

Neala start back to talk like we not suh nuffin'. "De pickney, him be walking, not strong but walking wid him new almost steady foots wen Mistress Olivia come to de cookhouse one day to suh wat her want mek fer a fancy ball dat she be having in a few days fer all dem white mans and white womans friends now dat she de proud mistress of Almars Ville and Fields plantation. Wen Mistress Olivia come in de cookhouse, de pickney in de cookhouse way him always be 'cause

Massa John suh dat it be fine wid him dat de pickney be in de cookhouse wid meh. Mistress Olivia she not like dat and her want fer Massa John to suh dat de pickney to go way de other pickney be; him suh it be him cookhouse and de pickney can be wid meh 'till it walking proper. I be mighty glad fer dat.

Mistress Olivia she try to get him to listen to her way, but him not listen so dat day wen she come to de cookhouse, she look at way de pickney be and her look at meh. I feel de hate in she fer meh and him. Him nigger but him beautiful and him look like Massa Fields. De pickney him not know'd dat she be a white womans, de mistress of de plantation, and dat she hate niggers, and 'fore I can stop him, de pickney mek him way to way she be and him raise him little fat hands up and pull on she dress, jis't de way him do wen him want fer meh, Sukey, or Eme to pick him up.

"Mistress Olivia face it be tighten up and 'cause she be so magra, de skin stretch tight tight ova de bones and it look like de bones gine tear she face wide open. She not have color to start but wat little she have left she face and 'fore I can mek de step to grab de pickney quick off she dress, she pick up her foot and she kicks him hard from off she big fancy dress. I hear and I feel de kick. De pickney him cry out. She kick de lil' pickney so hard it send him sprawling backward right in de hurf. Him land in de burning coals and him scream and him try to get out, and wen him try, him mek de pot of stew come down on him. I scream and I runs to him and wen I get him out de hot coals and I try to get de burning stew off him, it come off and some of him skin wid it too. Mistress Olivia she shout at meh, 'Neala! Put that pup down! Put it down now and get back here! I am talking!'

"I not put him down straight way and Mistress Olivia see dat I be planning to see 'bout muh pickney dat hollering from de burns and she suh, 'Nigger get here now!'

I not move. I wants to help muh pickney and I not know'ds way to start helping him. I want to begs him not to cry. I want to suh to him dat I be sorry dat she kick him and dat him burn up but Mistress Olivia she be screaming now and she suh, 'Nigger! I'm talking to you! Get over here now.'

I turns muh head and I looks at way she be but not at she since she suh dat no nigger is ever to look at she. I mek to suh something, I not sure wat it be, but she scream, "You insolent nigger bitch. Put that pup down and get over here now, nigger!"

I be crying and I wants to looks at Mistress Olivia and beg she to let meh look after him burns and I not mek to put him down and I suh wid muh head bow low, 'Please, Mistress, him burn mighty bad. Him jis't a tiny pickney. Please let meh, jis't fer a minute, look at him burns.'

Mistress Olivia she shout real hard at meh, 'I said put that pup down and don't none of you niggers touch him. I'm here to tell you niggers what I want fix for my ball and that's what I'm going to do. Put! That! Pup down now and come here and listen to what I have to say to you nigger.'

"I not wants to put him down. I wants to help him but I know'ds dat Mistress Olivia have nuffin' but hate fer meh and wid meh not moving right fast as she suh, I know'ds dat it be deff fer meh. I want to live to help muh pickney so I puts de pickney down and I starts to cry fresh. Him scream and scream wen I puts him down. Him cry fer meh and 'cause I be slave and she de Mistress, I nots be able to be muddah and help him 'cause she suh dat I gots to put him down. It rip muh heart to puts him back on de floor. Him try to stand wen I lay him down 'cause him burn all over and it hurt him mighty bad to lie down.

"Mistress Olivia she step to meh and she slap meh full in muh face wid she magra hand and she suh, 'Neala, shut your nigger mouth and listen to what I have to say.'

"I stop from crying out loud, but I not able to stop de tears from coming down muh face as I hear muh pickney on de floor hollering from de pain. I mek like I be listening, but I not listen to wat she suh. Mistress Olivia she tek longer dan need be to suh wat she want. I tinks in muh heart dat she talking long so dat de lil' pickney be suffer more wid de burns. Mistress Olivia tek 'till de pickney quiet 'fore she dun talk. Muh heart it beating hard in muh chest 'cause I tinks dat muh pickney dead from de way him gone quiet.

"Wen she dun talking, she turn and start walking out de cookhouse. Wen she get to way de pickney be on de floor, she mek like she gine kick de pickney again and I suh, 'Oh, Lawd, please, Mistress Olivia, I begs yuh please not fer kick de pickney again, him in plenty pain and him jis't a little pickney. Kick meh if yuh wants to kick a nigger. I come right now and fall 'fore yuh foots, kick meh, even in muh face, but please, Mistress Olivia, I begs yuh not to kick muh lil' burn up pickney, please, Mistress Olivia.'

"Mistress Olivia she step back from de pickney and she step to 'way I be and she tek she hand and she fold up all she magra fingers and she mek a hard magra fist and she box meh in muh face near by muh eyes wid all she strenf. Den she suh, 'Nigger, you dared to raise your voice to me, disobeyed me, and now you are telling me what to do in my house? I'm the Mistress of this plantation and no nigger will ever speak to me like that. What you've just done will never happen in this house again. I'll see to that, today. Now.'

"She walk back to way de pickney be on de floor and she fix she eyes on meh and den she pick her foots up and I shut muh eyes and wait fer de pickney to cry out from de kick. Him not cry out, and wen I open muh eyes, she jis't 'bout finish stepping over him like him be sleeping dog on de floor.

"She walk out de cookhouse and I know'ds dat de next time I seen Mistress Olivia dat it not gine be good fer meh. I mek in muh heart not to worry 'bout dat. I rush to way de pickney quiet to pick up muh pickney and I can see dat him burn mighty bad. Him burn ev'ry way but him face and him head. Him hands, legs, belly, and him back got big water blisters and way de skin dun fall off him pink. Muh pickney him pink, white, and nigger now. Some parts of him be burn so bad dat it look like cook pork fat: white. I not know'd how to pick him up and not burst de blisters and hurt him more so I jis't pick him up and beg de Lawd to not let him hurt too bad so dat I can get him to muh cabin. Wen I pick up de pickney, him cry out and Sukey and Eme dem crying and dem sorry fer meh and de pickney. I start to run wid de pickney to muh cabin and wen I gets to de yard, I see Mistress Olivia and she talking to Massa Fields and de Overseer. I not stop and dem not suh fer meh to stop."

"Neala she start to cry and muh belly it burning meh fer she. She crying but she suh, "I get de pickney to muh cabin and I do ev'ting I know'ds to do fer burns. I beg de Lawd to let de pickney live. I be in de cabin long enough to cover him burns wid hog fat and flour 'fore I hear de boots crunching outside. I know'ds who it be. I wait fer dem. De cabin open and it be de Overseer and Massa Fields. Massa Fields him suh, 'Neala, put the pickney down and come.'

"I put de pickney down, again. I puts him down as soft as I can on de bed and I go wid dem. I know'd already wat dem have in mind. I not know'd wat Mistress Olivia dun suh but I know'd dat it not matter to dem if it be true or lie. She suh it and it be good as de Lawd's own words fer dem. Dem tek meh back to de yard and I see Mistress Olivia. She standing on de porch and her gots her hand on her hip and she gots a smile on her magra hateful face. Soon as we be near enough to she, she suh, 'Whup her, Everett! Whup her for her infernal and insolent behavior to her Mistress!'

"I looks at de ground and all I be tinkin' is dat muh pickney back in de cabin and him in pain. De Overseer him reach and jis't 'fore him tear muh dress at de back, Mistress Olivia suh, 'Tie her here. Tie that nigger right here to the porch in front of me. I want to see her pay for what she has done to me.'

"De Overseer him tie meh hands and Massa Fields had him beat meh. Him hit meh and hit meh and I not cry 'cause I know'd dat muh pain not pain like wat muh pickney be feeling. Wen de Overseer raise him whip to hit meh again, Massa John him come in de yard same time and him suh, 'What in blazes is going on here? Why is the nigger Neala being whupped?'

"Massa Fields him suh, 'Mistress Olivia said that just now when she was in the cookhouse, Neala told her what to do in front of the other niggers.'

"Massa John him suh, 'Everett, how long has this nigger been cooking in the cookhouse? How long?' Him wait like him waiting fer Massa Fields to suh someting and wen him not suh nuffin', him suh, 'Very well then. Now,' and him turn to meh and him suh, 'Neala, why are you being whupped?'

"I mighty scared to suh wat fer but I not get a chance to suh nuffin' de pickney it must wake and it scream from de pain. Massa John him suh, 'Neala, is that your pickney? It's in your cabin by itself? Why isn't it in the cookhouse with Sukey and Eme?'

"Wen him suh dat, Mistress Olivia start to walk 'way and Massa John him look at she walking 'way self and him suh in him thunder voice, 'Some blasted body say something to me about what is going on here.' I not know'd wat mek him walk 'way, but de next ting I know'd him storming cross de yard to muh cabin way de pickney be screaming and screaming now. Him inside and outside de cabin 'fore I can tink and him coming back cross de yard and him gots de pickney in him hand and him shouting and him suh, 'Everett, this pickney is almost cooked. Neala, what happened to this pickney?'

"Young Massa Everett him look at him poppa and I know'd dat him know'd it gots someting to do wid Mistress Olivia, who by dis time dun walk off de porch and she inside de house. Him Poppa suh, 'Untie her now!'

"De Overseer him untie meh and Massa John him suh, "Neala, take your pickney. Go to your cabin and see about his burns." Him hand meh de pickney and I run back to muh cabin. I not tink to worry 'bout muh back or dat de tear up dress falling off meh. Wen de dress be get in de way of meh getting back to de cabin, I jis' step out de tear up dress and I runs de rest of de way naked wid muh pickney.

"All night I do all dat I know'd to do fer de pickney but it not be enough. In de early morning jis't 'fore de sun come up, yuh know'd dat time dat be night but it also be morning, well I be sitting on de bed watching de pickney wen him stretch out long, long in him sleep and, widout a sound him dead. I do like muh pickney. I stand and I stretch and I not mek a sound. I not holler, scream, run to tell Sukey, or Eme, nobody dat him dead. I picks him up from de bed and I holds him tight, tight to muh chest; I not worry now 'bout muh touch hurting him cook skin. I tek a deep breff and I tell muh pickney dat I sorry wid all muh heart dat Mistress Olivia kick him and send him in de fire. Den I begs de Lawd to give muh pickney rest eternal up in heaven, like de white preacher man suh, and den I sit wid him in muh arms. I looks at him beautiful face and I cry. I wash him face wid muh crying and I feel muh heart as it full up wid two tings: de pain from muh pickney deading and hate fer Mistress Olivia. By de time de sun be brek in de sky I be full too wid more hate fer Mistress Olivia dan I tink one nigger body can hold.

"I puts muh dead pickney back on de bed and I covers him so dat de flies not light on him while I be gone. Wen I turns muh back on muh dead pickney and walk out de cabin, I mek up muh mind 'bout two tings: not one more pickney gine ever roll in muh belly, and dat Mistress Olivia gine live long enough to feel same pain as meh.

"I go to de cookhouse and start to mek dem brekfast and muh heart it black. As I mek she brekfast, I see muh dead pickney in muh head and muh heart it suh fer meh to poison she but I know'd dat I gots to poison all of dem 'cause if I poison only she, dem gine know'd dat it be meh and dem gine kill meh. Muh head it still mix-up over Massa John Fields so I let dem live but I tell muh pickney dat him not gine be in de dirt by himself. I promise muh pickney dat I gine send all of Mistress Olivia's pickney to be him company. Dat be de furst morning I mek special tea fer she.

"Wen dem tell Massa John dat de pickney dead, him suh dat him sorry fer meh dat muh pickney dead. Him not suh it, but it clear dat him know'ds dat it be Mistress Olivia dat 'mek de pickney dead. Dem bury de pickney in de woods and I tek a piece of muh dress and I tie it near de tree way dem bury him so dat I be know'ds how to find de way back to way him be. I tek some dirt from him grave and I bring it back cross de yard wid meh, and wen I gets to way dem bury dem own, I throw'd de dirt in and I suh, 'Mistress Olivia, yuh gine bury all yuh pickney jis't de way I bury mine.'

"Massa John him soon tek sick and dead. I not know'd wat him dead from but since I be have a mix-up head over him, I cry fer him and I cry fer de dead pickney dat we mek. After dat, young Massa Field him be de Massa of the whole plantation. Him not mek meh to cabin wid no nigger mans. Him jis't left meh in de cabin, dat be jis't right fer meh since I not want to rut no more wid nobody on dis plantation or no other.

"I plan fer Mistress Olivia and I keep de wickedness she dun muh pickney in de front of muh head and I mek it muh business to fix and feed she special tea ev'ry morning to mek sure she not mek pickney. Mistress Olivia she cry ev'ry time she red river flow and wen 'bout a year pass, and she tinkin' dat I dun fergit dat she kick muh pickney and mek him dead, she come in de cookhouse and suh to meh, 'Neala, you niggers got your ways; do you have something you can give me to make Massa Fields and I have a child?'

"I not look at she. I keep muh eyes fix to de floor right 'bout de place way she kick muh pickney and I suh, 'Mistress, I not right know'ds if in it will wuk fer yuh, but if yuh wants I can try but, Mistress, wat if Neala not able to mek yuh to have pickney, is Neala goin' get beat again?'

"'No, Neala. I just want to give your Master an heir for this great big plantation. I'm his wife and a wife should give her husband a male heir.'

"I give she a different tea. Her woman parts dem open and I let it hold a pickney and jis't wen she belly start to rise up, I give she different tea and it fall out. Ev'ry time I let she get a little further along, so she hope harder and wish harder fer a pickney to mek it all de way to born so she can give Massa him heir. Den I let she get she wish. I let de pickney grow'd 'till it almost ready to be born and den I give she tea dat mek it come out whole, perfect, and dead. It be a boy: de heir she want fer de plantation. She heart it brek dat de pickney dead. Dem bury him near way I throw de dirt from muh pickney grave.

"Mistress Olivia she cry and she cry over she dead pickney and she come back to meh and she suh, 'Neala, Neala, I need to make a baby for your master, a son, an heir. He wants a child and if I don't give him one, he's going to find someone else. I love him, Neala. I can't lose him. Help me to make a baby, a son, an heir for my Everett.'

"She fix it in she heart dat she can get a pickney to live. I give she tea and I mek all she food. She eat and eat. By de time she get dis pickney in she belly, she fat fat. Dis one it come out perfect too: it be another boy pickney. Him de most beautifullest pickney I ever see. She happy and she crying 'cause now her gots a son fer Massa Fields: an heir fer de plantation.

"She proud of she heir and she fergit dat I be de one dat help she get de pickney. She go back to she ugly wicked ways and she suh dat she not want meh to touch she pickney, only Eme. So Eme be de one dat seeing him 'cause she suh dat she not want enough nigger breff blowing on she heir. She walking and sitting all day wid she heir in she hand like him be de next baby Jesus. One morning, her coming down de stairs wid de baby Jesus pickney in she hand wen her mek a few steps down de stairs, her miss and step on de hem of one of she 'too-good-fer-muh-pickney-to-touch' fancy dress and she trip and stumble a little way down de stairs: her not fall. De pickney she be holding drop from she hand wen she try to steady she foots. She try to catch him back but all she got be a handful of air. De pickney it fall down de steps, bup, bup, bup, bup 'most way to de bottom. Her scream and holler. De Massa him run to see wat be wrong and him come to find him pickney almost at de bottom of de steps. Him pick him pickney up and run up de stairs wid him, but 'fore him run, him suh fer meh to go get de Overseer. Wen him looking at meh, I run fast and I shout fer de Overseer but soon as I mek it way him not able to see meh, I stops in de cookhouse and I looks at de place way she kick muh pickney and I walk slow pass it.

"Wen I full pass it I quick muh steps to way it look like I be running and I starts shouting fer de Overseer. Him hear meh and him come and I suh dat Massa needs him right quick. Him hurry and him run to Massa, soon him running down de stairs again and him go and get de white doctor to come. De doctor him stay wid dem and she mek Eme to be in de room to run and fetch wat de doctor be needing, and since I not be in de room it be Eme dat suh she do like meh wen she not let meh touch muh burn up pickney. She sit, all night, jis't like me, by de bed of she pickney and jis't like meh, she beg de Lawd to let she pickney live but jis't like wid meh, 'fore de sun come up, yuh know'd dat time wen it not be night no more and it not be quite morning, well de pickney it dead jis't like muh pickney.

"She cry over she heir and den she heart it dry up and den ev'ry night she blame Massa Fields and she suh dat it be him fault dat her trip on de stairs 'cause board raise up and him not fix it. She cuss at him wenever dem be in de same room. A few weeks later, him bring yuh from over at Litchfield Plantation. I go back to giving she de tea but I not dry she up fer good 'till yuh belly raise up big and proud wid pickney. De day yuh birf de pickney is de day I give she de tea dat be mek she woman blood stop flowing, she be dry up fer good. I not have to give she de tea no more. Meh and she be even. I know'd nigger can never talk 'bout being even wid no white mans or womans, but in dis cookhouse where it jis't be meh, yuh, Sukey, and Eme, we can talk wat we want: I can suh dat she and meh be even, we even."

I want to cry fer Neala and she dead pickney but Neala she look at meh and she suh, "Him not be alone in him grave. I send him plenty company. I go where him bury and I tell him dat I be sorry dat I not be free nigger dat can jis't walk way from here. I not know'd wen it gine happen, but I know'd dat 'fore I be too old, freedom gine come and wen it come, I gine grab at it and I gine walk to muh freedom. I live fer dat. Muh heart it still black to Mistress Olivia, but wid ev'ry pickney yuh mek fer him and I see dem get big and strong, I be glad dat her living to see dem too and her not able to mek none. Meh and Mistress Olivia, we even, as even as nigger womans can be even wid white womans."

Chapter 27

Changing Who We Be In de Dark

A day I be mekking de biscuits and Neala she suh, "Here, drink dis and nobody goin' get a pickney to grow'd in yuh; not Massa nor Harold Joe, and wen yuh gets back to yer cabin yuh give dis to Harold Joe. Not worry 'bout Massa. Him nots be coming to yer cabin tonight. I got tea fer him too." Ev'rybody laugh and we went on mekking dem brekfast.

Dat night I do wat Neala suh. I give Harold Joe de tea and drink some more of de tea she suh fer meh to drink. Harold Joe as be him custom sing to de pickney. Him sing songs 'bout trees and birds and de Lawd up in heaven. De pickney dem used to him singing and one by one him sing dem to sleep. Den it be meh and him.

On nights other dan dis night, Harold Joe him wait fer Massa to come and chase him way. I can see him waiting fer Massa to come but de time wen Massa usually come and chase him come and pass. I lie down in front of de bed where de pickney be sleeping and soon I fall asleep. I not know'ds wen Harold Joe move from by de door but him come and him lie down next to meh. I feel him warmth 'fore muh head mek it clear dat him be next to meh. Den Harold Joe him whisper, "Milkweed, I know'ds dat Massa him suh dat him will cut Harold Joe up if in I rut wid yuh but, Milkweed, tonight if yuh let Harold Joe come closer to yuh, I go gladly tomorrow and let Massa Fields cut meh."

In de dark wid only de breaving of de sleeping pickney, I puts muh hand on Harold Joe's hand. Him hold muh hand 'till I fall asleep. I wakes up to find Harold Joe by de door on him mat. Meh and Harold Joe we go on like dat fer weeks. I would start de night out by muhself and at some time during de night, Harold Joe him come and touch muh hand. Little by little, meh and Harold Joe we reach de point wen him be hold meh. Him still never try to rut meh, but I drink de tea ev'ry evening jis't in case one night him do like Massa and him rut meh.

One night, Harold Joe him call muh name. Him suh it real soft dat only I can hear, "Milkweed, can I be yer mans? Not 'cause Massa suh so but 'cause yuh suh so. Milkweed, I wants yuh to want meh to be yer man and not Massa. Does yuh want meh to be yer tek-up-wid-man? It be us secret, Milkweed. I never tells a soul. It be 'tween meh, yuh, de Lawd, and him angels."

Harold Joe wait in de quiet and wen I not answer him, him suh, "Milkweed, I promise yuh dat Massa be never know'd. I be never look at yuh so him be know'ds dat Harold Joe love Milkweed."

Muh heart it jump. I suh, "Harold Joe, did yuh suh yuh love meh?"

"Milkweed, I loves yuh from de furst day I seen yuh, and I loves yuh still. I jis't wants yuh to want Harold Joe. Yuh not have to love meh, jis't suh it ok fer Harold Joe to love yuh in secret wen us be in dis cabin."

I turn to Harold Joe and I put muh head on him chest. I hears him heart beating hard enough to tear a hole in him chest and him suh, "I loves yuh, Milkweed."

Dat night, meh and Harold Joe start our secret life together. Muh pee-hole not be able to fit Harold Joe even though I dun mek seven pickney and even though Massa Fields got big cocky, him cocky be jis't like lil' boy cocky to Harold Joe. Harold Joe him not rush to rut meh de way Massa Fields do. Him wait and wait and den one night it happen. Meh and Harold Joe join. We be one. Him spill him seed on de floor ev'ry time. Him scared dat our secret it get out by him and meh mekking a pickney. I not be able to tell him de secret of we in de cookhouse, so I let him go on spillin' him seed on de floor.

Massa Fields him still come, but someting in him different. I not know'd wat it be 'till him suh him want meh to have another pickney fer him. Him pulling and tugging on meh like him be trying to figure out how yuh tek yer time wid a nigger woman, de way Harold Joe be doin'. I be expecting Massa to jis't rut meh de way him dun rut meh fer years, but Massa him not jis't drop him breeches and shove him cocky in meh. Him suh, "Milkweed, you've been here now more than ten years. Those years have been hard on your mistress. It was Olivia, Milkweed, that made me take Lilly from you. I didn't want to take her but your Mistress Olivia said that since I can't get a child of mine to stay in her long enough to born and live, then I'm to bring her the first daughter you have for me.

"At first, Milkweed, I protested. I reminded her that you are a nigger and your child would be a nigger, but she said that since you are making white-looking children, she wants your nigger white baby girl for herself. The first girl she said that could pass for a white baby. That's why I took Lilly, Milkweed."

Massa Fields him stopped talking like him waiting on meh to suh someting. I stay quiet. I 'member dat him be de Massa and as him dun said wen de furst one born, 'Milkweed not own nuffin' 'round here.' Den Massa him pull meh to him and jis't de way Harold Joe holds meh, him puts muh head on him chest and him suh, "Milkweed, you know you are the only nigger I've ever rut with."

I nots know'ds wat to suh to him 'cause meh and him not ever have no reason to talk in de ten years I be on dis plantation. Him come in and him rut wid meh. Dat's all we dun fer years 'fore Harold Joe and since I be in de cabin wid Harold Joe none of dat change. De only ting dat change is dat him mek Harold Joe go out de cabin like him be a dog.

I be wondering why Massa act like I matter to him. I get a bold feeling in meh and I suh, "Massa, why yuh talking to Milkweed?"

Him suh, "Because, Milkweed, I know a white man isn't ever supposed to care for a nigger but, Milkweed, you are special. Not just 'cause I brought you here, but inside of me is a place that gets all mixed up when I see you and I hear our Lilly call me daddy. Sometimes, deep in that place, I feel for you the way I used to feel for Olivia when I first met her and just before I made her my bride. Do you understand what I'm telling you, Milkweed?"

I stay quiet and him suh, "Answer me, Milkweed. Answer me. Do you understand what I'm telling you? Answer me and now."

I suh real soft 'cause I be scared. I never talk to Massa Fields in de ten years I be here so I suh, "No, Massa, I nots know'ds wat yuh be suhing but it not fer Milkweed to understand."

Den Massa him gets mad at meh and him suh, "What is wrong with all you niggers? Are you all really no better than animals? Is learning so hard for you niggers? Did we, so many years ago, waste time in killing those little niggers pickney over at Litchfield? What is so difficult for you to understand what I'm trying to tell you? What?"

I not suh nuffin', 'cause I know'ds dat if I suh wat in muh heart and in muh mind, it gine mek him do to meh now wat him not do to meh wen I be little gal pickney. Him gine kill meh so I jis't look at him.

Him suhs like him feeling sorrow fer meh, "You don't understand, do you?"

I not be able to let meh and Harold Joe's secret out so I suhs, "No Massa."

"Milkweed, do you know I have a name?"

"Yes."

"What is my name, Milkweed?"

"Massa."

"That's not my name. My name is Everett Michael Poole Fields. That's why this place is called Fields plantation and every nigger on this plantation is named Fields. Their name is Fields because they and you belong to me. Do you understand that?"

"Yes Massa."

Massa him pull meh to him and him suh, "Can you say Everett, Milkweed? Say it. Say Everett."

I look at him and I suh, "Yes Massa, Massa Fields."

Den Massa him start to laugh and him pull meh to him. Him suh, "Just say Everett. I want you to call me Everett."

"Massa, I nots be able do dat. If Massa Glasser hear meh, him goin' whip meh widin an inch of muh life, Massa."

"No one is going to whip you, Milkweed. Just say it. Say it for me tonight."

I look at Massa and I suh, "Everett."

Den Massa him pull meh closer to him and den him put him lips on mine. Furst him not move dem and I not move 'cause I not know'd wat to do. Den I feel Massa's hands sliding up muh sides and wid him lips on meh, him pulls meh even tighter to him, den Massa him open him mouth and put him tongue in muh mouth.

Massa kiss meh de way Harold Joe kiss meh. I not kiss Massa back and him stop. Him looks at meh and him suh, "What's the matter with you, Milkweed, don't you want to kiss me?"

I stare at Massa and I not know'd how to answer him 'cause I not wants to kiss him. I only wants to kiss Harold Joe since him be de furst person to ever kiss meh.

Massa Fields him push meh away from him a little and him suh, "Now you kiss me back the next time I kiss you or I'll snap your neck."

Massa him brings him mouth to mine and wen him put him tongue in muh mouth, I close muh eyes real tight and tinks dat him be Harold Joe and I kiss him back.

Massa him kiss meh harder dan even Harold ever kiss meh. Den Massa him start to moan and grab meh all over. Him pulling meh so tight to him I can hardly breave den Massa him stop kissing meh and hold meh even closer 'fore him suh, "God I love you, Milkweed. I've loved you from that first day I saw you standing there so scared over at Litchfield Plantation. I couldn't let them harm you. I couldn't. Something in you stole my heart. I'm not going to hide it from you anymore. I love you, Milkweed. Say you love me. Tell me you love me too, Milkweed. I want to hear you say you love me."

De way Massa Fields breaving hard, I not ever hear him breave like dat. It mek muh heart beat mix-up. I know'ds dat I nots be able to disobey him 'cause him be de Massa, but how I can fix muh face to suh I love him wen deep in muh heart I still wants him dead and more so fer tekking way muh only gal pickney. I suh, "But, Massa, no nigger woman 'pose to suh she love no Massa like de way yuh asking meh to love yuh."

"I'll give you whatever you want, Milkweed. Say you love me and mean it."

"Wat yuh goin' give meh, Massa?"

"Anything you want."

"Anyting, Massa?"

"Yes, Milkweed, anything, but you've got to say that you love me and I got to feel it in the deepest part of my soul that you mean it."

Him suh, "Tell me you love me, Milkweed, and look me full in my eyes when you say it because if I see fear or a lie in your eyes, I'm going to shoot you and that nigger I let sniff around you. Now tell me, Milkweed, and know that I'm going to know if you're saying the truth. Tell me you love me."

I look at Massa and mekking sure dat muh eyes not suh dat it be Harold Joe dem seeing, I suh, "I loves yuh, Everett."

Massa, him tek him time and him touch all over meh wid him hands, him fingers, and den him put him cocky in meh. Massa him not rush and wen him dun, him not roll off meh de way him usually be. Him let him cocky stay in muh pee-hole and den him grow'd again and again him teks him time. Massa keep dis up until de moon leave de sky and de early morning sun start to chase way de moon. I not sleep or even 'tempt to sleep all night 'cause each time Massa stir, him wants to rut meh. Wen Massa finally put him breeches on, muh whole body sore and sticky from de many times Massa dun release himself in meh. Massa him looks at meh and him suh, "What is it you want, Milkweed?"

Wen Massa suh dat, someting in meh run cold and muh head it suh, 'tell him nuffin'. Tell him yuh not want nuffin' 'cause love it not cost nuffin'.' But I know'ds dat I dun tolt him I love him and fer dat lie dat him mek meh tolt him, I gots to get someting dat gine mek muh telling him dat be worth it.

I fix it in muh heart to tek de biggest and bravest step since Mistress Litchfield suh she goin' give us book learning. I suh, "I wants to know'ds how to read." I suh it and I waits. I waits fer him to tek him gun and shoot meh. But Massa him nots shoot meh. Massa him not suh a word.

Him jis't stand looking at meh so I tinks him not hear meh so I squeeze de words out muh startin'-to-dry-up-from-fear throat.

I suh, "It be book learning I wants. I wants to know'ds muh letters, de numbers, and how to read de words dat letters mek."

Him walks 'way a little from meh and den him turns and him face it be different. It look like him not know'ds meh no more and den him suh, "Why? Why, Milkweed, did you have to ask for that? Why you didn't ask for a piece of cloth, some sweets for your pickney, something easy? Why book learning, Milkweed? Why?"

I feel fear from de way him suh it and I not answer. Massa him turns full 'round from meh and widout one more word, him walks out de cabin and him not look back at meh. I feel muh heart beat fast and den I feels it sink and sink and I not know'd where it sinking to, but I know'd dat wen it get to way it gine, ev'ting dat I know'ds gine be different by time it stop it travel.

Muh heart it go way hearts dat full of fear go and wen it get thar, it must be so dark it start to come back up. It coming back up but it not be 'lone. It bring more fear dan I ever know'd in muh whole life wid it. It got more fear wid it dan de day Massa Fields and him friends mek Tadpole's still warm blood mix in de dirt that I steps in.

De fear it not stop rising 'till it and muh heart stick in muh throat. I know'd dat I dun tolt muh deepest desire to a white mans, and not any white mans but de same white mans dat had kilt four of muh friends ten years ago 'cause dey mammas and Mistress Litchfield believed dat we could get a little book learning.

Soon as Massa gone, Harold Joe him ease in de cabin. Him not suh nuffin' at furst but den him suh wid fear all over him voice, "Milkweed, wat yuh suh to Massa? Wat yuh suh to him?"

"Why yuh asking, Harold Joe? Why yuh asking meh wat I suh to de Massa? Yuh nots ever ask 'fore now?"

"I not ever have to ask before 'cause Massa him not ever stay here 'most all de night and now I see him leaving and him walking like a man wid a purpose. Tell meh wat yuh suh to him to mek him walk 'way from here like dat."

I nots have it in meh to tell Harold Joe dat I lied and tolt Massa I love him so I tolt him de other truth. I tolt him dat I ask Massa fer book learning. Harold Joe him look at meh and him eyes jis't fill wid water. "Milkweed, why yuh dun gone and dun dat fer? Yuh know'd dat no white man gine give no nigger book learning. Yuh not learnt yer lesson from yer momma wanting book learning fer yuh over at Litchfield? It be wanting book learning dat brung yuh here and now yuh gine mek yer wanting book learning be de reason dat Massa finally kill yuh."

Muh whole body it tremble and de fear dat stick in muh throat it rise up some more and it mek it to muh eyes and I nots be able to stop it. It turn to water and it be tears. I starts to cry. Harold Joe him feel sorry and him frighten fer meh. Him stands right thar and him cry right along wid meh. It be jis't one blink from morning so de crying it gots to stop. No more time fer crying 'cause I gots to go to de cookhouse and mek de biscuits and bake de bread.

I 'most run to de cookhouse and it clear wen I walk in dat someting dun change. I feel it. It be Neala who mek it clear to meh dat I dun mek some big, big mistake. She suh, "Nigger Gal, wat yuh gone and dun? Wat yuh dun, Nigger Gal, tek Massa Fields and put him in de foul mood him be in? Nigger Gal, wat yuh dun?"

I be fixing to suh I not dun nuffin' wen Massa Fields storm in de cookhouse and him suh, "Milkweed, you getting around here thinking because I let you keep those nigger pickney out in the field that you and them are special, and the way you treating that first-born like you think you own him or he's special to me. He's not special, Milkweed. He's not white 'though he looks it. He's not. He's a nigger! A slave! Just like you and all the others: a fucking slave, Milkweed. A slave!"

I look at Massa and I tinking why him talking 'bout Isham like dat but I know'ds better than to suh a word. Massa Fields him suh, "Milkweed, let me tell you that you don't own anything around here nor can you just ask for whatever you think you want. It doesn't just happen like that, Milkweed. You are a nigger and no nigger ever just up and ask for things."

De same way him storms in, him storms back out. De whole cookhouse it quiet and I nots know'd how to look at Neala. I 'fraid that if I look at Neala, I gine see de hate dat she feeling fer meh 'cause I dun mek de Massa come in de cookhouse. Him never come in de cookhouse. It be de Mistress dat come sometime but even she not come so regular and now I dun mek de Massa of de house come in de cookhouse.

I go to mek de biscuits and Neala she suh, "Nigger Gal, I not wants yuh to touch nuffin' in dis cookhouse dis morning! Yuh dun mek de Massa of dis house come in dis cookhouse and him not come by himself. Him bring de devil wid him. I sorry fer yuh. Yuh dun tek a stick and stir up de hornet and de whole nest. I not want yuh in here. If de hornet gine bite yuh, den it best find yuh out in de field wen it come fer yuh."

I suh, "Neala, yuh want meh to go wuk in de field?"

"I not be de one to put yuh in de field, but I be de one dat can suh yuh not mekking biscuits in dis cookhouse dis morning. Him not suh fer yuh to go to no field so I nots be able to send yuh out. Yuh stay in here. Yuh is not to go outside. Yuh stay out him way. If in yuh lucky, him spirit gine calm down. If in yuh not have no luck and him not calm down, den it be yuh and only yuh to tek de sting from de hornet."

De day it tek ferever to end but soon de end come but no peace of mind come wid it. Neala she not suh nuffin' to meh all day and wen it be nighttime, she jis' walk pass meh like I not be standing way I be. Wen she mek it to de door, she suh, "I gots a feeling dat de sting yuh gine get from dat hornet gine mek yuh fergit ev'ry rutting him ever give yuh. I gine be sorry fer yuh, Nigger Gal. I not want to be yuh."

She walk 'way from meh and I be left standing thar on muh own. I not know'ds if to sit, stand, or go. I go. I go to de cabin wid Harold Joe and de pickney.

Massa Fields him not come to de cabin dat night. Him not come fer a few nights and ev'ry night Harold Joe and meh we wait fer him to come. Harold Joe him stop touching meh, spilling his seed, or even kissing meh. Him get it in him bones dat someting bad fixing to happen. Him suh, "I gots meh a real bad feeling 'bout de pickney."

Him ask meh over and over again, "Milkweed, wat mek yuh suh someting like dat to a white mans and a white mans dat kilt four nigger pickney 'cause dem mommas want dem to get book learning. Did yuh think 'cause him took yer nigger gal to live wid him and him wife in de big house dat yuh matter to him? Milkweed, I wish fer yuh, meh, and all yer pickney dat yuh be ask him fer someting like a lil' milk fer de pickney, or a handful more corn to cook and feed 'em. Lawd, Lawd, Milkweed I feels someting mighty terrible gine happen. I feel it deep in muh bones."

Somehow dat be furst time I tek a good look at Harold Joe. All along him jis' be Harold Joe, my secret tek-up-wid man, but now him be de man dat frighten right long wid meh. I look at him and I see dat him is ev'ting dat Massa Field not be.

Massa Fields him tall tall, and him white but not like other white mans, him skin it a little brown from de sun. Harold Joe him tall too, but him not tall tall like Massa Fields. Him brown and black at de same time; not molasses-black like Poppa Molasses, but him de same color as wood dat scorch but not burn all de way through. Him hair it not curly nor brownish red like Massa Fields, but it black, most like mine, and it got waves in it and it thick close to him head.

Him eyes dem wide apart and dem jis't like two deep black holes. Tonight, and most nights since I tolt Massa Fields I wants book learning, dem fill wid fear and got tears in dem waiting to fall, jis't like mine. Harold Joe him got nose dat thick and wide and him lips dem thick and wide too. Wen him kiss meh, dem cover muh nose and most times it hard fer meh to breave. I not suh nuffin' 'cause I likes wen him kiss meh. Meh and Harold Joe not kiss since dat night. I looks at Harold Joe and I suh, "I sorry fer de trouble I dun bring 'pon muhself. I sorry, Harold Joe."

Him suh, "It not be jis't yer trouble. I love yuh, Milkweed. It be muh trouble too." Him not come near meh but I know'ds dat if him not be frighten fer meh, him would come and hold meh. I let that be muh comfort. Harold Joe him hum, moan, and den him sing meh a comfort song. I drift to sleep. It not be a restful sleep. It be a sleep dat full wid fear.

Chapter 28

Wheels Keep Turning And Bringing Evil

De next day soon as I mek it to de cookhouse and 'fore I can get near de flour to mek de biscuits, I hears it. I hears it from far and I feels in muh heart dat wat Harold Joe be fearing coming true. I nots run outside to look. I not have to. I dun heard it enough times dat I know'd wat it be, but it never be fer meh. Never had nuffin' to do wid meh.

After it get near enough dat us all hearing it, I steals a look out de window and I watch it. Wat I dun be hearing all dis time dat be far 'way 'fore now it come right 'fore muh eyes. It be a wagon. De wheels on de wagon jis't stop turning wen Massa Fields him come in de cookhouse and him suh, "Milkweed, come outside."

I look at him and I wants to run 'way from him. I not know'd wat him want fer meh to come outside fer, but I know'ds in muh heart it not be fer good and if I run, it not gine mek de matter no better. I tink in muh head to drop to meh knees, wrap muh arms 'round him legs, and begs him not to mek meh go outside wid him, but de look in him face suh, "You are not to talk to me and you are best not to come near me." Him turns and him walk 'way and I follows behind him. Once we be outside, him suh, "Milkweed, go and bring the first pickney you birthed. Bring him, Milkweed! Bring him now!" I looks at Massa Fields and 'fore I move I begs him. I beg him, I suh, "Please, Massa, please Massa, nots sell muh boy from here."

Him turn sudden like him be weathervane and him caught in storm wind dat got hold of him. Him look at meh and him suh, "Your boy, Milkweed? I told you that you didn't own anything around here. Now get your ass to chipping and go and bring him! That little nigger is mine: my slave. Now go and bring the little nigger 'fore I have your ass tarred and feathered. Milkweed, I don't have time to waste over some begging nigger! Run!"

Wen him suh run I sees muhself hogs tied and him on him horse and behind meh on de ground Tadpole wid him guts cut open him, momma all crumble up like she be flour bag wid out flour, Lil' Theo wid him head cut off, him momma wid she mouth shoot way and Chem and Tiny in de tree, not swinging; jis't thar all dem dead. I nots turns to go and get de pickney, I do as him suh: I runs. I only gets to mek a few steps wen I sees Harold Joe. Him not like all de rest of de niggers standing 'round. Him gots muh de pickney Isham wid him and de pickney him know'ds dat I be coming to get him and him grab hold of Harold Joe's hand and him start to cry. Harold Joe him give de pickney a small shove and de pickney him walk to meh but it like him leg dem planting in de dirt wid each one of him steps.

I run-walk to de pickney. I meet him de rest of de way and I grabs him hand and I brings him to Massa Fields. Massa Fields not so much as look at meh as him tell de driver to put de pickney up on de wagon. De pickney him look at meh and him try to get off. Massa Fields him suh, "Milkweed! You tell that little nigger to sit down 'cause if he so much as gets off, I'll tear the skin off him. So you tell that pickney to sit his nigger ass up in that wagon!"

I begs de pickney sit. I suh, "Isham, sit still 'fore Massa whup yuh."

Him crying and I can see dat him mighty scared, but him sits still. Him listen. Dat's one ting 'bout Isham, him listen; wen no one listening, him listening, feeling, and understanding. Massa him not even look at de pickney like him know'd him. I look at Massa and wonder if him fergit dat dis be de same little pickney him call a son and de one dat him slap Neala and meh so hard fer. Him must fergit dat it because of dis pickney dat him put Neala and Sukey out to de field fer almost fifty days. Master him face it set and stern and den I know'ds how him can do wat him doing. Him be a white mans.

De wagon wid Isham in it start to pull off and Massa him suh, "Milkweed, get yourself off out of here. Go back to the cookhouse. I want my breakfast with my biscuits and I want it on time and I want it hot."

I suh, "Please, oh please, Massa, let meh least watch de wagon roll way."

Massa him suh, "Milkweed, you take the rest of them pickney and take them to the field or back to the cabin, but you get to moving with them now before I load them all up in that wagon. Now go!"

Furst time since I came to dis place, Massa him give meh choice: field or cabin. Him not ever give meh choice 'fore. I not have choice 'bout being dragged way from Momma Cornbread nor Poppa Molasses. I not have choice 'bout Massa mekkin' meh him bed warmer. I nots have choice 'bout wukking, cooking him food, being kicked, slapped, or punched by Mistress Olivia wen she feel like it 'cause she know'ds dat anytime she turn and she bed empty it's meh him rutting.

I tek de pickney and I starts to go to de cabin wid dem and Harold Joe him suh, "De Massa him dun tolt yuh dat him want him brekfast same time, so yuh best be rushing back to de cookhouse to get gine wid him food. I gine tek de pickney to de cabin and den I be getting to de field."

I not look at Harold Joe or de pickney 'cause dem be crying and dem wants to know'ds way Isham be gine. I not know'd wat to suh to dem so I not look at dem. I not want dem to see dat I be crying. I wipes muh face in de bottom of muh dress and I runs to de cookhouse. I mek it inside and Neala she be thar already. She dun start to mek de biscuits and from de time muh foots clear de threshold, she suh, "Nigger Gal, I not know'd wat yuh dun to mek him sell way him furst living pickney, but I know'ds dat him not dun wid yuh. Him not gine stop wid yuh 'till him sure dat yuh all bruk heart. Dat be de ways of white mans."

Neala she look at meh and I starts to cry and she suh, "Save dem. Yuh gine have plenty time fer dem so yuh might as well wait and cry yer big cry one time. Him suh him want him brekfast, so yuh better come over here and finish dese biscuits. And nots yuh get no snot in dem. Putting someting in dem food is not fer yuh to do. Dat be muh job. But today not be de day. All de food we send from dis cookhouse fer de next couple of days gots to be de best food dat dem ever eat. Now wat happen week from today dat be different story."

I looks at Neala and she look at meh and she smile. I not know'ds wat she see to smile at and like she know'd wat in muh head she suh, "I gots muh reason. I gots muh reason fer dis smile. Yuh go on and mek dem biscuits and brace yuhself. Yuh sorrow not over yet."

She shake she head from side to side and den she suh, "I not want to know'd wat yuh dun, but if I be yuh, I be tink hard on all de tings I dun and suh. Den I gine mek sure dat I never do dem tings ever again. Ever, ever again."

I put muh hand in de flour and I nots have a heart to mek biscuits, bread, or nuffin'. Neala she watch meh and she suh, "Mek em! Dat be all yuh gots to do now. Mek em and mek sure dem not burn. Lawd know'ds dis is not de morning fer any kind of mistake."

I talk fer de furst time since I walk in de cookhouse. I suh, "Neala, but Isham be him pickney. Him solt way him son. Him solt muh pickney from meh."

Neala she steps to way I be and she suh, "Stop dat damn foolish talk. Yuh not have no pickney. Isham not be him son. Isham be a nigger.

A slave to him. Him rut yuh; yuh mek pickney, dat be all. Isham him not be nuffin' special to him. Him be slave, Milkweed, jis't like meh and jis't like yuh: slave. Now if in yuh know'ds dat yuh not able to mek dem biscuits, yuh step way and let Sukey do it 'cause all de while yuh here suhing dat him solt yuh pickney, him and Mistress Olivia getting ready to come fer dem brekfast. Now move out de way and go sit some way and figure out wat yuh suh to turn dat hornet loose on yuh. Move! Sukey, yuh come here and mek these biscuits!"

I sit in de same corner way Neala mek bed fer Isham wen him furst born and I cry. Neala and Sukey dem get busy to mek up fer time dat lost wid de talking and soon it be like I not in de cookhouse. Dem gets de food dun and dem tek it out to Massa Fields and Mistress Olivia. De day go like dat. Neala and Sukey dem busy doing dem part and muh part. Dem left meh lone to cry and dats wat I do. I cry fer muh pickney. It not matter to muh head or muh heart dat Massa Fields suh dat de pickney not be mine; him be mine. I be him muddah. Him roll in muh belly and it be muh pee-hole dat him push him out. Him be muh pickney and I be him muddah. I cry fer muh pickney.

Dem furst nights widout Isham be de hardest on Harold 'cause Massa him not stay way. Him come de same night and de next night, and de one after dat, and de one after dat, and ev'ry time him come to de cabin, him tek one look at Harold Joe and him suh, "Nigger, get."

It get so dat from de time Harold Joe hear Massa Fields' boot crunching on de ground outside de cabin, him would get to de door and be stepping outside so Massa not have to tell him to get no more.

Harold Joe him never get far. Him suh dat him stay near, not to listen to de Massa rut meh but him suh, "I jis't stay near if in one night I gots to come in here and kill him fer yuh. I be kill him fer yuh, Milkweed. De furst chance him give meh, I gine kill him and let dem other white mans do wid meh wat dey please. I not care, Milkweed, 'cause him be dead and yuh, well, yuh nots have to put up wid him ruttin' yuh no more." I smile a little 'cause I glad dat Harold Joe hate Massa same as meh.

De sound of de wagon it never leave muh head, at night wen I sleeps I can see de wagon roll way. Wen I walk in de yard, I hear Isham crying. De sound it in de wind; depend on how it blow I can hear Isham calling fer meh. I nots look fer de wagon no more. I gets to know'ds dat de sound it only be in muh head. I looks at dem other pickney and I wants to stay in de cabin wid dem all de time. I fear dat Massa Fields gine solt dem way from meh. Even Harold Joe him be looking at de pickney and him sad dat dem be crying, missing dem brother.

Harold Joe him suh nuffin' wen it be jis't him, meh, and de pickney. Him jis't fix to moan a soulful kinda song. I not know'd wat to do. I not ever want to shut muh eye and sleep 'cause I gots to wait to see if de Massa gine come to rut meh and if him not come, I not want to sleep 'cause I see de wagon and hear Isham crying. Den wen I fall asleep, I see de wagon come and one by one, Massa him sell off muh pickney.

I not have long to wait fer de dream come true. Massa Fields him stop coming to rut meh and soon, one by one, soon as de pickney get high to way muh navel be, no higher. It be like Massa, him spend time watching de pickney grow'd and jis't wen him know'd dat muh heart not be able to loves 'em more, him looks at meh and suh, "Milkweed, bring em!" Sometimes I's not even see it happen. I come back from cooking and baking and de pickney him be gone and dem dat left behind suh, "Massa suh to bring him, Ma, and dem tek him to de wagon."

Soon all de pickney solt off and it be only meh and Harold Joe left. Him tek to holding muh at night. Fer a long time, we not do nuffin' but one night him reach fer meh and wid tears streaming down him face, him tek meh de gentlest tekking dat ever happen in all muh years and dis time him not spill him seed on de ground. Him 'lease it in meh. I prays to God dat it would tek hold and mek a pickney. I know'ds Massa will kilt meh and Harold Joe, but at least him pickney would had start to grow'd in muh belly. I holds Harold Joe de whole night and him let him cocky stay in muh pee-hole. It so big even after him 'lease himself it not fall out like Massa. I prays to de Lawd to let meh and Harold Joe mek a pickney. It be a nigger pickney and not be part of Massa Fields. Morning come and I gets up and I go and I mek de biscuits and bread.

De next night, jis't wen I come down from de cookhouse and jis't 'fore I step in de cabin, Massa Fields him come to de cabin and him suh, "Milkweed, go back now to your cabin. There isn't a reason for you to stay here anymore with Harold Joe. Go now!"

I not suh nuffin' I jis't do wat him suh. Soon as I step foot inside muh cabin, Massa Fields him come in 'hind meh. Him slams shut de door 'hind him and in one big step, him grab meh. Massa him push meh to de ground, him tek off him breeches, and him rut meh right thar on de floor. Him rut meh harder dan him ever rut meh 'fore. Him rut and slap meh and I nots cry. I stay still. Den Massa him grind hard into meh and 'lease himself. I stay more still. Den Massa him suh, "It's all your fault, Milkweed. All you had to do was say you love me and mean it. But you said it and you didn't mean it, and then you ask me for the impossible: book learning. Milkweed, you asked for book learning and you knew you didn't love me. I put you with that nigger and I told you not to rut with him, but you disobeyed me."

Muh heart it got to jumping all over muh chest. I wants to ask Massa how him know'd dat Harold Joe and meh be rutting, but I know'd enough to know'ds if I ask dat, him gine kill meh. Massa Fields him pull meh to him and him suh, "Go ahead, Milkweed, look at me and tell me you love me. Tell me you love me!"

Dis time I nots be able to lie. I wants him dead more dan anyting else. I not be able to lie even if in him gine kill meh like him be gine do wen him furst come to Massa Litchfield's plantation all dem years back.

"You can't say it, can you, Milkweed? I can say it to you, Milkweed. I, Everett Michael Poole Fields, a white man and owner of the biggest plantation in Promise Land, Greenwood, South Carolina, have fallen in love with a nigger. To make matters worse, the nigger hates me and wishes me dead. Isn't that true, Milkweed? You hate me. I know you hate me. Say it. Go ahead and say it, Milkweed. Say you hate me!"

Massa Fields holds onto meh and him be waiting and dis time him be waiting fer meh to tell him de truth. Him know'ds de truth him jis't wants to hear how much. I wants to say to him, 'Massa Fields, I dun been hating yuh since de furst day I seens yuh at Litchfield, and I dun spend ev'ry day since den wanting yuh dead.'

I nots suh nuffin'. I dun learn muh lesson. All muh pickney gone. I know'ds better in muh heart.

Massa Fields him suh, "I know you think it's 'cause you said you wanted book learning that I sold them pickney off, but I want you to know that's not why. It was Mistress Olivia. She said that the other children were looking too much like our Lilly and she wanted them gone so Lilly won't get to hear that Mistress Olivia wasn't her natural mother."

Massa Fields stop talking and in de quiet of dis cabin where him furst rut meh and I gave birf to all him pickney, de hate fer him dat had grow'd in muh belly all dese years start to come out. It not mek it all de way out 'cause Massa Fields pull meh to him. Him suh, "Milkweed, it would have been so easy for you here if you had found a way to get pass me being Massa Fields and loved me. I'm not ashamed to admit that I wanted you to love me, Milkweed. If you had loved me, I would have kept all those pickney here. I would have found a way to get 'round Olivia. I would have, but what did you do? You chose to love Harold Joe.

"That, Milkweed, was your biggest mistake and everything that has happened to all of you is your fault. You had a chance to love a white man, but you chose to love a nigger, a dumb fucking nigger. He doesn't even have a say about what his name is or should be. I, Everett Poole Fields, the master of this plantation, made that decision: I called him Harold Joe. As a matter of fact, you didn't even choose the nigger I chose him and sent you to him jis't the way I send all the other nigger wenches to breed on this plantation when I want to add to my chattel. That's all he is, Milkweed, a fucking nigger buck. He's just like one of my horses or one of my male boars. I bought him for the sole purpose of breeding because he has a big cock. He fucks and breeds when I say fuck and breed. He's not a man, Milkweed. I am a man, Milkweed. A white man is the only kind of man there is. Anything other than a white man is an animal; just a different kind but an animal nonetheless. Harold Joe, he's an animal, a nigger animal the same way pigs, horses, and cows are animals. Nigger man is just a two-legged, dumb fucking animal, no difference. I, Everett Poole Fields, on the other hand am white. I am a man."

Wen Massa Fields dun suhing wat him suh, him red, sweating, and him hair it not got one curl left in it. It be now sticking to him head and him shoulders. De hair on him chest it dun stick to him chest and him breaving hard and him look like mad dog. Him looking at meh and it like him waiting. I not know'ds wat fer so I bend muh head and I looks at muh toes. Dem be all dat I can see. Dem be all dat I want to see.

I gets to tinking dat him be tinking 'bout doin' someting really bad to meh, but him not sure wat de bad ting is him want to do. Him push meh way from him and him roll over and him not suh nuffin' else fer a while. Him not go to sleep, but him stay and jis't 'fore de sun start to come up, him turn meh on muh back, rut meh, and dis time him not pull out right away. Him stay and den wen him pull out, him suh, "I hope that baby will be the one that changes all that hate you have inside of you for me."

Massa him stay way him is. Him not touch meh and him not suh nuffin' to meh. I do like him, I not touch him and I know'ds better dan to suh anyting to him. De ting dat different is dat I try not to mek a sound, not even breave too hard.

De sun crack de sky and Massa Fields him get up, put him breeches and boots on, and him walk towards de door and jis't 'fore him put him foot outside, him suh, "I won't let a nigger have your heart, Milkweed. You are mine. Mine. No one else's. Mine and mine alone. Do you hear me, Milkweed? You are mine!"

Him put him foot out de door and him turn slowly and him look at meh fer a little while and den him step out de door widout suhin' another word. I hear him boots crunching de small rocks in de yard. I listen 'till

I not hear him no more. Wen I not hear him no more, I get up, put de frock over muh head, and I go and mek de biscuits and bake de bread. Dat be wat I know'd to do. I not let muh head tink on wat Master Everett suh bout Harold Joe or wat him suh 'bout I belong to him.

Chapter 29

Nothing Else To Lose But Muhself

I be jis't dun mekkin' de biscuits and be reaching to get de bread out de hurf wen I hears a wagon. Dis time I not let muh heart jump 'cause I not got no more pickney left to be solt. I know'd dat some other nigger womans gine have she heart bruk.

But soon as I gets de bread on de cooling board, Massa Fields him walk in de cookhouse and him suh, "Milkweed! Come here!"

I go to Massa and I suh, "Massa, Milkweed not got no more pickney."

Him suh, "Don't you think I know that Milkweed? Come."

I follow him outside and I not see nobody by de wagon and jis't wen it hit muh brain who be de one dat getting solt way, him suh, "Go! Get yourself on up in that wagon."

I looks at Massa and suh, "Yuh gine solt Milkweed?"

Him looks at meh and him suh, "Nigger, are you daring to question me, the Master of this plantation? Get your nigger ass on up in that wagon!"

I climbs on up in de wagon and I starts to look fer Harold Joe, I sees him way out in de corner by de cotton. I starts to plead and beg. I suh, "Oh please, Massa, not sell Milkweed from here. I be do and suh watever yuh wants meh to do and suh. Massa, please! Please nots sell meh way from 'round here!"

"The time for all that has passed. Move on, driver!"

De wagon it start to roll and I turns to keep muh eyes on Harold Joe. I sees him fixing to stand straight like a tree and den I see two white mans on horses headed to where him standing. I sees wen Harold Joe sees dem, and I not sees de fear in him eyes, but I get full of fear fer him. De white mans on de horses rides harder to where him be and den I sees it. Dem got rope in dem hands. Harold Joe him see de rope and him start to run. I wants to stands in de wagon and tells Harold Joe to run fer him life, but 'fore I can tink I sees dat one of dem him slow him horse down some. Him raise him hand up and wen I look, I see dat him be got a rifle and him aiming it at way Harold Joe be. Him fire and den him fire again.

De sounds dem loud and mek de horse dat drawing de wagon I be in bolt. Him run fer a few paces and den de driver get him back to how him be walking before. I not tek muh eyes from Harold Joe and I not see de bullet, but I look way de white mans look and I see wat de white mans see: de big gaping hole dat de bullet mek in Harold Joe's back. Harold Joe him not fall down same time. 'Cause him running him mek two more step and den him fall to de ground. De other white mans him ride up to where Harold Joe be on de ground, bucking in wat must be awful pain from de big hole in him back, and de other white mans, de one dat not shoot 'fore, raise him gun. I not see 'cause I turns muh head way from way dem be but I hears as him shoot Harold Joe two more times. I counts: one, two. Dat be four times dem shoot Harold Joe: one, two, three and four shots fer one nigger dat not be a man. I wonder right thar how many bullets it tek to kill a white mans, 'cause him after all be, as Massa Fields suh, a man.

I wants to scream but I know'ds dat if I scream dat de white man driving de wagon would jis't reach back and beat meh wid de horse whip. I wants to look back and see wat dey be doing to Harold Joe, but I know'ds it not matter. I not have to see. I know'd dat if him not dead from de four bullets dem shoot him wid, dem gine mek him dead time dey be dun wid him. I begs de Lawd to mek Harold Joe be dead so dat him not suffer no more.

It be only wen I be far 'way frum Massa Fields plantation dat I turns muh head. Twan't sure wat I be looking fer or why, but I keeps muh head turn in de direction where Harold Joe be last standing. I wants to cry but I know'ds I not be able to. I hate Massa Fields even more 'cause I know'ds it be him dat tell dem to kilt muh Harold Joe.

De wagon it keep rolling on and dis time wid muh head not cover by a sack, I can see muh way clear. I not know'd where de wagon be tekking meh but it not matter to meh. It be tekking meh 'way from de place where dem kilt Harold Joe and solt furst muh pickney and now meh. It feel like de wagon rolling long long, but soon it stop. I looks 'round and I start to remember some things and den I see de tree way dem swing Chem, and I know'ds where I be. I be back at Litchfield Plantation. Massa Fields dun solt meh back to de same place way him stole meh from. I be back where I be born, way Momma Cornbread and Poppa Molasses be.

I alone now, Lawd, but not all alone. Momma and Poppa be here but all muh pickney and Harold Joe, muh whole source of comfort be gone. But somehow even here on dis new plantation which is a old plantation and a hellhole, I got muh comfort. I can hears Harold Joe voice in muh head. I can hear de way him used to sing to meh. It still in all dem pieces of muh bruk heart. Dat's how I got through each time Massa sold off muh pickney and how I goin' have to get through dis time. But, Lawd, I swear I hear muh Harold Joe clear like him be right here. Him spirit dun follow meh to dis place and him singing meh one of him comfort songs.

A tired old woman she come to meet de wagon and she suh, "Massa Litchfield suh yuh is to get de cabin in de far corner near de willow tree. Come. Let meh show yuh where it be."

As de woman start to walk way, muh heart it jump all over muh chest, happy. It be Momma Cornbread. Her talking to meh and her not know'd dat it be meh; she gal pickney. I want to shout and suh to she dat it be meh, Milkweed, she gal pickney, but I suhs nuffin'. I follow she. She push de door to de cabin and she step in and wen she shut de door, she look at meh. She not look like de same woman. She eyes dem happy and she gots a smile on her face. She suh, "Dat be yuh, Milkweed? Suh it be yuh and mek a poor old woman's heart happy."

Muh brek heart bruk all de rest of de way and I rush to she and I start to cry. I cry ten years of hurt on she. Momma Cornbread she cry and cry and den she suh, "Hush, we nots be able to let dem know'ds dat it be yuh or Massa Litchfield him will fix to sell yuh way frum here. Can yuh manage, Milkweed, not to let on fer as long as possible dat it be yuh? Please, Milkweed?"

I bend muh head onto she head and I nods.

"I nots be able to stay wid yuh longer dan it tek to show yuh dis bed in dis corner, but ev'ry chance I get, I gine try to get de bits and pieces of yer life since dem tek yuh from meh."

"Poppa Molasses, where is Poppa Molasses?"

"Him gone. Massa Litchfield solt him off next day after dem kilt dem pickney. Massa Litchfield him suh dat yer poppa and de other male niggers should have dun someting to stop someone tekking a whip to him daughter. Him had dem beat and den him solt dem off. It not matter none to Massa Litchfield dat four nigger pickney got kilt and one nigger girl got drug way. Him solt off ev'ry nigger man dat had a pickney kilt or stole. Him suh it be dem fault fer mekking him daughter get treat bad. Him not bring none of dem back."

I start to cry and Momma Cornbread she suh, "Yuh not have to cry none. De Lawd dun seen it fit to bring yuh back to meh. I thankful for dis."

She suh, "In de morning, dem goin' come and get yuh and dem will figure out wat yuh good at. Yuh good at anything, Milkweed?"

"Bread, biscuits, and anything dat got to do wid flour, clabber, and potlash."

"Den yuh might do good in de cookhouse. Be sure and tell 'em dat in de morning."

She turn 'way and again I finds muhself alone in a cabin. Dis time it a little different. I near muh Momma Cornbread. I lie down on de bed in de corner and I talk to de Lawd. I suh, "Lawd, I so tired, Lawd, but if yuh fixin' to tek Milkweed from dis here place and brings meh to yuh pearly gates I… I welcome it. I jis' welcome it. Tired, tired, Lawd, but I's more bruk heart dan I's tired, Lawd. I've been through so much. Lawd, yuh dun know'd dat Milkweed been through so much. I now been solt back to de same plantation I'd been stole way from more dan ten years ago."

Wen I dun muh talk to de Lawd, I close muh eyes and I begs him to let meh sleep, but I nots wants to see de faces of muh pickney nor Harold Joe as dem white mans shoot him down like dog. It like de Lawd hearing meh 'cause Him let different tings come in muh head. Him give meh a peaceful sleep. I not see Harold Joe or none of muh pickney. I sees Momma Cornbread and I see she de same way she be jis' 'fore Massa Fields drag meh way.

Furst time I left dis here plantation I be fourteen maybe fifteen, and now dey dun solt meh back all broke, tired, and used up. I dun be used up by hard wuk and pickney mekking. I dun wuk so hard I feel like de mule dat dey dun brung meh out here by. I guess I could have pulled dat wagon by muhself had de mule up and dead rather dan pull one more nigger to or from another plantation. I guess nobody ever tink 'bout de mule and all dat it be hauling from one plantation or another. White mans care nuffin' fer nobody but white mans, white womans, and dem white pickney.

None of dem not ever admit it but some of dem white mans not plans to, but some of dem end up feeling someting strange 'bout nigger womans. I know'd. I had a white mans dat wen it twan't nobody but him and meh 'round him, treat meh like I be a white womans. No him not bought meh no fancy white womans hats, or none of dem fancy bags dem tek to town but, him, Massa Fields, well him sometimes be wants to hold meh. No, no; not hold meh down to beat meh, but hold meh and do meh like dem white womans suh to each other 'bout dem mans be holding and doing dem. It be him wanting dat wat got meh solt back. Him want dis nigger womans to love him same way white womans love white mans. Dat not be de way tings 'pose to be.

Sometimes wen I be back at Field Plantation and it not be nobody but Mistress Olivia and she white womans friends sitting around and dem have more dan one glass of sherry, dem gets 'round to talk 'bout mans and wat mans got between dem legs. Sometimes, and only after more dan one, two, maybe three glass of dat bright red sherry, dem talk 'bout nigger mans and wat nigger mans got between dem legs and how nigger mans fit dem tighter dan white mans 'cause white mans be no bigger dan wat dog got between dem legs but nigger mans; well nigger mans big like horse or elephant. Den dem laugh like whores, all dem but Mistress Olivia.

Mistress Olivia, she not laugh 'cause Massa Fields him be like a nigger man in him man parts. Him a nigger man in white man skin. Him big like horse or maybe horse and elephant between him legs. I know'd 'cause it be Massa Fields I dun mek all dem pickney fer. It be him wantin' to tink dat him could treat meh better dan a nigger dat mek Mistress Olivia 'mind him dat I be a nigger womans and she slave well as him. It be dat wat brung meh back to where him drag meh from.

I not 'member falling asleep but soon de sun be mekking a crack in de night sky and 'cause I use to being a slave, I gets up. Dat be time all slave get up; cookhouse nigger or field. Crack of dawn is wake up time fer nigger. I stands outside de cabin and I wait fer dem dat goin' decide wat place on dis plantation dem goin' put meh.

Jis't as Momma Cornbread suh, dem put meh in de cookhouse to cook, mek biscuits, and anything dat have to do wid flour. Time pass and 'cause I twan't tinking on Massa Fields no more but dis new plantation, I not notice muh whole body changing 'till one day Momma Cornbread she suh, "Milkweed, is yuh having a pickney?"

I look at Momma Cornbread and den I start to 'member wat Massa Fields had suh 'bout putting a pickney in meh. I look at muh belly and I not have to tink. I be mekking a pickney. I starts to hope in muh heart dat Massa Litchfield won't sell dis pickney from meh.

Momma Cornbread she suh, "Yuh not have to suh nuffin' to nobody. If and wen dem notice yuh wid pickney, yuh is to mek like yuh not know'd wat de matter wid yuh. Let dem tell yuh dat yuh gine have a pickney. White mans like to know'ds dat dem de only one can tink fer nigger."

I did jis't wat Mamma Cornbread suhs. I keeps on mekking de bread and biscuit 'till one day Phebe, she be de other nigger dat wuk in de cookhouse, suhs to meh, "Is yuh mekking a pickney?"

I look at she and I not suh nuffin'. I holds muh head down like I shame. She suh, "Mistress goin' want to know'ds how far long yuh be, 'cause her not like no nigger to birf no pickney in de cookhouse."

Again I suh nuffin'. I steady looking at muh foots. Den she suh, "Nigger Gal, wen de mistress come fer to tell us wat to mek fer she and de Massa's dinner, yuh is to tell she dat yuh is mekking a pickney."

Again I suh nuffin' and she left meh and went back to wat she be doing.

As de Mistress dun since de furst day I be in de cookhouse, she come to suh wat she want fer dinner fer her and her pappy, de Massa. Wen Mistress come, de nigger call Phebe she suh, "Mistress, de nigger gal from over at Fields plantation is wid pickney."

De Mistress she look at meh and she suh to Phebe, "How far along is the nigger gal?"

Phebe she suh, "I not know'd, Mistress, and I not tink de nigger gal she know'ds but from de look of she, I suh dat she got three maybe four months to go 'fore she mek pickney."

Den de Mistress she come over to meh and she suh, "I don't let any nigger that is with pickney touch anything that I'm to eat, so from now you are not to come near any food for me. If Phebe can find something else for you to do that doesn't involve food for me, you may stay in the cookhouse. If, however, Phebe's not able to find anything else for you to do, then you'll go to the field 'till you drop that pickney. You understand me, nigger?"

I know'ds dat I can get 'way widout answering Phebe, but I know'ds dat I not be able to play not talking wid de Mistress so I suh, "Yes, Mistress. Yes, Mistress."

Phebe, who 'till now not pay meh no mind or wat I suh to de mistress, suh, "Mistress, de nigger gal good wid she hands so I'm gine get she to wuk on de mending and fixin' if dat be 'ceptable to yuh, Mistress."

"I don't right care what the nigger does just as long as you don't let her near food for me or for the Master."

Dat be how dat went and how I got to be de one fixing and mending and soon I get good at it and Mistress she not notice anymore dat muh belly big. All she notice is dat I mek fine stitching on she clothes and dat is enough fer she.

De time fer de pickney come and since I dun birf so many pickney fer Massa Fields, it not worry meh none wen de pain start. I not suh nuffin' to nobody since I use to birfing by muhself or wid Neala so I go out de cookhouse where I be doin' some mending, and I walk 'cross de yard and I mek muh way to de cabin dey let meh share wid Momma Cornbread; dem not know'd she is muh Momma and dem dat 'member meh dem not suh nuffin'. It jis't like dem not know'ds meh at all.

Momma Cornbread she suh it fer de best dat dem see meh and go like dey not see meh.

Wen I mek it inside de cabin, Momma Cornbread she come soon after meh. She suh, "I see de way yuh walk over here and I can tell yuh ready fer dat pickney to come out. De Mistress she mek it so dat I be de one dat wid de niggers wen dem have dey pickney."

I look at Momma Cornbread and I feel like I wants to tell her wat Massa Fields dun to meh, but de pains dem start harder and thar be not time to tell she. I gets to tinking dat wen de pickney come out, she be see and she be know'd dat I know'd Massa Fields de way most nigger women know'ds white mans.

De pickney come out fast and Momma Cornbread she clean up de pickney wid de few rags dem give she. Wen Momma Cornbread give meh de pickney, muh heart got stuck in muh throat. De pickney it not white like all de rest. It be a nigger pickney wid wide-set eyes and skin dat look like it be wood dat burn jis't a little bit.

It twan't Massa Fields who put de pickney in meh. It be Harold Joe. I start to cry and Momma she not know'd why I cry. She tink I cry 'cause I happy. I look at Momma Cornbread and I know'd dat dem things I be planning to tell she 'bout wat I dun been through wid Massa Field if de pickney be white I not gine tell she now. I jis't fix dem deep in muh heart, never to tell, ever.

I call de pickney Haroldetta Litchfield since she born on Litchfield plantation. Massa Litchfield not care 'bout no nigger and she pickney. Him care 'bout wat dat nigger wuk be and how soon dat nigger gine get back to it.

Jis't like at Fields plantation, I gets back to wuk de next day but I not go back to mekkin' de biscuits and de bread right away. Mistress Litchfield suh she needs fer meh to keep fixing and mending, so I mek de bread in de morning and fer evening supper and in de middle I mend and fix.

Chapter 30

Slow Churning Memory

Time move slow on a plantation but one ting fer sure, it not change de things yuh 'member. In time, ev'rybody at Litchfield 'member meh. Some of dem like de mommas to dem dat be kilt on de day I be drag 'way want to know'ds wat happen to meh during de time I be gone. I tell some. I tell 'bout Neala and de biscuit mekking. I tell 'bout missing Momma Cornbread and Poppa Molasses and I tell 'bout de way Massa Field's Overseer and him temper, but I left out all dem parts dat jis't not bare repeating, mostly 'bout Massa Fields. I never tell dat I breed fer Massa Fields, nor did I suh to dem dat him suh him had love fer meh.

De part I keep deepest in muh heart is de part 'bout him and him wife tekking muh Lilly from meh. I not even tell Momma Cornbread dat part. I know'd wat life be like fer a nigger dat try to fit in to white mans world. I not want fer nobody to come and tek de good life from muh Lilly. I know'ds dat she not know'd dat her momma be a nigger so I not see de sense in mentioning to anybody dat I mek a pickney so white she passing fer white mans and white womans pickney. I jis't left dat part out.

Life it have a way of bringing tings back to yuh; I never figure on seeing Massa Fields, Mistress Olivia, or muh Lilly again, but life it not wuk like dat fer a nigger. It change 'pending on wat white mans want. Massa Fields him, it seem, not let go of things him figure 'long to him. Massa Fields had long figure meh to be one of dem things. Him come one morning, 'fore de sun can dry de dew off de grass, trying to buy meh from Massa Litchfield. Massa Litchfield him listen to wat it be Massa Fields have to suh den him suh, "Everett, my dear man, are you forgetting that the nigger was my slave when you stole her from my place?"

Muh heart near stop. I not ever figure dat all dis time Massa Litchfield know'd it be meh dat come back to him place. I start to wonder how long him know'd it be meh. But I not have long to try and figure nuffin' 'cause Massa Fields him suh, "I'm not forgetting that,

Litchfield, but I'm here to make you a generous offer for the nigger now."

"None of the niggers on my place are for sale, Fields. The place is running smoothly with young Mr. Rivers keeping them niggers in line as my new Overseer."

"Then surely you won't miss this one nigger, now would you, Richmond?"

"Fields, you are missing what I'm saying. What I'm saying is that I'm not selling back to you what was mine in the first place, and besides, you sold me the nigger with a pup growing in her and you know Miss Henrietta and how she feels 'bout niggers and their pups. Well, she's taken a fancy to this particular pup since the bitch was one of her playthings 'fore you took her."

"Child? Did you say dat Milkweed had a child?"

"I didn't say a blasted thing 'bout no child. I said that you sold the nigger bitch back to me knowing that she had a pup growing in her. You see the way I figured it, you selling her back to me with the pup in her was your way of making up for all the years you had her over at your place. You know, Everett, if I'd known earlier that it was you and your henchmen who had come to my place and put your accosted hands on my daughter and killed off her pets, I would have shot you. I should still shoot you for what you did, but selling the nigger bitch back to me with pup was ingenious on your part. But keep this in mind, Everett: the fact that I haven't shot you yet doesn't mean that someday I may not just up and shoot you for being here when my child was abused and doing nothing to stop it. But for now, just for now I'm not going to shoot you."

Massa Fields him not seem to know'ds wat to suh to Massa Litchfield, but dem him find him voice and him suh, "Then sell me the pup so it can be a plaything for my Lilly."

"Everett, Everett, I'm not selling you my property. Why don't you take yourself back to your place and see if you can find a pickney pup round your numerous cabins to make a suitable nigger pup for your girl to play with."

After Massa suh dat, it got mighty quiet. Dem stop talking like dem run outta tings to suh and den I hear dem boots crunching de ground and I can tell dat dem walking way from near where dem be standing. I hear only de crunching of de ground and soon I not hear dem talking no more.

I mek de mending last long, hoping dat dey be come back to where I be so I can get to hear more of wat dem suhing, but dem not come back. Soon I hear Massa Litchfield and him talking to de Overseer Mr. Rivers and him suhing, "Mr. Rivers, if I'm not here and Master Everett comes round here asking to buy any of my niggers, you are to tell him that the buying and selling of the niggers is done by me and me alone. Do you understand me? He's also not to make any request from you as far as the services of my niggers. Nothing. Do you understand me? Nothing is to be done about my niggers without my say so. Nothing!"

Massa Fields him not come back round de place fer a few months, but him name come up plenty one day wen Massa Litchfield had some white mans over fer smoking dem fancy, as him suh, Cuban cigars, and de drinking of wat him call, 'de finest brandy from de Colonies.' Him suh to him white mans friends wen dem dun had plenty to drink and dem laughing and talking like nigger wen nigger get a free day to dem self and Massa let dem get some corn whiskey.

Massa him had a lot to drink and him suh, "That fucking Everett Fields is an unrelenting stubborn son-of-a-bitch. Remember back 'bout ten years or so, my precious Henrietta was accosted and her pups were killed? Well, it was Everett and his fucking henchmen that did it. Well, in addition to killing my precious Henrietta nigger pups, he stole a bitch pup from here. He kept her over on his place all that time and now he's sold her back to me. Can you imagine the balls of that young son-of-a-bitch? He sold me back my property and now he's been bombarding me for months now wanting to buy her back 'cause his fat frog of a wife just realized that there isn't anyone that makes biscuits, flapjacks, or bread like the nigger bitch."

One of de white mans him start to talk and muh blood it run cold. I know'ds dat voice. It be de voice of de fat white mans dat kilt Tadpole and shoot him momma in she mouth right through she fingers dat she be using to keep from hollering. Muh knees dem start to shake and I can feel dat if I not mek muh head tink, dat I gine move muh bowels right here on Mistress Henrietta's fancy rug.

I wants to look to let muh eyes see wat muh ears know'd to be true. De fear too much fer meh and I jis't stay quiet and listen to him talk like him not know'd wat de Massa talking 'bout. I wants to tell Massa Litchfield dat him be here wen Massa Fields be here, but I know'd dat white mans not ever go 'gainst white mans and Lawd know'ds never fer a nigger.

Him talk. I hears him words but de fear not let dem sink in. Him suh, "Why with all the niggers he has over on his place can't Everett get one of his nigger bitches to learn how to make biscuits. It can't be that difficult to teach them dat. Nigger likes food and so they pick that up easily."

After him suh dat, all him white mans friends dem laugh and slap dem knees and one of dem suh, "Litchfield, you sure it's them biscuits he's after. You know what they say about fucking your niggers and Fields does have the most niggers here in Greenwood. He's probably done fuck the little nigger bitch and now he wants to be back in her nigger hole."

Wen him suh dat, dem all laugh and slap dem one another and one after de other suh dem joke 'bout fucking nigger womans and one of dem, I not know'd which one, suh, "Isn't it something how them niggers, despite how stink they smell, can get a white man's cock to jump up and be hard as blasted rock. The next thing you know, you want to rut them and it isn't just the women. If one of them nigger boys turns his ass to you, it makes you want to fuck him, even if it's just to teach him a lesson."

Dis time not all of dem laugh and dem dat laugh it not sound like full belly laugh. It be a laugh like dem not sure if dem should laugh or not. Wen dem nots be able to figure if dem should be laughing or not, dem stop from laughing. It quiet fer a while and de same one who had jis't suh 'bout rutting nigger boys him suh, "Not that I've done such a despicable thing, but I've heard that some of the male niggers are predisposed to this type of behavior. Mind you, it's just something that I've heard in passing."

One of him friends suh, "But, Richmond, what do you think Everett really wants with your nigger?"

Massa Litchfield him suh, "Like I said, I think it's his fat ass bitch of a wife, Olivia, and her greedy, greasy hands. She wants her hands on my nigger's biscuits and whatever she wants; Everett goes out of his way to get for her. Doesn't matter how long it takes."

Dat mek dem all laugh and de one who talk 'bout rutting wid nigger boys him laugh de loudest like him glad dat dem talking 'bout Massa Fields again and not 'bout him rutting wid nigger boys. De talk den turn to which one of dem cookhouses Massa Litchfield goin' let meh come to and mek biscuits and bread fer him and him family. While dem white mans try to figure out how each of dem goin' get meh to mek biscuits, flapjacks, and bread, I be figuring out too.

Mamma Cornbread never let go of de idea of meh and book learning, and wen I tolt her dat it be book learning I ask Massa Fields fer dat got meh solt back, she be mighty please. She suh, "After dem white mans kilt off dem pickney and tek yuh 'way and she Poppa solt off our mans, Mistress Henrietta suhs she wants to give us someting to tek de place of de pickney and de mans we lost. Mistress Henrietta, she try to teach we, and in even more secret how to spell and write de names of de pickney and mans we lost.

"Dem rest of womans tinkin' dat no book learning can tek de place of dem dat dead and dem dat solt way. Dey be mighty scared dat de white mans gine come back again and kilt de rest of we so dem not let she teach dem nuffin'. But yuh Momma, I finds a way each of dem times dat Mistress Henrietta wants to teach meh book learning to be way she suh to be. I lern how to do all dat Mistress Henrietta suh dat she be wanting to show you and de other pickney dat be from she Secret Schoolhouse Fer Nigger Pickney. I do ev'ting dat she want to mek meh know'd. I lern how to mek de letters to mek yer name.

"Wen Mistress Henrietta see dat I can mek de letters to mek yer name, she teach meh how to mek de letters to mek any name dat come to muh head. Den she suh I dun lernt so good she goin' mek meh know'ds numbers. I never mek book learning hard. I mek muh brain and muh hands do watever she want dem to do. So it not dat long 'fore she be showing meh how dem letters come together to mek words and wat dem words sound like. Mistress Henrietta lernt yer Ma to read dem white people's book.

"I, yuh muddah, is de only nigger know'ds letters, numbers, and I can read a bit. Not like Mistress Henrietta, but enough to know'ds wat on dem papers dat dem leave 'round de place 'cause dem know'ds dat nigger not even know'd nigger name even if it be on paper in front him face.

"I goin' teach yuh and yuh goin' teach Haroldetta but yuh must always keep de teaching as yer biggest secret; no matter where yuh end up. Milkweed, let ev'ting I tell yuh sink in yer brain. Mark it on yuh heart. 'member ev'ting. Fer wat we dun been through, sep'ration, beatings, and sights our eyes, brains, and heart nots ever gine ferget, yuh, meh, we gots to 'member but more dan anyting, fer wat I dun seen dem do to yuh and all dem tings dat too hard fer yuh to tell meh; we must 'member. All dat sufferin' nots to be fer nuffin'. 'member book learning is de most special ting. Dat's wat yuh must do; 'member and tell yuh own; 'specially yuh daughters. Tell 'em book learning 'fore anything, even love. Yuh hear meh, Milkweed, let nuffin' but de good Lawd come 'fore book learning."

Every morning wen it be meh and Momma Cornbread in de cookhouse, she be steal way and show me how to mek de letters and numbers. Her not tek no paper nor dem quilt to show me, Momma show'd me in de flour. She mek well in de flour way we gine put de lard, salt, and water and rising powder fer de biscuits and she suh, "Watch muh hand, Milkweed, watch." She tek she hand and she mek letter. Den she tek she hand and mek it go way and she tek muh hand in she hand

and she show'd me how to mek muh name. Over time, I come to know'ds dat:

M I L K W E E D is de letters to mek muh name.

De furst morning I see dem letters in de well of de flour, muh heart it full and de tears dem come to muh eyes. Momma Cornbread she suh, "Let dem be tears of joy. Book learning it gine mek all de difference fer niggers: it gine mean freedom." Den she write in de flour:

F R E E D O M and she suh, "Furst chance yuh gets at freedom, tek it and not look back. Promise meh dat yuh gine tek it and not look back, Milkweed."

I look at Momma Cornbread and 'membering Chem, Tiny, Lil' Theo, and Tadpole, I suh, "I promise yuh, Momma. I promise, furst chance I gets at freedom I gine tek it."

Chapter 31

Life Turn Upside Down

Massa Fields him stay way fer a long, long time but wen him think dat Massa Litchfield ferget dat him suh him goin' shoot him if him come back wid de same ole' song, him come back. Him talk fer a long time wid Massa Litchfield 'fore him bring up de real reason him come 'round de place, but soon him get to it.

Him suh, "Now, Richmond, you know I've been asking you for damn near, well… almost four years now to sell me the nigger Milkweed and you've so far refused me. But today I have a different proposition to put to you."

"Now, Everett, what do you think you can propose that will get me to reconsider my original decision not to sell her or to shoot you?"

"Cause this time I want to buy the nigger pup. What say you to this?"

"I'm saying what I said the first time, or have you forgotten that you asked me that already? The answer is still no, Everett. I'm not selling you any of my slaves. None. Not one!"

"Richmond, have you gone soft with all the talk of emancipation?"

"Emancipation? What in blazes are you talking about? Emancipation has nothing to do with me refusing to sell you my nigger or her pup. I'm just not selling either of them to you."

"I'm saying emancipation because you keep saying Milkweed's pickney. That pickney isn't Milkweed's. Truth be told, Richmond, half that little pup is mine and I want my half to come be pet to my Lilly."

As dem talk I gets to tinking dat mayhaps Massa is tinking him not be able to let Massa Fields shame him again 'bout de amount of freedom him give him slave on him plantation. Slave here at Litchfield Plantation still slave, but dem not slave like de way other Massas got dem slave. Massa Richmond him not chop, cut, burn, or none of dem tings dat other Massas do. Him will stand fer some beating, but no nigger goin' dead at de end of no beating wid him as de Massa.

I stop breaving waiting to hear how Massa goin' answer Massa Fields. I wait fer Massa Litchfield to suh what him gine do. Massa tek him good time 'fore him suh, "Everett, what is it about this nigger wench and her being on my plantation that doesn't give you any peace? First you and your kind trespass on my property, violate my daughter, kill four of my young niggers, steal and drag that young nigger slave near to her death. You have the balls to sell her back to my place, as if some old nigger 'round here won't eventually remember the nigger as the one you stole from me. Not only do you sell her back, but you sell her back with a pup growing in her belly and now you are standing on my property asking me to sell you the nigger pup 'cause you say half is yours."

Massa him tek a deep breff and him suh, "What, Everett, is your reason all these years for this? Tell me so I can finally have justification for shooting you. Go on, give me that good reason today so I can put us out of your misery."

Massa Fields him huff and grunt and I hear him breff suck back in him body deep wen Massa Litchfield suh him should shoot him. I smile a little bit. I start to think dat Massa Litchfield not goin' let no more sep'ration come 'tween meh, Momma Cornbread, and Haroldetta, but Massa Litchfield's next words mek de little smile I dun 'llow muhself to fall clean from muh face, and mek meh run to snatch muh heart dat had jump outta muh chest and be halfway through de door. Massa Litchfield him suh, "Good Lord, Everett, it's Milkweed you really want, isn't it? It's not her pup you're interested in. You want the nigger the way a white man wants a white woman, don't you? It's the wanting of the nigger that has kept you haunting my place all these years. Isn't it?"

Ev'thing went quiet. I wait fer even de flour on muh hand to fall off wid de hope dat it would mek a sound. De flour it fall off 'cause I be breaving hard and blowing it way, but it not mek no sound. Den Massa Fields talk him and him suh, "Richmond, that what you've just said is foolishness. What white man ever truly wants a nigger for anything more than to warm his loins and add a few niggers to his property?"

"What white man, Everett? What white man? You! You, Everett Fields, that's who. You are the white man. I can see the fire in your eyes for her. She has fire for you too. I knew there was something burning in her, but I didn't know 'till now what it was. Now I know. That blasted nigger has a fire for you the way a white woman has a fire for a white man. The fire in her is for you, Everett!"

Den Massa Fields him open him mouth' and him seal muh fate. Him suh soft and wid a surprise like it be him birt'day or something, "It is?"

Him suh dem two words and suh dem jis't like de night him tell meh to tell him I love him. Him not even suh it like him hear de scorn in Massa Litchfield's voice. Him suh, 'It is?' Like dem talking 'bout a white womans.

But Massa Litchfield him start to laugh real hard and him suh, "You are indeed a foolish son-of-a-bitch, Everett. You are longing for a nigger bitch and she's been longing over you too. You've fucked her, haven't you, man?"

Massa Litchfield him stop laughing wen Massa Fields suh, "Richmond, she haunts me. Awake, she haunts me. Asleep, she's there riding me. I go to bed and wake up wanting and needing her. I'm ashamed and damned for wanting and needing a nigger. But Milkweed is more than just a nigger wench to me. She's a beautiful poison that I can't seem to do without. Richmond, damn man, I'm drawn to her like a Monarch butterfly to the milkweed plant. What am I to do? I miss her and yes, I do, oh God, Richmond, love her. "

Him den laugh a strange kind of laugh and den him suh, "Even the way she smells, like a mixture of dirt, the air after a fresh rain, flour, and yes, her damnable hot biscuits."

Wen Massa Litchfield talk, him voice different. Before I know'd dat it be scorn in him voice, but I not know'd wat him voice full wid now. Him suh, "Good Lord, Everett, you are romanticizing over a nigger bitch, a slave! A fucking nigger bitch!"

Muh chest start to hurt and dat be wen muh brain suh, 'Breave, yuh gots to breave.' I try to breave but I nots be able get de air to come in muh body. I standing thar wid de flour and grease on muh hands, and I jis't wants to hear wat Massa Litchfield goin' suh and wen him talk, I know'd wat I hear in him voice before. It be worse dan scorn. It be hate. Him be hating de fact dat a white mans jis't tolt him dat him love a nigger womans same way him love a white womans. Massa Litchfield him suh through him teet, "Everett, you are a stupid fucking fool. Get off my property and don't you ever come back or repeat that damnable nonsense for anyone else to ever hear you, white man or nigger. You hear me, Everett? Repeat that nonsense ever again and I'll shoot you in your foolish fucking head, point blank, no mercy!"

I never hear wat Massa Fields suh 'cause no sooner dan Massa Litchfield suh wat him had to suh to Massa Fields, him be calling muh name. Muh name be barreling down de hallway towards meh wid Massa Litchfield pelting coming behind it. Him be shouting, "Milkweed! Milkweed! Bring your nigger ass out here!"

I stopped wat I be doin' which fer as long as I be listening to him and Massa Fields be nuffin', and I start running towards where muh name be coming towards meh like a mad dog. I be get to muh name 'fore Massa Litchfield mek it quite to way I be. Him be still shouting muh name, but muh name not use to coming from Massa Litchfield's mouth know'd dat someting mighty important had to be goin' on so it dun rush to reach meh way 'fore him.

I hurry close de space 'tween meh, him, and muh name and I suhs, "Yes, Massa Litchfield, yuh is call fer meh? I be right here, Massa Litchfield."

Him mek two steps to meh and 'fore him foots can steady on de floor, him grab at meh and wid one powerful jerk him had meh to him chest. I looks at him long as a nigger can look at a white mans, which be but less time dan it tek fer a nigger to blink. Him eyes be blazing de most hate dat I ever seen.

Him jerk meh so hard to him, de hair cloth I always have on muh head to cover muh hair fall off and muh hair, which I never let see de light of day far less anybody 'cept Momma Cornbread and Haroldetta, fall out from under and it fall to muh waist. Him eyes, which never seen muh hair 'fore, now blaze up wen him see dat I got de same straight down hair as him and him daughter. Only difference is dat dem own be like brown almost red, and mine it be black as midnight and it shine like one of dem stars.

Momma Cornbread she suh I gots muh hair from her momma, Lil' Mae, de Seminole Indian. But none of dat be matter now. Him eyes blazing like him goin' look at it and scorch it from right off muh head.

Him suh, "Is that it? Is that what you used to bewitch Massa Fields or did you use some kind of nigger magic on him. What? What? Tell me now or I'll tear it right off your head strand by bewitching strand. Speak, nigger or I'll skin you right here and now!"

A part of muh brain suh to suh to him dat I not know'ds wat him be talking 'bout, but I nots be able to get de words to mek in muh head. Him watching meh wid fire coming out him eyes. Den 'fore I can tink on someting, anyting to suh dat might mek de fire go outta him eyes, him reach back and, even furder dan wen Massa Fields slap meh and Neala dat day, and him slap meh hard 'cross muh mouth and him suh, "Curse you, nigger. Everett should have drawn and quartered you the day he stole you from here."

Jis't wen dem words be mekking through muh head, him grab hold of meh 'round de middle. I spin 'cause him grab meh so hard. I 'most fall but muh mind suh, 'If yuh fall, Milkweed, him goin' kick yuh to 'till yuh dead 'causing him tink yuh dun Massa Fields some evil wickedness.' I gets muh footin' and I stand and den I suhs, "Please, Massa, Milkweed is a good nigger. I nots know'ds no magic. I know'ds only how to mek biscuits and de bread. Have mercy on yer dumb nigger. I not know'ds no magic, Massa."

I sneaks quick to look at Massa Litchfield and wat I see mek meh wish I not sneak dat quick look. Him be almost foaming at de mouth and him be gone red, red, red. Him be red like him been riding, but I know'd dat him twan't riding nowhere 'cause him be jis't out in de yard talking to Massa Fields. I look at him eyes to beg fer mercy one more time and wen I look in dem eyes, I seen de same eyes dat Massa Fields had dat day wen him drug meh way from here. Muh knees dem be shaking and dem be shaking 'cause I know'ds dat him be shoot meh fer pissing on him floor, and den shoot meh again fer mekkin' him get holes in him good floor and nigger blood in him house, I be let all de fear in meh pour out muh body in piss.

I be waiting fer Massa Litchfield to hit meh again and move all muh features 'round on muh face, but him nots hit meh. Him look like him be tinking 'bout it fer a second, but in de same second dat him be tinking on it, someting shift in him brain and him change him mind. Him spin meh 'round and push meh forward but not towards nuffin' in particular dat I can see; but white mans not ever mean nigger good, so I move towards watever bad him be pushing meh to. I be moving fast as him be pushing meh and wen him had meh outside de house and half way cross de yard, him stop. I not be able to go forward no more.

Massa Litchfield den turns meh in another direction and him starts to push meh again. I not be moving fast enough fer him so him mek big long step in front of meh and him start to drag meh. I 'most running now to keep up wid him. De way I running now mek meh 'member how Massa Fields tie meh to him horse and suh run. Him slow him pace, up in front of where Massa be pulling meh be de place where dem keep dem dry goods. De place be bigger dan slave cabin, but smaller dan dem smallest room in dem house.

Wen him reach it, him stop pulling meh long enough to open de door. Him den turn and drag meh in and I not know'ds wat mek meh look to muh side, but I do and I see Momma Cornbread and in dat one look, I see she scared fer meh. I know'd dat if Momma Cornbread be able to, she would come and save meh from de sure enough hell she know'd dat Massa have in store fer meh, but Momma Cornbread she not be able to come: she slave jis't like meh. I also know'd dat nigger not ever get in white mans way. Dat is unless dat nigger fixing on deading dat day.

I look at Momma Cornbread and de look in she eyes is de same look she had de day wen Massa Fields drag meh way. I sorry dat she gots to see she pickney suffering at de hands of a white mans a second time. I scared fer meh, but I more sorry fer Momma dan I scared fer meh. I sorry 'cause she be muh momma. And though no white mans ever stop to tink how nigger feel 'bout other nigger, we nigger love we own. Momma Cornbread, she love meh and if she be able to, she would try to save meh from de fate 'fore meh, but all she love not be able to save meh now.

Massa Litchfield shove meh in and him shut de door back. De shove mek meh stumble but I do all I can nots to fall. I nots know'd what him have in mind but I not wants to add kicking meh 'till I be dead to de list. Him step to meh and suh through him teet, but not to meh, "Love? Love a nigger bitch?"

Den him reach and grab meh and him spin meh 'round and bend meh over someting. I not know'd wat because it be dark inside. Him reach and wid one pull, him tear de tin dress I be wearing right off meh. I be naked fer de furst time in front of Massa Litchfield. Fear and hate rise in meh like bile. I think 'fore now Massa Litchfield be white mans I hate 'cause him is a white mans, but now him is a white mans I hate 'cause him mek meh naked 'fore him eyes.

Bending naked over in de dark muh hand touch de ground and den it touch someting thin, hard, and cold. I let only muh hand move and de rest of meh stay bending over jis't as him bend meh. I hear Massa pulling at him breeches so I dun know'd wat him fixing to do so I mek muh hand separate from muh body and it move over de sharp ting on de floor. I can tell it long and hard and den muh brain suh wat it be. It be a knife. I not tink wen I mek muh fingers hold it and wrap 'round it. Meh and Massa finish we task same time. Him to free him cocky from him breeches, and meh to full wrap muh hand 'round de handle of de knife.

Wid one hard shove, Massa Litchfield had him cocky in meh pee-hole. Same time I wrap muh hand tighter round de handle of de knife. I tinking dat wid one hard shove jis't like how him jis't shove him cocky in meh, I gine put dis knife in him belly same way. I mek to raise muh hand and same time Massa Litchfield him stop and pull him cocky out muh pee-hole. Him not stop 'cause him spill him seed quick. Him jis't stop and him suh, "My Lord! Oh! My Lord!"

I can hear him backing 'way from meh and him boots crunch de floor. I stays bend over wid de knife in muh hand and muh mind suh, 'Rush at him now dat him not tinking or not 'pecting yuh to do him any harm. Rush him and cut open him gut, cut him neck, cut him cocky off.'

I mek too much time pass by tinking wat I gine do him and wen I start to raise up wid de knife in muh hand to gut him same way dem gut Tadpole, him suh, "Milkweed, get away from me before I kill you."

I drop de knife and I pull wat be left of de dress 'round meh and I runs to de door 'fore him change him mind and kilt meh.

Since him not suh way to go, I go to de cabin and 'fore I mek it inside, I see Momma Cornbread and she suh, widout suhing a word, dat she be sorry fer meh. Muh quick look suh, "I know'ds."

I runs inside de cabin and best as I be able, I put de ripped apart dress back together. I be more dan a lil' surprise wen I see dat some wet flour from de biscuits still be on muh hand. I wipe muh hands on de dress to clean muh hands 'fore running back to de cookhouse. No time or room to feel sorry 'bout wat Massa Litchfield dun to meh, or wonder why him change him mind and stop. Him stopping 'fore him 'lease himself in meh not mek wat him dun different from all dem times Massa Fields had him way wid meh. But none of dat is fer meh to spend time on since him goin' still be expecting him biscuits wid him brekfast. I shuts all dat tinking from muh head and I hurry cross de yard to get back to de biscuits and de bread.

I mek it half way 'cross de yard to de cookhouse same time Massa Litchfield come from de dry shed and him shouts, "Nigger, stop!"

Wen white mans suh, "Nigger stop!" All niggers near enough to hear him stop. I stop and looks at de ground while I waits to see if I be de nigger him want to stop. Him mek a few long steps and him standing in from of meh. I be de nigger him want to stop. I not look up; him not 'spect meh to look up. Him stretch him hand out so dat my eyes dat looking at de grass can see wat in him hand. It be de same knife I be tinking to kilt him wid. Him suh, "There is flour and grease on this here knife handle. Nigger, do you want to tell me how it got there?"

I see meh back in de dry shed holding de knife hard. I see meh spending too much time 'bout killing him and den him sets meh free and den I see meh fixing de dress in de cabin and I see de flour and grease on muh hand. I know'd dat him know'd dat I be de one dat put de flour and grease on de knife. I know'd him know'd dat I be tinking 'bout killing him. I not suh nuffin', but I can feel muh bladder letting loose.

I not be able to stop it dis time and right in front of de Massa holding de same knife I be holding jis't 'fore him turn meh loose, I piss muhself. I feel de piss run down muh leg to muh foot. Massa him not see dat I dun piss 'cause I can feel him eyes on meh. Him raise de knife and him put de blade right by muh ear and him press it straight way. I feel it starting to sink into muh neck and I see de way de white man's knife mek de line in Tadpole neck 'fore him head fall back and him dead.

I shut muh eyes to wait fer de feel of de knife cutting deeper into muh neck. Inside muh head, I know'd dat I not gine know'd wen him dun cut off my head. I tanks de Lawd fer dat. De wait fer him to start cutting off muh head be de ting dat be mekking meh worry. How long it gine tek him to cut off muh head? De knife it not move no more inside muh neck, but I can hear him breaving. Him breaving hard. Den I hear, "Poppa! Poppa! Dear God, Poppa! Don't! Please don't, Poppa!"

I not have to open muh eyes to know'ds it be Mistress Henrietta.

"Poppa, dear Poppa, don't let another nigger's blood be spilled on this land. Don't kill her, Poppa, please."

De pressing of de knife ease up. I want to breave but I 'fraid. Massa him suh, "This nigger here was going to take a knife to your poppa."

"But she didn't, Poppa. She didn't. Have mercy, Poppa. Punish her another way, but let her live, Poppa, please. Let her live."

De knife ease a little more. Den Massa tek de knife from 'hind my ear.

"Henrietta, this is none of your concern."

Massa be hardly breaving wen him suh dat. I tek a quick look at de Massa. Him be still red and him had foam at him mouth. Him look like dog dat drink poison. I not look up or move again. I wait. Mistress Henrietta she not move either. She stands and face de Massa. She suh, "Poppa, Milkweed, she's the pet pup you gave me. She's suffered greatly."

At de word suffered, Massa him suh, "Suffered! Suffered! She never suffered at Everett's hands. That fool wants her. He wants her! Did you hear me? He says he loves her!"

Of all dem words Massa suh to Mistress Henrietta, it like she only hear him suh one word and she suh back dat word to him like it be question, "Love?"

I look up quick to look at Mistress Henrietta and Massa, him see dat I be looking at de Mistress and him tek de knife, turn it round in him hand, and him knock meh real hard in muh head and him suh, "Insolent nigger!"

At de same time I feel de warmth of muh blood tekking it time to come out de gash dat de Massa jis't open in muh head, Mistress Henrietta suh again, "Love?"

My heart it beating faster 'cause I can tell dat Mistress Henrietta trying but she not be able to mek she brain see love dat someting a white mans can feel fer a nigger. De Massa stop being a Massa and him talk to she like a Poppa. Him suh, "He says he loves her and wants her, Henrietta."

I not look up again, but I not have to, I can hear right well. Mistress Henrietta, she suh, "Then let him have her, Poppa. She's my pup and I can do what I want with her. I don't want to see her ever again, Poppa. Don't kill her. Let her go, but leave Haroldetta here, Poppa."

I hear as Mistress Henrietta walk way. She walk way slow and soft. If not fer she dress moving over de grass and mek it sound like wind blowing through de trees, I not be know'd dat her move. Her move slow as de blood coming out de gash in muh head. Massa him suh to him walking way daughter, "I don't want her pup on my property."

Mistress and she dress dem stop moving and her voice thick as de blood dat dun mek it way to de ground at my foots, suh, "Then sell them all, Poppa. Sell them all to Everett. I don't care, Poppa."

Den she suh, "Love? He loves her, Poppa? Love like you love a woman, a real woman. A white woman?"

Her Poppa him not suh nuffin'. Mistress she den suhs de last words I ever hear from she mouth. She suh, "Imagine that. I live to see a pup bite the hand that feeds it. Sell them all Poppa… today… now!"

Her dress it start to move cross and over de grass again. Fresh blood start to come from muh head. Hate fer Massa Fields be wat pushing it out.

Massa him suh, "Walk."

I not know'ds where him want meh to walk so I mek a slow shuffle towards de gate but him suh, "Stop nigger!"

I stop. Him stay right where him be and him call loud to de Overseer, "Mister Augusta, come here now!"

I not see him come cross de grass, de field or come from nowhere. It like him be floating over Massa's head like dem angels de white preacher man talk 'bout; him jis't be in front of Massa. Him suh, "Yes, Mr. Litchfield?"

Him mek meh tink dat him angel wen him suh, "What you want done with her?"

Him suh dat like him dun been listening to Massa and Mistress Henrietta talk.

Massa him suh, "I want her, Cornbread, and her pup taken from here, today… now."

"Where you want me to take 'em, sir?"

"Cornbread, take her over to old man Talbert's plantation. Take this nigger bitch and the pup, I don't know what these niggers call her, but you know which pickney is the one she birthed since she came back over from Fields' plantation."

Hate fer Massa Everett in de form of bile rise up in meh. I wants to spit but I know'ds dat if I spit in front of two white mans, dey will jis't as soon see meh dead as dey would see meh sell. I swallow muh hate fer Massa Fields. It burn muh belly goin' back down.

We not own nuffin' so we get load on de wagon same as if we be bags of flour or feed fer de animals. Haroldetta she scared, but she more scared to open she mouth and ask meh anything 'cause she old enough to know'ds dat yuh not question white mans. Or ask question 'bout white mans in front of 'nother white mans. I wants to tell she not to be 'fraid but I know'ds dat not be de best or right ting to suh 'cause I 'fraid muhself. We sit quiet.

De wagon it start to roll way from Litchfield. I wants to look back to see if I be get a glimpse of Momma Cornbread. I looks but I not see she. I be glad dat I not see she. It best she not see de only family she got left tek way from she. A tear slip from de corner of my right eye. I not reach to wipe it. Den a tear slip from de corner of my left eye. I leave it. De two of dem dey meet at my chin and become one tear. Muh heart it suh dat dem two tears be meh and Momma Cornbread. We be goin' in different directions, but one day we meet back up and we be one again. Haroldetta she reach up and she touch de one tear from under my chin and she put she head on my lap. I nots cry no more. Crying not goin' change nuffin'. I nots turn my head to look back, never mind how much muh heart beg meh to look one last time just to see if I see Momma Cornbread. I keeps my head looking right in front of meh.

I nod off and I wake. De sun shift in de sky. It be hot. De wagon it keep rolling on. Meh and Haroldetta we nots suh one word. We jis't sit. Soon and it seem less time dan wen it tek meh from here I start to see de mekking of Field's plantation. De bile it come back in my belly.

Wid each turn of de wagon wheel dat bring meh closer to Massa Fields plantation and furda 'way from where dey tek Momma Cornbread, de hate I have fer Massa Fields, which I not know'ds could grow'd more, grow'd. I full up wid so much hate dat by de time de wagon come to a stop, I feel to jump down and head straightway to where Massa Fields be and kilt him wid my hands, but de fear in Haroldetta's eyes calm my hateful spirit. I stay right way I be 'till I hear, "Niggers, get down."

Chapter 32

No Time To Feel De Fear

I be back. Back at Fields plantation. Dis time I not alone. De pickney I'd left here wid in muh belly be standing next to meh and she be scared. I be scared too but I nots have no time to really feel it. I stands thar. I waits. Dats wat nigger do on white mans plantation. Yuh waits 'till dem suh wat yer to do. Nobody come to suh wat to do so I jis't stands. I nots has to tell Haroldetta not to ask nuffin'. Somehow, nigger and it not matter how small dem be, know'ds how to act 'round white mans. I stands thar and I nots look left nor right. I nots look straight ahead either because nigger know'ds dat white mans jis't waiting fer him eye and yourn to mek four so him can have reason to strip yer skin. I stands 'till I feel sweat start to run down muh back den, 'fore I see him, I smell him.

Massa Fields always smell one way. Like fresh scrub white mans. Him wear dem fancy water dat mek him smell good. Not dat all dem white mans smell fresh scrub 'cause plenty of dem from places other dan right here in Greenwood nots likes to wash dem ass. Nigger not have choice 'bout how often nigger wash, so nigger got excuse, but white mans who only have to holler, "Nigger, draw water for my bath and come wash me!" Dey not got no excuse fer why some of dem stink like dem roll in pig shit.

Massa Fields him come himself to de wagon, dat not be right. No Massa on no plantation ever come to no wagon wid slave on it. Him send him Overseer. Massa Fields him speak and him sound surprise. Him suh, "Litchfield sent you?"

De wagon man, figuring dat Massa Fields can only be talking to him, suh, "Yes sir! He said for me to bring these two nigger wenches to your place, sir."

"They are sweating. How long have you been here, man?"

De man not know'ds Massa angry so him suh, "Don't right know sir but they be niggers. Niggers sweat. That's what they do, sir. They be nothing more than some dumb nigger bitches."

Massa Fields him speak and him trying to sound like if him not be angry but 'cause I dun know'ds him so well, I hear it in him voice. Him suh, "Nigger, wenches, or bitches, that doesn't mean you have a right to treat my property however which way you choose. You were sent here to deliver these two niggers to my property. You have done so. Now take your wagon and be off my property."

De man him go to suh someting to Massa Fields, but watever mek him stop mek him 'cause next ting I know'ds is dat de wagon it rolling way and him de one mekkin' it. Dis time I not on it. I nots know'd if to be glad or not 'cause thar nots be no Momma Cornbread to go back to. I fix myself not to feel nuffin'.

Massa him start to walk way. I stand where I be. Him turn a little and him suh, "Come!" I give Haroldetta a little push and we follows him. Wen him near de cookhouse, him start shouting fer Neala. Neala she come running and she suh, "Yes, Massa."

Neala suh dis widout looking at Massa Fields. She not even know'd it be meh. She jis' come to do wat him want. Massa him suh, "Take Milkweed and her pickney with you to the cookhouse. Give them something to eat and drink."

Massa him turn and start walking back to where him come from. Wen Massa mek but a few steps, him stop and him suh, "Neala, find some work for the pickney in the cookhouse."

Wen I hear him foots gone far enough, I turn my head to watch him. Him steps dem slow like de one him mek wen him walk 'way from Massa Litchfield a few hours ago wen him went and mek things and life worser fer meh, Momma Cornbread, and Haroldetta.

"Nigger Gal, him suh fer meh to feed yuh. Him not suh nuffin' 'bout meh standing round in him yard in dis blazing sun and watching no nigger gal wid a mixed-up mind and feelings fer no white mans, especially one who is muh Massa. Now come, Nigger Gal and mek yer pickney follow 'fore him turn and see yuh looking at him wid expectations and turn back and tek de skin off all we."

I nots suh nuffin'. I follow Neala to de cookhouse. De minute we be inside, Neala be a different Neala. "Lawd, Nigger Gal, wat mek 'em sell yuh back to dis place?"

I nots know'ds how to answer she. I know'd better dan to open muh mouth and suh wat Massa Fields dun suh to Massa Litchfield. Neala nots need fer meh to suh nuffin', she suh, "Mistress Olivia nots goin' be pleased dat de Massa dun brun yuh back here. Lawd, Nigger Gal, yer life goin' be one bitter breeze after de other. She not goin' let one sweet breeze blow on yuh and yer pickney. I sorry, sorry dat him brung yuh back. I feel sorry fer yer pickney too 'cause it clear she a nigger pickney and she nots looks to be no older dan dem four or five years or so yuh left here."

Neala stop she talking fer a minute and she look and she look at Haroldetta and den she suh, "Lawd, Lawd, Lawd, yer pickney favor de slave Harold Joe. De one yuh be sweet on 'fore him solt yuh way. Yuh rut wid him and mek pickney. Massa Fields not goin' have no fergiveness in him fer yuh fer dat. Him goin' mek she and yuh suffer 'cause she proof yuh rut wid de nigger him suh yuh not to rut wid."

I look at Neala and I nots know'd which one of we, meh or Haroldetta, to feel sorry fer de most. Den I feel sorry fer Haroldetta de most 'cause she young and she nots know'd wat suffering like fer nigger. Neala nots give meh time fer sorry too long 'fore she suh, "Wat yuh call de pickney?"

I suh, "Haroldetta." Neala look at meh and she suh, "Yuh is a stupid nigger gal. Fancy name like dem nots belong to nigger and now wid she name so close to dat dead nigger man name, Massa goin' know'd fer sure it be him yuh rut wid. Yuh better come up wid different name fer yuh pickney 'fore yuh leave out dis here cookhouse. Yuh better get her to answer to it 'fore Massa mek him mind up wat him want dun wid she."

"Neala, I not know'ds wat else to call she. I dun call she Haroldetta since muh momma tek she out from meh."

"Well if yuh want she to live yuh better come up wid someting else to call she now and get she to hold it to she chest. Little as she be, she must know'd dat name not be nuffin' nigger hold on to. Look at yuh. Wat name beside Milkweed yuh have?"

"I nots have other name 'side Milkweed. I always been Milkweed. If muh name be someting else, I nots know'd wat it be."

"Well den if in yuh can live and not know'd wat yer other name be, she can be someting else now and learn to ferget wat her other name be too. Wat name yuh tink would fit she other dan Haroldetta?"

I look at muh pickney and I can see she even more frighten dan wen we be outside and I nots know'ds wat to suh. Den de surprise came from Haroldetta. She suh, "Sara."

'Fore I could get it in muh head dat Haroldetta be understanding all dat meh and Neala be talking, Neala suh, "She goin' live. She got sense. Pickney, way yuh get dat name from?"

Haroldetta look at Neala and she suh, "Mistress Henrietta she suh dat de name Haroldetta be too old fer meh. She suh dat I look like a Sara. She call meh Sara."

Neala looks at meh and she suh, "She name Sara from now. No more Haroldetta. Haroldetta be over at Litchfield's place in Greenville. She back here in Greenwood and she name be Sara."

Turning to Haroldetta, Neala suh, "Little Nigger Gal, wat yer name be?"

Haroldetta look right at Neala and she suh, "It be Sara. Jis't dat. Sara."

Muh pickney lose some she frightful look and inside of meh some of de frightfulness go down a little. I look at my Haroldetta and I suh, "Haroldetta…" 'fore I could finish suh to de pickney wat I be goin' tell she, which I twan't sure, she suh, "Momma, it not be Haroldetta no more, it be Sara. Sara, Momma, Sara."

I never got to suh nuffin' 'cause Neala suh, "Him 'specting meh to feed yuh so I bets be doing dat 'fore him come back."

Chapter 33

De Darkest Night

Muh furst night back at Fields plantation is de darkest night I ever see. It also is de quietest; it like ev'ting on and near dis place dead, even de night creatures dem quiet. I starts to feel frighten. Night too dark and quiet to mean anyting or anybody any good. I wish fer de sound of muh pickney but she not wid meh. Massa him suh dat she must go wid Nester and she six pickney. Haroldetta she cry 'cause she not ever been part from meh. I crys 'cause she cry, but den I see Massa standing off but not far enough off dat if him raise him voice yuh not hear him.

I beg Haroldetta to hush up and go wid Nester. I suh, "Sara, hush up and go on. Massa, him suh fer yuh to go so yuh go 'fore him sell yuh way from meh."

Haroldetta she see de fear in muh eyes and de way muh voice tremble and she hush up and follow Nester. I hear Nester suh, "Come, Sara, come."

I watch dem go cross de yard and I go to de cabin dat Massa tell Neala is fer meh. It not de one I had 'fore I left and it not de one I had wid Harold Joe. It not new, but it new to meh. Dem all de same so it mek no difference; cabin is cabin like white mans is white mans and nigger wuk is nigger wuk; all de same, no difference.

I lays down and I waits 'cause I know'ds Massa have reason fer sending way muh pickney. I wait and wait but Massa him not come. I let muhself start to believe dat him not goin' come den I hear de crunch of him boots outside. De sound come close and den it stop and den I hear it go way. I waits fer de sound to come back, but it nots. I not know'ds how long I waits, but it be morning and I gets up and do wat I know'ds to do. I go to de cookhouse to mek de biscuits and bread jis't like 'fore I left.

Dis, meh waiting at night, de sound of him boots coming and de sound of him boots goin', meh sleeping and not sleeping 'cause I be waiting fer him and den it be morning. I be tired but I still gots to do wat I know'd to do: mek de biscuits and bread. Dis same waiting, crunching, coming, goin', sleeping, not sleeping, mekking biscuits, and waiting go on fer three maybe four months. If I see Massa, him not suh nuffin' to meh.

Haroldetta, who ev'rybody calling Sara now, happy wen she see meh, but wen she not see meh she happy wid Nester and she pickney. I start worry dat soon she goin' ferget 'bout meh. I wants to ask Massa if she can come back and stay wid meh but Neala she suhs, "Nigger Gal, even yuh dat mek as many pickney fer Massa, and even get him to tek one fer him own, should tink more dan twice 'bout asking him or any other Massa 'bout decision dem mek." I tek wat she suh to muh heart.

One morning after I wait and wait all night fer Massa to come to muh cabin and him not come, I sleep pass time and so be I hurrying to de cookhouse to mek de biscuits. I see Massa and wen him sees meh dis time, him stop, look at meh, and I slow down 'pecting him to suh someting to meh but him nots. Him walk pass meh like him not see meh. Someting in muh belly it get mix-up wid de hate and it mek meh turn muh head and look back at him. Watching him walking pass meh mek meh want to run up to him and ask, "Massa Fields, why yer not talking to meh? Why yer not come to muh cabin no more?" But Neala's words dem fresh in muh head and I know'ds better. I turns muh head back and run de rest of de way to mek up fer muh slowing down. Him walking pass meh stay in muh head fer de rest of de day. Dat night I wait and wait, but him nots come. I fall into a trouble sleep.

Time on plantation can go by quick or it can go by slow. Wen yer mind mix-up over if yer hate yer Massa or not, or why yuh even wondering if yer hate yer Massa, or yuh waiting fer yer Massa to come rut yuh and him nots, time it go by slow. Wen yer busy cooking, mending and fixing dem clothes, time it go by fast, but time can change quick on a plantation. Even some tings can mek it stop. It stop fer meh de day I see Haroldetta playing wid de other pickney and she fall and she get cut. I nots know'ds how bad she be cut, but I hears she cry and I starts to run out de cookhouse to go see 'bout she. I mek it to de door wen I see de Massa right next to way she fall. Him call fer Nester, who be coming cross de yard. Him suh, "Go see 'bout yer pickney."

Nester she go where Haroldetta be and soon as Haroldetta see Nester, she suh, "Momma."

I wants to go out and tell Nester dat she not to have muh Haroldetta call she Momma. I not get to mek de furst step wen I looks and see Massa and him face look same way it look de day him and dem other white mans kilt off Tiny and Chem and de others. I looks way from him fast and I go back in de cookhouse. I starts to cry and Neala she suh, "Nigger Gal wat yer crying fer?"

I suhs, "Muh Haroldetta she fall and she get cut, and Massa suh to Nester fer she to go look after she pickney and she go to muh Haroldetta."

Neala she suh, "So wat yer cry fer Nigger Gal?"

I suhs, "But Haroldetta is muh pickney! She not Nester's pickney!"

"It be dat kind of talk dat mek yer pickney tek way from yuh and sell. Yuh nots 'member Massa telling yuh dat yuh nots owns nuffin' 'round here. Dat pickney, like de one him and him wife call dem daughter, her not yer pickney. She 'long to him and him can do wat him want wid she. Him suh Nesta is de muddah den she is de muddah, jis't like him wife de muddah to de one dey call Lilly. Now yuh not de muddah to no pickney. Yuh here to mek dem biscuits and fer him to rut yuh if him want. Dat be de way it be. Him suh wat him want and we do wat him suh fer we to do. Now yer stop dat crying wid yer mix-up nigger gal head and get back to wat yuh be doin'.'"

Time it start back to move from stop to slow to fast. Dem be waiting on dem food. I try not to tink on wat Neala suh, but it hard fer meh to know'ds dat one more of muh pickney now calling somebody else Momma.

Dat night I hear de sound of him boots crunching. Dis time de door open and him come in. I hears him boot as him cross de little space 'tween de door and de bed. One, den two, den three, den four. Him at de bed. I hear him pulling off him boots. Dem hit de floor, one, den two. Den I hear him pulling off him breeches. Den I hear him tekking off him shirt. I nots move or nuffin' not even open muh eyes. Him come next to meh. Him reach fer meh and him pull meh rough and mek me sit up. I move like life left muh body. De way him drag meh up clear muh head from de mix-up feelings. I hate him fer tekkin' way all muh pickney, bringing sep'ration 'tween Momma Cornbread and meh, and I hates him real deep fer killing Harold Joe. De hate fer Massa it move like pickney in muh belly.

I busy tinking on de hate I have fer him and I nots hear Massa's hand as it move. Massa him bring him face to muh face and him suh, "You have a nigger pickney! I told you and I told that nigger not to rut. You let a nigger rut with you."

I nots suh nuffin'. Massa him tek a deep breff and him hold it like him be tinking if him should let it out or not. Wen him figga wat to do wid him breff him let it out and him look at meh wid so much hate dat inside muh belly I feel de knots as dem tie muh belly string one at a time. Dem knots not stop 'till all muh whole belly strings tangle like watermelon or sweet potato vine on fence. Muh breff it stops.

I see Massa hand go from him side and him slap meh forward, and den backward. Him tek a deep breff and him slap meh 'gain sameway; forward and backward. Den him reach de farthest and slap meh again

I feel dis slaps deep in muh skin. It like him put branding iron to muh face. I count de slaps. One, two, three, and four. I waits fer de next slap but it nots come. I tek a breff. It not a deep one but enough to live. I wants to look at him and let him see dat though him slap meh hard enough to tek de skin off muh face, dat I not cry nor beg him fer mercy. It be de hate in meh dat keep way de crying.

Him wait like him waiting fer de cry to start and wen it not start, him suh in a voice dat sound like him not open him mouth but him talking through him teet, "Milkweed, if I so much as think that you've raised your eyes to look at another nigger on this plantation again, I'll skin your nigger pickney for you to see. Do you understand me, Milkweed?"

Again I suh nuffin'. Dat mek Massa huff and him slap meh again. Dis time it nots land on muh face exact as muh head bend down 'cause I know'ds better dan to look him in de eye. I feel de knock by muh ear and it mek a ringing sound go on ferever.

Him talk and him suh, "Milkweed, you are mine! You hear me! Mine! I can rut you, breed you, sell, or kill you if and when I want."

Massa him not wait fer meh to answer. Him push meh back on de bed and him lay next to meh. Den Massa, him not know'ds how dem slaps and words dun stir up de worse feelings I ever had fer him, tek him hand and shove it 'tween muh legs, den him push muh legs apart same time him roll 'top of meh and him push him cocky in meh and start to rut meh.

Massa him rutting and talking and I want to mek muh ears not hear him, but I hears him. I hears him breaving and I hears him suh muh name. I wants to tell him not to suh muh name but I nots be able to. Him is Massa over meh. Him rutting meh harder and den him 'lease himself. Dis time him nots call muh name. Him nots suh nuffin'. Him nots roll off meh. Him bring him face close to muh face and him suh, "By the time you make this child, you'll see that you belong here with me. Milkweed, you are mine. You belong to me. Accept that. You, me, Field's plantation, no separation ever!"

Massa him roll off meh, stands up, put him breeches and boots on and him left.

Jis't thar in de dark de hate fer Massa rise and rise 'till I nots be able to do nuffin' but cry. I nots want to cry but de crying it tek on a mind different to mine. It suh, 'cry fer Haroldetta, Momma Cornbread, Poppa, Lilly, Isham, Juba, Zack, Tuck, and yuh last one Willie.' I even cry fer de pickney girl I beg to dead. Den I cry de hardest fer Harold Joe. I cry 'cause I miss de sweet rutting, de soft touching, de gentle holding, and de deep kisses him use to give meh. I want to holler so hard dat de sound tek de dark and smash it open 'till it be like daytime. I nots holler 'cause I not wants to bring de Overseer or none of dem bitter breeze telling niggers to hear and tell on meh hoping to get favor wid de Overseer or de Massa. I try to quiet de hate but it rise too high to push down. I let it rise and I cry 'till I nots be able to cry no more. Dis be de longest and darkest night fer meh, ever.

Chapter 34

Lilly Thea Bess Willow Greenwood

The baby waited until Aunt Bess got to the part about her own grandmother, Rebeccah Fields, to decide she wanted to come out. Aunt Bess had been telling me for days that I was walking like any minute I was goin' have the baby. She just kept telling me that she knows everything has its time, but could I please ask the baby to know her time to come was when either she or Cousin Thea was home with me. Well the baby must have been listening because she waited 'till it was a Friday night. Both Aunt Bess and Cousin Thea were home.

I was feeling a bit more tired than usual and had gone up to rest. At some time during the night, and I don't know exactly when, I had a dream that I'd gone to the bathroom and the whole floor was wet; there was water everywhere. In the dream, water had soaked my slippers and was working its way up the hem of my nightgown and making me all wet and cold. As I tiptoed out the bathroom, I heard a baby crying. I searched all over for the baby but the water was rising and I couldn't find the baby.

I started to cry because I knew if I didn't find the baby, it would drown. The water was rising very quickly. Soon the water had reached my neck. I could feel my feet start to come off the floor. I became afraid and started to call for Aunt Bess to come and help me find the baby. I opened my mouth to scream and some of the water got into my mouth. I started to spit and scream very loudly for Aunt Bess.

The sound of my own screaming woke me. I was wet. My water had broken. I started to really scream and even louder for Aunt Bess. Both Aunt Bess and Cousin Thea came running. Not only was I wet, I was also in pain. I started to cry. Aunt Bess said, "Well there sure is a time for everything and the time for this baby is now. Thea, go get Deaconess Robins and tell her that Gina Pearl's water broke and the way her belly low it may not be long 'fore this baby get in the world. You remember which house is hers?"

If Cousin Thea answered, I don't know but all I remember is that the pain seemed to be coming from all over my belly. I wanted to stand. Then I wanted to sit and if Aunt Bess wasn't holding me, there was a minute or two when I wanted to run. That made Aunt Bess laugh. She said, "When you should've been running, you had your feet too wide apart for that; so don't shut them now. You need them open to get this baby out. That's one thing for sure 'bout babies. The same way you get them in, you almost got to get them out."

If I hadn't been in that much pain, I would have laughed 'cause it was funny but true. God was merciful to me. Deaconess Robins was in the room so quickly it was as if she were downstairs waiting on Aunt Bess to tell her come up the stairs. While Cousin Thea had me walking up and down the hallway, Aunt Bess and Deaconess Robins was fixing the bed for me to give birth. No sooner did they have the bed ready and me in it, than my baby started working hard, then harder on getting out.

Deaconess Robins must have done this a thousand times because in no time she had Aunt Bess and Cousin Thea holding and pressing against my legs. While they worked on pressing my legs back, she was pressing and pushing down on my belly and in between them pressing, and the baby struggling and me screaming, crying, and pushing. It took us three hours to help the baby make it into the world. It was a girl.

There was a mixture of excitement and worry on Aunt Bess' face. The room was so quiet. The baby wasn't crying. I looked from Aunt Bess to Cousin Thea and we all looked at Deaconess Robins, who was holding the quiet baby upside down. I started to cry. I wanted to hear her cry. She was supposed to cry. She wasn't supposed to be upside down and still in anybody's hands. She was supposed to cry. I heard a voice say, "Come on, baby, cry. You've got to cry. Please cry." The voice was mine but it was different. It was the voice of a mother pleading with a child to show she was alive and was goin' be alright."

"Gertrude, do something! What's wrong with the baby? Why isn't she crying? Make her cry, Gertie? Make her cry!" The voice this time wasn't mine. It was Aunt Bess' and she sounded afraid. "Oh Lord, Lord. Oh Lord, please let her to cry!"

Deaconess Robins didn't appear to be listening to anyone. She was busy with the baby. She still had the baby upside down and she was doing things I couldn't see. Then she brought the baby to her mouth and she blew a slow yet quick breath into the baby's mouth. I stopped breathing. The pain from a few moments ago was forgotten. The room, which had been busy with screaming and crying a few minutes ago, was now so still; had one hair fallen from the baby's head while she was being held upside down, the sound would have echoed a thousand times across the stillness of the room even though the room was fully carpeted.

We waited. Then the sound that had held us all hostage came. Faint and weak, but it came. She gasped, a deep but short breath that mirrored the one Deaconess Robins had just given to her. She held for it a second before letting it go and then, the best sound I'd ever heard; she started to cry. Just like that first breath, it was faint and weak but once her lungs got filled up, she let go a real cry. I started to cry, a different cry though; this was one of relief, a mother's relief. All of us except Deaconess Robins were crying.

Deaconess Robins was cleaning the baby and praying at the same time. It was then that I knew for sure what her name would be. She would be called Lilly. Great-Great-Grandmother Milkweed had had her Lilly taken away from her and I'd come real close to losing mine. A Lilly was coming back into this family. I called her Lilly Bess Thea Willow Greenwood

Aunt Bess said, "That's a lot of names for such a little tiny baby and, child, why you calling this baby Greenwood? Ain't your name Fields?"

I said, "It's just enough names, Aunt Bess, and when I work and save my money I goin' right down to the court house and change my name for real. Lilly will already be a Greenwood so I won't have to change hers."

Aunt Bess said, "Then she be Lilly Greenwood. That name suits her mighty fine. She be a Greenwood, not a Fields. I'm glad that you break 'way from that name. God Bless this child and her new name."

Although Aunt Bess didn't have any children she took over Lilly's care right after Deaconess Robins left. It was as if she didn't trust me to know what to do if Lilly should ever have a problem getting her breath again. She was right and I was glad she was looking after Lilly. Aunt Bess, always one for making you laugh or at least smile when she felt you were scared, said, "I may not have birthed no babies, but I done raised up so many white children in Brooklyn Heights they could fill a synagogue on them Simchat Torah. That, child, is their celebration once a year. They read their bible in public. Shoot, if all them praises I done said over them worked, they would even fill even a good ole' fashioned Baptist church. They would be so happy with all the good singing they goin' hear, they would get to throwing them funny little hats that they be wearing right out that good stained glass window. Next thing you know, they be shouting, 'Jesus, Jesus!'"

Aunt Bess got me to laugh so hard that soon I wasn't worrying about Lilly being so very tiny. Lilly was a tiny baby. She weighed all of five pounds ten ounces when she was born. Aunt Bess said it was Ma's fault that she was so small. She said if Ma had used good sense she'd figured out that a pregnant girl who had lost her man the way I'd lost mine needed her ma and she wouldn't have sent me away. Aunt Bess said, "Only that stupid sister of mine couldn't figure out that you more so than some stupid old man needed mothering, gentle care, and not being shipped way on a broken down piece of tin."

If Aunt Bess were different, softer, she would have cried. I saw the struggle, the tears trying to fall from her eyes and Aunt Bess doing all she could to make sure they didn't. I wasn't as strong as Aunt Bess. I didn't even struggle against my tears when I felt them welling up in my eyes. I let them fall, jump, or slosh from my eyes; whatever they wanted to do. I wanted to cry so I started to cry. It was a full-bodied cry. From the top of my eyes, the tears came. I was crying at the knowledge that I could not yet put into words. It was a knowledge that said so much of what I'd wanted, desired, or wished for was not goin' to be so I gave into the cry. It was, to me, like watching water run off a rooftop: a lot and sudden and it didn't care where or what it fell on.

I wasn't so sure why I was crying, but at the time it seemed like the only thing to do with Aunt Bess talking about Ma and all. Then I was crying because my baby was so small, then I was crying because she had no Poppa, and then I started to cry because she wasn't goin' to have anyone to call Nana.

Aunt Bess watched me crying for a little and when it seemed to her that my crying was lasting longer than what she would say, 'made good sense,' she said, "Gina Pearl or Promise Greenwood, or whatever you choosing to call yourself these days, let me tell you something. You ain't the only one to ever have a child without a man or Ma. Now I'm goin' ask you only once, 'cause that's all the time I've got or want to spend on all them tears you letting drip all over this house. What are all them tears for, and don't tell me that it's 'cause you ain't got Ma or man?"

I didn't have an answer. The truth didn't seem like it would make sense to say. So I said nothing. Aunt Bess said, "I thought so. Now that you figured out that all them tears don't make sense, help me to make sense of what we goin' do 'bout this little tiny baby and all her big clothes that falling off her."

I smiled. Aunt Bess knew it would make me smile. She said, "Now do some mothering and take this baby from me. Go make her happy and see if her little arms don't start to fill out. Filling out a baby don't just come from milk. Give her a lot of love and you'll see her fill out. Now it ain't goin' happen in a day or two, but watch: it goin' happen."

Poor Lilly, all the little clothes that Aunt Bess and Cousin Thea had made for her were so big, she did look, as Aunt Bess had said, as if she would fall out of even the smallest one. Aunt Bess didn't wait for Lilly to grow into them as she said she would. She spent all her free time, when she wasn't holding Lilly, making new smaller clothes for her. Before, where all our nights were taken up with needlework and Aunt Bess telling me and Cousin Thea about our family, the time was now taken up with caring for Lilly. Aunt Bess would sit and sew and either Cousin Thea or I would sit holding Lilly. Aunt Bess would look at us holding her and loving the smell of talcum powder and baby, and she'd say, "When the time comes, don't say I didn't warn the two of you."

"What time, Aunt Bess?"

"The time when you all goin' have to put her down and she, because she's done learn to love hands, ain't goin' let you. I ain't goin' break my night's rest to help you all with your little hand-held bouquet. Put that baby in her cradle and let her learn to love her own company."

We didn't and Aunt Bess was right. By the time Lilly was four months old, we couldn't put her down for a minute without her crying as if somebody was trying to steal her breath. Aunt Bess would look at us smile and say, "I warned the two of you. Now you all figure out who's losing their night's rest and, Thea, don't think that even if you stay up all night holding that spoiled child, you ain't goin' to work. You goin' to work even if you do so sleeping."

We learned and so did Lilly that we couldn't hold her all day and night. She learned how to love her own company, and Aunt Bess, not one for letting anyone to be idle too long, let me stay home with her 'till she could say a few words and had her legs, as Aunt Bess called it, but once she started walking stronger, Aunt Bess said that I had to find a job. I had that promise of a better life for her and myself to keep.

With Aunt Bess' help, I went to work in Brooklyn Heights. The people that I worked for knew me only as Promise from down south, 'cause that was all Aunt Bess said they needed to know. She gave me the same advice she'd given Cousin Thea, "Say little to nothing. The more they think you simple, the more they goin' get to forgetting you there. Keep your peace. Keep your business your business." I took Aunt Bess' advice. I didn't talk much to my work people. Wasn't no reason to let them into my personal, private business, or Promise Land, which was my most personal private business.

didn't have just one job. I had five. Each day of the week, I went to a different house. On Monday, I cleaned for the Baums on Pineapple Lane, on Tuesdays, I cleaned for the Levines on Cranberry Street, on Wednesdays, I cleaned for the Schwartzs on Montague Street, Thursdays and Fridays for the Levanthals on Henry Street, and on Saturday and some Sundays for the Kleins on Love Lane. I liked working for the Kleins. He was a doctor and she was the kind of white woman that talked to you like you were a person first and a Negro second. Although she talked to me like that, I still had to remember what Aunt Bess had said, "The more they think you simple, the more they'll say around you."

When all the other women had their one day off, I did their work. I cooked, cleaned, washed, starched, ironed, and of course, walked the babies. It was like a kind of exchange. I worked for them, I got paid, and they helped me hold Lilly. That was Aunt Bess' doing. I would take Lilly with me on the bus and whoever I was doing the work for that day met me at the bus and took Lilly with them to their house. When I was done doing the work for the day, I would go to their house, pick Lilly up, and head home.

If I had to spend the night, as sometimes happened when the white people went to their Broadway plays or operas, then Aunt Bess or Cousin Thea would get Lilly and watch her for me. On those times and nights, I would miss my baby and as soon as the sun rose up, I made their coffee and breakfast. I couldn't wait 'till their regular maid came through the door. I was gone. I hurried to my next job knowing that at the end of the day, I would get to hold and smell my baby.

The way we were living was like a song. It had a rhythm. The women that were housekeepers with us helped with babysitting Lilly for us. On the Sundays I wasn't working, we went to church. At night before we went to bed, Aunt Bess told us more about our family. For a long time, she hadn't talked about them because we'd been so busy with the newest link, but now that Lilly had filled out, was walking around and talking, the storytelling started back.

Chapter 35

Freedom, Soon Come—But Only Fer Some

We be but two years back at Massa Fields plantation wen word reach me dat Momma Cornbread had, wid help from a man dey be calling de Birdman, escaped from Talbert's plantation. De Birdman, him be what de white mans call a abolitionist. Dat word be too fancy fer meh. All it mean fer me is dat him help nigger get 'way from dem hard living. De Birdman had mek him way onto Massa Talbert's plantation pretending to be studying de birds round de place. Dey suh old man Talbert be so glad fer de company dat him let de man go all over him plantation like dem be long-lost brothers.

Talbert not know'd dat de man dun come on him plantation to help slaves escape. At night, de Birdman hold secret meetings and him tell de slaves 'bout de Underground Railroad and how to know'd de conductors from slave catchers and to trust de station massa wen dey mek it to dem house. De Birdman tolt Momma Cornbread who to trust and dey suh him give she a little money and some tings to help she escape. Wen Momma got de signal dat de conductors be coming through, she be ready. She escaped from Talbert's plantation and mek it all de way to Canada. Thar she be free woman: no more nigger slave; nigger yes, but not nigger slave, dey be a big difference. Freedom dat be de difference 'tween nigger slave and nigger free woman.

De one dat come wid de news 'bout Momma Cornbread him also suh dat Poppa Molasses had escaped jis' de same way, but wid a different man and even though Poppa Molasses be free, him suh him would never be truly free unless him know'd dat him Cornbread be free too and wid him. Poppa Molasses gets to be a conductor on de Underground Railroad and him mek trip after trip all over South Carolina, searching fer Momma Cornbread.

Poppa Molasses not get to bring Momma Cornbread over himself, but all de conductors know'd of de cornbread-yellow woman him be looking fer so wen one of dem set him eyes on Momma Cornbread at a camp meeting, him know'd dat she be Poppa Molasses' wife and thar got she passage on de Underground Railroad. Dey help she to steal way. Momma Cornbread escape and mek she way to Canada where she not meet up wid Poppa Molasses fer near two months 'cause him be a conductor on another underground trip.

Dey suh dat wen Momma Cornbread saw Poppa Molasses, she jis't cried and cried. Dey suh she never stop thanking de Lawd fer bringing she to she Molasses. Dem be back together after almost twenty years. Dey suh dat Momma Cornbread beg de Lawd not to shut she eyes 'fore she set dem on she Milkweed again. Muh heart bleed wen I hears dis part. Neala, who brung de messenger to see muh, suh, "Thar nots be nuffin' like de love of a muddah."

I cry and cry 'cause I wants to see Momma Cornbread and Poppa Molasses. I wants freedom from Massa Fields and him place more now dat I know'ds muh Momma Cornbread and Poppa Molasses free and together. In muh heart, all I can tinks is dat I wants Poppa Molasses to come find meh. I wants him to come and tek meh and muh pickney from here and if I can find de way, I goin' tek much Lilly.

I wants freedom fer meh, Haroldetta, Eve, and Lavinia. Eve and Lavinia dem be de two pickney I dun mek fer Massa Fields since I gets back on him place. De night him slap meh and slap meh and slap meh and him suh I be goin' mek pickney fer him, him be right. I not mek one pickney fer him; I mek two. Dem be Eve, her come out furst and den Lavinia, her come out right 'hind Eve. Neala mek him know'd dem born and dat dem be as white as muh Lilly. I waits fer Mistress Olivia to suh send dem, but she not suh fer meh to send dem so Massa, him let meh keep dem wid meh 'cause Mistress Olivia feeling poorly and she suh she nots wants no more of de nigger pickney him rut and mek wid meh.

I see muh Lilly from time to time 'cause Mistress Olivia feeling poorly and she letting Neala and Sukey care more and more fer she. Mistress Olivia dun suhs to Massa dat I is not to have a hand wid Mistress Lilly. Mistress Olivia holds plenty hate in she heart fer meh, 'cause Massa him rut meh and I mek pickney and she nots. Muh Lilly she mighty pretty. She gots de same brownish-red cornhusk hair as Massa Fields. She is de whitest pickney I mek. It hard to tell dat I is she muddah, but I can see dat she is muh pickney but I know'ds she nots know'ds dat she be muh pickney. She raise up in de big house and all she know'ds is dat Mistress Olivia is she muddah and she gets to call Massa Poppa, and dat burn muh belly 'cause I know'ds dat wen Eve and Lavinia get to where dem can talk, dem goin' have to call him Massa.

I wants freedom. I wants de same freedom dat Momma Cornbread and Poppa Molasses gots. I wants it so I nots have to watch one of muh pickney get to call Massa Fields Poppa and two other pickney dat mek de same way as she have to call him Massa. I wants freedom fer dem.

All day wen I doing muh wuk, I be singing a mek-up song in muh head. It be muh own song. Nots have no tune to it, but it mek muh heart happy. Muh song is Freedom Soon Come. "**F** is fer de fresh air I's goin' breave wid no Massa in muh way to suck way de good air. **R** is fer de running I's goin' do and know'd dat no Overseer goin' set dog to bite muh. **E** is fer ev'rybody dat is nigger who goin' walk 'way from Massa, Mistress, Overseer and plantation. **E** is for every good ting I goin' eat; same dat Massa and Mistress eat. **D** is fer de dance I goin' do wen I nots have Massa, Mistress, Overseer, nor no owner no more. **O** is fer de one shout I goin' mek wen I walk 'way from Massa and him plantation. **M** is fer de furst ting I goin' get dat goin' be mine; and not Massa, de Mistress, nor de Overseer nots be able to tek from meh.

Freedom I wants it same way I want de bref in muh body. Freedom it goin' be mine soon. I know'ds it; can feels it in muh bones.

Wen I dun sing muh song, I smile and I be happy in muh heart dat Mistress Henrietta still had it in she heart to teach Momma Cornbread to read and write. Mistress Henrietta she sell meh 'cause she poppa tell she dat Massa Fields suh him love meh, but dat nots matter to muh. She dun teach Momma Cornbread de letters and numbers and Momma she teach meh. Every time we wuk wid de flour, she show'd me in de flour how to mek de letters and numbers; den we smile as we mix de flour wid de water, all de letters and numbers gone.

I smile now I can spelt freedom and know'ds what it be. It not matter where I be. I know'ds muh letters, numbers, and I can read and write. Freedom is all I want now. I know'ds not to let Massa know'd wat in muh heart. Massa him nots know'ds dat I know'ds how to read or write. Him nots ask meh 'bout loving him anymore. Him come, him rut wen him want, and den him go.

Him nots let meh get muh Sara back. Him let Nester keep she, but Nester she let muh Sara know'd dat she be muh pickney. So fer dat I nots hate Nester like wen I use to feel in muh heart she be mekking muh pickney love she over meh.

Chapter 36

Mixed Up Mind And Feelings

Wid Mistress Olivia getting sicker and sicker, Massa him not wanting to be in de big house. Him suh him nots like de smell of sickness, sickroom, or sick people, even him wife. Him come every night now and him mek Nester have Eve and Lavinia 'cause him nots want dem cry and bother him wen him rutting meh. De pickney, like meh, 'long to him. Massa him stay longer and longer now wid meh. I sit and watch him, waiting to cough or mek noise if him look like him goin' fall in deep sleep.

Massa him know'd dat how I mek sure him nots falls sleep and stay wid meh 'till morning. One night, him start to drift off to deep sleep and I starts de coughing and him suh, "Milkweed, stop that infernal noise. You are not the watchman over me. I will leave when I am ready to leave. Now go to sleep."

Wen Massa suh him last words, him turn on him side and him pull meh close to him, put him hand on muh belly, and him suh, "Go to sleep."

Dat night I not sleep, stir, or nuffin'. I waits fer Massa to get up and go to him house. Him nots. Massa him get up jis't 'fore slave rise, put him clothes on, and him left. From dat night Massa mek dat de way him do. Him come, him rut meh, sometimes one, two, three times, and den him pull meh to him and him go to sleep. I nots worry none 'bout de rutting and mekking more pickney 'cause Neala she mek de tea fer meh, and I drinks it and so I nots mek no pickney. Massa him never ask why I nots mek no more pickney, so now after de rutting and wid him not mekking to go to him house, I learn how to fall asleep wid de Massa holding meh in him arms.

One night after Massa been spending de whole night in muh cabin, I dream dat I see Mistress Olivia looking down at meh and de Massa. In de dream, I goes to get up and runs 'cause it feel real dat Mistress Olivia in de cabin. I begs muh eyes to open same time I begs dem stay shut 'cause if it not be dream, den Mistress Olivia goin' kilt meh 'cause she hate meh almost more dan any white womans can hate a nigger woman dat de Massa pick to rut wid. Mistress Olivia's hate fer meh more dan ever 'cause I mek Massa him pickney and plenty pickney after dat, and she not able to mek pickney, not after de furst one fer him.

Mistress Olivia's hate fer meh dun grow'd more since she tek to she sick bed. It not help matters none fer meh dat Massa fix to spend most all de nights wid meh over dan be in de big house wid she. She stay alone and sick in she fancy big bedroom wid it big big, as she suh to she white womans friends, 'imported from Barbados Mahogany' bed. It mek wid four sticks dat go all de way to de ceiling. She even gots de soft cloth dat drop round it and shut yuh from seeing de big soft soft bed and de mountain of pillows dat she lay head wid, white as de cloud hair on.

It be dis same bed dat she talk 'bout to she white womans friends wen dem be laughing and talking dem private talk. Dem talk 'round meh like I not know'd wat dem be talking 'bout. Dem suh 'bout how dem husbands not know'ds how to rut dem good, and wen dem get chance, dem mek nigger buck show dem cocky to dem and den dem pick nigger wid de biggest cocky and mek him rut dem. Dem laugh at how dem suh dat de nigger buck be mighty scared at furst to rut dem but after a few times dem suh dat nigger buck be smelling 'round waiting fer de chance to rut, like a dog in heat.

Mistress Olivia she laugh and she suh, "I'll never have to find a nigger to rut with, my Everett, he's a nigger in his breeches and I'm so glad that the bed is strong or Everett would be buying a new bed each week the way he likes to climb between my legs with his big cock."

Dem laugh and now she all alone in she bed and she hate fer meh growing more wid she sickness. In muh dream, I nots want to looks at she, but she in muh head and behind muh shut eyes. All de hate Mistress Olivia gots fer meh mek she look like yuh can see right through she to de next side. I wants to let Massa know'ds dat Mistress Olivia not as sick as him tink she be since she dun come down from de big house and mek she way cross de yard to muh cabin.

I trys and trys but I nots be able to get my mouth to mek no sound come out. Mistress Olivia she point at meh and she suh in a voice dat soft but it come from all over de cabin, "Look at him sleep; comfortable the way he used to with me. He loves you now."

I wants to tell she dat it be she him love but muh mouth it nots mek no sound. Mistress Olivia come a little closer but she foots dem nots mek no sound 'cause dem not be touching de floor. It like she moves but her nots. Her jis't be de next place her tinking her wants to be, and dat be closer to where meh and Massa be; de bed. Wen she be right next to meh, she talks again and dis time it come from all over de cabin, but she mouth it still not open. She suh, "My Everett loves another. Not a white woman, but you, a nigger. Milkweed, you have my husband's heart."

Wen Mistress suh Milkweed, I want to piss but I not be able to piss; I not know'd dat Mistress Olivia be know'ds muh name. I want to wake up, but I nots be able to wake up. Mistress Olivia she come a little closer and she shake she head from side to side. Wen she turn she head, it pick up de moonlight and thar be tears on she face. Mistress Olivia crying and den she look at meh from where her not be on de floor no more, and she suh, "Keep him. He loves you, a nigger. Milkweed, I know that you hate me and you hate Massa Fields, but for the sake of Lilly, learn to love him. Learn to love him as he loves you. Love him, Milkweed."

Mistress Olivia stop talking. She mek she hand to go by she side and I blink to clear muh head from de bad dream. I try and muh eyes dem open. I looks and I look and her be gone. I starts to sweat. I wants to wake Massa and tell him dat Mistress Olivia be jis't here, but fear shut muh mouth.

I stay wrap in de Massa's arms and I never wants to see de sun as bad as I want to see it now, but morning it come slower dan it ever come in all muh years at dis place. Massa him not rise him usual time. Him sleep longer and deeper and I wants him to mek de slightest move and I would stir more and wake him de rest of de way, but him nots stir. Wen him rise, de sun dun crack de sky. Bit more and it be full morning. Massa him rush wid him breeches and him boots. I rush too 'cause I still gots to mek him biscuits and help Neala, Sukey, and Eme wid de rest of him brekfast.

I gets to de cookhouse and I can tell dat 'cause Neala dun start to mck de biscuits she in a cussing mood. She suh, "Nigger Gal, yuh getting' more mix-up in yuh head. I can tell dat yuh tink dat 'cause him stay wid yuh now after him rut yuh, dat yuh special, but Nigger Gal, yuh still a slave. Him can rut yuh one minute and 'fore him seed mek it way out yuh pee-hole, him can have yuh on a wagon."

I look at Neala and she looks at meh like I be somebody different. I wants to tell she dat I not think I special and dat Massa him stay wid meh 'cause de cabin is him own like ev'ting on dis plantation. I gets in muh head to suh dat, but den from de upstairs we hear de Massa. Him shout, "Neala! Sukey! Eme! Come!" Dem stop wat dem doin' and dem run to where him voice be.

Dem running and dem suhing, "Yes, Massa, Yes, Massa."

Him not call fer meh but I go to see wat him shouting fer. Wen dem in front of him, him suh, "Doctor… dead." Dem dun know'd not to question wat him suh so dem stand looking at him and him suh, "Your Mistress, Mistress Olivia… go… get… send… go… for the doctor."

Neala she de furst one to speak, she suh, "Which doctor, Massa, and where him be?"

Massa him suh, "Overseer. Get him."

Neala she turns way and starts to run. Sukey she jis't stands. Massa him suh, "Stay with Mistress Lilly. Don't let her go into her mother's bedroom."

Sukey she starts to go up de stairs. Massa him turns to go back up de long stair dat tek him to she fancy bedroom and jis't as him turn, him see meh and him pause. I frighten 'cause him not suh fer meh to come. I nots know'd wat to do so I stop. Him nots suh nuffin' to meh, him jis't turn and him go up de stairs. Him start to tek dem two at a time, den him jis't run de rest of de way. Him not suh nuffin' as him run. Sukey, seeing Massa run up de stairs, she start to run too. She go to where Mistress Lilly's bedroom be and Massa him go to where Mistress Olivia's bedroom be. I go back to de cookhouse.

I waits in de cookhouse fer dem to come from Mistress Lilly's bedroom. I tries to mek de biscuits but muh head it keep seeing Mistress Olivia in she long nightdress pointing at meh jis't as de moon be waxing and de sun be trying to mek it furst crack in de sky. My head it suh, "but how she mek it cross de yard and back to she bed so quick and she suh sick. If she mek it to muh cabin, how come she mek it back to she bed to dead?" Muh head it mix-up more dan it ever mix-up over Massa, but now it mix-up and it frighten.

De doctor him come and de Overseer him tek him up de stairs to where Massa be. De doctor him not up thar long. Neala she looking at meh like I dun someting wrong, and I wants to suh to she dat I nots do nuffin' wen Sukey she come in de cookhouse and she suh, "De doctor jis't tell Massa dat Mistress Olivia be dead."

Wen Sukey suh dat, muh throat it go dry and sore same time and muh head it start to spin. Neala she look at meh and she suh, "Why yer looking dat way fer? Dead him tek long to come fer she; it be 'bout time him come and mek she wicked, evil, magra heart finish dry up and stop."

I suh, "I had dream dis morning dat Mistress Olivia be in muh cabin jis't 'fore Massa left. She point at meh, talk and den she left."

Sukey she looks at meh and she look frighten. She suh, "But how come she dead wen him walk in?"

"But de doctor him jis't suh she dead, him not suh dis morning."

"Him have to suh jis't now. Him jis't be getting here. Him not be able to talk 'bout wen him not here."

Chapter 37

Muh Pickney Still Not Muh Pickney

Ev'rybody in de house busy. Some in doin' nuffin' but dem busy. Dem busy 'cause de dead come fer a white womans. De dead dun know'ds thar way to dis place, but dem not comes fer a white womans fer a long time so now dat dem dun find it to tek another white womans, Massa him nots know'ds wat to do. One minute him crying and de next minute him want ev'rybody to be doing someting. Wat dat someting is Massa himself nots know'ds, so de Overseer him sends fer Massa Litchfield and some of Massa's friends dem come and help de Massa. Dem fear dat wid Mistress Olivia goin' wid de dead Massa in him grief goin' lose hand wid him niggers.

Massa Litchfield him bring Mistress Henrietta 'cause dem suh dat nigger not know'd nuffin' 'bout grief and de way it can brek a pickney heart dat dun lost she muddah. Mistress Henrietta she send Sukey and Eme out from round muh Lilly. Wen dem come to de cookhouse, dem suh dat Mistress Lilly heart dun bruk 'cause she Muddah dead. I wants to go to muh pickney and tell she dat she muddah be meh and dat I full of life and wen freedom come, I gine get freedom fer she too.

Neala she look at meh and like she in muh head she suh, "Dat pickney nots know'ds nuffin' 'bout yuh. Yuh is jis't a nigger gal dat is a slave on her poppa's plantation. So, Nigger Gal, yuh gets it out yer head dat yuh have part in dat pickney grief. She muddah, not yuh, dead."

I looks at Neala and I suh, "She muh pickney and wen freedom come fer meh like it come fer muh muddah, I gine tek muh pickney from here. She muh pickney and I be she muddah same way I be muddah to Sara, Eve, and Lavinia."

Neala she tek two step to meh and she raise she hand to slap meh and I suh, "Neala, if yuh slap meh today, I gine tell Massa dat yuh tink yuh Massa over meh."

"Nigger Gal, watever mek yuh get dat thought to go in yer head, yuh best mek it go way 'cause today is not de day fer yuh to find out if Massa care one way or de other if him nigger kill dem one another in him cookhouse. So, Nigger Gal, yuh clear yer mix-up head of all dem foolish thoughts yuh be having. Him might rut yuh, and him might fill yer belly wid pickney, but today is as good a day as any fer yuh to know'ds dat yuh jis't a nigger gal wid a pee-hole to him."

I start to tell Neala dat she wrong, but den I 'member dat Massa Litchfield and Mistress Henrietta in de house and dem hate meh more dan Mistress Olivia. I look at Neala and I suh, "But she muh pickney."

"Nigger Gal, she not be yer pickney. She be de Mistress of dis plantation now, and yuh is she slave, not she muddah."

Neala look at meh and I can tell she sorry fer meh wen she suh, "She not been yer pickney since de day yer push she out dese fifteen years. She be a woman now and wid she muddah dead, Massa him goin' do like all dem Massas who wife dead. Him goin' get another wife and from de way Mistress Henrietta run over here so fast wid she poppa, yuh can bet yer nigger gal mixed-up head dat Mistress Henrietta goin' be de next mistress of dis plantation."

Wen Neala suh dat, I feels someting in meh move and it mek meh more mix-up in muh head. I want Mistress Henrietta to go back to Litchfield Plantation. I nots wants she to be de new Mistress here. Neala she look at meh and she suh, "Yuh is one mixed-up head, Nigger Gal. Yuh mixed-up over yer feelings fer de Massa. Him yer Massa! Him rut yuh and yuh mek pickney fer him and him even spend all night in yer cabin, but yer still him slave. Milkweed, un-mix-up yer head 'fore Mistress Henrietta un-mix it up fer yer. Mistress Henrietta not gine have him rutting yuh and she not goin' have him spending one minute in no nigger cabin, so yuh find a way to un-mix yer head. 'Cause soon as him get Mistress Olivia in de dirt, and Mistress Henrietta let wat dem call a 'spectable time of mourning pass, she goin' have she poppa tell Massa dat a young gal like Mistress Lilly needs a white womans to mek she a good white womans. Now dat is de ways of de white peoples. Nigger Gal, Mistress Henrietta goin' be a different mistress dan Mistress Olivia."

I looks at Neala and I nots know'ds why, but I starts to cry. Muh belly start to burn meh wen I tink dat another white womans gine mek muh pickney call she muddah. I suh, "Neala but she be muh pickney. She be muh pickney and I be she muddah."

"Milkweed, yuh gots to stop dat foolish talk. If yer miss and suh dat to Mistress Lilly Massa gine tek de skin off yuh and him goin' do de same to yer Sara. Wat happen' to yuh mix-up Nigger Gal? Yuh dun ferget dat yer gots a pickney who call yuh muddah? It be true dat Massa dun give she to Nester but Nester be let de pickney know'ds dat yuh is she muddah. And mix-up Nigger Gal, wat 'bout Eve and Lavinia? Dem not matter to yuh? Yuh goin' go get yerself skin fer one pickney, and leave three other pickney to suffer? Mix-up Nigger Gal, wipe yer face and 'member dat yuh is a nigger, a slave. Him rutting yuh nots mek none of dat go way. Yuh is a nigger, a slave, and him yer Massa and Mistress Lilly she be mistress over yuh. 'member dat."

Sukey and Eme dem look from meh to Neala, and Sukey she suh, "Milkweed, Neala she be right. If in yer nots get yer head un-mix-up over de Massa and Mistress Lilly, Mistress Henrietta wen she come and be him wife, she goin' know'ds dat yer head mix-up over him and she goin' mek him sell yuh and yer pickney 'way from here. Milkweed, nots let no more sep'ration come 'tween yuh and yuh pickney. Yer dun lost all yer boy pickney 'cause yuh love dem and Mistress Olivia hate dem 'cause yer mek dem wid de Massa. Nots let another white womans come sell yer pickney. Let Mistress Lilly go. She not been yer pickney fer all dese years. Let she go. Yer nots be able to be muddah to she. She only know'ds yer to be de slave name Milkweed who mek de bread, biscuits, and mend she clothes. Yer not she muddah. Yer is slave to she; a nigger; she be a white womans. A white womans wid white womans way."

"But she still muh pickney. She turn and roll in muh belly. Tell meh how to ferget dat it be meh dat push she out in de world. She white womans 'cause dem tell she dat she be a white womans. I be slave and nigger to she, but she always be muh pickney even if I nots be able to tell she dat. Muh heart and muh head know'ds dat she muh pickney and she nigger jis't like meh. She be a nigger too like all de pickney I mek fer him. I be dem muddah, so if dem be nigger; she be a nigger too!"

De cookhouse went quiet. It be like dem not know'ds wat to suh to meh. Den 'fore Neala can get she mouth to suh all dat she be fixing to suh, de quiet of de house it shatter like somebody hit glass to rock. It be Mistress Lilly. She suh, "Get out! Get out of my house! Get out! This is my mother's house, get out!"

We know'ds dis to be white mans and white womans matter so none of we move. Nigger know'ds better dan to run out to see wat be wrong in white mans house. Den we hear Massa and him suh, "Lilly, darling, she's here to help you."

"Poppa, I don't need Henrietta's help. Why wasn't she here when Mommy's health was failing? Where was she, Poppa? Where? Get her out of Mamma's house! Where's Sukey? I want Sukey!"

Den Massa him shout, "Sukey! Sukey!"

Sukey she runs to de Massa and 'fore she can suhs de furst word, Mistress Lilly she suh, "Sukey, my Sukey." And she starts to cry.

Massa him suh, "Go. Stay with Mistress Lilly. Don't let her be alone."

We hear as Sukey and Mistress Lilly foots dem go in direction of de stairs.

Neala she suh, "Did yer hear she. She be white womans. She be Mistress of dis plantation and she muddah not bury yet. Yer pickney is yer Mistress. Now yer tink she wants yer to get freedom fer she. She nots need freedom from yuh. She be white womans wid a plantation and slave. Yer not birf a nigger pickney, yer birf yer own Mistress."

I looks at Neala and thar be nuffin' to suh. My Lilly had, wid a few words, un-mix muh head 'bout who she be: she be a white womans wid a plantation and I be she nigger slave.

Soon de house be busy again. Thar be food to fix fer all dem white mans and white womans dat come to lie to de Massa and tell him how sorry dem be dat him wife dead. Dem all suh how sorry dem is dat she dead, but none of dem not one day set foot over de threshold to come and sit wid she wen she be feeling poorly in she big fancy, brought from Barbados mahogany bed, wid it four tall, tall reach to de ceiling posts, and soft cloth dat could be let down to hide de whole bed.

A few days later, all dem white mans and white womans come back and Massa, Mistress Lilly, and de preaching mans walk over to de place where all de white people dat dead on dis plantation be bury. Dem sing dem white people's song and den dem come back fer food and drink. Mistress Henrietta she come wid she poppa but dem left wid all de other white mans and white womans after dem eat and drink dem belly full. Sukey be de only one dat Mistress Lilly want to be near she 'cept de Massa. So Sukey is de only nigger to see Mistress Olivia bury. She suh dat Mistress Lilly cry and cry fer she muddah. She suh it mek de tears come from she own eye 'cause she in got no pickney and she know'ds dat I is Mistress Lilly's muddah and not de white womans dat dem put in de hole mek she sorry fer meh and fer Mistress Lilly. I suh to Sukey, "I glad dat yuh wid muh pickney."

Neala she look at meh and Sukey and she nots suh nuffin'. Thar be nuffin' to suh.

Chapter 38

In One Blink

Massa him stay 'way from meh fer a long long, long time. It be de longest him ever stay 'way from meh. Mistress Lilly be missing she muddah and 'though she got Sukey to stay wid she ev'ry night, Massa be de only one dat she turn to fer she comfort. So him stay in de house at night. Den one night Massa him come to de cabin. Him come in like him dun since furst time him come, but dis night him not rut meh furst. Him suh him come to tell meh dat tomorrow him goin' wid Mistress Lilly to a place call Wetherfield in Connecticut. Him suh him be tekking she to him kin where she gine be wid other young white womans. Him suh dat him be tekking Sukey and Eme to be she slave and dat him be back soon as Mistress Lilly be settle in dis place.

Den Massa him rut meh and wen him 'lease himself, him suh, "When I come back, Milkweed, I want my son to be growing in your belly. When he's born, call him Poole." I not suh nuffin' 'cause thar in no time Massa suh I gine mek pickney dat I nots mek pickney.

Massa, Sukey, Eme, and Mistress Lilly go to dis place call Wetherfield. Massa be gone near three months and by dat time, I know'ds dat Massa left him pickney in meh jis't like him suh. Dis pickney be not like none of muh other pickney. Dis one it nots move or nuffin', it like it not in muh belly. If not fer muh belly getting bigger, it like I not be mekking pickney.

All de time Massa gone meh and Neala keep de house ready. De Overseer suh dat we must have de house ready fer de Massa ev'ry day. So we dust, clean and have it ready. While de Massa gone I gets to have Eve and Lavinia wid meh. Sara she wid Nester so long now dat she like where she be. I nots mek she come. I mek she know'ds dat I is she muddah and dat be all.

Wen Massa come back him see meh same way him see meh all de time: crossing de yard. Him look at meh and dis time him let meh see dat him see meh. Fer de furst time since I know'd de Massa, him smile at meh. Him have same look in him eyes as I do wen I see Sara, Eve, or

Lavinia. I nots know'd wat to do so I look quick at de ground 'cause Massa is still a white mans and a white mans can smile at yuh while him putting rope over yer head to hang yuh. I wants to put muh hand over muh belly. I feel shame like Massa and meh got secret. Like him seeing muh belly big wid him pickney and him smiling at de sight of meh change someting. I looks way quick and hurry quicker to de cookhouse. Wen I mek it inside, Neala she suh, "Nigger Gal, why yuh look like white womans."

I suh, "Neala, wat yuh mean by dat? I be nigger gal. I nots be able to look like white womans."

"I know'ds yuh be nigger gal, but yuh got de look on yuh face dat white womans get wen dem white mans suh someting special to dem. Yuh nots have no mans on dis place and yer nots no white womans so why yuh got... wat dem call dat look dat dis mix-up nigger gal be got, Beck?"

Beck, de slave dat Massa brung to de cookhouse to tek over wat Sukey do, she suh, "Blush. White womans call it blushing. But Neala, nigger not ever have reason to blush so wat yuh tink got dis nigger gal wid she big pickney belly looking like white womans wid de blush?"

Flavia, de next one him brung in de cookhouse to do wat Eme be use to do, and who, never 'till now, have nuffin' to suh since she been in de cookhouse suh, "Jis't now I be looking through de window and I seen de Massa coming cross de yard and when him seen Milkweed walking like she be duck wid she big pickney belly him slow down, look at she and him smile; it be a big, big smile."

Neala looks at meh and she suh, "Nigger Gal, how long yuh gine have yer mix-up head over de Massa?"

I know'ds that her not really want answer so I nots suh nuffin'; I jis't mek de biscuits wid de mix-up feelings in muh head and muh heart.

Not long after dat morning de pickney be born. One minute muh belly high wid pickney and de next minute I got pickney. Him look jis't like Massa. I call him Poole like Massa suh. I look at de pickney and muh heart it wants to know'ds way muh other pickney dat him sell be. Ev'ry night I looks at dis pickney, and I nots know'd why dis pickney and he mek meh want to know'ds where dem other pickney be. I know'ds dat I not be able to ask Massa but someting in meh moving to ask him even if it mean him selling way Eve, Lavinia, and Sara. Muh heart suh it best to have no pickney dan to keep wanting to know'ds where de rest be. I let it rest 'till muh heart suh it be right time. Right time gots to come.

Talk start to mek it way to de slaves dat President Abraham Lincoln suhing dat all slaves should be free. Freedom like it gine soon come fer all of we, and because of Momma Cornbread I know'ds how to spell it and she had dun tolt meh wat freedom mean fer nigger, but it twan't someting dat we ever figure we be live long to see. Now ev'ryday de talk getting stronger and Massa Fields and him friends dey talking 'bout President Abraham Lincoln and dem suh dat wat him want fer nigger is wrong. Dem suh, "Why does he want to give niggers something they aren't going to know what to do with? Niggers have no idea what freedom is. Does Lincoln have any idea what kind of fucking mess he's startin? Free niggers? Congress will never let that happen."

Chapter 39

By De Morning Light—A New Life

After Poole born all de talk Massa and him man friends having be 'bout Abraham Lincoln and how him be talking in Washington and all over de country 'bout how nigger and slave should have dem freedom. Massa him not come to muh cabin no more. Him seeing meh and him not seeing meh; it be like wen him look at meh, him not like wat him see. Muh head it mix-up more so dan dat time wen I furst come bak and him not come to muh cabin.

Muh head it suh, 'If Massa be not smile dat smile at yuh 'fore now, him seeing yuh and looking like him not seeing yuh it not be matter.' But muh heart it suh, 'It matter dat him seeing meh and not seeing meh 'cause him smile mek meh warm. Him smile at meh once, him can smile at meh 'gain.' I feels bad inside 'cause I wants him to see meh again and smile at meh. Him not do it.

One morning, like all dem mornings I sees Massa and him seeing but not seeing meh, I fix it in muh heart to mek him see meh. I slow muh step and I kick at nuffin' in front of meh. I bends and I picks up de same nuffin' dat I be kicking. De Massa him slow him step too and him look at meh and him look 'way. In muh head, I begs him to look at meh. I wants wen I steal to look at him dat him got de same smile on him face jis't like 'fore.

I hold de nuffin' in muh hand and I mek a step and kick at another nuffin' and muh heart it suh, 'Look at de Massa.' Muh head it know'ds dat I not 'pose to look but heart suh, 'Wat worse ting him can do yuh? Him dun solt way yer pickney, him had dem to kilt yer Harold Joe, him tek way yer Lilly, give 'way yer Haroldetta, and most dun give 'way yer Eve and Lavinia, wat more can him tek from yuh?' So I mek muh eyes steal to look at him.

Wen I looks him jis't be standing de same place where him be wen I bends down and picks up de nuffin' I be kicking. Muh heart it beat all over muh chest wen him suh, "Is there something that you want, Milkweed?"

Him voice sound like Massa. Thar be no softness in it. Thar be no smile 'round him mouth. Him be de Massa and him face it suh I be de slave. I drops de nuffin' I be holding and 'fore I can mek meh mouth suh a word, him suh, "If there's nothing that you want, then you should be hurrying to the cookhouse. Or is it the field you want to be hurrying to?"

I nots look at Massa 'gain. I mek muh foots to run de rest of de way. Wen I mek it in de cookhouse Neala she suh, "Dat, wat yuh jis't dun in de yard jis't now be stupid mix-up Nigger Gal foolishness. Wat get in yer mix-up head to mek yuh tink dat yuh can jis't be all talky talky wid de Massa. Nigger Gal I dun tolt yuh dat 'cause white mans rut yuh and mek all dem pickney wid yuh nots mek yuh special to him over him dog. Next time yuh mix-up head tell yuh to be waiting fer de Massa to mek him see yuh more dan dirt, get yuh mix-up head to tink wat it feel like to have him tell dem to rip de skin off yer nigger gal self. Now get yer nigger gal mix-up head to do de only ting dat matter to him; him food."

I nots look at Neala. I nots suh nuffin'. Thar be nuffin' I can suh to Neala. Muh head it suh, 'Yuh stupid nigger gal.' But muh heart it suh, 'But him talk to yuh.'

Now inside I more mix-up. Him talk to meh it be true, but him nots have no softness in him voice like wen him suh him tekking Lilly to Wethersfield in Connecticut. Him sound cold like de white mans him is.

I mek de biscuits and Neala had meh to bake bread, cake, and sweet tings fer him and de white mans and womans dat be coming to de house dat evening. Wen I dun wid dat she mek meh start a fresh set of bread. She suh dat it plain dat I need wuk to do 'till I near drop dead and mayhaps den muh mix-up head it not have no strenf to be mix-up over Massa or no other white mans.

Dat day be de hardest I wuk since I be on dis plantation. I look at Neala and muh head suh, 'She wuk yuh harder dan white mans.'

Neala must know'ds wat I tink 'cause she suh, "Ev'ry time yuh mix-up head tink to slow yuh foots in front de Massa, tink 'bout how hard yuh wuk today. Thar be no Mistress on dis plantation, but Mistress or no Mistress, Massa him know'ds how him cookhouse be run. Him nots suh 'Neala, yuh be 'sponsable fer de cookhouse,' but him not have to suh it. It be wat I do since dem put meh here. So, mix-up Nigger Gal, tek tonight and clear yuh head."

I gets to de cabin 'pecting to hear muh pickney but it be quiet. I go in and dey not be thar. I step out and be goin' to mek muh way to Nester wen I looks and I see de Massa. Same time Nester she come cross de yard and she suh, "Massa him suh dat all yuh pickney to be wid meh from now."

I know'ds better dan to look at Massa. I turns from Nester and I go back inside de cabin. De quiet of de cabin burn at muh heart and I wants to cry. So tired of mekking pickney only to have next woman be muddah to dem. I lies down and I wants to dead. I wants to dead 'cause muh heart it full but empty same time. It full wid love fer meh pickney, and it empty 'cause Massa him tek 'way muh pickney one at a time 'fore and now him tek 'way all three of muh pickney. I miss all muh pickney, but I miss muh Poole wid someting so deep in muh soul I not be able to suh wat it be. Poole him be de quietest pickney I mek. Him not cry, fret, or none of dem tings small pickney do. Him jis't happy. Yuh touch him head; dat mek him happy. Yuh sing him mek up song; dat mek him happy. It nots matter wat yuh do or wat yuh suh him jis't happy. Him be jis't a sweet pickney. I miss him and him quietness even in all dis quietness.

In de dark I tinking dat jis't like wid Eve and Lavinia, Massa tek Poole and mek Nester have him and I tinks dat if Massa wants Nester to have him pickney more dan meh, why him not rut wid she and mek pickney. Wen muh head tink dat, muh heart it turn over in pain 'cause I nots want Massa to rut wid Nester. I stays in de dark cabin and I nots even wants to tink. Muh eyes dem start to get heavy and I glad dat sleep dun mek it way to muh cabin. I wants sleep, dis way I be able to ferget dat I nots have muh pickney no more. I miss de sound of dem breaving, de way dem do in dem peaceful sleep.

I know'ds dat I sleep, but den I wakes like it be morning. Massa him be in de cabin but I nots hear wen him come in. Him dun have him clothes and him boots off and him next to meh. Him nots suh nuffin' to meh. Him puts him hand on muh belly and den him let him hand go from muh belly to it near near muh pee-hole and den him suh, "Isham, Juba, Zack, Tuck, Willie, Lilly, Eve, Lavinia, Poole, and the little girl that died: ten children. Milkweed, you and I have made ten children together. Ten. Six boys and four girls. You've given me six sons and four daughters and what have I given you? What have I given you?"

Muh head it still mix-up, but it 'member what Neala suh and muh head is suh, 'Nigger Gal, yuh nots need Neala to tell yuh dat yuh nots answer Massa. Yuh nots answer him question 'cause if yuh answer Massa, morning goin' find yuh dead in de yard.'

Massa him tek him hand from by muh pee-hole and him suh, "After ten children, you are still my slave and eight of your children, eight of my children are slaves; three here and five over on Breckenshaw's plantation."

Wen Massa suh dat, muh heart it jump all over muh chest. Muh pickney dem be livin' and him know'ds dat dem living. I wants to ask Massa how dem be, but I know'ds dat even in dis dark, I better not let him know'ds dat I wants to know'ds more 'bout muh pickney.

Massa den suh, "I see them, you know. From time to time, I go over to Pursival's place and I see them. Of course, they don't know I'm their father but Breckenshaw and his Overseer knows they are my children. He doesn't work them hard. They don't work in the rice field. He has them working and caring for his horses, making the shoes. He says they are natural with the horses.

"The first one you had, Isham has grown into a fine man. He still has my coloring despite all that hot sun. He looks like you, Milkweed. He's just like you and he has this…" Massa him stop from talking and him tek de cover off muh head and muh hair it jis't falls all over de bed and Massa him tek him hand and I can feel dat him have muh hair in him hand. Him suh, "…hair. This much hair. He wears it like one of those Indians. The others they have hair that is the same color as mine, but Willie and Zack.…"

I not want to but muh head it turns to look at him 'fore I can stop it. Him stop from talking and muh heart it jump all over muh chest wid fear, but him not hit meh or nuffin'. Him suh, "I know all their names, you know. I learned them over time from Breckenshaw and the Overseer."

I turns my head from looking at him face and him suh, "Where was I? Yes, yes… I was saying that Willie and Zack has straight hair like yours, not a curl and, like Isham, they also wear their hair as if they were Indians. Juba isn't as lucky as his brothers though, his hair is brownish-red and curly just like mine."

Massa him start to rub muh belly. Den him tek muh bub bub and him put him hand over dem. Den Massa him turn meh on muh side 'till I face-to-face to him and much as I nots want to get muh head mix-up over Massa and wat him jis't suh to meh, I feel someting moving and sliding all over muh heart fer him. I not wants to feel fer him now. Him know'ds way muh pickney be all dis time and him nots suh nuffin' to meh.

Massa him keep touching meh soft and him hand dem mekking all inside of meh mix-up 'cause I be liking de way him soft touch feel. Den I feel Massa as him cocky start to grow'd on muh leg. I waits fer him to climb quick on meh, but Massa him not do dat. Him pull meh closer to him and him kiss meh. I now know'ds dat wen Massa kiss meh, him 'pect meh to kiss him back. I kiss Massa back and I know'ds dat de minute

I kiss him, I wants to kiss him. I let muh mouth kiss him and I stays kissing and kissing him.

Massa him feel fuller dan before. Him pressing hard 'gainst muh leg. I waits and waits fer Massa to climb and start rutting meh, but him nots. Him kiss and kiss meh and I kiss him back 'till I wants to beg him to climb and start rutting meh. I not have to wait long. Massa him climb on meh and soon as Massa get him cocky in meh, him start to shake and him 'lease him seed in meh. I waits fer him to roll off meh and get him breeches and him boots, but him nots move. Him stay right where him be and Massa do wat him never dun 'fore. Him start to swell in meh and him suh, "Damn you, Milkweed. You've bewitched me into loving you."

Him keep on growing and den him start to rut meh slow. Him moving him hand all over meh, and wid all him touching and rutting meh slow, him get muh pee-hole to feel him. Him pull back a little and to muh surprise, I push muh pee-hole to him. Him push him cocky back in and I not move again. Him still growing and still moving him hand all over meh. I push muh pee-hole to him again and him press deeper into it. I nots want to move, but him hands mekking muh pee-hole like de feel of him. Massa him suh, "You want me, don't you, Milkweed? Stop fighting wanting me."

I nots suh nuffin' and him not stop from touching meh slow and different from him ever touch meh before. Den him suh right in muh ear, "If you let yourself, you can forgive me all the wrong I've ever done to you, and you can love me. You can, Milkweed. You can."

Den him grab meh but not hard and him hold meh and him kiss meh de deepest and hardest kiss I ever had. It even deeper and harder dan any kiss Harold Joe ever give meh. I nots kiss Massa back dis time and him stop kissing meh, but him nots stop from moving 'round in muh pee-hole. Den Massa him do someting him never dun 'fore: him tek muh hands and mek meh hold him. Fer all dem times Massa rut meh, I nots one time touch him beyond wat him mek meh touch him, leg on leg, belly on belly, and him cocky in muh pee-hole, dat be all de touching we dun and now him mekking meh hold him.

Massa him suh, "Tighter. Hold me tighter and wrap your legs around me."

I nots wrap muh legs 'round him and Massa him tek him hands and jis't as him did wid muh hands, him do wid muh legs. Him tek muh legs in him hand and him suh, "Don't you take your arms from around me, Milkweed and hold me tighter."

I nots tek muh arms frum 'round him back and I hold him tight, tight.

Wid muh legs in him hands and meh holding him tight 'round him back, him start to kiss meh harder. Him start moving faster and faster and widout him mekking meh, I raise muh legs higher, I holds him tighter and I starts kissing him back. Dat mek him go faster and harder and den him calling, "Milkweed, Milkweed."

And this time muh hands hold him tight, tight and I feel someting in muh belly. I nots know'ds wat it be but I know'ds it not be hate. It pulling at muh and mekking meh hold him harder and I start to move under him. Muh head suhs fer meh to be still like all dem other times, but dat feeling dat I not know'ds wat it be suhing hold him tighter and open yer legs wider fer him. I do. Him suh muh name and den I hear a voice I nots know'd straightway suh, "Everett!"

I stops. It be muh voice. I lets him go and try to tek muh legs out him hands. Him grab meh tighter and him suh, "Don't stop, Milkweed. Love me back. Love me back. Love me, Milkweed."

Him rutting meh harder and him still gots muh legs in him hand. Muh hand reach and grab him on dey own and I holds him tight. Him suh in a voice I almost not hear, "You love me, don't you, Milkweed? You love me."

Massa him rutting, sweating, and him sweat fall on muh face. Him rutting so hard him hurting muh belly den Massa him holler like stuck pig. Den dat feeling dat I nots know'ds wat it be get all mix-up wid de warm feeling of him, and it mek meh grab him hard and it tek way muh breff. I now be de one rutting Massa. I moving under Massa and I nots be able to mek muh body stop, and jis't as him suh muh name again, I feel a rumble in muh belly and de sound of de rumble it come out muh mouth and it sound like, "Evvvv-veerrrr-retttttt!"

I grabs him and holds onto him tight hard and I rutting him back and de more I rut him back, de harder him rut meh and dis time I like de hard rut and want him to stay rutting meh. Him give a deep, deep rut dat I feel all de way at the bottom and top of muh belly same time and wen him 'lease himself, I feel it warm in muh belly. It feel like him peeing in muh pee-hole.

De feeling in muh belly suh it name to muh head and I not fight it no more, I hold de Massa and him hold meh. Him breaving it tek a long time to come back to wat it be 'fore him start to rut meh. Muh bref it come back and wid it coming back come de mix-up feeling in muh head, heart, and now muh belly. I wants to know'ds way all de hate I had fer Massa gone. No answer come. Massa, wen him bref come back, pull meh close to him and him suh, "The hate has left you, hasn't it, Milkweed?"

Him wait like him 'pecting meh to suh to a white mans dat it be true hate I had in muh belly and heart fer him. Him talk again and him suh, "None of that matters now. You love me, truly and passionately. Can you say it, Milkweed? Can you tell me this time that you love me?"

I, fer reason I nots know'd, starts to cry and him kiss muh whole face and him suh, "I'm sorry for all the ways and times I've hurt you, Milkweed. I'll show you that I mean it. I'll show you that a white man can truly love a nigger. I love you, Milkweed, and I'll never hurt you again. Never."

Massa him pull meh closer to him. Him put him mouth near mine and dis time I reach up wid muh head and I kiss Massa furst.

I not know'd wen mornin' come but it come, and wid it de sounds of de plantation and dat be wen I sees dat Massa still wid meh and all over outside de plantation it sound more alive dan ever. I nots feel fear dis time 'bout waking him so I touch him and I suh, "Massa, Massa, wake up. It be morning."

Him stir and wid him eyes still shut him stretch. When him dun stretch him open him eyes. Looks at meh and him smile. I wants to smile back but I never smile at white mans 'fore and 'fore I can gets muh mouth to mek de smile dat in muh heart, de sounds of outside mek dey way to him ears and him sit bolt upright. Him hurry and put him clothes and boots on. Him push de door open and all de sounds dem rush in. Dem be different dan any sound I ever hears on any plantation: niggers singing and not any nigger song I ever hear 'fore. Nigger song only got few words. Dem singing, "We free, we free, President Lincoln send de soldiers and dem suh we not slave no more. We free, we free, we be free. Still nigger, but not slave no more. We be free."

I rush jis't like Massa and I puts muh dress on. Massa him stand in de door looking out and I go to de door by him side and I looks out. I sees wat him seeing. Dem dat be him property, slave, bound and frighten fer de whip, knife, dog, and any white mans on a horse, wen him walk in muh cabin last night, now singing 'bout freedom and be fixing to jis't walk 'way from him plantation. Dem free and mayhaps scared, but not fer de whip but fer wat freedom mean fer nigger who not know'ds nuffin' but bound, beat, and broken.

I looks at de Massa and him jis't standing thar. Him not seem to know'd wat him to do wid dat many nigger singing, shouting, and not wukking. Massa him step in de yard and him walk jis't a few paces and him turn and him looking 'round. I steps in de yard after him but not go to way him be. I be looking fer Neala, Nester, and muh pickney. I nots see Nester but I sees Neala. She, like all de other niggers, jumping and singing. She runs to meh wen she sees meh and she suh, "Nigger Gal, de soldiers dem come and dem suh dat President Abraham Lincoln signs a bill and dat bill is mek nigger dat be slave yesterday free today. We free, Nigger Gal. Free. We not have to do wat dem suh no more. De soldiers suh we can walk 'way from here wid dem and no Massa or Overseer can stop we."

I looks at Neala and I suh, "Walk 'way from here to where? Where nigger goin' go and wat nigger dat only know'ds plantation living and slaving goin' do? Wat we goin' do, Neala?"

Neala, she suh, "I not know'd but dem soldiers suh we free and I is goin' to go and see wat freedom be taste like. I know'ds de taste of slaving, it be bitter wid no sweet. I know'ds doin' wat dem suh do. I know'ds dem whip, and dem hate fer nigger. I know'ds how dem tink 'bout nigger, but I not know'ds freedom.

"I be wanting freedom since I furst hear dat thar be such a ting. I born slave and now dat President Abraham Lincoln and him soldiers suh dat I not be slave no more, I wants wat dem suh we gine get: freedom."

Neala she suh, "Now go find Nester and get yer pickney from she. Now, today, because de President suh we free, dem pickney now be yuh own. Yuh can now suh dem be yer pickney and yuh can gets dem and walk 'way from here like de rest of we. Go, Nigger Gal, and get yer pickney."

In de time it tek fer Neala and meh to talk, niggers dun start to gather dem little bit of tings and dem walking. Dem nots know'd where dem goin' but dem singing dat dem free and dem walking off de plantation. I looks fer Massa way I seen him last but I not see him. I see de Overseer O'Brien and him jis't standing watching niggers singing and leaving. Him have him gun, but nigger not goin' near him, him gun, nor de house dat him and de rest of dem got gun to protect.

Neala she suh, "Milkweed, wat yuh standing thar waiting fer? Yuh nots have to mek biscuits, bread, nor help wid him brekfast. Yuh nots have to do nuffin'. Dat wat freedom be. It mean yuh nots have to do nuffin' yuh nots want to do. So go. Get yer pickney and come so we can find out wat freedom be like. It must be sweet like de cake dem be eating and de wine dat dem be drinking dat mek dem happy. Go. Get yer pickney and come."

I looks at Neala and I starts to cry. She suh, "Dem tears crying best be tears dat suh yuh happy dat yuh free 'cause yuh nots have no other reason fer dem. Nigger Gal why yuh crying and yuh not moving to go get yer pickney from Nester 'fore she move 'way from she cabin and yer pickney dem get mix-up wid other pickney and niggers leaving dis place?"

'Fore I can answers Nester she come to meh and she gots all muh pickney: Sara, Eve, Lavinia, and Poole. She suh, "I gots muh own pickney and I be gine wid dem. I nots right know'ds wat we goin' find but it be easier, I tink, fer meh if in yuh have yer own pickney. Ten pickney be a lot fer meh to fend wid."

De pickney dem come and dem stands by meh. Sara she crying and she wants to go wid Nester's pickney. She suh, "Momma, come. Come so we can go to freedom wid Nester."

Muh head it suh, 'Follow Neala, Nester, and she pickney and go see wat freedom be.' But muh heart it suh, 'Stay wid de Massa. Stay wid him.' I look at Neala and Nester and I suh, "Dis is wat I know'ds. I not know'ds freedom. I know'ds 'bout mekking anyting yuh can mek wid flour. I know'ds dis plantation and I know'ds…" I stops and I looks fer and find de Massa. Him standing now in front de big house near de Overseer. Him standing wid him hand on him hip. De morning sun it be shining on him and him brownish-red, shoulder-length curly hair it sending back de sun all over him, muh heart it get happy, I points and I suh, "I know'ds him. I know'ds him ways."

Neala she suh in a voice I never hear she use before, "Mix-up Nigger Gal, him is a white mans! Him be de one yuh suh kilt all dem small pickney wen yuh be but no more dan pickney yerself. Him be de one dat selt off yer furst set of pickney and him even sell yuh 'way from here and it be him dat 'cause sep'ration 'tween yuh and yuh momma. Yuh know'ds him? Yuh nots be able to know'ds him. Him is a white mans. Him kilt yer Harold Joe! Nigger should never, never want to know'ds white mans or feel dat dem wants to know'ds white mans or dem ways. White mans ways is not fer nigger to ever know'ds. Yuh know'ds him? Him is white mans Nigger Gal!"

Neala she look at meh and she voice it brek and tears start to come down she face. Fer de furst time since I know'ds Neala, she cry. She suh, "Come 'way from here. Come 'way from him. Come, Milkweed."

Sara she look at meh and she suh, "Momma, come. Come to freedom wid we. Leave here, Momma. Leave him. Him be slave-owner. Come, Momma."

I looks at muh pickney and 'fore I suh wat be in muh head, I know'ds wat be in muh heart. I be staying and I be staying wid him. I suh to she, "Sara, dis is wat I know'ds. I nots know'ds freedom."

Neala she look at meh and she shake she head from side to side and den she tek muh Sara by de hand and she suh, "Muh pickney him dead, but I know'ds how to love a pickney. If yuh staying wid him, den suh I can tek Sara and mch and she gine left dis place and go see wat life be like fer nigger off from dis place. Suh it Milkweed. Suh it and I gine wid dis gal pickney if she be want to come wid meh and see wat freedom."

'Fore I can find de words to answer Neala, Nester she suh, "De President suh we be free den I gine and see wat freedom be. I gine down dat long trail wid meh pickney and watever we find as free nigger gots to be better dan bound slave. Yuh Sara she be wid meh fer almost half she life and muh heart be hurt someting awful if she can be free and yuh mek she stay and be bound." Nester she look at muh pickney and she suh, "Sara, yuh wants to come and be free wid meh, muh pickney, and Neala?"

I stands looking at de Massa and de words Neala suh get all mix-up in muh head as I watch him. It clear him nots know'ds wat him can do 'bout nigger walking off him place singing songs 'bout dem free and no white mans goin' tell dem wat to do 'gain. Neala suck she teet and she suh, "Yuh is a foolish mix-up Nigger Gal. Dis pickney dun been solt once before and now freedom come fer she, yuh willing to mek she stay slave. Dats not wat a muddah do to she pickney. A muddah do wat she can to do de best fer she pickney even if she slave, but a muddah dat got chance to give she pickney freedom and choose to mek she pickney stay slave should be a dead muddah. Milkweed, wen I walks 'way from here, yuh be dead to meh 'cause yuh chose white mans over yer pickney."

Neala she stop talking to meh and she turn to Nester and suh, "Nester, get yer pickney and get wat food yuh have. I know'ds dat Massa nots gine let meh go back in him cookhouse so I dun gather all dat meh, Flavia, and Beck can get we hands on. Milkweed, we be tekking Sara and any of yuh pickney dat follow behind meh and Nester we gine tek."

Neala she grow'ds tired of meh and she suh, "De President, him be a white mans and him soldiers den be white mans and dat mean dem can up and change dem mind 'fore I gets to taste or know'd wat freedom be. Nigger Gal, de time is now. We gots to be moving on. So Nigger Gal wid yuh mix-up head go and gather yer other pickney and come or yuh let meh and Nester tek Sara here and and yuh other pickney be on we way."

Sara she crying and begging meh to come wid she to freedom. I looks at muh crying soon-to-be woman pickney and I suh, "Go. Go, Sara. Go to freedom wid Neala and Nester. Go." Wen I dun suh dat to muh pickney, I feel all in muh body dat tears filling up de inside of meh but I nots want none to come out.

Chapter 40

Freedom: Dis Way or Dat?

I looks from muh pickney to de Massa and inside muh head I be wondering if I can truly let muh Haroldetta walk ways from meh and I not know'd wat road she tek and way it tek she. Wen I looks at de Massa, I be wondering 'bout de road him on. Not dat him gine any way, but wid all de slave walking 'way from him and him not owner over dem no more him have different road to tek too.

Neala look at meh and she suh, "Him know'ds wat him be doin' wen him tolt yuh not to rut wid Harold Joe. Now yuh be turning yuh back on Harold Joe pickney fer de white mans dat kilt him."

I know'd in muh heart dat Harold Joe him be want freedom fer him pickney and so I be letting she go so she can go find wat freedom got fer she. Neala she suh, "In all muh born days, I never seen a nigger womans pick a white mans over she own nigger pickney dat she rut and mek wid she own tek-up-wid nigger mans."

Haroldetta she try one more time to gets meh to come to freedom wid she; she suh, "Come 'way from here, Momma, come wid we."

I looks at muh pickney and I suh, "Go. Go to freedom Haroldetta. I picks freedom fer yuh."

Neala she start to walk 'way and she suh 'fore she back full turn, "Nigger Gal, I hope dat in days to come, wen it jis't be yuh, Eve, Lavinia, and Poole who be slave to him and him white mans and white womans friends yuh mix-up head nots be sorry."

Now yuh gots 'till we start to walk to un-mix yuh head 'bout wat yuh gine do. Once I walk pass yuh, watever pickney behind meh I keeping as muh own. If yuh nots want none of dem to go, suh so now 'cause when I walk pass yuh wid dem yuh be dead to meh Milkweed; dead yuh hear meh; dead. It gine be like I never set eyes on yuh."

Sara she crying harder now and she suh, "Momma come. Nots mek meh go 'way from here widout yuh. Come, Momma, and bring Eve, Lavinia, and Poole. Come to freedom, Momma, come. Come 'way from him and dis place. Come and we not gine be slave no more. Come wid meh Momma; come."

Neala she turns she head full round and she, Nester and Nester pickney go to where de rest be goin'—through him yard to freedom. Dem looks jis't like how de white preacher mans suh dem people in de Bible looks de day dem get freedom from dem slave Massa and walk through de sea dat be red.

I stands watching and watching, mekking muh eyes see Sara walk to freedom. I be watching and den I hear muh other pickney wailing. Dem calling after Sara. Dem begging she nots to leave dem. I hears muh Haroldetta and she wailing too. Neala she stops. She not turns to looks at meh but I can see muh Haroldetta and she trying to brek free from dem to come back to meh. Neala and Nester dem be holding she hand. Neala she not turn 'round but she suh shout, "Nigger Gal, bring 'em and come! Come 'way from dis place!"

I mek de furst two step to dem and den over Neala shouting, Sara, and muh other pickney, who be holding onto muh dress crying and all de Nigger singing 'bout how dem marching to dem freedom, I hears de Massa's voice. Him voice big and him calling and hurrying come cross de yard same time. Wen him gets to meh him suh, "Are you leaving me and here?"

I looks at him and I feel de tearing in muh heart and I stop. Den I hears Neala and she shout even louder, "Nigger Gal, walk 'way from him!"

I grab hold of Poole and I look at Eve and Lavinia and not answering or looking at him I suh to dem, "Come."

We move as if we be jis't one body and him suh, "Milkweed, Stop!"

I not stop. Wid muh heart tearing de worse tear I ever feel I mek two more steps and Neala, she stop, turn and she be waiting. She got a smile on she face. She suh, "Come Nigger Gal! Come!"

I go to mek de next step and I nots be able to move. Him dun tek hold of Poole and him suh, "Go if you want, but the children, my children, are staying here with me. I looks at him and I 'pect to see him red and angry but him not be none dem tings him 'most look like him frighten but him suh, "You will not take my children from here. I am their father. The President says they are free, it's true, but these children, who just happen to have a slave as their mother, are mine. You needed his freedom. They needed his freedom, but I don't or won't ever need his freedom. I always had it."

Neala nots hear wat him suh to meh but she know'ds dat she in but a few minutes gone from being him slave so she turn she head and walk 'way from meh. Massa him suh, "Are you going to follow them?"

I looks at Massa and I nots know'ds wat to do or which way to go and him look at de pickney and him suh, "Come here. Stand here by me. I'm your father."

De pickney dem scared 'cause dem nots know'ds him as poppa. Dem nots know'ds nobody to be dem poppa. Dem jis't know'ds meh as dem momma. Dem eyes be wide wid fear 'cause him jis't be a white mans and de Massa to dem. I looks at de Massa and I suh, "I be stays wid de pickney."

Him suh, "Then take them away from this chaos; this infernal madness."

I suh to de pickney, "Come." And I starts to walk towards muh cabin but not 'fore I tek one more look to try and see muh walking to freedom pickney but I not see she; she dun get swallow up in de sea of walking 'way niggers. I turns muh head back and I mek a few blinds steps 'cause muh eyes dem full up wid tears so I nots be able to see muh walking-to-freedom pickney. Him suh, "Where are you taking my children?"

I nots looks at him but I suh, "De only place I gots to tek 'em."

"There are other places to take them."

"Way? Way to tek 'em? Way dis other place be?"

"Take them to the cookhouse. Feed them and stay there until I come."

I looks at de pickney who be crying and I suh, "Come." Dey come 'hind meh and I leads dem to de cookhouse. I mek dem sit on de floor. I cooks dem de same brekfast dat I be cooks fer him and I feeds and fulls muh pickney belly. We stays in de cookhouse fer most de day and since Massa him suh feed 'em, and dat be wat I do all day. Dem full like dem never full and one by one dem falls sleep and I sits on de floor wid dem.

Wen de furst cast of dark mek it way 'cross de yard, Massa him come in de cookhouse and him suh, "Your pickney; the one you call Sara has found her way back here."

Muh heart it start to run all over muh chest. I wants to run, but muh foots dem nots know'd way to run. Him suh, "You should go and see about her. She is blood-soaked. I didn't look to see if she's hurt or not. I don't want the other children to see her in the state she's in. Go to her."

I runs pass him and I calling, "Sara, Sara, where yuh be?"

In de almost dark, I see she eyes. Dem open wide 'till dem looks like dem goin' pop right out she head. She see dat it be meh and she starts to run to meh and she crying and hollering, "Momma! Momma!"

I hurry to where she be. I sees de dirt and de blood dat covering she from she head to she foots. I suh, "Sara, Sara, way yuh hurt? Yuh hurt bad?"

She crying and she suh, "It not be meh dat hurt, Momma. It be Momma Nester, Neala and …" She hollering so hard now she nots be able to get no more words out. I grabs muh pickney tight to meh and I starts to cry.

I tek she hand and I leads she way from de cookhouse since Massa suh not to bring she thar. I go to de cabin wid she. I starts to clean up muh pickney. I suh, "Haroldetta, way all dis blood come from?"

She suh, "De white mans dem turn loose dem big dogs. De dogs dem run we from de white mans place. Dem dogs be ev'rywhere. Momma Nester she runs and de dogs dem jumps, she falls and dem bite she ev'rywhere. Neala, she suh fer meh and Nester pickney to run from way de dogs be. She be trying to get de dogs off Momma Nester, but she nots be able to. She shouts fer us to run faster and faster. Some nigger mans dem runs to where Momma Nester and Neala be wid de dogs and dem tek sticks and dem beat de dogs 'cause de white mans not way dem dogs be. Wen dem gets de dogs off Momma Nester I mek Nester pickney stays wid some nigger womans dat on dem way to freedom wid we and I runs back to way Momma Nester be."

Haroldetta she crying and muh heart it hurt a deep pain fer she. I starts to cry and she suh, 'Dem dogs, Momma, dem kilt Momma Nester and dem bite Neala plenty, but Neala she not dead. I holds Momma Nester and I cry and Neala she mek it to her foots and she suh, "Sara, yuh Momma Nester she be gone. Run back to way yuh muddah be. Stay 'way from de white mans and even if yuh sees white womans; stay 'way from dem too, but finds yuh way back to yuh muddah 'fore it dark. I gine to freedom. Gotton, Abby, Gin, Beck, Pascal, and Jonas; dem be muh pickney now. Now yuh start running and yuh nots stop 'till yuh sees where yuh jis't left.'

"I suhs to Neala dat I wants to stay wid she and Momma Nester pickney but suh, 'Get from here, I be dey muddah now. Dem and yuh be different. Yuh gots a muddah. Yuh muddah she mek choice not to come to freedom, but she still be yuh muddah. Me and Nester we bring yuh so yuh get to taste freedom; Nester she be dead trying, and meh, I not know'ds how I get mek it wid dese dog bites so tek de little taste of freedom dat yuh get and let it tek yuh bak to yuh muddah. Use it, Sara, and start running now 'fore night come."

"Neala not listen to meh wen I suh, 'But, Neala, I like wat freedom taste like. I want to go wid yuh and get more freedom. I not want to go back to plantation living." But Neala she suh, "Yuh go back to yuh muddah and I gine use de time I gots to see that Nester pickney get other muddahs. Nester she dead 'cause she want freedom fer she and she pickney so I gine use my freedom and wat life I got to get she pickney dat chance at freedom. Sara, yuh got a muddah; yuh not need a next muddah, yuh go back to yer own muddah, now go, Sara, run."

"I nots know'd way to run so I looks at de ground and I run other way dat nigger foots be in de dirt. I finds muh way to here and I sees de Massa and I stands by him fence and I suh, "Massa, it be meh Sara. Please I beg yuh have mercy. I nots have other place to be." Him looks at meh fer a little while den him let Overseer O'Brien let meh in."

I clean up muh pickney den I gives she wat I gots in muh cabin to eats and I go back to de cookhouse and Massa him be thar watching de pickney sleeping on him cookhouse floor.

I mek two foots in de cookhouse and him suh, "Is she hurt?"

"No Massa. She not be hurt no way."

"Den where did all that blood come from?"

"It be from Nester. On dem way to freedom, dogs be set 'pon dem. De dogs dem bite Nester 'till she be dead."

"Nester is dead? What about her pickney?"

"Dem be wid Neala. She be hurt mighty bad."

"Where are they?"

"I nots right know'ds. Sara she suh dat Neala she move on wid Nester's pickney to freedom."

"Freedom. What does a nigger know about freedom? Where is she?"

"Which she, Massa?"

"Your pickney?"

"She be in de cabin."

"Since she's not hurt bring her in here. She is yours just as these others are yours."

I turns and walk out de door. I goes to de cabin and I suh, "Come, Sara, come. De Massa him suh yuh can come in de cookhouse wid de other pickney."

Massa him come in and out de cookhouse a few times. Last time him come in him got a gun. Him suh, "With all this freedom that Lincoln has given to slaves who have no idea what freedom is, or how to care for themselves, tonight is going to be a long night: dangers lurk everywhere. O'Brien is going to sleep here tonight. Take the children and go to his house."

"Massa, I nots be able to go to Overseer O'Brien's house. Him gine shoot meh and muh pickney de minute we mek it to him door."

"Milkweed, this is my plantation. O'Brien is not in his house nor is he going to shoot you. You and the children will be safe there tonight. Now go."

I gets de pickney and I go wid dem to O'Brien's house. I walks pass de smoke house and muh belly it start to burn meh at de smell of all de ham and sausages dat I know'ds be in thar. Dat be de furst time I 'member dat I not eat nuffin' all day. I swallow muh spit and be grateful dat muh Haroldetta mek she way back to meh, and dat dem white mans hounds not eat she 'way from meh. This gine be de furst night dat I be wid all muh pickney.

I looks 'round de house and it be a small big house. Him gots fancy desk wid chair, him have big hurf and it be warm in him house. Him have ev'ting dat de Massa gots in him big house. Him own jis't older or smaller dan Massa own. Him bed it be bigger dan nigger bed, but it be smaller dan Mistress Olivia, 'brung from Barbados' solid mahogany four-post bed. Him bed it have post like Mistress Olivia's bed but dem nots go to de ceilin'. Him own stop waist-high and dem post dem shiny like nigger spend all day mekking dem shine.

I can see dat de pickney fear dat Overseer O'Brien goin' come and find we in him house and shoot we. I not know'ds how to mek dem not fear wen I fear de same ting muhself. I find muh voice and I suh, "De Massa suh fer we to be here. So come lie down. Eve and Lavinia, yuh let Poole be in de middle. Sara, yuh mek yuhself fit at dem foots."

Dem climb in de bed like dem 'pect it to turns into white mans and kill dem. I tek one of him chair and I sits in it. I tanks de Lawd dat I can set muh eyes on muh pickney. Dem together fer de furst time fer meh to see dem sleep. I watch and soon, one by one dem fall sleep. I try to keep muh eyes open so I can be see wat de night gine bring but next ting I know'ds it be morning and de sun be mekking it way cross de sky.

It be quiet. Not usual sound on no plantation I ever be on. Den I 'member dat freedom come yesterday fer slave. I wakes my furst mornin' a free woman; but I not be truly free since I dun let love creep in meh heart and now I bound muhself here wid him 'cause of it. I dun let muh first chance to taste real freedom slip pass muh lips. I know'ds now dat I never gine know'ds wat de real taste of freedom be.

I sits and I be tinking if I gots to mek him biscuits and breakfast. Muh tinking not get time to finish 'cause same way muh pickney fall sleep dem wake, one by one. Dem nots move. Dem stay thar in de big bed looking at meh all sleep gone from dem eyes de minute dem open dem and 'member dat dem be in de Overseer's house.

Dem looking at meh like dem tink I know'ds wat to do fer dem; Den I hear de crunching of boots outside and de sound it coming closer and faster to way de door be. De pickney eyes dem come wider wid fear. De sound of de boots mek it to in front de house and dem stop. De door it open and it be O'Brien. Him step in and him mek two steps to meh. Muh heart it all over muh chest and it beat so hard dat it hurt meh. I suh, "Please, please, Massa I mighty sorry to be in yur house. I begs yuh nots to shoot muh pickney. It be Massa Fields dat suh fer meh to come here wid de pickney last night. I be sorry fer putting muh pickney in yer bed."

O'Brien him still be de Overseer but him nots mek to shoot meh nor de pickney. Him suh, "Massa Fields says that you are to come to the cookhouse now."

Him suh dat and him jis't turn and walk out de cabin like him never be thar. I suh to de pickney, "Come." Dey jump down and dey follow meh. I feel like chicken wid she lil' chick 'hind she. Wen I gets to be near de big house, I suh to dem, "Stay right here. I can see yuh from de cookhouse. Yuh all not go no way. Stay." I runs de rest of de way to mek up fer de time I tek to tell 'em to stay way dey be.

Wen I mek it to de cookhouse, Massa him be standing by de door. Him suh, "From this day until I say differently, you take what you want to feed my children and your daughter. Feed them this morning, but after you've made breakfast for me and O'Brien. You and the children will stay in O'Brien's house until I say otherwise."

Massa him start to walk way and him stop. Him turn to meh and him suh, "The children, where are they now?"

"In de yard, Massa, in de yard."

"Why?"

"I not know'd dat yuh wants dem in de cookhouse fer a second time, Massa."

"Milkweed, understand this. A lot has happened, a lot has changed, and a lot remains the same. What has happened is that a Republican President has said that slaves can't be slaves anymore and so there are now a lot of nigger people running around not sure what freedom is or what to do with it. That is what has changed. What remains the same is this: those children, with the exception of your Sara, are mine. They are all the children I have that I can see this morning. You are their mother and if you were a white woman we would make their parents, but you are a nigger that until yesterday was my slave, so we are not their parents. I'm their father and you are their mother. This is my plantation, my house and my cookhouse so feed my children and your child in my cookhouse until you figure out how to cook and feed them in O'Brien's old house."

Massa him walk 'way wen him dun suh wat him have to suh. I do in him cookhouse on dis morning wat I dun since de furst mornin' Neala brung meh here. I mek biscuits, bread, and him brekfast. Wat I be do different is dat dis morning I tek de brekfast out to him big fancy dining room and I feed him and Massa O'Brien. I waits and I serve dem wat dem want 'cause dey not be nobody else to serve dem. Wen him suh dat him nots need meh no more, I brung de pickney in de cookhouse and I feeds dem. I puts dem to sit on de floor and fer de furst time ever, I give muh pickney biscuits, ham, gravy, eggs and yes, I give dem milk. Dem quiet and dem sit and dem eat all de food.

Wen dem be eating de food Massa him come in de cookhouse and dem stop eating. Dem get all fearful like dem know'd dem be not to have him milk. 'Fore him speak, I suh, "Massa, I sorry. I never goin' feed dem none of yuh milk or eggs no more."

Him nots suh nuffin' 'bout de food, him suh, "I came to say that when you are done in here, you are to go to your old cabin and get what you need from it to make you feel comfortable in O'Brien's old house."

Him suh dat and him walk back out. De fear left de pickney faces and one by one dem went back to eating de food. I do as Massa suh. Wen dem dun eat, I tek dem wid meh and we get de little bit I had in de cabin and we move to Massa O'Brien's house. I gets to see it good in daylight. It be a strong-looking house. On de outside it got tabby but on de inside it got strong wood. Thar be two more rooms and dem all got fine furniture in dem. De furniture it like de furniture in de big house but dis furniture it look older. Like it be furniture dat Mistress Olivia not want no more. None of it mek like de furniture dat be in nigger cabin. Nigger furniture mek from leftover wood and nigger tek it to mek table, chair, and bed. Dis furniture, it be fine furniture. I nots tink be one other nigger anyway, free or near free dat gots furniture like dis. I looks and I nots know'ds how to live in such a big house wid such fine furniture. De pickney dem touch and looks at ev'ting and den I looks up and I sees muhself looking back at meh.

It be a mirror. It be a long time since I seens wat I be look like and now dat I seeing meh again, I be different but de same. I can see dat I older. I looks like muh momma 'cepting not as yellow, and I sees dat my nose it be de same like Massa's nose. I not notice dat 'fore nor did it much matter. I nots know'd why I mek it matter now. I looks too at muh mouth and I see de mouth dat only two nights ago kiss Massa Fields and 'though it be de same mouth dat kiss Harold Joe, it be different. Dis mouth dat kiss Massa Fields and liked it is also de same mouth dat open and send way Haroldetta and if not fer Neala, it be de mouth dat send she way to dead. I feel de same feeling I had wen I send she way in muh belly, and I wants to cry but not sure wat to cry fer since I gots all muh pickney and dem belly full.

I stops looks at muhself and I walks way. I nots have time fer crying or feeling sorry. Never had time 'fore now fer it and I nots have time now. I tek time to sits and I tink 'bout wat life gine be like fer meh and muh pickney now dat President Abraham Lincoln give nigger freedom. I tinks dat I nots know'd wat different tings dis day and night goin' bring so I pray to de Lawd dat it bring meh and muh pickney someting other dan fear.

It tek a fortnight, maybe jis't a bit more 'fore slave dat want freedom start finding dem way back to de plantation. Massa him letting dem dat want to come back come back. In all wen it be over, some twenty or thirty of dem come back. I watch and watch fer Neala wid Nester's pickney to come back; dem nots. I ask dem dat come back if dem see Neala and dem suh dem see she moving on wid de pickney and dat she join wid some niggers dat de soldiers walking way from 'nother plantation, and dem suh dat she suh, 'Only ting stopping meh from finding freedom is if I dead, and I be willing to choose dead over being slave again.'

I beg de Lawd, in muh heart, to look after Neala wid Nester's pickney 'cause she send back muh pickney, and 'though I be want freedom fer muh Sara, I still be glad dat Neala send she back. I know'ds in muh heart dat I never gine see Neala again, but I want Neala and Nester's pickney to find wat Momma Cornbread and Poppa Molasses dun find in Canada: freedom.

Chapter 41

Time After Freedom

Time after freedom it move faster dan before freedom come. Massa O'Brien him not Overseer no more since thar be no slave on de plantation, only nigger dat now wuk 'cause dem want to. Him still de one dat tell dem wat to do. 'fore freedom come, thar be near two hundred slaves on Massa Fields plantation. Now after freedom come, thar be 'bout sixty but dem not be sixty dat be here before. Some dat be here before come back, but most dem dat be here went to see wat freedom be. Dese dat be here now went from other plantation to see wat freedom be and days into weeks after dem gone looking fer freedom, wat dem finds mek dem not care fer freedom. Freedom bring dem hungry, white mans wid dogs dat chase dem from 'round dem place, and white mans dat from de Confederate dat hate nigger more dan white mans from de Union 'cause dem suh dat it be President Lincoln's love fer nigger dat mek dem lose de war wid de Union.

Massa O'Brien him be in charge and him different since him got him new house dat Massa let him build to 'place de one dat him give meh and muh pickney. Massa O'Brien him tek up wid a slave woman dat come on de plantation from other plantation. Massa O'Brien him move de woman in him house and she mek pickney fer him. Him woman she be like Poppa Molasses. Thar be nuffin' 'bout she dat can mek yuh tink she be white womans. She be all nigger. She tall, 'most tall as Massa O'Brien. She hair it be like rope and she not cover it like meh. She let it be open and wild. Massa suh fer she to wuk in de cookhouse wid meh. Massa him suh fur meh to bring two other womans dat suh dem wuk in cookhouse 'fore dem went to dem freedom. Tings near de same, but dem different.

In de big cabin, de pickney dem growing and I can tell dat it be soon time fer Sara to go get she own cabin and mek pickney. Sara she be good as meh at mekking de biscuits and bread; most anything she can do wid flour. Massa him suh she can wuk in de cookhouse wid meh. Time it like it mek Massa ferget dat she be Harold Joe pickney. Him nots come to de cabin now dat all de pickney wid meh, but wen him want to rut meh, him have him way of letting meh know'd.

Furst time Massa let meh know'd, him waits 'till him eating him brekfast and him suh, "Milkweed, this evening when you are done in the cookhouse you, not O'Brien's woman, fetch the water for my bath."

Dat evening I do wat him suh. Wen Anakey dun wat she have to do and she gets ready to go draw de water fer Massa, I suh, "Him suh fer meh to do it dis evening." Anakey she looks at meh and she suh not suh nuffin'. Wen I 'most dun draw de water fer him baff, him come in him quarters and him watch meh 'till I dun. Wen I dun and I puts all of wat him need fer him baff, him suh, "I need help wid the bath. Stay and scrub my back."

I stands and I waits on de Massa. Him tek him clothes off. I turns muh head and de Massa him laugh. Him suh, "Are you blushing at the sight of my nakedness? We've made ten children together. Milkweed, it's me; Everett. My nakedness is not new to you. Now come. Turn around, it will be hard for you to wash my back properly with your head down and turned."

I hears him step in de water and I turns muh head. Him be in and him such, "Scrub it good." I do wat him want and wen him dun wid him baff, him steps out de water and into de towel dat I be holding. Soon as Massa step into de towel, him grab fer meh. I jump back and him suh, "Milkweed, are you afraid of me? I promised you that I would never hurt you again. I mean that."

Him hold meh to him tighter and him kiss meh. I not tink I would kiss Massa back, but muh mouth open and it kiss him back and den muh hands dem raise up and dem hold onto him back. Massa him hold meh even tighter and kiss meh back even harder, and I feel him grow under de towel. Massa him start to walk backward jis't de way we be and wen him stop, him at him bed.

Massa him stop from kissing meh and him suh, "Come."

I mek de two steps to him bed and I climbs in. I wants to rut wid him. Him rut meh 'till him nots be able to rut no more and den him starts to fall asleep, and jis't 'fore him fall asleep, him pull meh to him belly and him suh, "Stay with me. I've missed sleeping with you. Stay. There's no one to make you go to your cabin."

Massa him pull meh to him and den him suh, "Do you think you can stop calling me Massa now. I don't have any more slaves, and besides you are a free woman; remember." I suh nuffin' and him suh, "If you call me Everett or not, you are my woman, Milkweed. Same way Anakey is O'Brien's woman, you are my woman. She calls him O'Brien, do you think then that if you can't call me Everett, you can call me Fields. I'll answer to Fields. It will be your special name for me."

I finds a voice I not know'ds I had and I suh, "And wat gine be muh special name dat yuh gine call meh?"

Massa him start to laugh and him suh, "What is your real name? I'll call you that."

I suh, "I not have other name. Milkweed dat be muh name."

"Then I'll call you Pearl. Pearl it is. That will be your special name when it's just you and me."

Soon as him suh dat, him gets out de bed and him gone fer a few minutes and wen him come back him gots a box. Him open de box and in it be rows and rows of white marbles jis't like Neala suh dem be look like. Him suh, "Pearls. Here, turn around and hold your hair up."

I do as Massa suh and den him come in front of meh and put de rows and rows of marbles by muh chest, den him suh, "Put your hand by your neck for a minute." I do and him come round 'hind meh and him fasten dem. I sits wid de pearls, as him suh dem be, resting on muh neck. Him step 'way again and wen him come back, him have a mirror in him hand. Him suh, "Look."

I looks and I sees a different meh. De pearls dem mek meh look special. I smile. Him suh, "You are smiling. You like them?"

I suh, "Yes. Dem be beautiful."

Him suh, "Then they are yours: pearls for my pearl."

Massa him gets back in de bed, pull meh right close to him belly and him put him hand round meh and him suh, "Pearl in pearls, go to sleep."

I press closer to him and I suh, "Dem be real beautiful, Fields."

Him kiss muh head and pull meh even closer. I close muh eyes 'membering dat Neala suh dat him faddah suh dat white mans give pearls to white womans to prove dat dem love dem, never a nigger; pearls not fer nigger womans, ever. I falls to sleep tinking dat pearls not fer nigger womans but I gots pearls on and I not be white womans; him faddah must not have tolt him dat pearls only fer white womans. Wen I wakes it be morning and de smell of de brekfast coming up de stairs. I rush to get up and him suh, "Pearl, where are you going?"

"I gots to go mek yuh brekfast. "

"You have my breakfast." And 'fore I can ask him wat him mean, him press him cocky on muh leg and him put him hand near muh pee-hole and him suh, "Here."

We rut and wen him dun him suh, "The pearls, take them off."

I looks at him and I feel shame come all over meh. Him suh, "I'm not taking them away from you, but you shouldn't wear them out this room. Pick the place you want to keep them and every time you come to me, get them and put them one."

I smile. Massa him kiss meh and him suh, "Now you can go and see about feeding your man."

I went to suh someting and him suh, "I am and there's nothing for you to say. I am your man and you are my woman. Just like O'Brien and Anakey."

I hurry to get to de cookhouse. Wen I gets to de cookhouse, Anakey she look at meh and laughing, she suh, "It never tek meh dat long to draw him baff. Wat yer do, Milkweed? Yuh spend all night wash him cocky? Him must have very big cocky dat it tek yuh all night to wash. O'Brien him got big cocky, but it not tek meh all night. Half de night most nights, but never all night."

I bends muh head in shame and dem all laugh. De way dem laughing it mek meh laugh too and soon I not shame no more and den I laughing too. After dat dem laugh wen I suh, "I have to draw baff fer de Massa."

Dem suh, "Wash him cocky furst and mek it hard quick dis way it not tek yuh all night and yuh have time fer other business."

Chapter 42

One By One By One

De night before de morning dat change ev'ting, Fields him rut meh like before. I goes to sleep jis't like I be doin' all de time, in him arms and wen mornin' come, nuffin' dat be de same de night we went to sleep ever be de same again.

De rider him come riding hard into de yard. Him calling fer Massa Fields 'fore him off him horse. Him shouting, "Get the Massa, get the Massa." Massa him be eating him brekfast and wen him hear de rider shouting, him rush to way de man shouting. De man soon as him see de Massa him suh, "A word in private with you, sir."

Massa him walk wid de man into him smoking room and no sooner dan de door close, dan I hears de Massa's voice. Him shout, "No! No! No! Not my Lilly."

Wen him suh, 'Not my Lilly!' muh heart it stop. Massa him be preparing to go Connecticut to bring she home and now him screaming, "Not my Lilly! Not my Lilly!"

I wants to run in way him be and ask wat be wrong wid muh pickney but only him and meh know'd dat Lilly be muh pickney. So I nots be able to go and ask him wat wrong. I wait 'till de man leave. De minute de man leave, Massa him come stumbling out and him suh, "Mistress Lilly! Mistress Lilly." Him stop and him crying.

I runs to where him leaning on de sofa and I suh, "Wat be wrong wid she? Wat wrong wid Mistress Lilly."

Him look at meh and him suh, "There was a coach accident three days ago. She was eloping to marry. The horse pulling the coach with her, Sukey, and Eme, got startled. He bolted, unhinging the coach and it went into a ravine. Sukey and Eme were thrown. They are dead. Lilly somehow managed to stay in the coach, but it flipped over many times. The driver, coward that he was, had tried to stop the bolting horse but realizing that he couldn't, he jumped just before the coach went over and into the ravine.

"Unable to get down into the ravine, he made his way back. They had not traveled far from where they'd rendezvous, and was able to get word back to that dastardly rag of a man she was running away to elope with. He sent aid to get the coach and my Lilly out the ravine and a rider to notify me. That was him that brought the news."

I suh, "Mistress Lilly, is she…?" I nots be able to get muh mouth to suh de words dat muh heart nots be able to even tink.

Him suh, "She is holding on. I must go now. Go get O'Brien."

I runs to de cookhouse and I suh, "Anakey, go get O'Brien. Massa need fer him to come now. Mistress Lilly she hurt something awful."

Anakey she tek off running and all de while she running, she calling, "O'Brien, O'Brien, Massa him need you come right now. Come right now!" O'Brien and Anakey come back together. O'Brien him come to Massa Fields and Anakey she stop in de cookhouse.

Massa him suh to O'Brien, "I must leave for Georgia at once. Get them to saddle my horse."

Dem get him horse ready so fast it like de horse it be always ready and waiting fer him to have to go someplace in a hurry. Fields him nots suh nuffin' else to meh, him jis't get on him horse and ride away. Dem days and night leading to weeks be de longest days and nights I ever know'd. I sleep little but I do de little sleep in muh house wid de other pickney. I wants to tell dem dat Mistress Lilly be dem sister, but I know'ds dat if I do, Massa him never goin' fergive meh and him most likely send me from 'round him place so I suhs nuffin' and I jis't prays in muh heart dat she not be hurt bad.

One morning jis't as de sun crack de sky and turn into early morning, I hears de sound of wheels and horses. De sound it get closer and closer and den it stop. It be de Fields. Him come back by coach. I nots wait fer him to call fer meh. I leave de pickney and I runs to de yard way de wagon be. O'Brien and Anakey dem already thar and Massa him gots Lilly in him arms. Her tek her arms and her put dem round him neck. It like it tek all she strenf to do dat. Him head up de steps leading to de big front porch and I watch fer a minute as him mek it to de big tall carved pole holding up de house. Him turn him body jis't a little bit and de light from de lantern dats still light shine on him and muh pickney in him arms and de light, it fall on her face and she look de whitest I be ever see she look: she look dead. I wants to run up de porch 'fore him and tek muh pickney from him arms. I wants to suh, "Give me muh pickney." But muh head it suh, 'But she him pickney too.' Muh heart it settle.

Him turn back and him go through de door dat O'Brien holding open. Him start to climb de long, long, winding steps dat goin' tek him to she room and each step him put him foot on, muh heart it beat double. Muh heart it frighten dat him goin' mek a mis-step wid muh pickney and dem goin' both fall. I 'fraid 'cause she not really moving in him arms. Massa him mek it all de way to de top and him turn and him suh, "Milkweed, come. Come give me a hand wid Mistress Lilly." I not wait fer him to suh a next word, I starts to turn up de steps. I wants to see wat wrong wid muh pickney.

I opens de door fer him and him put she on the bed. I looks at muh Lilly and she not be de same. Her skin it be looking like I can see to the bone, and I can see de color be gone from she. She lips dem be thin little lines on she face and she not mek a sound. Fields him bend him knee by de side of the bed and him suh, "She is hurt very badly. They don't think she's going to make it, Milkweed." Him start to cry and him suh through him crying, "She has to make it. She has to."

Den him cry and him crying so hard I feel de water come to muh eyes, and 'fore I know'd it I crying and I mix-up 'cause I tinks I crying 'cause she mighty sick and den I tinks I is crying 'cause him crying so bad. Den muh head it suh, 'It not matter why yuh tink yuh cry 'cause she be yuh pickney and him be she faddah so dat mek it alright; she both yuh all pickney.'

De doctor him come up de stairs. Him travel back wid Fields and Lilly. Him come in de rooms and him suh to Fields, "You must make her comfortable. Pull the drapes and have them make a fire in the hearth for her. When she stirs, I will be here to give her some medicine and then, later I will bleed her again. Know, Master Fields that I will do everything I can for her."

Fields him nots suh nuffin'; him get up from him knees and him sit in a chair. I nots know'ds wat to do so I mek a fire in de hurf and I draws de drapes to mek de room dark. De doctor him tek a seat near Lilly. I not sit down 'cause de doctor nots know'ds dat she be muh pickney. I waits and waits fer Fields to tell me wat to do. Den him notice dat I be jis't standing by she bed and him suh, "Sit. Wait. Be here so that you may go and get watever the doctor says to bring."

I nots suh nuffin'. I jis't grateful to be in de same room where she be. Day it go on and de sun is shift and she not mek a sound. Fields him suh, "She's so quiet. Shouldn't she be making some kind of sound?"

De doctor him suh, "I'm given her a strong elixir, it will be quite a while 'fore she stirs. Why don't you get something to eat? When she stirs, I'll send the nigger here to get you sir."

Fields him turn to meh and him suh, "Go fetch me something to eat and bring the doctor something as well. Also have Anakey to come and stay here while you fix the food."

I runs and gets Anakey and only wen she be up de stairs, I starts to gets de food fer him. I brings him de food and after him tek a sip of de coffee and a bit of de biscuit and ham, him stop from eating and him start to walk back and forth. Him want she to wake up, but she not waking up.

Lilly she stay like dat fer a fortnight and she not getting stronger, den de doctor him suh, "Master Fields, I'm afraid to say that your young daughter has taken a turn for the worse. There's nothing more I can do, sir. She has a day maybe two before she…" Him not finish wat him be getting ready to suh, him jis' look at Fields and bend him head. I stay waiting on Fields to shout at de doctor to mek she live, but him nots, him tank de doctor and him suh, "Thank you for all you've done for my dear sweet Lilly. Stay. Keep her comfortable. Don't let suffering be part of her leaving. If my child must leave me, then let her do so without further pain."

De doctor him suh, "She isn't feeling any pain, none at all."

Fields him nots looks at meh. Him jis' sits and him hold she hand. She a lot smaller dan wen she furst come back and him climb de stairs wid she in him hands. She jis' be a face dat got brownish red curly hair spread all over the pillow. Fields him suh to she, "You didn't have to run away, Lilly I would have allowed you to marry if that's what you wanted. You could have gone to the colonies. I would have missed you, but I would've let you go."

Lilly groaned, de furst sounds since him bring she back. It twan't much of a sound but I hears it and him hears it and him suh, "I love you, Lilly." And den him suh, "I've loved you from the first day I saw you and, Lilly, my precious sweet child, I love your mother very much. I love her, Lilly. I love her for giving me such a beautiful daughter."

She moan again and him suh, "Sleep my beautiful angel, I love you."

She moan one more time. Him kiss she cheek and him crying and him suh, "It's Ok my precious, sleep."

Her tek deep breff and it come out she mouth like she rush it out and den she jis' be quiet. Her not mek one more sound and I know'd dat muh Lilly dun tek she last breff. Muh Lilly dead right 'fore muh eyes. De doctor him come and him put a mirror to she nose. It not get cloudy. Him suh to Fields, "I'm so sorry, Sir. She's…" And jis' like 'fore wen him not be able to tell Fields wat him have to suh, him jis' let wat him be getting ready to suh hang in de air. It wait thar fer Fields to tek it down. Him not touch it. Him not have to touch it. Him know'd same way I know'd dat him be fixing to suh dat Lilly be dead. De doctor him walk out de room. Him left me and Fields wid Lilly.

I start to cry and I screams and I wants to beg she to live again, but I know'ds dat she be gone and I know'd dat Fields him let me stay so dat I can see muh pickney in she last days. Muh heart it sad, but it glad dat him let meh be thar wid she as she muddah and she not go way to she grave widout she muddah seeing she go. I waits fer Fields to scream and cry, but him nots. Him jis't sits holding she hand and him suh, "She wanted to sail with him to the colonies. She wanted to go to some wretched island in the West Indies called Barbados; some infernal place with naked savages running around eating each other. For that, life in the colonies and a sugar plantation that he promised my sweet innocent angel daughter, my child is dead. Damn him. Damn him and his entire family. Damn them, their sugar plantation, and damn their home; Farley Hill."

Fields him start to cry after him suh dat and den him suh, "He was older than me, you know. This Mr. Howell, he seduced my child and was goin' to steal her just the way he and his group do niggers. My child wasn't a nigger."

When Fields suh dat I look at him and I want to 'mind him dat Lilly, even now, 'though she dead, be a nigger. It be him and him wife dat mek she and all dem friends tink dat she be white, but she be nigger. She be nigger dat 'cause of who him be get to pass. Passing be de most dangerous ting nigger can do. But I not tell him nuffin', I let him go on. Him need to go on to get out how him feel 'bout dis man dat dun 'cause we Lilly to be way she be: dead.

"He killed my Lilly." Fields him crying and crying now and him turn to meh and him suh, "Come, sit with me. Sit." I go. Him suh, "We've lost a second daughter."

I reach and I touch muh pickney. It be de furst time I touch she since Mistress Olivia suh fer me to give she muh milk, and now dat I touching she again, she not know'ds dat I touching she. She dead and she not know'ds dat I be she muddah. I tek muh hand and I touch she face. I look at muh pickney and I wants to find someting on she dat show I is she muddah, and den I look at de hand I holding and I see it. Muh pickney got de same shape hand I gots. Her fingers dem long and dem point at de tip same way mine point, but it not matter now. She dead and I nots be able to tell de other pickney dat dem sister dead. Dat mek muh heart burn meh more. I cry fer dem dat not know'd dat she be dem sister.

Chapter 43

De Lawd Him Know'd Muh Pain

Jis't like wid Mistress Olivia, him friends dem come. De place busy wid all de coming and goin'. Him bury Lilly next to Mistress Olivia and dis time him let ev'rybody on de plantation come. I stands wid meh pickney and I cry. Dem tink I crying 'cause she be de Mistress of de plantation, but I crying 'cause dem nots know'd dat it be dem sister dat dead. After dem dun bury she, him friends dem stay and dem eat and drink. I look and I tinking in muh head, 'How dem be able to eat food and drink, him pickney dead, him heart broke, him crying, crying, crying, none of dem not feeling de pain dat him in. How dem can eat food?'

Fields him heart bruk and him sorry and sad all de time him nots call fer meh to mek him baff. Him nots do nuffin' but go day after day to where dey bury she and talk to she. Dis go on fer so long it be de way dat we come 'pect 'till one morning Anakey suh, "Him suh fer yuh to bring him brekfast in him room."

I tek him de brekfast up to him chambers and I find him in him bed. Him suh, "Milkweed, I'm sorry. I'm sorry that our daughter died not knowing the truth. She should have known that you, not Olivia was her mother."

Wen him dun talk, him look at meh and him be crying. I start to cry too and I suh, "But I know'd. In muh heart, she never stop from bein' muh pickney. She be muh pickney wen she be living and she still muh pickney now dat she dead. She always gine be muh pickney."

Him nots eat de brekfast. Him sip at de coffee and den him suh, "After supper come and draw my bath."

After supper I go and I fix him baff. I do wat I always do fer him and wen him dun, him suh, "Stay." Dat be it, "Stay." I wash like I do wen I be wid him and I gets in de bed. Him nots rut meh. Him hold meh and I go to sleep jis't like I dun so many other nights. It be in de fore day morning dat him rut meh. Him rut meh slow and him tek him time and wen him 'lease himself, him suh, "She's going to be our most beautiful child yet. You'll see. Our Rebeccah is going to be beautiful."

I suh, "Fields, I too old to mek pickney. I dun mek ten already."

Him suh, "Then make number eleven."

Jis't like him suh, I mek pickney number eleven. She be de most beautiful pickney we ever mek. She be Seminole, African, and white. She be brown like meh, long like Poppa wid him nose dat always look like it be smelling de road up ahead, and she got Fields' curly hair but her hair it twan't brownish-red, it be black like mine.

Fields him look at de pickney and him suh, "I told you we were going' to make our most beautiful child yet. Rebeccah Pearl Fields; that's her name." I looks at him and I smile. My furst smile since muh Lilly dead. Him smile back too and him suh, "Thank you for all my children."

Chapter 44

Different and Separate

After de last pickney born, him and muh life it different and separate yet it be de same life. In muh heart him be muh man, but in muh head I know'd dat him be de same man dat do to meh all dem cruel and hurtful tings. From time to time, muh head it 'member and it beg me not to ferget. Den it suh to meh, 'Why Haroldetta not know'd numbers and letters? Why yuh not tek time to show she how to mek de letter in de flour same way yuh momma show you?' I not have answer fer muhself. I tinks I 'fraid dat she not be able to keep dis secret and she might mek it be know'd dat she know'ds she numbers and letters. I not want de same wat happen to Tiny and dem to happen so I not teach Haroldetta nuffin'. She be all I have left from Harold Joe and I not wants to lose she. I wants muh Haroldetta more dan I tinks she need letters and numbers. So I nots let her know'd dat I know'd muh letters or muh numbers.

One night after him dun rut meh and 'fore I cans falls 'sleep, him suh, "Tomorrow after breakfast, there's something I have to show you."

"Wat it be, Fields?"

I waits fer him to suh wat it be but all him suh be, "Tomorrow. Now go to sleep, Pearl."

Him pull meh to him as be custom by now and him sleep. I fall sleep soon after him, but not 'fore I mek muh brain tink on Haroldetta, Eve, Lavinia, Poole, and muh Rebeccah. She be calls Beccah and she be walking now and pickin' a word here and there. Him git she to suh, "Dada." Dat mek him smile. Dem other pickney all be him own, but him not let dem call him 'dada' only Beccah get to do dat. I glad fer dat, but I be sorry same time.

Soon as him dun eat him brekfast, him suh, "Come. I want to show you something and bring the children. All of them."

I hurry out to de yard and I see muh Haroldetta. She be 'most a woman now. I suh, "Get Eve, Lavinia, Poole, and Beccah and come." Sara look at Fields and I know'd she see him as de Massa and she frighten. I suh, "Go bring 'em and come." Dem come and like de soldiers leading way de niggers to freedom, Fields him walk infront of we. Him walk far over to a place on him plantation dat it look like we never gine get to way it be him tekking we, den him stop and him suh, "Pearl, for you."

I looks and muh heart it jump. Right 'fore muh eyes be a house. Him suh, "It's yours. Your very own house. It's time you had something that was just yours; never having belonged to anyone else before."

I turns and I looks at Fields. Him have a big smile on him face. I starts to smile too. It be hard nots to smile wen I be looking at a house bigger dan O'Brien's old house but not as big as him own. Him suh, "Come, let's go inside."

We go in and it feel like I walks into some place dat I have no rights to be in. I look at Fields and I wants to ask him if him sure dat dis house be fer meh and muh pickney. I nots get time to suh nuffin' 'fore him suh, "Now all of you go on, look at the house then go on out back and look. There's a place for planting all that you want."

De pickney dem do jis't as him suh and dem go out to where dem see de land. De minute dem be outside, him step closer to meh and him tek meh in him arms and him suh, "Pearl, thank you for choosing to stay. Thank you for all my children and, Pearl, I know it's hard on you that our Lilly is gone. I miss her too, every day, but I'm so glad we have all these other children. I love them Pearl, each and every one of them. I know you don't think I love her, but I love your Sara too. I've learned. You have forgiven me all that I've done to you, and you've learned to love me. I learned to love her."

Him lift my face to look in muh eyes and him suh, "I know that you love me, Pearl. You may not say it but I know that you do. You do love me, don't you, Pearl?"

Him standing thar looking in muh eyes and him eyes dem begging me to suh I love him. I look at Fields and though I nots be able to get muh mouth to suh it, I close muh eyes and I nod. I nod muh truth to him. I not have to open muh eyes wen I feel him breaving on muh face. I wait 'cause I know'ds him goin' kiss meh. Him kiss meh. Not like wen we in him bed, but him kiss meh soft and him suh, "I promise you, Pearl, whatever I can do for you and the children to make your life easier, I'll do because I've never loved anyone as I love you and them. I love you, Pearl Fields. I know I can't marry you, but if I could, I would and you would be Mrs. Pearl Fields: not Milkweed. Pearl Fields, the wife of Everett Michael Poole Fields. I wish I could."

Him stop talking and den him tek muh hands and him suh, "If you could, Pearl, if we could, would you be my wife?"

I looks at him and I suh, "Fields, yuh know'ds dat I nots ever be no white mans wife."

"Yes you can. You can be my wife. If you say you would be my wife, I'll marry you right here and now on this spot. In the eyes of God, I'll promise to be your husband and treat you right. I'll treat you as my wife even if it's only between you and me. Say you'll marry me, Pearl, and all that I have: all of it, this plantation, these crops, these houses, I'll give it to you. I promise you. Say you will."

I looks at him and I nots know'd wat mek me suh it, but I suh, "Yes, Fields, I be yer wife, but not 'cause yuh suh yuh gine give meh wat be yourn."

Him grab me tight and him suh, "God, Pearl here has said she'll be my wife so in your presence I'm making her my wife, and in your presence, Lord, I'm doing as the good book says and I'm bestowing to her all that is mine." Him suh dat and dem him suh, "Pearl, in the presence of God do you promise to be my wife?"

I suh, "Yes."

Him suh, "And, God, in your presence I promise to be Pearl's husband. I promise more than Pearl: I have more. So I promise to take care of her, love and cherish her, in sickness and in health, and to bestow to her all my worldly goods. So, God, Pearl and I are now in your presence, husband and wife. I'm going to kiss my wife, God, in your presence."

Fields him bend him head and him kiss meh. I kiss him back and him suh, "Now you are my wife. Now you are Pearl Fields and when we go back to the house I'll bestow all my worldly goods to you."

I suh, "Bestow, wat dat mean, Fields?"

"It means that if anything happens to me, you own this plantation and all that is mine."

I laugh and I suh, "Nigger, dat be your slave, own plantation? Dat be never happen."

"I'll make it happen. I'll write it and I'll give it to you to store in a special place that only you will know where it be."

I not know'd wat to suh so I jis't smile. Him smile and him suh, "Today we should celebrate and tomorrow I'll do all the bestowing I just talked about."

"I suh, "We nots be able to do dat. It not like it we be married. It jis't 'tween meh and yuh. I nots be able to tell nobody and you nots be able to tell nobody. It jis't be meh and yuh dat know'ds, dats all."

"You are wrong. Three of us know: God, me, and you. So there'll be a celebration and it will be today. Today is Sunday, no one is working.

I'll tell O'Brien to see to it that there's plenty of liquor and extra everything for everyone. Then I'll have music and laughter and though I won't say what all the merriment is for, we'll know. You and I will know that today is our wedding day. Get the children and come."

I called de pickney and we all walk back to de yard. No sooner dan we in de yard, dan Fields call fer O'Brien and 'fore yuh can suh jump, him had de place alive and ev'ryone mekking merry all over de place. Anakey she suh to meh, "Wat yuh give him dat got him like dat?"

"Wat yuh talking 'bout Anakey? I not gives him nuffin'."

"Him like get new idea 'bout living or loving or like him had yer fronts fer de furst time. I nots know'd wat yuh give him or wat yuh do to him, but watever it be I be glads 'cause him feeding and giving nigger liquor like no white mans ever dun. It like a wedding widout bride and groom."

Wen Anakey suh dat, she looks at meh and I looks quick at de ground and den she suh, "Him giving yuh wedding celebration. Him mekking wedding feast fer yuh. Dat why him happy like dat. In him heart, him giving yuh wedding feast to go wid de big ole' house him had dem build fer yuh. I be wanting to tell yuh 'bout de house but O'Brien him suh dat Massa not wants fer yuh to know'd 'till it be dun and all de tings be in it. It be a beautiful house. I never know'd a nigger woman to have house like dat. Him love yuh someting fierce and now him giving yuh wedding feast."

I not suh nuffin' and Anakey she suh, "Yuh nots have to suh nuffin', but since I tink dat it be yuh wedding feast, I suh yuh should mek yerself look like de bride him mekking tink yuh is."

"I not have no wedding dress."

Wen I suh dat, Anakey she smile and she suh, "So it be yuh wedding day. I be happy fer yuh. It be muh secret 'till dem put me in de dirt. I gots a fancy dress dat O'Brien had dem send fer meh from him place call Ireland. We be de same, come and put it on. Den yuh be in yer bride dress."

Anakey let me put she dress on, and she put on a pretty one too and wen we come from she house, Fields and O'Brien dem be standing on him porch and wen Fields see meh, him smile big and him step down from de porch and him walk to meh. 'fore him can gets to meh, Anakey she walk 'way. Him gets next to meh and him suh, "Pearl, you look beautiful. Just as a bride should be. Did you tell Anakey?"

"Anakey she suh dat all de merriment like it be fer a wedding and den she suh dat yuh giving me wedding feast. I nots suh nuffin' and she suh dat I should look like de bride. I suh dat I not have no wedding dress and she suh dat O'Brien him bring she dress from Ireland and so she let me have it fer today."

"Then let's celebrate our wedding." Fields him walk back to where all de merriment be and him suh, "Everyone eat and drink: today is a good day for all of us here at Fields plantation. I've been sad a long time since I lost young Mistress Lilly. Today though I'm a happier man and I'm sharing my happiness with all of you. So eat, drink, and be happy because I am."

De merriment went on 'till de sun started to go down and den it be over. Ev'ryone go back to dem cabins and Sara she tek de pickney to O'Brien's house. Me and Fields we go to de big house. Dat nite to muh surprise, Fields him fix de baff and him suh, "You get in. Let me wash you. You are my bride, my wife. Let me do this for you, Pearl."

Him tek muh clothes off and him wash meh like I be a pickney and den him dry meh and him suh, "Wash my back and then you get in the bed and wait for me. I'll be right there."

Him hurry and wash and den him get in de bed wid meh and him suh, "Pearl Fields, my wife. I love you with all my whole heart. I don't remember when I didn't love you; I don't."

Den him kiss meh. Him rut meh and wen him 'lease himself, him suh, "Do you think we have one more child in us? I know you've made a lot of children for me, but you've never made one as my wife. Do you think we have another daughter in us, one as beautiful as you? We'll call her after my mother Charlotte Annabelle. What do you say, Pearl? One more on this our wedding night?"

Fields him never talk 'bout pickney 'till him feel in him bones dat him gine mek a pickney so I nots suh nuffin'. I jis't close muh eyes and fix muh mind fer de pickney dat I know'd him jis't put in muh belly. I not know'd wen night turn to morning, but by de time I open muh eyes, it be morning.

Sometime after and I nots know'd how long it be, but muh red river it nots flow and soon after dat, muh belly it start to rise and jis't like him suh, I wid pickney again. I be still living in O'Brien's house and one day him suh, "The house I built for you, why aren't you living in it? Don't you like it? Is there something else you need in it?

I suh, "No I likes it mighty fine."

"Then move into it before Charlotte is born. Let her be born in your new house."

Me and de pickney move in de house and him smile each time him see meh. Wen de pickney born, it be a gal piccaninny jis't like him suh and, jis't like him suh, it be like I climb in muh belly and den come back out as muh pickney: I born muhself. Him call she Charlotte Annabelle Fields. I 'member wat Neala suh 'bout him muddah and de hate she have fer nigger and I tink wat him muddah be tink to know'd dat him mek pickney wid nigger womans and call him de pickney after she name. I smile to muhself 'cause I know'd dat if Neala be 'round she be suh dat Mistress Charlotte be beg, fight and promise de devil to let she outta hell so she can go kilt him and drag him back to hell wid she.

Him see de smile on muh face and him smile. I know'ds that him tink dat muh smile got someting to do wid de pickney be looking like meh. I let him stay in him tinking. Thar be no sense in letting him know'd wat muh heart be tinking.

Wid de smile still on him face him suh, "All our children are beautiful and special but none are like her. She was born to my wife. I love you so much, Pearl, you'll never really know but I think somehow you do and some day, long after I'm gone, you'll find out how much."

I smile 'gain. Dis time dis smile be 'cause him looking at meh wid so much love dat I feel it deep in muh bones. I want to tell him dat I love him too but I still nots be able to mek muh mouth suh dat.

Chapter 45

Sara's Benjamin

Time it start to move differently. De pickney dem growing and changing and soon Charlotte she walking and talking, and it hard to believe dat she be pickney a few days ago. Time though it change quicker fer Sara de furst time wen she see Benjamin. She see him de day O'Brien bring him on de plantation to share crop, and it be like light go on in she. Sara she smiling and she wuking harder dan she wuk 'fore in de cookhouse. It like she hurrying time so dat she can gets to be in de yard wen him come through.

Benjamin him see muh Sara too and soon dem be courting. It nots tek too long 'fore she suh dat him wants to jump de broom wid she. One night wen I be in bed wid Fields, I suh, "De nigger Benjamin him wants muh Sara to be wife to him."

Fields him suh, "He's a hard-working nigger and if he loves her half as much as I love you then let them be. Let them be married."

I let dem. Muh Sara be seventeen and Benjamin be twenty-three. Fields him give muh Sara a fine wedding day. No nigger wuk dat Sunday. Wen wedding over, Fields him suh, "Sara, you and Benjamin can move to O'Brien's old house."

Sara she smile and she tanks him. I smile at muh Sara and I know'ds dat Harold Joe him be happy to see him pickney wid she jump de broom wid man. I be happy fer muh Haroldetta and I tinks 'gain on Neela and I be glad dat she send muh Haroldetta bak to meh 'cause now she get a chance to know'd life wid de love of a man jis't like she poppa.

Fields rutting me and him waiting fer meh to tell him dat one more pickney on de way, but dat news him be waiting on it never be coming and ev'r time muh red river run, him trying to figga why no pickney not coming.

One night him suh, "Shouldn't you be having another child by now? What's different now?"

I suh, "I not know'd. I be tinking dat dis not be time fer meh to mek more pickney. Wen de time be right, I be mek pickney."

Him look at meh and him look like him be tinking, but I nots suh nuffin' 'bout de tea. Dat be womans' business. We rut and hard and I not worry 'bout no pickney so de rutting it be better and better and soon him nots ask 'bout no more pickney. Wid muh Sara married, de only pickney I want in muh arms be de one dat she and Benjamin gine mek so wen it be jis't meh in de cookhouse, I brews de tea dat Neala show'd me to mek so dat I not mek no more pickney and I drinks it.

I keeps waiting fer news from muh Sara dat she and Benjamin mekking piccaninny, but dem not have luck wid mekking pickney. Soon as muh Sara get dem in she belly, dem fall out. She stop telling me wen she wid pickney. Soon I stops asking Sara 'bout de pickney, 'cause she be sad 'cause she want to give she husband de pickney dat him always talking 'bout.

It be five years 'fore she come in de cookhouse and she smiling. She suh, "Me and Benjamin we mekking pickney, and dis one it be staying in. It be four moons dat dun pass already, Momma. I gine get to keep dis pickney. Tank yuh, Lawd." She start to cry and we, meh and Anakey, we start to cry too and den we stop cry and gets mighty happy. Muh Sara gine be a muddah.

Benjamin him gets Anakey de night de birfing start. Dem not come get me 'cause dem know'ds dat I wid Fields most nights, and though dem be free nigger, dem still know'ds dat nigger business not reason enough to pound on de door of de Massa's big house. So dem not come fer meh. Dem waits 'till I come to mek him brekfast and wen I not see Anakey, dem suh, "Yuh Sara, she pickney coming, and Anakey be wid she 'fore day break."

I runs to muh Haroldetta. Soon as I gets near O'Brien's house, I can hear she screaming. I runs in and I see Anakey and her cover in blood. She see meh and she suh, "De foots coming out furst. Meh try to get dem back in but it be a big pickney.

I suh, "I gine tell Fields dat muh Sara she need de doctor to come."

Anakey she suh, "She be nigger. White mans doctor dem not come to help nigger woman birf no pickney."

"Fields gine mek him." I runs and I tells Fields dat muh Sara in trouble wid she pickney and she need a doctor. Jis't as I suh, him tell dem to go get de doctor. Him suh, "Tell him that Massa Fields needs him to come out right away. If he asks what for, tell him that I'm in need of him and for him to hurry."

I runs back to my Haroldetta and she trying to birf de pickney while we wait fer de doctor to come, but all dat coming out is blood and more blood, no pickney.

Wen de doctor come him fuss and cuss 'cause it be a nigger dat mekking de pickney and not a white womans like him be tinking. Fields him talks to him and him come in de house to help she. Him treat muh Haroldetta like she be a cow or horse. Him push him hand jis't so in way in de pickney foots dem be sticking out, and him suh, "Got to turn this little nigger 'round or it'll be dead just where it is."

I begs him to please help muh Haroldetta and nots let she pickney dead. Him nots suh nuffin' to meh, him jis't push him hand higher and muh Haroldetta she bawling fer him to jis't let she dead.

Him suh, "If it's dead you want to be, you can go on ahead, but you're going to leave a living nigger behind. No sense in Fields losing two of you. Now you do what I say, nigger, and leave all this talk about the dead 'till I'm done then you can go on and die. I don't care."

Him push him hand some more and him suh, "I've turned the little nigger. She's too weak to help. Come here and push on her belly. Right here." I do wat him suh and Haroldetta she bawl and bawl fer meh to stop. I stop pushing on she belly and him suh, "Nigger, if you do that, the little pickney it going die where it is in she. Now press down, nigger!"

I press down and de pickney it start to come out. Haroldetta like she feel it moving out and she trying to help, but she weak. Him suh fer meh to press down again and hard. I do wat him suh and de pickney it come out. Him suh, "This is one big nigger pickney." Him give me de pickney and him wipe him hands and suh, "I did what Fields asked me to do." And jis't like dat, him left.

I wants to run 'hind him and begs him to help muh pickney, but him left and de way him walk out de house I know'ds dat him not coming back. Him nots care if she dead. I care but I nots know'ds wat to do. She start to bawl again. She suh, "Momma! Momma! Someting else in meh." She sit up in de bed and she push and Lawd have mercy, another pickney it come out. Anakey she screaming, and Haroldetta, after she push out de pickney, she gone quiet and I looking at de two pickney. De boy him big, big like him near two or three months and de next pickney, a gal, she so small she look like him play ting. But she not a play ting. She crying and she crying hard.

Haroldetta, she suh, "Momma, it be two pickney I mek. Let meh see 'em."

I picks dem up and I let she look at dem. She suh, "Tell Benjamin to call de boy Benjamin Harold and to call de little gal Pearl Etta Mae."

She not suh nuffin' else. She jis't stay looking at dem. Den she suh, "Tek dem, Momma. I be mighty tired."

Anakey, who be cleaning she up, suh, "Milkweed, come. Look." I puts de pickney back on de bed and wents to way Anakey be at de foot of de bed. I looks and as I looks Anakey suh, "Milkweed, she like she pissing blood. It coming and coming. I dun help birf many a pickney and yuh dun birf 'bout a dozen of dem yuhself; yer eva see dis 'fore now?"

"No." Muh heart it sink so far I nots know'd way it gone. I fear fer muh Haroldetta. Why she bleeding like dis? I nots know'ds wat to do fer she. I suh to Anakey, "I gine beg Fields to see if him can mek de doctor come back and help she."

"Him jis't left. Dat doctor hate niggers."

I mek muh voice soft so dat Haroldetta nots hear meh and I suh to Anakey, "But she gine dead if him nots come back and help she."

"And yuh tink yuh telling him dat gine mek it matter to him?"

I starts to cry and I suh, "But she muh pickney. She muh pickney, Anakey. I gots to go and beg him fer she life."

"Den yuh beg she to live fer yuh and dem pickney 'fore yuh beg him. She gots to wants to live 'fore him can mek she. Him can do all de doctoring him know'ds, but if in she nots want to live bad enough, it in nots gine matter none, Milkweed!"

I try to get muh head to tink wat to suh to muh pickney dat gine mek she want to live, I look at de two pickney on de bed and den muh eyes dem 'most drop out muh head. De door it open and it be Fields and de doctor.

Fields him suh, "He said that your Sara is doing poorly and would most likely not …" Him stop from talking. Him tek a deep breff and him suh, "It took some convincing and I'm ashamed to admit quite a bit of money to persuade the good doctor here to come back and do what he can to make her comfortable, same as he did for my Lilly."

De doctor him suh, "She's a nigger, Fields. She's not your daughter; she not the same as your Lilly, your Lilly was a white woman. This here is a nigger, Fields, a nigger."

Fields him suh through him teet, "Make her comfortable."

"I can't stop the bleeding."

"Then do what you can; but make her comfortable."

De doctor him open him bag and him tek out a bottle and him go to muh Haroldetta and jis't fore him give she wat be in de bottle to drink, him suh, "Take these little nigger pickney off the bed. Put them someplace else."

Anakey she go and she pick up de boy and I pick up de gal and we put dem in de same box we had fer de pickney. Wen we had de pickney off de bed, him mek Haroldetta hold up she head and him mek she drink wat be in de bottle. She drinks it and she moans and she whole body it shake. Him open him bag and him tek two white tings dat look like muh pearls and him grind dem and him suh, "Nigger, get me some water."

I goes and I gets de water and I brings it back to him. Him tek de grind up powder and him put it in de water den him suh, "Nigger, get her to drink as much of this as she can."

I goes to muh Haroldetta and I suh, "Open yuh mouth and drink dis." Haroldetta she open she mouth and she bring she lips to de cup much as she can, and she drinks a little bit and she not want it.

Him suh, "Nigger make her drink more. She needs to drink more of it. It isn't going work if she doesn't drink more."

I beg she and I beg she 'till she drinks it. Den him suh, "Other than these niggers here cleaning her up, Fields, there's nothing more I can do for her. She's lost a lot of blood and there isn't anything I can do to give it back to her."

Fields him suh, "Try something else. Give her something else, anything."

"Fields she's a nigger, a nigger, Fields. This is what's wrong with President Lincoln setting them free. White people like you caring if a nigger dies or not. Now, Fields, I've done as much as I'm going to do for a nigger, your nigger or anybody else's nigger. If Booth had been a just a few months earlier, you and I wouldn't be here now. You would just let the nigger bitch die and buy you another one the next day."

Wen him dun suh dat him look at Fields and him walk out. Fields him march out after him and I hears him and Fields shouting outside. Muh Haroldetta she sleeping and I look at she sleep and I looks at de bloodstain. It getting bigger and bigger. It covering de bed almost to de middle of she back. I put all I can pon she woman parts to soak up de blood but it keep coming out and soaking through ev'ting.

Anakey she suh, "I gine get she Benjamin. Him should come and see him wife. It nots look good fer she and him should come." Anakey she nots wait fer meh to suh nuffin', she go and come back wid Benjamin. I nots know'ds wat to suh to him, but him look at de bed wid all de blood and him start crying. Him go to muh Haroldetta and him suh, "I tanks yuh fer de pickney. I tanks yuh fer all dem years dat yuh try. I tanks yuh fer all de years yuh be muh wife. Yuh is a good wife, Sara, and I loves yuh."

Him hold she hand and him crying hard loud wid de snot coming out him nose. Watching Benjamin cry like dat it be breking muh heart jis't as much as I know'ds dat another gal pickney of mine gine dead. Three dead gal pickney. One I beg to dead and two of dem dead fer de mans dem love. Muh Lilly, she dead 'cause she love a man and she be willing to go to de colonies, a place call Barbados, a place Fields suh be in de West Indies. Now muh Haroldetta she 'bout ready to dead 'cause she love a man dat beg she and beg she fer five years to mek a pickney fer him.

Den I hears it. It be de same breaving dat muh Lilly mek jis't 'fore she dead. I quick step to muh Haroldetta and I suh, "Haroldetta, yuh nots be able to dead. I loves yuh. Yuh pickney dem gine need dem muddah. Live fer dem."

Benjamin him start begging she too, but she not hearing. She mek another breff dat sound like de one 'fore it, and den she mek two or three more like it, den, like she cans get no air at all, she tek a deep deep breff. I hear it in she troat like a soft tunder and den she let it go like it be too hard to tek and keep, and den she quiet. She nots try to get another breff and I know'ds dat I dun see another one of muh pickney dead.

I wants to do like Fields wen him watch Lilly dead and nots holler, but I nots be able to. I be de one dat birf she so I holler and I holler and I beg she to try and tek one more bref. I suh to she, "Haroldetta, I not want yuh to be wid de angel in heaven! Come back to yuh muddah! I nots wants to be here widout yuh!"

She nots move. I picks she up from de bed and I shake she. I throws muh head on she chest and I begs and begs she to come back, but she nots. Benjamin him holler too and I hears him and him wants she to come back too.

Him suh, "Sara, I sorry I begs yuh fer pickney!" Den him holler, "Lawd, tek way one of de two pickney and give meh muh bak muh Sara." Wen him suh dat, I feel sorry fer de pickney 'cause dem faddah beg de Lawd to tek one of dem.

I looks at Benjamin looking at Sara like him tink dat de Lawd gine change him mind 'bout tekking Sara from him, and He gine let she come back from heaven. Wen Sara nots start breaving, him suh, "Den, Lawd, if in yuh not gine give meh muh Sara back, den tek way de two pickney! Tek dem! Mek dem dead too jis't like dem muddah. I nots wants dem; I jis't want dem muddah. Tek dem! Tek dem way from here, Lawd!"

I looks at Benjamin and I sorry in so many parts of muh heart at wat him begging de Lawd to do. De part dat love she 'cause I be she muddah it brek. De part dat love she 'cause she be muh Harold Joe's pickney, it brek. De part dat love she 'cause she love meh back wid de love dat suh she be glad I be she muddah, it brek. But de part dat brek de hardest be de part dat, 'till muh Haroldetta fight to birf and now dead birfing she pickney, be de part dat tek meh from muddah to Nana.

I be de two pickney Nana and wid Benjamin suhing him want dem dead mek meh want dem to live. I suh, "Benjamin, it nots be right to beg de Lawd to tek way yuh pickney. Muh pickney she dead 'cause she wants fer yuh to have pickney, and now yuh begging de Lawd to tek way de same pickney dat fer all de yers yuh beg him to let she mek."

Benjamin him bawling now, and Fields him come back in de house and him suh, "Oh my God, Pearl, I'm so sorry. I'm so sorry for you; for all of you."

Him suh dat and him left meh wid muh grief. I looks at de door where him gone out and I look on de bed where muh Haroldetta be dead and I suh, "Haroldetta, Haroldetta, yuh gots to live. I nots want yuh to be dead."

Anakey she suh, "She be gone Milkweed. She be gone. I sorry fer yuh and dese pickney here."

I looks at Anakey and I nots know'd wat to suh. She not wait on meh to suh nuffin' she suh, "We gots to tek care of dese motherless pickney and we gots to fix yer Sara up and mek she ready."

"Anakey, I nots be able to do it 'cause I nots know'ds wat I be mekking she ready fer."

Benjamin him look at Sara and den him do like Fields, him walk out de door. Him nots even looks at him pickney in de box. Him jis't be gone and it be meh, Anakey, and de two motherless pickney wid dem dead muddah, and den I know's dat I nots have nobody to leave she fixing up to. I gots to do it muhself. I looks at muh dead pickney and I suh, "Anakey, yuh know'ds dat she not Fields' pickney. She be fer muh Harold Joe. Him dead and him not know'd dat him had a pickney coming and now she dead and I feels like a part of meh dead now and gone ferever. Harold Joe him gone and him only pickney she gone, de only ting dat be holding him to meh gone now."

Anakey she suh, "But dat not be true, Milkweed. Yuh got dem two pickney. So dat mean dat yuh got two more pieces of Harold Joe and two more pieces of yuh Haroldetta back. Yuh not lost dem. Yuh gots dem back."

I looks at Anakey, muh pickney on de bed, and den I looks at she two pickney in de box, and I know'ds dat wat Anakey suh be true. I not lost muh Haroldetta altogether: I got she pickney and so I gots a part of she. I suh, "Anakey, yuh be right. I gots to do muh best fer muh Haroldetta and den I gine do de best by she pickney."

Chapter 46

Saying Goodbye And Hello At Same Time

J is't like de wedding Fields give muh Haroldetta, him send she off to heaven de same way. Him had dem build she a fine box and den him had a preacher man to come in and suh a few words 'bout how she be a good daughter, woman, wife, and how she dead bringing she pickney into de world. Him had dem to sing songs and wen dem be done, him had lots of liquor and food. De only body dat not be thar be Benjamin. Since de nite dat him beg de Lawd to tek de pickney, him jis't be gone and nobody know'ds way him be.

Dat nite, Fields him come to de new house fer de furst time after I start to live in it. Him lie down wid meh and him hold meh. Him nots try to rut meh 'cause I jis't crying fer muh pickney. Him suh, "Pearl, that Benjamin is one sorry son-of-a-bitch. Nigger or white man, you don't go off and not stay around to see your wife buried. Pearl, if he comes back around here again, I'm going to shoot him or have him shot. She was his wife. He talked about wanting children all the years they were married; she dies giving him the children he was so sure he wanted, and he goes off and leaves you with the pain. If you sees him 'fore I do, tell him I'm going to shoot him."

I suh, "I nots want yuh to shoot him, him be pickney faddah. It not mek fer dem not to have muddah nor faddah."

"But he left his pickney."

"And yuh sell your'n; way dat different, Fields?" I nots know'ds way dat come from but it out 'fore I can tek it bak.

Fields him quiet. Him not moving him hand, him not doin' nuffin'. It like him dead. Den him tek deep breff and him suh real soft, "Pearl, you're right. I did worse than Benjamin. Benjamin just left his, but I sold mine away from their mother and broke her heart. I am worse than Benjamin, worse."

Him voice be almost whisper time him suh, "Worse."

Den him not suh nuffin' and I feel deep in muh belly dat I right and I wrong at de same time. I right fer telling him dat him no different dan

Benjamin, but I wrong fer suhing it de way I suh it, so I suh, "Fields, I not mean it. I not know'd wat mek me suh dat. I mighty sorry."

Fields him stay quiet and him nots suh nuffin' more. Den him lets me go, get up, and put him clothes on. Wen him have all him clothes on, him walk to de door and him suh, "You know what's odd; until now, this very minute, I never thought of our sons as gone. I knew, always knew where they were, so to me they weren't lost. Lilly was different. In my heart, Lilly was the only child I'd lost. I never really, fully thought about your loss, it just was; you know the way things were, but now that I look back at it, your loss has always been greater than mine. What's sad here? Throughout your whole life, well from the day I met you, I've been and am the only one that has caused you your greatest pain. I'm so very sorry, Milkweed."

I listen to wat him be suhing and inside muh heart be fulling up wid de hurt over how and wat him be suhing, and I feeling ever more sorry dat I suh wat I suh to him but den him suh, 'Milkweed.' Up to wen him suh 'Milkweed', muh heart be crying fer how him sound so hurt, but den him suh, 'Milkweed' and de hurt fer him it stop like plow blade hitting a big rock. Him suh, 'Milkweed,' and den him left. Fields not call meh Milkweed since 'fore Rebeccah born. Wid him calling me Milkweed mek me 'member dat white mans is always white mans.

I starts to cry fresh. Muh heart it suh, 'Yuh always gine be a nigger fer him, why yuh had to mek de hate yuh had fer him go way? Why yuh had to go and love him more dan Harold Joe?' I cry more 'cause no answer come. I cry fer muh mix-up head and fer all muh pickney, de dead ones and de ones dat same as dead to meh 'cause I not see dem now 'most twenty-five years. Wen muh head suh twenty-five years, muh heart it holler, 'Yuh must hate him fresh, hate him like de day him tie yuh like log and drag yuh 'hind him horse. Hate him fer all de love yuh nots get to give yer pickney and dem not get to give yuh.

'Hate him fer mekking fear come in yer heart so heavy dat yuh not let Haroldetta know'ds she numbers and letters. Hate him dat she dead and she not know'd how to mek she name on paper, flour, or dirt! Hate him dat yuh got so much fear in yuh heart dat yuh got all dese pickney fer him and not one of dem know'ds dat yuh, demn nigger muddah, know'ds letter, numbers and writing!

'Yuh must hate him fer calling yuh Pearl so much dat now him call yuh by de name yuh muddah give yuh it hurt yer feelings. Yuh is a nigger, Milkweed! A nigger and fer him, it nots matter how many nights him rut yuh, nor how many pickney yuh dun mek fer him, yuh is a nigger. Yuh is de mix-up nigger gal dat wen chance come to gets to know'ds wat freedom be like, yuh let yuh mix-up head be so in love wid a white mans dat yuh let chance to taste wat freedom be like pass yer lips. Now look at yuh and yuh mix-up self. Three dead gal pickney, one of dem not know'ds dat yuh be she muddah, one yuh beg dead, and de one dat a nigger man give up him life to mek wid yuh now dead and all yuh boy pickney dat born 'fore she yuh not set eyes on all dese past year.

'Stop crying 'cause him call yuh, 'Milkweed!' Milkweed be yuh name. Yuh Momma not name yuh no Pearl. Yuh is Milkweed! Now if yuh must cry, den cry fer yuh pickney. Dat who yuh must cry fer. Nots cry 'cause in yuh mix-up head de white mans dat yuh had all rights to stay hating but yuh gone and love call yuh by name yuh momma give yuh.'

I crys and I crys and muh heart it pain meh so deep. I hold muh chest and I tell muh pickney I sorry, but I nots be able to get muh heart to get back to de place where it use to hate him. I looks and looks deep in muh heart and I nots be able to find nuffin', but love fer Fields. I ball muhself up like newborn pickney and I cry. I nots know'ds wen I falls sleep.

De next morning I wakes and I still all mix-up in muh head. I feel a weight in muh chest dat suhs, 'Wat yuh suh to Fields be de wrong ting to suh to him.' I hurry 'cause I nots be able to wait to see him and suh to him dat I sorry fer wat I suh, and dat I know'ds it be Mistress Olivia dat mek him sell way muh pickney.

I go to mek him brekfast but Anakey she suh him not here. O'Brien not know'd way him be either. I waits all day fer him to come back but him nots. Him not come back by nighttime. I goes to muh house and I waits fer de sound of him horse or anyting dat would suh him come back, but no sounds come. De place quiet. I waits and waits and den it be morning. Dat same ting go on day after day. Wen night come, I waits and waits and wen morning come, I tired but I goes to de cookhouse and I mek him brekfast and I waits fer him to come through de door and suh him ready to eat. Him never come.

After dis go on fer near a week, Anakey she suh, "Milkweed, it mek no sense dat ev'ry morning we mek him brekfast and we nots know'd if him gine come eat it. Him gone and him not suh way him gone so thar in nuffin' dat we nots be able to do but wait."

"But way him gone, Anakey?"

"Him be gone wen de morning come and him not suh nuffin' to O'Brien so I not know'd way him gone."

"But why him gone?"

"I nots know'ds why him gone. Wat yuh suh to him. Yuh tink it be someting yuh suh dat mek him go 'way?"

I look at Anakey and I nots know'd wat to suh. I turn muh head and I start to cry. I not know'd wat I crying fer 'cause I miss muh Haroldetta, but wid Fields jis't gone it got me mix-up more. I wants him to be here so dat I can jis't miss muh Haroldetta and cry fer she all I wants. I busy wid she pickney, but Rebeccah she good wid dem. Benjamin him never come back. Him jis't gone from de day after Haroldetta dead and nobody know'ds way him be. Benjamin him gone too, but him gone feel different to de way Haroldetta gone. Haroldetta she gone 'cause him beg she to mek him pickney and she mek him de pickney and dead to bring dem here, den him jis't left dem. Muh heart it hurting meh someting awful. It hurting fer meh two grand-pickney and it hurting fer muh Haroldetta and now, it hurting 'cause I nots know'ds way Fields be. I gets to tinking dat be a lot of hurt fer a heart dat dun know'd more hurt dan anyting else.

One morning wen I waiting fer Fields to come, O'Brien him come in de cookhouse and him suh dat niggers wukking in de indigo field find Benjamin. Dem suh him throw'd him head 'gainst a pitchfork and him dead. O'Brien suh dat it look like him be dead from de day Sara be dead, and him gine have dem bury de rest of him in de woods way dem bury niggers. Him suh fer meh and Anakey not to come, 'cause him not want fer we to see wat dem find, but wen dem dun, him gine mark de spot so dat later I can come and suh goodbye to him. I start to cry fer Benjamin and Anakey she suh, "Milkweed, yuh jis't nots be able to be crying and crying fer ev'ting and ev'rybody. Yuh gine get sick and den wat de pickney gine do wid yuh trying to sit at death door. Dem dun lost dem muddah and faddah; wat more yuh want dem lost?"

"But him dem faddah."

"Him not tink 'bout dat wen him go off and kilt himself. Dat be wrong. De Lawd suh dat nobody, nigger nor white mans, is to kilt himself. Benjamin him send him soul to hell. Pray fer him soul but not cry fer him body. Him body dun gone; it be him soul dat need help. Dat be wat yuh be needing to do, Milkweed. Leave dem tears fer someting else."

I look at Anakey and I not know'ds wat to do. Now I know'ds dat Fields be de only one of dem dat gone dat gine come back, but 'cause I not know'd way him be or wen him gine come back, it mekking meh sick. I nots be able to eat or sleep and I jis't wants to hear him suh, "Pearl." Not 'Milkweed' like him suh de last time I seen him. I want's him here and I wants him to call meh Pearl; I miss him.

O'Brien him worry dat Fields gone so long. Anakey she worry 'cause O'Brien worry and I finds dat I worry, but I worry different to de way dem worry. I miss him as muh man, and I miss him as muh pickney faddah. I wants to know'ds dat him be alright.

Den one morning at de start of de fourth or fifth week, him come back. Him come through de door and him calling, "Pearl! Pearl! Where are you? Come out here!"

I runs to way him voice coming from and I wants to jis't jump in him arms and tell him dat I miss him and dat I never wants fer him to go 'way like dat ever 'gain, but him not coming to meh. Him standing by de door and him waiting fer meh to get him. I gets to way him be and I not sure if to suh Fields or Massa. Him looks at meh and him can see dat I nots know'd if to suh Fields or Massa and him suh, "Come outside. There's something I want you to see. Come now."

I follow him outside and muh heart it stop. Him suh, "All!" Like him suh magic word, I see dem coming from de side of de house. Dem looks different but I know'ds dem. Dem look like Poole, Eve, Lavinia, Lilly, and Rebeccah. I looks and muh heart it beat and muh head it suh, 'Run, run to dem.' But 'fore I can run to dem, dem start running. Muh boy pickney, all of dem: Isham, Juba, Zack, Tuck, and Willie.

Dem all in front muh eyes and dem know'ds dat I is dem muddah. I starts to cry and I falls to de ground. Isham him gets to meh and him picks meh up from de ground. Him crying. One by one, de rest of dem come to meh and dem crying. Isham holding meh in him arms, him be big man but him suh, "Momma!" I looks at him and de words dem nots come pass muh neck and muh mouth it nots open, so I nods at him dat I be him muddah.

Fields him suh, "It took a lot of doing, searching, and money but I had to find them all for you. I had to get your children, our children, our sons back. I've told them, Pearl, that I'm their father and that I'm the one that brought separation between you and them. I've even, over the time that it took me to travel back here told them about Lilly, Sara, Eve, Lavinia, Poole, Rebeccah, and Charlotte, but most importantly, Pearl, I've told them about you."

I looks at Fields and him smiling and him suh, "Come. All of you. Come." We walk to de house and him shout, "Anakey! Anakey! Get O'Brien. I've found my sons: all of them."

Anakey she runs out de cookhouse and she calling, "O'Brien! O'Brien! De Massa him come back and him brung all him boy pickney! Him gots dem all. O'Brien! O'Brien come! Now! Look! See!"

O'Brien him come and him jis't standing looking at Fields and all de nigger mans standing next to him and Fields him suh, "O'Brien, these are my other children. Outside there's a wagon get some of the niggers to unload the things. Take everything to Pearl's house. When you are done, come and let me know."

O'Brien him jis't look at all muh pickney and him look like him nots be able to believe him eyes. I smile. Not 'cause O'Brien nots be able to believe him eyes, but 'cause I nots be able to believe muh own eyes. De Lawd bless meh to see all muh pickney.

Fields turns to Anakey and him suh, "Get them some breakfast; feed them in the dining room."

Dem looks at him and dem nots know'ds wat to really do 'cause dem seeing him as a white mans and not dem faddah so dem nots know'ds wat to mek of the way him be.

I suh, "It be alright. Come! Eat!" I touch dem one at a time and muh heart it jis't so happy, but I still crying.

Fields him come to meh and him suh, "I brought them back Pearl. I went to Breckenshaw's plantation and he said that some of them had left after the President said that all niggers were free and some stayed. He said he didn't know where the others had gone, but he didn't think that they had gone far. He said he felt that those that had stayed behind might know where the others were."

"Did dem know'd, Fields?"

"They did. It was just a matter of time, almost four weeks, before I was able to find them all but I found them and brought them to you. Now, Pearl, can you forgive me for having sold our children away from you? Can you, Pearl?"

I looks at him and I looks at de big mans eating de food and I know'ds dat I dun fergive him. Him show him love fer meh by gine and finding muh pickney. I stretch muh hand out to him. Him tek it and I suh, "Yuh brung muh pickney to meh; I can fergive yuh fer selling dem way. I can fergive yuh, Fields. I can."

Chapter 47

Hope In Dry Roots

It tek 'bout three weeks fer tings to change. I steady watch muh boy pickney but dem not boys, dem be big mans and dem be mans dat grow'd widout a faddah or a muddah. Dem grow'd only as slave. Dem know'd wat dem Massa Breckenshaw tolt dem to do and him, tank de Lawd, not be cruel to dem 'cause him know'ds dat dey be Fields' pickney. But now dem be looking at meh and I can see dat dem gots questions 'bout meh and Fields.

It be Isham dat tek de scabbing off de cut. Him come to meh one morning and him suh, "Muddah, I gots to ask yuh a question. I nots want fer yuh feelings to be hurt, but I gots to know'd how yuh stills be here on him plantation. Wen freedom come, why yuh not tek de chance to go see wat it be like. I wents and Zack, and Tuck, but Willie him suh dat him gine stay wid Massa Breckenshaw. We begs him to come but him stay way him be. We wents but we find it hard. Zack and meh we comes back to Massa Breckenshaw, 'cause we know'ds wat living 'round him place be. Tuck him not come back. Him suh him tek dead over slave and fer a long time, we not know'd way him be. Massa Breckenshaw him not suh nuffin' 'bout us gine to see wat freedom be like, but him ask way Tuck be wen we gets back and we suh dat Tuck gone and him look worry, but him be white mans so we know'ds dat him not really worry 'bout Tuck. And dats be how come we be at Massa Breckenshaw's plantation all dis time."

I look at muh man pickney and I speak muh truth, "I had chance same as ev'rybody else but I stays here 'cause like Willie, I know'ds him ways and him suh dat if I goes, I gots to leave de other pickney and muh heart it suh fer meh to stay. It suh, 'stay wid de pickney and stay wid him. Yuh know'ds him and yuh know'ds him ways.'"

"Muddah, him ways be white mans way, dem not ways dat suit nigger. Him dun tek way all yuh boy pickney and wen chance fer freedom come fer yuh, him suh him gine tek way de rest of yuh pickney. Dat be white mans ways. Nuffin' good fer nigger not even pickney dat nigger mek good fer nigger."

"But him yuh faddah, Isham."

Isham him gets to almost foam like Fields and I sees Fields in him, but him not trying to be Fields, him foam and him suh, "If I never had set muh eyes on yuh ever, I know'ds in muh heart dat if choice be your'n, yuh never let sep'ration come 'tween us. So yes, yuh is muh muddah, but him never gine be muh faddah. Him always gine be de white mans dat solt meh wen I be but a knee-high pickney. Him solt meh and mek meh know'd wat night be widout muh muddah. Wen him solt meh, I cry and cry fer yuh, Muddah. I cry and it be Breckenshaw, a white mans like him, dat send a slave name Becky to be muddah to meh. It be Becky dat tolt meh not to cry, it be Becky dat suh no nigger woman gots choice in sep'ration dat come 'tween she and she pickney. So him not muh faddah. Him be always white mans to meh and de worse kind. Him a white mans dat solt way him pickney from dem muddah, and wen him see dem, we be no more to him dan Massa Breckenshaw's chattel. Yes, Muddah, I know'ds dat word 'cause Massa Breckenshaw him suh we be him chattel. Dat be like animals, Muddah. Animal! It be Massa Fields dat solt we to him to be him chattel. Faddah? Never."

"But him wents and brung yuh bak to meh."

"Why, Muddah? Why him come now? Why him not come wen I be little pickney and wants de love of muh muddah? I had to get left over love from somebody dat had she own pickney. It be left over, Muddah, left over! It be not yuh love. Him tek meh from yuh and him tek way muh love. "

"Him not tek way yuh love. Him sorry. Him tolt me dat him sorry. I know'ds dat him sorry."

"Him tek way de love dat be fer meh, Zack, Tuck, and Willie. Him tek it fer himself so wat him sorry fer, Muddah?"

I starts to cry and Isham him look at meh and him suh, "Muddah, I looks at yuh looking at we and I sees dat yuh looking wid hope. Yuh hoping dat we can see pass de white mans dat him is and sees a faddah, but him be never faddah to we."

"Yuh tinks yuh can try, Isham?"

"Try, Muddah? It be 'most twenty-five years I not know'ds de love of muh muddah. Twenty years dat I spend nights looking at de stars and asking dem way muh muddah be. Twenty-five years dat I go from boy pickney to full nigger man and muh muddah not get to see dat. It not dat we be far from way yuh be, Muddah. I see him long 'fore him show up and suh him be muh faddah. Him come to Massa Breckenshaw's place;

dem drink and laugh and, Muddah, I fix shoe fer him horse and him suh dat I be a good nigger. A good nigger! And him know'd dat I be him pickney and dat muh muddah be slave at him place and him stay quiet. Try, Muddah? Try? It be de same as looking at dry roots and asking dem to grow'd trees and plants.

"De roots in muh heart dat go to way a faddah be, dem dead. Dem use to be living but dem dead now, and it not matter how much water yuh put to dem roots; dem nots be able to grow'd nuffin' but hate. It gine always be dat way wid meh wen I sees him. Him dry muh roots and thar in nuffin' him can do to mek muh roots grow'd again way him be. Him never gine be muh faddah and, Muddah, I nots be able to let yuh put yuh hope in dry roots. Dem dry, dry, dry! De only ting dem good fer now is mekking dirt good fer fresh planting. I sorry, Muddah."

Isham hold down him head and look at him foots and I looks at him foots too and I know'd in muh heart dat him gine tek him foots and him gine walk way from meh. I wants to holler and begs him not to walk way from meh, but I nots know'ds wat to suh. I looks at muh boy pickney dat be a mans and I suh, "I sorry Isham. I sorry."

"Wat yuh sorry fer, Muddah? Yer not solt meh."

"I sorry 'cause I can feel it in muh bones dat yuh fixing to walk 'way from here and from meh and yuh gine leave meh." Wen I suh dat, I cry out loud. I feel de cry tearing at de inside of muh belly. I wants to beg him to stay same way I begs Haroldetta not to dead, but I know'ds in muh heart dat it be de same way: him gine left meh.

Like wen I cry out loud, it be magic sound. I see de rest of dem. It like dem be off waiting 'till meh and Isham get to dis part so dem can come. Dem come walking together and I looks at dem foots and I know'ds in muh heart, dem walking way from meh too. I nots know'ds wen but dem not gine stay here. Dem hate Fields. I holler and holler fer dem not to leave meh, and Fields him come running wen him hears meh holler and him mek it to way him can see meh and muh grow'd up man pickney and him stop.

Him stop like wen horse get fright. Him nots bolt, but him stop same way and him looking at meh and muh grow'd up man pickney and him face it change. Him look like him nots be able to figga wat be wrong. Him know'ds dat someting be wrong wid meh, but him nots know'ds wat it be. I look at him and I want to suh to him to not come near meh and muh pickney. Muh heart want to shout at him dat if him come closer dat muh pickney dem gine go far from meh and dat muh heart nots be able to tek fer dem to go 'way. But him be white mans and dis be him place, so him come and him looks from meh to muh pickney and him suh, "Pearl, what's wrong?"

Him look de longest look at Isham and it be all over Isham's face dat him want to tell him wat him dun tell meh, but I begs Isham wid muh eyes to 'member dat Fields be a white mans. I suh to him, "Nuffin', nuffin' be wrong." Him looks and looks and him turns and walks 'way.

Wen him gone far enough way dat de wind not turn to bitter breeze and whisper in him ears wat we suh, Isham him suh, "Muddah, wen tomorrow come, I gine mek muh way back over to Massa Breckenshaw's plantation. I fix in muh heart to be free man over thar dan free man here wid de white mans dat solt meh way from yuh wen I be but a little pickney."

I holds muh belly way him roll and I suh, "Isham, I not wants yuh to suh dat. I not wants to hear yuh suh dat yuh gine leave meh. I beg yuh. I begging yuh not to leave meh in muh old age. It gine brek muh heart. Stay wid meh! I begs yuhs. I not be able to live if yuh go way from meh."

Isham him start to cry and him suh, "Find it in yuh heart to let meh go back, Muddah. I gine come regular; ev'ry Sunday, but I nots wants to be near him. I fear if I stay near way him be, dat muh heart it gine get blacker and I gine wants to see him dead fer all de hurt and sep'ration dat him brung 'tween us."

I look at dem and I suh, "Yuh all gine leave meh?" Dem nod dem heads like dem all on one string and Isham him suh, "We gine come back, Muddah. Ev'ry time Massa Breckenshaw suh we free to leave off him place, we gine come and see yuh, Eve, Lavinia, Poole, Rebeccah, and Charlotte."

"Stay wid meh! I begs yuhs. I not be able to live if yuh go way from meh. Stay. Stay wid meh."

Dem come to meh and dem hold meh and wen dem let meh go, I know'd dat nuffin' gine mek dem see Fields as dem faddah. Nuffin' gine let dem fergive him fer having solt dem way from meh, and nuffin' gine let dem fergive him fer not letting meh go wid muh other pickney and see wat freedom be like. I also know'ds dat muh grow'd up man pickney know'ds dat I love Fields, and dat I never gine left from 'round him, so dem gine left from 'round meh.

It tek same length of time dat it tek Fields to find dem fer dem to leave from 'round him place. One by one, same way him solt dem furst time, dem left. Sometimes, I be right thar wen dem walk way like Isham and Juba, and sometimes I be wid Fields in him house wen dem left. Dem two, Tuck and Zack be hard 'cause it be de one night dat Fields ask meh to come fix him baff dat Tuck and Zack left.

Willie him try to stay wid meh but de longer him stay, de harder it be fer him to be in de same place way Fields be. It be meh dat beg Willie to left from 'round Fields. I starts to feel in muh belly dat if him nots leave, den him gine ferget dat Fields be white mans and him gine get in trouble. I cry and I cry but I suh, "Willie, I know'ds dat yuh wants to stands and be de one to watch over meh and see dat no harm come to meh nor yuh bruddas nor sistas, but yuh heart it heavy wen yuh gots to be way Fields be. I nots want fer yuh to gets in nuh trouble so I gine begs yuh go 'way from here. Go way Isham, Juba, Tuck, and Zack be. Go wid dem and yuh come bak wen dem come on dem free days. Go, Willie."

Him look at meh and him got tears in him eyes. Him suh, "But, Muddah, I wants to be way yuh be."

"I not want yuh to go, but it be de best ting fer yuh to go from here."

Willie him try and him stay fer one more week but den I see de same look in him wen him look at Fields dat I see in Isham and I suh, "Go, Willie, go 'way from here."

Dis time Willie him not suh nuffin' and I knowd's in muh heart dat him gine soon. Wen Willie walk 'way, de only ting dat not stop dat day be muh heart. It brek, but it not stop. I stands and I watch him walk 'way, and wen I nots be able to tek it no more, I starts to cry and I runs to him. Muh head rag it fall off. I not stop to picks it up. I runs and runs. Him stops and let meh get to way him be. I suh through muh crying, "Willie, I know'ds dat I suh it best yuh go bak to Breckenshaw's plantation but I nots want yuh to go."

Him tck meh in him arms and him suh, "Muddah, nots weep like dis. If in yuh weeps it gine mek it so I nots be able to walk 'way from here. I gots to walk 'way frum dis place, Muddah. I gots to or him gine know'd dat muh heart bitter to him. It too bitter Muddah fer meh to see him day after day and not want to see him dead fer all dat him dun to yuh and we."

I use muh dress to wipe muh face and den muh Willie him squeeze muh tight and him suh, "I gine come furst Sunday dat I free. I gine come, Muddah."

I pats him back and I suh, "Go."

Him suh, "Muddah, tell him dat I be glad dat him brung meh to yuh. Tell him dat."

Him let meh go and him start de long walk back over to Breckenshaw's plantation. I watch him 'till him be dot and den I go back to de yard. I pass de rag dat tie muh head and I left it right way it be. I dun lost all muh man pickney, wat be a rag. I let de wind pass through muh hair. Only ting on meh dat be free. I gets back to de yard and Fields him be standing by de Magnolia tree dat mark sep'ration 'tween way him house be and way nigger cabin be. Him watch meh and wen I gets to where him standing, him suh, "They are all gone now?"

"Yes."

"They hate me; don't they?"

"Dem not hate yuh."

"Then why have they all left."

"Dem only know'ds Breckenshaw's plantation."

Fields him not suh nuffin' more and him start to walk 'way den him stop and him suh, "Does Eve, Lavinia, Pool, Charlotte, and Beccah hate me now too?"

"Dem nots hates yuh, Fields."

"What about you, Pearl, do you hate me?"

I looks at Fields and muh heart it gets fresh feelings dat I nots know'ds wat dey be, but dem be strange feelings. I suh, "I gine miss dem."

"I know you're going to miss them, but what about me, do you hate me too, Pearl?"

I looks at him and I suh real soft, "No. No, Fields, I nots hate yuh."

Fields him step to meh and him suh, "Tomorrow I'll have O'Brien take the other pickney to Breckenshaw's plantation."

Muh heart it jump all over muh chest and I step back from Fields and I suh, "Lawd, no, no, no, please I begs yuh let meh keep de rest of muh pickney. Please, I begs yuh not to sell dem way from meh."

Muh knees dem start to tremble and I nots be able to stands up no more. I feel muh whole body falling and I goes to de ground crying. I nots see him but same way de grass move de morning dat Mistress Henrietta suh to sell meh, Momma Cornbread, and muh Haroldetta, it move now. Dis time it be Fields. Him on de ground next to meh and him trying to pick meh up and him suh, "Pearl I'm not going to sell the children. I can't. They aren't my slaves anymore, don't you remember. They are our children. Oh my God, Pearl, you think I'm an animal?"

I raised muh eyes and I looks at him and I nots be able to suh nuffin'. It be him dat suh, "Please, get up, stop crying. Come. Come inside, Pearl."

I wants to get up and go wid him but muh legs dem weak and still trembling and I not trust dem to hold meh. I wants to stop crying now dat I know'ds him suh him not fixing to sell way muh pickney, but I not able to stop de feeling inside of meh. I feel frighten, alone, and bruk up in all muh belly, heart, head, and soul. I jis't wants to stay in de grass and get out muh cry. I start to cry fer ev'ry hurt I ever had. I cry fer Momma, Poppa, Chem, Tiny, Tadpole, and Lil' Theo. I cry fer muh three dead gal pickney, and den I cry fer de day dat bring sep'ration 'tween meh and dem dat I love. I holler fer all muh man pickney dat solt way from meh, and den I scream 'cause ev'ry pain I ever know'd in muh life dis white mans dat be holding meh be de one dat 'cause dem, and yet I dun grow'd to love him wid all muh heart and ev'ry drop of muh blood. I holler and holler 'till I feel like I gine get swallow up by de holler.

Fields him trying to get meh to stop from hollering and to stands and come wid him, but de holler and de pain it heavy and bigger dan muh wanting to go wid him, and it pulling meh to de ground. It suhing fer meh to stay in de grass 'till I gets all muh hurts and pain holler in de dirt. I wants to bury muh pain deep, deep in de dirt. Fields him lets meh go and him stands and him shouts, "Anakey! Anakey! Anakey!"

I nots see Anakey but de ground dat holding meh and telling meh to holler all muh hurt and pain deep, deep in it suh to meh dat she coming and she running fast.

Anakey she gets to way meh and Fields be and she suh, "Massa Fields, yuh calls fer meh?"

Fields him suh, "It's Pearl. Willie has walked away like his brothers and it's too much for her. She's taken with a 'bout of crying and I can't get her to stop, get up, or come with me. Help me to get her to her feet and then help me get her inside. Please."

De sound of Fields voice suhing, 'please' mek it to muh brain. Muh brain suh, 'De owner and Massa of dis plantation jis't beg a nigger please help him wid another nigger.' Dat tinking mek meh reach muh hand out to Anakey.

She bends to meh and she suh, "Come inside. Dem not gone from yuh ferever. Dem gine come back soon. Come, yuh not want de other pickney see yuh cry like dis. Come wid meh, Milkweed."

Anakey she starts to stands and wid she rising up, I feels muhself rising too. I holds on to she and together we stands. Fields him give meh over to Anakey and him walks 'sides us wen us walk 'way from way de ground dat begging meh to pour muh hurts and pains into it.

I walks wid Anakey holding meh, and Fields him jis't walk 'side Anakey. Anakey she goin' towards de cookhouse and Fields him suh, "Inside the house, not the cookhouse."

Fer de furst time since I set muh foots on dis plantation, I walks through de front doors of him big house. I dun been in dis room more times dan I cans count, but right dis minute I feels like I never seens it before. If de pains over all muh grow'd up man pickney leaving not be so deep, I might be pay mind to him beautiful fancy chairs dat look like dem got wings. To muh surprise, Fields tek meh to one of de wing chairs and him suh, "Sit. Sit, Pearl."

I sits in him chair and I waits fer it to do like bird and fly 'way wid meh. It nots move. I nots move either. Fields him, "Anakey, go and get Pearl some water."

Anakey she runs and I can hear she foots gine cross de floor. Fields him suh real soft, "Pearl, stop crying. You have to stop. I know that you thought I was going to send away the other children, but I've told you that I'm not. So can you please stop crying now? Trust what I've said to you. I'm not going to send our other children away."

I tek a deep breff and Anakey she come back wid de water and she hands it to meh. I teks a sip and it feel like I trying to swallow rock. De water it stick in muh neck and mek meh cough. De coughing it mek meh stop from crying. Fields him suh to Anakey, "You can go now." Anakey she walk way. Fields him suh to meh, "Pearl, do you want to go to your house or do you want to go upstairs to rest for a little while?"

"I wants to see muh pickney. I wants to go to muh house. Dem other pickney need to know'ds dat I not walk way from dem."

Fields him calls fer Anakey again and wen she come, him suh, "Take Pearl to her house and stay with her."

Anakey she tek meh by muh hand and we start to walk cross him hard wood floor. We keep walking 'till we out him house and we walk cross de yard and we keep walking 'till we at muh house. Anakey she quiet de whole time we walking and den she suh, "Yuh tinking dat yuh nots know'ds how yuh can love him even though yuh know'ds dat yuh grow'd up man pickney not wants to be way him be? Yuh all mix-up in yuh head 'cause yuh wants to hate him 'cause him solt way yuh pickney furst time, and now dat him go and finds dem fer yuh, dem be big mans and dem got hate in dem heart fer him. Yuh wants dem to love him as dem faddah, but dem nots know'ds how to find dem way pass de hate dem feel fer him as white mans, and dat got up all mix-up in yuh heart and yuh head 'cause yuh love him."

I starts to cry again and Anakey she suh, "Yuh nots have to choose. Love him wen him here, and yuh love dem wen dem here. Him gine figga it out fer himself and wen yuh man pickney come to see yuh, him gine not call fer yuh to come rut 'cause him not gine wants fer yuh to have to choose. A muddah gine pick she pickney over a mans any day. Him not gine mek yuh choose 'cause him love yuh and wants yuh to still love him. Him might not have set out to love yuh, but him love yuh someting fierce and I tinks dat wen him figga how much him love yuh, it mek him 'fraid. Him a white mans dat got de biggest plantation in dese parts and him love him a nigger womans maybe more dan him ever love a white womans."

"But him 'cause all muh pain."

"Yuh tink him de furst white mans to 'cause nigger womans pains."

"I know'ds dat him not de furst. But…"

"Save all dat but talk dat yuh fixing to give meh and let meh help yuh figga out some tings. Dese days white mans nots hate nigger any less now dat we free dan wen we be slave. Yuh dun got all dese pickney dat, other dan yuh Rebeccah, Poole, and Charlotte, can go up North and be white mans and white womans. Is dat wat yuh wants dem to do. Is dat way yuh tinking yuh gine tek all dese pickney and go?"

"I not suh dat."

"Milkweed, yuh got some place else to go?"

"No."

"So if yuh nots got no place else to go, den yuh gine have to find a way in yuh heart to be him woman again and let him know'd dat yuh is his womans, 'cause white mans dem got dem ways. If him tink dat yuh, a nigger womans, nots tinks him good enough to be she mans, den him might go get a white womans and bring she to dis plantation and wen she see dat all yuh piccaninny is him pickney, she gine tell him dat yuh nots be able to be here. Yuh gots to be here."

I slow down and I looks at Anakey and I suh, "Dis is way muh three gal pickney bury."

"Den yuh fix it in yuh heart to be him woman again. Him dun give yuh wedding feast. Him tinks of yuh as him wife."

"I not be him wife. I be a nigger. I nots be able to be no white mans wife."

"Him dun more dan O'Brien. Even though O'Brien never pretend dat I be him wife, I loves him and him loves meh back. I know'ds dat him does."

"Yuh really loves O'Brien, Anakey?"

"Yes. Now Fields suh dat I is to stay wid yuh, but I gots O'Brien and muh pickney and I wants to be wid dem tonight. So I gine beg yuh to finds a way to let him see dat yuh not tinking of leaving him or here."

"I not gine leave, Anakey. I gine stay here."

"But yuh gots to stay here and wid him. Him gots to know'ds dat yuh mek choice to stay wid him even after yuh man pickney walk way."

"But how I gine do dat, Anakey?"

"Milkweed, yuh not a pickney. Yuh dun rut him and mek twelve pickney wid him so yuh go to him and yuh rut him and rut him like yuh never rut in yuh whole life. Rut him and yuh rut him tonight."

"But him not suh fer meh to come to de house."

Anakey she laugh and she suh, "Go to him. Go like de preacher mans suh dat Queen Esther do. 'member him suh dat she suh, 'If I perish; I perish.' Go to him and see if yuh perish, if him send yuh way, or if him be happy dat yuh come to him."

De way Anakey laugh mek meh laugh and wen I laugh it like a cloud lift off muh eyes. I smile. We walk de rest of de way widout talking. Anakey she be singing a mek-up song and wen she dun, we at de house and she suh, "See 'bout yuh pickney and wen yuh dun, leave Eve and Lavinia to mek dem rest comfortable and yuh get bak up to dat house and yuh rut him like him is de woman and yuh be de mans."

We mek it to de house and Anakey she suh, "I be stay'ds wid yuh fer a short spell and den I gine to way O'Brien be and I gine rut him and let him know'ds dat I love him. I suh yuh go and let Fields know'ds dat yuh love him, yuh love dem and yuh not fixing to walk 'way frum here or him."

Book Seven

Lilly Thea Bess Willow
Greenwood
1929 - 1962

Chapter 48

From There To Now

By the time Aunt Bess reached this point of the story, it was as though I've lived every second and minute of Great-Great-Great-Grand-Nana Milkweed's life and I'm tired. Cousin Thea and I have, over the months of nights that Aunt Bess have taken to tell this story, cried every tear that Milkweed cried, and now I want to know the rest. I want to know what happened after all her sons went back, what happened to Charlotte, Rebeccah, Poole, and the twins; Eve and Lavinia.

"So Aunt Bess what happened to them after this?"

"One thing for sure is that Milkweed never left Fields. She stayed right there on that plantation until she was damn near a hundred. She lived to see even me born."

"You, Aunt Bess? Milkweed was around when you were born?"

"Well, child, what year do you think I was born? If you with your young and modern ways was born in 1909, when do you think your mother and I were born?"

"Aunt Bess, you don't have to say it like that; it's just hard to imagine that she went through slavery times and then was around when you were a little girl."

"Now I didn't say she was strong and sprightly, but I can say that I remember goin' down to the land where she was living and seeing her."

"Was Great-Great-Great-Grandfather Fields still living?"

"He might have been my Great or Great-Great-grandfather, but somehow nobody in the family ever called him that. Whenever anybody talked about him, he was just Fields. Not Grandfather, Great-Grandfather or nothing like that. He was Fields. Strange; until now I never really thought about him as my Great-Great-grandfather. He was just the man that stole Cornbread and Molasses' girl and their dreams for her to get book learning as well."

"But she loved him and he loved her. Didn't that amount to anything with the family?"

"Everybody that wanted to understand the love part understood, but most everybody got stuck on the killing of those little children, the stealing away of Milkweed, and all them children she had with him; breeding her like she was a sow or something."

"But they loved each other."

"Yeah and where did all that love get the family? We're still poor and he had all that money even way back then."

"But didn't he promise to bestow all his worldly goods to her?"

"You would remember that part, wouldn't you, but do you see us living high on any kinda hog; we're still poor, aren't we?"

"But did he leave it all to her, anything?"

"I don't know."

"Does anybody know?"

"Never heard nobody mention nothing 'bout this family owning any plantation. What I do know is that I don't know."

"But even if he didn't leave all his worldly goods to her, he still loved her and I guess because of how I loved Milton, I'm stuck on the love part."

"It's the love part that keeps doing the women of this family in. Look how much she sacrificed because she was in love."

"What do you suppose might have happened if she had stayed hating him?"

"I don't know because she didn't."

"She just loved him, didn't she, Aunt Bess? She loved him just like if he was a Negro."

"Child, you should shut your mouth. When is loving a white man ever goin' to be the same as loving a Negro?"

"A man is a man; ain't he?"

"Now that's some foolish talk coming from somebody who ain't lived yet. Come and tell me 'bout a man being a man when your Lilly grows up and the first man she falls in love with and gives herself to is a white man."

"That ain't goin' to happen. My Lilly never goin' love no white man."

"What makes you so sure? Do you think Milkweed, on the day she was hog tied and dragged away like if she was a log, was planning on falling in love with the same man who had done that to her. Nope. She hated him and was planning on killing him first chance she got."

"I know she wanted him dead but Aunt Bess, doesn't that prove the point that love is love? Look how she grew to love him. That's got to mean that love is love, isn't it?"

"I don't know 'bout all of that. I've only loved and had strong sweet loving from a Negro man and from what I see of white men I don't see no way on their little scrawny bodies where they goin' have no strong sweet loving stored up or the strength to give it to you. So if them don't got it store up and they don't have the strength I don't see how it goin' be coming out of none of them; sweet or otherwise."

"Aunt Bess!"

"Don't 'Aunt Bess' me. You ain't too young to hear this kind of talk. You forgetting that you got a daughter running 'round here. Well, how did she get here? And don't try to tell me that you are some new kind of Negro Virgin Mary and your Lilly is some new kind of baby Jesus. That only happened once and I don't see God finding another woman 'round here to have another child with. He made one; they strung him up and killed him. God ain't goin' send another child down here so this time they can what, swing him from a tree with some stupid rope? Naw, God is done with all His mixing with Earth women."

"Aunt Bess! That's blasphemy. You can go to hell for that."

"God ain't got man ways. God is God all by himself and He ain't goin' to send me to hell for that."

"But, Aunt Bess, I have another question though about Milkweed: did any of her children learn to read and write?"

"No. She stayed so afraid of then getting taken away from her that she never let on that she knew how. It was only after she died that Grandmother Charlotte came upon a box with her writings."

"So how did Great-Grandmother Charlotte know what was on the papers if she didn't know how to read or write?"

"Well, by then some Negroes were even goin' to college and Grandmother Charlotte got somebody to read them for her."

"What did she do then?"

"She got determination."

"Determination?"

"Child, how come you got so many questions now? I'd been telling you this story night after night and never once did you have questions like now. Why?"

"I just feel so sorry and sad in my heart for her. It's like Great-Great-Great-Grandmother Milkweed let down her momma and she did just what her momma begged her not to do. She forgot to etch learning in her heart and that of her children which is sad."

"Remember you are the one that just told me about love. Well, it was love that took that etched heart and covered it over."

"So how did we get back to everybody knowing the story?"

"Grandmother Charlotte; she was so mad at her momma for not teaching her to read, write, and do her numbers that she said it would never happen in her family again. She started right there to know her numbers, letters, and reading."

"She did?"

"She did and so she taught my momma and well, Momma taught me and your momma and now, most of us can read and write but we ain't been able to get one woman in this family through a college door."

"My Lilly is goin' to college."

"Oh! So you got an etched heart now."

"But it's like we cursed or something. How can we have come this far, through so much and not one woman in this whole family can find her way into a college. Everywhere you look, Negro women goin' to college and changing things. My Lilly goin' in and coming out and she's goin' to change things."

"How you know?"

"Cause I'm goin' tell her this story and I'm goin' help her keep her mind on books. I'm goin' tell her to stay away from boys and love."

"Oh, so you goin' to tell her about staying away from boys and love; I thought you loved a good love story."

"For Milkweed yes, but my Lilly has to go to college. She can find boys and love when she's done with college."

Laughing, Aunt Bess said, "Would them boys and the love they be bringing be white boys with weak love in their little scrawny bodies, or strapping Negro boys with strong sweet loving?"

I looked at Aunt Bess and, smiling, I said, "Negro boys, and yes, Aunt Bess, strong sweet loving."

"Then I think you best tell her and tell her early about the curse on this family."

"Aunt Bess, I was kidding about a curse, we ain't cursed… are we?"

"Well if we ain't, what happened to us then? Look at what Milkweed went through at first to get book learning and look how she was then able to keep that secret with her and not tell it once to all those children she had for Fields."

"Aunt Bess, I'm just wondering again… are you sure that Fields didn't give her the plantation? Did Fields have a will that gave it all to Milkweed?"

"Child, that's one thing that I don't know anything about nor ever heard about; if anybody in this family have the answer, then they are keeping it a secret just as tightly as she kept her knowledge of book learning."

"But, Aunt Bess, if Milkweed had all her children for him and she lived with him until they died, then who did he will all that land to?"

"I don't know. No one knows. He was just Fields the white man and plantation owner and she was Milkweed, the former slave that chose him, love, and the plantation over leaving and seeing what freedom had in store for her. It was his plantation and nobody ever got up enough caring to look into whether or not he left it to her. The family just went on living after Milkweed died."

"So how and when did we leave the plantation."

"Listen to you talking about we; there was no we. By the time I came along, my momma had long left Fields' plantation, and we were well settled in Promise Land."

"But how did Great-Grandmother get to Promise Land?"

"I don't have the answer to that. For all I know, it might have been love."

"Love?"

"Grandmother Charlotte never talked much about what happened to make them leave, but Grandfather Orrville was a peach farmer from Promise Land and that maybe how we ended up in Promise Land."

"Did they have a good love story too?"

"Not like Fields and Milkweed, but it was enough love to produce my momma and Uncle Juba."

"You had an Uncle Juba?"

"I guess it was because Grandmother Charlotte never forgot her brothers that went back to live and work on Breckenshaw's plantation."

"But I thought they came to visit every free minute they got."

"Child, times changed but white people stayed the same."

"What do you mean by that, Aunt Bess?"

"Child, after a while, white men had the Klan with all their anger and hatred for nigger and there was no safe place for a nigger. Hatred for niggers never got less. White men still hating Negroes 'till today. Look how we still can't go where we feel like, sit where we feel like, and God knows sleeping, living, and eating where we feel like ain't never goin' happen. So imagine what it was like for Grandmother Charlotte's brothers when all this was goin' on. They had to make choices and soon the choices meant they couldn't come see Milkweed when they wanted to. If Breckenshaw took them, then she got to see them; if he didn't, then it didn't happen."

"Couldn't Fields take Milkweed over to see them?"

"That would've been worse. Keep in mind, child, that Fields never remarried so people had to be talking 'bout him taking up with a nigger woman. Never mind that if and when his friend came to visit, she was like his house-servant, people ain't stupid. How anybody goin' miss all them white, half-white, and almost-white looking pickney 'bout the place?"

"But why didn't he marry again?"

"Because he loved her. He loved her and remember that he had promised her he would never hurt her again."

"But she would have been able to see her sons."

"He loved her and she loved him. They were "married" as far as the both of them were concerned, so she learned to live knowing that she could get word to her sons and by then, grand-children when they came along."

"You see, Aunt Bess, that's why Lilly is goin' to stay away from boys especially white ones."

Aunt Bess started to laugh and then she told me, "Child, you don't have to worry. I don't think there's another white man like Fields walking around looking for some poor Negro Baptist girl to love, and besides there are no plantations in Bedford Stuyvesant; plantation-thinking white people for sure, but no plantations, thank God."

"My Lilly is goin' go to college and when she's done with college, she's goin' to marry a fine strapping Negro man and have some strong Negro sons."

"Child, let your Lilly be a baby before you go marrying her off to some strong Negro man who himself must be someplace right now a baby and pooping on himself."

I started to laugh and Aunt Bess announced, "That's more than enough for tonight. We got work tomorrow. Go see 'bout your Lilly and make sure to tell her to stay away from white men."

"Aunt Bess, don't go and put no white man curse on my daughter."

"Why would I put another curse on my precious baby? What you got to do is tell her about the one we're dealing with now. That's the only curse you got to worry about."

"Aunt Bess, can I ask you something serious before I go up?"

"Is it goin' to keep me and you down here forever?"

"No. What do you think our life would've been like if Fields had left the plantation, the house, and all the land to Milkweed? I mean like what if we didn't have to be poor? What if Fields did leave all that land and stuff to Milkweed?"

"Why would he go and do a thing like that? The South was still the South, you know, and no white man, even one that lived the way he did with Milkweed, was goin' go against the way of white Southern men and do something like that, and besides, even if he did, there's no way that a bunch of Negroes goin' ever find out. It's been almost sixty years now so I don't think there's any way to find that out."

"But what if we could, Aunt Bess. What if we could find out? I don't think we should just let it die like that?"

"What you mean, die like that. That place belonged to a white man. He and Milkweed might have had their pretend marriage and wedding, but the government wasn't then or now goin' let a bunch of Negroes get their hands on a place that large. I think somebody in the family said it was about a thousand acres of land. Do you have any idea how big a place that is and what it would be worth today? A hell of a lot more than anybody goin' let some Negroes own."

"I was just wondering."

"Stop wondering about that. What you should be wondering about is your Lilly. If you are so moved by your grandmother's story, there's only one thing you should be wondering about and what you goin' do?"

"I know what I'm goin' to do, Aunt Bess. I'm goin' to see to it that Lilly knows what Milkweed went through, and I'm not goin' do like my momma. I'm goin' tell Lilly and see to it that Lilly gets to college. She's goin', Aunt Bess, you wait and see."

"Then you keep your mind on seeing that she gets into somebody's college and leave the ownership of Fields' plantation right where it is."

"It's still there?"

"It's a plantation. Where do you think it can go? Now stop with all the questions and go get some sleep. You got work to get to so your Lilly can get to college."

Aunt Bess, satisfied that we'd gotten most of the story out, took a break from her storytelling. She'd done it before, but this time the break had a good reason. Cousin Thea was getting married and it was all the preparation and wedding planning to do that got in the way of storytelling. Nothing was goin' to come before what Aunt Bess called 'our present time'. She said 'our past time' could wait. We had a wedding to plan. It was goin' to be beautiful.

Chapter 49

A Bitter Breeze

Cousin Thea, who had long stopped looking for Crawford to turn up and kill her, had learned to trust again; she was courting. She'd been courting him for two years when he asked her to marry him. She said yes and Aunt Bess got busy helping her plan the wedding. When Cousin Thea came into the church, I was shocked. Although the stinky woman had been gone a long time and I'd gotten used to Cousin Thea, I still wasn't ready for the proud beautiful woman walking down the aisle. She'd shed all her layers of fear and stink and had become a different woman. The woman she'd become wasn't fearful and the two years of being courted by Phillip Fillmore had completed her change. Cousin Thea was a very beautiful and happy woman.

Watching Phillip look at her as she came down the aisle, I could see he treasured her. She didn't ever have to worry about being beaten again. She would never have to keep a pot of hot water, oil, and grits simmering on her back burner waiting for the moment she would have to add lye to it and throw it on her tormentor and run.

Cousin Thea was walking confidently towards love and her new life. When Lilly saw her, she started to shout and clap her little hands with little girl pleasure. It took only a few moments and then Cousin Thea became Mrs. Phillip Fillmore. Our family quilt got bigger by a few more squares. Phillip's pieces were dark strong colors like him. Brown suede for his skin, silver velvet for the gray in his hair, and then there was all the red for the love he was showing and giving Cousin Thea.

Cousin Thea moved into Phillip's house on MacDonough Street. Though she was only a few blocks away, it felt as if she'd moved to another part of Brooklyn. The house on Chauncey Street became empty without her, but it wasn't empty for long. Cousin Thea and Phillip started making babies almost immediately. They weren't married a year before the first baby came. They had five in five years. At almost ten, Lilly loved it because she was the big sister. When Cousin Thea became pregnant with her sixth baby, Aunt Bess said, "Child, you stepped right outta that beautiful wedding dress right into a pregnant frock. You and Phillip over there acting like you all is Milkweed and Fields. When you all goin' learn that all your night times together don't have to be spent making babies?"

Cousin Thea laughed and replied, "I know, Bessie, but we want a lot of babies."

"A lot? Don't you'll think you all have a lot by now? How many more than these six do you want to make a lot?"

Smiling, Cousin Thea told us, "Three."

Aunt Bess shook her head from side to side and told her, "I think you listened too hard when I was talking about all them babies Milkweed had, but the two of you go on. Thea girl, you best remember that just like Fields, he's getting all the easy work. He putting in five or ten minutes of sweet work, if that much, and you got to put in nine months and all that time it takes to push 'em out. Just you remember that." We all laughed at that.

One more baby came the next year and with that baby, Bernard, came a bitter breeze. When that bitter breeze was done blowing, Aunt Bess had sailed out on it, leaving Lilly and me the most alone we'd ever been. I never learned to love Bernard and he was just on the outside of me liking him. I added Bernard to our family quilt with the thinnest of threads: I used black. No love went into thinking about him. Not that he needed my love; he had his parents to love him and they did because unlike me, they didn't hold him responsible for Aunt Bess' leaving. I did. I held him and Rawlins Fitzgerald responsible.

Rawlins Fitzgerald, a man I'd never met, didn't know, or had never heard about, had died and Phillip, the only Negro undertaker around went to pick up the body. Normally, it wouldn't have mattered to none of us 'cause that's what Phillip did. People, men, women, young, old, and some who didn't live long enough to tick off enough time to move the clock hands died and always, when called, he went for them. This time was different because Rawlins Fitzgerald, a Negro, had taken a swing at a tall, strong, Negro-hating Irish policeman; liquor would make a Negro do that.

With all the hate he had for Negroes, he shot Rawlins Fitzgerald dead and now the rest of them Irish policemen hated Rawlins Fitzgerald's dead body so much, they didn't want to release it to Phillip so he could take it away and dress it up for display for Negro people to come and see what being a drunk Negro with no good sense looked like after you took a swing at a white, Negro-hating Irish policeman.

The police said Rawlins Fitzgerald didn't deserve to be buried. They said that was too good for a no-good, drunken, take-a-swing-at-apoliceman dead nigger. He went back to being a nigger 'cause a Negro, they said, would've known his place. Phillip knew how to be a good Negro so he humbled the big, important, self-respecting, and well-respected by everybody that knew him man he was, and waited for them to be done killing Rawlins Fitzgerald over and over again.

Rawlins, in taking that drunken swing at a white and not just any white police but an Irish policeman, became a fucking-drunken-dead, too-good-for-burial nigger. They said the nigger deserved to be humiliated and be shown who was in charge even though he was dead from the minute the tall, strong, Irish policeman had shoved the gun in his mouth, splitting his top and bottom lips and knocking out all his front teeth; top and bottom, pointed the gun up towards Rawlins' brain, and pulled the trigger. There was no satisfying their anger. They did everything they could think of to humiliate the body of Rawlins Fitzgerald. When they were satisfied that he couldn't be killed anymore, they released the remains to Phillip; that was truly the first time, in a long time, a Negro had been reduced to remains.

Phillip Fillmore told nobody but his wife, and that wasn't until many, many years later when Agnes Fitzgerald, Rawlins Fitzgerald's mother, had died that he told Cousin Thea what the morgue gave him that night to go and make look like a man again so his mother could have something near what her son used to look like to say goodbye to.

Had Rawlins Fitzgerald picked a different day and a different night, I wouldn't have known nor cared, but he picked the same day Cousin Thea went into labor with child number seven, and it was because of him that a bitter breeze blew on Chauncey Street and took Aunt Bess with it.

Aunt Bess was rushing to be with Cousin Thea and never saw the milk truck. Being in a hurry and not wanting your cousin to be alone in her time of labor would make you do that. The milkman would never have struck and killed Aunt Bess if he'd seen her. It's true he was a white man and a Jewish one at that, and most of them didn't have any use for Negroes, but this Jewish white man was different. He was sweet on Aunt Bess and had been for years. Naum Glassberg would have been happy to hang his hat and coat on Aunt Bess' coat rack if she'd let him, but she never did and now he, the white Jewish man that loved her, had struck and killed her.

They said that from the way Aunt Bess fell and hit her head on the edge of the sidewalk, it was clear that she'd died the minute her head hit the curb. It was also the first time anybody had seen a white man cry like that over a Negro woman. Naum Glassberg didn't wait to see if anyone was goin' to try and help him get her to Evangelical Deaconess Hospital;

the only place he figured would help a Negro. He didn't know if they would or not and it didn't matter, he was goin' to try and get her the help she needed. But none of that mattered. Aunt Bess would never know of the effort he made 'cause she was already dead.

A bitter breeze blew two ways that day. One way it took Aunt Bess away, and when it blew the other way, it brought Bernard, whom it turned out didn't really need any help getting into the world; his six siblings had smoothed out all the rough paths, and left arrows pointing the way out into the world. He followed and if Naum Glassberg hadn't hit Aunt Bess with the truck, she wouldn't have made it there in time anyway. Bernard Fillmore came into the world hollering and screaming. It took him from the time his momma hung up the phone 'till Aunt Bess got her walking shoes on, grabbed her handbag, keys, and hat and made it to the corner of Decatur Street and Stuyvesant Avenue to get out; less than fifteen minutes because most of the way out was so smooth.

Naum Glassberg came by later that night to say how sorry he was. He offered to pay for the funeral but Phillip said he didn't have to. He would take care of it and he did, beautifully. Cousin Thea wanted to be at Aunt Bess' funeral and Phillip was waiting to give her a chance, but it was nearing one week and Cousin Thea still was in the baby's bed 'cause Bernard in his hurry and with his big head and wide shoulders had torn her. Phillip decided that Aunt Bess shouldn't have to wait no more for her final rest. Cousin Thea cried and tried, but in the end, she had to accept that she wouldn't be able to say her final goodbye to Aunt Bess.

The rest of us; people who had worked with Aunt Bess, people from her church, Lilly, and I went. Even Naum Glassberg came. He looked odd; sort of out of place being the only white face in a sea of Negro faces. He didn't seem to notice. He even went up to the casket, the first pink one I'd ever seen and the second casket I'd ever been this close to, the first one being the one that had Milton in it. Naum kneeled by the side and he said something that none of us knew what it was. It wasn't English. I guessed it must've been Jewish. When he was done saying his prayers, he reached in the casket, took Aunt Bess' hand, and said in a voice that was loud, loud, crying and cracking in between his words, "Miss Bessie, I'm so very sorry. I didn't see you. I didn't see you, Miss Bessie. I would never, never have done you no harm. My God knows that I'm telling the truth. Please, Miss Bessie, I need to know that you know I'm speaking the truth and I need your forgiveness."

Just as he said that, a rose that was part of the spray on her casket fell to the floor. It was white. Naum Glassberg quieted his crying and talking and picked it up. Putting it in his buttonhole, he said, "Miss

Bessie, I needed your forgiveness and you've given it to me. I'm glad that you know I would never have done anything in this world wrong to you. Thank you for forgiving me."

When he said that, another rose fell from the spray; this one was pink. He picked it up and placed it in Aunt Bess' hand. Touching her hand in a kind of patting motion, he said once more, "Miss Bessie, I'm truly, really sorry." He patted her hand one more time and walked away from her casket and out the door.

Chapter 50

Moving On Without Aunt Bess

A few weeks after Aunt Bess' funeral, a man I'd never seen before, came to the house. He said he was there to find out how much longer I planned to stay on in the house. I asked him who he was and why he was here asking me about my business. He said his name was Charles Cooper and he had papers to show that the house belonged to him and his family. According to the papers in his hand, his father, Charles Cooper, Sr., had been married a long, long time ago. When his father died just two years into the marriage, his will had said he was leaving his house to his wife as long as his wife, Bessie Fields, didn't remarry. Should she remained unmarried, when she died it was to go to his oldest son, this man who was not Aunt Bess' son. Now that Aunt Bess was dead, the house was his and he wanted it.

The shock that the house didn't belong to Aunt Bess confused me; I didn't know what to do. I asked him for some time to think. He said he would be back in a month, but when he came back, he would be coming back ready to move into the house since he was married and living with his wife in Harlem in a rented apartment. I said nothing; he didn't give me time to say anything. After he'd said what he had to say, he started walking out. It was clear that he held some kind of resentment towards Aunt Bess. I stood looking at the door wondering why Aunt Bess never mentioned Charles Cooper, being married, or the fact that this wasn't her house. I started to cry.

Once the tears stopped, I started to think. I made up my mind to move. I started looking for a place and asked everybody and anybody if they had a place I could get. Cousin Thea said that Lilly and I could come and stay with her and Phillip, but I couldn't do that. I couldn't bring myself to be that close to Bernard. The bitter breeze that had brought him into the world had taken Aunt Bess from me and now it was preparing to blow me out of the home I'd lived in these past fifteen, almost sixteen years. I found a place on Macon Street and Lewis Avenue and when Charles Cooper turned up with his almost-white wife and his four almost-white Negro children one month to the day later, I was ready to move. Actually I'd moved and was just waiting for him to show up so I could give him the keys.

The first night on Macon Street, both Lilly and I cried. Mrs. Ross, who was a Deaconess at St. Philip Church on McDonough Street and a long-time friend of Aunt Bess, rented me the apartment on the parlor floor of her house. She brought Lilly and me food and while we ate, she told me bits and pieces of the side of Aunt Bess I didn't know. She said she'd known Aunt Bess ever since she'd moved to Brooklyn from down South; Savannah, to be exact and although Aunt Bess had belonged to Mount Lebanon church when she died, prior to marrying Charles Cooper she had belonged to St. Philip's Church when St. Philip's Church was at 1610 Dean Street.

Mrs. Ross, with her deep brown skin, had eyes that looked as if they were searching for an important lost thing. Her hair, which was neither long nor short, was also almost all gray and had there not been an occasional strand of black hair here and there, her entire head would've been covered in a wooly mess of fuzzy and frizzy white hair. The only time it wasn't allowed to be fuzzy or in the two plaits was on Sunday. On Sunday, when she put on her Deaconess uniform and her little black pill box hat, her hair was pulled back and forced into a controlled bun and held in place by bobby pins and a hairnet. I would look at her hair and I could almost feel the struggle her tightly coiled hair, which she never ever hot-combed, was putting up against the pins and hairnet. It never won.

She was also very very short. Not so short as to look like a midget, but shorter than most women. It was as if as she got older, inches fell off from the top of her just the same way they were added on when she was growing up. I guessed then that's why they called it growing up. I wondered, as I looked at her, if they called what was happening to her 'growing down'. She was round, but not as round as Aunt Bess. Her roundness was in her middle, which made her look as if she ever fell, she would just wobble and roll away; like a child's toy.

The more she tried to understand why Aunt Bess would live in a house all these years and never let on to anyone that knew her that the house wasn't hers, didn't make any sense. I listened to Lizzie, she said it was short for Elizabeth and wanted me to call her that, and a part of my mind agreed, but I also didn't know that Aunt Bess had been married so I didn't know what to think of it all.

Mrs. Ross, who because she was Aunt Bess' age, was goin' to remain Mrs. Ross and not Lizzie, said there was something that didn't seem right about what this Charles Cooper had said because she didn't remember Aunt Bess ever mentioning Charles Cooper having a wife before Aunt Bess, or a child. She said I should search Aunt Bess' papers to see if any of them mentioned Charles Cooper having any children. I promised her that I would but because of my grief and the fact that I had Lilly to raise all by myself, I never got around to it.

What I did get was back to work in Brooklyn Heights and I remembered all that Aunt Bess had taught me. After I spoke to them and only so briefly about Aunt Bess' dying, I went back to being invisible right in front of their eyes. They themselves would forget I was there and when they talked, it would be, "A nigger did this or a nigger did that today, yesterday, the day before." Someone always ended up saying what should be done with niggers who forget that they were niggers. I looked at them and listened and kept right on remembering how to be there and not be there at the same time. Aunt Bess would've been so proud of me. I was a nigger in their house and I never did anything to ever let them think I'd forgotten that.

Cousin Thea, time permitting, would come by and visit with Lilly and me. Most times she came without the children and I was glad because when she came and brought Bernard, it was hard for me to be as nice to him as his beautiful face and sweet spirit called for. I was never outright mean, but I just wasn't as attentive or playful to him as I was with the other children. If she noticed, Cousin Thea never said a word. I think Bernard noticed because on those days when Cousin Thea brought him, he found play by himself and occasionally he'd look at me. Sometimes, I would swear his eyes asked, "Cousin Gina, why don't you like me?" I never answered those eyes; besides he was a child, how could he know or understand?

One evening when Cousin Thea was visiting and Lilly was at the Macon Street Library, I asked, "Thea, do you know any more about the family than what Aunt Bess got to tell us? I want to know more. The story feels undone. You know what I mean?"

"I know a little more, but Aunt Bess was the one that we all knew had the most bits and pieces."

"Bits and pieces?"

"Well, she was always the go-to person for questions. If anybody wanted to know anything, they said, "Ask Bessie, you know she knows." Cousin Thea laughed and I saw Aunt Bess so clearly in my mind.

"So tell me the bits and pieces you know."

"Well, Rebeccah was my great-great-grandmother so Bessie is my cousin twice or three times removed."

When Cousin Thea said, 'Cousin twice or three times removed,' I looked at her and she added, "There are cousins and there are cousins. Aunt Bess was an older cousin with good sense."

We both laughed and I said, "Or what, you would have scalded her too?"

"Gina, don't be stupid. Did Aunt Bess look like the kind of woman that would mess with some other woman's man or husband? No, she was more the 'scald your behind' type than the type that had to worry about getting her behind scalded."

"I guess it would've been hard to try that with her."

"Can we get back to what I know? I don't have years to talk like Aunt Bess, and besides I got to get home soon and get the children ready for bed."

"Ok, ok. I want to know what you know. Just so I won't feel like a big chunk is missing."

"Keep in mind, Gina, that Aunt Bess had a better source for her telling than my side of the family. So what we heard was different. Great-Great-Aunt Charlotte moved away from the plantation, but Rebeccah stayed, married, and grew up her children right there in Greenwood so she could be near to Fields plantation. She and most of her children cared for Fields and Milkweed as they grew older and feeble. Fields died somewhere around 1901. I was living with my mother in Cokesbury in the Abbervile district. I'd never met Fields, heard of him, but never met him. When we got word that he'd died, no one much really cared. He was as Aunt Bess said, just Fields most of the family never got pass what he'd done to Milkweed. She got pass it, but most of the family held on to it."

"But why? She chose to love him and stay with him."

"When those old people got to talking, it was like Milkweed didn't have a choice. They thought that she'd been a slave so long that she didn't know any better when she had a chance to go after freedom and see what it was."

"She knew better. She chose to be with him."

"I don't know; it's just how my side told it. So, anyway, no one much really cared if he'd lived or died. Great-Great-Grandmother Rebeccah went though. She was heartbroken. He was, after all, her father."

"Wasn't she old by then?"

"Yes, but back then old Southern women were strong."

"What about my Great-Great-Grandmother Charlotte? Did she go to the funeral?"

"I don't know all that much. I don't even know if she was alive or not."

"I don't think she was dead. I think she died when I was about six or so. I remember I was six because Grandmother Neala went to Cedar Springs for the funeral. Momma never really talked about her family, you know."

"Your momma was like that. She never talked about nothing that had to do with family. If not for Bess, most of us wouldn't know she was still living. She was so different from Bess. Bess was always about family and keeping our history alive. Your momma, hate to say it, was always looking for that great romance. She would see a man and the first things she did was check to see if his wedding finger had a ring or not; no ring, then she had hope that maybe this one would be the one. Not Bess; Bess didn't care what anybody had, she wanted her own."

"My momma was about romance?"

"Don't know why you're sounding surprised 'cause didn't she send you away so she could marry nasty old what-was-his-name again?"

"Threadwell. Ernest Threadwell. But didn't she love my father?"

"You can answer your own question if you can answer this one. Who is your father?"

"I don't right know. Do you?"

"No. No one in the family knows for sure. There were rumors but that was all, rumors."

"What was his name?"

"Bacchus Talbert."

"From the Talbert plantation family? Are you sure?"

"No. Neither he nor your momma ever admitted it and so the family let it go. You looked like a Fields and that was it."

I looked at Cousin Thea, took a deep breath and said, "It doesn't matter. None of that matters. I never knew him and, truth be told, I hardly knew her so who he was doesn't matter."

"You sure?"

"Yes, I'm sure. That chapter is closed and I want to close all the other chapters in this family history so that when I tell Lilly, I can have closure to all the chapters that make up this family book. Now let's move on."

"To what?"

"The rest of the family history."

"Child, that's all I know."

"It can't be. What about all of Milkweed's sons that went back to the plantation, Eve, Lavinia, and Poole? What about them?"

"I really don't know, Gina Pearl. It looks like you goin' have to go back to Promise Land, Cedar Springs, Cokesbury, and all them other places that we've lived to get your pieces of the puzzle. Maybe there you'll find some old members of the family who still have enough good sense in their brains to tell you."

"I ain't ever goin' back to Promise Land."

"Then I guess you are willing to live with what you know. Can you do that?"

"What?"

"Live with what you know."

"It's not like I have a choice is it?"

"Nope."

"Then we done."

When Cousin Thea said this, I had a feeling as though she was holding something back and I had to find out what it was. Had to get those missing pieces that she had, and for whatever reason wasn't willing to tell me. Looking at Cousin Thea and feeling like she was holding something important back from me made a dislike, not quite like the one I'd held for Bernard all these years, ooze into my bloodstream. I had to get that feeling out of my head. It wasn't right. Cousin Thea and I were now like sisters. If she didn't want me to know then, I'd just have to trust her and live with what I knew or make up in my mind to go back to Promise Land; I wasn't goin' back.

My thoughts went to Bernard; if not for him, Aunt Bess would be alive and I would get to hear all the other bits and pieces. I knew in my heart that there would never be any place in it for Bernard. I hated Bernard and his bitter-breeze-blowing self. I really did. I think Cousin Thea had finally figured that out and maybe that's why she held onto the bits and pieces that she knew. I guess if I ever warmed up to Bernard, she'd share those pieces with me. I decided she could keep them; I was never warming up to him.

Over the next two years, there wasn't much time to try and pick Cousin Thea's brain. Lilly was getting ready for college and that's all I had time for. I had enough of our history to give Lilly all the reasons she should get into college. I had the names of every woman in our history that mattered and Lilly knew them as well. She knew my name. I am Promise Greenwood (Gina Pearl Fields), the daughter of Etta Pearl Fields, who was the daughter of Neala Fields but not the Neala Fields that went to find freedom with Nester's children. Neala Fields was the daughter of Charlotte Fields, who was the daughter of Milkweed "Pearl" Fields, who was the daughter of Cornbread Beauford Litchfield Talbert, who was the daughter of Jennie Mae Beauford or Lil' Mae, who was a daughter of the Seminole tribe born sometime around 1795 or 1796. That was counting back seven generations of women and none of us, including me, had gotten nothing more in the line of schooling than a few numbers, letters, and some reading and writing. I had more reading and writing than most of them, but not enough to get me inside anybody's college. However, this child of mine, Lilly Bess Thea Willow Greenwood with the Seminole and Mandingo blood flowing in her veins, was goin' to somebody's college.

Chapter 51

A Change Is Coming

In New York, as in Promise Land, I was a Negro or nigger to white folk, but being called nigger in Promise Land wasn't the same as being called a nigger in New York. In Promise Land, most folk were white, and the rest of us were niggers. Me, Ma, and her people were niggers but we were niggers in Promise Land, where the white people knew you by your real name and used it if they felt like it and when they didn't feel like it; you was a nigger and you answered 'cause that was 'bout the best thing they was goin' call you anyway.

I might have changed my name, but I kept Gina Pearl Fields' dreams alive in my heart. It was the same dream I had when Milton and I were goin' to be married, and it was the same dream I held onto now that I was raising our daughter alone. Our daughter was goin' to do something that no woman in my family had ever done: she was goin' to college. I dreamed and worked. I knew, without really knowing, that no amount of dreaming was goin' to make a college drop out of heaven and just take my Negro child in. Therefore, every morning I sent her to Girls High School over on Nostrand Avenue and Macon Street, and I went to my various house-cleaning jobs in Brooklyn Heights.

I hated most of what I did, but I had dreams for my Lilly so I did what I had to do. I cleaned their houses, washed their dirty dishes and clothes, and I ironed whatever the white women put in their ironing basket. It never mattered if it was something that required ironing or not; if it was in the basket, I ironed it. I never asked any questions. When I was in one of my joking moods, I would tell Cousin Thea 'bout the white women I worked for. I would laugh and say to her, "Cousin Thea, if any of them white women ever fall in that stupid basket on ironing day, I goin' iron them. It goin' be up to her to shout, scream, or something to stop me. If she stays quiet, she's goin' wake up to find herself ironed, folded, and in a drawer or on a shelf somewhere." That was me; funny sometimes but serious most times.

I didn't really like taking their babies out walking either, but it gave me time to talk to God and get His grace to fall on me and if, when I was walking their white babies, some of God's grace fell on them, then so be it. Some of them babies didn't want God's grace because they would wait 'till the minute I got my talk goin' good, and then they would start crying. Sometimes I just wanted to keep right on talking and let them cry 'till they stopped, turned red, or whatever white babies did, but I couldn't just let them scream and cry; after all I was right in God's face trying to get His grace to fall on me.

I mostly went to God about my Lilly. Lilly was growing, learning, and along with that, she was getting prettier every day. The prettier she became, the more worried I became. She was the color of a shelled pecan. Her hair was thick and hung almost to her waist. Her cheekbones sat high on her face making it impossible not to notice her eyes. They looked like two little black holes that could, if you stared into them long enough, draw you in and lead you straight to heaven. Her lips were full like two tiny fluffy pinkish-brown oblong pillows, which, when she smiled, parted to show her unnaturally white teeth.

I did for my Lilly what my ma didn't do for me. I let her know that she was my everything, but that didn't stop me from reminding her that it would be her intelligence and not her looks that was goin' to open the door to college. I wasn't the only one talking to Lilly about college. Every evening when she came home from Girls High School, it was, "Ma, today Mr. Hirsh said this and Mr. Hirsh said that." Or, "Ma, would you believe that Mr. Hirsh says that I have a very good chance of getting into college because a lot of things have changed for Negroes."

Mr. Hirsh had been teaching at Girls High School for a few years before Lilly started there. One of the first things we heard that morning when Lilly and I walked through the halls of Girls High School was that Lilly would be lucky if she got into Mr. Hirsh's math class. Lilly's face brightened that morning because math was her favorite subject. She wanted to be an accountant and become the first female Negro to have her own accounting office with lots and lots of Negroes working there.

That was Lilly; not just dreaming for herself, but for others too. We heard of other math teachers, but we heard that Mr. Hirsh's math class was the hardest and the best. That day when we left, Lilly's goal was to make it into Mr. Hirsh's math class. She made it and from that day on, it was, "Mr. Hirsh said…" I lived with everyone or most everyone of her sentences starting or finishing with, "Mr. Hirsh."

I had never even been near a college, but I'd heard enough to know that it would be the difference for my Lilly. I told her everything I heard about college in the hope she would keep her mind on our dream; but with all the talking and telling, I forgot to tell her about the curse. I should have told her about the curse first and at least she would've had a fighting chance when she saw the first sign of it coming.

The news we were waiting on finally came. My Lilly was on her way to university and not just any university: my Lilly had gotten into Fisk University in Tennessee and they were even goin' to pay for her room and board. My daughter was goin' be at a school the very same year that an important Negro from Harlem was goin' be the first Negro President of Fisk University. I was so proud I told everybody up and down Macon Street, Chauncey Street, Stuyvesant Avenue, and Lewis Avenue. I even told strangers that I met, but never mind how my chest was bursting with pride, I never once let it slip from my lips to any of the white women's ear that my Lilly was on her way to that fine university.

That was my personal private business. No white woman was ever goin' to hear my personal private business from my lips. I kept my lips closed and opened them only when I prayed to God and thanked him for this blessing. A Greenwood, my daughter, was goin' to step over the threshold of not just somebody's college, but Fisk University. My prayers, which had gone to God before with a fair degree of regularity, now went without ceasing. I thanked and thanked Him each day for this blessing. I couldn't believe it: Fisk University with all its fine singers was ready to open its doors and let my Lilly in. Praise God.

As hard as I was working, Lilly was studying even harder. She wanted to prove to the college administrators at Fisk University that she was the right kind of Negro girl for their school. With me working extra days and hours and Lilly doing extra studying, there was little time for the two of us to do the things that made us a family. No bread got baked. There had been only one Sunday a few months ago, when I was able to make my special collard greens, macaroni and cheese, cornbread, and fried fish dinner. We both wished for more family time, but we understood the sacrifices. It had already proven that it was worth it. Each time I looked at Lilly, my heart would get so full. I was about to see my promise fulfilled. Aunt Bess was right, everything has its time. I only wished that in this time, Aunt Bess was around to see our Lilly on her way to a university for Negroes headed by a Negro.

Chapter 52

A Time To Love

Lilly

At first, I didn't really understand the feelings stirring my insides. When they started, I should have gone to Ma and said, 'Please help me, I'm feeling these funny feeling. It feels like a smile is in my belly." Unaware of a curse, I said nothing. The next time he was near me and that funny feeling started in my stomach, in my innocence I asked him about it, and all he did was smile. His smile made my stomach do a back flip and I closed my eyes from the feeling. When I opened my eyes, he was looking at me with the same smile that had just flipped my stomach. I wanted to run, but I didn't know where and if I told the truth, I didn't want to be too far away from him so I stayed and basked in his smile. It wasn't a long smile, but it was a smile and he was looking at me. I took that to mean that the smile was meant just for me.

I questioned what I was feeling and, not having gotten any more than a smile from him, I went to the one I was sure would give me the answer: I prayed to Jesus. I wasn't sure why I prayed, but I felt that I should. I waited for an answer, but none came. I prayed again. I prayed more than one prayer in the same night and waited for what seemed like an eternity for the answer to come. Still none came.

Then, remembering that Jesus was the son, I wondered if that might be the reason I hadn't gotten an answer yet. Deciding that my situation required immediate attention and I couldn't wait anymore on Jesus to go to his father on my behalf, I went directly to His Father; I went to God. That night I thanked Jesus for listening to my prayers and after I'd thanked him, I told God my problem. I even told Him that I'd been waiting on Jesus. Then I asked God that since I'd been waiting for a while, could He give me a sign so I would know that He'd gotten my prayer.

Just as I said that, my bedroom light flickered. I smiled. That was my sign. God was about light. In the beginning he'd said, "Let there be light," and there was light. He saw the light and it was good. Later, when the Israelites needed to escape from Pharaoh, God came as fire and gave them light so they could travel by night. So my flickering light told me that God had heard my prayer and I knew that I'd done the right thing by goin' straight to Him.

In both of these light situations, time was involved; making the Earth seven day, getting the Israelites to the Promised Land took forty years. I knew I wouldn't have to wait forty years because Ma had already seen Promise Land. I started counting down my seven days. While I waited for the answer to my prayer, I worked on avoiding the object of my distraction. I tried not to hear his deep beautiful voice or feel the chills it sent through me each time he spoke.

While I waited, I talked to myself. I told myself that what I was feeling was impossible. I even told myself that I was smart enough to know better. I went over in my mind all the things he was saying to me. When day seven rolled around and there still wasn't an answer or any more light flickering or any other signs, I stopped listening to myself. On day eight, I stopped waiting for an answer. I remembered that God's time was different to mine and by the time He got back to me, I might be away at college. I couldn't wait that long. I needed an answer today, not tomorrow, next week, in forty days, and God Himself had to have known I couldn't wait forty years.

I answered the yearning in my heart. My heart wanted him and all the good feelings that came with thinking about him. I followed my heart and fell. My fall was no different to any other Promise Land woman's fall. I fell fast, heavy, and hard. I fell in love and followed my heart to him. He saw me coming and smiled. I smiled back. Not unlike the smile that Nana Milkweed gave to Fields. He met me as I went to him. He held out his hands. I looked at his opened empty hands and took them. I took what he offered.

He offered me attention, affection, and finally himself. I, in turn, offered him my heart and after much soul-searching and no answer coming from God or His son, I offered him entry into my body. He accepted. As he tried to enter me, he realized I was a virgin. He stopped. I wondered why. I knew that it wasn't because he didn't think I was a virgin. His stopping had to be because he didn't want the taking of my virginity to be like this; in a storage room, on a cold concrete floor covered only by a jacket. I could tell that he wanted to stop; to wait for a better place and time, but he and his desire were too far-gone. He hungrily took all of what I offered. As he took it, and me, he promised me his undying love.

Swept along in our collective offering, we clung to each other. He whispered words of love and I listened and received every word, just as I received every thrust of his body into mine. As our passion peaked, we vowed to love each other forever. Done, we straightened our clothes, hugged shyly, hardly looked at each other, and then without as much as a word, we walked away.

He

I walked away with the knowledge that this wasn't just any virginity to brag about to my best friend, Charles Rancor, but it was the virginity of the person my heart had chosen to love. I didn't know it then, but this would be the last virginity to be lost at my hands. I'd taken my own a few years back, not intentionally but by curiosity and accident, and somehow ever since then, every woman I'd meet had already given hers to someone else. I found myself wondering if there was ever a husband who ever got the opportunity to receive that special gift on his wedding night. It was for that reason and the fact that I most sincerely loved her that she would remain the only woman I would ever love.

Lilly

I walked away, worried about what we'd done. I knew I'd given him the one thing Ma had told me that a woman couldn't give away twice. Ma had told me countless times how precious my virginity was and that I was to keep it for my husband. Ma had forgotten to tell me what to do if I should fall in love with someone that couldn't ever be my husband. She had forgotten to tell me what to do if that same someone made it all the way to touching the little black box that contained this precious jewel. I had lost it and couldn't go back to where I'd lost it to look for it. It had disintegrated into a crimson crown around his private parts and was, even as I walked away, no more now than a pinkish stain spreading across the seat of my panty. It was gone, lost forever.

We were both afraid. He was afraid because he was white, Jewish and rich, and I was afraid because I was Negro, Baptist, and poor as hell; but worst of all, I was his student and he, Matthew Hirsh, was my math teacher. He was supposed to be giving me extra help so I could get into college. He wasn't supposed to be climbing between my legs.

I was afraid because of what we had done and hoped that Ma would never find out. I hadn't counted on God and His ways of bringing those things done in darkness, even the darkness of a storage room, to light. Though I wouldn't know it for a few months, I'd walked away pregnant. My math teacher had truly taught me how to multiply.

A few weeks before Ma discovered I was pregnant, I'd figured it out for myself. I knew enough to know that in English class, a missing period meant a run-on sentence. But this was math. I saw the equation on the blackboard of my mind. It read: ***Solve this problem: One part male math teacher plus one part female math student plus one part missing menstrual cycle equals what?*** I went over the problem a thousand times in my mind and because I was really very good at math, my answer was always the same; the hypothesis never changed. I understood the unique element. It was the missing period. In the end, I wrote my answer on the blackboard of my mind. ***The answer equals one pregnant dead Negro girl when her ma finds out.***

I kept hoping that my math was wrong. My math was right. I was pregnant. I just had to wait for Ma to find out to have the dead Negro girl part completed.

As months went by and my belly began to grow, I got quieter. I had to find a way to tell Ma before she noticed and killed me. I didn't want to die. I wanted to live for the child growing in my belly. I came home from school and did my chores before Ma got home, and then I would just sit quietly in the living room with a book over my growing belly and once Ma fell asleep in her chair, I would ease off to bed. Ma never noticed my growing belly.

I eventually stopped talking. I was afraid that I would just break down and tell her my secret. Ma noticed the change in me, but figured that I was worried 'bout going away to Tennessee to college. As the months went by, I kept going to school and Ma kept going to her jobs; somehow not noticing I was getting bigger.

One evening, an evening it was raining harder than it had rained for months, Ma came home from work and found me just sitting, rocking, and crying. I wasn't crying because it was raining hard, but I was crying because that morning when I woke, I knew I couldn't hide my belly from Ma anymore. I had to tell her. As Ma came through the door and saw me sitting in the darkened room, I felt her tense up and I could feel her watching me. I also didn't have to look to tell that she was dripping water all over the parlor floor. She had to be. It was raining and Ma, for some reason she'd never explained, always walked in the rain. She wore a raincoat but would never carry an umbrella. I never heard the snaps of the coat, but instead I heard her, "Lilly, why you sitting in here crying like somebody told you I died. I'm standing right here so why you crying like that?"

"Ma, I'm sick."

"Sick? What's wrong?"

"I ..."

"You what, child?"

The bad feeling in my belly started to get worse. I slowly rose from the chair and looked down at my belly. Ma's eyes followed my gaze. I could tell she wasn't believing her eyes. I could tell she was hoping I was joking and had taken one of the cushions off the chair and put it under my clothes. The expression on my face said I wasn't joking and that roundish mound wasn't a cushion. Ma was shocked and though she could see I was pregnant, she still asked.

"Lilly, oh my God, are you ...?"

"Pregnant, Ma."

"I can see you're pregnant, but how you get to be pregnant?"

"It ain't my fault, Ma."

"Lilly, I ain't ask you about fault. I ask if you pregnant. You can't be pregnant."

"I am, Ma, but it ain't my fault."

"If it ain't your fault, Lilly, then tell me why you standing in front of me with a baby in your belly?"

"Ma, you ain't goin' understand."

When I said that she wasn't going to understand, I heard the snaps of her raincoat. It sounded like bullets going off. I closed my eyes. Then I heard as her bag dropped and her rain hat made a squishing sound as it hit the floor. The sound of her footsteps as she crossed the foyer echoed throughout the house. It sounded as if the thunder was rolling across the floor. I closed my eyes and waited. She was going to do the last part of the math answer. Ma was getting ready to kill the little pregnant Baptist Negro girl. I waited for the feel of her hands around my throat. It never came. Instead, through shut teeth and lips that I was sure weren't even moving, she said, "Lilly, don't tell me what I goin' or ain't goin' understand. I understand that there's only one way for a woman to get a baby in her belly. Somebody have to put what makes a baby in her. So who was it that put this baby in you?"

"Ma, I knew you won't understand."

"Lilly, you vexing my spirit. Now I ain't ever raised my hand to you, but if you keep on telling me what I ain't goin' understand and it ain't your fault, I goin' send you and that baby in your belly to meet your maker. Now tell me who did this to you and leave the understanding or not understanding to me!"

"I swear to you, Ma, it ain't my fault."

When I said it wasn't my fault again, Ma closed the space between us and pulled me to her. She was closing me in the folds of her arms while she cried, "Oh my God, my poor Lilly, tell me who did this to you, baby?" Her voice had gone soft almost like a whisper and there was fear there. Fear that someone had hurt me. She continued in that same voice. "Why didn't you tell me, baby? Lilly, we got to tell the police."

I tried to step out of her embrace because she'd gotten it wrong and I knew that I had to tell her. "Ma, we can't go to the police."

When she spoke, I could hear the hysteria rising in her voice, "What you mean, we can't? We got to go to the police!"

"It ain't like that, Ma."

Her hysteria was changing. Anger was mixing in with all that she was feeling. She spoke in a rush. "If it ain't like that, then what is it like, Lilly?"

"It ain't my fault."

When I said it wasn't my fault, all the hysteria and concern for me left. She was clearly angry. "Lilly, you said that already, and I'm understanding better how it ain't your fault. You was forced to do this thing. Who, Lilly? Who was the animal that hurt my baby?"

I bent my head slightly and said in a voice a little above a whisper, "Ma…"

The look on her face said she was understanding that if I wasn't raped as she was thinking, then I'd been with somebody deliberately.

Ma was screaming now and I could tell that she was starting to shake with anger. With tears in her eyes, she fixed her gaze on me and said, "Lilly, somebody had to put that baby in there so unless you tell me who it is, I'm goin' take you to the police and make you tell them! Who did this, Lilly?"

I couldn't tell her what she wanted to hear; all I could say was, "Ma, it wasn't like you thinking."

"Lilly, you aggravating me! Just tell me who did this to you and leave the understanding and the thinking to me. Now tell me 'cause I ain't goin' ask you no more after this time."

"Ma…"

"Lilly, don't be calling my name unless it is to tell me who got you like this so I can go and talk to him and his people."

"You can't do that, Ma."

"You right I can't do that 'cause you ain't told me who it is yet. Who did this to you!"

"Ma, help me."

"I want to help you, but you got to tell me who the boy is."

I raised my eyes from the floor and in one rushed breath I told her, "It ain't a boy, Ma, it's a man."

"A man, Lilly? You went with a man? You ain't but a child. What man brought himself to you? Who was it, Lilly? What nasty man brought himself to you?"

I looked at Ma and then I looked at the floor and mumbled, "He isn't nasty, Ma. He isn't nasty."

Ma was trembling and she grabbed me by my shoulders and she demanded, "Tell me his name and tell me now. Stop all this defending of this nasty dog. Now, what is his name?"

Ma's fingers were digging into my shoulders and she was staring at me; she was waiting. Lowering my head even lower and speaking just above a whisper, I told her, "Mr. Hirsh."

After I said his name, I raised my head slightly because I felt Ma's fingers release me. Ma looked as if she wanted to say something but her mouth had gone dry. Her throat had shut up. I could see from looking at her neck that her heart had changed its beat. Her throat was jumping all over the place. Ma looked as if her knees were goin' to buckle. I could tell she didn't want to believe what I'd said.

"Mister, Mister Hirsh? Did you say Mr. Hirsh? Which Mr. Hirsh this be?"

"Mr. Hirsh, Ma, Mr. Hirsh."

Ma forced the words out of her dry throat "Mr. Hirsh, your math teacher? Mrs. Hirsh's Matthew? Tell me that you know another Mr. Hirsh 'cause I know that you can't be standing here telling me that the baby in your belly is for Matthew Hirsh, your teacher."

I hung my head and nodded. The weight of my head made me feel as if my neck was broken. My little bit of stored up strength started to give. I started to crumble.

Ma was shaking all over and screamed at me, "Lilly, tell me that you lying on that man!"

"I ain't lying, Ma. I swear to God. I'm telling you the truth. It's Mr. Hirsh."

Ma sat down in a nearby chair. "Lilly, how did Matthew Hirsh get close enough to you to put something other than numbers in your head?"

"Ma, he loves me."

Ma screamed, "Love? Good Lord in heaven, you didn't just say that he loves you?"

"It's true, Ma, he told me so."

"Lilly, tell me that you ain't standing there with a baby in your belly because you believe Matthew Hirsh loves you. Didn't you notice that you be a poor Negro girl and he be a rich Jewish man? What made you think that he could really love a poor little Negro girl like you? Tell me that you didn't really believe it. Tell me!"

I looked at Ma and I could see the pain in her eyes. All her years of sacrificing and working hard was for nothing. Her heart was broken. I'd broken her heart because I'd given myself to a white man, and not just any white man, but one whose mother had no use for Negro people. Ma had told me from day one about Mrs. Hirsh. She hated Negroes. They could cook her food, clean her house, drive her car, but that was all. She made no secret that she hated Negroes just the same way the Germans hated Jews and if she had her way, she would do like Hitler and get rid of all the Negroes and everybody with dark skin and, as she'd said so often, 'nigger hair.'

"Lilly, when he was telling you he loved you, did he tell you that he was getting ready to marry some rich white girl? Did he, Lilly? Did he?"

I started to cry. Ma's news was a shock to me. He hadn't told me. I was hearing this news for the first time. Ma could see that the news was hurting me, but she didn't let herself feel sorry for me. My guess is she felt I needed to have a clear picture of what I'd given up college for.

"Now you see, Lilly, how it's your fault. You didn't have no better sense than to believe that some white man loved you. You gave your precious self away for nothing. If you had just kept your mind on goin' to college, none of this would've happened. Now you ain't goin' nowhere. Now you like all the rest of us Promise Land women. You goin' have a baby without a father, and this one is the only one that goin' have a white father by choice. Ain't that a laugh. White men ain't nothing new to Promise Land women, Lilly. But none of us, not since Milkweed, was ever foolish enough to believe their lusty ramblings 'bout love. Did you see this as some fairy tale where you were Milkweed and he was Fields? How did you come to believe that nonsense about love from a white man? How, Lilly? How?

"I wish you'd come to me, Lilly. I would've told you that all that talk about love was a lie. I would've told you to put all that love that you was starting to feel for him back in your heart. So, in a way you're right. It ain't your fault. It's mine for not telling you that something like this could happen. It's my fault. Now you standing there with a belly full of baby for a man who can never take you or his baby around his momma. I done told you since I started working for that woman how she feels 'bout Negroes; and what do you do, you pick her son. You listened to his lies and now your whole future is lost. Do you think a Negro child, even one that her son made is goin' live long enough to call her anything other

than Mistress or Mrs. Hirsh? Grandmother is out of the question. Mrs.
Hirsh would choose death first."

When Ma was done talking I said, "Ma, come to the school and talk
to him."

"Lilly, what you want me to come to the school and tell that white
man? You want me to tell him that you ain't got no way to support
a baby? Is that what you want me to tell him? Do you want me to tell
him that the next time I clean his house, I'm goin' tell his momma that
my daughter's making a baby for her son? Tell me, Lilly, so I can get it
right and do this thing for you that you didn't think about before you
gave yourself to him!"

"Ma, come to the school and ask him if he really loves me. Come,
Ma, let him tell you for himself that he really said it. He did."

Ma started to scream from where she was sitting in the chair, "Lilly,
stop! Stop saying that foolishness! That man don't love you! And if you
don't stop saying that nonsense, you goin' make me get up from here and
beat you like you're a stranger to me. So shut up with that foolishness
and let me tell you which part of this is your fault. I took the blame for
the part that was mine. The not telling you that something like this could
happen. But you got a part and you got to take the blame for the part
that's yours. It's your fault because you had one thing that was precious
to you. It was yours and it's true that only you could've decided who was
goin' get it, but if you had listened to me and done things right, it
would've belonged to your husband. A Negro man who was goin' work
himself to death 'cause you gave him your most precious gift. But what
did you do? You gave it to a white man! White men are used to taking
black virginities. They've been taking them from black women since and
before our people landed in this place. That part there; that's your fault.

"This part; our history, the one I spent all these years telling you.
The story that Aunt Bess told me and I told you; you know the story,
Lilly. Even if you'd forgotten about Momma Mae, Cornbread, Molasses,
and even Milkweed, then you should remember about them four little
boys that lost their lives because their mommas, like me, wanted book
learning for them. You got book learning so you know that a Negro
woman ain't never been nothing more to a white man than some big
grown-up doll.

"They come and play with you when nobody ain't looking and
when they done use up all your goodness, they just drop you anywhere
and leave you for some black man to come behind them and do the best
he can to make something good outta you. So since it weren't in none of
your books, then this is our fault for not letting someone be willing to

write it. But what you done, Lilly, is still wrong whether it's in a book or not. You let that white man take something he ain't have no right to take. He can't ever give it back to you. Now all you got to show for it is a baby that ain't goin' have no father. It is your fault! Lilly, you better…"

"Better what, Ma? Better what?"

Ma raised her eyes and lowered her voice as she said, "Get from my sight 'fore I move from here and try to take outta you what that wicked nasty white man left in you. Lilly! Go! Get! From! 'Fore! Me!" For the first time ever, Ma screamed at me. I dragged myself out of the room with all her anger-filled words bouncing all over me and making their way into my heart. My heart started to hurt. I thought I was goin' stop breathing, my heart was beating so fast.

I walked up the stairs hearing her voice say, 'Did he tell you that he was getting ready to marry a rich white woman?' I made it to my room and the second the door was closed, I started to cry. I cried out to God and the minute I did, I got my answer. I heard as plainly as if someone was in the room, "Wait. Wait on Me. You should have waited on Me."

Right there, I asked God to forgive me and begged Him to help me. I promised Him this time that I'd wait. I cried myself to sleep.

Gina Pearl

Soon as Lilly was gone, I let the tears I'd been trying to hold in since she dropped the news of the baby in my lap flow. The tears rushed from my eyes. They dripped from my chin to my folded hands and slid to my clothes. In the middle of my crying, I tried to figure out how her life could just up and change like that. I started to wonder if her life had let her know that it was getting ready to change. I thought I'd cried, my last cry on that falling apart tin can. Until this moment, I'd kept that promise to myself. Once I'd set foot in Brooklyn, I'd never cried again. Not even when months turned into years and I'd never heard from Momma. I hadn't cried when I figured out that Momma must have stayed true to her word and married Old Man Threadwell.

I hadn't really been listening to Momma and all her talk about marrying Old Man Threadwell because my mind had been on Milton Willow, and his joining rod. I'd taken to calling it that because it joined us together and made us one. I didn't want to think about Momma and Ernest Threadwell because I hated him. I hated Ernest Threadwell, his house, his screaming children, and most of all, I hated the way he looked at me whenever he came sniffing around Momma. He made me feel as if he was looking through my clothes and seeing me with them off. I didn't want to be anywhere near him and I couldn't believe that even after I'd told Momma about the way he made me feel, she would still think about marrying him.

Didn't Momma care that folks were goin' to talk about her rushing into marriage with him and just a few weeks after his wife had died. Why would Momma even want to marry a man who had kept his wife so pregnant that he'd finally managed to breed her to death? Poor Wisdom Threadwell; she'd so many children that it was hard to recall a time when her belly wasn't either high in the air or low dragging on the ground. Wisdom wasn't even forty and yet she looked a hundred. Wisdom was the only woman in Promise Land who had a baby or sometimes two every year.

Old Man Threadwell kept himself in her so much, people used to say he took his job digging in the dirt much too seriously. He was so used to digging in darkness that when he came home, he dug around in the only dark place that was close at hand: Wisdom. People in Promise Land believed it was having that last baby that had finally taken its toll on Wisdom's worn out body. It was said that she didn't even bother to look at the baby. She'd pushed it out and used the little energy she'd saved when no one was looking to open the gates of heaven and let herself in. She wanted rest and knew that in Old Man Threadwell's house, there was never goin' to be any for her so she chose the only way rest could be assured. She died.

I shook the thought of Wisdom Threadwell, who'd finally figured out how to use her name to her advantage to get away from him, Old Man Threadwell, and Momma, the new Mrs. Old Man Threadwell, from my head. I was my mother's daughter, but I wasn't my mother. I didn't have room in my life for nonsense. When I'd tried to love someone else, after being in Brooklyn for almost seven years, I discovered that he'd forgotten to tell me a very important detail: he had six children and a very pregnant wife with two more on the way, living on Duffield Street downtown Brooklyn with him. If I'd had enough time and if the way I found out was different, I'd have done like Cousin Thea; I'd have cooked his behind. There was no time for no cooking of anyone's behind because it was his very pregnant wife who'd walked up on us on Jay Street, just as we came out of the movies on Fulton Street. The way she looked at me made me feel cheap and nasty. I wanted to forget the day I'd met Delman Miggins.

On that day, I wasn't looking for a man. I'd gone to Abraham and Strauss Department store to get Lilly her Easter dress and some new shoes for Sunday school when he walked up to me and started talking. I was looking sharp with my hat, gloves, and pocketbook. I'd just started painting my face the way the other ladies were doing; making their eyes look doe-ish and lips so red: oh my God, I looked like a movie star or, depending on who was looking, a painted whore.

I didn't see where he'd come from but when I looked back on it later, he had to have just left home. Duffield Street was just around the corner from Abraham & Strauss department store. He was so sweet and the loving, yes there was some loving, it was so good it made me smile for days after he'd left. I'd been seeing him for about eight months when he started talking 'bout getting married and moving me and Lilly down south to Columbia, South Carolina, where his people were from.

I told him I'd had my share of the South and I wasn't goin' back. He started loving on me and soon I was ready to follow him anywhere just so I could keep on getting that good loving; I had just told him I would marry him when his wife saw us. She started to cry and I... well I didn't know what to do. I knew what I was thinking to do but at that time, I was too embarrassed. Right there on Fulton and Jay Street, his wife called me a painted whore and a home-wrecker. As the woman insulted me, he walked over to her and tried to take her hand at the same time as he was saying to her that it wasn't what it looked like. He told her that although it looked like he'd just come out the movies with me, he didn't know me at all. The fool then looked at me and said, "Miss, can you please tell my wife here that you were just asking me directions to some job place on Columbia Street in Brooklyn Heights? Can you please, Miss, tell my wife that: the truth."

I looked at the pregnant woman who I could tell wanted to believe anything but the truth and I said, "He's telling you the truth, Miss, I don't know this man. I'm sorry if it looks bad, but I got to get to this job. Do you know where 27 Columbia Street is, Miss?"

Stepping closer to her husband, my lover, she said, "I'm so sorry, Miss. It's just that I'm pregnant with twins, baby number seven and eight, and it's hard on me to think I could lose my sweet Del."

The lady turned to look at me and as she turned her back, he winked at me behind her back and had a smirk on his face as he mouthed a thank you. His wife said, "Walk 'till you get to Court Street and then..." I never heard what she said. I was choking on shame and disgust. I waited 'till she was done and because she said Court Street, I started to walk in that direction. My shame was real and deep. I wanted no woman's husband. I stopped seeing him and I never trusted anyone else, but none of that mattered when I discovered that he was a liar. I'd given my whole heart to Milton, and now that he was gone, I'd just keep on giving it all to our daughter.

Thinking about the name of Delmar Miggins made me have thoughts of Milton; thoughts that I'd hoped would stay buried, but they rose to the top of my once-again broken heart. Milton Willow and I were supposed to be married. All our thoughts were about being one with one another and then it was of our baby. All our being one had made us three. All Milton and I could think about was getting married and starting our life together. We were so happy.

I didn't want to remember hearing the frantic sound of Mr. Glover's hand pounding on the door to my momma's house as he tried to get our attention. There had been an accident. The truck that Milton was driving to take the peaches to town was, as usual, packed to overflowing, and the weight had caused it to blow a tire no sooner than Milton and Lloyd, his best friend and planned best man, had started off. Milton, not wanting to unload the truck and lose valuable time and money, had tried to get a jack under the truck so he and Lloyd could change the wheel. The weight had been too much for the jack. Breaking under the weight, the truck had collapsed, pinning them both under it.

Everybody had come running in the direction of the accident. Men tried frantically to get Milton and Lloyd from under the truck, but they couldn't do it. The truck was too heavy. The truck had to be unloaded. The wait was excruciating. The men tried to send us back to Momma's house to wait. We never made it. We made it as far as the giant oak tree a few yards away. There we stood; Milton's Momma, Lloyd's Momma, his wife, Momma, and me. We were all waiting with our love and hope now mingling with fear in our hearts. No one said anything. There was nothing to say.

Lloyd was pulled from under the twisted steel and broken wood first only because he, being thinner and more nimble than Milton and not being as far under the truck as Milton, had been able to scuttle back some before the truck had teetered over completely. Milton, because the truck was his, had been chuck up close to the wheel when the jack give way. The wait for them to get Milton out would be longer.

I didn't want to remember what Milton looked like when they finally got him out from under the twisted pile of rubble that used to be his truck. It was the first time that I saw what shattered hopes and dreams looked like. Shattered hopes are bloody. They make you shout and scream. And they make you vomit and want to shit at the same time. They sit on tips of splintered bones jutting through arms that once held you. Shattered hopes and dreams mock you as they swing from ripped tendons and sinew that struggle to holds limbs together. They reach out to you, teasing you, breaking your heart as they peek at you from places where eyes used to be. Shattered hopes and dreams climb deep into your soul. They break your heart and shatter your spirit.

For the second time in my life, I was shattered. I sat with my risen memories and accepted that my daughter was pregnant and wouldn't be goin' to college. I had no choice. Lilly Thea Bess Willow Greenwood was just like me, Momma, and all the Fields women before us. She had chosen love over a dream. She had let the bird in her hand named college go because she had listened to him and believed that there were really two named love and happiness in the bush waiting for her to come and get them. Her two birds in the bush could have come later. They were not worth what she'd let go; a good education at a first class Negro college and her dream of being the first Negro woman to have her own accounting office for Negro people where Negro people proudly came to work every day. Lilly had fallen victim to the curse. She'd have to do what all the others before her had done. She would accept her circumstances and live with the choice she'd made.

Book Eight

Andrea Matti Hirsh Greenwood
1947

Chapter 53

A Time To Be Born

Gina Pearl

Lilly stopped goin' to school. The school year was almost over anyway and a few weeks wouldn't make that much difference. She wasn't goin' back anyhow. She accepted that there would be no college for her. Matthew Hirsh never came by to see her. That was hard for her, so I tried to get her to understand why she was alone with her growing belly. This was Brooklyn and no little Negro girl was goin' to be allowed to have a Happy-Ever-After with no rich Jewish man; baby or no baby. There would be no house with the white picket fence. No husband to come home from work and say, 'Honey, I'm home. How was your day?' There also wouldn't be any cute little puppy running around in the backyard for her baby to play with. That was only in the picture books that white women read to their white children to give them hope of what was in store for them. None of them books was out there for a Negro girl. There would be no one wanting to protect her or be there for her. She'd made a hard choice and would need God to help her through the many bad days that were waiting for her and her baby.

Whether or not Lilly understood all that I was telling her didn't really matter because a few months after I found out she was pregnant, her daughter was born. She called her Andrea Matti Hirsh Greenwood. I didn't like the fact she named the child so close to Matthew Hirsh's name, but she'd made up her mind. It was her baby. I'd named my baby what I wanted. She could name her baby whatever she wanted, and so she did. I looked at my little grandbaby and remembered the conversation I'd had with Aunt Bess so many years ago when I promised her that I wouldn't let the story of what the women in this family went through to die.

Looking at my grandbaby, I could hear that conversation so clearly. We were sitting around in Aunt Bess' parlor and she was getting ready to tell me what the women in this family went through when she said, "I'm goin' take my time and when I'm done, you goin' see that this family get what my momma's great-nana felt was rightfully ours. Once you get it, you got to promise me that you never goin' let go of our history or of telling why the women in this family should be through suffering by now. One person slipping on a family history is all it takes for everybody to go back to the place they already left. I got your promise, Gina Pearl?"

I remember how Aunt Bess watched me; waiting on me to give her my promise. I remember how I looked at her and said, "I promise you, Aunt Bess, that I ain't goin' let what happened to us die with me."

Now, as Aunt Bess said then, "Gina Pearl, everything has its time." And now, well in about a few years once this baby starts to get understanding, I'm goin' start to tell her the same story I told her momma just in case her momma does like mine and let the story fade away. Can't let it fade away: Momma Mae, Lil' Mae, Cornbread, Molasses, Milkweed, Grandma Charlotte and even Ma had suffered and made sacrifices for this family. My ma's sacrifice wasn't really hers since it was me she sacrificed, but even that part got to get told. Don't want another daughter in this family sacrificing a child for a man, that can't happen again, shouldn't happen again; that kind of pain for a daughter is wrong, real wrong; I know.

Life was hard, but they weren't suffering because I was working. One day when Drea, that's what we called her, was about six or seven months old, things changed. I was at Mrs. Hirsh's house doing my usual cleaning when the hairs stood up on the back of my neck. I could tell someone was standing behind me. I turned around and he was standing there just watching me so I said, "Something I can do for you, Mr. Hirsh?" He just stood there looking at me and I started to feel frightened. He looked as if I'd done him something and it was making me uncomfortable so I looked at him and asked again, "Something I can do for you, Mr. Hirsh?"

"Yes, Mrs. Greenwood."

I almost fainted because I didn't know he knew my name so I just stood there looking at him.

"Mrs. Greenwood?"

"Yes, Mr. Hirsh, what is it you would like?"

"Mrs. Greenwood, how is Lilly? I heard that she had a baby."

"She's fine, but why you asking 'bout her. You ain't ever ask 'bout her before?"

"Lilly was my student."

"I know that, but why you asking me 'bout her and her private business?"

"I'm asking, Mrs. Greenwood, because I was her teacher."

"What does being her teacher have to do with you asking 'bout her business?"

He didn't answer me; he just turned and started to walk away, but before the sound of his shoes stopped echoing in the quiet of the house. I heard them coming towards me again. I thought for sure that he was coming back to fire me. He stood there looking at me for a while and then said, "You know, don't you, Mrs. Greenwood?"

"Know what, Mr. Hirsh?"

"About the baby."

"Sure I know about the baby, it's my grandchild, ain't it?"

"I guess you want to hear me say it. Is that what you want, Mrs. Greenwood? Would that give you some kind of vindication?"

"Vindi, vindi, vindi what? What you talking about, Mr. Hirsh?"

"Vindication."

"What would make you think that I need this vindi, vindi... whatever you call it thing?"

"The word is vindication, and it means like getting your justice or to have your name cleared."

"Meaning you no disrespect, Mr. Hirsh, but I don't need you to teach me nothing, and besides, I ain't needing no vindi-nothing."

"You may not, but Lilly needs to have her name cleared."

"Cleared from what?"

"It's been rumored around school that her baby is for the Negro janitor."

My blood started to boil, "The janitor? What foolishness you saying 'bout my child and her baby being for Mr. Thomas."

"Mr. Thomas? That's his name? How do you know him? Has he come to see you about the baby?"

"Mr. Hirsh, I don't know what it is you think you know but I wish you would stop saying this thing 'bout my child and Mr. Thomas. He ain't have to come and see me 'cause he ain't got nothing to do with my Lilly and no baby. He's a respectful, church-goin' family man. Now you may think you know a lot of things, but you ain't know nothing. You working right there with Mr. Thomas and you didn't even know that Mr. Thomas' name is Mr. Thomas, so how you goin' know 'bout my child and her personal private business concerning her baby and who the father of her baby is?"

"But I know."

"Mr. Hirsh, I don't know what you think you know, but whatever you think you know is wrong. My Lilly ain't that kinda girl. She ain't make no baby for Mr. Thomas."

"I know."

"What is it you think you know and how come you know?"

"Mrs. Greenwood, you and I could go on beating around the bush like this for a month of Sundays and we'll still end up in the same place so I'll just come right out and say it."

"Say what, Mr. Hirsh?"

"You know."

"Mr. Hirsh, I know a lot of things, but what is this particular thing you think I know?"

"About me."

"Again, Mr. Hirsh, I ain't meaning you no disrespect, but I don't know nothing 'bout you and for the sake of my job, I would like to keep it that way."

"What do you want, Mrs. Greenwood. What do you want from me?"

"I ain't want nothing more from you than for you to let me get on with my work 'fore your momma comes back and finds that I being too familiar with her son and send me home."

I was expecting him to walk away again, but he didn't; instead he looked me directly in my eyes and said, "Lilly and her baby is what we have to talk about. They are my business."

"Mr. Hirsh, I don't see how my Lilly and her baby is any of your business."

"Mrs. Greenwood, they are my business because I'm the baby's father."

Before I could open my mouth to say anything, I heard a sudden intake of air like somebody was suffocating. Both Mr. Hirsh and I turned around to see his momma standing behind us.

"Lilly? Baby? Father?"

"Oh my God, Mother. I didn't hear you come in."

"Matt, what are you talking about? Which Lilly and what baby are you talking about?"

I stood there and watched Mrs. Hirsh struggle with the truth that I had lived with for a little more than a year. She was struggling with what she'd just heard. It was sucking the air right out of her. She tried to speak, but it came out as a raspy whisper, the way people sound just before they die, but dying or not, she was determined to speak. She tried again. I was sure that Mrs. Hirsh was goin' use her last breath to tell me to get the hell out of her house. I was wrong. Mrs. Hirsh spoke, but not like a dying woman. Somewhere between her grappling with the truth and that struggle to breathe, she found her voice and spoke. "Matthew David Hirsh, is this Lilly you and Mrs. Greenwood are talking about her Lilly?"

"Yes Mother."

"Then tell me how her Lilly and her baby have anything to do with you? You've never even met the little nigger b..."

"Don't say that word, Mother."

Mrs. Hirsh was struggling to speak through teeth that wouldn't open. "Matthew! Don't you tell me what to say! If I want to call her a nigger bitch, I will!"

"Don't do that, Mother. Mrs. Greenwood is standing right here. Lilly is her daughter and that's very hurtful."

"Hurtful my ass! We aren't talking about a respectful Jewish girl, Matthew! We're talking about a nigger servant and her nigger daughter. I can call the little nigger a bitch if I want."

"Very well, Mother, as you wish. I did meet her; Mrs. Greenwood's Lilly. I do know her. I was her math teacher."

"So what does that have to do with anything, Matthew? For God's sake, what does her little nigger pup have to do with you?"

"I told you before, Mother, about those derogatory terms, but if you insist, I'll tell you then. It's true."

By this time, Mrs. Hirsh was screaming. "True! True! What is true, Matthew, and don't you toy with me? What is true?"

That boy looked his mother dead in her eyes just the way he'd looked me in mine and declared, "The baby, Mother. The baby, Lilly's baby, is also my baby. It's mine, Mother."

Mrs. Hirsh looked as if her eyes were goin' jump from her head, grow feet, and run down the hall. She was screaming so loud now that her voice was vibrating off her nice clean floors and wall. I was waiting for her head to bust and splatter blood and brains all over the curtains, carpet, and everything. I wasn't goin' to clean that up not after what she'd just call my Lilly.

"Don't you stand there and tell me that shit. None of it can be true, Matthew. You're white! You're my son! You're a Jew! It can't be true! Don't you dare open your mouth and tell me that you fucked some nigger bitch and fathered a nigger baby!"

"Mother, stop cursing and screaming like that."

"Don't you tell me not to curse. You fucked a nigger, Matthew? A nigger for God's sake, and you fathered a nigger baby!"

"I didn't father a nigger baby. I fathered a baby."

"Stop sounding so fucking pious and proud about you fathered a baby. How do you know it's yours? What makes you so sure she didn't sleep with the whole fucking neighborhood. You know how nigger bitches can be! They fuck…"

Before Mrs. Hirsh could finish, Matthew interrupted her. "Mother, stop with all this profanity and hatred. I realize this is a shock to you as it was for me when I finally figured it out."

"Figured? Matthew, you don't know what you're saying? Have you forgotten that you are married? Have you thought about what this will do to your future, and to Madeline, should she find out?"

"Why do you always have to be like that?"

"Like what, Matthew? Thinking about your future? Matthew, she's a nigger! A nigger, Matthew!"

"Mother!"

"Don't you 'Mother' me! You're the one that couldn't control your urges. Do you think you're the only one who ever had urges? Don't you think that I don't sometimes wonder what bacon and pork tastes like, but you've never seen me running to the butcher and bringing that stinking flesh in my home, have you, Matthew? Why couldn't you have done the same with your lust for nigger flesh?"

"Mother, this is useless. We can't get anywhere with you taking that attitude."

"Attitude, Matthew? It wasn't me who slept with the nigger bitch. It was you and now you're trying to bring shame into this family by standing there and admitting to fathering some nigger bitch's pup. What do you want me to do, Matthew? What?"

"I would like you to be a bit more understanding."

"Matthew, it is clear that you have lost your God-damn mind. A bit more understanding? Of what? The next thing I know, you will be suggesting that I hug Promise here and take her with me to Tiffany so we can pick out a silver spoon to put in the pup's mouth? Is that what you're expecting, Matthew? Well let me tell you something, Matthew, nigger pups don't use spoons; silver or otherwise. They are just good for lapping milk at the tits of the nigger bitch that birth them. I won't be accepting any nigger bitch or her pup in this family even if you think you can teach it to use a spoon. Not in this house! Ever! You hear me! If you want, you can go and see about the pup, but I don't ever want to hear one word of it ever spoken in this house again. Do I make myself clear, Matthew?"

I didn't hear what he said because I was already at the front door. While Matthew and his mother were having their sophisticated argument,

I'd gathered my things and was at the door. I had my hand on the knob and was about to turn it when I heard his footsteps.

"Mrs. Greenwood, wait a minute. Don't go."

"Don't go, Mr. Hirsh? Lilly may not mean nothing to you or your mother, but she's my whole life. I want you to be clear on one thing. Just now when your Momma was talking 'bout me and my daughter like we were some slaves on a plantation, it was only my fear of prison that kept me from closing my eyes and taking a swing at her. I done serve her and your whole family well all these years and she didn't have to pour out all her hate for us Negro people like that for me to hear. "

I started to cry. "She was talking 'bout my child and grandchild. So wait? For what Mr. Hirsh? To give her time to pile more of her hate on me and my child? No, Mr. Hirsh, there ain't nothing for me to wait for." Without another word, I opened the door and stepped out. To my surprise, he followed me.

"Mrs. Greenwood, wait a minute please. I realize you won't come back to work for us, but I also know my mother; before tonight is over, she will telephone half this neighborhood and tell them that you don't work for her anymore and not to let you work for them either. By tomorrow morning, you won't have any work. She's going to do it, Mrs. Greenwood. I know her."

Sniffling I said, "But, Mr. Hirsh, she can't do that. I have to work. I depend on them jobs to take care of me, Lilly, and the baby. If I don't have work, how am I goin' take care of us?"

"I don't have an answer right now, but may I offer you a ride home?"

"I don't need no ride. I can take the bus as I always do. I need those jobs."

"Please, Mrs. Greenwood. Let me take you home. I really would like to talk to you."

"Again, Mr. Hirsh, no disrespect, but what you and I got to talk about?"

"Lilly."

Before he could get one more word out, I took a deep breath, dried my eyes, and stopped him. "Mr. Hirsh, Lilly and her baby they are my business, not yours. Where was you when that baby was growing in her belly? All she had was me? Where was you, Mr. Hirsh? Don't tell me then that you didn't know it was you who got her like that. Don't tell me that it took gossip 'bout some janitor nonsense before you figured out it was you. Don't tell me that. I can tell that you know my Lilly was pure. So go on and tell me, Mr. Hirsh, what you think me and you got to talk about."

"Mrs. Greenwood, I need to let you know how afraid I was when I heard the other children talking about her being knocked up. I knew I was responsible, but I didn't know what to do. Please, Mrs. Greenwood, believe me, and please let me drive you home."

I didn't know where my fighting spirit went, but all I knew was that I didn't feel like fighting no more. I looked at him and just said, "Thank you."

"Mrs. Greenwood, when I get to your home, may I come in and see the baby?"

"I don't think that goin' be a good idea."

"Why?"

"Well, the baby you see, it's mighty fair-skinned and people would be talking even more if they see you."

"I would still like to see the baby. I've admitted that it's my child. I believe I have a right to see my child and I will one way or another."

"I can't fight with you. You want to see the baby; see the baby."

We drove the rest of the way in silence. When we got to the house, he turned off the engine and was out his door and opening my door before the sound of the engine had died down. He walked beside me as if he'd walked besides me and towards that gate a thousand times. I opened the door, let him in, and walked in behind him into the living room. I knew I didn't have to worry 'bout the house being clean 'cause it was all that Lilly had to do beside care for her baby.

"Mr. Hirsh, I'll go get the baby."

"Mrs. Greenwood, can I see Lilly too, please?"

I turned away without answering. I had only intended to bring Drea down. There was no sense in letting Lilly know that he was there; it would do her no good. Outside Lilly's bedroom, I stopped for a minute to say a quick prayer. I wanted to be sure I was doing the right thing. As soon as I was done, I gave a light tap on the door and walked in. "Lilly, there's someone here to see the baby and they've asked to see you as well."

"Momma, ain't nobody come see me since I had the baby. So who would come now?"

"It's Matthew Hirsh. He's downstairs. If you don't want to see him, I can tell him that you're sleeping or something, and I'll take the baby down to see him."

I watched as joy itself jumped all over my child. She looked the way I did every time someone said, 'Milton.' And then she said in a voice that sounded scared, "Ma, I want to see him and can I be the one to show him his daughter? I want to be able to remember it so that I can tell her. Can I, Ma? Can I be the one to take her to him, please?"

"Lilly, she's your baby, you do what you want with her."

"Ma, can you help me change her? I would like her to look and smell pretty the first time he sees her."

"Sure, Lilly and while I'm changing her, why don't you pull a comb through your hair and put on a brighter color dress on. Them dark color clothes you always wearing got you looking like you a widow wife or something."

I changed the baby while Lilly changed. I went to my room once Lilly took her baby and walked downstairs to where Matthew Hirsh was waiting for them.

Chapter 54

Father Behold Your Daughter, Daughter Behold Your Father

Lilly

Matthew was just sitting there looking as if any minute he would make a break for it. I walked slowly, not because I wanted to keep him waiting, but because I was scared. I didn't have time to worry about what I was going to say because at my next step the board under my foot creaked and he looked up. He looked up, smiled, and got up from the chair; with two giant-size steps he covered the distance between us. He was standing beside me just as he had on that day we'd walked away from each other; shy and afraid.

I guess he was afraid because in my arms was the product of that day. My heart swelled. I couldn't believe the torrent of emotions sweeping over me for him. As I stood looking at him, he could see I was afraid and nervous too. But I was sure he could see in those dark pools I call eyes; love. I still loved him. He breathed deeply. It was one of relief. I couldn't believe how much I wanted him to still love me. I spoke. His cocoon broke. The look in my eyes had freed him.

Nervously I said, "Ma said that you wanted to see the baby." Stretching my hand out with our daughter in it, I added, "Would you like to hold her?"

"A girl?"

"You didn't know?"

"No, your mother didn't tell me."

He stepped in a little closer and, taking the baby like he was being handed a gossamer angel, he took his daughter; our daughter. Looking into her uncovered face he noted, "Lilly, she's so beautiful."

"Thank you."

"Lilly, oh my God, Lilly, I'm so sorry. I never meant for you, for this, for…"

"You never meant for me to be pregnant? Is that what you're trying to say?"

"I don't mean that. Actually, I'm not sure what I'm trying to say, but you once said you loved me."

I didn't say anything, I just looked at him. A part of me was wondering why he was talking as if he knew what was going on in my heart. I knew that he couldn't, or he would never have said, "once said you loved me." There was nothing in the past tense about the way I felt for him. With him standing so close, I could hardly breathe. Past. If only he knew.

"Aren't you going to say anything Lilly?"

"Like what?"

"That's what I mean. You won't even say my name. Are you angry at me? Lilly, even if you're angry at me, I want you to look at our child. Look at her, Lilly, and then at me."

"What do you mean, look at her? I've looked at her. I've had seven months to do nothing, but look at her. So why are you asking me to look at her now. I know what she looks like."

"But, Lilly, you've never looked at her in her father's arms before? I know you had to give up on you and your mother's dreams of you going to Fisk but I promise you that I'll do all I can to help you with the baby. I feel stupid calling my daughter 'the baby'. What is her name?"

"Andrea Matti Hirsh Greenwood."

"Matti Hirsh?"

"Does that bother you? I called her Matti Hirsh just in case she never saw you; she would at least have your name."

"Thank you, Lilly."

"What's to thank me for?"

"Because you've suffered and given up so much and yet you thought enough of me to give her my name."

"I wanted to keep remembering you even though I knew you weren't goin' be around to help me take care of her."

"I'll help you, Lilly."

"What are you going do? Come over here and help change her diapers?"

"I can't do that, but I'll help you."

"How?"

"I don't quite have it worked out in my head yet, but I'm going to figure something out. I don't know when I'll see you both again, but you will hear from me. I may not come by, but I'll take care of the two of you."

"You make it sound like you going away forever."

"That's not it, but my situation is such that I won't be able to come by and see you regularly."

"Is it because of your wife?"

"You know?"

"Ma told me when I was pregnant."

"Lilly, believe me, I was telling you the truth when I told you I loved you. I really was."

"What about your wife? Didn't you love her?"

"The truth is I thought I loved Madeline, but then my heart fell for you and I followed. You are the only one that occupies my heart."

"What does that mean? Occupies your heart? What am I supposed to do with that, Matthew?"

"Let me occupy your heart. Can you still do that, Lilly? Can you let me occupy your heart?"

"But you're married."

"I know. I'm asking if you can do that even though I'm married."

"You're asking a lot. When me and you were together that time, I didn't know 'bout you getting ready to marry nobody, but you did and you let me be with you. Then I had a baby for you and I didn't hear one word from you. Ma had to figure out everything and now you standing there months and months after I ain't seen you and you got a wife yet you asking me to let you occupy my heart. That ain't fair."

"Love or life isn't fair, Lilly. It never is or …"

"Or what, it would've made me white, Jewish, and rich?"

"Don't make this about color, Lilly. It never was. So don't do this now. You are right, Lilly. I don't have a right to ask that of you just now. Let's leave it alone for now. I just want to sit here with you and my daughter. She's my only child, you know."

"I didn't know that."

We sat in silence. I sat quietly beside him watching him as he watched the baby. As the silence enveloped us, he looked at me and I could see he looked sad then he kissed the baby on her forehead and cheeks and gave her back to me as if something had suddenly pained him.

"Lilly, I have to go now. Thank you for letting me see her."

"It's no problem."

"I'm glad I came. I will always remember the first day I saw my first child. Lilly, I want you to know something and I mean this from the bottom of my heart: the love that created our child was real. I wasn't lying to you when I said I loved you. Never mind what happens from this point on, know that I mean it. I loved you then and I'll continue to love you, Lilly, always."

I wanted to cry. I wanted to beg him to stay with me and figure out a way, but I knew that he had another life. I said nothing more. Then Matthew reached into his pocket and took out a small thin book. He tore several sheets out then he wrote on each one and when he'd done this about seven times, he put them on the coffee table. He said, "Those are for you and our daughter." Then he got up and walked to the door and I followed. He was still holding the baby. With the baby still in his arms, he reached to open the door and just before he turned the knob, he stopped. He folded the baby into his chest as if he was making a permanent impression. Satisfied that he had a good enough impression, he kissed her again and handed her back to me. Then he touched my cheek and almost as if he didn't care that Ma was in the house, he closed the space between us and with the baby between us, he bent his head and whispered, 'Love her every day. On the days that I'm away, love her doubly hard. Love her always just the way we love each other.'

I said nothing. I couldn't or I would've choked. The words, along with all the love I felt for him, were bottlenecking in my throat. There was only enough room for the air to make it to my lungs. He stepped again to the door; this time he opened it and then just as quickly he shut it. He gathered us into his arms and kissed me hard and deep. I kissed him back. Again he reached for the doorknob. This time he opened it and stepped outside.

I closed the door but stood leaning against it until I heard his car drive away. Then I cried. I was crying so uncontrollably that I never heard Ma come in the room. Ma went to take the baby from me but I held her tight. Ma said, "I guess he left."

"Yes, he left."

"What did he have to say?"

"About the baby?

"No, about the man in the moon."

"Sorry, Ma. He thinks she's beautiful. He's likes her name, and Ma?"

"Yes, Lilly."

"He left these checks?"

"What he left checks for? Don't he know that you ain't got no banking account?"

"Ma, he didn't give them to me."

"He gave them to the baby? That's even dumber and he's a big-shot college man. You would think that his fancy foo foo Harvard school would've taught him more than that."

"No, Ma, he didn't write them out to the baby. He made them to CASH."

"Lilly, did you say cash?"

"Yes, Ma. All of them say 'pay to the order of CASH.'"

"Well, how much he paying to cash?"

"I guess, Ma, that it must be some joke as you was figuring 'cause he didn't fill in any dollar amount?"

"What you mean he ain't fill in no dollar amount?"

"Here look, Ma, all of them are blank."

Ma sat down on the sofa and as she sat down, I handed the baby to her and took the checks and counted them. He'd left seven.

"Lilly, do you realize what he's done?"

"No."

"Lilly, even though I ain't never have no banking account, I've been around enough white people to know that what he done is to give you a lot of money."

"Ma, how is it that you goin' say that he gave me a lot of money when he ain't write in no amount. Ma, he ain't give us nothing. He ain't write nothing on these checks so I'm right back where I started, Ma. Me and Drea, we still got nothing. We only got you and whatever you bring home."

"Listen to me, Lilly, it ain't like that. These blank checks mean you can write in the amount you want yourself and that's how much they going give you when you go to his bank."

"But, Ma, how he knows how much I'm going to write it for? What if I write it for more than he got?"

"I think, Lilly that he must not think you can write enough numbers there that he can't fill."

"So you mean, Ma, that tomorrow if I wanted to I could go and get fifty dollars."

"I would say so, but I wouldn't get fifty. That would be a waste of time going to the bank. I say that tonight after we bathe Drea and when she's sleeping, we sit down and figure out what it is you both need the most. Then when we know how much that is, then you goin' write in that amount. Tomorrow you goin' go to the bank and see if it they give you the money."

Ma had me make out the first check for $250.00. She said just in case Matthew changed his mind about the rest of them checks. I was scared about going to the white people's bank and getting all that money, but Ma wasn't in a frame of mind to listen to me and my fears. She said, "You ain't got time to worry 'bout them white people. You and your baby got a right to eat and if her white father wants her to eat proper, then she goin' eat proper." I said nothing.

Then Ma said something I didn't know before. "His wicked mother done made me lose all my house-cleaning work 'cause she's hateful and wicked; now through her son she's goin' pay me and feed us. You goin' to that bank and you goin' get money to take care of you and your baby: Mrs. Hirsh goin' take care of you and your baby." I didn't have no other choice but to go when she said go.

The morning I was going to the bank, Ma was up early helping me to look like I was used to going to a bank. Ma had me put on my best Sunday dress, gloves, and even a hat. She said that all those fine white women wore hats when they went out so I should wear a hat too. I looked like I belonged in the bank. I was just hoping that the white people would feel that way when I showed up at their bank and not call the police on me just for being bold enough to walk in.

When I got back home, I was smiling. I told Ma that them white people weren't exactly welcoming to me, but they didn't call the police either. That bank lady didn't believe me 'bout the check being mine and had me wait while she phoned Matthew. I could hear the woman saying, "Mr. Hirsh, there's a Negro girl her with a check of yours, saying you gave it to her. Do you want us to call the police, sir?" My heart stopped as I waited for her to finish talking, but then she hung up the phone and came back. She still wasn't smiling or nice, but she asked me how I would like the money.

I didn't even think that she might have meant something else so I said, "Fast."

I took the money from the lady and put it in my church bag, clutched it tight to my chest, and walked out the white people's bank praying. I never stopped clutching and praying 'till I walked through the doors and saw Ma. I took that money out faster than I'd put it in; it was the most money Ma and I had ever seen at one time.

About a month after I'd gone to the bank and cashed the last check, I got a package from Matthew. It was a fresh set of checks. Just as soon as I sat down with the checks and was trying to figure what I would do, a piece of paper fell out. It was a note asking me to meet him. He wanted me to bring the baby and meet him. He would tell me where later.

When Ma came home from work, she wasn't too happy, but since Matthew had helped her get a new job and he was taking care of us, she'd didn't object too much. The only thing that bothered Ma was that she couldn't understand how I was happy just staying home with the baby and not doing anything to better myself.

Chapter 55

And Unto Them A Son Is Born

Lilly

Almost nine months to the day after I came back from our little hide-away trip, I gave birth to a boy: Andre. Ma was upset that I'd become pregnant again, but she didn't really say anything because Matthew was taking care of us. None of us, including Ma, wanted or needed anything; he kept the money coming. He always sent enough to hold us over for about six months.

When Andrea was ten years old, just before her eleventh birthday, Matthew asked her what she wanted for her birthday, as he'd done every year. All of us went quiet when she said, "Daddy, I want a house."

"A house for your dolls?"

"No, Daddy, I want a real house with my own room and Andre can have his own room."

"And where do you want this house, Princess?"

"I want this house, Daddy. Mrs. Ross told Nana that she is ready to go down Savannah to be with her daughter, but she can't find anybody to buy her house. Daddy, will you buy it for me?"

Ma who usually had nothing to say when Andrea or Andre was talking to Matthew said, "Andrea! Mrs. Ross wasn't speaking to you. She was speaking to me and repeating something you overheard in a private conversation is rude. That was Mrs. Ross' personal private business, not yours."

"Ma, she didn't mean any harm."

"It's not about harm, Lilly; it's about repeating someone else's business. What if Mrs. Ross didn't want him to know she was having family or money trouble."

"Lilly and Andrea, your mother and grandmother is right. A person's private business is just that: private. None of us have a right to divulge another person's personal business unless they say that we can."

"So, Ma, when that man came so long ago and said we had to move from Aunt Bess' house, why didn't you tell him that? Why, Ma? You didn't question him or anything; you just packed up and walked away. Aunt Bess wouldn't have just packed up and walked away; she would have challenged him, fought him, made him bring more proof than one piece of paper saying this is my house, now get out."

"Lilly, what are you talking about?"

Ma started to get angry, but at that point I didn't care; well, I cared but now that it had come out I wanted to know, wanted answers about that part of our lives that had just gone unquestioned, and if Matthew could help us get answers, I was willing to talk about Ma's personal private business as she called it.

"Lilly, that's my business and it was Aunt Bess', so drop it. I mean it. Let's leave her business out of your daughter's business."

"Mrs. Greenwood, perhaps I can help; at least look into the matter. If it concerns, Lilly, it concerns me."

"So what are we teaching Andrea and Andre? Are we teaching them that they can just snoop into anybody's business if they feel like it and then go and talk about it? Is that what we are teaching them?"

At that point, Matthew said, "Andrea and Andre, why don't the two of you go to your room for a little while. Your Nana, Mommy, and I need to have some grown-up time."

"So, Daddy, am I going to get this house?"

"Let your Mommy and I talk and we'll come up with something very special for your birthday."

Andrea and Andre got up and as they walked out the room, Andrea said softly to her brother, "Nana isn't going to let him. She's going to ruin my birthday."

Ma said, "Andrea, don't be a fresh mouth. I heard you. Now, do you want me to come upstairs with you?"

"No, Nana."

No sooner were the children gone from the room than Ma started, "Mr. Hirsh." Ma had never gotten around to calling Matthew anything other than Mr. Hirsh. "I don't mean you any disrespect. You've been taking good care of Lilly and the children, but my business is my business. What happened so many years ago on Chauncey Street is my business and Aunt Bess' personal private business, and I don't want to discuss her business with you."

"I can understand that, Mrs. Greenwood, but what if there's something I can discover that would help?"

"How or what?"

"I won't or can't know unless I know what happened. If its bothering Lilly then I would want to do what I can to ease her concerns."

"But it's not Lilly's problem."

"Fine, Mrs. Greenwood. If you don't want to discuss it, that's your choice. It's just that I have many resources available to me now that I'm at the law firm."

"Law firm? I thought you were a math teacher."

Matthew smiled and then he said to Ma, "Mrs. Greenwood, I am qualified and certified to teach math, but I've also sat and passed the bar."

"The bar? What does sitting at or passing a bar have to do with helping me, Mrs. Ross, or Aunt Bess? That is assuming any of us wanted your help."

"Mrs. Greenwood, it's not a bar where you get drinks, but it's what you do to become a lawyer; just a bunch of test that say you paid attention at law school and now you can go and figure out how to help people solve their legal troubles."

"We don't have legal troubles, Mr. Hirsh, none at all."

"Ok, Lilly, we aren't getting anywhere. It's getting late and Andrea is expecting to hear something about her birthday gift."

"I'll take care of Andrea and her gift."

Ma was still sore at me so she got up, said goodnight to us and went to her room.

As soon as Ma left, I turned to Matthew and told him what I knew about the house on Chauncey Street and that this man just showed up and said we had to move and Ma, without even so much as questioning him, packed us up and moved us here to Mrs. Ross' house. Matthew had a lot of questions, more questions than I had answers for but he said he'd look into it.

Chapter 56

Right Arm Of The Law

Ma stayed mad at me for a few days, but soon she stopped being mad at me and the whole subject of the house on Chauncey Street never came up again. Andrea was another story, though. She'd set her mind on getting her own room and the closer it got to her birthday; it was all we heard about.

Matthew came by when he could and knowing that the house on Chauncey Street was a sore spot with Ma, he never asked anything else about it, well, not with Ma around anywhere. We were slowly approaching Andrea's birthday and with it being just days away, Andrea was turning up the heat. Every time Matthew called or had a chance to come by, Andrea hinted, and big, that her birthday was coming up, like if we could dare forget it.

That was Andrea's big thing: her birthday. It was to Andrea as if no one else in the house had a birthday. That wasn't really her fault because from the day she was born, she'd been the center of attention and Matthew was the one who spoiled her the most. So she was just being the child he'd made her. She was ready for her birthday gift and no doll's house was going to satisfy her. Matthew had his hands full with this birthday request.

On the morning of her birthday, Andrea got up almost as early as God did on the day of creation. She came bounding downstairs as if she expected to see Matthew sitting in the living room. When she got into the living room and saw that he wasn't there, I hardly got a good morning. It was, "Mommy it's my birthday!"

"Yes, Andrea, I know. I was there."

"Funny, Ma. Did you hear from Daddy? Did he get me a house?"

"Andrea Greenwood, listen to yourself, 'did he get me a house?' You are saying that as casually as if it's a normal request or one that you really believe your daddy is going to take seriously. Drea, people just don't get houses for birthday presents. So, let's make sure that you don't get your feelings all hurt when your daddy shows up this evening and he's not dragging a house behind his car."

I could see that Drea didn't believe me. Somehow she believed that her daddy was going to show up and bring her a house because she'd asked him for one. "Drea, I'm sorry that you've got your hopes all up like this. I should have let you know that it was not a fair thing to ask for from that day you asked your daddy for a house."

Drea waited 'till I was done talking and she took a deep breath, leaned all her weight on one foot and with just enough of a pout to her mouth where I didn't step from where I was and slap it off her face, she said, "Daddy always gets me what I want. Just you wait and see, I'm going to get a house for my birthday."

"You know what, Drea that's between you and your daddy. I'm going to stay out of it."

Drea looked at me as if she was saying, 'you should stay out of me and my daddy's business.' I took a deep breath and I felt sorry for her because Matthew had spoiled her and now here she was thinking there was nothing wrong in asking for a house and she wasn't even thirteen yet. I wondered what she would want for her twenty-first birthday. I let the thought leave my head as I said, "Birthday girl, are you ready for your big birthday breakfast?"

I saw the change in her. That was the magic question that brought her back from the brink of imagining a disappointment; her father not giving her something she'd asked for. But for now, she knew that her request, whatever she wanted for breakfast, would be fulfilled. I intended to satisfy whatever wish she wanted this morning; as long as it had to do with eggs, bacon, sausage, pancakes, waffles, or any breakfast food. After that she would go back to the edge of disappointment and try to imagine her unimaginable.

Smiling, she ran back to the bottom of the stairs and shouting up, she called, "Andre and Nana come on get up. It's my birthday; Mommy is making me my big birthday breakfast. Andre! Nana! Come!"

Ma and Andre came down the stairs and Drea started acting like the princess she believed herself to be. Breakfast was the same as if it were Christmas or New Year's Day; we ate and laughed. There were no gifts as was now the tradition. No gifts were ever given or exchanged unless Matthew was there. It was the one thing that he'd asked of us, that we wait and allow him to be a part of all our celebrations.

How Drea got though the day was beyond me. This was her big day and she knew that her daddy was going to give her this house for her birthday; she just knew it. At the first ring of the doorbell, Drea was at the door. It was Matthew. Drea's excited voice filled the house. She'd waited months for this moment and now that it was here, she was beside herself. Matthew was only able to get one foot through the door and then all her anxieties exploded in one long jumbled series of words that were supposed to be a question. Her excitement got behind her thoughts and just pushed them out; there was no order but Matthew, being Matthew, understood her. He should, this was the princess monster he'd created.

Matthew hugged her and as they walked into the house in their tight father and daughter embrace, I realized that I'd been holding my breath. I was nervous for her. I wanted and yet I didn't want her to get what she'd wished for. A part of me felt it would be wrong for Matthew to come through with such an enormous request now. What would she expect from him and life after this? The thought was scary, but it didn't have time to settle in my head as Matthew asked, "Well, Princess, are you ready to open your birthday presents?"

Drea was so excited, she just nodded. Matthew teased Drea, "Where do you want to start? Which gift do you want to open first?"

Before Drea could answer, Andre, holding his present out to her, said, "Mine, mine... open mine first, Drea."

Drea took it and it was the fastest present I ever saw opened. Paper and bows were flying all over the place; she had it opened and out and was moving onto the next box when Andre said, "But, Drea, you didn't even look at it. Do you like what I got for you?"

Drea put the next gift down, which was from me, and she went back to Andre and picking up the framed picture of the four of us on our last holiday. She smiled and answered, "Yes, Andre, I love it. It's beautiful. Thank you." He smiled but it was a different smile. She'd hurt his feelings by not taking the time to look at it before reaching for the next gift.

Holding the picture in her hand, she asked, "Mommy, can I open your gift next?" Andre's hurt feeling had slowed her absent-minded rush as she hurried to get to the one she believed was the most important one: the gift of a house from her daddy. She opened the next two gifts slower and she stopped at each one, looked, commented and said thank you. She looked at Matthew, she was ready, and she'd waited. He had to have her gift, the one she'd waited for: her house.

Matthew reached into his pocket and took out an envelope. He didn't give it to Drea, instead he handed it to Ma and he said, "Drea, I thought very hard about what you asked me for and I want you to know that I came very close to getting you just what you wanted, but I couldn't."

When Matthew said, 'couldn't, Drea started to cry and she said, "But, Daddy, it's my birthday. You always get me what I want for my birthday."

"That's true, Princess, but this wasn't an ordinary birthday request. I couldn't just go to the store and buy you a house. A house is a major investment and besides, you are eleven. Eleven is a little young to be a homeowner."

Drea was outright crying now. I moved closer to her and hugged her. She protested, "But, Mommy, I want my own room. I want to live in a house just like Daddy. I want to live in a house, Mommy. I want to live in a house."

By this time, Drea was wailing. Her eleven-year-old brain couldn't figure out why this was so hard for her giant of a daddy to do; after all, he'd done everything else. She just wanted a house: that wasn't something he couldn't do. She was sure of it.

I expected Matthew to come to Drea and try to comfort her but he didn't. Instead he turned to Ma and he said, "Go ahead, Miss. Greenwood, open the envelope."

When Matthew said that I became angry and I asked angrily, "Matthew, you didn't bring Drea a gift?"

Matthew looked at me and I could see disappointment in his face. He asked and in a much more controlled tone that the one I'd used, "Lilly, when have I not given Drea a gift for her birthday, Christmas, or any holiday? So why wouldn't I give her a gift today?"

A still crying Drea complained, "So Daddy, where's my gift then?"

Matthew answered, "Princess, please. In one minute. Mrs. Greenwood, please open the envelope and then I'll give my princess her birthday gift."

Ma opened the envelope without any questions. She took out a sheet of paper and as she started to read, tears came from her eyes and ran down her cheeks. She held the piece of paper out to me. I read it and I also started to cry. Ma spoke her first words since we started opening Drea's gifts. She simply said, "Thank you. Thank you."

Matthew replied, "You are welcome. Now, can I give Drea her present?"

Ma nodded and Matthew said, "Come on everyone, Drea's present is waiting."

I knew without asking where we were going. I followed Matthew out to the car. We got in and he drove the short distance to Chauncey

Street. We were in front of Aunt Bess' house. The lights were on. As we got out the car, he reached into the breast pocket of his jacket and handed Ma a key, telling her, "It works, Mrs. Greenwood. Let's go in."

Ma was crying so hard I don't think she heard anything that he said. Ma walked up the stairs and put the key in the lock. The door opened. She stepped in and we followed. Everything was the same, but different. The rooms were freshly painted, the huge mirror that stood in the hallway was shining as I'd never seen it shine, and everywhere you looked clean, fresh polished wood and mirrors shone back at you.

Matthew declared, "Let's go in the dining room. " We walked into the familiar dining room and on the brand new dining room table was the biggest birthday cake I'd ever seen and next to it was the biggest doll's house I'd ever seen. Drea saw the cake and house and she was over to the doll's house with as much excitement as if it were a real house. Matthew was smiling and Ma, well she was still crying and it was Andre who asked the question that helped to bring us all back to Earth, "Ma, whose house is this?"

It was Matthew who answered. "It's your Nana's house. It's the house where your mommy was born. This was your great-aunt Bess' house and has been your Nana's since January 1, 1930. That's the day your great-aunt Bess willed this house to her."

Ma sat in one of the chairs and looking at Matthew, she said, "Thank you so much, Mr. Hirsh. Thank you for caring enough to look into the matter even though," she added with a big smile on her tearstained face, "I told you that this was my personal private business."

Matthew replied, "Before we cut the cake, there's one more thing I'd like to show you all. Come." He headed up the stairs and we followed and at the top of the stairs there was a sign reading - *This Way Drea Hirsh Greenwood.* Drea looked at Matthew and was about to ask a question when he told her, "Follow the sign." Drea led the way and we followed down the hall. There was a sign on a door saying – *Enter Drea Hirsh Greenwood!* Drea pushed the door and was about to enter the darkened room when Matthew reached for and flipped the switch. The room was flooded with light and as our eyes adjusted, inside was the most beautiful little girl's room I'd ever seen. Drea let out a scream that was loud enough to bring down the rafters. Matthew looked at her and smiling he said, "Happy Birthday, Princess. Your very own room."

Drea ran back to her daddy and as she hugged him as she told him, "Thank you, Daddy. Thank you for my very own room."

"You are welcome, Princess. Be happy in your room."

"I will, Daddy, I will."

Chapter 57

A Change of Address

Andrea

All of us including Mrs. Ross moved from Macon Street. Nana, Mommy, Andre, and I moved to Chauncey Street; Mommy and Nana moved back in but Andre and I moved in for the first time. It was such a happy day for Nana. She went from room to room touching everything and crying. She cried the hardest when she went to Aunt Bess' room. Auntie Thea, who'd visited us regularly when we were on Macon Street, came by with her children, except Cousin Bernard. He was with Uncle Philip, she said. He was learning the business and was going to take it over with his two older brothers as she and Uncle Philip were getting ready to move to Virginia where Philip had some land and had built them a fine house.

Auntie Thea and Nana talked about Aunt Bess so much I almost expected to see her walk into the house, but she didn't. After Auntie Thea left, I couldn't wait to get to my room and spend my first night there. Daddy also had a room done for Andre and so for the first time ever, we were going to sleep apart. I was going to miss Andre, but I was glad to be alone in my own room. Daddy hadn't given me my own house, but he'd given me the next best thing: my own room.

As Daddy had done since before Andre was born, he planned our week away with him. Each year, we got a week out of Daddy's life. Somehow, Daddy always found a place where we could meet him and we could pretend to be a family. At the end of one of those weeks, when we'd been back at Chauncey Street about two years, we returned to the house and Nana, who hadn't been feeling really well but not sick enough for us to stay home with her, asked Mommy to take her to the emergency room.

Andre and I went over to Ms. Lewis' house. We were at Ms. Lewis for quite a long time, and when Mommy returned, Nana wasn't with her. Back at home, I went into the kitchen to see if Nana was getting me and

Andre something to eat 'cause she knew that while we were at Ms. Lewis' house, she never fed us. Ms. Lewis had told us that her house was no restaurant and if our mommy didn't feed us before she brought us over, then Mommy intended for us to stay hungry.

Nana had gotten so angry when I told her, she wanted to go over to Ms. Lewis' house and remind her whose grandchildren she was talking to. But Nana never did do that, instead she just made sure we had something to eat before we went and always had something waiting for us when we returned. Today, there was nothing. "Mommy, where's Nana?"

"Drea, your Nana didn't come home with me."

"Why not?"

"The doctors said they wanted to do some more tests to see why your Nana was feeling so sick."

"Will she be here when we get home from school tomorrow?"

"No and since I have to go back to the hospital tomorrow, I've asked Ms. Lewis to pick you all up from school, OK."

"You can't have Ms. Lewis pick us up."

"And why not?"

"Because Ms. Lewis said that her house ain't no restaurant and since Nana won't be here when we get home, me and Drea goin' be hungry 'cause Ms. Lewis don't give us no food."

"She doesn't?"

"It's true, Mommy, and Ms. Lewis said she don't feed no white man's children."

Mommy, who had been standing all this time, sat down. She sat down as if somebody had walked up to her and pushed her when she wasn't looking. Ma just sat there saying nothing and then she started to cry.

"Drea, how long ago did Ms. Lewis say this to you and Andre?"

"I don't know exactly when but it was a long, long time."

"So why didn't you tell me."

"'Cause."

"'Cause what?"

"'Cause Nana was always here to give us something when we got home, so we didn't care that Ms. Lewis didn't give us any of her food. Nana said she would see that we always had something to eat when we got in"

"Your Nana knew that Ms. Lewis talked about your daddy?"

"No, Mommy, I didn't remember to tell her that part, I just told her about the food 'cause we were hungry."

Mommy looked at me and Andre and said, "If anyone says anything to either of you again about your daddy, you're to tell me. Don't keep any kind of secrets from me, ok?"

We both nodded. Then Andre asked, "Mommy, so where me and Drea going be tomorrow when you got to go to the doctor?"

"I don't know, Andre, but I'll figure something out."

"Mommy?"

"Yes, Andre?"

"Can Daddy come and stay with us 'till you get back from seeing about Nana?"

"No, Andre, your father has to work."

"Mommy, why doesn't Daddy live here with us? If Daddy lived here with us, we would never have to go over to Ms. Lewis' house. Daddy could stay when you have to go and do things and when Daddy has to go and do things, you would stay with us, right, Mommy?"

"Now the two of you listen to me. Your father can't stay with you tomorrow, nor the next day, or the day after that, do you understand?"

"But why Mommy, and why doesn't Daddy come here ever?"

"Andre, he just can't. Just try to understand that he loves us all very much. He just can't live with us, but if he could, he would. Now, until things change, I don't really want to talk about your father not being here."

Andre could tell that Ma's patience was wearing thin so he didn't ask about Daddy anymore. Something in her voice said that tonight wasn't the night.

The following morning, Mommy made our breakfast and got us ready for school. She was rushing us, "Hurry up and eat that little bit of food, so we can get the bus."

We just hurried and ate. I don't remember tasting the breakfast. It went down so quickly. Outside Mommy said, "Hurry up. Why ya'll walking so slow this morning?"

We almost ran so that she wouldn't have to ask us to hurry again. When the bus stopped again, we didn't get off fast enough for her; she got off and she just started walking towards the school without us. We were trying to hurry, but Mommy was walking so fast that we were almost running. Then she stopped and through clenched teeth she said, "Why in God's good name are the two of you just so slow this morning? Just hurry up."

We ran even harder and when Andre reached Mommy, he put his hand in hers and because he hadn't learned yet to leave things alone, he had to say something. "Mommy?"

She stopped dead in her tracks and turned her head so slowly to look at him, it looked as if her head would never make it to face him. I held my breath. He was about to be knocked down by Mommy.

She answered him with one word. It sounded as if it came from nowhere and everywhere at the same time. "What?"

"When Mrs. Lewis treated us badly and didn't give us any food, Nana said she treated us that way 'cause we wasn't her children. So, Mommy, why you treating me and Drea like you is Ms. Lewis?"

Mommy let his hand go. Andre, who looked as if he were about to cry, just stood there looking at her. Ma bent to her knees and hugged Andre to her, and right there in front of our school, in front of all the parents and their children, she started crying.

"I'm sorry. Andre, your Nana was right. Mothers should never treat their children badly. I'm really sorry. I love you two more than the whole world."

Mommy took both our hands and we walked slowly the rest of the way to school.

That evening when she picked us up from school, her eyes were red. She'd been crying. Andre and I were quiet. Ma didn't ask us anything about school or homework or anything. She just hugged us.

"Mommy, aren't we going to the hospital?"

"No, Drea, we're going home."

"Mommy, are you taking us to Ms. Lewis'?"

"No."

We got home, changed, and started our homework. When we were done, we came downstairs and Mommy was sitting in Nana's chair where we'd left her when we went upstairs. There was no smell of food so I asked, "Mommy, is dinner goin' be ready soon."

"Dinner?"

Mommy said 'dinner' as if she wasn't sure what it was. I looked at Mommy and remembered Nana once saying, 'God helps those who help themselves.' I decided that I better do something and then God would notice that I was helping myself and he would come and help me. I went into the kitchen and made us sandwiches. Juice for me and milk for Andre. We were almost finished eating when Mommy came into the kitchen. She stood at the door watching us eat our sandwiches without her and Nana and she started to cry again. She just stood there with tears sliding down her face. Then the phone rang. Mommy jumped and then stared at the phone for a little while before she picked it up.

"Hello, Greenwood residence."

"This is Lillian Greenwood?"

"St. Mary's hospital?"

"Yes."

"Hold on. Drea, hold this phone and when I tell you to hang it up, hang it up."

Mommy walked out the kitchen and a few seconds later, she called, "Drea, hang up."

I hung the phone up and walked back over to my sandwich. I sat in silence trying to hear what she was saying but I couldn't hear. A few minutes of silence passed and then I heard Ma. She was crying. Then I heard her say, "Ok, thank you. I'll be there." Then she hung up. As soon as she hung up the phone, I could hear her dialing. Each number sounded as if it was taking a week to make it back around. Mommy was still crying.

"May I speak to Matthew Hirsh please?

"Ms. Lilly Greenwood.

"Thank you."

"Can you come over, Matt? I don't know what to do.

"In the kitchen.

"No, they are having sandwiches.

"Can't you change it?

"I've never asked before, not in all these years. Matt, it's my mother.

"Eight o'clock?

"Ok, see you then.

Sometime after we'd bathed and gotten ready for bed, the doorbell rang. It was Daddy. It felt funny to see him there. He looked as though he didn't belong. He belonged with us, but not in our house. He looked as if he belonged at the hotel. He wasn't a house-daddy. He was a hotel-daddy.

"Hi Daddy."

"Well, if it isn't my next two favorite people in the world."

"Daddy, why you saying the next two favorite people, who is your first favorite people."

"It's favorite person and your mommy is my first favorite person."

"But Daddy that can't be true 'cause Mommy, Drea, and Nana are my favorite persons and I never leave them the way you leave Mommy."

"Andre!"

Mommy shouted at Andre and he turned to run as if he'd done something bad when Daddy made two long steps and got to him before he could start his flight.

"Lilly, don't shout at the boy. He's young and he can only speak what comes to his mind. Don't be hard on him for things he doesn't understand."

"But, Matt, I've tried to explain to Andre."

"Then stop trying to explain. He's a boy and like all other boys, he wants his father around."

"Daddy, I just wish you were here with us all the time."

"And I wish that too, but I can't be here."

"Ms. Lewis said that you don't live here 'cause you is a white man."

Daddy looked at Andre as if someone had poured boiling oil in his shoes and told him to go ahead and put his foot in. "What did you say, Andre?"

"I said Ms. Lewis said you can't live here 'cause you is a white man and me and Drea is half-white, half-black, but we still be niggers. She says that you ain't want nobody to know you got nigger children."

Daddy sat down. He looked as if the hot oil in his shoes had burned his foot all the way to his heart.

"Good Lord, Lilly, who is this Ms. Lewis and why are my children around someone with such ugly prejudices and obviously no love for children?"

"Matt, I didn't know she was saying such things to the children."

"But who is she?"

"She's a neighbor a few doors from here." Mommy started to cry and Daddy got up from sitting beside Andre and walked over to where she was. He took Mommy into his arms as she cried. His holding her wasn't new to me, but here, in this house, it looked funny. I almost wanted to ask them why it looked funny, but then I understood. I'd always known he was Daddy, but he'd never been Daddy in this house. There had never been a daddy here in my house before today.

"Matt, I don't know what to do."

"Lilly, I don't want our children around that hateful ignorant woman ever again. If I wanted my children to be subjected to hatred, bigotry, and meanness, I would take them home to spend time with my mother, but since I haven't done that nor am I planning on doing that, I don't ever want that woman within a hair's breadth of my children. Are we clear on that, Lilly?"

Mommy took a little longer to answer than Daddy seemed to have the patience for and he repeated himself. "Lilly, do I make myself clear? Is that clear, Lilly?"

Mommy seemed too worn out to do anything other than nod and cry, but then she said, "I wasn't going send them back, Matt. I don't know what to do now that I have to be at the hospital every day and everything."

"Don't worry, Lilly, I'll figure something out. I'll take care of it. What time do they get home from school?"

"Matt, they don't get home from school, they are still too young to come home by themselves and if I get them here, who's going to watch them 'till I get home from the hospital."

"Don't worry, I'll figure something out."

I guess Daddy wanted to talk to Mommy alone so he pretended that he'd just noticed that we were dressed for bed, "Hey, are you two ready for bed?"

"You are a good guesser, Daddy. We were just going to bed when we saw you."

Andre and I walked towards our rooms. Mommy was crying again. She was talking into Daddy's shirt so I couldn't hear what she was saying, but something inside of me started to feel afraid. I could tell that something was going to be different and it had to do with Nana. I wanted to run back and hug her, but Daddy was holding her and that was enough. After Daddy let go of her, he took our hands and with a quick look back at Mommy, he walked us to our rooms. I looked back at Mommy before I went through my door and she was just standing there with her arms wrapped around herself. Mommy looked lost and lonely. I felt really sad for her because I knew that Mommy wanted Nana home and not at the hospital.

Daddy had never tucked either of us in and now he was getting ready to tuck us in the way we'd seen other white daddies do on TV. The only difference was that we weren't white children, but we were his children and that made all the difference in the world. Daddy sat with me for a little while and since I was now a big girl and didn't need a bedtime story, Daddy said, "Princess, let me go and see about Champ and once he's settled, I'll come back and see about you before I go back downstairs with your Mommy, OK."

Daddy walked out the room and down the hall with Andre and soon after he was in there, I heard his voice coming down the hall. He was telling Andre a story. I wanted to hear so I walked down the hall and sat on the edge of Andre's bed. Daddy had stopped when I walked in and once I was settled on the extra bed there, he started the story again. Daddy said it was a story he liked when he was a little boy. I was hearing the story but I wasn't listening. I was listening to the sound of Daddy's voice in the room. I'd never heard it in the house like this before and it seemed to be bouncing off the ceiling, sliding down the walls, rising up out of the carpeting, swinging off the curtains, and sitting on the edge of the bed. Daddy's voice sounded like music and it was a song I didn't want to end. I didn't want to fall asleep because I knew his voice would only be there as long as I was awake. As hard as I struggled, I couldn't keep my eyes open, and soon the voice in my head started to fade.

It seemed to me that I'd only blinked my eyes for a minute, but when I opened them again it was morning, I was in Andre's room, and Daddy and his voice were gone. Andre was still sleeping when I looked at him. I wanted him awake so we could talk about Daddy. I called his name and nothing. I got out of bed and shook him: nothing. It was always so hard to wake him. Nana always said that when Andre went to sleep, he turned into a cement boy and that's why it was so hard to wake him. She would always laugh and say, 'Oh, my little cement boy, I see you woke up. Now come here and let Nana brush that cement out of your eyes before it gets wet and you fall back to sleep on us again.'

This morning, there would be no Nana so I shook him and called his name 'till he woke. As I pushed the bedroom door, I smelled sausages so we ran to the kitchen. The closer we got, we could hear Mommy. She was talking. This made us run faster to see who she was talking to. As soon as we got into the kitchen, we could see who it was. Daddy was sitting at the table with a cup in his hand. He put the cup down just in time to catch Andre as he jumped into his arms.

"Good morning, Daddy, I'm so happy to see you."

"I'm happy to see you too, Champ."

"What about me, Daddy, aren't you happy to see me too?"

"Of course I am, Princess. I'm always going to be glad to see my Princess."

I jumped into the little space in Daddy's lap that Andre hadn't taken and I hugged Daddy. "Andrea and Andre Hirsh Greenwood are either of you glad to see me and where's my 'good morning Mommy' and my hugs and kisses?"

"I think the two of you better get over there and kiss her quickly before she turns into the wicked mommy monster."

Ma looked at Daddy and with a slight grin on her face she said, "Ha, ha, ha, that's very funny, Matthew Hirsh."

Daddy looked at Mommy with a grin that matched hers and replied, "Sorry, I just couldn't resist."

"Ok you two, now that all the hugs and kisses have been equally shared, how about some breakfast. Remember, this is a school morning."

We sat down and Mommy gave us eggs, sausages, and buttered toast and hot chocolate. Andre didn't have the first bite swallowed before he said, "Daddy, are you going to drive us to school?"

"Would you like that, Champ?"

"Oh yes, Daddy, more than anything in the world!"

"Then I guess I'm taking you."

"Matthew Hirsh!"

"Yes Ms. Lilly Greenwood, is there something wrong with me taking my children to school?"

"But Matthew?"

"But Matthew what? I'm tired, Lilly. I'm tired of not... Never mind."

"Matthew, it's just that I don't think it's such a good idea, you know."

"I know, Lilly, but I'm so tired."

"You're being tired doesn't change the fact that this is still 1959."

Daddy said nothing, he just kept looking at Mommy. We left the table. We could tell that they were going to have grown-up talk. When we got back to the kitchen, Mommy wasn't looking pleased but she had our school things in her hand. She was looking from Daddy to us and then back to Daddy again. There was no smile. It was as if she'd lost her smile when we went to the bathroom. Mommy walked over to us and kissed us. Turning to Daddy, she said, "Matt, drop the children off a few blocks and let them walk in the rest of the way. Drea knows how to cross the street with Andre." Turning to me, she added, "After your daddy drops you all off, take your brother's hand and walk the rest of the way. Do that. Just that. Nothing more."

Daddy just kept on looking at Mommy. He said nothing. As we all walked towards the door, he asked, "Lilly, how many doors down did you say this Ms. Lewis lives?"

"Why, Matthew?"

Before Daddy could answer, Andre shouted out, "Daddy, Ms. Lewis lives four doors down from us. You got to ring the middle bell. Are we going to give Ms. Lewis a ride to her job, Daddy?"

Daddy never really answered Mommy or Andre. He walked over to where she was standing, he wrapped his arms around her, hugged her and then he told her, "Remember you're the Lilly that makes my pond beautiful and I love you."

That always made Mommy smile but today there was no smile. She looked afraid. "Hurry, Matthew, before the children are late." With a trembling voice, she quickly added, "A few blocks from the school, Matt, a few blocks."

Daddy pretended he was a soldier and saluted her. She laughed for real this time and told him, "Matthew Hirsh, you're one silly man."

We walked out the house and then Daddy said, "Andre, take me to Ms. Lewis' house."

"Sure, Daddy, it's right over here." Daddy's steps got longer and we had to hurry to keep up. Daddy walked through the gate, up the stairs and rang the bell. We waited. It seemed as if the door was never going to open, but soon it opened and Ms. Lewis was standing in the doorway.

Daddy said, "Good morning, are you Ms. Lewis?"

Ms. Lewis looked at me, then Andre, and then she looked at Daddy. Ms. Lewis' mouth got real slack as if the bottom piece was going drop the way puppets do when the string is broken. Daddy asked again, "Are you Ms. Lewis?"

"I be Ms. Lewis. Something I can do for you, mister."

Daddy then said, "Yes, actually there's plenty. I believe you know these children?"

"I know them. Them be Lilly's children."

"That is mostly right," Daddy answered.

"What you mean by mostly?"

"It's true that there are Lilly's children, but by now I'm guessing you have already figured out that these are my children as well."

Ms. Lewis' puppet mouth got even slacker. She just stared at Daddy. She looked like she wanted to run back in the house and nail her door shut. Daddy stepped closer to Ms. Lewis and then he said in a real soft voice, "Don't you ever again open your ugly, hateful mouth and tell my children anything about them being half-white, half-black or half-anything else. Do you hear me?"

"What you talking 'bout, mister? I would never tell children such things."

Turning to us, Daddy asked, "Did you tell your mother and me the truth about what this woman called the two of you."

Together, me and Andre said, "Yes Daddy."

Then Andre stepped between Daddy and Ms. Lewis and pulled on her arm, "Ms. Lewis, don't you remember telling me and Drea that day when we was hungry at your house that your house ain't no restaurant and you don't feed no white man's children?"

"Andre baby, you know Ms. Lewis ain't said nothing like that to you all."

"Ms. Lewis, you don't remember saying that to me and Drea?"

Ms. Lewis looked at Daddy and she could see that he didn't believe her. "Mister I, I…"

Daddy looked at Ms. Lewis and told her, "It's true I'm a white man. It's true these are my children, but what isn't true or ever will be is this: my children will never be niggers. Don't you ever open your hateful mouth and say such mean things to my children ever again. Do you hear me?"

Daddy didn't wait for Ms. Lewis to answer; he turned away from her and headed down the steps. We followed. Daddy never turned around to look at her but I did. I turned around and she was standing in her doorway like Daddy's words had turned her into a cement person. I was happy that Daddy had told her never call us half-white niggers again.

Daddy drove to our school but he didn't do as Mommy had asked. He didn't stop the few blocks so we could get out. He kept right on driving until he was at the gate of our school. Then he got out, walked over to my door and opened it, then he opened Andre's door. Daddy took our hands as we held our schoolbags and our lunchboxes. He walked us right into the schoolyard. My heart was beating really fast. I wasn't sure why I was feeling scared, but I was thinking that maybe Daddy should have listened to Mommy.

Turning to Andre, Daddy asked, "Champ, where does your class line up?"

"Over there, Daddy." Andre pointed to the far side of the wall where the third graders were. Still holding our hands, Daddy walked Andre over to his teacher. Ms. Madison was standing there just staring at Daddy. She looked as if she'd never seen a daddy before. Daddy didn't pay her staring at him any attention; he just put his hand out as if to shake her hand as he said, "I'm Matthew Hirsh, Andre's father."

Ms. Madison stood there looking at Daddy. She never answered and Daddy never seemed to notice. He bent down and gave Andre a hug and then he walked with me to my line. All the children in the yard were looking at Daddy and me. I tried to walk taller because I was happy, but something inside me had me scared and pressed my shoulders down to the ground.

Daddy got to my line and he did the same thing he'd done at Andre's line. He walked over to my teacher and put his hand out. Just like Ms. Madison, Ms. Wright stared at Daddy but unlike Ms. Madison, she took Daddy's out-stretched hand and shook it. She didn't say anything so I said, "Daddy, this is Ms. Wright, she's my teacher."

Daddy took his hand from Ms. Wright's and said, "Matthew Hirsh. It's my pleasure to meet you. Drea talks about you often."

With Daddy letting go of Ms. Wright's hand, she went back to being like Ms. Madison. She just stood there. You would think that teachers had never seen a daddy before. Everybody was watching me with Daddy. I wanted to smile because now everybody could see that Andre and I had a real daddy but when Daddy bent down to kiss me goodbye, I was afraid to put my arms around his neck and give him a kiss. Daddy smiled. It was like he understood what I didn't understand. He bent down and kissed the top of my head. As he walked away, he said, "Love you, Princess."

I wanted to say, 'love you too, Daddy,' but neither my throat nor my lips would work. Daddy smiled, waved, and walked in the direction of the car.

The thing that had me scared when Daddy was in the schoolyard left me when Ms. Madison and Ms. Wright treated me and Andre as if we were new children at the school. Andre and I had the best day at school we'd ever had. I was glad that Daddy had come to school with us. When school was over Andre and I were getting ready to walk to the gate to wait for Mommy, Ms. Madison called, "Andrea, your father called. You and Andre are to wait here."

"Daddy is coming to get me and Andre?"

"Apparently."

I didn't know why she said 'apparently' like she was mad or something, but I guess she was mad because now we had a daddy; she couldn't call us fatherless pups no more. We sat in the chairs outside the office to wait. We waited for a long time and then Daddy finally came. With him was a woman I'd never seen before. She was almost tall to Daddy's shoulder, but she was roundish and had a nice face. She was wearing a hat so I didn't see her hair but a few strands with minds of their own, were peeking out from under her hat trying to see me. They found me. I looked at them and smiled. They were like strands of silver, happy to be in the sunlight, which was bouncing off the strands. I looked at the lady and thought her hair would make a nice sweater for Christmas because it was all silvery. Her face looked as if it would smile anytime without her asking it too. I liked her right away.

Daddy brought the lady with the nice, smiling, roundish face and silvery hair with him into the office and told Ms. Madison that her name was Mrs. Peters and from now on she would be coming to the school every evening to pick me and Andre up. Then he turned to the lady and said, "Mrs. Peters, this is Andrea and," turning to where Andre was sitting on the floor putting away his reading book, he added, "this big man here, he's Andre."

Mrs. Peters smiled at us, walked over to where our things were and picked them up. Daddy took our hands and we walked out the office with him and Mrs. Peters. When we got outside, we didn't see Daddy's car. Instead we walked to a different car and a man was standing by the driver's side. Daddy said the man was Mrs. Peter's husband and from now on he and Mrs. Peters would be helping Mommy take care of us.

Mr. Peters would be bringing us to school and picking us up and Mrs. Peters would be staying with us until Mommy got home from the hospital. Andre, Daddy, and me got into the back of the car and Mr. and Mrs. Peters sat up front. Daddy told Mr. Peters which way to go to our house. When we got to our house, Ms. Lewis was in her yard and when she saw me, Daddy, Andre, and Mr. and Mrs. Peters, she waved. Daddy didn't wave back but turned to Mr. and Mrs. Peters and told her, "That woman isn't to be anywhere near my children. She's called my children nigger white children. She's not allowed near this house. Do I make myself clear?"

To my surprise, both Mr. and Mrs. Peters said, "Yes Mr. Hirsh We'll see to it."

It sounded to me as if they had been practicing it for a school play. To our surprise, Daddy had keys and opened the door. When we were all inside, he said to Mr. Peters, "Neal, bring the groceries in."

It seemed as if Mr. Peters was used to taking orders because he said, "Yes sir."

Daddy turned to us and asked, "Now what are the two of you supposed to be doing?"

"Daddy, we take off our school clothes, change, and do our homework while Mommy cooks dinner."

As we walked towards the bedroom, Mr. Peters came in with the first set of groceries. Daddy walked Mr. Peters to the kitchen as if he'd walked there a thousand times before. We changed and were back downstairs by the time Mr. Peters had finished bringing the groceries in. I'd never seen so many groceries in our kitchen before. It looked as if Daddy had bought out the whole supermarket. Mr. Peters was standing by the door and he looked like a statue. Daddy turned to him and said, "Neal, that's all for now. The children's mother will be back around 9:00 P.M. come back for Noreen then."

"Yes, Mr. Hirsh."

Daddy let him out and then came back to help us with our homework. When dinner was ready, Mrs. Peters came and told us. It looked like just the way Nana would set it for Sunday dinner. We were glad that we weren't at Ms. Lewis' house. She wouldn't feed us anyway. After we were done, Mrs. Peters cleared the dishes away. I could hear the water running in the kitchen. I couldn't believe it. Someone other than Mommy or Nana was in our kitchen washing dishes. When Mrs. Peters was done, she came into the living and sat in a chair opposite where we were on the couch watching TV with Daddy. When it was time for bed, Andre and I went upstairs to get ready. Mommy must have come home when we were taking our baths because to our surprise, both she and Daddy came in to tuck us in. I was happy. I'd never had both Mommy and Daddy in my room before. Mommy's eyes were red from crying. She looked really tired. "Mommy, did Nana come home with you tonight?" Andre asked.

"No, baby, your Nana has to stay at the hospital for a little while longer. The doctors need her there so that they can take care of her."

"Mommy, when you see Nana tomorrow will you tell her that I miss her?"

"Sure, Andre, I'll tell her."

Mommy sat on my bed. As Daddy talked, some of the tired on her face went away. When Daddy was finished, we were still awake, but Daddy didn't start a new story. He kissed us and told us, "Now Andre, off to your room, then you both close those little peepers and go to sleep."

"But Daddy we ain't sleepy."

"Now I don't remember asking if you were sleepy."

Daddy walked Andre out of my room and back to his. Mommy kissed me and followed them. In the morning when we woke, there was the smell of breakfast cooking again. Again we rushed to the kitchen, but Daddy wasn't there. Mrs. Peters and Mommy were in the kitchen. They were making breakfast and talking. I liked the smell of the breakfast, but I didn't want to see Mrs. Peters and Mommy making our breakfast. I wanted to see Daddy drinking coffee and Mommy making our breakfast. I looked at Mrs. Peters and I missed Daddy and Nana. My house had changed because Nana was in the hospital. Mrs. Peters was nice, but she wasn't Nana. While Mommy drank coffee, Mrs. Peters made us lunch. Watching Mrs. Peters make our lunch was making me sad for Nana. I wished she didn't have to stay with the doctors.

"Mommy is Nana coming home soon?"

"Andrea, I told you last night that your Nana has to stay at the hospital because the doctors have to run tests."

"Excuse me, Mrs. Greenwood, Mr. Peters is here to take the children to school."

It looked funny to have such a big car for just us, but I was glad we didn't have to take the bus. Mommy kissed us goodbye and Mr. Peters drove us to school.

The weeks that Nana was in the hospital went by very slowly. We got used to Mr. and Mrs. Peters. Daddy never came back. Mommy was getting real tired and I could tell she was missing Nana more and more. She was always sad and crying. Soon, in the mornings it was Mrs. Peters who made the whole breakfast, made our lunch, and even walked us to the car. Some mornings, Mommy would come to the door to say goodbye, but most mornings she just sat in Nana's chair and let us hug her goodbye. She didn't even bother to stand. Standing seemed to be an effort she didn't want to think about or make.

Some evenings when Mommy came home from the hospital, she came to our rooms and kissed us goodnight, but most evenings, she just opened the doors as if she was just making sure that we were still there and then she would just close them without saying anything. We started to miss her too.

Chapter 58

A Time To Die

After Nana had been in the hospital for six, maybe seven weeks or more, Mr. Peters brought us home from school one evening and Mommy was already there. Seeing Mommy there was unusual 'cause since Mr. and Mrs. Peters had started taking care of us, Mommy was never there when we got home from school. She was always at the hospital. This day, however, Mommy was home. She was sitting in Nana's chair and beside the chair was the suitcase she had taken to the hospital with Nana's things. I looked at the suitcase and took off running to Nana's room. I was running and shouting, "Nana! Nana! I'm so glad you're home." I pushed Nana's door without knocking and was in her room and almost to her bed before I noticed it was empty. "Nana, where are you?" I didn't hear an answer so I ran to the bathroom and called from outside the door, "Nana, you in here?"

Then I heard Mrs. Peters voice. "Your Nana isn't here."

"But Mrs. Peters, I see her suitcase and if the suitcase is here, Nana has to be here."

I ran pass Mrs. Peters to Mommy, who was sitting and holding Andre. She was rocking back and forth with him as if he were a baby. She was crying softly. The tears were falling on Andre's head.

"Mommy, what are you crying for?"

Mommy didn't answer me but started to cry louder. Mrs. Peters took my hand and made me sit next to her on the sofa. She said, "Andrea, your Nana isn't here."

"Then where is she? Is she still at the hospital?"

"No, baby, she went home to be with the Lord."

When Mrs. Peters said that Mommy started to scream. She was screaming and shouting, "Oh God! Oh God! Ma! God, why did you have to take Ma from me? Why? Why? Why my Ma, Lord?"

Mommy got up from the chair. Andre held onto her neck. She pried him loose. He kind of fell to the floor. Once he was off, Mommy started to run. She was moving so fast she looked like a baseball that had been hit really hard and she was well on her way to being a home run. She ran to Nana's room screaming. We could hear her as if the wall was gone. Mrs. Peters got up from the chair and went after Mommy into Nana's room.

Mr. Peters, who had come to take Mrs. Peters home, took her place on the sofa beside Andre and me. We were crying. Andre turned to Mr. Peters and asked, "Mr. Peters where is God's house? Is it far? Can you drive me, Drea, and Mommy there so that we can be with Nana? I don't want Nana to be at the Lord's house alone. She's going to want us to be there with her because we've always lived in the same house."

Mr. Peters didn't answer. All he said was, "Shhhh, shhhh, don't cry. Your Nana won't want to have all of you crying like this."

Then Andre started crying for Daddy. "Mr. Peters, I want Daddy. Can you please go and bring Daddy here?"

I started to cry more because I knew that Daddy couldn't come.

"Andre, Daddy can't come over."

"But, Drea, if you called Daddy he would come. Drea, call Daddy. Call him and tell him that Nana is at the Lord's house. Tell him that Mr. Peters won't drive us there, please, Drea. I want Nana and Daddy. Please, Drea, call Daddy."

Mrs. Peters came out of the bedroom and said to Mr. Peters, "I think you better call Mr. Hirsh. Tell him that Ms. Greenwood's Mommy has gone on to be with the Lord. Tell him that Ms. Greenwood is taking it mighty hard."

Mr. Peters just sat there looking at Mrs. Peters as if he didn't understand what she said.

"Neal! Either you call him or I'll call him myself. I don't care much now 'bout losing no job. Ms. Greenwood needs to have somebody here with her that she knows. She knows us, but she ain't know us to the point where she can pour her sorry on us, so call him. Call him now, Neal."

Mr. Peters got up and went to the phone and Mrs. Peters sat down beside me. As soon as Mr. Peters put his hand on the phone, it rang. He jumped back and watched the phone as it rang a second time. At the third ring, Mrs. Peters said, "Neal! Pick up the phone and say something."

Mr. Peters picked up the phone and said, "Greenwoods residence, may I help you?

"Very bad. Everybody is crying.

"She's the worse.

"Mrs. Peters is sitting with them.

"Yes, we can sir.

"An hour?

"That won't be a problem.

"Goodbye."

Mr. Peters hung up the phone, as he walked back to where we were sitting we could hear Mommy in Nana's room. She was screaming and crying. Mrs. Peters, turning to Mr. Peters asked, "Neal, who was that on the phone?"

"Mr. Hirsh. He called the hospital and they told him. He's on his way over, but wants us to stay."

"Neal, did he think for one minute we were going leave these children and their mother in all this pain?"

"Noreen, you go in the room with her and I'll sit with the children until he gets here. She don't need to be alone. You ain't her Ma, but you know what it's like to lose a Ma."

Mrs. Peters got up and no sooner was she up, than Mr. Peters sat down. Andre was still asking Mr. Peters to drive him to the Lord's house and Mr. Peters didn't have an answer. I sat by Mr. Peters' side and listened to Mommy. I could hear Mrs. Peters talking to her. Trying to soothe her just the way Nana would've, but that only seemed to make Mommy cry harder. We were sitting quietly on the sofa when we heard keys in the door. It was Daddy. Daddy looked as if he'd been crying. We ran to him. He hugged us tightly. Then Andre said, "Daddy, Mrs. Peters said that Nana is with the Lord and Mommy is in Nana's bedroom just crying."

"I know. I know."

"Daddy, tell Mr. Peters to take us to where the Lord's house is. I want to be with my Nana."

"Andre, Mr. Peters can't take you there. The Lord's house is in a special place. You can't get there by car. You can only get there when He calls you to come live with Him and He only calls the person that He needs."

"So Daddy, when is God goin' call us to come to be with him and Nana?"

"I don't know, Champ but I don't think it's going be right now. You see your Nana was sick and was in a lot of pain. That's why the Lord took her to be with Him. He can take better care of your Nana if she's with Him."

"Daddy, will he send her back once he fixes her and she gets better?"

"No, son. Once you're with the Lord, you stay there forever and ever."

"Forever?"

"Forever."

Daddy turned from Andre to Mr. Peters and said, "Neal, stay with the children. I need to go and see about their mother."

"Yes, Mr. Hirsh, no problem." For the third time that evening, Mr. Peters sat between me and Andre. Daddy looked at us as we clung to Mr. Peters and he said, "Thanks Neal."

Daddy walked down the hall into Nana's room and Mrs. Peters came out. We could hear Mommy screaming and Daddy's voice as he tried to quiet her. His voice sounded as if he was talking to someone who would break apart at any minute. Daddy sounded afraid. It was as if Mommy's screams was going to shatter her and he would never be able to gather all her pieces together. Daddy's voice was begging Mommy to remain whole.

Mr. and Mrs. Peters took us into the kitchen and gave us hot chocolate and cookies. Mrs. Peters talked to us about God and his love. She told us about how he protected little children and that he would send angels to watch over us all night. Then Mrs. Peters started to sing to us. She sang a song about how Jesus loves us and that little ones belonged to him. The part that said that we were weak but Jesus was strong made me feel a little better. I didn't want to be strong. I was glad that Jesus was strong and I belonged to him.

When Mrs. Peters was done singing, Andre was looking sleepy and I was feeling a little sleepy too, but I didn't want to sleep. I was afraid that if I went to sleep, God would call Mommy, Daddy, or Andre to be home with him. Mrs. Peters must have guessed that I was afraid because she took my hand and said, "Andrea, God loves you and wants only the best for you. He will watch over your Nana until the day comes when you will see her again in His home in heaven. It's ok to go to sleep. Trust in God. He won't trick you and take your whole family away from you while you're sleeping. God doesn't work like that. He always does what's best for you."

Mrs. Peters took my hand. I liked that hers were big and warm. She took us to Andre's room with the two beds, but I climbed in with him. Daddy didn't come to tuck us in. It was Mrs. Peters who tucked us in. She kept on wrapping words of comfort and love around us 'till we felt safe. She sat in the room until we fell asleep. I don't know when Mr. and Mrs. Peters went home but when I turned during the night, I was beside Andre and beside Andre was Mommy and beside Mommy was Daddy.

Daddy had come and gathered us all close together. He was here and keeping us safe. I closed my eyes and went back to sleep. In my dreams, I saw my Nana in the Lord's house and she was showing the angels how to make biscuits. She also had a plate next to her with a whole pickle on it. I became afraid.

The days leading up to Nana's funeral were a blur. Mommy went to bed and stayed there. Mr. and Mrs. Peters and Daddy took care of us. It was mostly Mrs. Peters. Daddy came sometimes but he couldn't stay every night. He called every day and he trusted Mr. and Mrs. Peters to look after us and the house.

We missed Nana a lot, but we were missing Mommy more. Sometime we would go into Mommy's room and sit by the side of her bed. Sometimes, she would lift her head up from the pillow, look at us and smile, and other times, she would lift her head up, look at us looking at her and cry. We were missing Mommy, but Mommy didn't seem to be missing us.

The day of Nana's funeral, Mommy didn't want to come out of her room. She didn't want to eat, bathe, get dressed, or nothing. It was Mrs. Peters who went into Mommy's room and helped her get ready. Daddy, Andre, Mr. Peters, and I waited in the living room. When Mrs. Peters and Mommy came out of her room, you could tell that Mrs. Peters had tried, but Mommy didn't look right. Her face didn't light up when she saw Daddy. She neither hugged nor kissed him. She looked at him and it was if she wasn't really seeing him. Daddy walked over to Mommy and took her by the hand. We walked out of the house to go to the funeral. It was time to say goodbye to Nana.

Daddy drove his car. Mommy sat beside him and Andre and I sat in the back. Mr. and Mrs. Peters followed in their car. There were no more cars following us. It was just us going to say goodbye to Nana. Andre and I were crying silently because we didn't want Mommy to hear us and start crying again. I kept waiting for Mommy to start crying, but she didn't. She was the quietest in the car. It was as if she didn't know we were going to Nana's funeral.

When we got to the funeral home, there were lots of people who knew Nana. Mommy didn't say anything to any of them. Daddy shook hands with many people for the first time. Daddy didn't seem to notice or care that some people were looking at him surprised because he was holding Mommy and we were walking together like a family. When we walked in, Daddy was holding Mommy as if she was made out of cobwebs and he didn't want anybody, their gossip, curiosity, or misspoken words of sympathy to get near her because he knew that it would stick and hurt her. Daddy was being Ma's knight in shining armor. From where I was standing, I could see Nana in the coffin. I didn't want to see her like that so I sat down right where I was. Andre sat beside me. His eyes were wide and wet. Fear and tears were mixing together in his eyes. I did like Daddy; I put my arm around Andre to protect him. Mr. and Mrs. Peters came and stood beside where we'd sat down. Mr. Peters took Andre's hand and Mrs. Peters took mine. We stood up and began walking towards the casket.

Daddy was walking Mommy down towards the casket and Mommy didn't want to walk. Her legs looked like the string that was holding them to her hip had become broken. At one point, Mommy just stopped and looked at Daddy and all she said was, "No Matt, no Matt." Daddy tightened his arm around Mommy's waist and waited until she was ready to walk again. She started again but very slowly. Her broken string legs went in every direction they felt like going. Mommy went wherever they went. Slowly, Daddy got her straight again and walked Mommy towards Nana. The closer Daddy and Mommy got, the heavier Mommy seemed to become. I looked at Daddy and knew that he didn't mind. He walked slowly and carefully with his fragile string and straw doll. The journey ended at Nana's casket.

Mommy was holding onto Daddy's jacket so tightly, she'd almost pulled it fully around so the buttons were almost at his back. She leaned into the casket and gently kissed Nana on her powdered cheek. She took her free hand and, still holding tightly to Daddy's jacket, wiped some of the powder off Nana's face and then she fixed Nana's hair. She also smoothed her dress and finally she patted her hand. The pat had the look as if she was saying, "You go on. It's ok. I'll be there soon." It scared me worse than the dream of Nana in the Lord's house with the pickle on the plate.

Then with a look that I'd never seen in her eyes before, Mommy turned and looked at Daddy and said, "Matt, I want to go home too." Daddy didn't say anything. He walked Mommy away from the casket and sat with her at the front row. Although Andre and I were afraid, we walked with Mr. and Mrs. Peters to look at Nana. Andre said, "I love you, Nana." When Andre said that, it made me cry and I turned my head into Mr. Peters' side and cried. He smelled like mothballs. Mothballs reminded me of Nana. I was trying to be brave and not cry out loud, but I couldn't help it. The smell of the mothballs finally made me holler out for my Nana.

When everyone had walked pass Nana's casket, it was time for the funeral to begin. Cousin Bernard, who was a funeral director now that Uncle Philip was no longer in the business, stepped to the casket, looked oddly at Nana, almost with a little smirk on his face then closed the casket. Mommy closed her eyes tightly and pulled on Daddy's jacket.

A lady that knew Nana from her first days of working in Brooklyn Heights sung a song for Nana that none of us had ever heard before. She said she'd written it herself and it was a based on Nana's hometown, life, and people in general. She said she that although it wasn't a church song, Nana would understand. She unfolded a piece of paper she had the words to her song on and before she started, she said the name of her song was 'Promised Land'.

The lady sung it soft and sweet. It was louder than a whisper and just that but it was loud enough. We could all hear her. It wasn't a jump-around song. Hearing it just made Mommy shout and scream. Daddy had to do everything he could to keep Mommy from running to Nana's casket. When the lady was done singing her made-up song, she placed the piece of paper on Nana's casket and said, "Gina Pearl Fields, you is my one true, true friend. I hope when my time comes, I get to see you in the Promised Land."

It was the first time that someone had called Nana by something other than Promise Greenwood. Had Nana not told me what her real name used to be, I wouldn't have known she meant Nana. By this time, Mommy was leaning against Daddy like she was a wet towel waiting to get wrung out. Mommy wasn't filled with water 'cause she'd been crying forever. Mommy was filled with pain and she wanted it gone. I wanted it gone too. I wanted her back too, but every time somebody said something about Nana, more pieces of Mommy fell off. The pieces were slowly piling up at Daddy's feet. Mr. and Mrs. Peters said that although they didn't really know Nana all too well, they knew her well enough. Mrs. Peters said that a long, long time ago they had once worked in the same house with her. Then I understood where Mr. and Mrs. Peters knew Nana from. They had worked for Daddy's mother at his house before coming to work for Daddy at our house.

Mr. and Mrs. Peters looked directly at Mommy as they sung *His Eye Is on the Sparrow*. They sung as if they'd been singing to her their whole lives. I half-way expected the pieces of Mommy that were piling up at Daddy's feet to become one giant heap and exchange places with Mommy at his side. It didn't happen. Mommy's already fallen off pieces stayed at Daddy's feet and what was left of Mommy stayed clinging to Daddy's arm. By the time Mr. and Mrs. Peters finished singing; Mommy had calmed down and had almost stopped crying. The funeral service ended. Mommy didn't cry anymore. Not even when Cousin Bernard stood up, re-opened the casket, and offered everyone their last chance to come and say goodbye to Nana.

I really didn't want to go back to look at Nana, but I wanted to take the song home with me. So I stood up and as soon as I made the first step, Auntie Noreen stood up and took my hand. She walked with me to Nana's casket and just before I looked at Nana one last time, I picked up the piece of paper with the lady's song on it. Cousin Bernard hadn't even noticed it sitting in the flowers that were spread all across where Nana's lap would've been. I squeezed the piece of paper tightly in my hand. I felt a little like I was taking something that was Nana's, but I didn't think that Nana would mind. After all, Nana always said, 'No sense letting things go to waste if you can use it.' Nana's song was going to go to waste, maybe even get blown away once her casket was moved from inside the funeral home. I didn't want to lose her song. I'd keep if for her. It was the first and last song anyone had ever written for her.

Neither Andre nor Mommy came up for the final viewing. Andre was crying into Mr. Peter's jacket and Mommy just sat next to Daddy watching the people walk pass Nana's once-again opened casket. Mommy was making sounds like a puppy with a broken leg. I looked at her from where I was and her eyes were dry. Mommy had either simply cried out all her tears or they had dried up. Either way, she wasn't crying no more. Cousin Bernard closed Nana's casket once everyone had walked pass and then the preacher came down and he started to walk down the church aisle. Cousin Bernard followed with Nana's casket and the rest of us followed. Mommy walked very slowly beside Daddy. If Mommy was thinner, she would have looked like one of Daddy's scarves that was too long and was dragging on the floor.

We drove the short drive to the cemetery. I looked at the words of the song. I read them and every now and again I would look at Mommy. She was still clinging to Daddy's jacket. At the graveside, Mommy seemed to be in a deep trance. She walked up to the casket and touched it gently as if it was one giant bubble and she didn't want to be the one to touch it and make it pop. She started to, then changed her mind about putting the rose she'd been holding on the casket. When the graveside service was over, they said that we could say our goodbyes and leave. That didn't sit well with Mommy. She told Daddy that she didn't want to leave Nana like that. She wanted Cousin Bernard and the people at the cemetery to lay Nana to rest while she was there.

Daddy told Mommy that the cemetery people would take care of Nana. I was watching Mommy, expecting her to start hollering or trying to climb into the grave. She didn't. She just looked from Daddy to the casket and from the casket back to Daddy. I could tell that Mommy's feet wanted to walk away, but the rest of her body wouldn't follow. Slowly,

Mommy sank to her knees and started to rock. Daddy sank to his knees and rocked with her. Andre and I just stood there crying at the sight of our Mommy and Daddy on their knees rocking. Daddy was crying, but not as loudly or sadly as Mommy.

Mommy rocked and rocked 'till she was still. Daddy, along with Mr. Peters, got her to stand. The two of them led her away from the grave and towards the car. I looked at her and I could tell that if either one of them loosened their grip, she was going to run right back and throw herself in the hole that had Nana's casket sitting over it. Daddy and Mr. Peters must have figured it out too because they held her tighter. Daddy got into the back seat of his car with Mommy and without a word, Mr. Peters got into the driver's side. Mrs. Peters walked Andre and me to Mr. Peters' car. We didn't know she could drive. Andre and I got into the car. Mrs. Peters followed behind Mr. Peters. All the way home, I read the words to Promised Land. By the time we got home, I almost knew all the words by heart.

Promised land

Chorus: When I'm walking on the water over shifting sands,
Won't you shine on, shine on me?
I'll be one step closer to the Promised Land,
Won't you shine on me?
When I'm looking for the promise of a helping hand,
Won't you shine on, shine on me?
I'll be one step closer to the Promised Land,
Won't you shine on me?

Time stands still but it's just another season,
Everybody's looking for a place to be.
If we do all the wrong things for all the right reasons,
We'll be struggling to get upstream.

Repeat chorus

Waiting for a journey in the shadow of adventure,
Everybody wants to sail the seven seas.
Fly across the oceans, climb every mountain,
Taking every chance and opportunity.

Repeat chorus

All the dreamers dreaming, all the schemers scheming,
All the players playing with a perfect hand.
If we do all the wrong things for all the right reasons,
We'll be one step away from the Promised Land.

 I kept reading the song over and over and wondered why the lady would put words like that in a song for a funeral. Then I guessed that the song wasn't really meant for Nana after all, but for all the living people that she knew who should stop all their scheming, and doing all their wrong things, or they wouldn't see the Promised Land. Nana had done all the right things so I knew for sure she was in the Promised Land. I was glad for Nana. Not because she was dead, but because she'd done enough right things to get into the Lord's house.

Chapter 59

Sorrow Rains Down Again

All of us came home from Nana's funeral except Mommy. At first I didn't notice or realize, but little by little I started to. Mommy stopped helping Mrs. Peters with anything. Even the slightest thing seemed too much for her. Soon Mrs. Peters was doing everything for us except coming to the school to talk to the teachers, and then one day I had a problem at school and Mrs. Peters came. She said that Mommy wasn't feeling well. After that, Mrs. Peters was everywhere doing everything. Daddy came by for a little while, but soon things went back to whatever normal can be when your Nana has gone home to be with the Lord and your Mommy is sad all the time. Daddy went back to being the daddy he was before Nana got sick. Mommy didn't notice.

When the week came for us to vacation with Daddy, Mommy asked him if Mrs. Peters could go instead. Daddy said no so we didn't go. Mommy stayed in her room and Andre and I cried the whole week. Mrs. Peters tried to stop us from crying but she couldn't. The week was the only time we ever got to be a family. At first, we cried because we didn't get our week and then we cried for everything else, including missing Nana and Mommy. We had nothing else to do but cry because it was summer vacation. Things weren't the same after that.

One day it was Mommy, Nana, Andre, and me. Then Nana was gone and Mommy never stopped crying. She came out of her room a few minutes each day just to walk to Nana's room. After Nana's room had stayed empty for a long time, Mrs. Peters asked Mommy if, since she was staying most nights now, she could use the room. Mommy agreed yet when Mommy missed Nana too much, she would go to Nana's room. She would look at Mrs. Peters and shake her head as if she was confused about who she was and why she was in her ma's room. Mrs. Peters soon moved the few things she'd moved into Nana's room out. She fixed up a room in the basement and on the nights she stayed over, she slept there. That move made Mommy feel better because now she could walk into Nana's room and touch her things whenever she felt like. It was hurting me to see the way Mommy looked at me. I knew she knew who I was, but sometimes she gave me the same confused look she used to give Mrs. Peters when she was in Nana's room. The look said, 'I know I know you but I'm not so sure from where.'

The truth was Mommy didn't really know who I was anymore because while she was in her room mourning Nana, Andre and I had grown and changed quite a bit. I was getting ready for tenth grade and Andre was going to seventh. Mommy had missed almost three years of our lives. We had grown and she'd missed it all. She made no effort to come out of her grief because she didn't want to be with us. She only wanted to be with Nana. There was nothing any of us could do. Daddy tried the hardest; he had Mommy go and talk to someone about why she was so sad but it didn't help. Mommy didn't try to stop from missing Nana.

The doctor told Daddy that Mommy needed to try; she needed to want something other than the pain that was sucking her soul away. We wanted her to want something else too. We wanted her to remember that we were her children and that we needed her. Sometimes she tried but the effort always seemed to be more than her spirit could handle. Eventually, we started to accept the Mommy that she was. She was a Mommy that never stopped being Nana's daughter and now that Nana was gone, Mommy was lost in her grief. We wanted our Mommy; that was our wanting; it wasn't hers. She wanted her Mommy more than she wanted to be ours.

Over the years as Mommy withdrew from our lives, Daddy would come by a bit more regularly. He didn't come by every day but he came often enough for us to know that we weren't alone. We still had one parent, but each time Daddy visited, he tried to coax Mommy out of the house, her room, her grief, her pain, her shell; anything—just join us in living. He failed more often than not. Each time he couldn't get her to come out of her grief, the pain of his failed effort showed on his face. He would look so sad. That look never left his face, but he was never sad enough to leave without saying to her, "Don't ever forget you're the Lilly that makes my pond beautiful. I love you."

Sometime Mommy would smile and other times it was as if she didn't hear him. Daddy would then kiss her gently and leave. I was sad for me, but sadder still for Daddy. Mommy was stopping from loving all of us. She only loved Nana.

Chapter 60

If You Love Someone Set Them Free

Mommy ate enough so that the law wouldn't charge Mrs. Peters with starving her to death. Actually it seemed that Mommy tried less and yet harder at the same time. She tried harder to join Nana and less to stay with us. You could see it in her face when she looked at us. She was waiting on us to accept that she didn't want to be with us anymore. She wanted us to let her go. We accepted. We loved her enough to let her go. It was Daddy who told Mommy that it was OK. He sounded just like Nana when he said, "Lilly, I've loved you for an eternity but I can't keep begging you to want to stay here with me and our children. I want you to want to be here with us. To be a family but, Lilly, I don't know what else to do for you. What do you want me to do?"

Mommy looked at Daddy with eyes that were now deep-set in a thin face with jutting cheek bones and said, "Let me go, Matthew. Let me go." That was it. She'd finally told Daddy what she wanted. She wanted to be gone.

"Is that what you really want, Lilly?"

"Yes, Matthew. Let me go home."

That night, Daddy came out and talked to us as if we were grown. He didn't try to sugar-coat anything. He told us about sending Mommy to doctors about her depression and the only other thing left would be to send Mommy away to a hospital for the mentally insane and he couldn't do that. He said he didn't think that even if he sent her to a hospital it would change anything. It might, he said, make it worse. He then told us that our Mommy's heart was broken and she didn't want it mended. He told us to try and find a way to accept that Mommy believed her heart was too broken to ever be mended again. Daddy said Mommy wanted to be with her ma and there wasn't anything we could do.

Right after all of us accepted that fact, we tried letting go but that was hard. There was no real way to let Mommy go. No one had ever written a book on letting go of a living person that wasn't really sick, but wanted to be in heaven. We loved Mommy so we did everything we could to pull her back to us. Mommy didn't let herself be pulled. She continued to fight us; to pull back more and more. When Mommy noticed that we hadn't stop from trying to pull her to us, she pulled back in a way that none of us anticipated: she shut herself away from us. She didn't let us in her room anymore and when we begged and begged and she did let us come in, she still pulled away: she didn't talk to us. She was just there.

We started to go in less and less and tried harder to accept that she was going and wasn't coming back. Daddy started taking Andre and I to the same doctor that had told him that Mommy wanted to go. The doctor told us we had to make our peace with her and let her go. He worked with all of us; Daddy, Andre, and I on letting go of Mommy. We finally got there or as much there as you can let go of someone you love as much as all of us loved Mommy.

Nana must have realized that we had let Mommy go because Nana stayed right there in the Lord's house and asked Him if Mommy could join her now. He said, "OK."

Mommy gladly went.

I stopped loving Nana and wasn't too sure about God after that for quite some time.

Daddy came to the house the morning Mrs. Peters couldn't wake Mommy. When Daddy let himself in, he looked tired. He looked the way Andre and I'd looked the first time we didn't get our week with him. He'd been crying. He loved Mommy and wanted her to stay, but Mommy didn't love him or us enough to do that. I think that's what hurt Daddy the most. If it were Daddy whose heart was broken, he would've stayed with us and found a way to fix his broken heart if Mommy had asked him to. Daddy just couldn't understand why Mommy hadn't done the same for him and for us. When Daddy came into the house, he took a quick look at us sitting with Mr. and Mrs. Peters and went to Mommy's room. He stayed there a long time. He didn't rush out in a panic or anything. He just stayed there.

Alone with Mommy, I could hear him crying and screaming. He sounded angry with her. I'd never heard Daddy raise his voice to Mommy and now that he was raising it; it was loud enough that if Nana was around she would've said, 'He sure loud enough. He so loud he could wake the dead.' But I guess Nana was wrong about that. Daddy was loud; really very loud. Mommy was dead and not even Daddy with all his pain and screaming could wake her.

I started to wonder if Mommy's ears were really closed to Daddy's pain and suffering. Then I started to think that Mommy might not be really dead and that she was hearing him, but was so determined to join Nana that she was just lying there faking it. Daddy was loud enough. She could hear him. She just refused to wake up. He was trying with those screams to wake Mommy, I knew it. Mommy was the one being stubborn. She stayed still and stubborn and allowed Daddy to go on trying to wake her. He talked to her, he begged her, and finally he became angry with her again. He reminded her that he'd loved her from the first day he saw her. Then Daddy just came right out and said, "Damn you, Lilly, why couldn't you have stayed; if not for me then for our children? Lilly what are our children supposed to do without you? What, Lilly? What are our children to do, Lilly? What are they to do, Lilly?" Then Daddy screamed louder. Mommy didn't wake up. She stayed dead.

I took a piece of my broken heart from Mommy and Nana's side and added it to Daddy's side. I knew then that I would stay angry at Nana, Mommy, and God for a long time because of what they'd done to him. Mommy had no right to leave Daddy or to break his heart. He was shouting louder and louder and just when he started shouting at God, the police and ambulance arrived. Daddy calmed down. He continued crying though. He stayed with Mommy even after Mrs. Peters brought the ambulance people and the police to Mommy's room.

Daddy screamed at God, "How much? How much pain do you want me and my children to endure? Punish me for my sins, but not my children. They are innocent. Please don't take them away from me too."

The emergency people made Daddy leave Mommy's room. He came out and sat on the couch with us. He was moaning and saying her name softly. He kept saying, "Lilly, Lilly, my sweet Lilly. What am I to do without you?"

Andre and I were crying. Our Mommy had died because she couldn't live without her Mommy and I didn't know what to do. But I knew that even if I didn't want to live for me, I would live for Daddy and Andre. I would be stronger than Mommy. I would live

When the emergency people were done, they said we could come in for a minute. We went into Mommy's room to say goodbye to her. It felt strange to be in a room with Mommy and for her to not know we were there. She was Mommy, but she wasn't really. The Mommy before Nana died would have found a way to stop our pain. The one on the bed hadn't worried about us or our pain. She'd only worried about herself and her love for her mommy. Leaving us was easier than living without her mommy. Our mommy had sacrificed all of us so she could be with her mommy.

I looked at Mommy; in her death she'd become beautiful again. I let her go. I let her go because she hadn't wanted to be with us and she'd already been gone a long time anyway. I closed off the part of my heart that was hers. I'd loved her more than she'd loved me. I loved her enough to let her go, but she hadn't loved me enough to stay.

Daddy didn't want us to see when they took Mommy out of the house so he had Mr. and Mrs. Peters go with us to our rooms. He stayed with Mommy. Once he called for us to come downstairs, he didn't have to tell us Mommy was gone we could tell. The house had an unusual quiet feeling. There was a silence that, despite our crying, hung over the house like a big tent. It was covering, shielding, muting, quieting, and absorbing our pain. I was glad for the tent. It kept our pain private. Watching Daddy cry and pace made us cry harder.

I started to become afraid of God even though I'd decided to stop loving him. I told him that I wouldn't do like Mommy and die. I was going to live. I knew that my living didn't have anything to do with me if he decided that he wanted three generations of Greenwood women up there in his house, he would just go on and do whatever he pleased. He was, after all, God. As Nana would say, "The God I believe in is an awesome and omnipotent God." I stood right there and became truly afraid of this awesome and omnipotent God who would take children's Nana and then their mommy.

"Daddy, what did me and Drea do that would make God take away Nana and Mommy?"

"Champ," Daddy said through his tears, "Neither you nor your sister did anything wrong. It's just the way God is."

"Well, Daddy, doesn't God know that we are young and need our Mommy just the way Mommy needed her mommy? Doesn't God know that you don't live here with us? Daddy, what is God expecting me and Drea to do now without anybody?"

"God has his ways and all we can do is accept them."

"You know something, Daddy; I got a small problem with God and his ways. Right now, Daddy, God's ways ain't right. They just ain't, Daddy." Andre started to cry really hard.

Daddy just hugged him. He hugged him hard as if he hoped in hugging him he could absorb all of his hurts and pain. Andre was almost as tall as Daddy but right at that moment he looked like a little boy. I wanted to climb into Daddy's lap and never move, but I just couldn't. I was feeling robbed, and inside of me, I could feel the pieces of my soul, spirit, and heart being taken. I wanted to find a way or something to stop the pieces of my heart from leaving. I walked into Mommy's room. The bed had been stripped. The linens, like Mommy, were gone. I lay right in the spot where Mrs. Peters had found her. I knew Mommy's spot because for almost three years or so, Mommy hadn't really moved from it, and so I laid down in it.

I closed my eyes and let all my brokenness float to God. I hoped that when He saw all my broken pieces, he would see what His answering Mommy's prayers had done to me. I hoped also that He would see them and realize He shouldn't answer everybody's prayers before He fully thought through the consequences of what His actions would do to other people.

I kept my eyes closed and tried to imagine what it was like for Mommy to lie here night after night and ask Him to take her to her ma. There, in the spot on her bed, in the space and place where God had answered her prayers, I again promised myself that I wouldn't do what she'd done. I would never pray that prayer. I would never ask Him to take me to be with her and Nana.

I decided that despite this pain or any other that I may feel in the future, I would be strong. I would live. I had to live. I wanted to live. I had to. I would never wish to die. I would survive always. I would always find a reason to live. Dying was never going to be an option or solution to any of my problems.

Chapter 61

Saying Goodbye

Once Mommy had taken her love for me, Daddy, and Andre, her spirit, joy, and everything that was hers to the Lord's house, what she left behind was an empty shell. Since Mommy didn't have any grown up family, the hospital gave Daddy Mommy's empty shell. They called it a body. Mommy, who only that morning was a Mommy in her bed, was now a body, released by the hospital and laid out in a coffin. Mommy wasn't Jewish, but Daddy was and since the hospital had released the body to him and there wasn't anything he could really do with it, he gave it a Jewish funeral. Cousin Bernard wanted to have a Baptist funeral, but Daddy said that while Mommy lived, she was his life and now that she was gone he would take care of her. The funeral was quick and quiet.

It was Daddy, Andre, Mr. and Mrs. Peters, me, Cousin Bernard, and a few of his brothers and sisters, Aunt Thea and Uncle Philip couldn't get to New York in time so they missed it. A few people from the block and our teachers came. Mommy had never worked so there were no work people. She'd never pushed any white babies other than me and Andre, and we weren't really white, just half, so there were no other women who had pushed babies with her to come and say anything about her.

Mommy didn't belong to a church so they were no church people. She didn't party or hang out, so they were no party or hanging out people. Mommy had just belonged to me, Daddy and Andre, and so we were there. Ms. Lewis tried to come, but Daddy told her she couldn't. He told Mrs. Peters to tell her to stay 'the hell' away from him and his children. Daddy had never forgiven Ms. Lewis for calling us nigger white children.

When it was time for a member of the family to speak, Daddy spoke. He spoke about his love for Mommy and that even now in her death, it wouldn't diminish. He said that all the love in his heart, with the exception of what was mine and Andre's was Mommy's and that's how it would remain until the day he joined her. I prayed very quickly to God that if He heard Daddy, He should ignore that part; Daddy didn't mean what he was saying about joining her. Andre read a letter he'd written and he cried from the time he said, "Dear Mommy," until he said, "'till I see you in God's house."

I read Mommy a poem. I tried really hard not to cry and almost wouldn't have had Mrs. Peters not started moaning. I cried and I read. I didn't want to stop so I just cried through it like Andre. When I was finished, Mr. and Mrs. Peters each sung a song. Mrs. Peters sung *I Won't Complain* without music. When Mrs. Peters was finished, a man we had never seen before delivered Mommy's eulogy. He spoke as if he'd known Mommy her whole life. From the way he spoke, I gussed he was Daddy's Rabbi and he had in fact known of Mommy and us even if he'd never seen her and us until today. Mommy's funeral was almost over and Cousin Bernard had re-opened the casket and was allowing us to say a final good-bye when an old white woman came in. She walked right up to Mommy's casket and looked at Mommy, and then she looked at Daddy who was hugging Andre and me.

The old white woman sat down without saying anything to anybody. When Cousin Bernard closed the casket and we got ready to leave, we had to walk pass her. When we got beside her she reached out a wrinkled hand that was weighed down with rings and things and she touched Daddy's arm. He stopped. He looked first at the wrinkled hand with all the rings and things and slowly raised his eyes from the wrinkled hand to the woman's face and then he demanded, "What are you doing here?"

"Rabbi Stein called the house this afternoon, he thought I knew her. I didn't say anything to the contrary Matthew. I had to come."

"Why did you come? Did you want to make sure that Lilly was gone? Well, are you satisfied now? Now that you have verified it, you can go and tell Madeline that Lilly is really gone. Go and tell her that my Lilly is truly dead. Also remember to tell her this and you keep it in mind for yourself as well; death won't stop my love for her." Daddy paused, took a deep breath, and then he continued, "Right now, I have to go and see about her and then I have to take care of our children."

Andre and I were standing quietly beside Daddy. He never took his hand from around my waist or off Andre's shoulder. The oldish white woman with the wrinkled hand with the rings and things spoke again. She said, "Matthew, I didn't come here to argue with you."

"So why did you come?"

"I'm your mother. I couldn't let you go through all this alone."

"Alone? I'm not alone, Mother, or didn't you notice? I have my children and over there are Neal and Noreen, you do remember them, don't you?"

"Matthew, let me help you. Let me help you through this."

"You see, Mother, that has always been part of our problem. You saw things one way and I saw them another. For you, Lilly's dying is a "this"; a thing you feel you can help me get through. Losing Lilly is not a "this" Mother, that you can help me get through. It's not a thing to 'get through'."

"Please, Matthew, let me help you."

"I don't need your help, Mother. The woman I loved and who is the mother of my children has died. How are you planning on helping me, as you put it, get through this? Mother, this is not something that you can throw Daddy's money at. You can't bargain with God or purchase her out of heaven, Mother. This one is in God's hands so can I please go, Mother? I have to see about my Lilly. I'm going to sit Shiva for her."

The oldish white woman looked at Daddy as if he'd cursed at her and at the same time spat in her face.

"Don't look so shocked. In my heart, she was my wife. After I've sat Shiva, and after I've figured out what to do for our children, I'll return. You may call me then and you may say or do anything you feel like. Right now, I have to take my children so they can say their final farewell to their mother."

"Matthew?"

"Yes Mother?"

"Are these the children? Introduce me to them, please. What are their names?"

"See, Mother, that's what I'm talking about. You can never come right out and say something nice the first time. Listen to what you asked me, Mother, 'are these the children?' "These" children, Mother? No, these are not "the" children? This beautiful young lady is Andrea Matti Hirsh Greenwood, she's the oldest, and this handsome young man is Andre Matthew David Hirsh Greenwood. These, as you called them, are my children, our, Lilly and my children, not 'the' children."

Before the oldish white woman could speak, Daddy said, "Princess, Champ, this is Mrs. Esther Hirsh, my mother. That makes her your grandmother."

Andre and I just looked at her. We didn't know what to say. It was she who spoke. She said, "Children." Seeing that Daddy was getting ready to correct her, she quickly said, "Andrea, Andre, I'm sorry for your loss and I'm sorry that I never met you before. I should have. I should have met you all before today."

Again we didn't know what to say so we said nothing. It was Daddy who spoke and he sounded very upset, "Yes, Mother, you should have."

The oldish white woman looked as if she wanted to cry, but I knew she didn't know Mommy so I guess she was crying because her only grandchildren didn't exactly look like what I guessed she'd imagined her grandchildren would look like. The oldish white woman sat down. Daddy walked out. We followed. I looked back to see if she was following us. She wasn't. She was just sitting where we'd left her. I could see her lips moving. I guess she was talking to the Jewish God. I wondered if she was telling him she was sorry about not meeting us before or asking him to make room for Mommy as she was on her way to Him. I didn't have a lot of time to wonder anymore about what she was saying 'cause it was time for us to leave.

We drove out to the same cemetery where Mommy had buried Nana. Daddy had arranged for Mommy to rest right next to Nana. Just as we'd done with Nana, after we'd prayed some more and asked God to receive Mommy into His kingdom, we left Mommy in her casket over a hole covered with some fake grass just the way we'd left Nana a few years back. We drove back to the house in quiet.

It felt strange being back in the house. Last night Mommy was here and alive. This morning she was dead and this evening, not twelve hours since Mrs. Peters couldn't wake her, she was buried and we were even more alone. The question that came to my mind was how do you live without your mommy? The minute it came into my thoughts, I understood immediately what Mommy had gone through. She couldn't imagine or think of living without her mommy. What I didn't understand was how Mommy expected me and Andre to live without her. Did she expect us to wish to be with her the way she'd wish to be with Nana?

We just sat there, the three of us, and then Daddy looked as if someone had lit a match under him, not for it to burn right through his clothes but as if it was something that until that second he hadn't thought about. Daddy turned to Mr. Peters and said, "Neal, come here for a minute please."

"Sure, Mr. Hirsh, what can I do for you?"

Daddy looked at Mr. Peters as if what he had to say was a matter of life or death. "Neal, you know the phone numbers to my house and my mother's? Please call both Mrs. Hirshes and let them know that I'll be sitting Shiva here for Lilly and if there's an emergency, they should call you at your home. Please leave them the number, and by no means give them this address or phone number."

Mr. Peters walked over to the phone and made the two phone calls. Daddy never asked what was said, nor did Mr. Peters say. He just walked into the kitchen and left Daddy with us.

Andre was the first one to talk. He asked, "Daddy, what is Shiva and why you sitting it?"

"Son, sitting Shiva is what we, in the Jewish faith, do for our loved ones that have passed on. For seven days we stay in the home of the loved one that has gone to be with the Lord. We talk and think about them. If we want, we cry, or laugh or anything that would help us with our grief and mourning, that is what we do. In the Jewish faith, we believe that this will help us not hurt as much. Mr. and Mrs. Peters will do all the work."

"But, Daddy, they do all the work now anyway."

"It's a little different this time."

"But how is it different, Daddy? How is this different from their regular work?"

"Well, during Shiva we, the ones that have lost our loved ones, are not supposed to do anything at all. I won't shave; change my clothes, use hot water to bathe; nothing that would give me pleasure. My only job is to think about your mother. It is a way, we believe, to help us with our hurting and pain of missing your mother."

"But Daddy, Mommy wouldn't want me and Andrea not to bathe or change our clothes."

"You don't have to do that part. I'll do that part. I understand this better and we won't want to do anything that would displease your mother. So you may sit with me."

"Is that all we do. We just sit here and stuff."

"No son, there's more to it, but Mr. and Mrs. Peters knows what to do. They will prepare the se'udat havra'ah."

"That's a hard word. I don't think I can say that one."

"It's ok, Champ. It just means a simple meal of lentils and eggs or eggs and bread. We eat the lentils and eggs because they are round and remind us that life goes on. This meal is the meal of condolence or consolation."

"I understand that, Daddy. You get the consolation prize when you don't win."

"No, son, in this case the consolation meal is a meal to help us feel better. Kinda help ease away some of our hurt."

"Daddy, that's the same thing. You get a consolation prize just so that you won't feel so bad about not winning."

Daddy didn't spend any more time trying to get Andre to understand. He just said, "I knew you would understand, son." Then daddy went on to explain the rest of what would happen during the Shiva. While Daddy was talking to us, Mrs. Peters came out of the kitchen and she had a white candle in her hand. It was lit and without a word, she put it on the side cabinet. Daddy said that the candle was to remember Mommy's spirit.

Seeing the candle started to make me feel really sad. I watched the candle burning and each time it flickered, the more I missed Mommy. This Shiva thing sounded like a good idea to help us get our pain out, but Mommy wasn't Jewish so I didn't see how it could help her. "Daddy, Mommy wasn't Jewish so how come she can get a Shiva?"

"You're right, your mother wasn't Jewish but in my heart, and because I loved her so much, she was my wife and therefore, although my faith says that I shouldn't sit Shiva for her, I will."

Andre looked at Daddy and said, "Then, Daddy isn't that like breaking the rules?"

"It's kinda, but different because our love had no boundaries. We didn't abide by the world's rules. We had our own. She loved me and I loved her."

"So, Daddy, if you and Mommy loved each other so much why didn't you live here with us?"

"If things were different, I would've."

"Daddy, did Mommy know that if you could have, you would have?"

"Yes, Princess, I never hid the truth from your mother. She understood and continued to love me anyway."

I'm not sure what it was that Daddy said but Andre started to cry. He started to cry so hard and loud that Daddy wrapped him into his chest as if Andre was a wet baby and Daddy was a great big fluffy towel. Andre got lost in the folds that were Daddy and his loud cry became a muffled sound. I looked at Daddy and my brother, wrapped in each other's arms, one protecting and the other being protected, and I missed Mommy even more.

Again I promised myself that I would live. I would never ask the Lord to take me to be with Mommy and Nana. I started to cry, but it wasn't for Mommy. I was crying because my father and my brother were falling apart and their pieces were starting to fall on the floor. Through blurry eyes, I looked at their pile of pieces and I didn't know what to do. I wanted to tell them that it would be all right, and we would be fine, but I wasn't sure, so I collected all their pieces. I sorted Daddy's pieces and put them in one pile and Andre's in another pile. As I picked up Andre's pieces, I figured out what Shiva was.

Shiva was a time that let you fall to pieces in private with someone who knew what your pieces looked like, so they could pick them up and keep them safe. I began to appreciate the Shiva as I watched more and more pieces fall from Andre and Daddy. I picked them up, sorted them, and kept them safe. Daddy said it was going be a whole week. I looked at how many pieces had already fallen and figured that it was going to be a long week. I decided to get something special to keep their fallen pieces in until I could figure out how to make them whole again.

The week of the Shiva went by slowly. The pieces continued to fall and I continued to pick them up and sort them. Then the seven days were up and Daddy said that we had to walk around the block because it would show everyone we were returning to our daily lives and that we were taking Mommy's soul out of the house.

We did just as Daddy said. Daddy, Andre, Mr. and Mrs. Peters, and I walked out of the house. Daddy walked in front and alone. I guess he did because he was walking with Mommy's soul. Andre and I walked in the middle, side by side, and Mr. and Mrs. Peters walked behind, also side by side. We walked around the block. I didn't care who saw us or thought that we looked odd or that Daddy looked like the Pied Piper leading us away.

We walked because Daddy said it was how we would finish Mommy's Shiva. We had to see that her soul was escorted to wherever souls went. We got back to the house and Daddy went into Mommy's room where he'd been staying and then he came out and went to the bathroom. He showered, shaved, changed, and ate a little something and then, because we knew that he would be leaving us all alone, we got sad. He said, "Don't look like that. I'll be back in a little while. I have to go and take care of some business, but I'll be back. I promise. Mr. and Mrs. Peters will stay with you."

Daddy kissed us goodbye and left. Andre and I started to cry. This was the first time since Mommy died that we didn't have our daddy. We had no family; we were truly alone.

Chapter 62

Too Young To Live Alone

It was only after Daddy was gone that I started to realize how all alone we were. While Andre was sitting on the couch, I walked into Mommy's room. It was so empty. Mommy's room had gone from being her room to being Daddy's room and now it didn't belong to anyone. Soon Mr. and Mrs. Peters would go back to their own house and we would be all alone. This had me worried because I knew that we were too young to live alone. I walked over to Mommy's bed that for the past week was Daddy's bed and now belonged to no one. I sat on it. I must have sat there forever 'cause soon Mrs. Peters knocked gently on the door. When I didn't answer, she pushed the door a little and called my name. My name floated to me as if it were on a cloud yet I didn't want to answer, but I didn't have a good reason not to answer so I said, "Yes, Mrs. Peters, you want me?"

"Well, child it ain't so much as wanting you, but it's worrying about you that I am. I'm worried about the two of you little ones."

"Mrs. Peters, I'm worried about me and Andre too. What's going to happen to us? Is the state going to take me and Andre and put us in an orphanage now that we don't have Mommy and Daddy has gone back to his house?"

"Child, don't fret yourself. Me and Mr. Peters won't let that happen. We love the two of you like you was our own two grandchildren. We raised your daddy and we sure ain't going turn our back on his children now. We'll figure something out. Yes, sir, we'll figure something out."

"Mrs. Peters, I feel so empty. Why did Mommy and Nana have to go away and leave us so alone?"

"Child, I don't have an answer, but I know one thing for sure and that's the Lord has His reasoning and our job isn't to ask Him why but to accept His will."

"Mrs. Peters, I have a problem with a God that can take away two little children's Mommy and Nana. Mrs. Peters He must know that once He took away our Mommy, that we were going be all alone."

"Andrea, this is where you're going to have to start growing your faith in the Lord. You have to believe that He has a plan and that in the midst of all this pain, He's working something out."

When Mrs. Peters stopped from talking, I threw myself into her arms and I started to cry. I cried and cried and Mrs. Peters just held me. The harder she held me, the more it started to feel like Nana was holding me. Mrs. Peters never let me go. I knew then that Mr. and Mrs. Peters would look after us because she understood that we were too young to live alone.

When she was sure I was through crying, she walked me to the living room and just as she'd said Mr. Peters was sitting with Andre. He looked just like the grandfather we'd never had. Mr. Peters was sitting on the couch and Andre was sitting right up close to him. It looked like Andre was just absorbing Mr. Peters' warmth and Mr. Peters was letting him. That night, Mr. and Mrs. Peters stayed with us. Mr. Peters stayed on the couch and Mrs. Peters put a folding bed in my room. Andre didn't want to be alone so he brought a blanket into my room and slept on the floor. Only Mr. Peters was alone.

Morning came the quickest it had ever come to our house. It was just like one minute I was saying my night prayers, and the next; just like that it was morning. I looked outside and a morning like none I'd ever seen before was spreading itself all over Chauncey Street. I felt it in the air. Things were going to be changing for Andre and me. I wasn't sure what it was, but it was going to happen today, and it was going to change everything we'd ever known.

I got out of bed, washed up, changed my clothes, and waited. I didn't have long to wait 'cause soon everyone else was waking up. There were waking like God had whispered in their ears that today He was going do a special thing. We were still a little sad, but it was different. It was the first night after Mommy's Shiva and I was wondering if that had anything to do with it. We'd spent a full week being just sad; a full week talking about Mommy.

Today everyone was waking up different. I started to wonder how Daddy was waking up on Pierrepont Street. I missed him and wanted to know how this morning had found him but I knew had to wait for him to call. We never called Daddy. Mrs. Peters went to see about Mr. Peters while Andre took his stuff into his room. Soon, the smell of bacon filled the air. It was the first time in a long time we were smelling bacon. Mrs. Peters never cooked bacon when Daddy was around. Today Daddy wasn't around so she didn't have to cook Jewish.

I looked at Andre and for the first time in a long time, he smiled. He hurried up, dressed, and we went out to the kitchen. "Well, good morning, you two. I guess you like what you're smelling?"

We smiled and nodded.

Mrs. Peters said, "Sit down. There's plenty for everyone."

"Mrs. Peters, can I have lots and lots."

"Why?"

"Because when Daddy comes back, we can't have bacon. I just want to store it in my belly just in case he stays long again."

That made us all laugh; it was the first time there was laughter in the house that didn't have to do with a happy memory about Mommy. Mrs. Peters looked at Andre and said, "Well I better hurry up and give this fine gentleman his chocolate 'fore he chokes trying to stuff that bacon down his throat."

Andre took the hot chocolate and began blowing into the cup so he could take a sip. The sip seemed to be enough to help him work the bacon down his throat. Andre looked happy eating all that bacon. We were all glad to see him eat. We ate breakfast and talked. Mr. and Mrs. Peters talked about Barbados. Mrs. Peters said that when she and Mr. Peters were young like me and Andre, they made friends and they had been best friends ever since. Mr. Peters made Mrs. Peters smile into her hands when he winked at Andre and said, "Yup, I took one look at her and knew that she and me was going be together the rest of our days. I knew it then and I'm still sure after these fifty-five years."

"Fifty-five years!" Andre noted. "That's a long, long time. Mr. Peters, does that mean that you two are old as dust?"

"Boy, what you know 'bout somebody being old as dust?"

"Only what Nana said. She said that if you're past your prime, then you're old as dust. Is fifty-five past your prime?"

"I guess your Nana had a point there, son. Fifty-five sure is past your prime and so I guess that makes us old as dust."

Mrs. Peters just burst out laughing so hard that she nearly fell off her chair. She said, Neal, we're old as dust. Ain't that something? All these years with you and now I done turned into dust."

Every time somebody would say dust we would all get to laughing. Then Mrs. Peters tried to make a serious face and said, "Neal, I guess from now on I won't be dusting the chairs and tables here."

"Why, Noreen?"

Laughing, Mrs. Peters said, "Because, Neal, if I dust the furniture too clean, I might be cleaning way parts of you or me."

"Noreen, I don't get what you mean."

"Neal, since we're old as dust and I dust the furniture, I may be dusting way part of you and me. You don't get it, Neal. Me and you are old as dust. The furniture got dust, little bits of me and you spread all over them."

Mr. Peters wasn't laughing so Mrs. Peters just said, "Forget it, Neal. You done missed the joke and now it ain't funny no more."

"Sorry, Noreen; you know me. I don't always get it first time. I bet you when I ain't thinking about it I'm going get it."

"You right, Neal, long after no one else ain't remembering this joke you going get it and you going to laugh."

"See, Noreen, that's what I always liked about you. Things that would make other people mad ain't never no big thing with you. You leave it alone and we never have fuss."

Mrs. Peters just looked at Mr. Peters and smiled. I watched them and was glad that they were thinking of us like family. Suddenly, I didn't feel so alone. I felt like I was a part of a family again.

Chapter 63

A Time To Pluck Up That Which Is Planted

Daddy called every day but it was a week before he came back. We came home from school, had dinner, and were getting ready to take our baths when he came in. We were all glad to see him. Mrs. Peters asked Daddy if he was hungry. Daddy had never said no to Mrs. Peters' cooking and so she went into the kitchen to fix him something to eat. Daddy ate quietly but we could tell that he had something on his mind. Daddy looked as if what he had to say was going to hurt us worse than Mommy and Nana going to be with the Lord. He ate slowly, I guess to build up his courage.

Andre and I had learned not to question Daddy when he had that look on his face. Daddy finished eating and went into the living room. We followed. "Princess and Champ," Daddy started, "I've been talking to Neal and Noreen about your continued care and I've reached a decision. Over the next few months, while you guys are out of school, Princess, we will move your things to Mr. and Mrs. Peters on Bainbridge Street."

At the mention of my things, Andre started in, "Daddy, why only Andrea's things? What's going happen to my things? Am I going to stay here in the house all by myself?"

"Whoa, Champ, slow down. I was getting to you as soon as I'd explained to Princess what we had decided, but since you're anxious, I'll give Princess a chance to think about what I'm saying and I'll tell you what plans I have for you."

I wanted to stop Daddy and tell him to finish talking about me. I wanted him to tell me why I had to leave home, but I knew that it wouldn't be right or sound right. I said nothing. As Daddy talked to Andre, I looked over to Mr. and Mrs. Peters; they looked pleased at the idea of me going to their house so I started to feel a little less scared.

"Champ, I've found a new school for you."

"But, Daddy, what's wrong with the school I'm going to now. I know everybody there remember?"

"I know, Champ, but the two of you to take care of every day is a handful. Princess can almost take care of herself, but you need more attention. So that's why I've found you a new school."

"Where's my new school going to be, Daddy?"

"It's in a place called Pennsylvania"

"Why so far. Daddy, how's Andre going to get home every day and then get back to school in the morning? Is Mr. Peters going to drive him, Daddy?"

"Ok, Ok let's see which of those questions I'm going to answer first. Princess, your brother won't come home every day."

"Daddy, you mean I have to stay at the school all the time."

"Yes, Champ. That's why it's called a boarding school."

"But, Daddy, why do I have to go to a boarding school? Couldn't you have found a perfectly good school here for me in the city? I don't want to go away. I want to stay here and live with Mr. and Mrs. Peters and Andrea. I won't give them any trouble."

"Champ, you are almost fourteen. That's a wonderful age to make new friends. I went to boarding school and some of the fellows I met there are still my friends."

"Then, Daddy, I guess your decision is final?"

"Let's just say for now, because of the circumstances it's not open for discussion. I believe that this is best for you. Know Champ that I'll always do what I believe is best for you and Drea."

"Daddy, I don't really want to go but I understand. It has to do with what's best for me. If you say this is the best school for me, then I'll do what I can to make it the best thing for me. But, Daddy, I have a question."

"What's that, Champ?

"Have you chosen a boarding school for Drea?"

"Daddy, if Andre has to go to a boarding school, I want to go to a boarding school too."

"Andrea and Andre! Stop this whining now and listen to me! Listen and hear me out. This isn't easy for me. I'm doing what I think is best for the both of you; to give you both the best chance at the best future I can provide. Andre, you need the best opportunity available so that you can go out into the world and make something of yourself. Andrea, you need a mother's nourishing and guidance. Noreen is the only one I know that can give you that."

Andre and I stopped talking. It was the first time Daddy had ever raised his voice to us. He sounded frustrated.

"Daddy, I'm sorry. It's just that…"

Daddy stopped me before I could finish. "Princess, this isn't easy for me, but Mr. and Mrs. Peters can't continue with the disruption of their lives to accommodate me. I've appreciated everything that they've done these past three years but everyone has their limits and I don't want to stretch Neal and Noreen to the point where they don't want to be bothered. Now they have agreed to take you in and let you live with them and see about you. I'll be around to come visit you and take care of you. You both know that I can't take you to live with me. If I could, I would have done that already. "

We didn't interrupt Daddy with any more questions. He talked and in his talking, he laid out the plans for us. It was decided and we accepted. Andre would be going with Daddy in a few weeks to see his new school and Mrs. Peters would be helping me pack Mommy's and Nana things. Daddy said he would put anything that I couldn't take to Mr. and Mrs. Peter's house in his office basement. He said that this way when I wanted it, he could get it for me. Over the next few weeks, we packed boxes and marked them. As soon as we had a room finished, Mrs. Peters and I moved on to another room. Soon we had all that was going to be stored away packed up. Mr. Peters called his friends and they came and took the things; some to Daddy's office building and the rest to Bainbridge Street.

Andre went with Daddy to see his new school and he came back happy. He liked it and was glad that he would be with other fourteen and fifteen-year-old boys. He talked about a boy named Tony Adams and said that he and Tony were going to be sharing the same room. Andre just went on and on about Tony. It was 'Tony said this' and 'Tony said this'. Daddy just looked at Andre and smiled. I could tell that Daddy knew he'd made the right decision.

We had no sooner started to packing than we were finished. I stood in the middle of the empty house and missed Nana, Mommy, and everything that was part of the family we used to be. It was all gone now. All stored away in boxes. Mrs. Peters had helped me fix up my room at her house. She had Mr. Peters bring a bookcase into my room and on it; she'd help me put my favorite things that belonged to Nana and Mommy.

My furniture was hodge-podge and Daddy said it was ok. I had Nana's angel headboard, Mommy's dresser, and Andre's chest of drawers. I had the fancy oval beveled-shaped mirror from the hallway that Nana had said belonged to her Aunt Bess. Mr. Peters hung that over Mommy's dresser for me. I had one night table from Nana's room and one from Mommy's. I wanted to take a lamp from Nana's bedroom and one from Mommy's bedroom, but when Daddy came by to see my room at Mrs. Peters' house, he said I should at least have something matching and new in my room. He bought me a set of lamps.

Soon it was August. The house on Chauncey Street was empty. Years of living was packed up in boxes and stored away for another lifetime. Andre was ready and excited to go away to school and I was ready to move into my new room. Mrs. Peters and I had worked really hard to make the room feel like home.

We all went with Andre the day he went to his new school. Andre showed us everything as if he'd been there a long time. I was sad that Andre was going to be so far away, but I was happy for him. We met Tony and Troy Adams. Tony was fourteen like Andre, but Troy appeared to be about seventeen, almost eighteen. Tony had the same complexion as Andre and I. We all looked like chocolate with a little too much milk.

Troy, on the other hand, looked like a piece of cedar that someone had dipped in honey. His hair was very light and in some places it looked as if the sun was playing hide and seek and was shining through from underneath. His hair also looked as if it had never had a comb in it, nor needed to. His hair was soft enough for just his fingers. Where Andre's nose and mine was pointed like Daddy's, Troy's was a combination of straight and flared. It wasn't a very wide flare, but it wasn't straight either. That nose belonged on his face. It matched his eyes, which seemed to be looking deep into your soul. Troy didn't just stop at your skin when he looked at you; he traveled deep within to places he had no right being or seeing.

If Nana was around and she had met Troy, she would've said, "That boy looks at you like he goin' snatch your soul." Nana always had a way of calling people out just the way she saw them. I think Nana would've liked Tony and she would've kept an extra eye on Troy. He looked as if he could steal your heart and you wouldn't notice it was gone 'till you stopped from breathing and even then it wouldn't matter because he had it.

I knew that I still had my heart because it was beating so hard my breathing didn't have any rhythm. It was out of control and making me sound as if I'd been running. I noticed that Mrs. Peters was watching me watch Troy. I looked away, but my breathing remained like I was running. Troy stayed around long enough for me to get a picture of him imprinted on my brain and heart and then he was gone. I remembered Troy the rest of the day. I even hoped to get another glance of him. He never came back around.

We left Andre at his school and Daddy drove us back in his car. Mr. and Mrs. Peters drove back in their car. They went ahead to Bainbridge Street and Daddy took me over to Chauncey Street. I wanted to walk around the house one last time. I was going to miss my old life. Daddy walked with me from room to room. There was nothing there that reminded me of my old life. The carpet was gone. In its place were new wooden floors. Daddy had replaced the carpet in my room and it was no longer pink. My room was now just a plain old white room. It didn't look like my room anymore.

In Mommy's room, everything that reminded me of her was gone. Andre's room, like mine, was just plain white. I walked into the kitchen and our fridge, stove, and sink were gone. Daddy had replaced them too. He said in a very matter of fact voice, "Those were your mother's things. I didn't want anyone else using her fridge or cooking on her stove." I asked Daddy where he'd put the fridge and he said that Mr. Peters had put them in his basement kitchen. I was happy. I could go and touch them whenever I wanted. We stayed a few minutes then it was time to go. I walked out the house on Chauncey Street. I doubted that I would ever walk back in it again, but in my heart I was glad that Daddy hadn't sold it. He said that he wouldn't or couldn't since the house now belonged to Andre and me.

Daddy and I drove to Bainbridge Street. We didn't really talk. There was nothing much really to be said. All our lives had been changed because the person we loved had died and left us to go on without her. Daddy was doing the best he could. Outside Mr. and Mrs. Peters' house, Daddy and I sat and looked at each other. I felt as if I would never see him again. I felt as if once I got out the car and walked up the steps, he was just going to be gone. He would disappear into the night and I would be all alone with just Mr. and Mrs. Peters. Daddy must have read my mind because he said, "I'm always going to be here, Princess. You're a big girl now. You call me at the office if you need anything and know that as soon as I can, I'll be here. I'm not going away, Princess. I knew your mother very well, and she would never have gone away if she didn't believe that I would take care of you and your brother. I promise you, Princess that I'll always be here, always."

I didn't know what to say so I just looked at him. I took every detail of Daddy's face in as if I were seeing him for the first time. I made sure that my hazel eyes found his pale blue eyes and recorded them. I made my eyes see his nose, the same nose that was mine and Andre's. I looked at his hair and made sure that my eyes remembered the thick wavy sea of light chocolate frosting that was his hair. Hair that was just like Andre's, or that Andre's was just like, and was responsible for me having the kind of hair that was as Nana used to say, "A whole lot easier to comb than Mommy's used to be." I watched Daddy as he watched me. His eyes got all misty. Daddy reached to open his door and I opened mine. I walked towards my new home. Tonight would be my first real night alone. Mr. and Mrs. Peters would be there, but I would still be alone.

I reached up to ring the bell when Daddy asked, "Princess, don't you have a key."

"Yes, Daddy, I just forgot."

Before I could get the key, the door opened; it was Mrs. Peters. She was standing there and smiling her usual smile; the one that welcomed you back even if you had gone into the kitchen for some water. The smile always said, "So glad to see you. Welcome back."

We stepped in and the smell of Mrs. Peters' food filled the house and our noses. I became instantly hungry. Mrs. Peters had anticipated that we would want something to eat and had the food in the oven keeping warm. Daddy washed his hands in the kitchen and I went to the bathroom. I knew better than to ever wash my hands in the kitchen sink. Daddy was Daddy and neither Mr. nor Mrs. Peters would've said anything to him about washing his dirty hands in the kitchen sink. I also knew better than to say anything about it. I knew what to leave alone when it came to Daddy and Mrs. Peters. The four of us sat down to eat. No one mentioned Andre, but it was clear we were all thinking about him. Mr. Peters couldn't take it anymore and when he reached for the plantains, he said, "Now who's going eat Andre's share of plantains tonight?"

Daddy smiled and said, "Well, since that boy got his appetite from me, I guess I can split them with you." Mr. Peters smiled and he and Daddy took extra plantains.

After dinner, Mr. Peters and Daddy had some things to talk about so Mrs. Peters and I went to the kitchen. It was decided that I would help Mrs. Peters with the house chores. Mrs. Peters was no longer working for Daddy. I was living at them. I had to help out. Mrs. Peters said that my room would be my responsibility, but she would continue with the rest of the house. The dishes and kitchen work she said was different. In the kitchen, she said she would teach me things so the kitchen was never housework. Mrs. Peters and I finished up in the kitchen and went out to the living room where Daddy and Mr. Peters were watching TV and talking. I sat next to Daddy and Mrs. Peters sat in her chair, which was next to Mr. Peters'. Daddy stayed until The Dick Van Dyke Show was finished and then he said that he would be leaving. I walked with Daddy to the door, kissed him goodnight and I turned and walked back to the living room where my guardians and family were waiting for me. I silently let Daddy, Andre, Nana, and Mommy know that I was OK.

Mrs. Peters smiled and welcomed me back. I'd only gone a few feet but to her I'd been gone long enough to be welcomed back. I was glad for her welcoming smile and walked into the radiance of it. The warmth wrapped me like a heated blanket in the winter and I settled in. My heart felt happy and I smiled. I smiled because I knew that as long as Mr. and Mrs. Peters lived on Bainbridge Street, Andrea Matti Hirsh Greenwood would have a home to come to and a smile that welcome her back to it.

I sat and talked with Mr. and Mrs. Peters for a little while and then when upstairs to my new bedroom. I read Nana's bible, which used to belong to Aunt Bess. I went to Nana's favorite passage: Ecclesiastes 3:1-8: for everything there truly was a season. I read for a little while and just as I started to become sleepy, I put the bible down, turned out the light in the new lamp and went to sleep.

In my mind, I'd slept a short peaceful sleep, but when I woke, I was almost eighteen years old and was on my way out the twelfth grade. I'd been with the Peters for two years. During that time, I'd grown into a young woman with long coltish legs and breasts that made all the clothes that were fitting me the night before I went to sleep too small. My waist, which until I went to bed was the same width as my shoulders with a nice round mound in the middle that I used to be so proud of once I filled it with Auntie Noreen's rice and peas, fried chicken, cheese and macaroni or as she called it; macaroni pie, and potato salad, was now gone. In its place was this tapered area and the mound; well that was completely gone. I was as flat as cardboard. My hair, which had never had any problems growing, was now at my waist. Mrs. Peters had never allowed anyone to cut it because I'd never wanted it cut.

Andre had fared no better in the two years. He was sixteen and getting ready to go into eleventh grade. During the time he'd been away at school, he'd grown taller than Daddy's six-foot-one inch. Andre now stood a full three inches taller than Daddy. This, his towering height over Daddy always made Daddy laugh. "The son," he said each time he saw Andre, "has become the man." There we stood, Andre and I, not quite man or woman but no longer children.

We weren't orphans in the true sense of the word but because we no longer had Mommy and Nana, we felt that we were. I know because Andre and I kept this shared secret. Yes, we had Daddy, but Daddy, try as much as he wanted to, he couldn't be ours totally. So for his missing times, we mourned him and it was that missing part that orphaned us.

We didn't tell Daddy, Auntie Noreen, or Uncle Neal how we felt because we knew how that would hurt. So we kept our secret and now with our heels in our past, and our toes on the threshold of our futures, we stood children of a mother who had grieved herself to death and a father, resolute that he, despite his circumstances and society's frown was going to see us through the doors of the future he'd planned and laid out for us. College for me and a partnership with him in his law firm for Andre.

Chapter 64

The Tail-end Of Time

I was in the twelfth grade when a new boy moved in a few doors down from Mr. and Mrs. Peters. His family, like Mr. and Mrs. Peters, was from the West Indies. His name was Hamilton. Unlike Troy, who never noticed how hard I was trying to get him to see me, Hamilton noticed when I saw him. I saw him from the first day he moved on the block and then I saw him more when he started attending my school.

Mrs. Peters, who I now called Auntie Noreen, saw that I'd seen Hamilton and she said, "Now tell me why you looking at that ugly boy so hard?"

I'd been watching Hamilton play ball in his yard. I was looking at the way he never seemed to miss one basket; every ball he pointed at the basket it went in. I was so absorbed in my Hamilton-watching that I never noticed or heard Auntie Noreen when she'd stepped out on our tiny front porch.

"Auntie Noreen, why are you saying that he's ugly? He's not that ugly."

"Child, now I know you don't wear any glasses, but what's wrong with your eyes that you can't see all them faults in that boy."

"Auntie Noreen, you ain't even talked to Hamilton and you're finding fault with him."

"Oh, it's Hamilton. Now when did you have time to find out that that big ole' gorilla looking boy's name is Hamilton?"

"Auntie Noreen, he ain't no gorilla. Hamilton goes to my school and he's very nice."

"Now tell me, young lady, why do you think this Mr. Hamilton is so nice?"

"Because he just is."

"No sweetness. He's nice because he don't have no other choice. Everything else about him is taken up with ugliness."

"Auntie Noreen, that's not nice. You'll see that if you ever talk to him, he's nice."

Laughing, Auntie Noreen said, "I guess I ain't ever going find out that he's nice 'cause I don't know how to speak gorilla. Tell me, Drea, when did you learn to speak gorilla? Are they teaching that in twelfth grade?"

Auntie Noreen started to laugh harder and make gorilla sounds. It was when she turned her hands like she were going to drag them on the ground and started to sway from side to side and even went as if she was going to beat her chest that I became upset. I couldn't even figure out why her laughing at Hamilton was upsetting me, but it was. Auntie Noreen noticed that I was getting upset and stopped. Walking over to me, she hugged me and said, "I'm sorry, sweetness, I was just teasing you 'bout your friend. I don't mean no harm. None at all, if you want to like your little gorilla boy, you go right on and like your gorilla boy. I guess somebody got to be kind to the little gorilla boy."

"Auntie Noreen, you said you were just teasing. Then if you're just teasing, stop calling him gorilla boy."

Auntie Noreen pretended she was a soldier and said, "Yes, sir, aye aye, sir. No more gorilla boy. It's Hamilton you want me to call him, then Hamilton it will be."

I laughed at how silly Auntie Noreen looked pretending to be in the army. Then she gave me her welcome back smile and I came back. I came back from the place I was going where I'd become angry and upset for no real reason. She welcomed me back as if I'd been really gone. That was Auntie Noreen, always providing me a place to return to.

With college just around the corner, Daddy was busy. He was busy looking at colleges for me. He said that it had been my mother's dream to go to college and he was sure that if she were around, it would've made her happy to see the day I would be going off to college. Daddy wanted me to go away and I wanted to stay right here. Hamilton and I had become real close and since his mother couldn't afford to send him to college, nor did he want to go anyway, I wanted to stay to be with him. I couldn't tell Daddy, Auntie Noreen, or Uncle Neal the real reason I wanted to stay. I just kept finding excuses after excuses each time Daddy mentioned an out-of-state college. I almost fainted when Mr. Peters suggested to Daddy that I go to school in Barbados at the University of the West Indies.

Then Daddy stopped asking me and one day when he came over he said it was decided. I could pick between a small girl's college in Virginia or a small college in Georgia, but either way I was going away to school. It was decided and the decision had nothing to do with me anymore. As summer vacation drew near, I approached it with dread. I knew that at the end of summer I would start the year that meant I would be going away. I would be going away from all that was familiar and unlike Andre, who loved his time at boarding school, I didn't want to go. I believed that I loved Hamilton and wanted to stay where he was.

Auntie Noreen tried to talk to me about what it would mean for me to go away to college. She kept telling me it would mean a brighter future and a chance for a better life, but she didn't understand. Hamilton had become my every reason for everything. His mother was nice to me and said she didn't see why my father had to keep pushing me to go away to college. She said, "Well, it ain't like it's something that everybody round here doing. How many people 'round here other than you are rushing off to some stupid college?"

Hamilton was no better than his mother. He'd already dropped out of high school because Coach Hinds had told him if he didn't bring his grades up, he was going to cut him from the basketball team. Hamilton, didn't pay Coach Hinds no mind because he felt they couldn't win without him. Hamilton's grades didn't improve and Coach Hinds kept his word and cut him from the team. Hamilton's pride got in his way and he told Coach Hinds to kiss his black Grenadian ass and left basketball and school and his dream of playing in the NBA behind.

When I tried to talk Hamilton about going back to school, even offered to help him with his missing assignments, and to do what he would have to so that Coach Hinds would take him back, he told me, "Drea, I ain't going back. He don't know how to treat his star. Making me want to do the same shit as everybody else; I ain't going back. You wait. You wait and see. Coach Hinds going come running back to me when Jerry Rivers make them lose the championship game and when they come looking for me, I'm going tell them all again to kiss my black Grenadian ass. You wait, Drea. You wait and see. They goin' come begging."

Hamilton kept waiting for someone to come. No one ever came. They didn't have to. Jerry Rivers wasn't only winning, but I'd heard that he'd gotten a scholarship to go play at a big university in Virginia. This made Hamilton mad and bitter. Hamilton then went from mad and bitter to disappointed and full of blame. He blamed everyone for everything that went wrong. He even blamed me for not making him go back to school. Even when I reminded Hamilton that I'd begged him to go back, he said that I'd not begged him hard enough and now here he was a failure and it was my fault.

I didn't know what to do. Auntie Noreen heard that Hamilton was no longer in school and she told me she didn't want that don't-want-nothing, good-for-nothing boy hanging around me. Even Uncle Neal, who for the most part was always quiet and left all the talking to Auntie Noreen and Daddy, had something to say. He was sitting real quiet in his chair while Auntie Noreen was going on and on about Hamilton being just a blight. When she was done, he said, "Drea, your Auntie Noreen is right. I don't smell nothing good coming out of that boy. He's headed for trouble and it would do you well to listen to your Auntie Noreen and me and stay away from that boy. He's trouble, Drea, just plain old trouble."

"Auntie Noreen and Uncle Neal, he's not like that. It's just that right now things aren't working out for him."

"But Drea, why you think things ain't working out for that boy? Things ain't working out for him 'cause he's hard-headed and his mother don't make him want nothing. That's the problem right there. If she made him want something bad enough so that he would be willing to get up and go get it, then life would work out some for him, but it can't work out if he ain't willing to get up and go fight for something. You got to be willing, in this man's country, to fight for something, Drea."

"Listen to your Auntie Noreen, she knows what she's talking about. We came here and had to fight. We even had to fight to be domestics. But your Auntie Noreen had a plan and she worked real hard at it. In her plan, she would get us both hired together all the time. I listened to her. I learned to drive and she learned how to cook what they ate and soon everybody in Brooklyn Heights and some places in Manhattan knew that if you had Noreen and Neal Peters working for you, you had two hard working people. Listen to us, Drea, he's big trouble."

I told Hamilton most of what Auntie Noreen and Uncle Neal said about him. Hamilton had an idea. He said, "Ask your daddy if he'll help me get a job down in his big-shot law office."

I wasn't sure what to say and he started to get mad at me. He said, "See, can't count on you and you're here and telling me about me not wanting nothing. Well I'm telling you that I want something now. I want that job with your father. Now are you going talk to him for me or not?"

I started to get afraid. Hamilton was getting angrier. I couldn't ask Daddy to help Hamilton because Daddy would want to know how, when, and where I'd spoken to him. I got up and started to leave.

"Where you going Drea?"

"I have to be home before Auntie Noreen and Uncle Neal gets home."

"See, that's what I'm talking about. You always got to be doing whatever everybody wants, but you can't do that one thing for me."

Then Hamilton got up from the floor and sat beside me. He put his arms around me and started to kiss me. I'd kissed Hamilton before, but I didn't want to kiss him while he was like this. So I told him to stop and let me go home. Hamilton stopped, but he didn't let me go home. He looked like he would cry.

"You see, Drea, you keep proving me right all the time. You can't do nothing for me. Not even something that would make me feel like somebody, Drea."

Hamilton started to put his hand under my skirt and all the while he was saying, "Make me feel good, Drea."

Then I felt Hamilton's hand go between my legs. I wanted to stop him, but he'd said that I wouldn't do anything for him. So I let him. I wanted him to see that I would do something for him. When he pushed me back on the couch, pushed his hand into the leg of my panty and with his other hand unzipped his pants and shoved his thing in me, I didn't stop him.

I experienced the worst pain I'd ever felt in my life and yet, I didn't stop him. I stayed silently crying and let him even though I felt like somebody was shoving a hot poker in me. I let him because he'd said that nobody would do anything for him. I stayed still while Hamilton pushed and shoved his way into me. Even when he shoved really fast and hard, I said nothing. In a few minutes, he stopped, pulled himself away from me and with a spiteful look on his face, he said, "Look what you made me do."

I didn't understand why he was angry. Pulling my skirt down, I asked, "What did I do?"

Hamilton's face twisted. He put his hand over his mouth like he was going to vomit and said, "Don't go trying to make me feel bad for your shit. This, all of this, was your fault."

I started to cry. I was so confused. "Fault? What are you talking about? I didn't make you do anything?"

Hamilton stepped further away from me and with an even more twisted and disgusted look, he said, "See what I mean, you going blame me now for what just happened, right, you going blame me? But, Drea, I'll tell the whole world that what just happened here wasn't my fault."

Through my tears I asked, "What blame, Hamilton? What are you talking about?"

"This shit that just happened is on you 'cause I didn't call you over here. You came over here by yourself."

"But, Hamilton, you said that I didn't do anything for you. You said that you wanted to feel better and you, you were the one that went on about me not doing anything for you and now, now you blame me for what just happened between us."

"Between us? What us you talking about? We ain't no us. I see what you trying to do. You trying to shift the blame."

"Hamilton, why you have to curse and talk like that. Why you always got to point the blame away from you to somebody else?"

"That's right; go on preach the word according to Drea, the used-to-be virgin!"

At the sound of his words, 'used to be virgin' I started to cry harder. I stood up and stepped back from him. I wanted to be away from him. He was ugly and hateful. I walked towards the door and once I reached it and was sure I could get out, I said, "Hamilton Trindle, my family was right; I should have stayed away from you."

Hamilton pounced just so he could get to the door. He stepped in front of me as if he wanted to slap me, but he didn't, he just looked at me and said, "Mrs. High and Mighty, are you getting ready to run home and tell your family that the useless Grenadian boy down the block just fucked you? Are you? Go on, Ms. Andrea half-Jewish, half-white, just got poked in your hole Hirsh Greenwood, and tell your white daddy that the 'Want Nothing' down the block just screwed you."

I pushed pass him to the door. I opened the door and before I went through, I looked back at him and I saw what Auntie Noreen had seen the first day she'd seen him. Hamilton was one ugly gorilla and he had hateful ugly primitive ways. I opened the door and he shouted in a very hateful voice, "That's right. Run home and tell them that the same Hamilton Trindle who can't do nothing just filled you full of baby. Tell them that I did that. That I fucked you and filled your half-Jewish cunt with a baby!"

Hamilton's words stopped me in my tracks. Until that second, I hadn't thought about a baby. I was only doing something to make him happy, now he was shouting nasty hateful curses at me and screaming about filling me with a baby. Leaving the door open, I ran out the house. I stopped when I'd made it out the gate. I turned and looked at him standing in the doorway and I hated him. I knew in that second that this feeling would last for the rest of my life.

I didn't do as Hamilton thought I would. I didn't tell anyone anything. I rushed home and as soon as I was in my room, I got undressed, balled the clothes up, and put them in a bag to throw in the trash and then I showered. I showered repeatedly. I hoped to wash away the hurt, anger, and deep hatred I was feeling. It didn't. The hatred was growing and taking root.

I told no one what had happened at Mrs. Trindle's; not even when I missed the first period. When I missed my second period, I shopped for looser clothes so no one could see the change in me when it started. If Auntie Noreen noticed, she said nothing, but a few weeks after I'd missed my third period, I came home from school and Auntie Noreen called me as soon as I came through the door. "Andrea, come up here. I'm in your room."

"I'll be right up."

Auntie Noreen being in my room wasn't that unusual, but her being there by herself was unusual. I walked to my room. She was sitting on my bed and I could see she was very upset. "Drea, why didn't you come to me?"

"Come to you about what, Auntie?"

The way Auntie Noreen looked at me; I thought she would get up and knock me to the floor.

"Don't play dumb or stupid with me. Why would you go and tell Mrs. Trindle that you were pregnant and not come to me first? Mrs. Trindle? Andrea, why would you go to that ignorant woman for advice?"

I looked at Auntie Noreen and I wanted to run. She was looking so disappointed. I'd disappointed her. I didn't know what to say. How could I have thought that Mrs. Trindle wouldn't say anything to Auntie Noreen?

I was thinking of something to say, but Auntie Noreen stopped me. "Don't say anything, Drea. I'm trying to understand why you would've gone to that woman. She can't tell you what's on either side of a penny. How was she going be able to help you with something like this?"

"I…"

"How could you go to her before you came to me? She don't know nothing 'bout you, Andrea. Beside your father and brother, me and Mr. Peters is the only family you got. Andrea, how did you let something like this happen to you?"

"It just happened."

Auntie Noreen looked as if she would explode. She stood up and in two steps she had me by the shoulders. Auntie Noreen had never laid a hand on me before unless it was out of kindness and love, but now she was squeezing my arms and she was angry.

"Child, I would take that foolishness from somebody like Mrs. Trindle who ain't never had nothing, or been exposed to nothing, but not from you, Drea; not from you. Drea, you got too much sense for this. Your father gave you every opportunity. He ain't ever one day let you want for nothing, and now when he's expecting you to start college, you're pregnant. Who you think going tell him that you getting ready to have a baby? How you going to look your father in the face and tell him that you ain't going to college 'cause you're pregnant."

I started to cry and Auntie Noreen loosened her hold on me. She pulled me into her arms and the same woman who only a moment ago was shouting at me, was now holding me. She was holding me and welcoming me back. I couldn't see her face, but I knew she had spent her anger. I hugged her back hard and cried. Then Auntie said the words I'd feared for almost four months, "Andrea, you must tell your father."

I clung even tighter to her. "Auntie Noreen, I can't. I'm afraid."

"I know that this is going to be hard for you, but I've already called your father and he'll be here as soon as he leaves his office this evening." I let Auntie Noreen go and walked to my bed and sat down. I couldn't look at her. I was ashamed.

"Drea, I'm guessing that you went over to Mrs. Trindle's because that baby that you're having belongs to that useless son of hers, right?" I never raised my head or eyes to look at Auntie Noreen, I just nodded my head.

"Mrs. Trindle said that you're four months pregnant, is that true?" Again I nodded my head.

I don't know how long Auntie Noreen and I stayed in my room, but I could tell that it was a long time because outside started to darken. The darker it got, the more afraid I became. Soon Daddy would be here and I would have to face him. Auntie Noreen never left me and when Mr. Peters came home and called for her, she simply said, "Neal, I'm up here. I'm with Drea." I'm not sure if it was what she said or if it was the tone in her voice, but Uncle Neal came quickly. I stole a peek at his face and saw concern painted all over it.

"Noreen, what's wrong with Drea? What's so wrong with Drea that it has brought a quiet to the house?"

Auntie Noreen in her very straightforward way, said, "Neal, Drea has gotten herself pregnant. It's for the Trindle boy down the block. His mother told me today."

Uncle Neal sat down in my one chair and said nothing. I could tell from how heavy he sat in the chair that I'd added a ton of weight to his shoulders. I couldn't bring myself to look at him so I kept my head lowered as far into my chest as I could get it. The three of us just sat there. Each one of us was weighed down by the baby in my belly.

Daddy, as he had always done when Auntie Noreen called, came, no questions. She had called; that was enough. As the three of us sat in the now darkened and quiet room, the doorbell rang. It rang and I wanted to run. I wasn't sure where I wanted to go, but instinctively I knew I had to go someplace. I couldn't face Daddy right away so I went to the bathroom. Uncle Neal went down the stairs to let Daddy in and Auntie Noreen stayed seated on my bed where the news of the growing baby in my belly had pushed her earlier. It seemed like an eternity ago. From the bathroom, I could hear Daddy and Uncle Neal's footsteps coming up the stairs. I looked around my bathroom for a place to hide. Finding none; I washed my hands, dried them, and stepped out.

With Daddy, Auntie Noreen, and Uncle Neal in my room, it felt very small. I felt even smaller. I stood at the bathroom door unsure of what to say or do. I looked to Auntie Noreen and Uncle Neal for help; they offered none. I thought to go back in the bathroom, but something in Daddy's eyes said that it wasn't such a good idea. I stood just where I was, found a spot on the carpet to focus on, and told Daddy that I was pregnant.

I braced myself for whatever the news of my pregnancy would turn Daddy into. He didn't turn into anything. He remained Daddy. I wanted to go to him, but my feet wouldn't move. Daddy's moved. He crossed the floor and came to me. I braced myself for a slap. It never came. Instead, Daddy folded me into his arms. With each fold, he shut the world out. I hugged him back and told him I was sorry and asked him to help me.

My family accepted the fact that I'd made a mistake. Daddy wanted to go after Hamilton for statutory rape. I was only seventeen. Auntie Noreen said that Mrs. Trindle had told her that Hamilton had moved out a few months ago and was now living somewhere in North Carolina. Daddy decided to leave it alone, but he added, "For now."

Daddy turned to Auntie Noreen and said, "Noreen, you're going to have to let me give you something now. Drea is going to need a lot more care, there are going to be visits to the doctor, and soon there's going to be a baby in the house."

"Matthew Hirsh, we raised you, raised this child of yours, and you don't think we can't take care of your grandchild."

"It's not that, Noreen, but it's different now."

"Tell me how it's different. Are you, like Andre, going to tell us that we're old as dust?"

Suddenly Uncle Neal started to laugh. He started to laugh the strangest laugh and none of us could see what he was finding funny then Auntie Noreen turned to him and said, "Well, well, Neal. That's the longest it ever took you to get a joke. How many years ago did that boy say we was old as dust and you just now getting it. You just went and proved to Matthew Hirsh right now that we need help. It took you all these years to get that joke."

Uncle Neal was still laughing and the fact that he'd either just gotten it or just remembered it made Daddy laugh. "Noreen, you're right. I'll leave you to decide if and when you need help. However, know that when you decide, all you have to do is let me know, OK." And that was it. Just like that, Daddy had come over and fixed everything.

In the morning, Auntie Noreen took me to St. Mary's hospital and registered me in the clinic. When I had to go, Uncle Neal and Auntie Noreen would take me. I never had to go by myself. Daddy never came though. He either called the evenings after my clinic visits or he would come by.

Daddy hired someone to come by and give me lessons. I never went back to school. The next few months went by quickly, and one night while I was sleeping, I dreamed I was swimming only to discover that I was in a pool of my own creation. My water had broken. My baby was ready to be born.

Chapter 65

Let There Be

One minute I'm pregnant, and the next my bed is soaked and Uncle Neal is taking me to St. Mary's hospital. It was late so no one called Daddy, but Auntie Noreen told me that as soon as she could, she would call him and let him know that I was at the hospital. There was no one else to call. Hamilton had been gone almost five months and I didn't have much of a relationship with Mrs. Trindle after she'd betrayed me.

My labor was intense. It seemed as if the baby was fighting to stay in more than it wanted to come out. The baby couldn't or wouldn't come out. I was doing everything that the doctor told me to do and yet the baby won't budge. My belly was twisting and contorting, and it was then I realized why the baby wasn't coming out. The baby wasn't helping; it was making me suffer.

I'd been angry, hateful, and resentful towards this baby and its father the whole pregnancy and now the baby was getting back at me. When it was time to push, I pushed. I pushed 'till I was practically sitting upright but nothing. I continued to push and wait. While I waited, I watched my belly; it looked as if both sides of my belly, as well as the top were being pushed outward simultaneously. It looked like a square with a mound in the middle. There was only one way that my belly could look like that. The baby was spread-eagle. It had to be stretching its arms and legs right across my belly and touching the inside of my belly with its palms and sole of its feet. This baby was fighting against my wanting to push it out of me.

We continued to struggle and fight each other. I wanted one thing and the baby wanted another. I wanted the baby out and the baby wanted to stay in as long as it could and make me suffer. The doctor started talking about cutting me and as angry as I was at Hamilton and his baby, I didn't want to get cut, so when the doctor said push, I pushed. I didn't push as if I were trying to get a stubborn baby out of me. I pushed as if I were the void that was there at the beginning of creation before God said 'Let there be light" and illuminated me.

I pushed as if God himself was speaking into me and He was saying, "Let There Be!" I pushed as if the baby was the stumbling block that was preventing me from letting whatever God wanted me to be. I stopped trying to give birth to a simple thing like a baby and concentrated on giving birth to the whole world. I focused only on what was blocking my way from creating this miracle for God and since I had some more "Letting There Be" to do, I pushed and shut my mind against how badly I was hurting

I pushed and each time I pushed, I said, "Let there be!" I never said what, but I knew in my heart what I was thinking. The doctor would say, "Come on, little lady, push." And I would scream, "Let there be!" I'm sure they heard me but no one asked anything. I think they understood. I wanted the baby out and I didn't care how; well I didn't want to get cut. The fight continued. The baby would come down a little and then it would go right back up. Soon the doctor and I were having our own re-enactment of the creation. He would say, "Push!" I would say, "Let there be!" And he would say, "That was good." Finally after I was beginning to become exhausted, I realized that I'd said enough of "Let There Be!" to create several universes and the doctor said that the baby had eased down enough that soon I would be able to birth the baby.

The very next time the doctor said push, I remembered how much I hated Hamilton and pictured that I was trying to push the baby, along with Hamilton, out of the world's way. I put my hatred for him at the top of my womb and pushed the hardest I'd ever pushed. That worked because the doctor said one more good push like that and we were going have a baby. My mind was a little numb from all the pushing and trying but when he said "we", my mind realized that for the first time someone had said "we", and was sharing ownership of the baby with me. That was all I needed to hear. The next time, the doctor said, "This should be your last one, now give a good push."

On the outside, I raised my head up, pressed my chin down on my chest, and through teeth that were pressed so hard together that I was sure calcium powder was going to come out of my mouth when I tried to speak, I said, "LET THERE BEEEEEEEEE!"

Inside, where I'd mentally climbed, I stood right above the space holding the womb that contained that little angry baby, I placed my hands at the top of my chest, placed my feet on the top of the womb, and pushed down. I was going to push Hamilton and his little angry baby all the way into the vast darkened void that was waiting to receive the world inside of me. I pressed down and pushed. I felt them moving out of the way of the world. This time I was going to win. I was going get them out of my belly and out of the world's way.

When it was all over, I'd pushed out a child who came with the whole world and all its weight on her shoulders. I looked at her with that giant globe attached to her and wondered how they were going to cut the steel umbilical cord that had her and her world attached to me. She'd inherited the world, its weight, and all its problems because she was a Trindle.

After she'd been cleaned up, I looked at her and I cried. I cried because after the many times that I'd said, "Let There Be" I couldn't look at her and say, "It was good!" I'd given birth to Hamilton all over again. Auntie Noreen was right; Hamilton was one ugly gorilla boy and he'd push an ugly gorilla baby into me and I, in turn, had pushed an ugly gorilla baby girl out into the world. I looked at Hamilton's gorilla baby and tried very hard, because I was her mother, to find some beauty on her; even a birthmark would have been acceptable. I could find nothing, not one little tiny thing.

I cried even harder because I knew, as I looked at her, that the world was going to see her just as I was seeing her at this moment. No one would ever see a beautiful baby. I, with my new mother's eyes, couldn't work that miracle, so how did I expect the world to do it. Hamilton's baby looked just like him and his mother. She was smaller and more wrinkled and that wasn't help her disposition any. I cried for her and the life she was going to have.

Auntie Noreen and Uncle Neal came to see the baby. I knew by the look on their faces they were thinking that some mistake had been made because baby girl Hirsh Greenwood, as she was being called, had nothing of me, Mommy, Nana, Andre, or Daddy in her. Baby girl Greenwood looked as if she belonged to Mrs. Trindle and Hamilton alone. I'd picked out a lot of beautiful names because I'd somehow imagined that I would give birth to a child that would look like it needed a pretty name, but she turned out be a Trindle and I didn't know what to do. I looked at her little Trindle gorilla face and wondered where names for babies that looked like her came from.

The nurse came in and asked me what her name was going to be. I didn't know what to say to the nurse so I lied. I told the nurse that I didn't have a name picked out yet. Then I asked the nurse, "What's your name?"

She said, "Leela P. Brown."

That sounded better than anything that I could ever come up with so I said, "That's what I'm going to call her. Her name is going be Leela Phoebe Hirsh Greenwood."

The nurse looked at me and said, "Ms. Hirsh Greenwood, you sure there ain't nobody in your family you want to name your baby after?"

I said, "No, there ain't. I think Leela Phoebe is a pretty name. It's going to suit her just fine. I like Leela. She looks like a Leela."

The nurse wrote it down on a piece of paper and left. A few days later, Uncle Neal and Auntie Noreen came to take us home. Daddy, who for whatever reason had never made it to the hospital, was there when we arrived. He came and took the baby as if he was afraid she would float away. He sat down with her and then he started to look her over. Daddy just sat there smiling and beaming as if I'd put an angel in his hands. He looked at me with his eyes brimming with tears as he told me, "Princess, she's so beautiful."

The tears that had been brimming on the lids of his eyes slid down his cheeks. I sat beside him and looked at the baby again. I'd looked at her in the hospital for almost a week and could find no beauty in her. I looked again to see if in Daddy's arms a miracle had happened. Again my mother's eyes failed to see any beauty. All I saw was a tiny wrinkled Hamilton.

As Daddy sat with the baby in his arms, the doorbell rang. Uncle Neal went to the door and it was Mrs. Trindle. She'd seen us come home and wanted to know if she could come in and see the baby. Auntie Noreen started to say no, but Daddy asked Auntie Noreen to let her come in. He said that there would be no harm in it. Mrs. Trindle came in and walked softly over to where Daddy was sitting with the baby. She sat down next to Daddy and he handed the baby to her. Mrs. Trindle's face took on the same look that Daddy's had a few minutes ago and she said the same thing, "She's beautiful."

As with Daddy, I sat down and looked again at the baby that to them was so beautiful she was making them cry. I looked and the results were the same as before: a tiny wrinkled Hamilton. I looked at Mrs. Trindle and I could understand her thinking that the baby was beautiful because the baby looked like her and Hamilton, but Daddy, there was no excusing him for the trick he'd allowed his eyes to play on him.

While Daddy and Mrs. Trindle succumbed to the blindness of love and sunk deeper into their state of blissful denial at the beauty of the baby in their hands, I was wondering what would become of me and my life with a baby and not even a high school diploma. This was not what my life was supposed to be like. I was supposed to be on the threshold of fulfilling the dream of a slave who was willing to sacrifice everything for book learning.

As I watched Daddy and Mrs. Trindle sinking deeper and deeper into their murky abyss of grandparent-hood, the more my hatred for Hamilton grew. If only for the child's sake, I wished to stop hating Hamilton but at the very thought of his name, a searing pain of anger and resentment went through me. This baby, his child, would be a constant reminder that he, with one cruel, hate-filled act had snatched me from the path of my destined journey of getting into college and fulfilling Cornbread and Milkweed's dream and placed me at the tail-end of time. I determined in my heart, and with the same tenacity that this child had struggled with me to be born to find a way to get back to the place where I would break this generational curse that had deterred the dream of every woman of this lineage.

There was a way back. I had to find it even if it meant searching on my hands and knees or with this very fiery child strapped to my hip. Either way, there was a way back, and I was going to find it. I had to. A lot of people, including this mirror of Hamilton, were waiting on me. I closed my eyes and prayed. I let them stay closed for a long time. I was hoping that when I opened them again, I would be in my room the day before I tried to make Hamilton happy. I heard a faint cry. I opened my eyes. I wasn't in my room. Daddy and Mrs. Trindle were still sitting in their own abyss and in their hands was the child that had fought me every inch of the way to be born. She was crying a demanding cry.

I got up, walked over to Daddy and Mrs. Trindle, and as I extended my hands to Daddy to take her, I wished there was a void, unseen but present that would suck both she and I away. There wasn't one. Daddy placed her in my outstretched arms. I took her and as I looked into her tiny wrinkled Hamilton face, I tried to find the map that would take me back to the path I was on. Her little eyes fluttered open and in them, her fiery determination burned back at me. I would have to find the path back to my destiny somewhere else. It wasn't going to be with this child or through this child. Even if she knew the way, something told me she wasn't about to tell me. As I made my way to sit with Leela in my arms, I silently asked the Lord to help me. I could tell I was going to need it with this child.

I took a deep breath and as I exhaled, I thought, "Lord, what did you mean when you said, "Suffer the little children to come unto me and refuse them not? Did you mean Leela as well?"

Leela didn't give the Lord time to answer. She let out a loud wail and snatched me back to my present reality: her. The road back was going to be a long one. A very, very long one but I, with my Mandinka, Seminole, and Jewish blood was making it back and Leela, with her Mandinka, Seminole, Jewish, and that additional blood I didn't have, Trindle blood, was coming along and from the way she was carrying on right now, it would be kicking and screaming. I was OK with that because the only thing that mattered is that I find the road back.

I sat down and started to feed her. She was going to need something on her stomach for this journey. It didn't make sense starting out with her hungry.

Glossary

Abolitionist: An individual who was opposed to slavery and often times, at great risk to self, worked to help slaves escape from the plantations and their owners.

Bitter breeze: An expression used in this context to refer to anyone or thing that comes in negatively and takes something out with it. A bitter breezing slave was like a snitch. He or she would 'take' news to the Master or Overseer about or against a fellow slave. This would gain that slave a few 'points' and show that they are indeed a 'good nigger/slave'.

Branding: Slaves were often branded/marked with their owners mark. This was done by heating an iron that had the slave owner's identifying 'logo' and that 'logo' was heated and burnt into the slaves skin. It usually didn't involve a prolong scorching or burning of the skin. A red hot iron was held to the skin long enough for the 'logo' to make its mark. Slaves were considered property. Same as cows, horses or other livestock.

Clabber: Milk that was intentionally allowed to spoil/curdled. Major ingredient added to make biscuits

Comfort Songs: These songs were like spirituals. They were intended to ease pain, soothe hurt and give the listener hope that the bad feeling or experience would pass and better days/times were coming.

Conductor: Code word for anyone who assisted in helping slaves to escape from their masters. These conductors often came through/onto the plantation; held secret meeting and took the slaves away, at great personal risk, to freedom.

Drivers: Slaves that were trained to 'handle' other slaves. Often times these slaves were equally as cruel as the white Overseers. A Good example of a 'bitter breeze' would be a driver who wanted to show how truly 'good' he was.

Emancipation Proclamation: The Executive Order used by President Abraham Lincoln to free the slaves in 1862

Hill-up the ground: A process of hoeing and weeding to keep the area around the rice free of weeds.

Lick: In the context used a form of physical punishment. Sometimes a stick, whip or even a belt would be used to administer the beating.

Mortar: Part of a two-part 'tool' set- the bowl. Used during slavery in the processing of rice. These tools, mostly made of wood, were huge and used to pound the rice in order to separate the rice from the chaff.

Magra: Thin to the point of appearing emaciated

Nappy Hair: The short and tightly curled hair of most slaves

Nigger pup: It's a derogatory term used to refer to a small child of a negro slave. Often times a child less than but almost at toddling age.

Passing: Some slaves (mostly those of mixed-race who possessed all the physical and facial characteristics to be mistaken for a white person) and later the descendants of slaves and white people would 'pass' as white people. This was a very dangerous thing to do because if that individual was found out it could mean physical harm or even death.

Patrollers: A group of usually 3 - 6 white men who enforced discipline during slavery. They returned run-away slaves and were very cruel to all 'blacks' --slaves and free persons alike.

Pestle: Shaped like a baseball bat and used (along with the mortar) to grind the rice shaft to get the grain out.

Pickney: Derogative name for a slave baby but adapted by slaves as reference to their own children

Poking: Sexual intercourse akin to rape/sexual intercourse without emotional attachment.

Pop: To break by pulling or forcing apart

Potash: The term "potash" comes from the old-Dutch word potaschen. The old method of making potassium carbonate ($K2CO3$) was by leaching wood ashes and evaporating the solution in large iron pots, leaving a white residue called "pot ash".[2][3] Later, "potash" became the term widely applied to naturally occurring potassium salts and the commercial product derived from Potash along with hartshorn was also used as a baking aid similar to baking soda in old German baked goods such as Lebkuchen (ginger bread). - (Wikipedia)[17]

Rut: Term used for sexual intercourse.

Rutting: See rut

Seasoning: Newly 'acquired' slaves were taken from Africa to the West Indies: Barbados, Jamaica and St. Thomas to be 'seasoned.' This 'act' ensured slave owners that the slave would be properly indoctrinated and 'knew' the ways to be on a plantation. It also meant that the slave seller received a higher price for this 'well-trained' slave. Some slaves did not survive this seasoning.

Shiva: A period of mourning that last for seven days. During this time the family or person sitting Shiva will do nothing of pleasure. The individual, if it's a man, will not shave, have sexual intercourse, use hot water for bathing or even listen to music. There's a special meal that's prepared the first day. This meal is call the se'udat havra'ah--the meal of condolence (eggs and bread or eggs and lentils because of the roundness symbolizing that life return) is prepared by someone else other that the bereaved. In the household where the Shiva is being observed all mirrors in the house are covered.

Simchat Torah: A Jewish festival celebrating the public readings (end of Deuteronomy and the beginning of Genesis). The first five books of Moses (the Torah).

Slave Pass or Pass: A document issued to slaves that enabled them to travel from their master's plantation to other parts of the region and not be thought to be run-away slaves. Sometimes this pass did not stop a person from being kidnapped and resold into slavery.

Sluice Gate: This gate was used to control the flow of water to the rice field. It was important that 'just' enough water was used in the rice growing process.

Underground Railroad: A vast connective system of people, homes and tunnels used to help slaves escape slavery and get to a friendly state (North) or country (Canada) that had more tolerance for equality or fairness.

Winnowing: The process employed by slaves to separate the rice grain from the chaff. This task was mostly performed by the women slaves.